THERE ARE SPIRITS BURNING
IN THE AIR

With wings of flame and eyes as brilliant as knives, they move on the winds that blow above the sphere of the moon, and now and again their gaze falls like the strike of lightning to the earth below, where it sears anything it touches. Their voices have the snap of fire and their bodies are the conjoining of fire and wind, the breath of the sun coalesced into mind and will.

All this she sees inside the vision made by fire. Here she runs as would a mouse, silent and watchful, staying in the shadows. She braves the unknown passageways and the vast hidden halls where other creatures lurk.

She needs help so desperately and she does not know where to turn.

Through the endless twisting halls she seeks the gateway that will lead her to the old Aoi sorcerer.

There! *Seen in shadow, in a dark dry corridor walled in stone, she sees two people walking, searching as she is.*

There! *A boy sleeps with six companions, heads pillowed on stone, feet and knees covered by heaps of treasure, armbands of beaten gold, rings, gems, vessels poured out of the silver of moonlight, and smooth scarlet beads that are dragon's blood turned to stone with exposure to the air.*

There! *Creatures move and crawl among the tunnels, misshapen knuckles tamping down soil clawed from the dank walls. Like the Eika, they seem fashioned more of metal and soil than of the higher elements, trapped forever by the weight of earth that courses through their blood and hardens their bones.*

When she at last finds the burning stone that marks the gateway to the old sorcerer, he no longer sits beside it. He has left that place, and she does not know where to find him.

A whisper of breath touches the back of her neck. She shudders. Her back stings as if, simply by closing in on her, the creature blisters her with its poisonous intent.

She begins to run through the halls. But the creature is stronger than she is, here, in this place. It knows these paths, and it is looking for her.

"Liath."

It knows her name. . .

Prince of Dogs

VOLUME TWO
OF
CROWN OF STARS

Kate Elliott

DAW BOOKS, INC.
DONALD A. WOLLHEIM, FOUNDER
375 Hudson Street, New York, NY 10014

ELIZABETH R. WOLLHEIM
SHEILA E. GILBERT
PUBLISHERS

http://www.sff.net/people/Kate.Elliott

First Paperback Printing, February 1999
2 3 4 5 6 7 8 9

To Jay

WENDAR AND VARRE

RECENT RULERS OF WENDAR AND VARRE

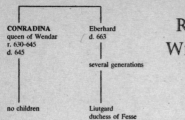

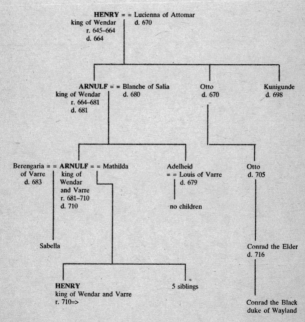

CONRADINA
queen of Wendar
r. 630–645
d. 645

Eberhard
d. 663

several generations

no children

Liutgard
duchess of Fesse

HENRY == Lucienna of Attomar
king of Wendar   d. 670
r. 645–664
d. 664

ARNULF == Blanche of Salia
king of Wendar   d. 680
r. 664–681
d. 681

Otto
d. 670

Kunigunde
d. 698

Berengaria == **ARNULF** == Mathilda
of Varre   king of
d. 683   Wendar
              and Varre
              r. 681–710
              d. 710

Adelheid
== Louis of Varre
      d. 679

no children

Otto
d. 705

Sabella

Conrad the Elder
d. 716

HENRY
king of Wendar and Varre
r. 710=>

5 siblings

Conrad the Black
duke of Wayland

== married
r. reigned
d. died

12/-

CONTENTS

PART FOUR

SEEKER OF HEARTS

PROLOGUE

1

ALL spring they managed to stay alive by hiding in the abandoned tannery quarter, coming out only at night to scrounge for food. After a few nights, running from the dogs, hiding in the pits, they became accustomed to the stink. Better to stink like the tanners, Matthias pointed out to his sister, than be torn to pieces by dogs.

Anna reflected silently on this. It gave her some small satisfaction to know that if they were caught by the Eika savages, if they were run down by the dogs and rent arm from shoulder, leg from hip, at least they would smell so badly of chicken dung that surely not even those hideous dogs would eat them. Or if the dogs did eat them, then maybe their flesh, immersed so many times in oak bark tannin that their skin had begun to take on a leathery cast, would poison the creatures; then, from the Chamber of Light where her spirit would reside after death in blessed peace, she could watch their writhing, agonized deaths.

All spring there was food to be scrounged, for those who had escaped the city had fled without having time to fetch anything and those who had not escaped were dead. Or so at least observation told them. Half-eaten corpses lay strewn in the streets and alleys, and many houses stank of rotted flesh. But they found stores of vegetables in root cellars and barrels of ale in the common houses. Once, they foolishly ventured to the kitchens of the mayor's palace where they found sweetmeats that made Anna, who stuffed herself with them, violently ill. Matthias forced her to run, gagging, with a hand clapped over her mouth to keep it in and in such pain she thought her stomach was going to burst, all the way back to the tanneries so she could throw

1

it up into the puering pits, a stew of chicken dung mixed
with water that would, he prayed, hide the smell of fresh
human vomit.

No dogs came 'round the tanneries for a long while after
that. Perhaps the Eika had given up hunting their human
prey or deemed there were none left worth hunting in the
empty city. Perhaps they'd sailed down the river to hunt in
greener pastures. But neither child dared climb the city
walls to the parapet to see how many Eika ships lay
beached along the river's edge. Now and again they saw
Eika walking those parapets, staring north toward the sea.
Now and again they heard the keening and howling of the
dogs and, once, the screams of a human, whether man or
woman they could not tell. They kept to familiar haunts
and stayed mostly in the little shed where Matthias had
slept after he had been apprenticed to a currier the winter
before the Eika attack. Left behind, forgotten, in the confusion of the attack and the hopeless street-by-street defense
of the city, he had had the wits to take refuge with his
younger sister in the foul tannery pits when he saw the
dogs hunting through the city. That was why they had survived when so many others had died.

But come summer, they used up their last stores and had
to dig in untended gardens for those half-grown vegetables
that had fought past the weeds. They learned to hunt rats,
for there were rats aplenty in the empty buildings, fat ones
well fed on dessicated corpses. Anna found herself with a
talent for stone throwing, too, and brought down seagulls
and complacent pigeons and once a feral cat.

Come summer, more Eika came, and these Eika brought
human slaves with them, gleaned from a distant harvest.

When one fine summer's morning the Eika returned to
the tanning quarter with slaves brought to work in the tannery, the two children fled to a loft and cowered behind
tanned hides which had been hung to dry from the crossbeams. When they heard voices, the creak and scrape of a
body climbing the ladder, Matthias boosted Anna up to
one of the great beams. Her terror added strength to her
tugs, and with him scrambling on the uneven plank wall
and her pulling, they got him up beside her. There they
huddled, clinging to the beam and shaking with fear. The

stink of the tannery protected them no longer. The trap-door opened at the far end of the loft.

Anna sucked down a sob when they heard the first whispery soft words—an Eika speaking a language they could not understand. A dog yipped and growled outside. As if in reply a human voice—below, from over by the puering pits—yelped in pain, then began screaming and pleading pointlessly and unintelligibly, screaming again until at last, mercifully, the screams cut off with a gurgle. Matthias bit his lip to keep from crying out. Anna's eyes filled with tears that slipped down her cheeks; she grasped the wooden Circle of Unity that hung on a leather cord at her thin chest—her mother's dying gift to her—and traced her finger around its smooth circle in silent prayer as she had seen her mother do many times, though this wordless prayer had not availed her mother against her final illness.

Footsteps shuddered on the rungs. A body scraped, half metal, half cloth, heaving itself up and over onto the loft floor. A man grunted, a human sound, curt and yet familiar in its humanity.

The Eika spoke again, this time in recognizable if broken Wendish. "How soon these is ready?"

"I will have to look them over." The man enunciated each word carefully. "Most likely all are ready if they've been here since—" He broke off, then took a shuddering breath. Had he witnessed that killing just now, or only listened to it, as they had? "Since spring."

"I count, these," said the Eika. "Before you come, I count these skins. Less than I count come to me when they ready, I kill one slave for each skin less than I count. I start with you."

"I understand," said the man, but the children could not see him, could only hear, and what emotion they heard in his voice they could not interpret.

"You bring to me when ready," said the Eika. The ladder creaked, and this time they recognized the slight chime of mail as the Eika left the loft and climbed back down, away, to wherever Eika went when they were not hunting and killing.

Still the children clung there, praying the man would go away.

But instead he moved slowly through the loft, jostling

the hides, rubbing them, testing them. Counting them. A
loose plank creaked under his foot. The quiet rustle of a
hide sliding against another marked his progress, and the
huff and stir of leather-sodden air in the dim room, spreading outward from his movements, shifted and swirled about
them like the exhalation of approaching death, for discov-
ery would indeed mean death.

Finally it was too much for Anna, who was three winters
younger than Matthias. The sound got out of her throat,
like a puppy's whimper, before she could gulp it back. The
man's slow quiet movement ceased, but they still heard his
breathing, ragged in the gloom.

"Who's there?" the man whispered, then muttered a
Lady's Blessing.

Anna set her lips together, squeezed her eyes shut, and
wept silently, free hand clutching the Circle. Matthias
groped for the knife at his belt, but he was afraid to pull
it out of its sheath, for even that slight noise would surely
give them away.

"Who's there?" the man said again, and his voice shook
as if he, too, were afraid.

Neither child dared answer. Finally, thank the Lady, he
went away.

They waited a while and climbed down from the beam.

"I have to pee," whimpered Anna as she wiped her nose.
But they dared not leave the loft and yet, sooner or later,
they would have to leave the loft or starve. She peed in
the farthest darkest corner and hoped it would dry before
anyone came back up. There were other chores for the new
slaves in the tannery—hides to be washed and hair and
flesh scraped from them, new pits to be filled for puering
or drenching, hides to be layered in with oak bark, satu-
rated in the tannic acid, or, tanning completed, rinsed off
and smoothed before drying. There were other lofts where
hides waited, drying, in silent darkness, until they were
ready for the currier. No reason anyone should come up
here again this day.

But that evening they heard steps on the ladder. No time,
this time, to scramble up on the beam. They huddled behind the far wall, wrapping themselves in a cow hide.

They heard, instead of words, the soft tap of something
set down on wood. Then the trap closed and footsteps

thumped down the ladder. After a bit Matthias ventured out.

"Anna! Quietly!" he whispered.

She crept out and found him weighing a hunk of goat's cheese in one hand and a dark, small, misshapen loaf of bread in the other. A rough-hewn wooden bowl sat empty beside the trap. She stared at these treasures fearfully. "If we eat it, then he'll know we're here."

Matthias broke off a piece of cheese, sniffed it, and popped it in his mouth. "We'll eat a bit now," he said. "What difference does it make? If we don't get out of here tonight, then they'll discover us sooner or later. We'll save the rest for after we've escaped."

She nodded. She knew when to argue, now, and when to remain silent because argument was pointless. He gave her a corner of cheese; it tasted salty and pungent. The bread was dry as plain oats, and its coarse texture made her thirsty. He divided the rest of the food into two portions and gave half to her. Both carried leather pouches, tied to their belts, for such gleanings as this. Such necessities the ruined city provided in plenty, taken from empty houses and shops or—if valuable enough—pried from the dead. Water, clothing, knives or spoons or even an entire timbered house furnished with fine painted furniture and good linen, none of this they lacked; only food and safety.

They waited until no crack of light gleamed through the plank walls onto the warped floorboards, until gray shadow became indistinguishable from black. Then Matthias eased open the trap and slid over the edge as quietly as he could.

"Lady!"

A man, not Matthias, spoke. Anna froze. Matthias grunted and dropped to the ground.

"There now," said the man, "don't pull your knife on me. I won't hurt you. Lady Above, I didn't think any soul had survived in this charnel house. You're just a child."

"Old enough to be apprenticed," muttered Matthias, stung, as he always was, because this man's voice was like their uncle's and his taunt the same one. Only perhaps, Anna thought, this man had spoken with awed pity, not with contempt, when he called Matthias a child. She had a sudden rash intuition that this man could be trusted, unlike their uncle, and anyway, if Matthias was now caught, it was

better to die with him than to struggle on in a fight she
could never win alone. She swung her legs out and climbed
quickly and quietly down the ladder.

Matthias swore at her under his breath. The man gasped
aloud, then clapped a hand over his mouth and stared furtively around, but they remained alone. No one moved
through the tanning grounds this late. The quarter moon lit
them, and thin ghostly shadows cut the pits with strange patterns. Anna grabbed her brother's hand and held on tightly.

"Ai, Lady, and a younger one still," the man said at last.
"I thought you was a cat. Are there more of you?"

"Only us two," said Matthias.

"Lord in Heaven. How did you survive?"

Matthias gestured toward the pits, then realized the man
might not be able to see his movement. "There was food
enough to be scrounged, until now. We hid here because
the dogs couldn't smell us."

The man squinted at Anna in the dim light, stepped forward abruptly, and took her chin in his hand. Matthias
started forward, raising his belt knife, but Anna said, "No,"
and he stopped and waited.

After a moment the man let go and stepped back, brushing his eyes with a finger. "A girl. You're a girl, and no
older than my little Mariya. The Lady is merciful, to have
saved one."

"Where is your daughter?" asked Anna, bold now. This
man did not scare her.

"Dead," he said curtly. "In the Eika raid that took my
village not a month ago. They killed everyone."

"They didn't kill you," said Anna reasonably, seeing that
he looked alive and not anything like the shade of a dead
man—not that she had ever seen such a thing, but certainly
she had heard stories of them such as come back to haunt
the living world on Hallowing Eve.

"Ai, they killed me, child," he said bitterly. "Killed all
but this husk. Now I am merely a soulless body, their slave,
to do with as they will until they tire of me and feed me
to the dogs." Though he spoke as though living exhausted
him, still he shuddered when he spoke of the dogs.

Anna sorted through this explanation and thought she
understood most of it. "What will you do with us?" she
asked. "Won't the Eika kill us if they find us?"

"They will," said the man. "They never leave children alive. They only want grown slaves strong enough to do their work. But I heard tell from one of the other slaves that there are no children in Gent, no bodies of children, simply no children at all. It's a tale they whisper at night, in the darkness, that the saint who guards the city led the children away to safety or up to the Chamber of Light, I don't know which."

"It's true," muttered Matthias. "All the children are gone, but I don't know where they went."

"Where are your parents, then?" asked the man. "Why were you not taken to safety, if the others were?"

Anna shrugged, but she saw her brother hunch down as he always did, because the misery still sank its claws in him although she did not recall their parents well enough to mourn them.

"They're dead four summers ago," said Matthias. "Our da drowned when he was out fishing, and our ma died a few months later of a fever. They were good people. Then we went to our uncle. He ran, when the Eika came. He never thought of us. I ran back to the house and got Anna, but by then there was fighting everywhere. You couldn't even get to the cathedral where most folk fled, so we hid in here. And here we stayed."

"It's a miracle," murmured the man. Out of the night's silence came sudden noise: dogs barking and a single harsh call, a word neither child understood. The man started noticeably. "They come 'round in the middle night to count us," he said. "I must go back. I won't betray you, I swear it on Our Lady's Hearth. May Our Lord strike me down with His heavenly Sword if I do any such thing. I'll bring more food tomorrow, if I can."

Then he was gone, retreating into the night.

They relieved themselves quickly in one of the stinking pits filled with dung and water, and paused after to look up at the strangely clear sky, so hard a darkness above them that the stars were almost painful to look upon. They heard the dogs again and Matthias shoved Anna onto the ladder. She scrambled back up, and he came up behind her and closed the trap. After a hesitation, but without speaking, they devoured the rest of the cheese and bread—and waited for tomorrow.

2

THE next night, long after sunset, the man came again and tapped on the door softly and said, "I am your friend."

Cautiously, Matthias opened the trap and peered down. After a moment he climbed down. Anna followed him. The man gave them bread and watched silently as they ate. She could see him a bit more clearly tonight—the moon was waxing, and its quarter face slowly swelled, bubbling toward the full. Not particularly tall, he had the broad shoulders of a farmer and a moon-shaped face.

"What are you called?" he asked finally, hesitantly.

"I am called Matthias, and this is Anna, which is short for Johanna. Our ma named us after the disciplas of the blessed Daisan."

The man nodded, as if he had known this all along or perhaps only to show he understood. "I am called Otto. I am sorry the bread was all I could bring. We are not fed well, and I dare not ask the others for a share of their portion. I don't know if I can trust them, for they're no kin of mine. Any one of them might tell the Eika in return for some reward, more bread perhaps."

"It is very kind of you to help us," said Anna brightly, for she remembered that their ma had always told her to be polite and to be thankful for the gifts she received.

The man caught in a sob, then hesitantly touched her hair. As abruptly, he backed away from her. "Or perhaps, like me, the others would gladly help, if only it meant finding a way to see two more brought free of the savages. It isn't as if the Eika play favorites. I've never seen them seek to turn their slaves against each other by handing out special treatment. They despise us all. All are treated the same. Work or die."

"Is it only here," asked Matthias, "in the tanneries, that they've brought slaves?"

"They've opened up the smithies, too, though they've no one trained here in blacksmith's work. But we're slaves and expendable." His voice was hard. "It's fortune's chance I was sent here to the tanneries, though it stinks like nothing I've smelled before. It's whispered that at the forge men are burned every day and the Eika as likely to slit a burned man's throat as to let that man heal if he can't get up and keep working. I saw those Eika. I saw one pushed into a fire. It didn't burn. The heat left no scar on its body. They don't have skin, not like us. It's some kind of hide, like a snake's scales but harder and thicker. Dragon's get." He hawked and spat, as if to get the taste of the word out of his mouth. "The spawn of dragons and human women, that's what they say, but I don't see how such an unnatural congress could take place. But we should not speak of this in front of the child."

"I've seen nothing she hasn't seen also," said Matthias softly, but Anna felt at once that the man's simple statement, protecting her, confiding in the boy, had won over her brother's trust.

She finished her bread and wished there were more, but she knew better than to ask. Perhaps he had given them his entire ration. It would be rude to demand more.

"Fortune's chance," the man whispered bitterly. "Fortune had smiled more sweetly on me had she let me die with my children. But no." He shook his head, shifting, casting a glance back over his shoulder nervously, for surely he had reason to be nervous, as did they all. "For everything, a reason. I was spared so that I might find you." He took a step forward, clasped Matthias by the hand and with his other hand touched Anna's hair gently. "I will find a way for you to escape here, I swear it. Now I must go. I tell them I use the privies each night at this hour, so I must get back. The Eika are strange creatures. Savages they are, surely, but they are fastidious; but perhaps that only goes to show that 'the path of the Enemy is paved neatly with well-washed stones, for the waters cleansing them are the tears of the wicked.' We may make soil only in one place, no pissing even except where they tell us to or on the new skins. That is why we may come out for a few moments' freedom in this way, even at night, for they cannot bear the stink of our human bodies near their own. But I dare not stay longer."

He came again the next night, and the next, and the next

after that, bringing them pittances of food but enough to stave off starvation. Ale he brought also and once wine in a flagon, for there was little water to be found in and about the tanning pits and all of it foul-tasting.

He quickly discovered that Matthias had more knowledge of the tannery and its workings than any of the slaves set to work here; in three months' apprenticeship, Matthias had learned the rudiments of currying and tanning, enough to know what went on at each station and with each tool. The boy he treated politely, even kindly, but it was Anna he truly doted on. She sat on his lap and he stroked her hair and once or twice forgot himself and called her "Mariya."

No one disturbed the hides in their loft. Otto explained that he was in charge of overseeing them, and no slave had time to look into another's business. After several more nights passed, he began bringing more food.

"The Eika have increased our rations. They brought in more slaves to work the bakeries, but also, my boy, what you have told me and I have told the others is helping us work. They are pleased with us, so they feed us better." The moon was full, now, and Anna could see his expression, which was, as always, grim. "No good fortune for those taken to the smithies, or so I hear. As many are dragged out dead as walk in alive. Beasts!" He hid his eyes behind a hand, but she could see the anguished line of his mouth. "Soon the hides will be dry and they will be carted off, and then there will be no place for you to hide."

"They'll hang up more hides, won't they?" asked Anna.

"Ah, child." He pulled her tight against his chest. "That they will, but I can't hide you here forever. I've asked here and there, but I don't know how to get you out of the city, except—"

"Except what?" demanded Matthias, for he, too, Anna knew, had been talking to her about any possible way for them to escape from the city. Perhaps they could have done it during the spring, had they not been so frightened, but they had been frightened, and the dogs had roamed the city every night. Now, with slaves in the city and all the gates watched—or so he assumed—it would be even harder to escape.

"I don't know. It's just a story, and I don't know whether to believe it." But he clutched Anna, his lips touching her hair, a father's kiss. "I've heard some say there's a creature, a daimone, held prisoner in the cathedral. They say the Eika enchanter lured it from the heavens above where such creatures live and imprisoned it in a solid body like to our own. He keeps it chained to his throne."

Anna shuddered, but she felt safe on Otto's lap; he was holding her so securely.

"I am thinking," continued the man slowly, "that the magi say daimones know secrets hidden from human ken. If it is true the saint beloved of this city saved the children, if it is true she led them by hidden ways out from the cathedral to safety, then might not this daimone know of that hidden way? For can daimones not see into both the past and the future, farther than mortal eyes can see? If you offer the creature some gift, and if it hates the Eika as much as we do, might it not tell you of this secret way? It is a small chance, surely, but I can think of no other. The gates are guarded day and night and the dogs roam the streets." He shuddered, as they all shuddered, at the thought of the dogs. "You are children. The saint will smile on you as she did on the others."

"You will come, too, won't you, Papa Otto?" Anna rested her head on his chest.

He wept, but silently, tears streaming down his face. "I dare not," he said. "I dare not attempt it."

"You could escape with us," said Matthias. "God will show you mercy for your kindness to us, who are no kin of yours."

"God might, but the Eika will not. You don't know them. They're savages, but they're as cunning as weasels. They mark each slave, and if one slave goes missing, then others get staked out in front of the dogs and the dogs let loose on them. That way if any slave tries to escape, he knows what will happen to those left behind. I will not cause the death of those I work beside. I could do nothing to save my family. I will not save myself and by so doing kill these others who are as innocent as my dear children. But you two might escape, if you can find and speak to this daimone."

"But what could we bring it?" Matthias asked. "We have nothing—" Then he halted and Anna saw by his crafty look that he had thought of something. He reached into his boot and drew out the prize of their extensive collection of knives, secreted here and there about their bodies. This one, looted from the corpse of a stout man richly dressed in the kind of clothes only a wealthy merchant or a noble could afford, had a good blade and a finely wrought hilt molded in the shape of a dragon's head, studded with emeralds for eyes. By this measure Anna saw Matthias trusted Otto fully; the knife was too valuable to show to anyone who might covet it and easily take it by force from a lad and his young sister.

Otto's eyes widened, for even by the moonlight the knife's quality was evident. "That is a handsome piece," he said. "And a worthy gift, if you can get so far."

"But how will we get into the cathedral?" asked Matthias. "The Eika chieftain lives there, doesn't he? Does he ever come out?"

The slow quiet brush of summer's wind, the night breeze off the river, stirred Otto's hair as he considered. Anna smelled on its wings the distant tang of iron and the forge, a bare taste under the stench of the tanning pits so near at hand. The man sighed at last, coming to some conclusion.

"It is time to trust others. This information I cannot gain on my own. Let us pray, children, to Our Lady and Lord. Let us pray that we weak mortal folk can join together against our heathen enemies, for now we must trust to others who are no kin of ours except that we are humankind standing together against the savages."

With this he left them.

The next night he brought a woman, stooped, scarred, and weary. She stared for a long time at the children and said at last, "It is a miracle they could have survived the slaughter. It is a sign from St. Kristine." She went away again, and he gave them their nightly ration of food.

The next night he brought a young man who had broad shoulders but such a weight on them that he looked as bent with age as a man twice his years. But seeing the children, he lifted up and became a man proud of his youth and strength again. "We'll show those damned savages," he said in a low voice. "We'll never let them have these. We'll beat them in this. That will lend us strength in the days ahead."

The next night Otto brought a robust woman who still wore her deacon's robes though they were now stained, torn, and dirty. But she nodded, seeing the children—not surprised, for surely she had by now heard tell of them. She bent her head over clasped hands.

"Let us pray," she murmured.

It had been a long time since Anna had prayed. She had forgotten the responses, but she traced around the smooth wood of her Circle of Unity carefully with a finger as the deacon murmured the holy words of God, for that was the prayer she knew best. Otto watched her, as he always watched her: with tears in his eyes.

"This is a sign from God," the deacon said after her prayer. "So will They judge our worthiness to escape this blight, if we can save these children who are no kin of ours and yet are indeed our children, given into our hands, just as all who live within the Circle of Unity are the children of Our Lady and Lord."

Otto nodded solemnly.

The deacon rested a hand on Matthias' shoulder, as if giving a blessing. "Those who get water from the river and bring it here have spoken now with those who get water for the smithies, and of those in the smithies some carry weapons to the cathedral, where the chieftain sits in his chair and oversees all. Other slaves who sweep and clean the cathedral meet at times with those who carry weapons from the smithies, and this information they have given us."

She paused at a noise, but it was only the wind banging a loose shutter. "The chieftain leaves the cathedral four times each day to take his dogs to the necessarium—"

"The necessarium?" asked Anna.

This question stirred the first faint smile Anna had seen on any of the slaves' faces, even on Otto's. "Pits. Holes dug in the ground where such creatures relieve themselves, for even such as they are slaves to their bodies. As are all of us bound to mortal matter. Now hush, child. Though it was a fair question, you must listen carefully to my words. Once each day all Eika leave the cathedral, with their dogs and the few slaves who attend them there. They go to the river to perform their nightly ablutions—" She raised a hand to forestall Anna's question. "Their bath. At this time, which is the time Vespers would be sung each evening, the cathedral is empty."

"Except for the daimone," said Otto.

"If such a creature truly exists. So say the slaves who clean there, but it may be that their minds are disordered by their proximity to the savages, for none has been allowed close to this creature, which is said to be chained with iron to the holy altar. By their description it seems to be more of a dog than a man. One man said it has human speech, but another said it can only yip and howl and bark. To this plan, if the saint grants us a miracle, we must trust. Now do you understand?" She asked this of Matthias and studied him carefully in the moon's waning light as he nodded, once, to show he understood. Anna nodded also and took Matthias' hand because she was so frightened.

"Tonight," said the deacon. She looked at Otto and he nodded, though his hands clenched.

"Tonight?" asked Anna in a whisper. "So soon—?" Impulsively she darted forward and clasped her arms round Otto's body. His clothes hung on him, a once stout man made thin by privation and grief, yet still he felt sturdy to her. He held her tightly against him, and she felt his tears on her cheeks.

"We must move immediately," said the deacon. "You might be discovered any day. It is indeed a miracle you have not been found before this." She frowned, and the moonlight painted her face in stark, suffering lines. "We know not if some fool will betray us all, thinking to gain favor in the eyes of the Eika. But there is no favor to be gained with the savages. They are no kin to us. They have no mercy for their own kind, and less than that for us, and so shall we have no mercy for them. Now. Make your farewells, children. You will not see Otto again."

Anna wept. It was too hard to leave him behind, the only person besides Matthias who had shown her kindness since her parents died.

"Take news," said Otto. He still held Anna, but she knew he spoke to Matthias. "Take news to others that some are yet alive in this city, that we are made slaves. Tell them the Eika are massing and building their strength, that they are using us to forge weapons and craft armor for them."

"We'll come back for you," said Matthias, his own voice choked with tears. Anna could not speak, could only cling. Otto stank of the puering pits, but they all of them stank

of the tannery; it was a good scent to her now, a familiar
one that promised safety. Out beyond the tanning pits lay
the great wide world which she no longer knew or trusted.

"Ai, Lady," whispered Otto. He kissed Anna's hair a
final time. "Perhaps it is worse this way: that you have
given me hope. I will wait for you, as well as I can. If
you live, if I survive, if we are reunited, then I will be as
your father."

"Come, children," said the deacon, taking their hands
after gently prying Anna free from Otto's grasp.

Anna cried as she was led away. She looked back to see
Otto staring after them, hands working at his sides, opening
and closing, and then his face was lost to her, hidden by
night and distance.

The deacon took them to the edge of the fetid trench
where the slaves relieved themselves. "Wait here," she said.
"A man will come for you."

She left and returned to the building where the slaves
slept. Somewhat later, the young man they had met before arrived.

"Come," he said, hoisting Anna onto his back. "We must
run all the way to the forge." So they ran, hiding once for
the man to catch his breath and a second time when they
heard the howling of the dogs nearby, but they saw nothing.
Only ghosts walked the city at night. It had been so long
since Anna had ventured out into the ruined streets that
the open spaces and angular shadows, the simple emptiness,
made chills crawl like spiders up and down her skin.

The young man left them, quite unceremoniously, by another trench, this one equally filled with the stink of piss
and diarrhea. But it was yet a good, decent, *human* smell,
not like the dry metallic odor of the savages.

A woman found them there. She stared at first, then
handled them, touching their lips, their hair, their ears.

"You are real," she said. "Real children. They murdered
mine. Come. There is no time." She led them at a loping
run farther into the labyrinth of the city, on to another
trench, another group of slaves. By this way, from trench
to trench, they passed through the city.

"That is our only freedom," said the man who took them
at last within sight of the cathedral even as they saw the
first stain of light in the eastern sky. "They are savages, the

Eika, but they cannot stand the least stink of human piss
or shit near them. I've seen a man killed for loosing his
bowels where he was not meant to, though he could not
help himself. So we may come out to relieve ourselves, one
by one, and if we say we are having the cramping, then we
are allowed a little more time. Now. This is as far as I or
any of us can take you. Hide here, under these rags next
to the trench, for the Eika never come near these trenches.
Do not move, do not stir, even if you hear the dogs. Perhaps they will discover you and kill you. We all will pray
that they do not. Be patient. Wait out the day. You will
know by the light and by the horn they blow and by the
great size of the procession when they go down to the river.
Be careful, though, for they do not all go; some remain
behind to guard the slaves who sleep in that building across
the way, which they call the mint. For all I know, some
may remain behind here in the cathedral as well. What is
inside the cathedral I do not know. That you must discover
for yourselves. May God go with you."

He clasped their hands in his, first Anna and then Matthias, as the sign of their kinship. Then he directed them
to lie flat and covered them with the stinking, filthy rags.
Anna heard his footsteps recede. Something crawled over
her hand. She choked off a gasp. She dared not move,
hardly dared breathe. But for the first time in so many days
and weeks she held an odd, light feeling in her heart. It
took a long time to decide what it was, and finally she
recalled Otto's last words to them:

"You have given me hope."

Amazingly, even almost smothered as she was by the
foul-smelling heap of rags, she slept.

3

HOWLS woke her. She jerked up and at once Matthias shoved her down to keep her still. She made no sound.

Rags slipped, giving her a view of the steps of the cathedral and avenue. Not five paces from her, a man stopped, turning his back to the pile of rags, and pissed into the trench. Then, straightening his clothes, he edged closer and crouched down. Of all the slaves she had seen he looked best kept; his tunic was not encrusted with dirt, though it was not precisely clean either. He toyed with the rope belt hung low on his thin hips and glanced back once over his shoulder, toward the cathedral steps. Through the gap in the rags Anna could see on those steps another slave. This person—she could not tell if it was a man or a woman—washed the gleaming white stone steps with rags and a bucket of water.

The man cleared his throat and spoke in a rush. "As soon as all have gone down the road, run inside into the nave. Stay in the shadows if you can and go to the end, where you will find the altar. There you will find the daimone. Approach it softly. It can be violent, or so we have seen. None of us speaks to it. That is forbidden."

He stood and walked away, and that was the last they saw of him, for first he vanished from their restricted view and then, coming back into sight on the steps, he was suddenly engulfed by dogs.

A horn blasted, a sharp, painful sound. A swarm of dogs surged down the stairs, growling and barking and yipping and howling like mad things. Anna whimpered and then stuck a hand in her mouth, biting down hard, to stop herself from crying out loud. They were monsters, huge hulking things as tall at the shoulder as she was, with long lean haunches and massive shoulders and yellow eyes that sparked with demon's fire. Their mouths hung open perpetually to display their great teeth and red, lolling tongues.

They bowled over the two slaves, overwhelmed them until all she could see was a frenzy of dogs, roiling and leaping and biting each other and only God knew what else. She shut her eyes and groped for her Circle. Matthias choked down a sob; his grip on her tightened. She dared not look. She did not want to see.

A voice roared, a great bellowing powerful shout. She squinched her eyes shut as hard as she could, but Matthias tugged on her and her eyes opened. Eika strode down the steps now, sickly things with their scaled hides. Yet each one, though a savage with nothing of humankind in it, had a brutish strength and the gleam of animal cunning in its bearing and in its sharp ugly face. They grabbed the frenzied dogs by their back legs and yanked them away, struck them hard blows with their clawed hands or the hafts of their spears. The Eika yipped and howled at the dogs as if they were kin and could understand each other in their beast's language.

Behind them came the oddest looking pair of Eika she had yet seen. The first was a huge brawny creature dressed in gold-and-silver chains studded with bright gems, and its companion was an Eika as scrawny as the human slaves and itself clothed only in a single rag tied about its hips. A leather pouch hung from the belt around its waist; it carried a small wooden chest braced against one scrawny hip. The huge Eika waded into the seething mass of dogs and proceeded to strike about himself, roaring and laughing as he tossed dogs aside and beat them away from their prey.

One dog at last broke away and bounded down the steps. Many of the Eika warriors followed after it. As if this defection signaled their defeat, the rest of the dogs retreated from the Eika chieftain's wrath—or his humor, for why else would he station slaves on the steps right then, knowing what the dogs would likely do to them?—and loped away down the steps, turning to follow the others down toward the river. As they cleared the steps, their passing revealed two ravaged, red heaps of—

This time she clamped her eyes shut and did not look, willed herself not to look, and heard only Matthias gulping under his breath, trying to keep silent because any noise would doom them.

Finally he whispered, "They've gone. They've carried the

two—them—away. Come now, Anna. Don't lose heart now when we're so close."

He scrabbled at the rags, dug himself free, and jumped to his feet, then yanked her up. He ran and she ran behind, stumbling, gasping for breath because she was so scared and because she had almost forgotten how to run and because her legs were stiff from so many days lying still. They came under the shadow of the cathedral wall and ran up the steps. Blood still stained the stone next to an overturned bucket of water, and runnels of pink water seeped down the steps toward the avenue below. Rags were strewn everywhere, stained with blood.

The great doors stood open, but because the sun set behind the cathedral, little light penetrated the interior by this, the eastern entrance. They ducked inside, and at once Matthias threw himself against a wall and tugged Anna down beside him. He put a finger to his lips. They stood there in shadow and listened.

And heard . . . the music of chains, shifting, whispering, as some creature tested its bonds and found them as unyielding as ever.

Matthias crept forward to hide behind one of the great pillars of stone that supported the great roof. Here, in the side aisle, they remained in shadow. The nave itself, the vast central aisle of the cathedral, was brighter, lit by windows built high into the towering walls that faced north and south. Brightest of all was the altar, lying in a wash of light from seven tall windows set in a semicircle at the far end of the church, encircling the Hearth.

A heap of refuse lay next to the altar.

Matthias slipped forward to the next pillar, using it as cover to get close to the altar. Anna followed him. She wanted to grab hold of his belt, to cling, but she did not. This she had learned: They must both be free to move quickly.

It was silent. The stone muffled sound, and the outside world seemed far away in this place—once a haven but now the camp of savages. She felt their musty scent against her the way dry things dragged against the skin cause a tingling in fingertips and neck; she smelled it the way a storm announces itself by a certain feeling in the air long before the first rolling peal of thunder is heard and the first slash of lightning seen in the dark sky. *They* ruled this space now, which had once been sacred to God.

She caught up to Matthias and leaned on the cool, stippled stone. He touched her briefly, then darted forward to the next pillar.

The refuse heap by the altar stirred and came to life.

Not rags but dogs, starting out of sleep, scrambling up, alerted.

"Run," moaned Matthias. He shoved her back, toward the door, but it was too late, the door was too far away. They could never run as fast as the dogs, only hide from them. And there was no place to hide here.

The dogs bolted toward them. Anna ran, stumbled, jerked herself up.

"No!" she screamed, for Matthias had run out into the nave, out into the path of the dogs to try to distract them so that she could run free.

"Go! Go!" he shouted.

But she ran to him. It was better to die with him, torn to pieces by the dogs, than live if he were dead. Ai, Lady. What did it matter? There was no way to live in this city except as a slave of the Eika, if that could be called life.

She reached him just before the dogs did, the hideous dogs. She flung her arms around her brother and braced herself for the impact, for death. Please, Lady, let it be quick.

A hoarse cry—not human words, not any words she recognized—came from the direction of the altar, punctuated by noises that sounded like growls and yips. The dogs clattered to a halt, nails slipping and sliding on the stone paving, and they stopped a body's length from the children, growling, glaring with sparking yellow eyes. Then, when more of those hoarse words came, they slunk away, tails down, still growling but now submissive to the creature that rose out of the heap of rags by the altar, a heap which was not rags after all but the daimone itself.

Not human, certainly not that. This much Anna saw easily in the fading light that penetrated the cathedral nave. It was tall and human-shaped, but the Eika were human-shaped and they were no kin to humans. It had covered itself modestly with clothing, though cloth and tunic were shredded by teeth marks and as ragged as if strips had been torn off at random. Gold cloth bound its forearms, this also torn and ripped in many places as though the dogs had gnawed and worried at it, seeking flesh underneath. It wore an iron collar around its neck; to the collar was fastened a thick iron chain, and that chain was fastened to the heavy block of stone that was the altarstone, the Hearth of Our Lady.

It stared at them with eyes as inhumanly green as the emeralds that studded Matthias' fancy dagger, and as if that stare reminded him of the chosen gift, Matthias slipped the dagger out from his boot and held it forward, hilt first, in offering.

"Come," said the daimone in its hoarse voice.

They dared not disobey, for it spoke in the tone of a creature used to obedience and, in any case, it controlled the dogs by some daimonic magic. And why not? It was not human, it was an aetherical creature, something that flew bodiless through the vast impenetrable heavens far above the mortal earth, far above the changing moon; it would not fear human children nor hesitate to command them.

They crept closer, and this time Anna held tight to Matthias' belt with one hand and her Circle with the other, chewing at her lower lip. She sniffed back tears, but she did not flinch as the dogs circled them, smelling their feet and nipping forward only to be brought to heel by the harsh words of the daimone.

Closer yet, then close enough that Matthias could reach out and hand the knife to the daimone. It took it and with sudden furtive haste glanced around the shadowed nave, peering into the colonnades, then tucked the precious weapon in among the filthy rags it wore to cover itself. It stood there silent, listening, and they grew silent as well, but Anna heard nothing and Matthias made no sound.

Anna stared. She thought that, perhaps, when the enchanter had called the daimone down from the heavens and when the magic had imprisoned it in a body made of earth, the daimone had tried—given now no choice—to form itself into a human body. For it was very like a human: human eyes though they were of a stark green color and somewhat pulled at the corners, as if distorted; human skin though it had the tint of bronze as if the metals hidden

in earth had leached out to the surface; a human face
though with broad, prominent cheekbones; and no trace of
beard though it was clearly male. But had not God made
humans both male and female? Why should They not make
daimones likewise?

And it spoke human speech, though slowly, as if not
much practiced at it. To the dogs, in that other language
of beasts, it spoke more fluidly.

"Why have you given me this knife?" it asked. Its voice
likewise, she thought: a human voice but with that hoarse
edge to it, not quite formed.

Matthias dipped his chin for courage and faced the creature squarely. "In trade for the secret of St. Kristine, who
led the other children to safety."

"Who led them to safety," it echoed.

It stared at them for what seemed forever until Anna
thought it had not understood what Matthias said, only
mimicked the sounds. The dogs sniffed at her feet, and a
hundred prickles ran like poisonous creatures up and down
her back. The Eika procession would return at any moment.

The creature flung up its head as a dog does at a sudden
sound. "Quickly," it said. "Beyond the tower stair lies a
door to the crypt. In the crypt lies the path you seek. *Go
free.*" That fast, it changed before their eyes to a mad thing.
It grabbed the heavy chain that bound it and yanked violently. It threw back its head and howled, and the dogs set
up such a yammering and howling and barking that Anna
was deafened.

Matthias grabbed her hand. Together they ran into the
shadow of the colonnade and all the way back along the
nave while the daimone hammered the chain against the stone
paving like a wild beast and the dogs leaped and barked
around it, some nipping in at its body to be met by elbow
or fist.

"God help the poor creature," muttered Matthias. They
came to the end of the colonnade and into the long entryway which ran perpendicular to the nave, itself now
draped in shadows as the sun set outside and the interior
darkened and the poor mad daimone finally ceased its frantic and useless efforts to free itself. Magic it might have, to
control the dogs, but not magic enough to free itself from
the Eika enchanter.

The door that opened onto the stairwell which led to the crypt stood before them, dark, somber wood scored with deep scratches as if someone had clawed at it, trying to get in. Matthias set a hand on the latch, jiggling it tentatively to make sure it wasn't stuck or squeaky.

In the new silence Anna heard the noise first, the scuff of a foot on stone. She whirled and then, because she could not help herself, let out a low moan of fear. Matthias looked back over his shoulder. She felt him stiffen and grope for the knife he always tucked in at his belt.

Too late.

An Eika stood in the shadows not ten strides from them, next to the great doors. It stepped out from its hiding place and stared at them. It was tall, as most of the savages were, but more slender than bulky; its body winked and dazzled in the last glint of sun through the high windows because it wore a girdle of surpassing beauty, gold-and-silver chains linked together and bound in with jewels like a hundred eyes all staring at them, who were at last caught.

She was too terrified even to whimper. She loosened her hand from her Circle and traced it, a finger all the way around the smooth wood grain, the Circle of God's Mercy, as her mother had taught her many years ago: the only prayer she knew.

The creature moved no farther, not to retreat, not to charge.

But Anna saw the strangest thing she had yet seen in her entire life, stranger than slaughter and death and the horrible dogs and rats feeding on a bloated corpse. The creature wore a necklace, a plain leather thong knotted in several places as if it had broken more than once and been tied back together, and on that leather thong, resting against its gleaming copper-scaled chest, hung a wooden Circle of Unity, the sign of the church. Just like hers.

Still it did not move, nor did it raise its head and howl an alarm. But, just like her, it lifted a single finger and traced the round shape of the Circle, as she had done.

Matthias shook himself as if coming out of a dream. He lifted the latch, grasped Anna by the arm. "Don't look," he said. "Don't look back. Just follow me."

He dragged her inside, shutting the door after them

though there was no light to see by. Together they stumbled down the stairs into the black crypt.

No one—no thing, no creature, no sound of pursuit—came after them.

"It's a miracle," she whispered, and then stumbled as she took a step down only to find there were no more steps; the impact jarred her entire body. She lost hold of Matthias and groped frantically, found him again, and clutched his hand so tight he grunted in pain, but she would not lessen her grip on him. She could see nothing, not even her hand in front of her face.

"Look," whispered Matthias, and his whisper faded into the blackness, and she heard it filter away into some vast empty unknowable expanse.

She saw it first as luminescence, a faint glowing light. Then, as her eyes adjusted, she gasped and gagged, for the crypt before them was filled with skeletal corpses and all of them in the same stage of decay although they no longer stank of rotting flesh.

"Look there," whispered Matthias. He pointed, and she could *see* his arm lifted in the gloom and see beyond it a throbbing light as faint as the soul's breath might appear if it were visible to the human eye. "Come!" he said urgently, and they began the gruesome task of picking their way through the litter of corpses.

"Fighting men, these were," he said. "Look. Some are still wearing surcoats, what you can see of them."

Some indeed wore gold surcoats bearing the sigil of a black dragon. Anna did not know what this meant, only that the one time she had seen a procession go by, bearing a banner to mark the passage of a noble lord or lady, it had not been this one but some other creature, a hound perhaps or a horse. This mystery—who were these soldiers? Had they died in the last battle, when the city was overwhelmed? How had they come to be dumped in this holy crypt like so much refuse?—she could not answer.

Gaping skulls grinned up at them, but Anna no longer feared them. They were dead; they had fought to save their kin, their human brothers and sisters, and so they would not disturb her and Matthias now. In this way she was able to find a path through their bodies, to nudge them gently aside when necessary. Once, when she saw a knife protruding from a rib cage, she carefully pried it out and took it for herself, thanking the poor dead soul who had in this way saved it for her. You never knew when you might need another knife.

Beyond the dead soldiers they followed the light farther into the crypt, past the gravestones of the holy dead, those who were once biscops and deacons and good men and women who labored for the church, until they came to a secret corner and found there what the daimone had promised them: a staircase leading down into the earth, illuminated by the whisper of light that had led them there.

Anna felt hope swell in her heart, of itself a light against the darkness of despair and dread.

Matthias hesitated and then, not looking back, started down the stairs, testing each one carefully before he set his full weight on it. Because he still held her hand, because she feared more than anything else in the world losing him, she had to follow. Yet she looked back over her shoulder—though she could see nothing but darkness behind them—and spoke a solemn vow:

"We'll come back for you, Papa Otto, for you and all the others but especially for you."

The stairs led down a long way and all of it in darkness. They felt their way along, groping along the wall with the flats of their hands, and when at last the stairs ended and the wall curved and then straightened, a breeze caught her lips and she tasted something strange on it, something she had not tasted for many months: fresh air untainted by a city's death, and green things growing in plain good earth, not in the crevices between fallen stones.

They walked for a long while, resting a few times although never for long.

When they emerged from the tunnel, it was dawn.

They came out of a cave's mouth to see a field of oats run wild and a few buildings that looked abandoned. Behind the narrow cave mouth rose a ridge of rock and up this Matthias scrambled, Anna right behind him. From the ridge they looked back over the empty countryside to the city below, resting like a jewel on an island in the middle of the broad river. From this distance one would never guess what lay inside. It looked like a perfect toy model of a city, untouched, gently gleaming in the early morning sunlight.

"I should have killed it," said Matthias.

"Killed what?" she asked. "The Eika?" Without thinking, she clasped her Circle of Unity. She could not stop thinking about the Circle of Unity that had hung at its chest.

"The daimone," he said. "I should have killed it with the knife. Then it would have been free of the mortal body and able to go home to the heavens. Wouldn't that have been a better trade?"

Anna shook her head. "I don't think any human can kill a daimone. They aren't like us, they don't have our blood, and maybe they don't have blood at all the way we do. You would just have made it mad."

He sighed. "Maybe so. But I pity that poor soul. If it has a soul."

She hesitated, but then she asked, "Do Eika have souls?"

"Of course not!"

"But that one—it saw us, and it let us go. It wore a Circle, Matthias. If it wore a Circle, isn't it kin of ours because it also believes in God?"

"It just stole it from a body and wears it as a trophy. I don't know why it let us go. Maybe St. Kristine watched over us and blinded its eyes." He turned his back on the city and began to climb back down the hill. "Come, Anna. I don't know how far we'll have to walk before we find people."

But St. Kristine, while surely saving them, had not blinded the Eika's eyes. Anna knew that. It had seen her touch her Circle, and it had copied her movement. It *had* let them go, knowingly, deliberately. Just as every human slave in the city had conspired to set them free, which was only what they would have done for their own kin.

It was a beautiful summer's day and they walked free through bright woods and drank from free-flowing streams and ate, carefully, a few moist berries. At dusk Matthias saw a campfire. The astonished woodsmen—set here in the forest to hunt and to keep an eye out for Eika incursions—gladly traded them food for one of the extra knives, and let them sleep huddled by the coals. In the morning one woodsman escorted the children to the nearest village.

"Let me give you some advice," said the woodsman, who was small and wiry and cheerful, and who had lost one finger on his left hand. "There's little room in Steleshame these days, with all the refugees. But you've value in the news you bring, so don't sell it cheap, and you might get to stay there. Ask for an apprenticeship, lad, and something to keep your sister busy with and cared for until she's old enough to marry. Lady's Blood! It *is* a miracle. We never thought to see any other folk walk alive out of the city. How did you survive? How did you get free?"

Matthias told a brief version of the story, but when he got to the end, he didn't mention the Eika. For the Eika was not part of Matthias' story. And yet the Eika puzzled Anna most. But she kept silent. All humans hated the Eika. They had every reason to, for the Eika were savages and their dogs the most hideous creatures living.

"Your brother will no doubt find work with a tanner, child," the woodsman said to Anna. "Have you any skills?"

She did not mean to say it. It popped out unbidden. "When I'm old enough, I'll travel like the fraters do. I'll bring the Holy Word and the Circle of Unity to the Eika. They can't be meant to be savages."

He laughed, but not unkindly, only shaking his head as adults did when children said something they considered silly. Matthias shushed her and made a face.

But the day was very beautiful, and they were free, and perhaps if they brought news that slaves still lived in the city, someone—some noble lady or lord—might lead an expedition to free the others. If only Papa Otto and the rest could hold on for that long.

She thought for a long while as she walked through the woodland. She and Matthias had lost both father and mother and been given into the callous care of their uncle. Yet it was not their uncle—their only remaining kinsman— who had saved them. He had tried only to save himself and she supposed she would never know if he still walked among the living or rotted among the forgotten dead. It was Papa Otto—no blood father of theirs—and the other slaves who had saved them. If they, who were not her true kin, could act as kin, then was it not possible that even an Eika could become kin? This thought she held like a gift in her heart. Matthias had given the daimone the knife, which it could use to defend itself or free itself if such were possible, and in exchange it had given them freedom.

But in the end, after all that had happened, it was the solitary Eika who had stayed its hand and let them go.

PART ONE

DIVINATION BY THUNDER

I
THE MUSIC OF WAR

1

HE smelled the storm coming before the first rumble of thunder sounded far in the distance. The dogs stirred restlessly and nipped at him, but he slapped them aside until they whined and hunkered down at his feet.

Bloodheart appeared not to have heard the distant thunder. The Eika chieftain sat on his throne, just out of reach of his captive's chains, and measured leg and arm bones that had been scraped clean of flesh. Tossing aside those he did not want, he sawed off the knobby joint ends of the bones until he had half a dozen smooth white lengths of various sizes collected in his lap. With a sharp stick he hollowed out the bones, cleaning out the marrow. Then, using a stone burin mounted on a stick, he drilled holes down the length of the hollow bones. All this he worked in silence, except for the hasp of the ob-

31

sidian saw, the rasp of wood scraping, and his muted
grunting breaths as he twirled stick between palms to
drive the drill through.

Beyond, other sounds made a counterpoint to Bloodheart's task: The old priest crouched on the marble floor
as he tossed out finger bones into a random pattern read
and swept aside; outside, Eika soldiers played a game on
the cathedral steps which involved a head in a sack; thunder
muttered far away, and the Veser River, a low roar too
faint here for human ears to hear, sang its constant familiar chant.

The dogs, slinking away, gnawed at the discarded bones,
cracking them open for the marrow inside. The most faithful brought a few bones back to drop at his feet, his portion
as their lord. God knew he was hungry all the time now,
but never let it be said he had stooped to this: eating
human remains.

He fought back the shattering despair. It came on him
in waves as out of nowhere, out of the shadows or out of
Bloodheart's enchantment that shackled him here, bound
by more than iron. Caught in a sudden fit of uncontrollable
shaking, he clutched chains in his hands and scraped them
violently against the marble floor until his skin was rubbed
raw and the chains polished to a shining gleam but with no
least weakening of their heavy links.

Only then, when the dogs began to growl around him
sensing his weakness, when his blood dripped on the pale
marble to form little rosettes of agony against cold stone,
did he remember himself, cuff them into submission, and
look up.

Teeth bared, Bloodheart grinned down from his chair.
"Prince of dogs," he said, his voice as whispery as the flut-
ter of birds in the eaves. "Shall I make a flute out of your
bones when you are dead?"

"You will never kill me," he replied in his hoarse voice.
Some days, these were the only words he remembered how
to say.

But Bloodheart was not even listening. Instead, the Eika
chieftain lifted the smooth white tubes one by one to his
lips, testing their tone. Some breathed high, some low, and
on them, switching from one to the next, he played a rag-

ged melody while at last lightning flashed, seen through the great cathedral windows, and thunder broke overhead, and the Eika soldiers outside laughed uproariously in the sudden drenching rain and continued their game.

2

"TWO months!" King Henry paced under the awning while rain drizzled beyond the overhang, dripping down the sides of his tent, curling down tent poles in slow streams. "I have wasted two months on these damned stubborn Varren lords when we could have been marching on Gent!"

Liath had taken shelter under a wagon; with night watch ahead, she had been permitted an afternoon's nap. Thank the Lady the rain had not drenched the ground. She was still dry, and now she listened as Henry's advisers rallied around him, soothing his temper.

"You could not have left Varre behind that quickly," said his favored cleric, Sister Rosvita, in her usual calm voice. "You have done the right thing, Your Majesty, the only thing you could do. Your anger toward the Eika is justified, and when the time is right, they will suffer your wrath."

"The time will never be right!" Henry was in one of his rare sour moods. Liath could see only legs and torsos from this angle, and while any soul would have known Henry by the belt he wore embossed and painted with the badges of each of the six duchies whose princes owed allegiance to him as king regnant, on this day he was also recognizable by the sheer irritable energy he projected as he paced from one corner of the carpet to the other. "Five sieges we have laid in, in the last two months."

"None of them lasted more than five days," said Margrave Judith with disdain. "None of these Varren nobles had any stomach for a fight, knowing Lady Sabella was defeated."

"Your Majesty." Now Helmut Villam weighed in, and the others paused to listen respectfully to the words of a man whose age and experience of hard campaigns eclipsed even that of the king. "Once Lady Svanhilde surrenders to your authority, we can turn east. You have sent what Eagles you can to the Wendish dukes and nobles, to raise the alarm. But do not forget that after the battle we fought near Kassel, your forces are too weak in any case to attack the Eika at Gent. It will take time to assemble a new army."

"Damn Sabella," said Henry. "I was too lenient with her."

"She is our sister, Henry," said Biscop Constance. Though the rebuke was mild, only one of Henry's powerful younger sisters would have dared utter it.

"Half sister," muttered the king, but he had stopped pacing.

"She is safely confined under my authority in Autun, where I will soon return," added Constance, who despite her youth had the grave authority of a much older woman. He grunted, acknowledging this truth.

They began to talk about the disposition of this latest siege, invested yesterday afternoon, and what route they would take when they at last marched east through northern Arconia back into Wendar.

The rain slackened and stopped. Liath wormed out from under the wagon, strapped on sword and quiver and draped her saddle-bags over her shoulder, then went hunting for food. Rations had been scarce the past several weeks. Hard as it was to feed the king's progress, it was more difficult still in these days of summer before the harvest came in. That they marched through lands hostile toward the king did not help matters any. Although the former kingdom of Varre was by right of succession under Henry's rule, the number of recalcitrant nobles and reluctant church leaders in Varre amazed even Liath, who had long ago gotten used to being an outsider.

Yet despite the hardships, she was as content as she could be. She had food, most of the time, and such shelter as a wagon or tent awning afforded. She was *free*. For now, it was enough.

The camp sprawled in a ragged half circle around a wooden palisade, the outer ring of Lady Svanhilde's fortress. The two siege engines and three ballistas sat just out of range of an arrow's shot from the wall; hastily dug ditches protected their flanks, and a wall of mantelets shielded the men who guarded and worked the machines. On either side of the mantelets a picket of stakes stood,

protecting the camp from a charge of cavalry. The first line
of mud-streaked tents, some listing under the weight of rain
puddles caught in canvas, stood somewhat back from these
stakes, and the tents of nobles and king yet farther back,
almost into the trees. The patchwork of tents and wagons
left many gaps and wide stretches of open ground, but
Henry had been careful to avoid trampling the ripening
fields. He needed grain to feed his retinue.

Certain of the camp followers had set up stalls or brought
wares from nearby villages to sell. Indeed, the army's camp
resembled a large disorganized autumn market more than
it did any other army Liath had ever seen.

In Arethousa, a precise order of march prevailed and
every tent had its specific site rated in order of proximity
to the emperor.

In Andalla, the Kalif had his own compound made of
manteletlike frames draped with bright fabric. Only the favored few were allowed inside this compound, and the Kalif
himself from his place of seclusion ordered the generals
who led his troops into battle.

In that almost fatal passage across the deserts west of
Kartiako, so many years ago now, she remembered a silent
and deadly army whose robes were the color of sand and
who seemed to move as with the wind's speed and sudden
gusting shifts of direction. She and Da and a dozen others
were all that had survived of the one hundred souls who
had started the trek in a vast caravan. She had been so
hungry, and too young truly to understand why there had
been no food toward the end of that terrible journey.

Now she stared, caught by the enticing smell of a rack
of pig meat roasting over a fire. The robust woman tending
it looked her over.

"Any coin?" she demanded. Her accent had the broad
Varren lilt. "What do you have to trade?"

Liath shrugged and made to move on. She had nothing,
only her status as a King's Eagle.

"Here, friend." A Lion halted beside her. Ragged around
the edges of his well-worn tunic, still, he had a friendly
smile. "Don't just walk away. We serve the king, and such
as her must feed the king's servants."

The woman spit on the ground. "If I feed the king's

servants all that I have, for no return, then I'll have nothing
to feed my own kin."

"You came to take coin off of us, good woman," said
the Lion with a laugh, "so don't complain if you must feed
those of us who have no coin. We only came here because
your Varren lords rebelled against the king's authority.
Otherwise we'd not have been graced with the vision of
your beautiful face."

This was too much. She smiled at his smooth flattery,
then recalled her irritation. "It isn't *my* fault the nobles
quarrel. And it wasn't Lady Svanhilde that followed the
king's sister, it was her reckless eldest son, Lord Charles.
Poor woman. She had only boy children and loved them
too well."

"My mother had only boys," retorted the Lion, "but we
none of us gave her reason to be ashamed. Come now, give
this loyal Eagle something to eat."

Grudgingly, the woman did so, a fresh piece of pork spit-
ted on a twig. The Lion handed her a round of flat bread,
coarse flour mixed with a paste of dried berries, their usual
rations when all else was gone. It was still warm from
baking.

"Thank you," she said, not quite knowing how to respond to his kindness except to identify herself. "I'm
called Liath."

"I'm known as Thiadbold. You're the Eagle who rode in
from Gent," he added. "We remember you. Those of us
who serve the king, and who don't have noble kin—" Here
he grinned. He had a shock of red hair and part of one ear
missing, the lobe sliced cleanly off and healed now into a
white dimple. "—must watch out for each other as we may.
Will you drink with us?"

The camp of Lions, sited near the king's tent, was much
reduced. The first King Henry had commissioned ten centuries of Lions. In these days, at least five of those centuries
served in the eastern marchlands, protecting market cities
and key forts from the incursions of the barbarians. Two
Lion banners flew at this camp, marking the two centuries
who marched with the king. But even considering those
men who stood watch at this hour, Liath could not imagine
that more than sixty men out of two hundred had survived
the final battle with Lady Sabella.

"I can't," she said with some regret. She was not used to sitting and chatting in the company of soldiers—or anyone else, for that matter. Even some of the other Eagles thought her aloof and had told her so, being by nature an independent group of souls who had no reluctance to speak their minds when in the company of their own kind. "I stand watch tonight."

He nodded and let her go.

In the woods beyond she heard the bleating and lowing of livestock, kept well away from the tempting fields. Some soldiers, too, had been commandeered from those recalcitrant Varren lords who had fled home after Sabella's defeat and hoped to avoid the king's notice. These sat sullen in their own camps, watched by the king's men. A few brace of young noble lordlings and a handful of their rashest sisters had come along as well, some as hostages, some for the hope of war and booty at Gent or farther east in the marchlands. At least some of these had gear and horses but, all in all, Henry's army had lost much of its strength.

By the time she got back to the king's tent, she had licked every last spot of grease off her fingers. The king had gone to his bed and his noble companions had retired to their own tents.

Hathui handed her a skin filled with ale. "You'll want this," she said. "If we don't take this damned city by tomorrow, we'll be forced to drink water. Now I'm to bed." As the king's favored Eagle, she slept just inside the entrance to his tent, along with his other personal servants.

Liath got the night watch because she could see so well in the dark, but she also liked it because it left her alone with her thoughts. Some nights, though, her thoughts were no fit companion.

Gent.

She could not bear to think of Gent and what had happened there. Sometimes, at night, she still dreamed of the Eika dogs. It was better to remain awake at night, if she could.

With the sky overcast, she could not observe the heavens. Instead, she walked through her city of memory. Only standing alone through the night, freed from Hugh and no longer under the eye of Wolfhere, dared she risk the intense concentration it took to order her city and remember.

The city stands on a hill that is also an island. Seven walls ring the city, each one pierced by a gate. At the height, on a plateau, stands the tower.

But on this journey into the city, she crosses under the threshold of the third gate, which is surmounted by the Cup of Boundless Waters. She enters the fourth house to the left, passing under an archway of horn.

Here resides her recollection of Artemisia's Dreams, and here she walks into the first hall and enters the second chamber, first book, second chapter. Why do these dreams of the Eika dogs torment her? Do they mean something she ought to interpret, or are they just the memory of that awful last day in Gent?

But Artemisia gives her no respite, once she has read the various symbols installed in the little chamber, each one a trigger for some portion of the words written in the book.

" 'Let me tell you that if you want to make sense of your dream, it must be remembered from beginning to end, or you cannot interpret it. Only if you remember it completely, can you explore the point to which the vision leads.' "

But she never recalled beginning or end to the dreams, only the sudden madness of the dogs feeding among the pale tombs of the dead, in the darkness of the crypt at the cathedral in Gent.

Wind soughed through the trees. She shook herself and shifted. Her knees ached from standing so stiffly. Down by the siege engines several campfires burned. Figures shifted, a change of guard. She watched as a man's figure stooped, adding wood, then straightened and moved out of her sight into darkness. Drizzle started up, pattered for a little while, and gave way to a weighty night's stillness, more sticky than hot. One of the servants emerged from the tent, staggering with sleep, relieved himself, and went in again.

Slowly the clouds began to break up. Stars shone here and there through the rents, ragged patterns formed and concealed as quickly as she could recognize them. The waning crescent moon appeared in a gap, then vanished. Above, the wheel of the heavens turned and winter's sky rose—the sky seen in the late autumn and early winter evenings, here marking the advent of late summer's dawn. The first hint of light colored the tents and palisade wall a murky gray, gaining tone as, above, the faintest stars faded from view.

A man's figure moved down by the siege engines, scurrying along the wall of mantelets. One of the campfires was doused. She started forward in surprise, then saw half a dozen shadowy figures heave themselves over the mantelets and drop to the ground behind.

Raiders from the fortress.

"Hathui!" she cried, then drew her sword and dashed down the slope, shouting the alarm as she ran.

A horn sounded, and men began to yell. "To arms! To arms!"

As she ran through the foremost tents, soldiers fell in beside her or hurried before, all running to protect the front line. Below, a man screamed in pain. Swords rang, the clash of arms and the pound of blade against shield. A sudden fire bloomed at the base of the leftmost siege engine and by its unruly light she saw the skirmish unfold and spread as men leaped forward to beat down the flames while others took up blazing brands to look for their enemy—or start new fires.

Dawn grayed the horizon. As if in answer to the call to arms now ringing through camp, the gates of the fortress swung open. More than a score of mounted riders, pennants held high upon their up-raised spears, galloped through the yawning gate and drove down toward the engines.

Liath saw them coming, heard voices beyond her shout warnings, heard the shrill of horns from King Henry's camp as they blared a warning, but she had more pressing matters before her.

The raiders had put one ballista to the torch with a flaming pitch that refused to yield to water or blanket. A solitary Lion—one she didn't recognize except by his tabard—defended another ballista from three of the raiders. With torch and sword he held them at bay. Another raider lay dead, nearly decapitated, at his feet. They had not yet trapped the Lion against the ballista, but they would in a moment.

"Eagles don't fight, they witness." So Hathui always said. But he would die without her help.

She plunged in, parrying blows, and took up a position

to his left. He greeted her with a slurred "gud morn'n."
Despite the odds, she sensed he was smiling. The raiders
hesitated, faced with two where there had been one. She
shifted, feinting to attack, when the Lion changed position
beside her and his face fell within her view. His cheek had
been split by a slash; a permanent toothy grin showed
through the rivulets of blood. For an instant too long the
ghastly grin caught her eye. One of the raiders rushed her
from the left. She turned, catching his blow on her quillons,
but the weight of his charge drove her to her knees. She
strained up, locked in a test of strength as the man tried
to force her down. The injured Lion thrust his lit torch into
a second raider's face, stunning him, and then two more
Lions ran up.

One was Thiadbold. She recognized him by his red hair;
he had not had time to put on a helmet. That fast, he drove
his sword to its hilt through the abdomen of the raider who
grappled with her. They stood embraced above her, the
impaled man flushing and twitching, his sword arm pinned
to his side by the body of the man who killed him. Thiadbold had wrapped his free arm tight around his prey, holding him as he would a shield, until he was sure that all of
the fight had drained from the body. The raider's sword
fell from his limp hand. Thiadbold stepped back to let the
corpse fall, twisting his own sword free.

Liath rolled out of the way of the body, then jumped to
her feet as the two remaining raiders gave ground—but
not fast enough. Cut down, they dropped, screaming, and
lay still.

The injured Lion turned to beat again at the fire that
scorched the ballista. Blood dripped down his tabard.

"Fall back!" cried Thiadbold, his words underscored by
a heavy drumming throb, the pound of hooves and the
ominous call of a low-pitched horn. "To the camp! To
the king!"

She saw at once what the ruse had been. The raid on
the siege engines had diverted their attention from the
picket of stakes that protected the flanks of the camp. The
horsemen from the fortress pressed forward at full charge
and with spears lowered. With the stakes now uprooted or
cut down, they had a clear sweep into camp.

"We have too few to repel the charge!" cried Thiadbold. "Eagle! Fall back!"

She obeyed, and they made room for her behind them, for of all the men hacking around at the remains of the raiding force, falling back to set a position against the charge of heavy horse, she was the only one without some kind of armor.

The injured Lion had salvaged bolts from the ballista and these he handed to his fellows. "Brace with these," he shouted, his voice heavily slurred. "It's our only chance to stop the charge. Eagle!" He nodded toward her, his sliced cheek still seeping blood. "Shoot into the faces of the horses. That might hurt their charge."

Men stumbled forward through the dawning light, forming a line where once the pickets had stood. New raiders, emboldened by the defensive posture of the king's troops, set to work on the now undefended engines.

"The king!" voices shouted far behind her. "The king rides forth!"

She hunched down behind the line of Lions and men-at-arms, a few of whom held the long ballista bolts inclined forward like spears. While the others braced themselves, spear butts dug into the ground, she sheathed her sword and readied her bow. Her mind had gone still and quiet; empty. She nocked, drew, and shot, but lost sight of the arrow in the gloom. The pounding of hooves drowned her; she could not even hear the Lions next to her speaking. Beyond, the fortress lay still. No footmen or archers had followed the lord's charge out the gates. She nocked another arrow, drew—

The horsemen were upon them. She had only an instant to register their tabards, sewn with the device of a swan. The lead horseman, made bright by his shining mail and gleaming helm and the white coat of his horse, cleared them with a great leap. His fellows broke through, some of the horses jumping, some simply shattering the line with their weight. Only one horse faltered, screaming in pain as a spear caught it in the chest, and went down. A Lion dragged the rider from his horse.

She followed the charging horsemen with her nocked arrow but could not release it for fear of hitting the king's people. By now, all was chaos in the camp. The lord leading the charge had little interest in the infantry who hurried forward. His *milites* behind him, he headed for the tent that flew the king's banner: a huge red silk pennant marked with an eagle, a dragon, and a lion stitched in gold. His charge carried him through camp, scattering the disorganized troops who lay in his path.

King Henry had not waited for his lords. With a quilted jacket and steel cap he had mounted, taken up St. Perpetua's holy lance, and now, with no more than a dozen mounted riders at his back, he raced toward the fray. The king broke from a cluster of tents into the small parade that separated the high nobility from the rest of the camp. Henry drove his horse into a charge, lance lowered, and galloped forward in a headlong fury. Others, shouting, tried to divert his charge, but the king's horse was evidently possessed by the same fury that, smoldering for so long, had finally burst into full flame. These riders would feel the wrath that Sabella, as his kinswoman, had been spared.

From the opposite end of the parade, the lord and his retinue approached, also at full gallop. As they passed the last tent of the lower camp, the right leg of the lord's mount caught the guy rope, toppling the tent and throwing lord and horse to the ground with terrific force.

"Up, you!" cried Thiadbold, jerking Liath to her feet. A few men lay moaning or quiet on the ground around her. The rider, pulled from his horse, was dead.

She ran up the hill with the others.

Henry barely had time to pull up his charge as the lord's companions scattered in confusion. The king laid his lance against the man's chest. The lord's face was hidden by mail that draped down from the nasal of his gold-trimmed helmet.

"Yield!" cried the king in a voice that carried across the camp and caused a sudden stilling hand to press down on the battle. The man did not stir but, one by one, his companions were slain, disarmed, or forced to surrender.

"Liath! To me!" Liath ran over to Hathui and stood panting beside her. "Eagles don't fight," added Hathui in an undertone. "They witness. But you did well, comrade."

Henry did not move, simply sat his patient horse with the lance point pressed up under the mail, hard into the lord's vulnerable throat.

In this way he waited as his Wendish lords hurried to form up around him, the crippled Villam chief among them. Margrave Judith directed the mopup: prisoners herded into a group, horses tied up, the fires put out—although two of the ballistae had already collapsed into ashy heaps.

As the sun rose, the gates of the fortress yawned open again. A great lady, mounted on a brown mare whose trappings had as much gold and silver woven into them as a biscop's stole, rode between two deacons dressed in simple white and two holy fraters in drab brown. Her retinue, all unarmed, crowded behind her. Already a wailing had risen from the back of their ranks, keening and mourning.

Henry gestured with his free hand and his men parted to let Lady Svanhilde through his lines. She approached, was helped to dismount by one of her stewards, and knelt before the king.

"I beg you, Your Majesty," she said, her voice shaken with grief. "Let me see if my son yet lives. I beg you, grant us your mercy. This was no plan of mine. He is a rash youth, and has listened too long to the poets singing the music of war."

"You would have been better served to come before me yesterday, when first we arrived," said the king, but he withdrew his lance from the body.

Lady Svanhilde unbuckled the helm and drew it back. Her sudden gasp made clear what was not yet apparent to all. The young man was dead although no mark of war stained his body. He had died in the fall from his horse. His mother began to weep, but in a dignified way.

"This gives me no pleasure," said the king suddenly in a voice made hoarse by remembered grief. "I, too, have lost a beloved son."

She pressed a hand to her heart and stared down for a long time on the slack face of the young man. She was an old woman, frail, with thin bones. When she stood, she needed help to rise. But pride shone in her face as she regarded the king who sat above her, still mounted, his holy lance given into the care of Helmut Villam. "He followed Lady Sabella, although I counseled against it."

"And your loyalties?" demanded Biscop Constance, who had come forward now that the fighting was over.

"Your Grace." Lady Svanhilde inclined her head, showing more respect to the biscop than she had to the king. "We bow to the regnant."

Margrave Judith snorted. "Now that you are compelled to!"

"Necessity breeds hard choices," said the lady without flinching. "I will do what I am commanded, because I must."

"Let her be," said Henry suddenly. "Feed us this night, Lady Svanhilde, give us the tithe I ask for, and we will be on our way in the morning."

"What tithe is that?" Several Wendish lords gasped to hear a defeated noble question terms.

"I need men, horses, and armor to retake the city of Gent, which has fallen to the Eika. This is the tax I set upon you and all the other Varren nobles who followed Sabella. Her fight cost me much of my strength, which you and your countryfolk will return to me."

Lady Svanhilde poured the king's wine and served him with her own hands at the feast. Her children served his children, the two margraves, the biscop, and certain other high nobles whose rank demanded they be served with equal honor to the rest. Liath, standing with Hathui behind the king's chair, tried not to listen to the rumbling of her own stomach. As one of the lucky ones, she would get leftovers from the feast fed to the nobles.

As usual, Lady Tallia had pride of place beside her uncle, King Henry, but the young princess merely picked at her food, contenting herself with so little that Liath wondered how she could keep up her strength.

"As you see," said Henry to Lady Svanhilde, indicating Tallia, "Sabella's only child rides with me." He looked carefully at the three children serving at the feast. One, a girl of about twelve years of age, had a face pale from crying; as her aunt's heir, she served the king's children, Theophanu and Ekkehard. Svanhilde's two sons served the other high nobles. One was a boy of no more than eight, so nervous that a steward hovered at his elbow, helping him to set platters down without breaking them and to pour without spilling. The other was a boy somewhat older than Ekkehard, not yet at his majority. His manners were perfect and his expression grimly serious.

"These are your remaining children?" asked Henry.

Svanhilde gestured to a steward to bring more wine. "I have a son in the monastery my grandmother founded. This boy, Constantine—" She indicated the elder of the two boys. "—is to join the schola at Mainni next spring, when he turns fifteen."

"Let him join my schola instead," said the king. "Sister Rosvita supervises the young clerics and the business of the court. She would be glad to attend to his education."

"That would be a great honor," said the lady without emotion, glancing toward Lady Tallia. She, like everyone else there, understood that her son was now a hostage for her good behavior and continued support.

Hathui cleared her throat, shifting to stretch her back. "Indeed," she murmured so that only Liath could hear, "the king's schola has increased vastly in numbers in these last two months, so many young lords and ladies from Varre have come to join us. They almost make up for the lack of Princess Sapientia."

These sudden and occasional outbursts of sarcasm from Hathui never failed to surprise Liath. But since Hathui always grinned after speaking them, Liath could not be sure whether she disliked the nobles or merely found them amusing.

Liath followed the movements of young Constantine as he was brought before the king to kneel and be presented to Henry. He was even allowed to kiss the king's hand. Would she have wished for such a life? To be given into the king's schola, where she might study, write, and read all she wished—and be praised for it? If Da hadn't died—

But Da *had* died. Da had been murdered.

She touched her left shoulder, where, when she wasn't riding, she usually draped her saddlebag. She felt light, almost naked, without it, but she had to leave her gear wrapped in her cloak in the fortress stables. She hated to leave the bag anywhere, for fear someone would steal both it and, more importantly, the precious book hidden inside, but she'd had no choice. At least this time one of the Eagles had been left behind to guard all their various possessions while the others came to stand attendance on the king and remind these Varren lords of the king's magnificence and his far-reaching strength.

Lions stood here, too, ranged along the walls. She caught sight of Thiadbold, by the door that led out of the great hall to the courtyard and kitchens. He was chatting with one of his comrades.

Above the buzz of conversation she heard Margrave Judith address the king. The imposing margrave terrified Liath even though Liath was certain that Judith could not know who Liath was and had no reason to connect an anonymous Eagle with her own son. Hugh was abbot of Firsebarg now, which lay west of here in northern Varingia. He had no reason to attend the king's progress. At first, she had been afraid that Henry's progress through Varre might take them that far, but it had not because on this journey, Henry did not need to visit a place loyal to him.

"I will take my party and ride east to my marchlands," Judith was saying. "I will raise what levies I can, Your Majesty, but with the harvest coming, with winter after and then the spring sowing, it will be next summer before I can march on Gent."

"What of this marriage I've heard you speak of?" asked the king. "Will that delay you?"

She raised her eyebrows. A powerful woman of about the same age as Henry, she had borne five children, of whom three still lived, and had outlived two husbands. Unlike Lady Svanhilde, these travails had not weakened her, and she could still ride to battle, although she had sons and sons-in-law to do that for her now. Despite herself, Liath had to admire Judith's strength—and be grateful that strength wasn't turned against her.

"A young husband is always eager to prove himself on the field," she said. This statement produced guffaws and hearty good wishes, to which she replied, in a stately manner, "I see no reason he can't fight at Gent, once we reach there. But I must return to Austra to marry, and I promised I would collect my bridegroom this past spring." Her lips quirked up, and she looked rather more satisfied at the prospect than Liath thought seemly. "The delay brought on by Sabella's rebellion was unexpected. I hope his kin have not given up on me."

"It's hot in here," muttered Liath.

"And not just because of the conversation," retorted Hathui with a grin. "Go outside for a bit. You won't be needed."

Liath nodded and sidled away from the high table. Pressing back along the wall, she got caught in an eddy of servants bringing the next course, roasted pheasants arranged on platters with their feathers opened like a fan behind them. From this vantage she could hear the conversation at the nearest table, where Sister Rosvita sat with her clerics.

"I hope he's as handsome as they all say her first husband was," one woman was saying.

"Her first husband wasn't handsome, dear Sister Amabilia," said the plump young man sitting beside her. "He was heir to considerable lands and wealth because his mother outlived her sisters and gave birth to no daughters. It was the margrave's famous Alban concubine who was so handsome. Isn't that right, Sister Rosvita? You were with the court then, weren't you?"

"Let us keep our minds on Godly subjects, Brother Fortunatus." But after uttering this pious sentiment, Sister Rosvita smiled. She was famous at court for her great learning and wise counsel, and for never losing her temper. After two months with the king's progress, Liath could not help but admire her from afar—especially having heard Ivar sing her praises so often in Heart's Rest. "I can't recall his name now, but in truth, he was memorably beautiful, the kind of face one never forgets."

"High praise from you, Sister Rosvita," said the one called Amabilia. "Even if you do remember everything."

The stream of platters and pheasants passed. Liath hurried on and made it to the door.

"Thiadbold." She stopped beside the red-haired Lion. "What of the man this morning, whose cheek was cut so horribly? Will he live?"

"He'll live, though he won't be charming any of the women with his handsome face, alas for him."

"Will he still be able to serve as a Lion? What will happen to him if he can't?" She knew all too well what it meant to have neither kin nor home.

"A Lion who is unfit to serve because of a wound in battle can expect a handsome reward from the king, a plot of land in the marchcountry or fenland."

"Aren't those dangerous and difficult places to farm?"

"In some ways, but you're free of service to the lordlings who demand tithes and labor. The king only demands service from you to man the marchcountry watchforts. Even a man as scarred as poor Johannes will be can find a wife if he has a plot of land to pass on to their daughters. There's always a strong woman to be found, a younger sister, perhaps, who'd like to forge out on her own and will overlook an unsightly scar." He hesitated, then touched her, briefly, on the elbow. "But mind, Eagle, we Lions will remember that you came to his aid."

Behind them, at the table, the king rose and lifted his cup, commanding silence. "In the morning we march east, toward Wendar," the king announced. Several of the younger lords cheered, happy at the prospect of marching nearer to those lands where fighting might be expected. "But let us not rejoice in a hall of mourning. Let us remember the lesson of St. Katina."

Since St. Katina had been tormented by visions of great troubles lying in wait for her village in the same way a beast of the forest lies in wait for an innocent fawn, Liath wondered that King Henry would want to remind his retinue of her story. But this *was* her feast day, and her visions *had* proved truthful.

" 'Do not let fear draw a veil across your sight,' " said Biscop Constance.

" 'Do not forget that which troubles you.' " The king stared past his cup toward a vision only he could see. "It has been sixty-seven days since I learned of the death of—" Here he faltered. Never could he bring himself to say the name out loud. Better that he never do so, thought Liath bitterly, so as not to bring pain blooming fresh out of her own heart. "Since the Dragons fell at Gent."

Certain of the young lords in the back of the hall called out a toast to the bravery of the fabled Dragons. Some of them, no doubt, had hopes that Henry would name a new captain and form a new troop of Dragons, but he had not once spoken of such a thing in Liath's hearing. They drank, toasting the dead Dragons, but Henry only sipped at his wine.

Villam changed the subject at once, discussing the road back. They would ride southeast until they linked up with the Hellweg, the Clear Way, that began in easternmost Arconia, then cut through northwestern Fesse and from there into the heartland of Saony.

"It is too late to hope to reach Quedlinhame for Matthiasmass," the king said, "for the harvest will be over. But we may reach there in time to celebrate the Feast of St. Valentinus with my mother and sister."

Quedlinhame. Wasn't that where Ivar had been sent? Liath glanced toward Sister Rosvita, who was smiling at some comment made by Sister Amabilia. Thinking of Ivar made her think of Hanna. Where was Hanna now? How did her journey prosper, she and Wolfhere? Once Hanna had spoken of Darre as if it were a city built from a poet's song, all breath and no substance. Now Hanna would see it herself.

"Then," the king was saying, "we will swing south, to hunt."

"What are we hunting?" asked Villam.

"Troops and supplies," said King Henry grimly. "If not for this year, then for the next." The thought of Gent was never far from his mind.

3

ANNA had to walk farther into the forest than she ever had before in order to find anything to harvest. The woods nearest to Steleshame had been picked clean by the refugees from Gent. Matthias didn't like her to go out into the woods alone, especially as the border of the forest itself steadily shrank back as refugees culled what they could in berries and roots, let their livestock graze away the undergrowth, and then cut down the trees themselves for shelter and fuel.

She and Matthias had survived in Gent for a long time, all alone. Surely she could survive a few expeditions into the forest, where the worst predators were wolves and bears—if any still roamed here now that the forest had been hunted clean by the foresters who guarded the pathways against Eika scouts and who supplied Mistress Gisela and the refugees in Steleshame with fresh meat.

But there was not enough for everyone. There was never enough for everyone.

She used a stick to beat a pathway through the leaves and undergrowth. Burrs stuck to her skirts. Sharp thistles pricked her feet. She had a welt on one cheek and a tear in her shawl where it had gotten caught on a dead branch. Fearful of losing her direction, she scored a line in the trees she passed so she could follow this trail back; she and Matthias had plenty of knives, four of which they had so far traded for canvas and a steady supply of eggs. But stopping to score every third or fourth tree made slow going—and her feet hurt from stones and stickers.

Ahead, a dense thicket glistened with berries, bright red balls no bigger around than the tip of her little finger. She bit into one carefully; its sour bite made her wince, and a sharp tang burned her tongue. But she picked every last one nevertheless, dropping them into the pouch she had brought along. Maybe they were poison, but certain wise-women in the camp knew which could be eaten raw, which eaten if cooked, which could be used for dye, and which were simply useless. Scrambling through the thicket looking for more of the berries, she found the real treasure. A tree had fallen and left space and enough sun for a garden of wild onions.

She got down on hands and knees to dig them up. Matthias would be so proud of her.

When the twig snapped, old reflexes kept her still. She dared not even raise her head. Only that stillness saved her. They walked past on the other side of the thicket, and when they whispered, one to the other, she knew by the whispery flute of their voices and the harsh unintelligible words that Eika stalked these woods.

Ai, Lady. Were they hunting for Steleshame? Would they never let the refugees rest? Would they find her? She knew what they did to children.

But she kept her hands buried in the dirt, the smell of onions sharp in her nostrils, and prayed to the Lord and Lady, lips forming unspoken words. If she could only stay still, and hidden, they would pass by without seeing her. Then she could run back and warn Matthias—and all the others.

She heard the snick, like a nail flicking against a kettle, heard a hiss of air and then a sudden grunt. A howl of rage pierced the air not ten paces from her, at her back. She dared not move. She stifled a sob, grasping onions and dirt in her hands as, behind her, foresters converged on the Eika and a bitter fight ensued.

"Don't run," Matthias had always counseled her. *"If you run, they'll see you."* And anyway, if she ran, she'd probably never find this trove of onions again.

A man shrieked. Branches snapped and splintered in a wave of sound, and a heavy weight hit the ground so hard and close behind her that she felt the shudder through her knees. An arrow thunked into wood. Metal rang, meeting another blade. A man shouted a warning. Many feet crashed through the undergrowth and someone cursed.

Then came many voices raised at once, running feet, undergrowth torn and broken, and a drumming like many blows thrown down upon the earth—or on some object.

Silence.

She dared not raise her head. A thin liquid puddled by

her left hand, lapping over and wetting her little finger. It stung like the kiss of a bee. Moving her head a bare fraction, she risked a glance back over her shoulder.

An outflung hand reached for her. Eyes stared at her, and lips pulled back from sharp teeth, a mouth opened wide in a last grimace. Every part of her that was not her actual physical body bolted up and fled, screaming in terror—but her training held. She did not move, and after an instant of such terror that her stomach burned, she realized the Eika had fallen, dead, almost into her hiding place.

Farther away, she heard foresters talking.

"I only saw two."

"They scout in pairs."

"Where's their dogs?"

"Ai, Lord, have you ever seen their dogs, lad? Scout with them dogs and you tell everyone where you're passing. They never scout with their dogs, and it's just as well for us. I swear the dogs are harder to kill than the damned savages."

"What do we do with these two, now?"

"Leave them be and let the maggots and flies have them, if such creatures can even eat Eika."

Shuddering, she picked herself up, wiping her fingers clean of the greenish liquid that had oozed from the wound where an arrow had embedded itself in the Eika's throat. She had harvesting to do. The onions came up easily, but she trembled as she worked, even knowing the Eika couldn't hurt her now.

"Hey there! What's this?"

Men thrashed through the undergrowth and she glanced up to see two of them hacking at the thicket, then peering over the broken and crushed leaves, at *her*.

"Ai, I know you," said one of the foresters. "You're the child what came out of Gent early summer." He didn't ask what she was doing; he didn't need to. "God's blood, but you came close to having your throat slit, lass. You'd better get back to town." He waved his companion away. "What have you found there, child?"

"Onions," she said, suddenly afraid he would take them away from her.

But he merely nodded, pulled a colored stick from his belt, and stuck it beside the tree to mark the find. "Don't take them all, now. That's the problem with you folk, you take everything and don't leave anything to go to seed for next year. You must husband what you find, just as a farmer saves seed to sow and doesn't use it all for bread."

She stared at him, waiting for him to move off, and he sighed and stepped back. "Nay, child, I'll take nothing from you. We're better off who live out here than you poor orphans nearby the town. That Gisela, she's a cunning householder and would indenture you all if she had room for it. Go on, then."

She jumped up and scuttled away, clutching the precious onions against her. After she could no longer see the foresters, she stopped to make a fold in her skirt, laying the onions in the fold and tucking the fabric up under her belt, a makeshift pouch for her new treasure. She peered up through leaves at the sky. It was hot, if not unpleasant, but well past noontide—time to be heading back so that she would not be caught out after dark. She arranged her shawl on her back to drape over one shoulder and around the opposite hip. With a practiced backward motion she filled this sling with firewood: anything loose, dry, and not too heavy for her to carry.

Thus laden, she arrived back at camp in the late afternoon. She drew her sling of firewood over the lump in her skirt, hiding her trove of onions as she cut across the camp on her way to the tannery. Once this stretch of ground had also been woodland, harvested under the supervision of Gisela, mistress of the holding of Steleshame which sat on the rise above. Now Anna saw only stumps where there had once been scrub forest. Goats had eaten the last of the greenery except in the carefully fenced and hoarded vegetable patches. All the scattered seeds had long since been eaten by chickens and geese, and any least stick or twig had gone to cookfires. When the rains fell, mud washed every pathway into a river of filth that wound through the maze of shelters and huts.

Here, at Steleshame, many of the refugees from Gent had encamped last spring, washed up like sticks and leaves after a flood. News of so many children had excited the concern or greed of folk living west of the holding, and about a third of the orphans had been taken away to towns and villages, some to good situations, some, no doubt, to bad.

But hundreds remained behind. Most had nowhere else to go. Some refused to leave the vicinity of Gent, while others were simply too weak to attempt to walk to more distant settlements. Not even Mistress Gisela's displeasure could force them to move on.

Into this camp Anna and Matthias had wandered just after midsummer. Matthias had been lucky to trade intelligence about Gent for employment at the tanning works, which lay outside the Steleshame palisade next to the sprawling refugee encampment.

Now as late summer heat became stifling, a sickness afflicted the weakest in camp. Certain wisewomen called it a flux, a curse brought on by the enemy's swarm of malevolent helpers. Others called it a spell called down on them by the Eika enchanter, while yet others blamed the presence of malefici—evil sorcerers—hidden in their own camp. Every day a few parties of desperate souls trickled away, seeking their fortune elsewhere. Yet for every person who left, another would likely wander into the camp a day or week later telling tales of Eika atrocities in some other village within reach of the Veser River.

At the tannery, where Anna and Matthias slept in a crude shelter strung up behind the drying sheds, the sickness had not yet taken its toll. But they had cider and bread as well as eggs to eat every day, and Anna supposed the stink of the tannery drove away evil spirits.

As she scurried through camp, she prayed the pungent smell of earth and onions would not give away her secret good fortune. She was not big enough to fight off any but a smaller child, if it came to that.

"Settle down, now, children. Sit down. Sit down. My voice isn't what it used to be, alas, but if you will all be quiet, I will tell you the tale of Helen."

Anna paused despite knowing she ought to hurry right back to Matthias. With the aid of a stout walking stick, an old man shuffled forward and laboriously seated himself on a stool set down behind him by a girl. Many young children crowded 'round with gaunt faces upturned. She recognized him, just as she recognized the children: They, too, were refugees from Gent, the only ones who had escaped the

Eika attack. No older children sat here; like Matthias, they
had taken on the responsibilities of adults or been adopted
by farmers to the west. They worked the tanneries and
the armories, assisted the blacksmiths, chopped and hauled
wood, built huts, broke virgin forestland to the plow, sowed
and tended fields, and hauled water from the stream. It was
children Anna's age or younger who were set to watch over
the very smallest ones, even those toddling babies whose
nursing mothers had to spend all of their day working to
make food and shelter.

The old man had been an honored guest at the mayor's
palace in Gent; he was a poet, so he said, accustomed to
sing before nobles. Yet if this were true, why hadn't the
mayor of Gent taken him along when he had traded some
part of the wealth he had salvaged from Gent to Mistress
Gisela in exchange for her allowing him to set up
housekeeping within the palisade wall of Steleshame? The
old man had been left behind to fend for himself. Too
crippled to work, he told tales in the hope of gaining a
pittance of bread or the dregs from a cup of cider.

He cleared his throat to begin. His voice was far more
robust than his elderly frame.

" 'This is a tale of war and a woman. Fated to be an exile
not once but twice, first from her beloved Lassadaemon and
then from her second home, red-gated Ilios, she suffered
the wrath of cruel Mok, the majestic Queen of Heaven,
and labored hard under the yoke of that great Queen's
fury. High Heaven willed that she walk the long path of
adventure. But in the end she succeeded in founding her
city, and thus in time out of these tribulations grew the
high walls and noble empire of Dariya.' "

The poet hesitated, seeing his audience grow restless,
then began again—this time without the stiff cadence that
made the opening hard to follow. "Helen was heir to the
throne of Lassadaemon. She had just come into her inheritance when usurpers arrived. Ai, ruthless Mernon and his
brother Menlos marched with their terrible armies into the
peaceful land and forced poor Helen to marry that foul
chieftain, Menlos."

"Were they like the Eika?" demanded a child.

"Oh, worse! Far worse! They came out of the tribe of
Dorias, whose women consorted with the vile Bwrmen."

He coughed and surveyed the crowd, seeing that he had their attention. Anna liked the story much better told this way. "They made Helen a prisoner in her own palace while Mernon went off to conquer—well, never mind that. So Helen escaped and with her faithful servants fled to the sea, where they took ship. They set sail for Ilios, where her mother's mother's kin had settled many years before and built a fine, grand city with red gates and golden towers under the protection of bright Somorhas. But Mernon and Menlos prayed to cruel Mok, the pitiless Queen of Heaven, and since she was jealous of beautiful Somorhas, she cajoled her brother Sujandan, the God of the Sea, into sending storms to sink Helen's ship. 'How quickly night came, covering the sun! How the winds howled around them! How the waves rose and fell, first smothering the bow of the ship, then sinking so low that the very bottom of the sea was exposed!' "

Beyond the old man's shoulder Anna could see the palisade and heavy gates of Steleshame proper. The gates were always shut, even during the day. Some in the camp grumbled that it was more to keep out the refugees than to guard against an Eika attack, for everyone in camp knew that within Steleshame they ate beans and bread every day, even the servants. Now, one of the gates to this haven of plenty opened, and five riders appeared. They rode out on the southeast track, along which part of the refugee's settlement had sprawled.

The poet's story—even as the storm-tossed ship ran aground on an island filled with monsters—could not compete with such an unusual event. Anna followed the others as they ran to line the road, hoping for news.

"Where are you going?" children shouted to the riders as they passed through the camp. "Are you leaving?"

"Nay," shouted back a young woman outfitted in a boiled leather coat for armor, with a short spear braced against her stirrup and two long knives stuck in her belt. "We're riding to the stronghold of Duchess Rotrudis, down to Osterburg where it's said she holds court at Matthiasmass."

"Will she come to rescue us?" demanded several children at once.

The other riders had gone on, but the young woman lingered, eyeing the crowd of children with a frown, shaking her head all the while. "I don't know what she'll do. But we must ask for help. More Eika scouts are sighted every day. More villages are burned. Their circle is growing wider. Soon they will engulf all of us. There are too many people here already. Mistress Gisela can't support them all."

Her comrades called to her and she urged her horse forward, leaving the camp behind.

Most of the children wandered back to the old poet and told him what the rider had said.

He snorted. "As if Mistress Gisela *supports* any but her own kin and servants, and those with coin to pay for food and protection. Alas that there is no biscop here to feed the poor." Anna noticed all at once how thin he was. A film of white half-covered his left eye, and his hands had a constant small tremor.

"Who is Duchess Rotrudis?" she asked.

Trained as both listener and singer, he found her in the crowd and nodded toward her, acknowledging her question. "Rotrudis is duchess of Saony. She is the younger sister of King Henry. Alas that the Dragons fell. That was a terrible day."

"Why hasn't the king come to rescue us?" asked a boy.

"Nay, lad, you must recall that the world is a wide place and filled with danger. I have traveled over its many roads and paths. It takes months to get news from one place to another." Seeing their expressions shift from hope to fear, he hurried on. "But I have no doubt King Henry knows of the fall of Gent and mourns it."

"Then why doesn't he *come?*"

He only shrugged. "The king may be anywhere. He may be marching on his way here now. How can we know?"

"Have you ever seen the king?" Anna asked.

He was surprised and perhaps taken aback by her question. "I have not," he answered, voice shaking and cheeks flushed. "But I have sung before his son, the one who was captain of the Dragons."

"Tell us more of the story," said a child.

"Tell us something that happened to *you,* friend," said Anna suddenly, knowing she ought to return to the tannery but not quite able to tear herself away.

"Something that happened to *me,*" he murmured.

"Yes! Yes!" cried the other children.

"You don't want to hear more of the lay of Helen?"

"Did it happen to you?" asked Anna. "Were you on the ship?"

"Why, no, child," he said, half chuckling. "It happened so long ago that—"

"You were a child then?"

"Nay, child. It happened long before Daisan received the Holy Word of God and preached the truth of the Unities, bringing Light to the Darkness. It happened long, long ago, before even the old stone walls you see in Steleshame were built."

"I've never been inside Steleshame," Anna pointed out. "And if it happened so long ago, how do you know it's true?"

"Because it has been passed down from poet to poet, line for line, even written down by the ancient scribes so it would be remembered." Then he smiled softly. Amazingly, he still had most of his teeth, but perhaps a poet took better care of his mouth, knowing that his fortune rested there and in what he could recall from his mind. "But I'll tell you a story that happened to me when I was a young man. Ai, Lady! Have you ever heard of the Alfar Mountains? Can you imagine, you children, mountains that are so high that they caress the heavens? That snow lies thick upon them even on the hottest summer's day? These mountains you must cross if you wish to travel south from the kingdom of Wendar into the kingdom of Aosta. In Aosta you will find the holy city of Darre. That is where the skopos resides, she who is Mother over the Holy Church."

"If the mountains are so high," asked Anna, "then how can you get over them?"

"Hush, now," he said querulously. "Let us proceed with no more questions. There are only a few paths over the mountains. So high do these tracks rise along the rugged ground that a man can reach up and touch the stars themselves at nightfall. But every step is dangerous. No matter how clear at dawn, each day may turn into one of blinding storm—even at midsummer, for summer is the only season when one may cross the mountains.

"Yet some few attempt the crossing late in the season. Some few, as I did, try it even as late as the month of

Octumbre. My need was great—" He raised a hand, forestalling a question. "It had to do with a woman. You need ask no more than that! I was warned against attempting the crossing, but I was a rash youth. I thought I could do anything. And indeed, as I climbed, the weather held fair and I had no trouble . . ."

He leaned forward, his voice dropping to a whisper that still carried easily over the crowd. Every child hushed and leaned forward, mirroring him. "The blizzard hit without warning. It was the very middle of day, a fine day, a warm day, and between one footstep and the next I was engulfed in storm. I saw nothing but howling white wind before my eyes. The cold pierced me like a sword, and I staggered and fell to my knees.

"But I would not give up! Nay, not when *she* awaited me in distant Darre. I staggered forward, crawled when I could no longer walk, and yet the storm still raged about me. The cold blinded me, and I could not feel my feet. I stumbled, fell, and tumbled down a slope to my death."

Here he paused again. Anna edged forward, hand tight over the bulge of onions. No one spoke.

"But alas, the fall hadn't killed me. I tried to open my swollen eyes. As I groped forward, I felt grass under my hands. A stream ran not a man's length from my body, and there I crawled and drank my fill of its clear water. I splashed it on my face and slowly I could see again. Above me, beyond the steep slope down which I had fallen, the storm still raged. A few flakes of snow drifted down on the breeze to wet my face. But in the vale it was as warm as springtime, with violets, and trees in bloom."

"Where were you?" Anna demanded, unable to keep still.

But now memory made him look down. His old shoulders hunched, and he sighed heavily, as if sorry to have remembered this tale. "I never knew. Truly, it was a miracle I did not die that day. There was a ring of trees, mostly birch, and a little grassy meadow, but beyond that I never managed to go. A hut stood at the edge of the meadow. There I slept and recovered my strength. Every morning I would find food and drink outside the door, sweet bread, strong cider, a stew of beans, tart apples. But no matter how I tried to stay awake, I never could. I never saw what creature brought me the food. When I was strong enough, I knew it was time to leave, so I went."

"Didn't you ever find it again?" asked Anna. Other children nodded their heads, marveling at the thought of an enchanted place where food appeared miraculously each morning.

"Nay, though I traveled three times more over that pass. I searched, but the way was closed to me. Now I wonder sometimes if it was only a dream."

"Could we take him in?" she demanded at dusk as she and Matthias feasted privately on onion stew and roasted eggs. "He's just a frail old man. He can't eat much, and he hasn't anyone else to take care of him. There's room for him to sleep here." With the flap pulled down snug to protect them from wind and rain, their little lean-to did indeed have room for one more to sleep—just barely.

"But what good would he be to us, Anna?" Matthias had gulped down his portion more like a dog than a boy, eating the egg first and the stew after. Now he wiped the sides of the blackened pot clean with a dry hunk of bread he'd saved from his midday meal.

"We weren't any good to Papa Otto!" she retorted. "Oh, Matthias, he knows the most wonderful stories."

"But they're not true." Matthias licked the last crumbs off his lips and eyed the old pot with longing, wishing for more. Then he took Anna by the wrist and shook her. "They're just tales he made up. He as good as admitted it was a dream—if the whole thing even happened at all! That's how storytellers make their stories sound true, by pretending it happened to them." He shook his head, grimacing, and let her go. "But you may as well bring the old man here to us, if he's no other place to sleep. It's true enough that Papa Otto and the other slaves in Gent helped us for no return. We should help others as we can. And anyway, if you have him to care for, maybe you won't go wandering out into the woods and get yourself slaughtered by Eika!"

She frowned. "How do you know his stories aren't true? You never saw such things or traveled so far."

"Mountains high enough that their peaks touch the sky! Snow all the year round! Do you believe that?"

"Why shouldn't I believe? All we've ever seen is Gent—and now Steleshame and a bit of forest." She licked the last spot of egg from her lips. "I bet there's all kinds of strange places just as fantastic as the stories the poet tells. You'll see. I'll bring him here tomorrow. I bet he's been to places no one here has ever heard of. Poets have to do that, don't they? Maybe he knows what the Eika lands look like. Maybe he's seen the sea that Helen sailed across. Maybe he's really traveled across the great mountains!"

Matthias only snorted and, as the last daylight faded, rolled up in his blanket. Exhausted by his day's labor hauling ashes and water and lime, he quickly fell asleep.

Anna snuggled up against him, but she could not go to sleep as easily. Instead, she closed her eyes and dreamed of the wide world, of a place far from the filth of the camp and the lurking shadows of the Eika.

II
IN THE
SHADOW OF
THE MOUNTAINS

1

THE hawk spiraled far above, a speck against the three mountain peaks that dominated the view. It sank, then caught an updraft and rose, wings outstretched, into the depthless blue of the sky. Here, where human paths arched closest to the vast and impenetrable mystery of the heavens, Hanna could believe that anything was possible. She could believe that the distant bird, hovering high overhead, was no hawk at all but a man or woman wearing a bird's shape—or else that it was a spirit, an angel disguised in plain feathers, surveying earth from the heights.

Or perhaps it was only a hawk, hunting for its supper.

A thin crest of breeze touched her ears, and she thought she heard the bird's harsh call; its slow spiral did not alter. As she waited, the heavens shaded from the vivid blue of afternoon into the intense blue-gray of impending twilight. Shadow crept up the stark white peaks as the sun sank in the western sky.

Where had Wolfhere gone, and why was he taking so long to return?

The path wound farther up into heather and gorse, side-tracked by heaps of sharp boulders and the high shoulder of a cliff face. Beyond, the dirt track lost itself in a narrow defile. Wolfhere had bade her wait here while he walked on ahead, disappearing through the narrow gate of stone and crumbling cliff into the vale that lay beyond. Through the gap Hanna saw the rippling tops of trees, suggesting a cleft of land that ran lush with spring-fed plants. She had seen other such valleys in these mountains, sudden gorges and startlingly green vales half hidden by the jagged land-scape. Beneath the scent of gorse she smelled cookfires and a distant whiff of the forge.

Why had Wolfhere wanted her to accompany him this far, and no farther?

"Stay here and watch," he had said. "But on no account follow me and let no other follow me."

What was he hiding? What *other* did he expect to follow them up here, on this goat track he called a path? She turned to look back the way they had come. At first she thought they *had* been following a goat track along the heights towering above the ancient paved road that marked St. Barnaria Pass. But no goat's track sported a thin trail of wagon wheels, although how a wagon could possibly be dragged up here was more than she could imagine.

It was very strange.

A few steps back, an outcropping gave her a good view down onto the pass below. The road had been built during the old Dariyan Empire by their astoundingly clever engi-neers. In the hundreds of years since then, not even winter storms had washed it away, although many of its stones were cracked or upturned by the weight of snow, the thaw-ing power of ice, or the simple strength of obstinate grass. Its resilience astonished her.

The hawk wafted lazily above. She blinked back tears as

her gaze caught the edge of the sinking sun. Specks swam before her eyes; then she realized that two more birds had joined the first.

Her neck hurt from staring upward for so long, but in her seventeen or so years of life she had never imagined there might be a place like *this*. She knew the sea and the marsh, rivers and hills and the dark mat of forest. She had now seen the king's court and the glittering parade of nobles on his progress. She had seen the Eika raiders and their fearsome dogs so close she could have spit on them.

But to see such mountains as these! The peaks were themselves presences, towering creatures hunched in sleep, their shoulders and bowed heads covered by drifts of snow deeper than anything Hanna had ever seen. Last winter she would have laughed at any poor soul foolish enough to suggest that she, Hanna, daughter of the innkeepers Birta and Hansal, would herself journey across those mountains wearing the badge of an Eagle. Last winter her mother and father had arranged for her betrothal to young Johan, freeholder and farmer, a man of simple tastes and no curiosity, his gaze fixed on the earth.

Now, as summer flowers bloomed alongside the high mountain pass, she—mercifully *un*betrothed—was on her way south across the Alfar Mountains, an agent of the king on an important errand to the skopos herself. Truly, her life had taken a sudden and surprising turn. How distant Heart's Rest seemed now!

From the outcropping she could see down to the road and, farther back, partially hidden by the thrusting shoulder of a ridge, the hostel where their party had halted for the night. The stone buildings nestled into the ridge's spine. Under the protection of the skopos, the hostel was run by monks from the Order of St. Servitius. According to Wolfhere, those monks stayed up in these inhospitable heights through the winter. A merchant in their party had been snowed in one terrible winter, or so he claimed, and he had regaled the party with a horrific story of fire salamanders, cannibalism, and avenging spirits. The story sounded so true when he told it, but Wolfhere had stood in the shadows of the campfire that night, shaking his head and frowning.

She had seen heaps of snow in shadowed verges beside

the road and huge fields of ice and snow on the slopes above, giving credence to the tale, but she had also seen flowers aplenty, pale blue, butter yellow, scarlet and orange, scattered across tough grass and ground-clinging shrubs. She had seen sky so deep a blue that it shaded into violet as if brushed with a stain of beet juice. She laughed at herself. Their party included a bard journeying to Darre to make his fortune, and he never used such prosaic images as beet juice to describe the sky.

No one traveled the mountains alone, not even King's Eagles. They had found a party assembling in the city of Genevie and joined it. Now they counted among their companions the bard, seven fraters, a high and mighty presbyter returning to the skopos with an important cartulary and his train of clerics and servants, and a motley assortment of merchants, wagons, and slaves—and the two prisoners she and Wolfhere and ten of King Henry's Lions escorted to the palace of the skopos in Darre.

A breeze skirled down from the heights, and the sun slid behind a low-lying ridge. The moon's pale disk gleamed softly against the darkening sky. Dusk. She shuddered.

Where was Wolfhere? How was she to make her way back down that path in darkness? What if he had fallen and hurt himself?

A bird called. She had a sudden, awful feeling of being watched.

She spun and *there,* perched on a stub of rock jutting out from the cliffside that demarked one side of the narrow defile, sat a hawk. She let out a nervous chuckle and fanned herself, abruptly flushed though the day was cooling fast. The hawk did not stir. Uncanny, with eyes as dark as amber, it stared unblinking at her until she felt chills run up her back.

And there was something else . . . a suggestion of something hovering just where the path dipped out of sight. Something there and yet not there, a figure glimpsed out of the corner of her eye, a pale woman creature whose skin had the color and texture of water. But when she looked directly, she saw nothing, only shadows sliding along the rock like the ripple of water over pebbles in a stream.

The hawk launched itself up in a flurry of wings. She

ducked instinctively and heard a gasp. Was it her own or someone else's, someone hidden?

The hawk was gone. A light bobbed into view. Wolfhere, whistling, came up the path around the shoulder of the cliff face.

"Lady Above!" she swore. "I thought you weren't coming back."

He stopped and looked around, then cocked an eyebrow and resumed walking past her and down the path toward the hostel. To keep in the light she had to hurry after; the moon was not yet half full and did not give enough illumination for her to negotiate the hillside track.

"Where did you get that lantern?" she demanded, angry that she had waited for so long but would evidently get no explanation.

"Ah," he said, hoisting the lantern a little higher.

He did not intend to answer her. Fuming, she followed him down the path, stumbling now and again over a rock or a thick tuft of grass grown untimely in the middle of the track. By now the hostel appeared below them only as a dark encrustation against the blacker ridge; a single lantern burned at the enclosure's gateway. So did a light burn all night, every night, a beacon for any lost traveler caught out and struggling toward safe haven just as after the body's death the soul struggles upward to the Chamber of Light— or so the bard had said, thinking it a poetical conceit.

"Where did you go?" Hanna asked, not expecting an answer. Wolfhere gave her none. She watched his back, his confident walk, the gray-silver gleam of his hair in the twilight, his ancient, seamed hand steady on the lantern's handle.

Hanna did not distrust Wolfhere, but neither did she precisely trust him. He kept his secrets close by him, for secrets he clearly had. Starting with the one he had never answered: How had he come so fortuitously this past spring to the inn at Heart's Rest just in time to save her dear friend Liath from slavery? He had freed Liath and taken her away from the village, made her a King's Eagle like himself. Like a leaf drawn in the wake of a boat, Hanna had been dragged along also. She, too, had been made a King's Eagle, had left the village of her birth to begin these great adventures. Wolfhere was not a man of whom one

asked questions lightly, but Hanna was determined to see
Liath remain safe. So she had asked questions, which was
more than Liath was willing to do. How had he known
Liath was in Heart's Rest and in danger? From what was
he protecting her? Wolfhere had never taken offense at
those questions; of course, he had never answered them
either.

They left the narrow defile and mysterious valley behind
and, soon enough, the hillside path deposited them on the
smooth stone of the old Dariyan road a few hundred paces
from the enclosure's gateway. Stars bloomed above, a sudden harvest of bright flowers; ahead, a lantern flared as it
swung back and forth in the breeze.

On a bench beside the gateway sat a monk, brown-robed,
hooded, and silent. The lantern hung from a post, illuminating
him in a pool of soft light. He lifted a weather-roughened
hand at their approach and without speaking opened the
gate to let them in. Because she was a woman and thus
could not be admitted to the innermost cloister, she had
seen few of the monks. Of those, only the genial cellarer—
the monk in charge of provisions—and the guest-master
seemed willing, or permitted, to speak to visitors. Many
monks and nuns took a vow of silence, of course. The
brothers at Sheep's Head were rumored never to speak at
all once they had passed out of the novitiate, communicating only with hand signs.

Wolfhere opened his lantern and blew out its flame. Together, they trudged in pale moonlight past the ripe-smelling
dung heap. A fence scraped her thigh and she smelled the
rich tang of plants as they walked alongside the garden.
Beyond this enclosure stood half a dozen squat beehives.
Finally, they came in among the outbuildings: stables,
kitchen, bakery, kiln, and forge—dark and empty at this
hour except for a single form sitting beside the dull red
coals, tending the fire. The hostel of the monks of St. Servitius was famous, Wolfhere had told her, not just because
some of them lived here the winter through, despite snow
and ice and bitter cold, but also because they kept a
blacksmith.

As they came up to the guest house, a young monk,
unhooded, hurried out the door and away to the right,
toward the infirmary. His reddish-pale hair and coltish gait

reminded Hanna abruptly and painfully of her milk brother Ivar.

Was he well? Had he forgiven her for choosing to stay with Liath rather than go with him?

Wolfhere sighed suddenly and squared his shoulders. Shaken out of her thoughts, Hanna heard shrill voices from the entryway. They mounted the wood steps into the entry chamber, now lit by four candles, and right into the middle of an argument.

2

"THIS guest house is reserved," said a sallow man Hanna immediately identified as the insufferable manservant to the presbyter, "for those who arrive on horseback. It is quite impossible that these common soldiers be stationed here."

"But the prisoners—" This objection, raised by the inoffensive guest-master, was quelled at once by the presbyter himself, who now stepped out of the shadows.

"I will not let my rest be disturbed by their shuffling and muttering," said the presbyter, his Wendish marred by a thick accent. He had a thin, aristocratic voice, fully as imperious as that of the nobles she had observed during her weeks attending King Henry's progress. But of course he, too, was a man of noble birth; with a perpetually curled-down lip, soft, white hands, and the imposingly portly demeanor of a man who feasts more days than not, one could never have mistaken him for a farmer or a hard-working craftsman. "The two guards who are standing watch over the prisoners must be moved. If that means the prisoners must be moved, so be it."

Wolfhere responded blandly. "Are you suggesting Biscop Antonia and Brother Heribert be quartered in the stables with the servants?"

The presbyter's eyes flared, and he looked mightily irritated, as if he suspected Wolfhere of baiting him. "I am suggesting, Eagle, that you and those you are responsible for do not disturb my rest."

"Your rest is of supreme importance to me, Your Honor," said Wolfhere with no apparent irony, "but I swore to King Henry of Wendar and Varre that I would deliver Biscop Antonia and her cleric to the palace of the skopos, Her Holiness Clementia. This building—" he gestured to stone walls and tight shutters—"grants me a measure of security. You know, of course, that Biscop Antonia is accused of sorcery and might be capable of any foul act."

The presbyter grunted. "All the more reason to remove her from this guest house." He signed to his manservant, turned with a swirl of rich fabric, and climbed the steps into the gloom above where another servant waited to light him to his chamber.

Wolfhere turned to the guest-master. "My apologies for inconveniencing you again, good brother. Have you any other chamber that might serve our purpose?"

The guest-master glanced at the presbyter's manservant, who sniffed audibly, steepled his fingers, and tapped his thumbs together impatiently. "At times it happens that a brother or traveler is disturbed by evil spirits who have insinuated themselves into his mind, and at those times we must isolate him in a locked chamber in the infirmary until an effusion of herbs or a healing can extricate the creature from his body. It is not what I would choose for a biscop, even one accused of such, um, undertakings, but—" He hesitated, perhaps fearing that Wolfhere's reaction would be as explosive as that of the presbyter, but in the end he glanced again toward the manservant. Worse to insult a presbyter than one of King Henry's Eagles, especially considering—Hanna reminded herself—that they were not in Henry's kingdom now.

"That will do very well," said Wolfhere easily. "But will it inconvenience the Brother Infirmarian?"

"I think not. At this time we have only one aged brother resting there who is too feeble for our daily rounds."

"Hanna." Wolfhere nodded at her. "Go fetch the other Lions. Once the Brother Infirmarian has made all ready, we will transfer the prisoners to their new cell."

Satisfied, the manservant hurried up the stairs to deliver this news to his master. The guest-master grimaced, then quickly smoothed the expression over as he retreated out the door. Hanna moved to follow him, but Wolfhere said her name softly. She turned to see him open the lantern's glass shutter and reach inside. He murmured a word under his breath, and the touch of his fingers to the dark wick ignited a flame. She started back, surprised, but he merely handed the lit lantern to her and waved her away. Outside, Hanna hoisted the lantern to light her way to the stables.

The guardsmen had already bedded down for the night on the straw in the loft, wrapped in their cloaks. They rousted easily enough. King's Lions all, they were used to night alarms and swift risings for an early march, and they followed her back to the guest house without grumbling. They served the king and did not complain at the tasks given them. Such was the strength of the oaths they had sworn to Henry.

At Hanna's entrance, the guest-master nervously shook his ring of keys and led the way into the back passage where two Lions stood guard at a locked door. Inside the chamber, Biscop Antonia sat, wide awake, in the room's only chair while Brother Heribert sat on the edge of one of the two beds, fingering the silver Circle of Unity that hung on a chain at his chest. A carpet, thrown down as a courtesy, covered the plank floor; the windows were closed and shuttered, barred from the outside.

"Your Grace," said Wolfhere. "I beg pardon for disturbing you, but it has become necessary to move you to different quarters."

A stout woman of respectable age, Biscop Antonia wore her episcopal dignity with gentle authority and a benign expression. "No unbearable hardship afflicts the faithful," she said mildly, "for is it not said in the Holy Verses that 'thy daughters and sons did not succumb to the fangs of snakes?' "

Wolfhere did not reply but merely signed for her and the cleric to precede him out the door. Heribert rose and went out first. A quiet, attractive, neat young man, he had the soft, delicate white hands of an aristocrat born, one who had never put those hands to labor more taxing than prayer, the folding of vestments, and the occasional writing of a deed or royal capitulary. All the monks here in the hostel of St. Servitius had, like Hanna, work-roughened hands, but Heribert was a cleric whose duties were to pray, read, and act as scribe in the episcopal chancellery or the king's chapel. With her hands folded quietly in front of her, Antonia followed after him, smiling and nodding first at Wolfhere and then at Hanna.

The single mild glance she gave Hanna made the young Eagle horribly uncomfortable. Biscop Antonia appeared as kindly and wise as an old grandmother who had lived her life in perfect harmony with the God of the Unities and been blessed with a prosperous family and many surviving grandchildren. But she was accused of base sorcery, such as even the church could not countenance, and Hanna herself had heard the biscop speak words of such searing contempt at the parley before the battle between King Henry and his sister Sabella that she knew Antonia's kindly mien disguised something dark and unpleasant beneath.

Better not to be noticed by such folk. Or, as the saying went in Heart's Rest, "Let well enough alone and turn over no rock unless you care to be knowing what's underneath it."

But after one glance, Antonia no longer appeared to notice Hanna. As the guards escorted them out of the building and down the stony path to the infirmary, she kept up a one-sided conversation with Wolfhere. "I have been reflecting on the words of St. Thecla, in her *Letter to the Dariyans,* when she speaks of the law of sin. Is not God's law higher than the law of sin?"

Wolfhere grunted. His lips twitched as if he were restraining words. He turned so that the lantern light hid his expression in shadow.

"And yet do we not, in our ignorance, in our flesh, remain slaves to the law of sin?" she continued. "By what means do they judge who have not wholly united themselves to the life-giving law of the God of the Unities and the Holy Word?"

Wolfhere made no answer. They came to the infirmary steps. Here the Brother Infirmarian met them, lantern in hand, and showed them to a small cell where he had hastily erected a cot next to the single pallet. He bowed several times, bobbing up and down so that the lantern light rose and dipped nauseatingly; he was clearly distraught at the idea of closing a holy biscop into such mean quarters, but he obeyed the commands of his superiors—and Wolfhere carried letters from both King Henry and Biscop Constance as proof of his authority to carry out his mission.

Antonia and Heribert walked into the cell. The Brother Infirmarian shut and locked the door behind them and hung the key on a ring at his belt. Two Lions stationed themselves on either side of the door. Wolfhere directed two more Lions to sleep outside on the ground beneath the shuttered and barred window that let air into the cell.

"On no account," Wolfhere finished, looking sternly at

the Infirmarian, "is any person to enter into that cell without me beside him."

Then he and Hanna and the other six Lions returned to the stables. In the loft, Hanna kicked hay into a pile, threw her cloak over the prickly mound, and pulled off her boots before lying down and shaking her blanket open on top of herself. Wolfhere bedded down in the hay beside her. Already she heard the snores of the soldiers from the other end of the loft.

She waited for a long while but was not sleepy. The loft door stood open to let in air. Through it she saw the black hulk of mountain, a blot against the night, and a single patch of sky brilliant with stars.

"You don't like her," she whispered finally, thinking that Wolfhere, too, did not sleep.

There was a long pause and she began to think the old man was in fact asleep, that she had mistaken his breathing.

"I do not."

"But if I didn't know what she had been accused of, if I hadn't heard her speak that one time, at the parley with Lord Villam, then I would never suspect she was—" She hesitated. Wolfhere made no comment, so she went on. "It's just hard to imagine she could do such terrible things—murder a lackwit in cold blood so she could raise creatures to control Count Lavastine's will, cast a spell on the *guivre* to put it under her power, *and* send her servants to catch living men for it to feed on. It's just that she seems . . . such a good and generous soul, so mild and compassionate. And she is a biscop besides. How can the Lady and Lord allow a person with such an evil heart to be elevated in Their church?"

"That is indeed a mystery."

This answer did not satisfy Hanna, who frowned and shifted on her makeshift pallet. Under the cloak, hay poked through the cloth against her back, tiny blunt pinpricks. She wiped the dust of old hay and last summer's straw from her dry lips. "But you must have *some* idea!"

"She is related on her mother's side to the reigning Queen of Karonne, and her kin on her father's side had land near the city of Mainni, where she was some years ago elevated to the episcopal chair. Do you suppose the skopos nominates only the most worthy?"

"I thought women and men who entered the church entered to serve God, not their own desires and ambitions. Deacon Fortensia cares faithfully for our small village though she herself resides a half day's walk farther north, at the church of St. Sirri. The monks at the monastery at Sheep's Head are—*were*—" For had not Eika killed them all? "—famed for their devotion to Our Lady and Lord."

"Some do enter the church to serve God, and do so faithfully throughout their lives. Some see in the church an opportunity for advancement. Others are put in the church against their will."

As Ivar had been.

"Are all who serve in the church faithful to God alone?" Wolfhere continued. "What of Frater Hugh? You were acquainted with him, I believe."

Hanna shut her eyes and turned her face away, ashamed to remember so clearly and with still a betraying warmth in her throat. Only Wolfhere's unheralded arrival had saved Liath from a lifetime of servitude to Hugh. Beautiful Hugh.

Wolfhere grunted, but he might simply have been settling himself more comfortably on the hay. He said nothing more and for once she did not want to ask any more questions. He had an odd, perhaps a deliberate, way of turning questions back on the one who asked them. She set her cheek against the folds of her cloak and shut her eyes. The light snores of the men-at-arms, the rustling of mice scurrying on their nightly rounds, and the quiet noises of the horses stabled below lulled her to sleep.

3

THE rats came out at night to gnaw on the bones. The whispering scrape of their claws on stone alerted him, brought him instantly out of his doze. Most of the dogs slept; one whined in a dream and thumped his whipcord tail against the cathedral floor. The Eika slept, sprawled across the stone as if it were the softest of featherbeds to them. They loved the stone the way a nursing child loves its mother's breast, and nuzzled near it whenever they could.

Only *he* did not sleep. He never slept, only napped, caught moments of dream and then bolted awake as a muzzle nudged him, testing, or as Eika laughed and poked him with their spears, or if he heard a human voice cry out in agony and hopeless pleading. That was the worst, the slaves—for he knew the Eika had brought human slaves into the city when summer came and that he could do nothing to help those poor souls.

Gent had fallen, and he would have died protecting her, only he could not die. That was the curse his mother had put on him at his birth: *"No disease known to you will touch him, nor will any wound inflicted by any creature male or female cause his death."*

He could not sleep, and when he was lucid, he wondered if the periods of madness, the shaking, the fits of insensibility when he would come to suddenly and realize it was night when last it had been dawn, were a mercy set on him by the Hand of Our Lady. An educated man might have known disciplines of the mind with which to combat this prison that was as much of spirit as of chains. But he had only been trained for war. That was his lot, the bastard son of the king, the child whose birth gave Henry the right to be named Heir to the throne of Wendar and Varre: to become a fighter and defend his father's realm.

He had always been an obedient son.

Would his father send soldiers to rescue him? Yet surely Henry thought him dead. It was *Gent* they must rescue. No king could leave such an important city in barbarian hands.

And even if he were rescued, what if his father no longer wished to acknowledge him, seeing what manner of creature he had become?

He vaguely recalled a dream in which two children had visited him—except there were no children in Gent, not any more. *She* had led them to safety, long ago.

Once children had flocked to him, but these two children had been afraid of him. They had seen not a prince but an animal; he had seen their reaction in their eyes. Were they only mirrors created in his mind? A vision through which he could see himself and what he had become? Or had they really been here?

As rats scurried through the refuse, he searched under the rags that were all that was left of his clothing—and found knife and badge. *Their* knife. *Her* badge, the badge of the Eagles. Only it was not her badge, it was another badge, that of a man who had fallen and whose name he could not recall. But it represented her, it held her warmth, for she had been like a warm thing, like a star fallen to earth and trapped in a human body as he was trapped in these chains.

The rats scrabbled among the bones. Slowly, he eased the knife out from under his torn and ragged tunic. This knife had been a gift, of sorts, an exchange—though he would have told the children the secret of the saint's tunnel without any gift. He would have told them because it was his duty to aid them, to aid all of the king's subjects. He was captain of the King's Dragons and obliged by his oath to the king, his father, to protect and defend the king's possessions and everything and everyone that the king ruled.

Rats were not subject to the king.

The bones lay within reach of his chains, and he was quick and silent but for the scrape of chains as he moved, sticking one on the point, grabbing another by the tail. It squeaked wildly and scrabbled helplessly at his fingers. He killed them. The dogs stirred, waking. The Eika slept on.

He growled the dogs down, and they subsided. They fed better than he did, because they did not scorn human flesh. He skinned the rats and, because he had no fire, ate them raw.

No better than the Eika, less than a man, more than a

dog, he would have wept at his own savagery, but he had no tears. He never got enough to drink. Sometimes the priest remembered to set out water for him. Once a slave had done so, and been killed for her pains.

The Eika slept on. He sawed at the chains with the knife, but the work only dulled the blade. At last, he tucked it away again and curled up among his chains. The iron collar at his neck chafed his skin, and he shifted to ease the raw ache. The Eagle's badge lay cool against his skin, next to his heart.

Ai, Lady, if only he could sleep for one night, soundlessly and without dreaming, without interruption. If only he could rest. But the dogs panted, wakeful now, smelling death.

4

AWAKE.

Something was wrong. Hanna knew it instantly, but it took her three breaths to identify what it was. A cold hard wind blew into the loft, scattering hay and chilling her limbs, and a soft cold *thing* settled on her lips. Without thinking, she licked it. *Snow.*

More snow settled on her face, blown in from outside as the wind rose and moaned in the beams. The unlatched loft door banged incessantly. A dog barked. Distantly she heard voices shouting an alarm, and then the wind gusted so hard it shook the very timbers of the stables and jarred the Lions awake.

She rolled up onto her hands and knees, groping in the blackness for her boots. She found Wolfhere's blanket with her hand.

He was gone.

A bell began to toll, a dull reverberating sound that shook through her. It seemed to call in a thick oppressive voice: *Fire! Storm! Attack! Awake! Awake!*

She got hold of her boots and tugged them on, then crawled, found the trapdoor and the ladder by touch, and eased herself over and climbed down. Above, one of the soldiers called to her, but the wind howled and screamed at such a pitch outside that she couldn't make out his words. She found the floor and stood, clutching the ladder, trying to get her bearings. The horses had gone wild with fear; the voice of the monk in charge of the stables was a murmur running beneath the roar of the storm as he attempted, in vain, to calm them. The bell tolled on and on as if for a hundred newly dead souls being rung up through the seven spheres of Heaven to the Chamber of Light above.

"Hanna."

She jerked around but could not see Wolfhere, for it was utterly black inside.

"I'm at the door," he said.

Gingerly, she crossed to him. Bitter cold air streamed in through the cracks in the plank door. With each gust the door shuddered and shook and even, once, bent inward as if the wind were trying to break it down. Wolfhere had to lean hard against the door to keep it closed. Upstairs the loft door stopped banging abruptly.

A heavy object slammed against the stable door. Wood ripped and splintered, but the door did not give way, though she felt Wolfhere press farther into the door to hold it shut. Then, like the whisper of mice in the walls, she heard a voice from outside.

"Please. I beg you, if any are inside, let me enter." It was the guest-master.

At once Wolfhere unlatched the door. Wind blew the door open. It smashed into Hanna, a haze of pain all along her right side, and as she stumbled back, it slammed all the way open and hit the inner wall so hard the top hinge tore free. A hooded figure staggered in, propelled by the tearing wind.

No *wind,* this. No *storm* either, not as she knew storms. Half stunned, Hanna stared in disbelief. Outside she could not even see the shadows of the other outbuildings or the cloister. She could see neither sky nor moon. The world was a ghastly gray-white. They stood isolated in the middle of a howling blizzard.

She could no longer hear the bell.

Snow spun into the stables, blasting her face. Within, in the darkness of the stables, a horse broke free. She heard the swearing of the stablekeeper as he fought the animal back to its stall.

"Hanna!" Wolfhere had to shout to be heard above the gale. "Help me!" They grasped the shattered door and together yanked it back to the broken hinge to shove it closed against the cold hand of the wind. Despite the cold, she was sweating with fear and exertion. Her hand slipped on the weathered wood, and a splinter jabbed in just as Wolfhere grunted and put the pin through the latch.

"I can't risk light," he said, turning. "A broken lantern in this storm would burn this place down around us."

The guest-master had crumpled to the floor, and now Hanna could faintly discern his shape, made manifest more

by the thin coating of snow on his robe and hood than by
his own substance. He was muttering a prayer in Dariyan,
the language of the church. She could not follow the words.
He sounded half delirious, like a man raving with fever.

A man cursed above; one of the soldiers, a bulky shadow
in armor, came down the ladder, swearing with such a foul
string of curses that it took her a few shocked moments
before she realized he was not angry but terrified.

"Did you see them?" he demanded as he thudded into
the ground. Outside wind screamed, and hail peppered the
walls like pebbles flung in volleys; the stables, the very
wood structure of them, groaned under the onslaught.

"*Things,*" said the guest-master in a terrified voice as the
wind battered at the stables and hail pounded on the roof
and walls. "Ai, Merciful Lady protect us from such visions.
Protect us from such creatures. Such creatures as must be
conceived in feculence and expelled from their dam's soiled
flesh in base darkness. So came they down from the moun-
tainside. So fell they down upon the wind. And such a stink
they had to them that the hair on the back of my neck
stood on end and my body shook with terror and the guests
came rushing out of their chambers all crying and sobbing
and one indeed could only babble like a child and he
glowed as if he had been lit afire."

"Brother, take hold of yourself," said Wolfhere sternly.
"Tell me what you saw."

"I have told you! They were living beings and yet like
no creature I have ever seen. They had no limbs but only
a thick dark body like an incorporeal staff as thick around
as my own poor flesh. They sang in dire voices but in a
language most foul-sounding if it was language at all. The
wind bore them down from the mountain and the storm
came with them as if they had raised it out of the air or
from corrupt magics, for it is like no storm I have ever
seen and I have lived here at this hostel for almost twenty
years and served God in Unity faithfully, so help me. Ai,
Lord in Heaven. That this terrible sight had never been
given me for I have not the strength. . . ."

"Hush," said Wolfhere. He shifted. "Lion. Watch over
this good brother. Hanna. Dare you walk outside with
me?"

Her shoulder and hip throbbed from the pain of being

struck by the windblown door. Shifting to her right leg brought stabs of pain bad enough to make her wince.

"Hanna?"

"I can go," she said.

First Wolfhere found rope hanging on the wall, which he tied round his waist and then, by touch, round hers. The Lion braced himself against the door as Wolfhere unlatched it, but even so, the wind flung the soldier backward, and he skidded back, dragging his heels against the dirt floor. Wolfhere tugged Hanna after him. Together they forged out into the blizzard.

They staggered under the press of wind. Not six steps out Wolfhere began shouting at her, though she could scarcely hear him over the roar of the wind. She looked behind. She could not see the stables; night and storm buried them in darkness. Panic gripped her. She could not breathe. Her hands curled tight, so cold so fast she could no longer feel them.

Wind struck. She had to lean, hunched over, in order not to be thrown down by the force of wind and snow and—more than that—a peppering against her skin, stinging and harsh, as if the gale were stripping the mountains themselves of all their earth, scraping soil and rock off them to reveal the bones beneath.

Something brushed her. She screamed. She could not help herself. Some *thing,* some creature, but like no creature she ever seen or dreamed of. Then it was gone, vanished into the night, but there was another, and a third, streaming past her, borne on the gale. Towers of darkness, they were blacker even than the night itself, like a glimpse of the Abyss, the pit of the Enemy in which the wicked fall endlessly, never reaching bottom. With them, *of* them, around them swirled the stench of burning iron. Hanna heard their voices like the muttering of bells beneath the tearing wind, wordless and yet sentient.

From out of the blackness she heard a low rumbling roar that surged and swelled to a terrible crashing booming shuddering thunder that went on and on.

The rope at her waist pulled taut as Wolfhere reeled her in and shoved her back toward the stables. "Go!" he cried. "We dare not—"

She stumbled back. Groping, she found the door; shaking, she fumbled with the latch, and at last they got it open and fell inside. The soldier slammed the door shut and latched it behind them. The roar deafened her; it filled the air as if it were itself part of the air. Then, slowly, it subsided, faded, until once more the wind was all the sound they heard, the endless tearing wind and the hail of rain and snow and pebbles against the wood walls.

Inside, it was warm and dark. The nervous horses stamped; the stablekeeper spoke in a soothing voice. Hanna heard, also, others of the Lions moving 'round the stable, calming the animals. The guest-master sobbed softly.

"What was that noise?" she asked as the building creaked and groaned and the wind shook the rafters and the low throb of bells numbed her down to her boots. Her hip and shoulder ached. She rubbed her hands to warm them.

"Avalanche," said the guest-master through his tears. "Ai, Lady, I know that sound well, for I have lived in these mountains twenty years. And close by, it was. I fear me that the cloister—" No farther could he go. He began to weep again.

"What were those creatures?" she asked.

Wolfhere untied her. "*Galla,*" he said. The word had a hard, foreign, ugly sound, the "g" more of a guttural "gh."

"What are galla?" she asked.

"Something we should not speak of now, with them walking abroad, for they might hear their name spoken a third time and seek us out who know of them," he said in such a tone she knew he meant to say no more. "We must wait out the storm."

It was a long night. She could not sleep, nor did Wolfhere, though perhaps some of the Lions did. That the guest-master did sleep, fitfully, she knew because his weeping slackened at last.

Just as the gale slackened at last. Come dawn, Wolfhere ventured out with Hanna right behind him. It was a cloudless morning, the sky a delicate, washed-out blue. The mountains stood in all their glory, white peaks gleaming in the pale new sun. There was not a breath of wind. But for the debris scattered everywhere, the gate and much of the fence enclosure knocked down, the woodpile torn apart and scattered, shutters torn from hinges, and goats milling in confusion in the middle of the garden, she would never have guessed there had been a storm at all. Oddly, the beehives stood unscathed.

But the infirmary was gone.

There monks and merchants scurried, a swarm of them buzzing round the huge pile of boulders and earth that covered what had once been the infirmary. Built of stone and timber, it was obliterated now, melded with the great bank of mountain that had slid down on top of it.

They hurried over. The monks had managed to pull from the rubble the bodies of their ancient brother and of two Lions. Of the other two soldiers—Hanna recognized these as the two who had been posted outside, along the wall behind the cell that had imprisoned Antonia and Heribert—one had a broken leg and the other lay on the ground, moaning, his skin unbroken but something broken inside him. The Brother Infirmarian knelt beside him, probing his abdomen gently. Tears wet the monk's face.

"It happened so fast," the monk said, looking up when Wolfhere knelt beside him. "I ran outside, hearing the noise, and then saw—nay, I did not see it but *felt* it, felt its power. Then the avalanche came. Lady forgive me, but I ran. Only when I saw it was too late, only when I saw the infirmary would be overwhelmed, did I recall poor Brother Fusulus, who was too weak to save himself."

"You were spared," said Wolfhere, "because you have yet work to do in this world. What of this man, here?"

The Infirmarian shook his head. "God will decide if he is to live."

Wolfhere rose and paced over the edge of the avalanche. Hanna followed him but kept back, not wanting to venture too close. She could see the bones of the infirmary underneath rock and rubble, mortared stones torn up by their roots, planks strewn like so much offal, a bed overturned but its rope base untouched, a three-legged stool with one leg broken, dried herbs once tied in bundles now scattered every which way on the torn grass.

"What of the prisoners?" asked Wolfhere when he turned back to the others.

The abbot himself came forward. He had been soothing the presbyter, who had already sent his servants to the stables to make ready to leave. "We cannot find their bodies," he said. "This is most distressing. The rocks have buried them utterly. We will try to dig them out, but—"

"No matter." Wolfhere surveyed the huge scar, the trail of the avalanche, that now scored the side of the ridge. Something shifted in the rubble and a few pebbles bounced down to land at his feet. He backed away nervously. "Search only if it is safe. The prisoners are lost to us now."

"What will you do?" asked the abbot. "What of the two injured men? Brother Infirmarian says this poor man must not be moved any distance, and the other will not be able to walk for many weeks."

"Can they remain here until they are healed?"

"Of course." The abbot directed his monks to move the injured men away.

"Come, Hanna," said Wolfhere. He walked back toward the stables, leaving the Lions to help.

"Why did you say it in that way? That the prisoners are 'lost to us.' Not that they're dead."

He looked at her curiously. "Do you think they are dead? Do you believe she lies there under the rocks? That someday, if the monks can dig the building out, they will find their two crushed bodies or their shattered bones?"

"Of course they must be dead. They were locked in the cell. How could they have escaped—" Seeing his expression, she broke off. "You don't think they're dead."

"I do not. That was no natural storm."

No natural storm. A blizzard blown up in the midst of mild summer weather. Strange unnatural creatures he had named galla walking abroad, stinking of the forge.

"Where will she go, Hanna? That is the question we must ask ourselves now. Where will she go? Who will shelter such as her?"

"I don't know."

"Sabella might, if she could reach Sabella. But Sabella is herself in prison, so Wendar and Varre are closed to Antonia, for now." He sighed sharply and stopped at the stable door, turning back to look up at the mountains, so calm, so clear, above them. "I should have known. I should have prepared for this. But I underestimated her power."

"Where will *we* go?"

He considered. "Alas, I fear we must split up. One of us must continue on to Darre to lay the charges against Biscop

Antonia before the skopos. That way we remain prepared, whatever Antonia means to do. One of us must return to Henry and warn him, and hope he believes us." He smiled suddenly then, with a wry expression that made Hanna remember how much she liked him. "Better that one be you, Hanna. You will take four of the Lions, I the other two—when I journey back this way, I will pick up the two who remain here, if they survive."

She had grown used to Wolfhere and now, abruptly, was afraid to travel without him. "How long will it take you? How soon will you return to Wendar?"

He shrugged. "I cannot say. I may be able to get back across the pass this autumn, but most likely I won't be able to return until next summer. *You* must convince Henry, child." He touched her, briefly, on her Eagle's badge, newly made and still as bright as if the memory of Manfred's death lit it. "You have earned this, Hanna. Do not think you are unequal to the task." He went inside the stables.

Hanna lingered outside, staring up at the three great peaks so beautiful, so silent, so at peace in their vast strength, their sheer living force, that it seemed impossible to believe at this instant that three—brief—human lives had been extinguished in the shadow at their feet. What was it the bard had called them? *Youngwife.* Monk's Ridge. Terror. She shaded her eyes against the rising sun and looked for the hawk, but no birds flew in the sky this fair morning.

She would return to Wendar, to the king's progress, without seeing the city of Darre and the palace of the holy skopos. Without seeing, perhaps, a few elves or other strange creatures not of humankind. And yet, this also meant she would return to Liath sooner.

Thinking of Liath made her think of Hugh, though she did not want to think of Hugh. Beautiful Hugh. And thinking of Hugh made her remember what he had done, and so she thought of Ivar. Ai, Lady, where was Ivar now? Had he reached Quedlinhame safely? Did he like it there? Was he resigned to his fate? Or did he still fight against it?

III
THE CLOISTER

1

IVAR hated Quedlinhame. He hated the monastery, he hated the daily round of monotonous prayer, and most of all he hated the novices' dormitory, which was a narrow barracks of a building where he spent all of his nights and much of his day in miserable silence along with the other novices. Worst, because of the careful reckoning of days at Mass and in prayerbooks, he knew exactly how many days he had been imprisoned here.

One hundred and seventy-seven days ago, on St. Bonfilia's Day, he had knelt before the postern gate in a cold rain and after a night of utter wretchedness had been admitted onto the grounds of Quedlinhame. They did not even give him a tour of the famous church. Instead, his new keepers immediately led him to the novitiary and locked him in with the rest of the poor souls consigned to this purgatory.

The poor male souls, of course. Quedlinhame was a double monastery; the abbess, Mother Scholastica, ruled over both monks and nuns who lived apart but prayed together. The novices' dormitory let out onto a small cloister, a courtyard marked off by trim columns. A high wood fence ran down the center of this cloister, dividing it into two smaller courtyards, one for the male novices and one for the female novices whose dormitory lay on the opposite side.

Ivar prayed briefly at that fence every day unless the weather was awful, once in the morning just after the service of Terce and once in the afternoon before Vespers. Or at least, he appeared to be praying. In fact, in these, his only unsupervised moments of the day, he studied the wood planks. In the last five months, he and the other three first-year novices had examined that fence finger's breadth by finger's breadth, each upright plank, each horizontal beam, each crack and warp and weathered knot. But he could not find any chink through which to see onto the other side.

Were the female novices young? Almost certainly. Like him, most of them would have been put into the church—most willingly, some not—by their families when they reached adolescence.

Were they pretty? Perhaps. This goal he had set himself soon after he arrived: to identify each female novice by name and face. It kept him from going crazy, even though he knew it was wrong and against the rules. Or perhaps *because* it was against the rules.

Right now, his fellow first-year novice, Baldwin, had finished digging dirt out from under his nails with his shaving knife and now he stuck that knife into the minute gap between two warping planks. He wiggled the blade back and forth in what Ivar supposed would be a vain attempt to try to widen the gap enough to peer through. Baldwin, however, would not give up. In all things, fair-haired Baldwin knew that eventually he would get his way.

Ermanrich lumbered up and plopped down beside Ivar. He shivered in the cool autumn wind, which Ivar found pleasant after a hot summer confined within walls, but Ermanrich, though stoutest in body of their band of four, was also most susceptible to fevers and runny noses. He coughed now and wiped running eyes and squinted at Baldwin's handiwork.

"There must be a weak spot," Ermanrich muttered. He picked at his nails, which were dirty from turning over soil in the garden now that all the vegetables were harvested. "Hathumod says the first years all think Baldwin is very handsome." Hathumod was Ermanrich's cousin and in her second year as a novice. She and Ermanrich had mysterious ways of communicating which Ivar had not yet divined the nature of.

"What does Hathumod think of our Baldwin?" Ivar asked.

"She won't say."

Baldwin glanced at them and grinned, then went back to his work.

He had every reason to be vain of his looks, but of course, according to his own account, it was those looks that had landed him in the monastery. He was, indeed, the handsomest fellow Ivar had ever laid eyes on . . . with the exception of Frater Hugh.

Ai, Lady! Even thinking of that bastard Hugh made Ivar angry all over again, trapped by helpless fury. He had tried to free Liath but had been made to look a fool and then gotten condemned to this life in the bargain. All of it Hugh's fault, that damned arrogant handsome bastard. What had happened to Liath? Was she still Hugh's concubine? At least, if reports were true, Hanna was with her.

Ivar could not begrudge Hanna her choice—service with Liath rather than with him. Liath needed Hanna more than he did, and anyway here at Quedlinhame he was not allowed to converse with any woman except Mother Scholastica. He had brought two male servants with him, and they tended to his clothing and his bed and with the other servants tidied the dormitory and in general did whatever manual labor he himself did not have time for, since as a novice his main duties were to pray and to study. Had he brought Hanna, she would have been sent to work as a laundress or cook, and he would never have seen her. Better that she stayed with Liath.

He sighed heavily.

Ermanrich touched a hand to his elbow, though novices were not supposed to touch, to form bonds of affection and sympathy. They were meant to devote themselves only to

God. "You're thinking of *her* again," said the stout boy. "Was she really as pretty as Baldwin?"

"Utterly unlike," said Ivar, but then he smiled, because Ermanrich always made him smile. "She was dark—"

"Dark like Duke Conrad the Black?" asked Baldwin without looking up from his scraping at the fence. "I met him once."

"*Met* him?" demanded Ermanrich.

"Oh, well, not met. I saw him once."

"I don't know if they look anything alike," said Ivar. "I never saw Duke Conrad. How did he get to be so dark?"

"His mother came from the east. She was a princess from Jinna country." Baldwin had a treasure trove of gossip about the noble families of Wendar and Varre. "She was a present to one of the Arnulfs, I forget which, from one of the sultans of the east. Conrad the Elder, who was then Duke of Wayland, took a fancy to her and because King Arnulf owed him a favor, he asked for the girl. She was just a child then, but very pretty, everyone said. Conrad had her raised as a good Daisanite, for she came of heathen fire-worshipers. When she was old enough, he took her as a concubine, but of all his wives and concubines only *she* conceived by him, so perhaps she knew some eastern witchery, for the rumor went round that Conrad was infertile because of a curse set on him by one of the Lost Ones he raped when he was a young man."

Ermanrich coughed again and cocked one eyebrow up.

"You don't believe me?" demanded Baldwin, cheek ticking as he tried to suppress a grin.

"Which part do you wish to know that I believe?" asked Ermanrich.

"And then what happened?" asked Ivar, trying to imagine this Jinna girl but only able to see Liath in his mind's eye. The thought of her made his heart ache.

"She gave birth to a baby boy, the second Conrad, whom we now know as Conrad the Black. He succeeded to the duchy when his father died. She still lives, you know, the Jinna woman. I don't know what her old name was, her heathen name, but she was baptized with a good Daisanite name, Mariya or Miryam. Something like that."

"They let a bastard inherit?" asked Ermanrich, looking skeptical.

"No, no. At the end of his life, when it came time to name his heir, Conrad the Elder claimed he had been married to her all along. The first tame deacon he got to say she was present at the ceremony then turned out to have been only ten years old when the marriage was supposed to have been solemnized. So Conrad finally made a huge bequest of land to the local biscop and *she* agreed that God had sanctified the union before the child's birth. Look! I've made a crack!" He leaned down and stuck his perfectly-proportioned nose up against the wood, closed one eye, and peered through the tiny gap with the other. Then he withdrew, shaking his head. "All I can see is warts. I *knew* they would have warts."

"Dearest Baldwin, doomed by warts to a life in the monastery," said Ermanrich in a sententious voice. "Now move and let me try." They changed places.

"Hush," said Ivar. "Here comes Lord Reginar and his dogs."

Lord Reginar had a pack of five "dogs"—the other second-year novices—and a thin face made ill-featured mostly because of its habitual sour expression.

"What's this?" he said, pausing beside the three first-year boys. He touched a scrap of very fine white linen to his lips as if the stench of the first years offended him. "Are you at your daily *prayers?*" That he meant to insinuate something was clear, though what exactly he meant was not.

Ivar stifled a giggle. He found Reginar's conceit so pathetic, especially compared to that of Hugh, that he always wanted to laugh. But a count's son never ever laughed at the son of a duchess and one who, in addition, wore the gold torque around his neck that symbolized he came of the blood of the royal family and had a claim—however distant—to the throne.

Ermanrich clasped his hands tight and leaned against the fence, covering the telltale signs of cutting. He began to murmur a psalm in the singsong voice he used at his prayers.

Baldwin smiled brightly up at the young lord. "How kind of you to deign to notice us this day, Lord Reginar," he said without any obvious sign of sarcasm.

Ermanrich made a choking sound.

Reginar touched his lips again with the linen, but even he—youngest son of Duchess Rotrudis and nephew of both Mother Scholastica and King Henry—was not immune to Baldwin's charms. "It is true," he said, "that two march-landers and a minor count's son are unlikely to receive attentions from such as myself every day, but then you are entitled to sleep near me, as are all these others." He gestured toward his sycophants, an indistinguishable collection of boys of good family who had had the misfortune to be dedicated to the monastery last year, together with Reginar, and had by necessity—or by force—fallen into orbit around him.

"Pray you," said Baldwin sweetly, "do not forget our good comrade Sigfrid, Mother Scholastica's favorite. I am sure he, too, is not insensible to the favor you show us."

Ermanrich fell into a fit of frantic coughing. One of the boys hovering at Reginar's back tittered, and the young lord turned right around and slapped him hard. Then he spun and stalked away, his "dogs" scurrying after him.

Fittingly, at that moment Sigfrid came running out of the dormitory, his sharp face alight, his novice's robes all askew. He did not notice Reginar. He never did. And that was the worst insult of all, although Reginar never understood that Sigfrid noticed nothing except his studies, his prayers, and—now—his three friends.

"I heard the most amazing news," Sigfrid said as he halted beside them. He knelt with the practiced ease of a person who has spent years moving into or out of a kneeling position, as indeed Sigfrid himself cheerfully admitted he had, having come at age five to his vocation: monk-in-training.

"That was cruel," said Ermanrich.

"What was?" asked Sigfrid.

Baldwin smiled. "Poor Reginar. He can't abide that his own dear aunt, Mother Scholastica, favors a mere steward's son and lavishes her favor—and her private tutorials—on that lowborn creature instead of on her nephew."

"Oh, dear," said Sigfrid. He looked concerned all at once. "I do not mean to make anyone envious of me. I have not striven for Mother Scholastica's attention, and yet—" His face took on an expression of rapt contempla-

tion. "—to be privileged to study with her and with Brother
Methodius—"

"You know what they say." Baldwin cut in before Sigfrid
could launch into a long recitation—by heart, of course—
of whatever horrific matristic text written centuries ago he
had studied today in Mother Scholastica's study.

"Why, no," said Ermanrich. "What do they say?"

"That Lord Reginar was put into the monastery only
because his mother detests him. Had she allowed him to
become ordained as a frater and then be elevated to the
rank of presbyter, he would have had to visit her every
three years as is traditional, as long as she lives, and she
decided it was better to put him in the monastery where
she'd never have to see him again if she didn't wish it."

Ermanrich snorted, gulped, and began to laugh helplessly.

Sigfrid gazed sorrowfully at Baldwin and only shook his
head, as if to remind the other boy that the Lord and Lady
looked ill on those who spoke spitefully of others.

"I believe it," muttered Ivar.

"I'm sorry, Ivar," said Baldwin quickly. "I didn't mean
to remind you of your own situation."

"Never mind," said Ivar. "What's done is done. What
was your news, Sigfrid?"

"King Henry's progress is coming here, to Quedlinhame,
for the Feast of St. Valentinus. They expect the king today
or tomorrow!"

"How do you know this?" Ermanrich demanded. "Not
even Hathumod knows, for if she did, she'd have told me."

Sigfrid blushed. He had a sensitive face, his expressions
made interesting by the conflict between his studious nature
and solitary soul on the one hand and the very real and
passionate liking he had taken to his year-mates on the
other. "Alas, I fear I overheard them. It was ill-done of
me, I know—but I couldn't wait to tell you, for I knew you
would want to hear! Imagine! The king!"

Baldwin yawned. "Ah, yes. I've met the king."

"Have you really *met* him?" demanded Ermanrich,
laughing.

The schoolmaster appeared under the colonnade and
they all leaped guiltily to their feet and with contrite faces
made their way to the line. As first years, they took their

place at the end, matched up in pairs. Before them walked Reginar and his sycophants, and in front of Reginar—although Reginar hated *anyone* to walk in front of him—stood the humble third years.

As they marched out of the dormitory and made their way along the path that led to the church, Ivar craned his neck when the brown-robed female novices came into view. For his pains he got a sharp whack on his shoulders from the schoolmaster's willow switch. It stung, but in a way the pain helped him. The pain helped him remember that he was Ivar, son of Count Harl and Lady Herlinda. He was not truly a monk, not by vocation as Sigfrid was, nor was he resigned to his fate as was Ermanrich, sixth of seven sons of a marchland countess who, to her horror, had never given birth to a girl and had perforce made her eldest son her heir and after that hastily dedicated the superfluous boys to the church so they would not contest their brother's elevation to the rank of count after her death. Unlike Baldwin, he had not escaped an unwanted marriage by begging to be put in the church.

No. He had been forced to take the novice's hood. Forced because he loved Liath and she loved him and he would have taken her away from Hugh, and this had been Hugh's way of revenging himself on Ivar.

No. He never minded the pain or the austerities of a novice's life. The pain, even of the willow switch, reminded Ivar daily that he would, somehow, avenge himself on Hugh and save Liath from Hugh's clutches. No matter that Hugh—bastard though he was—ranked far above a minor count's youngest son. No matter that Hugh's mother, a powerful margrave, was an acknowledged favorite of King Henry.

By hating Quedlinhame, Ivar kept himself strong enough to hate Hugh. Somehow, some way, Ivar would have his revenge.

2

BLOODHEART had sons. As time passed, Sanglant learned how to recognize them: by their ornamentation. Only the sons of Bloodheart could stud their teeth with gems; the mail skirts they wore, as intricate as lace, were gilded with gold and silver and woven with bright stones and flashing jewels; a stylized red-ocher arrowhead, symbol of their father's hegemony, figured prominently in the pattern of colorful painting with which they decorated their torsos.

As summer passed into autumn and the vast nave of air in the cathedral grew steadily colder, sons came and went from their favored place in front of Bloodheart's heavy chair. They left for expeditions whose fruit brought gold, cattle, slaves, and a harvest of endlessly fascinating small items: an eagle-feather quill, a length of sky-blue silk, a sword with an ornamented gold hilt, vases carved out of horn or marble, an arrow fletched with the iron-gray feathers of a griffin, a turquoise pendant engraved with six-pointed stars inlaid with gold, a silver paten, a bloodstone cameo ring, a linen tablecloth embroidered with silk, slivers of ossified dragon's fire sharpened into thin blades, a hoard of green beads, translucent angel's tears polished and strung together as a necklace, silk bed-curtains, and silk-covered pillows. Bloodheart tossed one of the pillows to Sanglant, but the dogs ripped it to pieces and bits of its feather stuffing floated, spinning in the still air, for the rest of the day.

One son haunted the cathedral more than the others, favored or in disgrace, Sanglant could not tell. He was easily distinguished from the others: He wore at his chest a wooden Circle of Unity, no doubt a trophy ripped off a corpse, and he had taken upon himself the odd habit of, once a day, overseeing the slave who brought bucket and rags to clean up the spot where, at the limit of his chains, Sanglant relieved himself. This humiliation Sanglant endured in silence. It was, in its own way, a mercy not to be left to fester in worse filth than what he already had to suffer.

But Bloodheart was fickle, or perhaps it served his purposes to act so.

Day by day more Eika trickled in until their numbers swamped the cathedral. They were like a swarm of locusts, all of them pestering him with pricks of their spears, with spit, with dogs sent to fight him until the tunic he had wrapped his forearms in lay in shreds on the floor and his skin was a mass of bleeding scrapes and bites. But it would heal. It always did, cleanly and without infection. Some of the dogs died, to be eaten by his pack and, finally, by him as well; this food he could not scorn, because he had so little. The dogs that fled him were quickly killed by their pack brothers.

The Eika cheered on these battles, ringing him and shouting and calling out encouragement. Since he understood so little of their language, he could not tell whether they hoped he died, or whether his living was entertainment enough. They sang until all hours of the night and seemed to have no need of sleep, nor could he sleep in any case, with the dogs testing him and the curious coming to stare and point and howl with laughter at the sight of a half-human prince among the dogs.

Bloodheart sat and surveyed all from his throne, and his priest crouched at his side, scratching the scars on his scrawny chest now and again, rolling bones to read the future, caressing the little wooden chest which he kept always beside him.

But at last, on a day made warm by the press of bodies and cold by the gloomy light that filtered in through the windows, Bloodheart rose and howled them to attention.

"Which of you has brought me the greatest treasure?" he cried, or so Sanglant assumed, because at once the sons came forward with magnificent treasures, some of which Sanglant had seen before, some of which were new: gold chalices; a necklace of emeralds; a sword of such terrible beauty and slender killing sleekness that it must have come from the forges of the east; a woman's veil woven so cunningly that it could have been a spiderweb unfastened from branches and gilded with silver and pearls; rings made gaudy with precious stones; a reliquary of ivory and gold and pearls; a Quman bowcase—

Sanglant shut his eyes. He had to lean forward onto his hands, swept by such a powerful memory of Liath walking ahead of him through the stables, her body ornamented by a bowcase incised with a griffin devouring a deer, that he trembled. His dogs growled, always alert to weakness. Bloodheart barked out words, and Sanglant jerked up, ready to fight. Never let it be said that he did not fight until his last breath.

But Bloodheart's attention was on another. He called one of his sons before him, the one who wore the Circle. This one, young and straight, had less of the bulky mass of his brothers, but there was yet something about him that was different, something Sanglant recognized but could put no name to, unless it was intelligence.

Bloodheart gestured to the treasures scattered like leaves at his feet. He spoke, indicating this last of his sons. What had he brought?

The other Eika howled and dogs began barking and howling in response. Never allowed to leave the city, this Eika son could hardly have been expected to find and bring home treasure. But perhaps he was in disgrace, and this, finally, was the moment Bloodheart had chosen to make the point.

The young Eika stood calmly under the storm of their howling and derision. At last, seeing they had not made him cower, they quieted. He did not speak immediately. He waited, and when he did speak, he spoke only to his father and, amazingly, in good Wendish.

"I bring you the most precious treasure," he said, his voice as smooth as the tone of the bone flutes Bloodheart played each day. "Wisdom."

"Wisdom!" Bloodheart grinned, flashing gems. "What might that be?"

"Which of your other sons can speak the tongue of the human kind?"

"Why should they? What use are the humans to us? They are weak, and being weak, will die. We will take what we want from them and go on our way."

"They have not died yet." He did not look toward Sangiant. "The humankind are as numerous as flies on a corpse. Though we are stronger, we are fewer."

Murmuring, the others grew restless at an exchange few of them could understand.

"What matters it if we are fewer," said Bloodheart, "if they are weaker?" But he still spoke Wendish, to Sanglant's surprise. "What matters it as long as we kill twenty for every one of our brothers who dies?"

"Why must we kill so many if we could gain more with less killing?"

Bloodheart's laughter sounded long and ominously in the echoing nave. Abruptly, he spat at the young Eika's feet. "Go back to Rikin fjord. You are too young to bide here any longer. Your captivity weakened you, and you are not strong enough to fight this war. Go home and rest with the Mothers. Prove yourself there in the fjordlands, bring the other tribes under my heel, and perhaps I will let you return. But while *you* are under my displeasure, let none among my sons speak to you in the language of true people, but only in the language of the Soft Ones. I have spoken."

He turned, spat toward Sanglant, and seated himself on his throne. The priest translated his words in a quavering voice, and then the hubbub began, so loud with howling and laughter and harsh words, with the scraping and banging of spear hafts on stone, and with the stamping of heels to the ground that Sanglant was deafened.

The Eika princeling stood his ground, oblivious to the taunts and the abuse. When at last Bloodheart began to distribute gifts to his favored soldiers, he alone left quietly, without looking back—out to the lit world beyond this stone and timber prison. A breath of wind touched Sanglant's lips. He licked it, moisture from rain almost painful on his dry tongue.

Free to go, even in disgrace.

The madness came as a cloud covers the sun. But he fought it this time, fought succumbing to it. He did not want to fall into madness in front of so many, an animal in truth. But the dogs circled in, and the black cloud descended, and he forgot everything except his fear that he would be chained here forever.

3

A rich autumn light streamed in through the schola windows, bathing Ivar in such a soporific warmth that he nodded, then jerked himself back to attention as the schoolmaster paused beside him.

"Mundus, munde, mundi, mundo, mundum, mundo, Ivar. Certainly *if* you would bestir yourself, you could master Dariyan easily. Ermanrich, pay attention. Ah, yes, Baldwin, of course you are doing well; it just needs more practice. See, it is mundi here, not mundo, in the vocative."

The schoolmaster moved forward to the second-year novices, whose study of Dariyan, the language of the old Empire and now of the Daisanite Church, was more advanced than that of the first years—all but Sigfrid, who spoke and read Dariyan fluently.

Ivar yawned and painstakingly impressed the word into the wax tablet. He was a slow writer and reader, having only learned the alphabet upon leaving the world and entering the monastery. *Mundus,* the world. Ivar very much wanted to be out in the world right now. He shifted, trying to get comfortable on the hard wooden bench, but of course it was impossible to get comfortable. One was not meant to be *comfortable* in the monastery but rather and always discomforted by one's own unworthiness in the face of God's majesty.

However, if he slid forward just so, he could lean a little farther into the sunlight that spilled over the table. The heat of the sun melted through the coarse fabric of his robe. The warmth was too powerful a spell. Ivar dozed off over his tablet while the schoolmaster, lecturing to the row of third-year novices, droned on about the elegant style on display in St. Augustina's *City of God.*

Something nudged Ivar's foot, and he snorted and started awake, losing his grip on his stylus. It fell to the stone floor, and the sound of its impact in the silent chamber resounded in his ears at least as loudly as if one of the huge stone pillars in the church had just crashed down.

But Fortune was with him this day, as She had not been yesterday when he had been caught trying to look at the female novices. Ermanrich—for he was the culprit who had nudged him awake—made a quick sign with his free hand: *Look.*

The schoolmaster had walked to the door and was now speaking in a low voice with Brother Methodius, prior of the monastic half of Quedlinhame as well as Mother Scholastica's deputy. Finally he turned back to survey his pupils and signed: *Stand.*

Dutifully, they stood. Ivar stooped to grab the stylus off the floor and set it next to the tablet, for once free of the punishment that would normally attend his carelessness.

"Come." Brother Methodius stepped forward. "You are to be granted the honor of attending the adventus of King Henry. Keep silence, I pray you, and keep your heads bowed humbly." His eyes glinted, and Ivar thought the good brother suppressed a smile. "No doubt Our Lord and Lady will forgive you a single glance at the magnificence of the king's progress as it passes by, if you are not yet strong enough to resist such temptation."

He signed in the hand language learned by all the monks. *Come.* The novices formed rows quickly, for they had by now much practice in obedience. But even Sigfrid's eyes were wide with awe at the thought of seeing the king.

Ivar had never seen the king, of course. Heart's Rest and the North March of Wendar was too far north, too remote, and too poor to be of much interest to the king; the counts of the North March were left to rule as they wished, unless that rule came into direct conflict with the king's authority. During Ivar's lifetime such an incident had never happened, but his father, Count Harl, could dimly recall an expedition by the King's Dragons—his elite cavalry—to put down a northern rebellion in the time of the younger Arnulf many years ago.

Here at Quedlinhame, of course, they could expect to see the king frequently. King Henry preferred to spend Holy Week at the foundation ruled over by his sister, Mother Scholastica, and inhabited by his widowed mother, Queen Mathilda, now a nun. In autumn, as it was now, the king and his court often rested here on their way to the royal hunting lodges in the Thurin Forest.

The king! Even Ivar, who tried very hard to dislike everything at Quedlinhame excluding his new friends, could not help but be excited. As they walked down the steps from the schoolroom and out of the dormitory, he noticed as if for the first time what a veritable hive of activity the great monastery had become. Servants swept pavement or whitewashed exterior walls. Women aired out blankets and featherbeds at the guest houses. By the kitchens, wagons waited in neat rows, their beds heaped with vegetables, casks of ale, baskets of ground wheat and rye, and crocks of honey. Cages of chickens stood stacked by the slaughter pit and a half dozen servants worked feverishly, chopping off heads, while others carried the dead chickens to huge vats of boiling water and threw them in to scald off the feathers. Butchered pigs and cattle hung, draining, from the beams of the slaughterhouse shed. The bakery fires roared, and the smell of cooking permeated the air.

The line of novices joined that of the assembled monks and they walked out together under the great archway that spanned the gate. Up until the time of the first Henry, Quedlinhame had been a fortress, part of the vast inheritance his wife, Lucienna of Attomar, had brought to their marriage. Together they had dedicated both the fortress and their only daughter Kunigunde to the church, and at age sixteen she had become first abbess—first "Mother"— of Quedlinhame Convent. During her long rule the foundation had expanded to include monks—which unfortunate ambition had transpired in the end to bring Ivar here to this prestigious foundation against his wishes.

Not even these troubling thoughts could dampen Ivar's excitement as the entire community left the enclosure in dutiful silence and walked down the hill on the stone-paved avenue that led through town. They walked out beyond the town walls and along the road for at least a mile. They passed townsfolk, standing at the side of the road, who had left their tasks and brought themselves and their children to witness the arrival of the king. Out here, newly sown fields of winter wheat wore brown earth laced with shoots of tender green as their autumn garb. The view behind was dominated by the great hill on which stood the ancient fortress that was now the monastery; the towers of the church pierced the deep blue of the heavens, reaching

toward God. They halted on either side of the road, two
lines of simply-clad brothers and sisters of the church and
the many layservants who served them and God both—
perhaps two hundred souls in total.

   Ivar heard the king's progress before he saw it. He heard
a muttering as of many feet and hooves and rolling wheels,
felt the subtle vibration as a tremor rising up through the
soles of his feet. He heard them singing, many voices raised
in a joyful psalm. The strength of their combined voices,
the sheer power of it, made him shiver with joy; not even
a full prayer service and the chanting and singing of the
monks and nuns in unison at Quedlinhame made him feel
this sudden pull to be torn away from his own person and
become some other one, one who could join in the *concordia*, the power that attended upon the king's presence.

> *I sing of loyalty and justice.*
> *I will raise this psalm to Thee,*
> *Our Lord and Lady Who are God in Unity.*
> *I will follow a wise and blameless course*
>   *whatever may befall me.*
> *I will go about my house in purity of heart.*
> *I will set before myself no sordid aim.*
> *I will hate disloyalty.*
> *I will silence those who spread tales*
>   *behind men's backs.*
> *I will not sit at table with those*
>   *who are proud and pompous.*
> *I will choose the most loyal for my companions;*
> *my servants shall be folk whose lives are blameless.*
> *Morning after morning I will put*
>   *all wicked men to silence*
> *and I will rejoice in all on God's earth which is good.*

   The schoolmaster always enjoined his pupils to keep
their heads bowed and their eyes toward the ground, for
in this way they made themselves smaller and indicated
their insignificance. But as the cavalcade drew near enough
that he could hear the small noises of a hundred or more
souls in movement, Ivar could not help himself. He had
to look.

   Ermanrich stirred beside him, and Baldwin drew in a

sharp, surprised breath. Only Sigfrid kept his head dutifully bowed.

A King's Eagle rode in front, as herald. She wore the scarlet-trimmed cape and the brass badge of an Eagle, and she stared straight ahead at the road before her; she had a hard, interesting face, broad shoulders, and the look of a person sure of her position and name in the world. In her right hand she held a staff, its haft wedged against her boot. The king's banner draped from the staff, curling down to hide the hand itself, for there was no wind to lift the banner.

Behind her rode six young nobles honored this day with a position at the head of the procession. They, too, carried pennants, one for each of the duchies under Henry's rule: Saony, Fesse, Avaria, Varingia, Arconia, and Wayland. Ivar guessed the four boys and two girls to be about the same age as himself; the girl holding the standard of Arconia had hair as pale as wheat and fingers so delicate that he wondered how she had the strength to grip the banner pole. He wondered whose child she was. If only he had been sent to court, instead of to Quedlinhame, then he might have ridden proudly at the front of such an adventus—an arrival—as this! His gaze skipped back to the riders who followed directly behind the pennants.

In this group of nobles, each one attired magnificently in fine embroidered and trimmed linen tunics, in fine leather riding boots, with handsome fur-trimmed capes or richly colored wool cloaks thrown over all, the eye still leaped immediately to King Henry. Ivar had never seen him before, yet he knew instantly that the middle-aged man riding in the center was the king though he wore no crown. He needed no crown. The weight of his authority was like a mantle cast over his shoulders. He wore clothing no plainer and no richer than the others, one prince among many, but the leather belt that girdled his waist, embossed with the symbols of each of the six duchies that made up the kingdom of Wendar and Varre, and the many small and subtle gestures of the others as they deferred to him, proclaimed him *prima inter pares,* first among equals. From the back of a handsome bay mare, he surveyed the hooded monks and nuns, most of whom still stared fixedly at the ground, with stern approval for their humility.

Just as he passed the ranks of the novices, his eye caught Ivar's gaze. One royal eyebrow arched, intrigued or censorious. Ivar blushed and dropped his gaze.

He saw booted feet march by, heard the renewed voices of many men lifted in song: The King's Lions had been granted the honor of marching directly behind the king. They halted suddenly and their song cut off, to be replaced by the stillness of a fine autumn day, the creak of leather, the restlessness of horses farther down the line, the barking of a dog.

Ermanrich shifted next to Ivar and whispered to Baldwin. "If only I were closer."

Startled, Ivar glanced up at the same time as did Sigfrid. Their view was partly blocked by the ranks of Lions, sturdy men clothed in fighting gear and gold tabards marked by a black lion, but beyond the *milites*—the fighting men—and the nobles, the king had ridden forward with only the Eagle in attendance to greet Mother Scholastica.

She was also mounted, as befit a woman of royal birth come to greet her brother; she rode on a mule whose coat was so polished a gray as to be almost white. In her dark blue robes, adorned only with the gold Circle of Unity hanging at her chest, with her hair drawn back under a white scarf and her face guileless and calm, she appeared every bit as regal as her elder brother. Of course it was not fitting that a woman of her ecclesiastic rank dismount to greet anyone except the skopos, but neither could the king dismount to greet her. So the king had ridden forward on his mare to meet her, and now, with the two animals side by side, the royal siblings leaned across the gap and gave each other the kiss of family, once to each cheek, as greeting.

"And if," continued Ermanrich in that whisper, "you took Master Pursed-Lips' willow switch—"

Baldwin started to snicker.

"—and gave a quick twitch of it to the mare's hindquarters, what do you think would happen?"

Sigfrid snorted and clapped a hand over his mouth. Ivar was so aghast at Ermanrich's imagining either Mother Scholastica or the king made ridiculous by a bolting horse that he started to giggle.

That same willow switch lashed hard against his rump

and he yelped. Then Ermanrich gulped down a yelp as he, too, was disciplined.

"Keep silence," hissed the schoolmaster, stationing himself behind the four boys. He did not, of course, switch either Baldwin or Sigfrid, and poor Sigfrid looked horrifically guilty, for had he not responded by laughing at Ermanrich's jest? Ivar bit his lip as he blinked back tears; his buttocks stung. Ermanrich had his usual sly grin on his face. He had unknowable reserves and rarely showed any visible sign of feeling pain. The schoolmaster cleared his throat and Ivar hastily looked down just as the king and his sister parted, her mule being brought around by a servant so abbess and king could lead the procession up to the monastery together.

On past Ivar's station marched the Lions, then the rest of the train, a stamp of feet and hooves and rumble of wagons. Beyond, toward town, people shouted and cried out praise to the king.

Ivar's rump still smarted. He could practically feel the schoolmaster's breath on his neck, but the schoolmaster had moved on. A sudden feeling like the whisper of elfshot made his neck prickle. He glanced up, or he would have missed her.

"Liath!" He almost fell forward. The three other boys jerked their heads up and stared. Baldwin whistled under his breath.

Liath! He could never mistake her for someone else: dark hair, golden-brown skin, her height and slender frame. She wore the cape and badge of a King's Eagle. *She wore the badge of a King's Eagle!* Somehow she had gotten free of Hugh.

Envy pierced him, as ugly an emotion as he had ever felt. *Who had helped her?* He did not want to share that victory, share her gratitude, with anyone. Had she freed herself? Surely not. Hugh would never let her go. Perhaps Hugh was dead; yet not even that thought satisfied Ivar. He, Ivar, son of Harl and Herlinda, must be the one to kill Hugh—or, preferably, to humiliate him.

As wagons rumbled by, he could only stare at her receding back, at the braid that hung in a thick line to her waist. She looked closely at the ranks of hooded monks, their heads bowed modestly so none might see their faces. She knew he was here, didn't she? Surely she remembered he had been sent to Quedlinhame, only because he had tried to help *her*.

As he watched her ride away, he almost wept, yet was so filled with joy that he thought he must shine with it. Now, as she passed the last line of layservants, she stopped looking. She stared straight ahead instead, gaze fixed on some unseeable point, perhaps on the church towers whose gilded roofs glinted in the noonday sun. She was lost to him as the king's progress rode into Quedlinhame and the train—wagons, produce, servants, spare horses, tents, furnishings, the entire ponderous cavalcade that attended the king—trundled past, kicking dust up into his teeth.

Still he stared after her, keeping his head lifted defiantly as the long train passed, the last of the courtiers and their attendant servants at the end. He searched them all, looking for Hanna. Hanna had sworn to stay by Liath. But of Hanna he saw no sign.

The willow switch surprised him. This time it landed on his shoulders and he actually grunted out loud, it hurt so badly.

"It is unseemly to stare," said the schoolmaster coldly. "You bring notice on yourself."

Ivar clamped his lips shut over a retort. Now he could not get angry. Now he must plan. Liath had come to Quedlinhame and though the novices rarely stirred outside their dormitory and courtyard, though they were always heavily supervised, he would find a way to let Liath know he was here. He would find a way to see her, talk to her. To *touch* her.

Even thinking such a thing was a sin.

But he didn't care.

The last of the train rolled by. The monks and nuns fell into place behind the king's progress. Bells rang in Quedlinhame. Someone at the head of their procession began to sing and the others joined in as they walked back toward town, following the king.

> *O God, endow the king with Thine own justice,*
> *and give Thy righteousness to the king's heir*
> *so this one may judge Thy people rightly*
> *and deal out justice to the poor and suffering.*

By this time the road was a swirling, choking mass of dust made no better by the hysterical townsfolk who swarmed in behind the line of monks and nuns. Their excitement was itself a creature, huge and perilous and joyful. Was this not the king? There would be a ceremony later, after the king had washed himself and greeted his sainted mother in quieter rooms. Queen Mathilda was not strong enough for a public greeting. Then Mass would be sung in the town's church, and as many townsfolk as could manage would crowd into the church to see the king robed and crowned in royal splendor, his sacred presence a reminder of God's heavenly grace and Henry's earthly power. After the Feast of St. Valentinus tomorrow, townsfolk could bring their grievances to the king's personal attention, for he would rest in town for Hallowing Eve and the holy days of All Souls and All Saints which followed. Only then would he and his retinue ride on to Thurin Forest, where they would hunt. Ivar envied them the freedom to hunt.

But he had his own hunting to do. Somehow, at some time in the excitement during the next three days, Master Pursed-Lips would stray from his attentiveness. He would forget to watch quite as closely. Somehow Ivar would find a way to contact Liath.

4

LIATH had searched the line of monks along the roadside, but their heads had remained bowed, their faces hidden. So she rode on into Quedlinhame, through the town, and up a winding road that led to the top of the hill where thick walls protected monks and nuns from the temptations of the world; so Da had said to her. Had he been a brother here once?

Beyond the monastery gate, layservants took the horses and led them away to the stables. She started after them, swinging her saddlebag off the horse and draping its weight over her shoulder—then heard her name above the clamor of horses and wagons.

"Liath!" Hathui hailed her.

Liath threaded her way through the mob, avoiding a whippet hound snapping at the end of a leash, stepping over a fresh pile of horse manure, waiting as a noble lady still mounted on a fine gray gelding crossed in front of her.

"Come. We are to attend the king." Hathui smoothed down her tunic and straightened the brass badge that pinned her cloak. Then she frowned at Liath. "You should have left your gear with the horse. It'll be safe in a convent, I should think!"

Liath attempted a smile. "I didn't think. I just grabbed it."

Hathui crooked an eyebrow. She was not a woman easily fooled nor one to succumb to nonsense. "What's in there so precious that you'll never let that bag leave your side?"

"Nothing!" It was said too quickly, of course. Liath shifted the saddlebag on her shoulders, shrugging the back pouch aside where it had gotten tangled with her bow quiver. "Nothing special except to me. Something Da left to me. The only thing I have left of him."

"Yes, so you've said before," replied Hathui in the tone of someone who doesn't believe what she is hearing. "But if Wolfhere minds not, than neither shall I. He may settle this with you when he returns."

Which, Lady grant, might be many months from now. Though she missed Hanna bitterly, Liath did not regret that she would not see Wolfhere until next year, when he and Hanna could cross back over the mountains from Darre and return to the king's progress. She *liked* Wolfhere, but she could not trust him.

Monks walked through the gate. She looked for Ivar's pale, familiar face.

"Come, come, Liath. We wait upon the king. He does not wait upon *us*. Why are you staring so?"

Liath shook off the older woman's hand and followed beside her as they crossed the field. Ahead, the king and a few of his most trusted retainers gathered by the stairs that led up to the church's portico. "I know someone who is a novice here—"

"Ivar, son of Count Harl and Lady Herlinda."

Liath glanced sharply at her. "How did you know?"

"Hanna told me. She told me all about Ivar, her milk brother."

It stung, the dart of jealousy, that Hanna had formed such a friendship with this tough marchlander woman. Liath liked Hathui but could never be comfortable with her. She dared not trust anyone she had met after Da's death. Trusted no one now, except Hanna. Except possibly Ivar, if she could find him.

No one else, except Sanglant—and he was dead.

"Never meant for me even if he had lived," she muttered.

"What?" asked Hathui. Liath shook her head, not answering. "Hanna said Ivar loved you," Hathui added in an altered tone of voice. "Do you feel guilt for it still, that Frater Hugh condemned him to a life as a monk though it was no wish of the boy's? Only because he interfered with what Hugh wanted?"

"Hanna told you a great deal," said Liath, voice choked.

"We are friends. As you and I might be, but you are such a strange, distant creature, more like a fey spirit than a woman—" Hathui broke off, not because she wished to avoid offending Liath—Hathui said what she meant and intended no offense by it—but because they had reached the king. King Henry caught sight of Hathui and indicated with a gesture that she should walk behind him as they proceeded into the church. Liath stumbled over her own feet and hurried to catch up, not knowing where else to walk except behind Hathui. In the midst of so many fine nobles she could nurse her pain in private because, to the noble lords and ladies, she was merely an appendage of the king, like his crown or scepter or throne, not a real living person they had to take any notice of. She was simply an Eagle, a messenger to be dispatched at the king's whim.

Hanna had every right to tell Hathui whatever she wished, had every right to count Hathui as a friend. Wolfhere and Hathui and poor dead Manfred—the three Eagles who had rescued her from Hugh—surely knew or guessed the truth of her relationship to Hugh, knew that he had kept her warm in his bed though he was a holy frater and dedicated to the church, that he had gotten her with child and then beaten her nearly to death for defying him, after which beating she had miscarried. In the end, worn down by exhaustion and fear, she had given him *The Book of Secrets* and all it represented: her submission to him.

Only the arrival of Wolfhere and his two companion Eagles had saved her. *They* had rescued her from Hugh; she had not truly escaped him. Liath glanced up at Hathui's sturdy back, she who walked directly behind the king. Hathui had not once treated Liath with disrespect or scorned her, even knowing she had been a churchman's slave and concubine. Hathui might be only a freeholder's daughter, but the freeholders of the marchlands were notoriously proud. The king himself had seen fit to bestow on Hathui his favor. In the four months Liath had ridden with the king's progress, she had seen how Hathui was called frequently to the king's side, how he now and again asked her advice on some matter. This was indeed a signal honor for a woman born of common farmers.

Yes, Hanna had every right to count Hathui as a friend. But that endless niggling fear pricked at Liath: What if Hanna came to prefer Hathui? What if she loved Liath the less for liking Hathui more? It was a weak, unkind thought, both toward Hanna and toward Hathui. Liath could even now hear what Da would say were he alive to hear her confess such a thing: *"A rosebush can give more than one bloom each season."*

But Da was dead. Murdered. And Hanna was all she had

left. She wanted so desperately not to lose her. *"No use fretting about the donkey,"* Da would say, *"when he's safe inside the shed and you've loose chickens to save from the fox."*

At that moment Hathui glanced back at her and gave her a reassuring smile. They entered the church. It was surprisingly light inside the nave, a long lofty space with a wooden ceiling made of a checkerboard of crossbeams. A double row of arched windows set high in the wall, well above the decorative columns that lined the nave, admitted this light. The party walked forward solemnly so that Henry and his sister could kneel before the Hearth. Liath admired the parallel rows of columns, two round columns alternating with every square one to form the central nave. Eagles and dragons and lions adorned the capitals, carved cunningly into stone; these symbols of power served to remind visitors and postulants alike whose authority reigned here, second only to God in Unity. The floor was paved in pale yellow-and-dun granite. She tried, superstitiously, not to step on any of the cracks seaming the blocks into a larger whole.

The king mounted the steps at the far end of the nave and knelt before the Hearth. Liath knelt with the others, many of whom perforce had to get down on their knees on the stairs in all manner of awkward positions. Her knee captured the trailing end of Hathui's cloak so that the poor woman could not kneel forward comfortably, but it had become so very quiet in the church that Liath dared not shift even enough to loosen the cloak from her weight.

Mother Scholastica said a prayer over the Hearth to which the assembled nobles murmured rote responses. Liath could not keep her eyes from the Hearth, where a sparkling reliquary cut entirely from rock crystal and formed into the shape of a falcon rested next to Mother Scholastica's hand. Beside the reliquary stood a book so studded in gems and coated with gold leaf that it seemed of itself to emanate light.

Blessed and sanctified, King Henry rose, shook off his cloak into the hands of a waiting servant, and beckoned to Hathui and his two most trusted advisers: the crippled margrave, Helmut Villam, and the cleric, Rosvita of Korvei. Hathui beckoned to Liath, and the two Eagles hastened to follow these notables as they descended the stairs and exited the church by a smaller door that led into quarters reserved for the mother abbess and her servants.

In an insignificant room just off the abbess' private cloister, King Henry knelt beside the low bed on which his mother lay. He kissed her hands in greeting, as any son gives his mother the honor due her. "Mother."

She touched his eyes gently. "You have been weeping, my child. What is this grief for? Do you still mourn the boy?"

He hid his face even from her, but not for long. A mother's demands must be acknowledged. At last he set his face against the coarse wool blanket—fit for a common nun but surely not for a queen—and wept his sorrow freely while the others turned their gazes away.

They had all knelt in emulation of the king. Liath, at the back, studied their faces. Hathui stared steadily at the rough flagstone floor of the cell, her expression one of mingled pity and respect. The old margrave, Helmut Villam, wiped a tear from his own cheek with his remaining hand. Mother Scholastica frowned at the display—not at the sight of a grown man crying, for of course the ability to express grief easily and compassionately was a kingly virtue, but at the excessive grief Henry still carried with him at the death of a son who was, after all, only a bastard. The cleric had no expression Liath could read on her intelligent face, but she glanced Liath's way, as if she had felt her gaze upon her, and Liath looked down at once. *"Don't let them notice you,"* Da had always said. *"Safety lies in staying hidden."*

"Now, child," the old queen was saying to Henry. Though her body was weak and her voice tremulous, her spirit clearly had not quailed under the burden of her illness. "You will dry these tears. It has been half a year since the boy died—and an honorable death he had, did he not? It is time to let him go. Is this not the eve of hallowing? Let him go so that his spirit may ascend, as it must, through the seven spheres to come to rest at last in the blessed Chamber of Light. You bind his soul to this world with your grief."

"These are heathen words," said Mother Scholastica abruptly.

"It is a heathen holy day, is it not, though we have given

it a Daisanite name?" retorted the queen. Married young,
she had borne at least two of her ten children before she
was Liath's age, or so Liath calculated. She was at most
fourteen years older than Henry, who was her eldest child.
Her hair, uncoifed in the privacy of her cell, had a few
brown strands still woven in among the white. Whatever
sickness ravaged her came not only from the assault of
time but also from a more physical malady. "We speak of
Hallowing Eve still and pray to all the saints on these days
when the great tides of the heavens bring the living and
the dead close together—bring them so close that we might
even touch, if our eyes were open."

Liath caught in a sob. As she listened to the old queen
speak, she recalled Da so vividly that it was almost as if
she could *see* him standing beside her, glimpsed out of the
corner of her eye.

"It is a form of respect," continued the old woman, "that
I think God will not begrudge us."

Mother Scholastica bowed her head obediently, for although she was mistress of Quedlinhame and Mother over
all the nuns, including Mathilda, she was at the same time
this woman's daughter. Mathilda had been queen once and
was a powerful woman still, queen by title though she no
longer sat upon a throne.

"Henry, you must let him go, or he will wander here
forever, trapped by your grief."

"What if he can't die as we do?" asked Henry in a rasping voice. "What if his mother's blood forbids him entrance
to the Chamber of Light? Is he then doomed to wander as
a shade on this earth forever? Are we never to be reunited
in the blessed peace of the Light?"

"That is for Our Lord and Lady to judge," said Mother
Scholastica sternly, "not for us to trouble ourselves over.
Many books were written by the ancients on this question—
whether the Lost Ones had souls—but this is not the time
or place to debate that issue. Come, Henry. You are tiring
our mother."

"No," said the old queen. "I am not tired. If you speak
to me of your grief, Henry, perhaps that will ease it." She
looked up, her gaze sharper than Liath had expected from
a bedridden woman. "Villam is here."

It struck Liath suddenly that Helmut Villam was as old

as Queen Mathilda. Despite his crippling injury, he had far more vigor, the energy of a much younger person. The margrave came forward, kissed her hand, then retired to the door. The queen acknowledged Rosvita next, clasped the cleric's hands in her own in the sign of fealty. "My *History?*" she asked with a gentle smile. "How does it progress?"

The cleric's smile in answer was brief but sweet. "I hope to complete the First Book this year, Your Majesty, so that you may have it read to you and learn of the illustrious deeds of the first Henry and his son, the elder Arnulf."

"Do not tarry too long, my sister, for your words interest me greatly, and I fear I have not too many more days upon this earth."

Rosvita bowed her head, touching her forehead to the old queen's wrinkled hands. Then she stood and retreated.

"Who are these?" the old woman asked, looking at the two Eagles.

Henry glanced back. At first he appeared surprised. Then he registered Hathui. "My faithful Eagle," he said wryly. He looked beyond Hathui—Liath flinched when his powerful gaze focused on *her.* For an instant it was like Hugh's gaze, penetrating, absolute; like the strike of lightning, it could obliterate her. But Henry only marked her and looked away without further interest. "This other Eagle was at Gent. Together with Wolfhere she witnessed the destruction of the Dragons and the death of—" His voice broke, unable to speak the name of his dead son.

"Together with Wolfhere," said the queen thoughtfully, as if the name meant something to her. Liath stared at the gray stone, at its uneven surface and rough grade. No polished marble or fine granite blocks graced this common nun's cell. "Come forward, child."

One did not disobey a queen, even one who now professed to be a nun, not when she used *that* tone of voice. Liath hooked a foot under her body, stood, took seven small steps forward, and knelt again. Only then did she look up.

Gray eyes as cool as winter storm clouds and yet with a deep calm beneath them met Liath's gaze. "You are some relation to Conrad the Black, perhaps?" Queen Mathilda asked. "I have seen such coloring nowhere else, except per-

haps in—" She made a tiny gesture with one hand, a scis-
soring of fingers quickly made and quickly vanished.
Mother Scholastica rose and left the cell. Henry still
gripped his mother's other hand, the one that lay so still
upon the rough wool blanket. Mathilda had the most delicate wrists Liath had ever seen on an adult. Her small
hands were weathered with work, for Queen Mathilda was
famous for serving in common with the other nuns, such
was her humility. "You are no relation?"

Liath shook her head, not trusting herself to speak.

"You were in Gent?"

Liath nodded. Lady Above, please let her be satisfied
with this knowledge; please let her not demand that Liath
tell the entire awful heart-wrenching tale again, so that she
had to live through it again: that last vision seen through
fire, Sanglant struck down by an Eika ax and Bloodheart
gloating above his fallen body, holding aloft in his bare
bloody hand the golden neck torque that signified the
prince's royal kinship.

At that moment Liath realized Queen Mathilda did not
wear the golden torque, though her son and daughter did.
But she was not born of the royal lineages of Wendar and
Varre. She had only married into the family. At this moment, under that calm gray but utterly penetrating gaze,
Liath could not remember where Mathilda came from, of
what kin, of what country—only that she had ruled as
queen beside Arnulf the Younger, his second wife, and that
she now examined Liath with keen interest and not a little
understanding.

"You knew Sanglant," she said.

Liath nodded, dared say nothing in answer. *I loved Sanglant.* But the prince was not for her; even Wolfhere had
warned him away from her. *"Down that road I dare not
walk,"* Sanglant had said to her, for was he not an obedient
son? *"Be bound, as I am, by the fate others have determined
for you. That way you will remain safe."*

But the fate that had bound Sanglant, captain of the
King's Dragons and bastard son of a king, was nothing like
the fate she struggled against, whose bonds she could not
even recognize. Just as well, she thought bitterly, that he
was killed. It was only safe to love someone who was already dead.

Her expression betrayed her.

"The last," said the queen, comprehending the whole, "if not the first. Pretty enough that any might understand why he was tempted. That is enough, child. You may go."

Liath was mortified. To be discovered, to be seen through so easily, and by a woman who did not even know her! Henry was staring morosely at the far wall, idly twisting the signet ring on his right hand, not paying attention. Villam had gone outside to the sun. Only Hathui and Rosvita witnessed. Perhaps the queen had spoken too softly for them to hear. Liath dipped her head obediently and retreated, still on her knees, back to the safety of the door and Hathui's shadow.

But a queen—a girl brought from foreign lands to marry an older and possibly indifferent man—surely must learn to study faces and puzzle out intrigue from every line and utterance. After all, she had gotten *her* son onto the throne of Wendar and Varre despite the claim of the elder half sister—Arnulf's only living child from his first and some said more legitimate marriage. It would not do to underestimate a woman like Mathilda, no matter how weak she looked now.

Liath was allowed to leave, although Hathui remained with the king and the king appeared determined to remain for some while with his mother. Outside, no one asked her to run errands or carry a trifling message. She couldn't enter the innermost cloisters, of course, but when the king's progress had come to Quedlinhame it was impossible to stop visitors from wandering the grounds and gardens of the monastery. She climbed the outer wall and found a vantage point from which to look down over the foundation.

All monasteries—whether housing monks or nuns—were built on the same general plan, one laid out three centuries ago by St. Benedicta, founder of The Rule. Liath had seen plans of various monasteries, and once she had seen a thing and committed it to memory, it was the work of a moment to dredge it up again. *Mathilda.* She searched in the city of memory. Past the gate surmounted by the Throne of Virtue stood the halls of the kingdoms. She found the one inscribed with the Dragon, Lion, and Eagle of Wendar and went inside. On the dais Henry sat alone now that his queen, Sophia, had died. Behind him, through a curtain, lay the chamber of Arnulf the Younger, flanked on the right by his first wife, Berengaria of Varre, and on the left by Mathilda. This seated statue of Mathilda held in its right hand a scroll bearing the names of her nine children and in its left, signifying her descent, a small banner embroidered with the sigil of the kingdom of Karrone.

Liath backtracked to the hall of Karrone. There among the gathered dead and living nobles of the royal house, all cast in stone, she found Mathilda. Granddaughter of Berta, princess and later Queen of Karrone, the first Karronese prince to defy her Salian overlords and style herself regnant. Daughter of Berta's only son, prince and later King Rodulf, the last of Berta's five children, all of whom had held the throne, each in succession. Having seen the chronicle of the monks of St. Galle, Liath could even recall the dates of their reigns and their deaths. Rodulf had reigned from 692 until 710. His death had brought forth two claimants to Karrone's throne: his niece Marozia and his grandson, Henry. Marozia had seized the throne by right of proximity, and Henry, newly crowned king of Wendar and Varre, was too young in power to contest her. Instead he had married his younger brother Benedict to her daughter, also called Marozia; these two now reigned in the mountainous kingdom of Karrone as Queen Regnant and King Consort.

All of this Liath remembered, and much more besides. It was only in the central tower, the highest point in the city itself, that a door stood which she could not unlock—behind it rested *Da's secrets,* all he had kept hidden from her. She shook her head impatiently and scanned the monastery, searching for a small building with its own cloister, set apart from the others: the novitiary.

Eventually the novices would have to emerge from the novitiary, to pray, to attend to their bodily needs, to perform manual labor. The Rule enjoined that all nuns and monks spend some part of each day in labor, "for then are they truly laborers for God when they live by the labor of their hands."

She hunkered down to wait, finding a patch of warm autumn sun and tugging her cloak tight around her. The sudden cold autumn wind on her neck made her shudder, and she was abruptly seized with an unreasoning panic, heart pounding, breath caught in her throat and her hands trembling as if with a palsy. But Hugh wasn't here. *He wasn't here.* She still had the book, and other weapons besides. To calm herself, she touched them one by one, like talismans: Her short sword rested easily on her left hip; her eating knife nestled in a sheath; the weight of her bow, quiver and arrows made a comforting presence on her back.

Ai, Lady! Surely she was safe from Hugh now.

The door to the novitiary opened and a double line of brown-robed novices, heads bowed humbly, emerged from the novitiary and walked in strict columns by paved paths, then dirt ones, out to the gardens. Liath jumped up to follow them. Certain of the noble lords and ladies lounged at their leisure on the withering autumn grass or admired the late flowers in the herb garden; unlike Liath, they ignored the novices—all, that is, except the wheat-haired girl Liath recognized as Lady Tallia.

As the column of novices passed Tallia, she knelt on ragged grass and bowed her head in prayer. Liath found the girl's piety grating and excessive, but others praised her for it. Liath had been on the road for too long to find it admirable that Tallia ruined her gowns by using them to wash the Hearths of churches, scraping her pale fine hands raw in the process. That was all very well for a noblewoman who could replace such fine stuffs, but something else again for those who had little to spare. Tallia might fast at every opportunity and turn away fine meats and soft breads and rich savories, but at least she had such food to turn away. Liath had traveled the roads with Da for eight years. She had seen faces gaunt with starvation because the last harvest had run scant; she had seen children scrabbling in the dirt for precious grains of wheat and rye and oats.

Some among the novices did not ignore the nobles. Some looked up, curious—as she would have been curious, in their place. The watching schoolmaster scurried down the line and applied his willow switch to shoulders. They plodded out to the gardens where a ridge of soil lay dry and crumbling on one side from a summer under the sun and fresh and moist on the other where the novices had turned it up the previous day. With hoes, pointed sticks, and shovels, they commenced digging the unturned earth.

Liath picked her way down the steep stone stairs and

took a circuitous route across the grounds. Lady Tallia had ventured to the edge of the garden and Liath saw her pleading with the schoolmistress—for both male and female novices worked in the gardens this day, though at separate ends as was proper. After a bit, the schoolmistress relented and handed the girl a stick. With this in hand, she promptly climbed over the little stone fence that served to keep vermin out of the vegetables and with more enthusiasm than skill commenced digging beside the other female novices, oblivious to the stains that now accumulated on the hem and knees of her gold linen gown.

Liath circled in and took up a stance east of the novices, where she pretended to study the towers of the church. She busied herself with her cloak, flashing its scarlet trim.

Of a sudden she saw him, caught with his astonished gaze on her and his hoe frozen in the dirt. He nudged the boy next to him. Ai, Lady! Even from this distance Liath could see that his friend was remarkably handsome. The handsome boy elbowed another and that one the next until four faces stared at her while she stared back.

Ivar! He gaped at her for long stunned moments, then straightened, yanked his hoe out of the earth as if he meant to run over and greet her—and suddenly hunched over again to strike his hoe back into the dirt. All of them did, dutiful novices attending to their labor just in time for the schoolmaster to pass them by, willow switch in hand, and glower first at them and then, briefly, at the Eagle who was making a spectacle of herself so close by sheltered novices.

It would be impossible to speak to Ivar.

Impossible.

At that moment she noted the long narrow shed with many plank doors which sat out away from the cloister: the necessarium. Even holy church folk must attend to the needs of the earthly body. She looked back toward Ivar. He was chopping the hoe onto the dirt with one hand, pointlessly but enough to make it look as though he were working, and with his other hand making signs. Though Da had taught her the silent hand language used by nuns and monks, she stood too far from Ivar to read what he said, and she dared not move closer since the schoolmaster had already marked her. Instead, knowing Ivar watched her, she ostentatiously stretched one arm up over her head and slowly lowered it until her hand pointed toward the necessarium. She turned her back on the gardens and walked over to the long shed.

Picking a door at random—not at the very end, not in the middle—she pulled it open, paused so that Ivar had time to mark her, then stepped up onto a rough raised plank floor and closed herself into the gloom.

Lady Above! It stank of piss and excrement. But there was room to turn around and also, because this was a *royal* monastery, a sanded wood bench with a hole cut in the middle on which to sit. She sat on the edge of the bench, extremely careful to make sure no trailing end of cloak snaked down the hole to the pit below, and covered her nose and mouth with an edge of that cloak. In this way, shielded somewhat from the ripe smell of human waste by the honest scent of good plain wool, she waited.

She waited for a long time, so long, in fact, that the smell began not to bother her as much, and the occasional sounds as doors banged open or shut and folk—monks, nuns, and courtfolk alike—went about their business in the long shed began to have a kind of monotonous lulling pattern to them. Suddenly, a hand scraped at the rope handle. She shrank back into the corner as the door opened.

As quickly, a brown-robed figure slipped inside and closed the door behind him. She stood up, and because the space between bench and door was so narrow and because her left foot had gone numb, she staggered. He embraced her, steadying her, and clasped her hard against him. His hood fell back. She stood there, stiff and dumb, and he began muttering her name over and over as if he knew no other word and kissed first her neck and, as he got his bearings, her ear, her cheek and finally her mouth.

"Ivar." She slid a hand between them. He was taller than she remembered, filled out, broader in the shoulder. His embrace—so unfamiliar and yet utterly familiar—reminded her of long-ago nights in Heart's Rest when she and he and Hanna would run laughing out of a rainstorm and huddle together in the shelter of the inn stables. But they had so little time. "Ivar!" she said urgently, pulling away.

"Say you will marry me," he said softly, lips moist against her skin. "Say you will marry me, Liath, and we will escape from here somehow and make our way in the world. Nothing will stop us." He took in a sharp breath to speak more passionate words yet, then grunted. "Ai, Lord! What a stink!"

She muffled her giggles in the coarse fabric of his robe; he buried his face in her hair. In moments she was crying softly and he was, too. She closed her arms about his torso and hugged him tightly. Kinless, she had no one left her but Ivar and Hanna.

"Ai, Liath," he whispered. "What will we do? Whatever will we do?"

5

NIGHT came as it always did, whether this day's night or the next one he did not know. He no longer had any conception of time, only of the stone beneath him, the rain—or lack of it—on the roof, the dogs growling around him, the slaves scurrying about their tasks, bent and frightened, and the Eika on their way in and out of the cathedral, always moving. Sometimes they left him alone through days and nights he could no longer keep track of, for there was still a world outside although he had long since forgotten what it looked like. Most of the dogs went with them, then, although some few always stayed beside him. He was never truly alone. Perhaps it was better that he was never truly alone. Without the dogs, he would have forgotten that he existed.

Sometimes when they left him, he could only stare at nothing, or else at the stippling in the marble stone with its veins running away into nothing, or else at the scars on his arms and legs which were in all stages of healing, some still oozing blood, some pink, some scabbed, some the white of a cleanly healed wound.

Sometimes he was seized with such a restless surge of energy that he paced in the semicircle that was the limit of his chains, or lunged, or ran in place, or sparred with imaginary sword or spear against an imaginary opponent, the old drill he had learned so well that his body knew it by heart though he could not now put words to its movements. Only the chains hindered him. Always the chains hindered him, the iron collar, the heavy manacles chafing his wrists and his ankles.

"Why aren't you dead yet?" Bloodheart would ask with irritation when he returned, or in the mornings when light flooded in through open doors and the painted windows shone with stories from the Holy Verses: the blessed Daisan and the seven miracles; the Witnessing of St. Thecla; the *Vision of the Abyss* of St. Matthias; the *Revelation* of

St. Johanna: 'Outside are dogs and murderers, fornicators and sorcerers, and all who love deceit; only those whose robes are clean will have the right to enter the gates of the blessed city.'

Dog he was now. Murderer he had once been named by the mother of a young nobleman who had rebelled against the king's authority and paid for that rebellion with his life and the lives of his followers; no doubt the families of the barbarians who had invaded Wendar's borders and been killed by his Dragons in fair combat felt the same, but they never came to court to face him or his king. Fornicator—well, he could not regret a single one of the women he had slept with, and he had never heard that they regretted the act either.

He would have used sorcery to escape this torment had he known how. But that gift, said to be the life's blood of his mother's kin, he knew nothing of. She had abandoned him, and he had taken up instead the birthright of his father's people. Trained to fight and to die bravely, he knew nothing else. He had nothing else.

The brass badge pressed painfully against the joint where arm met shoulder as he shifted, trying to find a comfortable position so that the chains did not rub him raw.

The Eagle's badge. Her image came to his mind's eye as sharply as if he had seen her yesterday. Her name he remembered, when he had forgotten so much else: *Liath*.

"My heart rests not within me but with another, and she is far away from here." Was it true? Or had he only spoken those words as defiance, as a shield against Bloodheart's enchantment? What if it were true? What if it could be true?

There was a world beyond this prison, if he could only imagine it. But when he imagined life, he imagined war, battle, his brave Dragons dying around him. That imagining always led him here, chained to the altar stone in this cathedral. What was the name of the city?

She would know.

Gent. It was in Gent he waited, imprisoned, scraping sometimes at his chains, sawing at them with the knife when the Eika were absent, but he could not get free.

Yet as the holy man is freed from the world by contemplating God, surely he could free at least his mind from this prison by contemplating the world outside. He was not a holy man, to meditate on Our Lord and Lady, although surely he ought to. He was too restless for that holy peace, and uneducated in the disciplines of the mind.

The world outside waned from autumn to winter. It was cold. The dying sun would be reborn, as they sang in the Old Faith, and then spring would return. And he would still be chained.

She had led others to freedom. If he only imagined himself walking beside her through a field of oats, then Bloodheart could touch him no longer.

6

YOUNG Tallia, her wheat-colored hair and wheat-colored gown rendering her almost colorless, knelt on the hard stone floor before Mother Scholastica's chair. The girl carefully avoided the carpet laid on the floor, as if she dared not succumb to the luxury of padding beneath her much-abused knees.

"I beg you!" she cried. "I want nothing more than to dedicate my life to the church in memory of the woman I was named after, Biscop Tallia of Pairri, she who was daughter of the great Emperor Taillefer. If you would let me pledge myself as a novice here at Quedlinhame, I would serve faithfully. I would humble myself as befits a good nun. I would serve the poor with my own hands and wash the feet of lepers."

The king, pacing, turned at this. "I have had several marriage offers for you, none of which I am tempted to act on at this time—"

"I beg you, Uncle!" Tallia had the dubious ability to make tears spring out at any utterance. But Rosvita did not think this entirely contrived: The girl had a kind of tortured piety about her, no doubt from living with her mother Sabella and her poor idiot of a father, Duke Berengar. "Let me be wed to Our Lord, not to the flesh."

Henry lifted his eyes to heaven as if imploring God to grant him patience. Rosvita had heard this argument played out a dozen times in the last six months—indeed, Tallia seemed to have memorized the speech—and the cleric knew Henry wearied of it and of the girl's dramatic piety.

"I am not opposed to your vocation," said the king, turning back finally and speaking with some semblance of patience, "but you are an heiress, Tallia, and therefore not so easily removed from the world."

The girl cast one beseeching glance toward Queen Mathilda, who reclined on a couch, then clasped her hands at her breast, shut her eyes, and began to pray.

"However," said Mother Scholastica before the girl could get well-launched into a psalm, "we have agreed, King Henry and I, that for the time being you will reside with the novices here at Quedlinhame. But only until a decision has been made over what will become of you."

By this means, of course, Henry and Scholastica placed Tallia as a virtual hostage in the middle of Henry's strongest duchy. But Tallia wept tears of gratitude and was finally—thank the Lady—led away by the schoolmistress.

Queen Mathilda said, into the silence, "She seems fierce in her vocation."

"Indeed," said Henry in the tone of a man who has been pressed too far. "Her privations are legendary."

Mother Scholastica raised one eyebrow. She studied the owl feather—her quill pen—that lay by her right hand; touching its feathers briefly, stroking them with the tip of a finger, she looked at her mother. "Excessive piety can itself be a form of pride," she said dryly.

"So did I observe in you," said the old queen with the barest of smiles, "when you were young."

"So did I come to observe in myself," said Mother Scholastica without smiling. Here, in her private study with only family and clerics in attendance, she had let slip her white scarf to reveal hair, rather lighter than Henry's, liberally sprinkled with gray. Only three years younger than Henry, she looked perhaps ten years younger. This contradiction was much debated in the matristic writings. Women, blessed with the ability to bleed and to give birth, suffered from that birthing if they took advantage of the blessing, while those who pledged themselves and their fertility to the church, living their lives as holy virgins, often lived much longer lives. Mathilda, who had given birth to ten children and been widowed at the age of thirty-eight, looked as ancient and frail as Mother Otta, the abbess of Korvei Convent, but Mother Otta was ninety and the queen only fifty-six.

Now, later that same day, these thoughts came back to Rosvita as she knelt with the congregation in the Quedlinhame town church. Thunder rumbled in the distance as Mother Scholastica intoned the final words of her homily.

"The Lady does not give out her blessing freely. This is God's way of teaching a lesson to humankind. Although the gift of bearing children is certainly a blessing, the means by which we mortals can in some measure know immortality, all earthly beings are tainted with the infinitesimal grains of the primordial darkness that mixed by chance with the pure elements of light, wind, fire, and water. That intermingling brought about the creation of the world. And those of us who live in the world are thereby stained with darkness. Only through the blessed Daisan's teaching, only through the blinding glory of the Chamber of Light, can we cleanse ourselves and attain a place at Our Lord's and Lady's side. So ends the teaching."

The brethren—monks and nuns from Quedlinhame—sang the *Te Deum,* the hymn to God's glory. Their voices blended with the fine precision of a choir used to singing in concord. With this music as accompaniment, King Henry entered the church in formal procession.

Rosvita stifled a yawn. It was so very muggy for this late in the year, and she was not as young as she once had been. It was no longer easy to stand—or kneel—through an entire service. For how many years had she traveled with the king's progress? How often had she seen the banners representing the six duchies carried in and displayed, symbol of the king's earthly power? How many times had she watched the ceremonial anointing, robing, and crowning of the king on feast days? Yet even now as King Henry ascended the steps that led to the altar stone and Hearth, the familiar quaver of awe caught in her throat.

Bareheaded but clad in a robe woven of cloth-of-gold, his shoes detailed in gold braid, King Henry knelt before his sister, Mother Scholastica, offering himself before the Lady's Hearth. Every soul knelt with the king. The abbess combed his newly cut hair with an ivory comb encrusted with gold and tiny gems. She anointed him with oil, on the right ear, from the forehead to the left ear, and on the crown of his head.

"May Our Lord and Lady crown you with the crown of glory, may They anoint you with the oil of Their favor," she said.

Assisted by certain local nobles singled out for this honor, she placed the robe of state over his shoulders; trimmed with ermine, woven of the finest white wool, the cloak bore the emblems of each duchy embroidered across its expanse: a dragon for Saony, an eagle for Fesse, a lion

for Avaria, a stallion for Wayland, a hawk for Varingia—
and a *guivre* for Arconia.

"The borders of this cloak trailing on the ground," the
abbess continued, "shall remind you that you are to be
zealous in the faith and to keep peace."

Rosvita shuddered, thinking of the *guivre*—the terrible
basilisk-like creature—whose presence had almost won the
Battle of Kassel for Sabella.

But Sabella had not won. A monk and a boy had killed
the *guivre,* surely a sign of God's displeasure at Sabella's
attempt to usurp her half brother's power. Henry's luck—
the luck of the rightful king—had held true.

Now Mother Scholastica handed Henry the royal scepter,
a tall staff carved out of ebony wood and studded with
jewels, its head carved into the shape of a dragon's head
with ruby eyes gleaming.

"Receive this staff of virtue. May you rule wisely and well."

On this staff the king leaned as Mother Scholastica
crowned him in the sight of all the folk who were present.

"Crown him, God, with justice, glory, honor, and strong
deeds."

A great sigh swept through the crowd, mingled awe and
pleasure at the rare sight of their king crowned and robed
in the sight of God and his countryfolk.

From the gathered host a single voice cried out: "May
the King live forever!" Other voices from the crowd answered the first with the same words until the acclamation
was a roar of approval.

From her station on the steps below the Hearth, Rosvita
surveyed the assembled courtfolk, brethren, and local nobles come from their estates to watch the ceremony and to
feast after with the king and his retinue. She sought in their
faces some clue to their state of mind. Few of the nobles
here would harbor any sympathy for the recently imprisoned Sabella. But in other duchies the king's position was
not so strong. That was why he had to travel constantly
across his kingdom: so that his people could see him; so
that his nobles would be reminded in ceremonies like this
one that *he* was king and therefore had authority to rule;
and so that Henry, appearing before them, could demand
troops and supplies for his wars—in this case, for an assault
on Gent.

The boom of thunder rolled, shaking glass windows and causing one child in the back of the nave to start crying.

What did the thunder portend? Those called fulgutari claimed they could divine the future by observing the sound and appearance of storms and the direction of thunder and lightning. This display now, with great booms of thunder rattling the church and lightning scoring bright flashes against the lowering sky of late afternoon, seemed to underscore Henry's power, as if God in Their Unity reminded the assembled people that he had received God's grace.

But perhaps it portended other things. Divination by thunder was condemned by the church as were all forms of divination, for women and men must trust to God and not seek knowledge of what is to come. It was sacriligious even to think of heathen practices.

Rain lashed the windows. The side doors were opened to allow the poor to process through in an orderly line. None complained that, waiting outside, they had gotten soaked through. They waited gratefully for this chance to be blessed and touched by King Henry himself, for was it not true that the anointed king's touch might bring healing?

Rosvita yawned again. She ought to be watching the holy blessings, but she had seen this same scene, albeit rarely with the dramatic background of thunder and lightning, so many times before on the endless itinerant progress of the king. Could the heathens foretell the future from the sounds and directions of thunder? Surely not. Only angels and the daimones of the upper air could see into the future, and back into the past, for they did not live in Time in the same way humans did. But, alas, she could never help thinking of such things, sacrilegious though they might be. She would be damned by her curiosity; Mother Otta of Korvei Convent had told her that so many times, although not without a smile.

Thunder rumbled off into the northwest, and the rain slackened as the last of the poor and sick shuffled past King Henry for the ritual blessing. The nobles shifted restlessly—as restless as the weather or as their fears that Henry would demand large levies from them in the coming season of war.

At last the final hymn was sung. A happy babble of voices filled the church as the king led the procession out of the church. In the royal hall, the Feast of All Saints

would be celebrated. Rosvita followed the king together
with the rest of his retinue, nobles and townsfolk crowded
behind, all eager to partake in some way of the meal, even
if it was simply bread handed out from the doors. Her
stomach, like a distant failing echo of the thunder, rumbled
softly, and she chuckled.

In the morning, still driven by nagging thoughts of thunder and portents, she availed herself of Quedlinhame's excellent library. She ought to be working on her *History of
the Wendish People*, but she knew from long experience
that until this nibbling curiosity was satisfied, she would be
able to think of nothing else.

Rosvita turned first to Isidora of Seviya's great encyclo-
pedia, the *Etymologies*, which contained descriptions of various forms of sorcery and magic. But Isidora's book had
only a passing reference to the fulgutari.

Dissatisfied, Rosvita replaced the volume in its cabinet
and latched the door. The library had long since outgrown
its original chamber and now several smaller rooms contained the overflow books. She stood in one of these chambers now; the *Etymologies* had been consigned here not
because the work was unimportant—far from it—but because, Rosvita thought uncharitably, Quedlinhame's librarian was incompetent and disorganized. There was no logical
order to the placement of the books, and in order to find
which cabinet any book might reside in, one had to consult
the catalog—which sat on a lectern in the central library
hall. Rosvita sighed. *In wrath, remember mercy.* No doubt
her own faults were greater than those of the librarian.

As she crossed back through the warren of dark rooms,
she saw a cloaked figure standing in the pale light afforded
by a slit of a window high in one stone wall: one of the
King's Eagles.

She paused in shadow and stared—not at the young
woman, for this Eagle was instantly recognizable for her
height and coloring, but at what she was doing. Clerics took
little notice of Eagles, who were recruited from the children
of stewards, freeholders, artisans, or merchants. Clerics
wrote the letters and capitularies and cartularies which
were handed over, sealed, to the king's messengers. Eagles
carried those messages; they did not read them.

A very few, like the infamous Wolfhere, had been educated—as had, evidently, this strange young person as well.

The young Eagle stood and, in light surely too dim for any human eyes to see finely written calligraphy, *read* a book. Her finger traced the lines of text and her lips moved, her profile framed by dust motes floating downward on the thin gleam of light. So intent was she on her reading that she remained oblivious to Rosvita's presence.

In the silence of Korvei Convent, where nuns communicated by hand signs, Rosvita had learned the trick of reading lips. She had even used this skill to learn things forbidden to novices. Now, curiosity piqued, she tried to puzzle out syllables and sound from the movements of the young woman's lips—

—and was baffled. The Eagle read not in Wendish or in Dariyan, but in another language, one Rosvita could not "hear" through seeing. Where had such a young person learned to read? What on earth was she reading?

Rosvita glided softly out of the room, passed through an arch, and emerged into the library hall, blinking at the sudden shift in light. Here, at individual carrels, several nuns read. Cabinets stood along the walls, shut and latched. The catalog rested on a lecturn carved with owls peeking out from oak trees. It lay open. Rosvita skimmed the titles listed on the page: St. Peter of Aron's *The Eternal Geometry,* Origen's *De Principiis,* Ptolomaia's *Tetrabiblos,* Abu Ma'shar's *Zīj al-hazārāt.*

Rosvita blinked back amazement. Could it be this book that the girl read? She recognized the language, here transposed into Dariyan script, though she could not read Jinna herself. Did the girl claim Jinna ancestry, revealed in her complexion? Had she been trained to read the Jinna language? This was a mystery indeed. The young Eagle would bear watching.

Given the company it kept, the book appeared to be about matters astronomical. Surely even the librarian here, for all her faults, would catalog books about the weather— which took place in the sky—near to those about the heavens. Rosvita flipped idly through the pages, searching for *what* she was not sure, but could find nothing that seemed to be what she wanted.

Distracted, she shrugged and stretched and examined the

room. From here she could see into the scriptorium, where nuns and monks worked in silence writing correspondence and making copies of missals and old texts. The monastery had recently received from a sister institution six ancient papyrus scrolls written in Dariyan and Arethousan. These were being recopied onto parchment and bound into books.

Drawn by the light pouring in through the windows and the quiet murmur emanating from the scriptorium, Rosvita wandered past the cabinets and out under a wall set with arches into the scriptorium. Here some of the novices had assembled to obscrve the scribes at work—work they would themselves be engaged in once they became monks. One restless boy, his hood slipped back to reveal curly red-gold hair and a pale freckled face, sidled up to the schoolmaster and made a hand sign: *Necessarium.* With obvious disgust, the schoolmaster signed assent. No doubt the poor boy had been consigned to the monastery against his will and now chafed at the discipline: Rosvita had seen such novices in her time at Korvei.

With a sudden and violent start she recognized the boy. Ivar had not yet been born when she entered Korvei Convent, and she had actually only met him on two occasions. Perhaps she was mistaken; perhaps this was not Ivar at all but merely a northcountry boy who resembled him in coloring. But their father, Count Harl, had written to her not six months ago telling her that Ivar was to be pledged as a novice at Quedlinhame. It had to be him.

Ivar hurried out of the scriptorium, not noticing Rosvita. But he went on into the library rather than going outside. And meanwhile, three other novices distracted the schoolmaster, asking him about a parchment laid on one of the desks. Clearly they meant him not to notice where Ivar had gone.

So Rosvita followed him.

He hurried through the library hall and vanished into the warren of dim rooms beyond. She entered cautiously and was quickly rewarded by the sound of voices, so soft that had she not been listening for them she might have thought it the sough of the wind heard through the windows. By listening for direction and sound, as the fulgutari were said to observe the movement of storms, she managed to creep close enough to overhear without being seen.

"But your vows—"

"I care nothing for my pledge! You know that. My father forced me to become a novice here, just because of—" Here he bit off a word. "I'm not like Sigfrid, I have no vocation. And I won't be like Ermanrich who resigned himself long ago—"

"But is it so easy to be released from that pledge? Ai, Lady. Ivar, I'm flattered—"

"You don't want to marry me!"

Rosvita almost stumbled and gave herself away, but she had just enough presence of mind to lay a palm against the carven door of one of the cabinets: the same one, she noted with a dry smile, in which resided Isidora's *Etymologies.* She recognized the image carved into the oak door. It was St. Donna of Pens, the famed librarian of the first convent founded by St. Benedicta, holding scroll and quill pen. If only Quedlinhame's librarian had followed the good saint's example, this fine collection of books would not be arranged in such disorder.

Lady and Lord! Her little brother, now a novice, wanted to marry some unknown and unnamed woman! Their father would be furious.

"Ivar," said the unknown and unnamed woman in a calm voice. Her accent was slight but peculiar. "Ivar, listen to me. You know I have nothing, no kin—"

This was all it took, that he would become infatuated with a kinless woman! No wonder Count Harl had sent him to the monastery: to get him out of trouble.

"—or none who know me. I have safety in the Eagles."— The Eagles!—"Surely you understand that I can't marry you unless you offer me that kind of safety."

The Eagle Rosvita had seen loitering in this chamber earlier had waited here for this very assignation! At that moment, groping as for a stone, Rosvita could not recall the young woman's name. Instead, the cleric leaned against the carved cabinet doors and settled herself for a long wait while she listened to her brother launch into an impassioned, if whispered, plea for love, marriage, indeed every part of the world which six months ago on entering Quedlinhame he had sworn to renounce forever.

7

"I'LL leave the monastery," Ivar concluded. "We'll travel east and find service in the marchlands. There's always need for soldiers in the east—"

"But don't you understand?" she said with fine disregard for his sincerity. Did she not think he could do what he pledged? Did she not understand that he would do *anything* for her? "Until you had such a place, until I was assured of such a place, I can't leave the Eagles. How can you ask me to?"

"Because I love you!"

She sighed, brushing a hand across her lips, breathing through her fingers. He wanted to kiss those fingers but dared not. After their first embrace—in the privies—she had become, not cooler but more distant.

"I love you as well, but as a brother. I can't love you—" Here the hesitation. "—in *that* way." Her second hesitation was longer and more profound. "I love another man."

"You love another!" Angry, he said the first name that came to his lips. "Hugh!"

She went still and cold and deathly rigid.

"Ai, Lord, forgive me, Liath. I didn't mean to say it. I know—"

"It doesn't matter." She shook herself free. Dim light sifted in through the stout cabinets of books, books upon books upon books, so many that their weight alone felt like a pile of stones crushing him. Just as Liath's words crushed him. "This man's dead. I trust you, Ivar, but if it ever came to pass that all obstacles were put aside and we married, you must understand I could never love you in the way I loved him."

If. "If" sounded to Ivar like a very good word.

"Lady!" She rested a hand—too briefly—on his shoulder. The warmth of her flesh burned him through his coarse robes. "I sound so selfish. But I'm alone in the world. I have to protect myself."

"No, *I* am here." He gripped her hand in his, the clasp of kinship. "I am always here. And Hanna is with you, surely." In the privies, he had not had time to ask about Hanna, only time to arrange this meeting—only time to kiss her. He had dreamed of Liath last night and embarrassed himself in his sleep, but the others, Baldwin, Ermanrich, and Sigfrid, had helped him hide the traces.

"Hanna was sent south with Wolfhere, to escort Biscop Antonia—" She shook her head, impatient with herself. "You wouldn't know about that. I beg you, Ivar, understand that—it's not just Hugh I need to be safe against. It's . . . it's other things, things that chased Da and me for years until they finally caught up and killed him, and I don't know *what* they are. Ai, Lady." She leaned forward, against him—but not to embrace him as he wished, only to whisper as if she feared the walls themselves, the books in their silent waiting, might hear. "Do you understand?"

A year ago, Ivar would have dismissed all these concerns with a wave of the hand and with grandiose plans that came to nothing. But he was older now, and he had, amazingly, learned something.

"All right, then," he said, as calmly as he could, for she was still leaning against him. "You will marry no man but me."

She gave a caught-in laugh, more a sob perhaps. "I could never have married *him*. If not him, then you, because I can trust you." But she said it wistfully, as if she still mourned that other man whose name she dared not utter out loud.

Ivar felt he might float, he was so happy. She *trusted* him.

In time, he thought, she would forget the other man. In time she would love Ivar alone and only remember as a kind of hazy dream that she had spoken so about another man, a dead man. A dead man was no rival to a living one. And, because he had learned, for the first time he *thought* rather than acted impulsively. She was kinless, so needed kin, clan, family. There was Hugh to deal with; but Ivar *wanted* his revenge on Hugh, and he understood Hugh well enough to know that if Ivar had Liath, then, sooner or later, Hugh would appear. There remained only how to get out of the monastery. He must find a way to escape. But this would take planning.

"It will take time," he said at last and with reluctance.
"Will you wait for me?"

She smiled sadly. "I will stay an Eagle. That much I can
promise you. They are my kin now."

"Hush," he said suddenly, pressing her away from him.
A rustling more like mice than wind sounded from the
hidden corner of the room. "Who's there?" Ivar demanded.

She came out quietly from behind a row of cabinets. It
took Ivar a few moments to recognize her in the dim room,
and then his mouth dropped open in astonishment.

"Are you my sister Rosvita?" he demanded.

"Ai, Lady," swore Liath. She jerked away from him.

"Yes, Ivar." As soon as the cleric spoke, he knew it for
truth. "My brother," she continued, expression bland and
eyes bright with—laughter? anger? He did not know her
to be able to judge. "My brother novice," she went on,
gesturing toward his coarse brown robe, "this is most irregular. I will have to report you to Mother Scholastica."

But at those words, Ivar exulted. "Very well," he said,
drawing himself up. "I will go willingly." Brought to Mother
Scholastica's notice for the sin of consorting with a woman,
surely—*surely*—the mother abbess would throw him out of
Quedlinhame once and for all time.

It was a serious enough offense that Ivar had only to
wait through Sext, the midday prayers, kneeling like a penitent on the flagstone floor in front of Mother Scholastica's
empty and thereby imposing chair, before the door opened
behind him and the abbess entered her study. Rosvita
walked with her. Ivar could not read his sister's expression.
He wished he knew her, so that he might guess what she
had told the abbess, might guess whether Rosvita was sympathetic or hostile to his cause. But he did not know and
dared not guess.

"I gave you no leave to look up, Brother Ivar," said
Mother Scholastica.

He flinched and dropped his gaze, watched feet shift, a
dance whose measure and steps he could not follow. To his
horror, Rosvita retreated from the room to leave him alone
with the formidable abbess. He clenched his hands together, wrapping the fingers tightly around each other, and
bit down on his lower lip for courage. His knees hurt. There

was a carpet, but he had been strictly enjoined not to kneel upon anything that would soften his penance.

Mother Scholastica sat down in her chair. For a long while, though he dared not look up, he knew she studied him. A knob, an uneven hump in the stone, dug into his right knee. It was so painful he thought he would cry, but he was afraid to utter any complaint.

She rules with a rein of iron, so they all said. She was the king's younger sister. Why had he ever ever thought, in that wild liberating moment in the library, that he could face her down?

She cleared her throat as a prelude to speaking. "In our experience," she said, "when the king visits Quedlinhame with his court, there runs in his wake like the wash of a boat on the waters a shiver of restlessness through those of the novices and some few of the brothers and sisters who are not at that moment content in their vows. Always a few, seduced by the bright colors and the panoply and the excitement, mourn their loss of the world and seek to follow the king. It is our duty to rescue these fragile souls from their folly, for it is a fleeting temptation, dangerous but not, I think, unforeseeable."

"But I never wanted—"

"I did not yet give you leave to speak, Brother Ivar."

He hunched down, nails biting into knuckles. She did not have to raise her voice to make him feel humiliated and terrified.

"But I do mean to give you leave to speak. We are not barbarians, like the Eika or the Quman riders, to enslave you for no cause but our own earthly enrichment. It is your soul we care for, Ivar. Your soul we have been given charge of. That is a heavy burden and a heavy responsibility." She paused. "*Now* you may speak, Brother."

Given leave to speak, he also took the chance to shift his right knee off the digging knob of rock. Then he took a breath. Once begun, he could not hide his passion. "I don't want to be here! Let me go with the king. Let me be a Dragon—"

"The Dragons are destroyed."

"Destroyed?" The news shook him out of his single-minded fury.

"They were overwhelmed by a force of Eika, at Gent."

Destroyed. Trying to make sense of this, he looked up at her. He had never actually seen Mother Scholastica from this close before; only the rare novice, like Sigfrid, came into contact with the abbess. She had a handsome face, her hair tucked away inside a plain linen scarf draped and folded over her head and twisting in neat lines down over her shoulders. She wore dark blue robes to distinguish her from the other nuns, a gold Circle of Unity studded with gems on a gold chain that hung halfway down her chest, and the golden torque that signified her royal kinship around her neck. Her gaze remained cool; she was not one bit flustered by this meeting or by the circumstances which had brought him here. He had a sudden, awful notion that she had judged many a boy or girl whose complaint was similar to his.

He would not let himself be overawed by her consequence! He was also the son of noble parents, if not of a king. "Then—then they'll need more Dragons," he blurted out. "Let me go, please. Let me serve the king."

"It is not my decision to make."

"How can you stop me if I refuse to take vows as a monk when my novitiate is ended?" he demanded.

She raised an eyebrow. "You have already pledged yourself to enter the church, an oath spoken outside these gates."

"I had no choice!"

"You spoke the words. I did not speak them for you."

"Is a vow sworn under compulsion valid?"

"Did I or any other hold a sword to your throat? *You* swore the vow."

"But—"

"And," she said, lifting a hand for silence—a hand that bore two handsome rings, one plain burnished gold braid, the other a fine opal in a gold setting, "your father has pledged a handsome dowry to accompany you. We do not betroth ourselves lightly, neither to a partner in marriage—" He winced as she paused. Her gaze was keen and unrelenting. "—nor to the church. If a vow can be as easily broken as a feather can be snapped in two—" She lifted a quill made from an owl feather from her table, displaying it to him. "—then how can we any of us trust the other?" She set down the feather. "Our oaths are what make us honorable people. What man or woman who has forsworn his noble lord or lady can ever be trusted again? *You* swore your promise to Our Lady and Lord. Do you mean to forswear that oath and live outside the church for the rest of your days?"

Said thus, it all sounded so much more serious. No man or woman who made a vow and then broke it was worthy of honor. His knees ached; his back hurt. His hood had slipped back, and the hem of his robe had doubled up under his left calf to press annoyingly into the flesh.

"No. I—" He faltered. Had he actually imagined scant hours ago that he could get the better in a debate with Mother Scholastica?

"Why now, Ivar?" She, too, shifted in her chair, as if her back hurt *her,* and for one uncharitable moment he hoped it did. "You are a good boy and never rebellious, never like this. *Was* it the king's arrival?"

He flushed. Of course she must already know.

"You are tempted by the presence of so many women who are not bound by vows," she went on, as if toying with him, though her voice remained level and her expression clear and calm. "Do not be ashamed to admit such to me, Ivar. I understand that we who pledge ourselves to the church have to battle the temptations of the flesh in order to make ourselves worthy. Those who remain in the world do their part as well, but theirs is a different path. We in the church strive to set the darkness behind us, to make of ourselves an immaculate chamber, to set aside the taint of darkness that lies within each of us, that is part of each of us. For did the blessed Daisan not preach that although we are bound by our nature, God's goodness to humankind was in giving us liberty?"

" 'Keep clear of all that is evil,' " responded Ivar dutifully, for these sayings had been drilled into the novices, " 'which we would not wish to befall ourselves.' "

"Good is natural to us, Ivar. We are glad when we act rightly. As the blessed Daisan said, 'Evil is the work of the Enemy, and therefore we do those evil things when we are not masters of ourselves.' "

"But—but I don't want *this* path. Not this one. I want—"

"Can you be sure?"

"It isn't *women*—it isn't just any—"

"*One* woman?"

He betrayed himself, but surely that did not matter. She already knew. He caught in his breath abruptly, a stab of pain in his lungs. What had happened to Liath? What if she was thrown out of the Eagles?

"A woman who traveled with the king's progress," continued Mother Scholastica in that same emotionless voice. Not emotionless, no—she spoke without being torn by emotion, without the violent feelings that ripped him apart from within.

Ai, Lord. The memory of embracing Liath—even in the stink of the privies . . .

"This, too, will pass, Ivar. I have seen it happen so many times."

"Never!" He leaped to his feet. "I will always love her! Always! I loved her before I came here, and I will never stop loving her. I promised I would marry her—"

"Ivar. I beg you, take hold of yourself and remember dignity."

Panting with anger and frustration, he knelt again.

"As the blessed Daisan said, 'For desire is a different thing from love, and friendship something else than joining together with evil intent. We ought to realize without difficulty that false love is called lust and that even if it gives temporary peace, there is a world of difference between that and true love, whose peace lasts till the end of days, suffering neither trouble nor loss.' "

He could not speak. He stared fixedly at one of the paned windows which let light into the study. A branch scraped the glass as it swayed in a rising wind, and the last remaining leaf dangled precariously, ready to fall.

"You must have your father's permission to marry. Do you?"

There was no need to answer. He wanted to cry with shame. None of this had gone as he had planned.

"Do not think I take this lightly, child," she said. He risked a glance up, for a certain note of compassion had surfaced in her tone. She did indeed have an expression on her face that he could almost call sympathetic. "I can see you are firm in your resolve and passionate in your attachment. But I am not free to let you go. You were given into my care by your father and your kin, you spoke your vows—willingly, I thought—and were taken into this monastery. It would be unwise of me to let every young person walk free at each least impulse toward the world."

"This isn't an *impulse!*"

She lifted her ringed hand for silence. "Perhaps not. If it is not an impulse, as you claim, then time will not dull it. I will send a message to your father, and you will wait for his reply. What you propose is not an undertaking to be entered into lightly, just as we should not any of us enter into the church lightly." By this mild rebuke she scolded him. "There remains also the young woman to be considered. Who is she? She has a name, I have discovered—an unusual name, Arethousan. Who are her kin?"

"I don't know anything about her," he admitted finally. "Not really. No one in Heart's Rest did."

"Is she of noble birth?"

He blinked. Perhaps silence was the better choice. Liath and her father had been close with their secrets. And her father *had* died—although only Liath had claimed it was murder; Marshal Liudolf had decreed the death came of natural causes.

"Answer me, child."

He did not like the stern look Mother Scholastica fixed on him. "I—I think so. Her father was educated."

"Her mother?"

He shrugged. "She never had a mother. I mean—we never knew of her mother."

"Her father was educated—? Was he a fallen monastic, perhaps? Ah, yes, I see it in your face."

"I don't *know* that he was. But we all thought he must have been a monk once, or perhaps a frater—"

"If he left the church, he would scarcely speak of such an act out loud. Educated in and then fled from the church. You are sure she was *his* child?"

"Yes!" he exclaimed, indignant on Liath's behalf.

"Not his concubine or servant?"

"No! Of course they were father and child."

"It might explain all," said Mother Scholastica, musing now; she appeared to have forgotten Ivar's existence, and certainly cared nothing for his indignation. "Why she could read Jinna."

Read Jinna? What else was hidden in Liath that she had

never shared with him? He had a sudden sick intuition that
Frater Hugh might not have been interested in Liath only
for her beauty and youth.

"Dark of feature. A fallen churchman. Perhaps my
mother was right. A frater may travel as a missionary to
the four quarters of the world, even unto the Jinna heathens who worship the fire god Astereos. Such a man might
have been seduced by the potions and perfumes of the east,
such a man might have forsworn his oath to the church and
gotten a child on an eastern woman and then, as an honorable Daisanite, refused to leave the child behind to be
raised as a heathen. That would explain her complexion
and her ability to read. Well, Ivar." The abrupt change of
subject startled him, her sudden cooling of interest in him.
"It is good you confessed this to me. Return to the novitiary. You will study. You will obey. In time, *if* you do your
duty and remain meek and humble, I will call you here
again and let you know what answer your father has given."

The interview was over. She signed with her hand the
gesture for departure, and he knew there was no point in
protesting. But he could not leave one question unasked,
even if he was punished for asking it.

"What will happen to Liath? Because of what I did, I
mean."

She favored him with a sudden smile, and its power—its
approval—struck him as if he had been granted a glimpse
of the Chamber of Light in all its brilliance through a crack
in the gates. "That is the first time in this interview you
have spoken of *her* need and not your own. She serves as
a King's Eagle, and I have heard no complaint of her service there. It will continue. Now." He bowed his head over
clasped hands, was allowed to kiss her opal ring, and
backed out of the room, stumbling down backward over
the doorstep.

Master Pursed-Lips waited outside, as glowering as any
looming storm cloud. Mercifully, he withheld the willow
switch.

"You may be certain," said the schoolmaster in his dis-
agreeable voice, "that you and your fellows, whose conniv-
ance in this matter has been duly noted, will be confined
in the novitiary for the remainder of the king's visit, and
closely guarded thereafter. Take no notion in your mind to

escape and run after them. We have dealt with these kinds
of things before."

Spoken ominously, the schoolmaster's threats proved
true. The king's progress left the next day and although the
other novices got to leave the barracks and line the road
to lend pomp and dignity to the departure of king and
court, Ivar, Baldwin, Ermanrich, and Sigfrid were left behind. They waited out the dreary interlude in the courtyard,
taking turns with their knives at the fence.

"*She's* really in love with you?" demanded Baldwin.

"Why should that surprise you? Am I *that* ugly?" Ivar
wanted to slug his friend.

Baldwin looked him over consideringly, then shrugged.
"No."

"But if she's an Eagle," pointed out Ermanrich, "then
she can't be of noble birth. Why would your father ever
allow you to marry a common-born woman?"

"But her father was in the church, and educated," Ivar
protested. "He must have come out of a noble lineage!"
Thinking about it only made it worse, but he couldn't help
thinking. Mother Scholastica had promised to send a message to his father. He would *have* to be patient—and Liath
had promised to wait.

Sigfrid had been given his turn with Baldwin's knife and
he was trying to wiggle the little gap into a wider gap,
something they could actually *see* through. Now he glanced
over his shoulder toward the empty courtyard, then leaned
forward to the others. "While I was waiting for my lesson,"
he said in a low voice, "I heard that Lady Sabella's daughter is going to be held here until King Henry decides to
marry her off or let her become a novice."

"Ah," said Baldwin. "The young Lady Tallia. I met her
once."

Ermanrich snorted.

"Oh!" said Sigfrid in the tone of man who has opened
the door only to find a snake in his room. "I didn't think
it would *work*."

"Hush," said Baldwin. "Move this way, Ermanrich. Ivar,
get on your knees as if you're praying. Move over here."

Sigfrid had accomplished the deed. Pressure had forced
one thin plank to slide behind another, and now they had

a gap through which they could see a thin strip of the other side of the courtyard.

Baldwin hunkered down and flattened his face against the fence. He gasped and jerked back. "There's someone there!" he hissed. "A novice!"

"Does she have warts?" asked Ermanrich.

"Be serious!" Baldwin stuck his right eye against the gap again, closing his left and squinching up his face to see better. After a pause, he backed away and spoke in a whisper. "She's kneeling just opposite us. I think it's Lady Tallia!"

Ermanrich whistled under his breath.

Even Ivar was impressed. "Let me look," he demanded. Baldwin scooted back and Ivar pressed his face up against the fence. The wood scraped his skin. Ermanrich's breath blew against his neck as if, with enough force of will, the other boy could see through Ivar's eyes.

She had thrown back her hood and he recognized her at once: the wheat-haired girl who had carried the banner of Arconia—her father's duchy—at the forefront of the procession the day King Henry had arrived at Quedlinhame. Only three days ago! How much had happened since then.

She prayed, thin hands clasped before her breast, pale lips touching her knuckles. Then, abruptly, her eyes opened and she looked straight at him. She had the palest blue eyes, like a many-times-washed indigo tunic bled so fine that only the memory of blue remained in the threads.

"Who are you?" she whispered.

Ivar jerked back from the fence.

"She said something!" exclaimed Ermanrich. He stuck his face up against the fence. "Are you Lady Tallia?" he whispered.

Baldwin pulled Ermanrich back from the wall and wedged himself in as Ermanrich made a grunt of protest.

"You must not look upon me," she said in that same quiet voice, as soft as the wind brushing Ivar's hair. His hood had fallen back, and he hastily jerked it up over his head, looking guiltily back toward the barracks. The layservant left to watch over them was not in sight. "It is not seemly for you to stare so," she continued. In the silence of the courtyard they could hear her words clearly. She hesitated, then went on. "But that we have stumbled upon this opportunity to converse—that, surely, is God's doing, is it not?"

"Oh, certainly," said Baldwin blithely, although, obedient to her wish, he had now drawn back from the gap in the fence. "Are you to be a nun?"

Sigfrid made a choked noise in his throat and immediately assumed a position of prayer. The layservant had walked back into view, a surly, stout man no doubt angered at having to watch over four disobedient novices rather than the colorful departure of king and court. All four boys hunkered down in attitudes of contrite prayer.

From the shelter of the colonnade, the layservant could not hear Tallia's faint voice, but the four boys could. "It is my most devout wish to become a nun. Unless I can be a deacon, but they will not let me out into the world except to marry me to some grasping nobleman."

"Why would you want to be a deacon?" asked Sigfrid. "In the cloister, we can devote all our hours to study and contemplation."

"But a deacon who lives in the world can bring the true Word of God to those who live in darkness. If I were ordained as a deacon, I could preach the Holy Word of the Redeemer as it was taught me by Frater Agius, he who was granted God's favor and a holy martyrdom."

A low rumble of thunder sounded in the distance, like drums beating for the departure of the king. Ivar smelled rain on the wind. Dark clouds scudded overhead.

"Who is the Redeemer?" asked Ermanrich, his bland, friendly face bearing now a confused expression.

"That's a heresy," whispered Sigfrid, but he did not move.

Baldwin did not move.

Ivar did not move. He wanted to hear her speak again. She had a kind of monotonously fascinating voice, pure and quietly zealous. And she was female, and young.

"For the blessed Daisan was born not of earthly mortals but out of Our Lady, who is God. He alone was born without any taint of darkness. So did he suffer. By the order of the Empress Thaisannia, she of the mask, he was flayed alive because of his preaching, as was their custom with criminals and those who spoke treason against the Dariyan Empire and its ruler. His heart was cut out of him, and where his heart's blood fell and touched the soil, there bloomed roses."

Sigfrid made the sign of the Circle against what is forbidden—against this most erroneous and dangerous heresy. But he did not move away. None of them moved. They were caught there, spellbound, as the thunder rumbled closer and the first drops of rain darkened the dirt around them.

"But by his suffering, by his sacrifice, he redeemed us from our sins. Our salvation comes through that redemption. For though he died, he lived again. So did God in Her wisdom redeem him, for was he not Her only Son?"

She would have gone on, perhaps she did go on, but the wind picked up and lightning flashed bright against lowering clouds and thunder pealed overhead. The stinging bite of rain drove them to the shelter of the colonnade. Whether she ran in as well Ivar could not know, but he imagined her, kneeling still, soaked and pounded by rain as she prayed her heretical prayers. That image disturbed him greatly for many nights to come.

IV
ON THE WINGS OF
THE STORM

1

THE king and his entourage rode south from Quedlinhame. Liath rode northeast through scattered woodland amid rolling hills with a message for Duchess Rotrudis, the king's sister. She followed the Osterwaldweg, a grassy track that ran north from Quedlinhame and slanted east-northeast at the confluence of the Ailer and Urness Rivers, themselves tributaries of the Veser. In the morning the track, crisp with frost, glittered in the cold sun as though an angel had blown its sweet breath over the rutted road. By evening, wagon traffic, sun, and the usual passage of a swift autumn storm overhead had turned the path to a sludge that would refreeze over the long night.

It was always windy and sometimes quite chill, but in the

late afternoon the sun would often shine brightly. During those times Liath would find a patch of sunlight while her horse foraged along the verge of the track. Sometimes, if the way lay empty, she would open *The Book of Secrets* and read words she had long since memorized or puzzle over the brief Arethousan glosses in the inner book, the most secret ancient text. Alas, without time to study or preceptor to continue her teaching, she had already forgotten much of what little Arethousan she had learned from Hugh. But perhaps if she forgot everything he had taught her, she would truly be free from him.

Other times, frustrated by her ignorance, she would simply close her eyes and imagine Da beside her on the quiet road. The sun's warmth was like his presence, soothing and secure; oddly, she could never imagine him by her on cloudy days. Perhaps his spirit, looking down on her from the Chamber of Light where he now resided at peace, could only see her when his view down through the seven spheres was unobstructed.

"*Do you suppose,*" she imagined him asking now, "*that souls have sight? Or is that sense reserved for those who wear an earthly body?*"

"You're trying to trick me, Da," she would answer. "*Angels and daimones don't wear earthly bodies. They wear bodies made up of the pure elements, fire and light and wind and air, and yet they can see with a sight that is keener than that of humankind. They can see both past and future. They can see the souls of the stars.*"

"*Some have argued they are the souls of the fixed stars.*" Thus would the argument be joined, over free will and Fate and natural law. And if not that argument, then a different one, for Da had a fine treasure-house of his own, knowledge earned over many years of study, and though his "city of memory" was not as finely honed as Liath's—for he had taught her skills of memory which he had only mastered late in life—it was yet impressive. He knew so much, and all of it he meant to teach to his daughter, especially the secrets of the mathematici, the knowledge of the stars and of the movements of the planets through the heavens.

A sudden gust of wind fluttered the pages of the open book, set on her knee. Snow swirled past, but there were no clouds in the sky now. The cold wind brought memory.

*Wings, settling on the eaves. A sudden gust of white snow
through the smoke hole, although it was not winter.*

*Asleep and aware, bound to silence. Awake but unable to
move, and therefore still asleep. The darkness held her down
as if it were a weight draped over her.*

*A voice of bells, heard as if on the wind. Two sharp
thunks sounded, arrows striking wood.*

"*Your weak arrows avail you nothing,*" said the voice of
bells. "*Where is she?*"

"*Nowhere you can find her,*" said Da.

"*Liath,*" said a voice of bells, coming from everywhere
and nowhere at once.

Heart beating wildly, she dared not move, but she had
to look. Snow spun past like the trailing edge of a storm,
flakes dissolving in the sun. A feathery gleam lit the track
where it bent away northward, a roiling in the air like the
fluttering of translucent wings as pale as the air itself.

Something came toward her down the road.

The fear bit so deep, like a griffin's beak closing on her
throat, that she could not draw breath. Certainly she could
not run. Da's voice rang in her ears: "*Safety lies in staying hidden.*"

She did not move.

"*Liathano.*"

She heard it then, clearly, the voice made of the echoes
of bells ringing away long into an unbroken night. She saw
it though it was not any earthly being. It did not walk the
track but rather floated above it, as if unable to set its
aetherical being fully in contact with the dense soil of the
mortal world. It came down the track from the north, face-
less, with only humanlike limbs and the form of a human
body and the wings of an angel to give it shape.

It called her, alluring, not unmusical, with that awful
throbbing bass vibrato in its tone. It wanted her to answer.
It *compelled* her to answer.

But Da had protected her against magic. Silent, as still
as stone, she did not move. She held her breath. A leaf
blown free by the wind fluttered over her arms and came
to rest on the open book, and then a second, as if the earth
itself collaborated in hiding her.

The creature stalked past her, still calling, and went on
up the road to the south and, at last, out of her sight. A

single white feather swirled in the eddy left by its passing and drifted down to the ground. It was so pale that it shone like purest glass. Where she had tied it to a leather cord to hang around her neck, the gold feather left to her by the Aoi sorcerer burned against her skin as if in warning.

Still she did not move. She was too stunned to move. She sat so still that eventually a trio of half-wild pigs, all tusks and bristles and sleek haunches, ventured out onto the path to investigate this bright interloper. But as soon as the lead pig nudged the white feather with its snout, the feather spit sparks, flashed and, with a whirlpool of smoke, dissipated into the air. The pigs squealed and scattered.

Liath laughed almost hysterically, but as soon as the fit passed, she was swept by such anger that she could barely get the book back into the saddlebag because her hands shook so. Was it such a creature that had murdered Da? Even that very one? Anger and terror warred within her, but anger won out. It hadn't seen her. Da's magic still protected her; whatever spell he had laid on her long ago had not died with him.

With anger came revelation: All those years she had thought him a failed sorcerer when instead he had poured that power into keeping her hidden.

"I swear to you, Da," she whispered, standing beside her horse with her eyes turned to the heavens where, perhaps, his soul looked down upon her, trapped on the mortal earth, "that I'll find out what it was that killed you."

"*Nay, Liath, you must be careful,*" she imagined him saying to her. He was always so afraid.

And for good reason. Was it the aetherical daimone itself that stalked them, or a human sorcerer, a maleficus, who had drawn it from its sphere above the moon and coerced it to do his bidding?

"I'll be like a mouse," she murmured. "They'll never see me. I promise you, Da. I'll never let them catch me." With that, in her imagination, he seemed to be content.

A distant flock of sheep crested a rise and disappeared out of her view, an amorphous body herded by unseen dogs and a single shepherd. She did not want to stay here, where the creature had come so close. Apprehensive now and still unnerved by that unearthly sight and by the horrible, sick fear that had come over her when its inhuman voice spoke

her name, she mounted and rode on. On this, her third day
out of Quedlinhame, she could expect to come by nightfall
to the palace at Goslar, so Hathui had told her. Please the
Lady that she did; she did not want to sleep alone this
night. And from Goslar, if the weather held, another four
days of steady riding would bring her to Osterburg, the city
and fortress favored by Duchess Rotrudis.

But when she rode into Goslar that evening, it was to
find a large retinue already inhabiting it. A groom took her
horse and she was brought at once into the great hall.
There, seated on a chair carved with dragons and draped
with gold pillows embroidered with black dragons whose
curling shape and fierce demeanor echoed those of the
King's Dragons, waited Duchess Rotrudis herself.

"What message does Henry send to me?" she asked
without preamble as soon as Liath knelt before her. She
did not resemble those of her siblings Liath had seen:
Henry, Mother Scholastica, and Biscop Constance; she was
not handsome nor had she any elegance of form. Short,
stout, and with hands as broad and red as a farmer's, she
had a nose that looked as if it had been broken one too
many times, and old pockmarks scarred her cheeks. Even
so, no one would have mistaken her for anything but one
of the great princes of the land.

"King Henry speaks these words, my lady," began Liath
dutifully. " 'From Henry, King over Wendar and Varre,
to Rotrudis, Duchess of Saony and Attomar and beloved
kinswoman, this entreaty. Now that winter is upon us, it is
time to think of next summer's campaign. We must drive
the Eika out of Gent, but for this endeavor we will need a
great army. Fully half of my forces died at Kassel. I have
taken what I can out of Varre, and asked for more, but
you, as well, must bear this burden with the others. Send
messengers to your noble ladies and lords that they will
increase their levies and send troops to Steleshame after
the Feast of St. Sormas. From this staging place we will
attack Gent. Let it be done. These words, spoken in the
presence of our blessed mother, represent my wishes in
the matter.' "

Rotrudis snorted, took a draught of wine, and called for
more wood on the hearth. "Fine words," she said indig-
nantly, "when it is my duchy that the Eika ravage now.

They are not content with Gent. My own city of Osterburg has been attacked!"

"Attacked!" The memory of Gent's fall hit Liath as hard as a sword's blow, and she swayed back, horrified.

"We drove them off," said the duchess bluntly. "It was only ten ships of the damned savages." She handed the gold cup to her cupbearer, a pretty young woman dressed in a plain gown of white linen. With a grunt, she heaved herself up and walked over to look down on Liath. Pressing the tip of her walking stick under Liath's chin, she lifted the Eagle's head up so she could examine her face. "Are you some relation to Conrad the Black?" she demanded. "His by-blow, perhaps?"

"No, my lady. I am no relation to Duke Conrad."

"Well-spoken, I see," said the duchess. "Too old to be his get, in any case." She had a limp and one swollen foot, and when she sat heavily down in her chair, the pillows sighed beneath her. A servant hurried forward to prop the foot up on a padded stool. All along the walls rich tapestries hung, a sequence depicting a band of young ladies on the hunt, first after a stag, then a panther, and last a griffin. "You tell this, then, to my dear brother Henry. Good God, where is he now, dare I ask?"

"He and the court have ridden south—"

"To hunt in Thurin Forest, no doubt!"

"Yes, my lady."

"While my villages burn under the raids of the Eika! Ah, well, no doubt he'll claim he must meet and trouble every southern lord in order to get them to pledge troops for next summer's war. A war every summer, *that* is Henry for you." She put out her hand and her cupbearer placed the gold cup in her hand. The duchess examined its contents, then frowned. "Here, child, my cup is empty." A boy dressed in a neat white linen tunic rushed over, took the cup away, and returned with a full one. A cleric leaned over and whispered into the duchess' ear.

Liath wished the noble lords would think of placing carpets or pillows down in front of their chairs so that her knees might have some respite.

"True enough," commented Rotrudis to the cleric before returning her attention to Liath. "Tell Henry that I expect more help from him. These Eika are like flies swarming around fresh meat. What if I can't wait for next summer?"

"I have no further message from the king, my lady. But—" She hesitated.

"But? But! Go on. I'm no fool to think Eagles don't notice that which others might miss."

"It's true, my lady, that Henry's forces were badly hurt at Kassel. His complement of Lions went from perhaps two hundred men to a bare sixty, and though he has sent for more centuries from the marchlands, there is no guarantee those men can march so far so fast or that the marchlords will be able to let them go."

"Huh. The Quman haven't raided for years. I think there's no threat there. But go on. What of the Varren lords?"

"They, too, suffered at Kassel, though under Sabella's banner. But the king has collected levies from them and expects more to be sent in the spring."

"That isn't good enough! I've had to send my own son Wichman and his band of reckless young gadflies to Steleshame to restore order. What has *Henry* risked?"

This was too much. Furious, Liath lifted her gaze to stare straight at the duchess. "King Henry lost his son at Gent!"

Courtiers murmured, shocked at her tone, but the duchess only laughed. "Here's fire for you! Well then, it's true enough that Prince Sanglant died at Gent together with the Dragons, but that's what the poor boy was bred for, wasn't it?"

"*Bred* for?" said Liath, appalled.

"Quiet! You have spoken enough. Now you will listen to my words and carry them faithfully back to my dear brother. I need more help, and I need it soon. According to my reports, there's not a village left standing within a day's ride of Gent, and half the livestock stolen from the villages within three days' walk likewise and my people slaughtered, frightened, and running with a scant harvest to feed them this winter and no chance to sow in the spring, if the Eika aren't driven out. These Eika raid up the Veser as they wish, although winter's ice may dull their oars in the water, and none of the waterways are safe—nor will they be after the thaw come spring. Tell Henry this: I know where our royal sister Sabella is. If he cannot help me, then she will—and bring me those lords who pledged loyalty to her, if Henry can't."

She paused, sipped wine, winced as she shifted her foot on the stool. "Now then, have you understood it all?"

Liath could barely speak, she was so astounded at the reference to Sabella. "That's the message you wish me to take back to King Henry?"

"Would I have spoken it if it were not what I wished delivered to him? Your duty is not to question, Eagle. Yours is to ride. Go on, then. I am done with you."

Liath rose, backed away, and retreated to the farthest corner of the hall. Was she meant to ride out immediately into the twilight? Where anything might await her? But a steward led her to a table placed in the back of the hall while the nobles began their evening's feast. Here, with some of the other servants, she was fed royally, a fine meal of goose, partridge, fish braised in a tart sauce, mince pie, and as much bread as she could eat together with a sharp cider. The nobles' feast went on forever, what with singing and dancing and tales, and even when the last platter of food was taken away, they still drank so heavily that Liath was surprised they hadn't emptied the cellars.

She crept away from the table at last and curled up in the corner, and yet woke intermittently throughout the long night, roused by their laughter, each time seeing through the haze of smoke and torchlight the nobles still drinking, singing, wrestling among the young men, and boasting while they paced the floor and drank again. Only at dawn, when she struggled to her feet and made ready to ride, had they at last given up the night's carousing and themselves gone to their beds.

2

KING Henry and his court were out hunting when she rode into the broad enclosure that formed the northernmost of the royal hunting lodges in the Thurin Forest. It had taken her seven days to ride here, pushing her pace and changing horses at Quedlinhame. This time, at the monastery, she had been restricted to the stables; she'd had no chance to contact Ivar again. On the road, she'd seen no trace of the mysterious creature who had passed so close by her before.

Great hall and barracks, kitchens, smithy, storerooms, stables, and a few guest houses made up the hunting lodge. A large grassy field surrounded these buildings, bounded by a steep-bedded, narrow river on one side and the palisade wall on the others. Servants scurried here and there about the lodge. Liath heard the squeal of pigs being driven to slaughter for the night's feast. A veritable army of servants swarmed around the cookhouse—set well away from the great hall in case of fire—and farther, down a grassy slope to the river, servants aired linen and featherbeds and washed clothes.

Once she crossed under the palisade gate, a groom took her horse and informed her that the king was gone for the day. Liath was glad to miss the hunt. She could take no pleasure in hunting some poor, terrified creature—it reminded her too much of her own life.

She settled her saddle and harness in the same empty stall where she found Hathui's familiar gear, saddlebags and rolled-up wool blanket. Hathui had gone out with the king. She crouched to open the bag, set her hand on the book within—and hesitated. Had the daimone appeared— tracked her down—because she had opened the book out on the road? Or because she had, in her thoughts, recalled Da's death? Or had it only been coincidence that the creature had appeared then? She closed the flap and tied the pouch shut, shoved the saddlebag under her saddle, then went outside.

It was a fine blustery autumn day with clouds aplenty and the scent of cooking fires heavy on the wind. Brittle leaves of faded yellow and orange rolled across Liath's boots, blown by the wind. Goats grazed on the verge of the forest on the other side of the river, attended by a solitary shepherd. No one marked her. They were all too busy.

The morning's sun which had shone on her earlier had now vanished, shrouded by the wings of a coming storm. This was the season of storms, blown in one after the next. She shivered, thinking of the Eika, themselves a storm blown in from the north; it was still painful to remember the fall of Gent.

Yet the world beyond seemed far away, here deep in the heart of the forest. No one lived here, no freeholders or peasants working a noble lady's estate or church lands farmed the steep hills and densely wooded valleys. The Thurin remained a forest wilderness, and here the king hunted most autumns.

The cool bluster of the day drove her to seek shelter in the great hall. But to her surprise and dismay, clerics tenanted the great hall, half a dozen garbed in neat robes. She had thought they, too, would be out hunting.

Instead, they sat quietly at the long tables where, in the evenings, the king and his court feasted. They went about the king's business while the king went about his pleasure. Goose quills bobbed evenly, dabbed in ink, letters curving across parchment or vellum.

Liath took a step back, but it was too late. At the chair nearest the door sat Ivar's sister, Rosvita. She looked up, caught sight of Liath, and beckoned to her. A bound book, parchment pages folded into a quire, some of them not yet cut, lay open on the table before her. Her fingers were stained with ink.

Cautiously, Liath ventured closer.

"You are back, Eagle," said the cleric.

"I am, Sister. I bring a message from Duchess Rotrudis for the king."

"You left Quedlinhame swiftly," observed Rosvita, "and must not have tarried there long on your way back."

Ai, Lady! In all that had happened since, Liath had scarcely thought about poor Ivar. What was it Da had always said? *"When the wolf has your arm in its jaws, then use the other to tickle its belly."*

"What are you writing?" Liath asked, but the words written in fresh ink caught her in their spell and she read out loud:

"Then Henry, born to Kunigunde, Duchess of Saony, and her husband, Arnulf of Avaria, became duke by reason of his mother's death and his elder sisters having died before him. But Queen Conradina, who had often tested the valor of the new duke, was afraid to entrust to him all his mother's power. By this attitude the queen incurred the indignation of the entire Wendish army. She then spoke many words in praise of the new and most noble duke, promising to bestow on Henry great responsibilities and to glorify him with honor. But the Wendish soldiers were not deceived. The queen, seeing that they were more unfriendly than usual, and realizing that she could not destroy the new duke openly, tried to find a way to have him slain by treachery.

"She sent her brother with an army into Wendar to lay it waste. But when he came to the city which is called Gent, it is related that he boastfully stated that the greatest trouble he anticipated was that the Wendish would not dare show themselves before the walls so that he could fight them. With this boast still on his lips, the Wendish came rushing upon him and once the battle was joined they cut down his army of Arconians and Salians and Varingians with such slaughter that, as the bards tell us, the Abyss must indeed be a large place if it can contain so great a multitude of the slain.

"Eberhard, the queen's brother, was freed from his fear that the Wendish would not put in an appearance, for he saw them actually before him, and he fled from them."

"A history!" Liath exclaimed. She turned her gaze to Rosvita only to see the older woman staring at her with an ominous smile touching her lips. All the other clerics had ceased their writing to stare at this oddity, a King's Eagle who could read the language of educated church people, Dariyan.

Ai, Lady. She had betrayed herself again, and this time in front of the king's schola, his retinue of educated clerics.

"I am working on a history of the Wendish people," agreed Rosvita without any sign of astonishment, unlike the others. "I am relating here the story of how the first Henry, Duke of Saony, became King of Wendar upon the death of Queen Conradina."

"What will you write next?" Liath asked, hoping to distract her.

Rosvita coughed politely, and the other clerics hastily and obviously went back to their work. She set down her quill—a magnificent eagle's feather, surely the mark of great favor from the king or his mother—beside the book. "Queen Conradina was herself wounded in battle, and thus finding herself burdened with disease as well as the loss of her earlier good fortune, she called her brother Eberhard to her side and reminded him that their family had every resource that the dignity of the rulership demanded—every resource except good luck. She gave to Eberhard the insignia of their royal ancestors—sacred lance, scepter, golden torque, and crown—and told him to take the insignia and give them to Duke Henry along with his allegiance. Soon after this she died, a brave and valiant woman, outstanding both at home and in the field, well known for her liberality—"

"Both in and out of bed," said one of the clerics, and others laughed and then quieted when Rosvita signed for *Silence.*

"Eberhard offered both himself and the treasures to Henry, made a peace treaty with him, and established friendship. That friendship he kept faithfully to the end. Then, at the city known as Kassel, in the presence of all the great princes of the realm, he made Henry king."

"Of course," said Liath. "And now the first Henry's great-grandson, our Henry, is King of Wendar *and* Varre." She bowed slightly, backing up. "I beg pardon for disturbing you, Sister. I will leave you and these others to your work."

She turned and hurried out the door, then leaned against the wall and thanked Lady and Lord that she had escaped their scrutiny. The faint lime scent of freshly washed plaster burned in her nostrils and with it burned a wash of envy. Had events transpired differently that dimly recalled day nine years ago, she might have taken orders herself and become a cleric. She could have sat together in the company of others like herself, and written, and read, and talked. How strange that Ivar chafed where she might have found happiness. But it was not to be.

Still, seeing the clerics made her wistful—and bold. She walked back to the stables, feeling a sudden urge to touch the book again, even if the act itself of touching the book brought her into danger.

The dim light in the stables draped like a cloak of secrecy thrown over her shoulders, giving her courage. She pulled *The Book of Secrets* out of the saddlebag and opened it delicately. She waited a moment, but no cold wind disturbed the stillness of the stables. Even for her salamander eyes, it was too dark in the stables to read. Instead, she simply sat touching the book, the binding, the grain of the leather, the parchment leaves and the fragile touch of the innermost book, ink on papyrus.

She laid her check against it, breathing in its dry perfume. Da's book. All she had left of him and everything he had given to her. Ai, Lady. He had given her all that he had, literally; all the power that was in him. She had only doubted him because she hadn't understood.

It *was* never safe, not for her. She no longer wondered at Da's exaggerated vigilance, his fastidious wariness, his attention to each least detail at every monastery guest house, at every isolated inn or farmer's shed they had bedded down in. Not any more.

Hugh had understood Da's power better than she had, it seemed. Wind rattled the stable doors and she started around, but it was natural wind. She could smell rain, though none yet fell, could hear the clatter of bare branches outside as the storm's breath, running before it, stirred the trees in anticipation of its coming. *Hugh.*

That suddenly, as if the name itself had magic, she shuddered, trembling violently, and caught the book against her chest as she fought back tears. She must not, could not, give in to the old fear. She had escaped him.

"Eagle. *Liath.*"

She jerked, startled, and spun around, but it was too late. She had been run to ground, cornered, and cut off.

Rosvita had come after her.

3

ROSVITA knew she would be damned for her curiosity, so she had given up trying to stop herself from succumbing to its lure.

She had blotted the fresh ink carefully and left the book open to dry, pushed back her chair, and risen to follow the young Eagle. Since the incident in the library at Quedlinhame, she had not been able to stop thinking about the young Eagle.

Once out in the courtyard she saw the young woman vanish into the stables, so she followed, tracking her to an empty stall where she sat alone in the gloom.

"Eagle. Liath."

As soon as she spoke the words, she saw the object the girl clutched to her chest like a frightened child. It was a book. Surprised and puzzled, Rosvita acted before thinking. She stepped forward and plucked the book from the Eagle's grasp. The girl gasped out loud and jumped up, but Rosvita had already retreated to the door and thus the Eagle had perforce to follow her outside as a starving dog slinks at the heels of a woman gnawing on a succulent rib of pork.

"I beg you—" stuttered the girl, face washed gray with fear. She was of good height but so slender that she appeared frail.

At once, faced with such an expression of abject misery and terror, Rosvita relented. She handed back the book and yet, as the young woman locked the book under her left arm, immediately regretted her own act of generosity. The title was lost in the folds of the Eagle's cloak. What on God's earth did an Eagle mean by carrying a book? And what kind of book was it? But Rosvita was too wise to attempt a direct assault.

"I can't help but wonder where a woman such as yourself learned to read Dariyan so fluently," she said. "Are you church educated?"

The girl hesitated, her fine mouth turning down stubbornly. Then, with an effort, she smoothed her expression. Rosvita had studied faces for too many years not to recognize a person who wanted to remain unnoticed and unremarked—although how, with such a striking face, this young person thought she could remain unnoticed, Rosvita could not fathom.

"My da educated me," she said at last.

"You mentioned him to Queen Mathilda, did you not? He was in the church?"

She shrugged, not wanting to answer.

"Perhaps he left the church after you were born," suggested Rovita, trying to sound sympathetic, trying to worm her way past the wall the girl had thrown up. "Does he have kin? Do you know who your people are?"

"I have been told he has cousins at Bodfeld. But they disclaimed the kinship after—" She broke off.

That, Rosvita saw, was the girl's weakness. Once begun, she would forget to stop. "After he acknowledged you as his child? Or had he already left the church?"

"I don't know," said the girl, a little rudely.

"I beg your pardon. But then, I was often told by my mother abbess that my curiosity is unpardonable." Rosvita offered a smile. The girl *almost* smiled back, but did not. The fierce blue of her eyes, as brilliant as sapphires or the blue depths of fire, shone bright against her dusky skin. "Your mother?"

"Is dead. These many years."

"And now Wolfhere has taken you on as his discipla. Perhaps you knew him before?"

"No, I didn't—" She shook her head impatiently. "He took me into the Eagles. He saved me from—" She winched her right arm more tightly against her side, concealing the book.

Lady Above! Had she *stolen* it from the library at Quedlinhame?

It was time for the direct approach. "What book is that?"

Rosvita had never seen anyone look quite so fragile and terrified. *Had* the girl stolen it? Ought she to seek justice in this case, and force her to tell the truth—or was it better to be merciful and let her confess in due time?

"It—My da gave it to me," the girl said at last, in a rush. "It's the only thing I have left of him."

A rumble of thunder sounded closer now. Rain brushed the cleric's cheeks and struck her hands like thoughts falling from the heavens to disturb what little peace of mind she had ever managed to secure. So many thoughts distracted her, like the drops of rain increasing in frequency now: old Brother Fidelis and his legacy, the *Vita of St. Radegundis,* which he had given to her; his last whispered mention of Seven Sleepers, daimones or humans or some other creatures whose power he feared; the terrible and mysterious disappearance of Villam's son, Berthold, and his six companions, in the stone circle in the hills above Hersford; her *History,* which she really must continue working on so that it might be finished before the old queen died; the book that this vulnerable girl clutched to herself so tightly.

The book. Rosvita knew at that instant, as if the sound of thunder divined it, that she would somehow, in some way, get a look inside that book.

Suddenly, as lightning flashed and a fresh peal of thunder cracked and roared in response, the girl spoke. "Do you know how to read Arethousan?"

Rosvita arched one eyebrow. "Yes, I do. I learned from Queen Sophia herself." The girl remained silent, quite unlike the unrolling turmoil in the sky. Seeing an opening, Rosvita continued. "Would you like to learn Arethousan? You read Dariyan very well."

She bit her lip. She was tempted.

Tempted. This Rosvita understood. This fault she knew how to nurture, although surely it was a sin to do so. "I can teach you Arethousan. I saw you reading in the library, a Jinna work, I believe, one of the astronomers. That was just before Ivar—"

"Ivar," whispered the girl, looking embarrassed.

"My brother Ivar," agreed Rosvita, and saw at once the wedge through which she could penetrate this girl's defenses. "Did he ever speak of me? You knew him in Heart's Rest, I believe, before he entered the church."

"He always spoke of you with respect," she admitted, "though he never wanted to emulate your vocation!"

"So he gave me reason to understand."

The Eagle flushed and looked away, embarrassed either to replay that scene in the library in her own mind or to remember that another had witnessed the whole. "He trusts you."

Rosvita took in a careful breath, measuring her words. This moment was the crucial one. Here might all be won, or lost.

"Sister!"

She almost cursed out loud, managed not to. She glanced toward the sound of the voice and grimaced. A middle-aged man with dark hair and undistinguished features—a King's Eagle—led his horse through the gate into the courtyard.

"I beg you, Sister, I bring an important message." He led the horse forward—it was limping—and halted before her. "Sister," he repeated respectfully.

Lady's Blood! Granted this distraction, the girl escaped, slinking away like a hunted creature escaping the hounds. It was too late to call her back, and in any case, Rosvita knew her duty: The man looked worn, weary, and as if his feet hurt him.

"Where have you come from?" she asked politely. It was not, after all, *his* fault, not precisely, anyway. By such means did God remind her of her duty.

"I am the herald for Princess Sapientia."

"Sapientia!"

"I was meant to ride in half a day before her, to make sure her lodgings were properly prepared, but my horse came up lame, so I am—" He halted, silenced by the ring of harness and by the laughter and animated cheer of voices carried on the wind in a sudden lull. Lightning brightened the darkening sky; thunder, almost on top of them, cracked and rolled, shaking the shutters. It began to rain.

The riders appeared in the gate, laughing, untroubled by storm and rain. It was a small retinue, not above twenty riders together with several wagons and a number of servants walking beside, but clearly a noblewoman's party. A banner sodden with rain fluttered limply in the wind. The horses wore rich caparisons, and the soldiers were outfitted in good armor.

The princess rode at the front. Rosvita judged she could

scarcely be more than four months gone, given that she had only ridden out on her heir's progress some six months ago, but the princess was of such a slight build that even through her heavy wool traveling tunic Rosvita could see the telltale swelling of her belly.

But the cleric's gaze skipped almost immediately away from the princess to the man riding with easy grace beside her.

Rosvita's mouth dropped open. Without any words being spoken, she *knew* this man was the father of Sapientia's as yet unborn child. Knew it, as she was meant to know, as all were meant to know, by the little gestures of intimacy he and the princess exchanged. Truth to tell, she was scandalized, although after so many years in the king's progress she had thought herself inured to scandal.

The Eagle, still beside her, grunted, acknowledging her surprise. "Not quite what anyone expected."

And yet, after a moment's consideration, Rosvita realized she was not at all surprised. Henry's grief had rendered him incapable of sending his eldest legitimate child on her way for her heir's progress, as was traditional. He had left that duty to another, to Judith, margrave of Olsatia and Austra.

This, of course, was the inevitable result.

4

SHE jammed the book into the saddlebag, cursing herself under her breath. *Why* must she continually betray herself? Wouldn't it be better to stop pretending to be what she was not—a simple, uneducated Eagle? Why not confide in the woman? She looked trustworthy enough, and she was Ivar's sister.

Yet Rosvita had lived for many years in the circle of the king's progress. She could not be a simple woman, uncomplicated in the way Ivar was; she might involve herself in many intrigues unknown to Liath, dangerous to Liath. As a good churchwoman, surely she would not be sympathetic to tales of daimones and the forbidden knowledge of the mathematici.

I would never know. I can never know whom to trust. That is why Da told me to "Trust no one."

Thunder boomed. The entire stables shook under that great crack and rumbling roar. She jumped, startled, hating herself for being scared all the time. If only Hanna would return, but she could not expect Hanna for months. And with Hanna would come Wolfhere and his damnable questions and his watching eyes.

And yet, was not Rosvita more likely to be trustworthy than Wolfhere? Liath liked Wolfhere—that was the worst of it—but she could never trust him. He had known both her mother and father. He knew what she was, and he wanted something from her, just as *Hugh* had wanted—

But she was not going to think about Hugh. She could not. Hugh looked like someone who could be trusted. Beautiful Hugh. She touched a hand to her cheek, remembering the pain when he hit her.

"You are free of Hugh," she whispered, if only to stop this pointless endless fruitless speculation.

Thunder cracked and rumbled on and on and on, directly overhead. She shuddered, seized by a sudden intense wave of fear, as if fear were a living being, a daimone that had

set its claws into her and tightened them, drawing blood
and entrails and sucking all the spirit out of her. Rain
drummed on the roof.

Abruptly the doors to the stables opened and servants
and horses flooded in. They talked all at once, chattering,
excited, exuberant. She shrank back into the stable where
her and Hathui's gear lay together. Hiding in shadow, she
listened: Sapientia, sent off on her heir's progress after the
battle at Kassel, had returned to the king's progress trium-
phantly pregnant with the child who, if born alive and
healthy, would guarantee her claim to become ruler after
her father.

On the heels of their arrival the hunters returned, escaping the full force of the storm. Every stall was needed to
stable horses. Liath gathered up her and Hathui's meager
bundles and hauled them up to the loft where she arranged
them in a safe corner. It took time. It kept her out of the
way. It made her just another anonymous servant, someone
who would be overlooked.

But not, alas, forever.

Hathui, wet through, came up the ladder and onto the
plank floor. She wrung water out of her cloak. Her hair lay
matted to her head and in streaks down her neck.

"You're back!" she said with surprise.

"I am."

"You should have been waiting for the king," scolded
Hathui. Then, distracted by the stamp and bustle of folk
below, she added, "I hear Princess Sapientia has returned,
though I haven't seen her."

"I haven't seen her either," said Liath. "She and her
party must have been riding just behind me."

"They came in by the western road." Hathui gathered
her saddlebags and bedroll. "I'm off to Quedlinhame to
announce the news to Queen Mathilda and Mother Scholastica. You must go now and attend the king. *At once.*"

Liath nodded dutifully. She nudged her saddlebags into
the corner and threw her bedroll over them to conceal
them. Hathui hoisted her bedroll over her shoulders and,
with a brisk nod at Liath, climbed back down the ladder.
Liath followed.

Rain pounded outside. She paused as Hathui got a new
horse, freshly saddled. Ducking out by a side door, she

hesitated under the eaves as water coursed down from the thatch roof and puddled at her feet, as rain pummeled the dry-packed earth of the courtyard into a shallow sea of mud. Hathui, coming outside by the main stable doors, swung onto her horse and forged out through the open gate into the teeth of the storm. Liath gazed across the courtyard at the whitewashed wall of one long side of the great hall, where all the living and feasting and sleeping went on. It looked no different than it had an hour ago, when she had entered hoping to find solitude there. But now, as if brought by the storm, she felt that wave of fear again, such a hideous swell of dread that her knees almost gave out under her.

She must not give in to the old fear. She touched the hilt of her sword, her "good friend," and shifted her shoulders to feel the comfortable weight of her bow, *Seeker of Hearts,* and her quiver full of arrows.

She braced herself against the wall, then thrust forward into the storm, dashing as fast as she could across the sloppy ground. She reached the other side without being too thoroughly drenched, and a Lion standing guard under the protection of the eaves gave her a smile for her trouble and opened the door. Warmth and smoke roiled out. She stepped up to enter the hall.

It was much changed now. The industrious clerics had been overwhelmed by loud, wet, laughing, bragging courtiers, noble folk newly ridden in from the hunt. Though a large chamber, the hall seemed cramped, reeking with the smell of wet wool and sweaty, jovial men and women. Liath weaved her way through them toward the hearth at the other end of the hall, where the king's chair stood. With each step, dread clawed in her, a sharp-fingered hand digging through her soul, groping up the paved streets of her city of memory on the track of her sealed tower. She had to force each foot forward, one step after the next.

What was wrong with her? Why had this fear come on her?

How much easier it would be to turn and flee. But that was what Da had done, and in the end it hadn't saved him. In order to live, she was going to have to do better than Da.

They parted before her, making way for the King's Eagle. Henry sat in his chair, looking tired. With one hand

he toyed with a hound's leash, knotted and tangled. His
other hand rested on a thigh; he opened and closed it over
and over. He looked distracted, staring without seeing
toward his two younger children who sat on stools beside
the fire. Sapientia stood beside him, shifting restlessly from
one foot to the other, glancing again and again toward a
knot of people kneeling to her left. These, her courtiers,
stooped over a finely carved chest in which she probably
had stored her fine clothing as well as mementos of her
sacred progress, whose successful outcome would mark her
as fit to rule as Queen Regnant after Henry's death.

Thunder boomed, rattling the timbers and shaking the
barred shutters, and hard on top of that came a second
crash, resounding through the hall, stilling their chatter.
The princess' courtiers rose and transformed themselves
into a new pattern, one made bright and focused by the
man who stood at their heart, the man at whom Sapientia
stared, her gaze fixed avidly and jealously on his face.

His beautiful face.

As the thunder faded, Liath heard the gentle snap and
rustle of the hearth's fire.

Hugh.

PART TWO

CAPUT
DRACONIS

V
THE HAND OF
THE LADY

1

WIND *scours his skin but he minds it not. Mere cold, mere sting of blown snow, cannot drive him from the stem of the ship. He sails on the wings of the storm, driving down on the northcountry to tear out the throats of those warleaders who have refused to bare their throats to his father, Bloodheart. This was the duty given him.*

His nestbrothers laughed and howled their derision, for they see this as his punishment. Did he not prove himself weak when he got captured by the Soft Ones? Does he not further display his weakness because he wears the circle at his chest, the circle that is the mark of the God of the Soft Ones?

He knows that Bloodheart meant the duty as punishment.

Sent back to the northcountry, land of OldMother and the WiseMothers, he will not gain booty and glory by raiding all-winter into the lands that lie near the city the Soft Ones call Gent but which Bloodheart has renamed Hundse, "to treat like a dog."

But his nestbrothers cannot think more than two steps before their eyes. They do not understand, and he does not tell them, that he wears the circle not because he believes in the God of the Soft Ones but rather as a mark of his link to Alain Henrisson, the human who freed him. They do not understand that their brother, who returns in disgrace to the northcountry, will be the one who holds his claws to the throats of the rebellious warleaders.

Someday, somehow, Bloodheart will die. It is the way of males to die. It is the way of the OldMother to stiffen and grow old and climb at last to the fjall of the WiseMothers. There, with her mothers and grandmothers and great-grandmothers unto uncounted generations, she will dream of the past and of the future and of the stars that lie like thoughts strewn across the fjall of the heavens far above, too steep a climb for mortal legs.

And when Bloodheart dies, who will the warleaders of the northcountry remember? The ones who raid and burn in the southlands, far away from the homelands? Or the one who drove into their halls and plundered their gold and stole and slaughtered their slaves? The one before whom they bared their throats?

The mewling and sobbing of a slave disturbs him. The dogs are restless, but he no longer lets them feed on obedient slaves. This lesson he learned from Alain: Impulse must not govern action. The other RockChildren, rowing, glance his way with their bitter eyes; they want to challenge him but dare not. They did not fight their way to a man's form out of the nestlings sired by Bloodheart. They come from other nests, other valleys, other dams. They serve Bloodheart and his litters. They do not contest him.

But they still watch. He dares show no sign of weakness in front of them, or else they will not fight for him when it comes time to bring the rebellious warleaders to heel, the independent ones who raid as all the RockChildren did before Bloodheart's hegemony: as they wish, with no coordination, with no greater vision leading them. They are no better

than dogs! How they matured into men puzzles him sometimes, but he does not worry himself about it. That is a
question only OldMother and the WiseMothers can answer.

He steps down from the stem and makes his way across
the rocking ship. The beat and rise and fall of the waves is
like a second breath to him; he does not falter although the
swells are steep here where the seas sing with the joy of
coming storm.

He stops at the stern where the slaves huddle. Miserable
creatures. One—bearded as all the older males are—stares
defiantly at him for a moment; then, remembering, the male
drops his gaze swiftly and hunches his shoulders, waiting
for the death blow. Another would kill the male simply for
that glance. But he knows better.

Nurture the strong ones. In time they can become useful
tools.

He leans down and presses the tip of a claw gently but
firmly into the edge of one soft eye of the defiant male, as
if to say. "I have noticed you."

Then he shoves aside the others to find the one who moans
and mewls and groans. This one has the stink of blood and
feces about her. She is a female of middle years, haggard of
face, thin, her skirts stained with blood and diarrhea, the
sign of an illness he has learned to recognize. Every Soft
One he has ever seen excrete such a foul combination of
blood and pus and stink dies after a day or three of agonizing pain. Some of his nestbrothers in Gent would wager over
how many days one stricken by the disease could live. But
he has also noticed that this disease can pass itself on to
others if not eradicated quickly. What good does it do the
miserable creature to lie there in pain and her own fetid
mess?

He does not, of course, want to stain his claws with her
tainted fluids. He fetches a spear, its iron point honed into
a fine instrument of death. He places the tip of the spear
against the female's breast. She whimpers and sobs, still
clutching her belly, and the others draw away, but no one
tries to stop him. They fear him. Surely they know she is
doomed. Not even the prayers they mouth to their god can
save her.

This is the other lesson he learned from Alain: to be merciful. With a single thrust, he pierces her chest.

*   *   *

Alain started up, gasping, hands clutched to his chest.
The pain that stabbed into him faded as Rage and Sorrow
stirred, woke, and licked his hands until he calmed. The
dream had been so real. But all the dreams of Fifth Son
seemed this real. Somehow the blood they had exchanged
so many months ago linked them now irrevocably. He saw
with Fifth Son's eyes and knew his thoughts. He lived, in
those sleeping hours, in Fifth Son's metal-hard skin.

Shuddering, he let the two black hounds nuzzle him until
the wave of revulsion passed. The revulsion brought in its
wake shame. What right had he to judge another creature,
even an Eika?

A flame lit suddenly, seen through the gauzy veil that
separated his side of the tent from his father's.

My father.

The veil was pushed aside. Count Lavastine looked in,
candle and holder gripped in one hand and the other still
caught in the thin fabric of tent wall.

"Alain? I heard you cry out."

Alain swung his legs off the cot and looked up at his
father. If he stood, he would top Lavastine by half a head;
at this vulnerable time of night, with the count dressed in
shirt and linen drawers, he remained seated. Lavastine let
the fabric wall fall behind him and crossed to Alain.

"Are you well?" He placed the back of his hand against
the boy's cheek. It was not precisely a tender gesture—
Lavastine did not have tender impulses—but the simple
display of concern moved Alain deeply.

"I am well. I had a bad dream."

Terror padded in from the other room and nipped at
Rage. Lavastine cuffed them gently, almost absently, and
they both settled down comfortably together, a quivering
mass of black hounds.

"You are concerned about the battle."

Ai, Lady, the dream had been so vivid that Alain had
forgotten about the work they meant to do at dawn.

"No," he said truthfully. "I am troubled by dreams of
the Eika prince."

Lavastine began to pace. Terror yawned, stretched, made
as if to rise and pad after his master, and then bared teeth,
nipped sleepily at Rage again, and settled back to sleep.

"Do not fear *my* anger, Alain. You were honest with me, and I have forgiven you for freeing the savage. Is it the Eika you fear? Perhaps you're afraid the prince you let go will be among them and you don't know if you can kill him, if it comes to that?"

"He isn't among them. He's sailing north. He was sent back to his own country by his father to bring to heel all the warleaders who haven't yet accepted Bloodheart as chief over all the Eika. King, I suppose we might say."

As soon as he spoke, Alain realized how strange this statement must sound. Lavastine turned and, in the warm light of the candle, he gave that grimace which was his smile, not an expression of warmth, precisely, nor yet of amusement. "Son." Always, these past months, he savored the word, *son.* "If it is true you have dreams that are also true visions, I wish you never to speak of them to anyone but me. Never to a deacon or any person in the church."

"Why not?"

"They might claim you have been touched by God and try to take you away from me. I will not let you go, not as long as I am alive."

Alain shivered. "Don't say that," he whispered. "Don't speak of death."

Lavastine reached, hesitated, then touched the boy on his dark head, laying his hand there *almost* tenderly, certainly possessively. "I will not let go of you, ever, Alain," he repeated. With a shake of his head as a dog shakes off water, he pulled away and crossed to the other side of the tent, hooking the fabric wall up over a post. "I smell morning," he said. "Come, son. It is time to arm for battle."

The hounds roused and with their waking roused the servants, who hurried to bring lit lanterns and clothing. They dressed the count and his heir in padded jackets to cushion their bodies from the weight of their armor. Alain had spent the summer training in armor, becoming accustomed to its weight and feel along his body: heavy mail hauberk, soft leather hood over which a servant slipped and tightened a mail coif and, on top of that, a conical helmet trimmed with bronze. Another servant bound his calves with leather strips wound from ankle to knee. This was far better armor than anything he could have hoped to wear as a man-at-arms.

He did not think about battle—if it came to that—as the servant hung belt and short sword at his hips. Outside, he took a spear from the rack set up beside the tent. The long haft of oak was strengthened by a twining ribbon of blue leather that wound from butt to lugs, the "wings" projecting out on either side just below the blade. Grooms brought their horses. Without too much trepidation, Alain swung up on his. He was a natural rider—Lavastine had stated more than once, in his emphatic way, that this was clearly a sign of Alain's noble blood. He might well have been *born* to the saddle, but he had truly only learned to ride after that day in the month of Sormas when Lavastine had acknowledged him as son and heir. He was untried and inexperienced, especially when it came time to ride into a skirmish where he might see actual fighting. But a count's son did not *walk* into battle. So he would ride.

Lavastine mounted his fine gray gelding, Graymane, and nodded at Alain as if to say: "*Are you ready?*"

Alain nodded in turn. He would not disappoint his father.

Wasn't riding to war what he had dreamed of all his life? His foster father, Henri the merchant, and his Aunt Bel had pledged him to the church, to live out his life as a monk at the Dragon's Tail Monastery. But the Lady of Battles had appeared that stormy spring day when Eika had burned the monastery and slaughtered all the monks. She had given him a rose that never wilted and could never be crushed, a rose he kept wrapped in a little cloth bag and wore on a leather thong around his neck. She had taken a pledge from him. "*Serve me.*" He had sworn to serve her in order to save Osna village from the Eika attack but also because what she promised him was his heart's desire. For that, knowing that the man who raised him had promised him in good faith to the church, he still felt guilty.

Birds chirped, and the gray light that heralds dawn rose around them, etching the skeletal lines of trees against the seamless expanse of sky. Above the trees stars shone. Trained by a navigator, Alain could not help but note stars and constellations and wonder at their omens. The wandering stars moved on the backdrop of the sphere of the fixed stars, the highest of the seven spheres beyond which lay the Chamber of Light. Their threads wove power that

guided Fate and could be wielded by hands trained in that
craft. Or so it was claimed, though such teaching was condemned by the church.

The pale rose beacon of Aturna, the Magus, shone near
the zenith in the constellation known as The Sisters, and
Mok, planet of wisdom and bounty, made her stately way
through The Lion. Beyond Aturna to the west, the jewel
of seven stars clustered closely together and known as "the
Crown" glittered so brightly he thought he could see the
mysterious seventh sister among her six bolder siblings.
Bow and Arrow, the arrow tipped with the bright blue brilliance of the star Seirios, pointed toward the Hunter with
his belt of gems and his left shoulder tipped with red—
the star called Vulneris. But as Alain stared, recalling the
knowledge taught him by his foster father, the stars faded
with dawn. Soon the light of the rising sun would obliterate
this sight, as Lavastine meant to obliterate the Eika camp.

Lavastine lifted a hand for silence. His men-at-arms
quieted to gather around him. These were the cavalry,
some twenty experienced men, the best of his fighters. The
infantry was already in place. The scouts, by now, would
be creeping down to the shoreline to do their duty.

Lavastine left nothing to chance, not when he could
help it.

They started out slowly, each armed servant holding on
to a horse's bridle and leading them across the rough
ground. It grew lighter as they crossed down through forest,
picked their way across a blackened field that had once
been ripe oats, and came out on a sandy hill that overlooked sea and shore. There, on a rocky rise just above a
river's mouth, Eika had built a winter camp.

The sea shone and glimmered in the east where the first
line of light touched it, spreading over the waves. From the
beach down by the river, as if it were an echo of the sun's
light, fire sprang up among the ships

"Forward," said Lavastine calmly. He was always calm.

Alain was sweating with excitement. Someday, perhaps,
the bards would sing of this battle. He followed his father
down, the other mounted soldiers ranged around them, protecting them. No nobleman sent his soldiers into battle
alone; that would be dishonorable as well as disloyal. So
must his son—his bastard son, only recently proclaimed as

his legitimate heir—be seen capable of riding to war and fighting in battle.

Lavastine glanced, just once, toward Alain, as if to say: "*Don't fail me.*"

An alarm shrieked—the howling of dogs and the blast of a horn—from the Eika camp. Like hornets, Eika rushed from their shelters and out of their palisade to save their ships.

Archers hidden in the brush on the steep slopes of the ridge lit arrows from coals concealed in hollow tubes they had carried with them and began to shoot into the enclosure. The infantrymen, who had waded out along the shore, closed in on the surprised Eika from the river's mouth. And from behind, the claw that closed the pincer's mouth, rode Lavastine with his cavalry.

It took every ounce of skill Alain had to keep his horse running with the rest, to keep his balance, to simply stay with them and keep hold of his spear—not be jounced off or have his attention wrenched away by a hundred distractions. The cloth shelters in the enclosure burned with a spitting, furious flame. The ships did not burn as brightly, but shapes swarmed over them, dousing the flames and howling their rage while the lightly armed scouts scuttled away to safety.

Then the cavalry hit the first rank of the Eika, those who had seen them coming and turned to fight. Alain rode right over one. He did not even tuck and thrust with his spear, did not even parry, just rode, hoping the horse knew what it was doing. *He* did not. He was dimly aware that beside him Lavastine thrust and stuck with his spear, striking home into an Eika chest, tugged, then gave up the spear and rode on. Soldiers pounded after them, leaving behind a mass of trampled Eika. Beyond, a larger clot of Eika struggled with the infantry. On foot the Eika had the advantage over the smaller, weaker men. With axes hacking and shields used like weapons, striking and punching, Eika clawed and fought their way through the foot soldiers. But even in the fury of battle some turned, alerted by the cries of their brothers and the pounding of hooves.

He was upon them. Skin of copper, of bronze, of gold or silver or iron, they resembled creatures poured out of metal into a human mold, and yet they were not human at

all. One cut at him, its teeth gleaming sharply white, its
hair the dead color of bleached bone. He parried with his
spear, felt the ax blade cut and hang up in the leather-
bound haft. He tugged, suddenly frantic, and the Eika
dropped its shield and drew its knife. Horrified, Alain released his hold on the spear and, as the creature staggered
back with its lips frozen in a ghastly grimace, he jerked his
sword from its sheath, lifted it high—

—and in that moment, with the Eika off-balance before
him, with the skirmish swirling forward as other horsemen
pressed Eika back and Lavastine shouted to urge them on,
in that instant before his father looked around, before his
father would see him frozen, a coward, he knew he could
not do it.

He could not kill.

The Eika cast away ax and spear and leaped forward
with its knife, a wicked obsidian blade. Alain tried to lift
his short sword to parry, but he was paralyzed with that
revelation.

He could not kill.

He was not worthy. He would never be a soldier. He
had failed his father.

He was going to die.

The sun flashed fire in his eyes, blinding him. Or was it
death that he did not yet feel, a knife buried in his eye or
throat, that blinded him? He dropped his reins and instinctively held up a hand to shield his eyes from the sun. A
shadow swooped down over him. An iron-gray broadsword
cut down across his sight. The Eika fell, cut down in mid-
leap, and collapsed to the earth.

Alain gasped and groped for his reins before the horse
could feel he had lost control; but this was a trained warhorse. It moved forward with the others. Who had come
forward? Who had saved him? *Who had witnessed his
cowardice?*

He turned. *Her* gaze was at once distant and utterly
piercing. The rose burned at his chest like a hot coal
pressed against his skin.

She spurred her horse forward, his horse responding not
to his limp control but somehow to *hers,* though she did
not touch it, though she did not hold its reins.

"Stay beside me," she said, whether words spoken

through her lips or ringing in his mind he could not tell. *I am the Lady of Battles.* She had a terrible beauty, seared by hardship and agony and the wild madness of battle. She drove her white horse, and with him beside her, surged forward through the Eika, striking to each side, so smooth in her movements that he knew she had ridden to war for so many years that she no longer had to think in order to kill.

Beyond her rode Lavastine, face grim and focused on his task. He took no pleasure in battle; this was duty. He parried a blow and cut in his turn, striking down a silver-scaled Eika; in that instant, as the Eika fell before him, Lavastine looked right past the woman and with that glance marked Alain and went back to the fight.

Now the cavalry drove the Eika back into the waiting line of infantry. Crushed between foe and foe, the Eika fought with hopeless fury or struggled to run free. But Alain, with the Lady of Battles at his side, remained untouched. She struck down any of the savages who lunged at him or hacked at him with ax or spear. He managed to stay seated on his horse. On her other side, Lavastine fought with the same steady imperturbable calm.

Alain jerked his horse left to avoid trampling an infantrymen. The two lines had met at last. Lavastine peeled aside and with a shouted command led Alain and a dozen others down toward the shore. Some Eika ran flat out for the ships; others fought as the horsemen came up behind them. But the savages were broken now. Each one fought only for its own life, or for death. Down at the beach one ship was halfway into the water; Eika jostled each other for a place in its belly, grappling for oars, shoving it out into the current. The other two ships burned with an oily smoke that stung Alain's nostrils, bringing tears to his eyes and a cloudy haze over his vision.

"Rein in!" cried Lavastine.

Alain blinked back tears and passed a hand over his eyes. "Well done," said the count.

Alain wiped tears from his checks and looked at his father with surprise. *Well done?* To whom was he speaking?

Soldiers circled them, weapons held at the ready. They waited on that verge where sandy soil turns into grassy beach and watched a single ship as it hove to into the current, watched as oars beat the water and the ship was swept out to sea. A few arrows, shot harmlessly from the rocking belly of the boat, splashed in the shallows or skittered away into the reeds.

The Lady of Battles was gone. At his chest he felt only the cool, soft lump that was the little leather pouch.

The soldiers ranged 'round as they shook themselves free of the last eddies of skirmishing. A few Eika had plunged into the river to swim after the receding ship. Most lay dying on the ground. A few men were wounded, one or two with mortal wounds, but Lavastine's tactics had worked with that same blunt effectiveness with which Lavastine himself approached life.

"Well done, my son," repeated Lavastine. He lifted his sword; a viscous fluid the greenish-blue color of corroded copper stained the blade. With it held high, he addressed his soldiers. "My trusted companions, now you have seen this boy prove himself in battle."

One of the cavalrymen spoke. "I saw him strike down four with his own hand, my lord. He had the battle fury on him. He shone with it. I will follow Lord Alain gladly." To Alain's horror, he saw *respect* in the soldier's eyes.

As soon as this was spoken, others began to talk. Others, too, had seen a kind of unearthly glow around the lad.

"But I did nothing," he protested. "I was afraid. It was the hand of the Lady of Battles which protected me, which struck down those Eika."

As soon as the words passed his lips, he wished he had not spoken. They misunderstood him utterly. *They none of them had seen her.* They took his words as modesty, and as piety. They believed he had accomplished those deeds when in fact he had proved himself unworthy and only been saved by *her* intervention.

Some of the men drew the Circle at their breasts. Some murmured with awe and amazement. Others bowed their heads. Lavastine stared at him hard, and then, as if he could not help himself, he gave that grimace which to him was a smile.

"God in Unity have set Their Hand on you, my son," he said with pride. "You are meant to be a warrior."

2

LAVASTINE and his retinue celebrated the Feast
of St. Valentinus at the holding of Lord Geoffrey's wife,
Lady Aldegund. All summer Lavastine had drilled Alain in
the art of war and the rules of proper conduct, both of which
were necessary—more than necessary, given the particulars
of Alain's birth—for Alain to impress those noble families
and other stewards and servants who gave allegiance to the
counts of Lavas. Wealth Alain would inherit from his father,
but there were many other virtues he must display in abundance in order to rule as count after him. All of these
virtues Lavastine had and to spare: shrewdness, military
prowess, boldness, liberality, and a stubborn and dogged
determination to defend his possessions and prerogatives.

"They are treating you well?" Lavastine asked that evening as they made ready for the feast, which would be held
in the great hall.

"Yes, Father." Alain stood very still, admiring the fine
brocade that trimmed Lavastine's indigo tunic while a servingman wrapped strips of linen around Alain's calves, binding his loose hosen tightly against his lower legs. A buckle
worked of tiny panels of cloissonne interspersed with gar-
nets mounted in gold cells clasped the narrow leather belt
he wore to hike his tunic up around his knees; its richness
still stunned him. The tunic itself, woven of wool, was dyed
with woad to a rich afternoon blue. He recognized the color
from cloth dyed and woven in Osna village by his Aunt
Bel and old Mistress Garia, both of whom had daughters
and distant kin and servantwomen trained in weaving.

*But she's not my Aunt Bel, not any more. She's only the
common woman who raised me.*

So had Lavastine decreed. Alain had heard nothing from
his old family since the count had sent a reward of sceattas
to Bel and Henri, payment for the years they had fostered
Alain. Had they forgotten him so quickly, not even to send
word of how they and Stancy and Julien and little Agnes
and the others fared?

This thought, and the traitorous wrench of sorrow it produced in his heart, he kept to himself.

All was ready at last; in the company of kin they need wear no weapons. The hounds had been penned outside, since it was not safe—to the others—to bring them indoors in an unfamiliar hall. Alain followed Lavastine down the stairs from the loft where they, as honored guests, would sleep with their servants this night. Together, he and his father came into the long hall. Every tapestry in the holding had been aired and now hung to decorate the walls. Fire burned in the central hearth where six months ago Lavastine—under Biscop Antonia's spell—had set his hounds on his own kinsman, Geoffrey, and on Geoffrey's young wife.

Now, Alain felt that every eye there turned to measure *him*. Lavastine they had forgiven for the madness set on him by another, but Alain did not think Lord Geoffrey and the others quite believed that Lavastine truly intended to make this unknown and illegitimate boy his heir.

They were all terribly polite as he took his place on his father's right side. That place, the one of greatest honor, had once been given to Lord Geoffrey; of all Lavastine's kin, Geoffrey was his nearest blood relation—or had been, until Alain.

Lady Aldegund, as hostess, sat on Lavastine's left. After a prayer, she directed her servants to pour wine at the upper table and cider to those at the lower tables. She handed Lavastine the cup that she, as hostess, and he, as honored guest, were to share; he bowed his head and offered it back to her, so she might have the first taste.

"Let us give this toast," said Lord Geoffrey with that same polite smile fixed on his face, "to the newly discovered son and heir of my cousin, Lavastine." He drank and handed his cup to Alain.

Lavastine's men-at-arms toasted heartily, with cheers. From Aldegund and Geoffrey's people the salute was subdued, even perfunctory. Lavastine studied the assembled crowd—quite fifty people—with narrowed eyes and his habitual half-frown, but he made no comment. He was no fool. He must know that many folk would not gladly accept the illegitimate son over the legitimate third cousin. Servants brought in the first course, a variety of fowl, chickens, geese, moorhens, and quail, all steeped so heavily in spices that Alain feared he would get sick to his stomach.

"You found no more winter camps?" asked Lord Geoffrey, leaning past Alain to address Lavastine.

Lavastine lifted his cup to lips and made a small gesture with his free hand.

Alain started. "Why, no, Lord Geoffrey," he said dutifully, seeing that his father meant for him to answer, "we found no more. It is not usual for the Eika to winter in these lands."

Geoffrey's mouth twisted into a smile. "Indeed not, Lord Alain. This is the first time we have seen any Eika on our shores after Matthiasmass, and yet my own men burned a winter camp a month ago. Now you bring news that not one week ago you destroyed another. I wonder if the Eika mean to begin a new campaign. What if they want our land as well as our gold?"

"Do they farm?" asked Alain.

Geoffrey blinked. Aldegund took the cup from Lavastine and answered for her husband. She was a year or two younger than Alain, and her first child lay asleep in a cradle upstairs. "I would suppose that savages know nothing of farming. My kin have held estates in these lands since the time of the Emperor Taillefer. All the Eika ever want is gold and whatever other wealth—slaves, iron, coins, jewelry—they can carry away."

"But why would they want land, if not to farm it?" asked Alain. "Or to pasture sheep and cattle?" He saw at once he had asked the wrong question. He had asked the sort of question Aunt Bel would ask. The other noble folk ranged along the table turned to listen—to see him make a fool of himself.

He refused to oblige them. And he refused to be ashamed of the common sense Aunt Bel had taught him.

"If the Eika are now making winter camps, then we must ask ourselves why they do this now, this year, when they did not before. Isn't it true that there is one who stands as king among them, this Bloodheart? They have always been raiders before. Each ship is ruled over by a separate war-leader. Now one Eika unites many tribes, and he has taken Gent, the very city where King Arnulf the Elder crowned

his children and laid his claim for them to be rulers over
Wendar and Varre together."

The nobles grumbled, forgetting their distrust of Alain
when reminded of their grievance at old King Arnulf,
grandfather of the current king, Henry. Once, as princes
and counts and noble ladies and lords of Varre, they had
crowned their own sovereign ruler and fought their own
private battles for influence in the Varren court. Now, out-
siders in a court dominated by nobles of Wendish blood,
they waited, discontent. Some of these men had ridden with
Sabella in her rebellion against Henry. Some of these
women had sent supplies and gold to enrich Sabella's war
chests and maintain her army. Now Sabella was a prisoner
and her rebellion ended; Lavastine had pledged himself
loyal to King Henry, and in return Henry had acknowledged Lavastine's bastard son as the count's heir.

The bastard son who had to prove himself worthy, in
their eyes. "Now some of the Eika acknowledge a king,"
he continued, "while others build winter camps in Varren
lands. What does this mean?"

"Indeed," said Lavastine. "What does it mean, Lord
Geoffrey? Have you thought on this puzzle, cousin?"

By his expression, Geoffrey clearly had not. He took a
gulp of wine to cover his discomfiture and set the cup down
hard on the table. A few soldiers, at a lower table, laughed;
Lavastine's men, they had seen Alain in battle and now
seemed as willing to follow where he led as were Rage and
Sorrow and the other black hounds.

I am not worthy.

And yet, if the Lady of Battles had appeared to him and
not to the others, was that not a sign of his worthiness?
Did he not carry the rose, the mark of her favor?

A servingwoman, refilled Lord Geoffrey's cup and lingered just long enough to look over Alain impertinently
but with obvious interest; he flushed, suddenly warm. And
why shouldn't he be? The hall was certainly warm enough
to suit the coldest heart.

"Have you formed some opinion yourself as to the Eika's
reasons, Lord Alain?" asked Aldegund with a sharp tinge
to her voice, like malice. A sweet-faced woman, scarcely
more than a girl, Aldegund had not accepted Alain and,
except for her marriage to Geoffrey, Lavastine had no

claim over her. Her kin had their own lands and estates, their own connection to Varren nobility and to the Wendish kings. She made a gesture and the servingwoman moved away to tend to other cups.

"I have." His flush deepened as he heard his own words. It sounded so very—*proud.* But a count's son was allowed some arrogance; indeed, it was expected of him.

"Go on." Lavastine gestured with his cup.

Alain allowed himself a drink of wine for courage—such very fine wine, carted in from Salia, and so *much* of it—before he continued. "I think Bloodheart means to make of himself a king to rival King Henry, or King Lothair of Salia. But when a king or queen is made, there are always princes who chafe under this rule. Some of these warleaders might not like being under the hand of another Eika, even one said to be a powerful enchanter. Yet if their own people wish to gain Bloodheart's favor, those warleaders and the men loyal to them might be driven out of their own lands because they are rebels. Perhaps that is why they winter here. They may have nothing to go back to."

"It is possible," said Geoffrey grudgingly, finishing their shared cup. His wife sent a servant at once to refill it.

"Is it not just as likely," asked an older man whom Alain identified as Meginher, one of Aldegund's many maternal uncles, a fighting man who had a considerable reputation, "that these winter camps have been built at the order of this Bloodheart?"

"Why do we suppose," asked Aldegund sharply, "that these Eika behave in any manner like ourselves? They are savages, are they not? Why should they act as we do? What do we truly know of them?"

I know what I see in my dreams. But he could not speak of those dreams out loud. His father had forbidden it. He bowed his head before her superior wisdom, for though she was young, she was a woman, lady of this estate and fashioned in the likeness of Our Lady, who orders the Hearth of Life. Men were fashioned for rougher work, and though certainly they were usually skilled beyond women in combat and hard labor, everyone knew, and the church mothers had often written on, the greater potential of women for the labors of the mind and the arts. These blessings, like that of childbirth, were granted to them by the grace of Our Lady, Mother of Life.

"We know little of the Eika," said Lavastine curtly. "While we still have good weather, however, myself, my *son,* and these of our men-at-arms who accompany us will patrol the coasts for as long as we can. We will march west to Osna Sound next. The last and worst incursion of the Eika came there two springs ago, as you know."

"Ah." Lord Geoffrey leaned forward with new interest. "There is a village at Osna Sound. Isn't that where you were fostered, Lord Alain? I remember when you came to Lavas town along with the other laborers who owed their year's service."

"You do?" asked Alain, surprised that as important a man as Geoffrey had noticed an insignificant common boy like himself.

But Geoffrey looked down swiftly, and Alain glanced at his father to see that Lavastine had fixed an expressionless—yet for that very reason intimidating—stare on the other man.

Meginher snorted and turned to his cup, taking a swig of wine. Servants staggered in under the weight of a roasted boar and several haunches of venison decorated with pimentos. Alain could not help but think of Lackling, who had eaten gruel all his life with a few beans or turnips if there were extra. Poor bastard . . . just like Alain, only how different Lackling's fate had turned out to be. He had never been given leave to eat food this rich, except the last scraps taken from the table if he could grab them before they were thrown to the pigs.

"Of course," said Lavastine, relinquishing the cup to his hostess, who had it filled once again with wine, "any person would have noticed your quality at once, Alain, for it was preordained that you take your place among the magnates and potentes, was it not? Twice now you have distinguished yourself in battle." He said this firmly and clearly so that every person in the hall heard him. He gestured toward the captain of his cavalry. "Is it not true, Captain?"

The soldier stood. He, like the others, had bent his knee before Alain four days ago after the battle—and not just because Lavastine wished them to do so. "I have fought for the counts of Lavas since I was a lad, and I have never seen anything like this. I remember when the boy killed the *guivre* at the battle outside Kassel. Even so, to see him ride through his first battle as a true soldier, to see him strike to either side with no sign of fear, with such strength, with such fury that it shone from him as if he had been touched by the saints and God Themselves, to see him slay Eika on his right hand and on his left, I could see he had been born to the life of a warrior." The other men—those of Lavastine's soldiers who had survived the battle— pounded cups and knife hilts and empty platters on the table as they roared their approval.

Alain leaped up. "It was the hand of the Lady of Battles, not my own," he insisted, "which killed those Eika."

"Sit," said Lavastine softly and, as obedient as the hounds, Alain sat.

The others murmured, but Lord Geoffrey made no more comments about Alain's service as a laborer at Lavas Holding, and Lady Aldegund turned the talk to more innocent subjects: the year's harvest, the new wheeled plow, and how the mild summer and autumn presaged a good growing season which would, in turn, presage a rich harvest of taxes.

A third course was brought in, veal and lamb spiced with cumin and pepper and other exotic flavors and condiments. A poet, trained in the court chapel of the Salian king and now singing for his supper at the lesser courts of nobles, sang from an old and lengthy panegyric in praise of the Salian Emperor Taillefer as Alain picked at his food.

"*As did the mariners of old, I set sail to test my weary limbs against the storms of the sea, to try my ship against the ocean waves. I set my gaze to that beacon which gleams from afar. That light is the name of Taillefer. Look! The sun shines no more brightly than the emperor, who illuminates the earth with his boundless love and great wisdom.*"

The poet went on in this manner, extolling the virtues of the long-dead emperor while Alain wondered how the noble lords and ladies could possibly eat as much food as they were stuffing into their bellies at this feast. He had gone hungry from time to time—everyone did—but he had never suffered; Aunt Bel was prosperous enough to be able to set aside some portion every year against a catastrophically bad harvest. But he had seen the poor who lived from hand to mouth, their children in perpetual want, begging at the church with legs and arms as thin as sticks and faces bleak with hopelessness. In good years, of course, such people found day labor and managed, but in bad years even the prosperous stared into the gaunt face of hunger.

"For although the sun knows twelve hours of darkness, Taillefer, like a star, shines eternally. He enters first among the company, and he clears the way so that all may follow. With heavy chains he binds the unjust and with a stiff yoke he constrains the proud. With a stern hand he teaches the impious to love God."

The servants brought in a fourth course of clear soup together with a bread so white and fine it seemed to dissolve on Alain's tongue.

"Taillefer is the fount of all grace and honor. His achievements have made him famous throughout the four quarters of the earth. He is generous, prudent, just, pious, affable, handsome, outstanding at arms, wise in conciliation, compassionate to the poor, and gentle with the weak. Never before did there speak such an eloquent lecturer; the sweetness of his words surpasses those of Marcia Tullia, the orator of ancient Dariya. He alone has penetrated the hidden paths of knowledge and understood all its mysteries, for to him God revealed the secrets of the universe. He has discovered every secret of the mathematici and the secret hidden words and the ways of the stars in their courses and the means by which their powers may be drawn down into the hands of humankind. No navigator has studied the heavens with greater keenness."

After the soup came apple tarts, pears steeped in honey, and a custard. The creamy mixture of milk, honey, and eggs melted on Alain's lips like nectar, and he thought that perhaps he could endure another entire poem cataloging the dead emperor's virtues if only he could make room in his belly for several more helpings of custard. Mostly, however, he wanted to go to sleep. It was well into night now;

candles and torches burned, illuminating the feast and the faces of women and men eating and drinking their fill, passing cups from mouth to mouth, sharing bites of apple tart, getting up to stretch their limbs. A constant stream of people went to and from the forecourt, so sodden with wine that they had to relieve themselves. Some of the soldiers, made restless by the long court poem, called for a stanza from the *Gold of the Hevelli.* Instead, the learned poet launched into a long digression—evidently part of the poem—in which Taillefer oversaw the construction of a new palace at the city of Autun, where he had most often lingered with his court. His workers labored eagerly, raising straight columns and a high citadel, digging into the earth to find hot springs for the baths the emperor loved; the most favored workers built a church fit for a hallowed king. "They labor as do the bees in summer"—at which point the poet went into a second long digression, this one on the nature of bees.

It was time to go outside. Alain excused himself and left the hall. As he came out into the cold autumn night, he sucked in a deep breath of clean air. Inside, smoke from hearth and torches had wreathed the air with a heavy perfume; he was dizzy from it and from the wine. Aunt Bel had never served such wine at her table! Or such a plethora of dishes, each one as exotic as if it had been itself carted to this land from the fabled East. But he was becoming accustomed to feasts.

Feeling suddenly guilty for his good fortune, he walked farther out into the night and relieved himself against a tree. The chill air had the effect of sharpening his senses, and he heard the crack of a branch under a foot and the long scrape of cloth pulled across twigs before he saw the shadow slip toward him. He hastily tied his hosen and stepped back, then let out a breath; it was only one of the servingwomen who had lost her way or also come out to relieve herself.

"My lord Alain," she said. She stumbled and gave a little cry. He started forward and put out an arm to catch her. She pressed herself against him. She had firm breasts and a provocative swell of belly and hip beneath her long gown. "It's a cold night. The hayloft is much warmer than it is out here."

He was suddenly much warmer than he had any right to
be on such a cold night. Somehow, her moist lips nuzzled
his neck; her breath smelled of sweet custard. Somehow,
her hand slipped around the curve of his buttocks.

"My—my father expects me inside."

"Inside you shall be, my lord, if you wish it."

The sudden heat that transfixed his body scared him, and
yet, the more she stroked his body, the more he felt it.
He fumbled at her shoulders as she maneuvered him back,
pinning him up against the tree.

"You're very handsome," she murmured.

"Am I?" he asked, surprised. No woman except the
bored Withi had ever shown interest in him before he became Lavastine's heir. But the thought vanished as does
mist under the sun when she kissed him, moving her body
against his and taking hold of his hands, guiding them.

If this was the fire of lust, then it was no wonder people
succumbed to it. But, kissing her, he made the servingwoman in his mind into an image of Tallia, and the
thought of kissing *her*, of being free to do so, of meeting
her in the marriage bed . . .

"Ah!" sighed the woman. "That's better. Not as inexperienced as you look, my lord." She deftly slid her hands
along his belt and unfastened the buckle. "I've a brother
who will be ready for service next spring. He's a good
strong boy." The belt, and extra length of tunic held up by
it, slipped down to around his knees. "He'd make a fine
man-at-arms."

At this moment, she could have asked for anything and
he would have given it to her. She took his hands and
helped them slide her own tunic up, to her knees, to her
thighs, baring pale legs, to her hips . . .

From the kennels erupted a sudden uproar of barking
and maddened howls and men's shouts, punctuated by a
scream. Alain knew those howls: Lavastine's hounds. *His*
hounds.

"I beg you," he said, so out of breath he might as well
have been running. He tried to slide out away from her,
caught his back on a branch that stabbed in just below his
shoulder blade. He stumbled, took a step, tripped over his
not-quite-fastened belt, and fell hard to his knees. The jolt
brought tears to his eyes. His skin was on fire.

"My lord Alain!" She came to his rescue, helping him up, fumbling with the belt.

"I don't mean—I'm sorry—but the hounds—"

Her face was a flash of pale skin and dark eyes in the light of a thin crescent moon. "Of course you must go." She had remembered the hounds, and what he was. Now she was frightened of *him*, she who had held all the power moments before.

He hastily tucked his tunic in over his belt so he wouldn't trip on its length, then ran for the kennels, which lay out behind the great hall in the lee of the stables.

The hounds had gone mad, ravaging a man who lay like a rag doll in their midst. Alain waded in and dragged them off the poor man, who by now bled from a score of bites and ragged tears.

"Back! Back!" Made strong by anger and fear and the still coursing memory of the servingwoman's caresses, Alain hoisted the man up and hauled him out of the kennel, kicked Terror back, scolded Rage and Sorrow, who slunk together to a corner and hunkered down as if ashamed of themselves. As they should be! One of the handlers slammed the gate shut behind him. He let the man down onto the ground and examined his legs and arms, which had taken the worst of it from the hounds. The man writhed on the ground, moaning and crying and begging for mercy.

It was one of Lord Geoffrey's men.

"How did this happen?" he demanded, looking up at the others, a ring of Lavastine's soldiers who were obviously drunk.

"He said such things, my lord," said one, young enough and drunk enough to be brash. "He said things about *you*, my lord, but he never saw you in the battle against the Eika. He never saw you kill the *guivre* and save Count Lavastine's life. He had no right to say such things and he wouldn't believe us, what we said, so it came to—"

Those weren't shadows on the soldiers' faces, but bruises. "It came to a fight?"

"Yes, my lord."

"How did he get into the kennel? Ai, by our Lord! You." He gestured to one of the handlers. "Run and get the herb-woman who lives here. There is such a one, surely? Ask at the stable." The handler obeyed, dashing off.

The soldiers did not answer at once. But he could guess how it had all happened. While he allowed himself to be seduced, this other game had unfolded here. Even now, watching the man weeping with pain before him, watching as blood pooled on the ground, running his hands over the man's skin to find the gaping wounds, he knew this man could die. If he did not succumb to loss of blood or the simple trauma, he might well die later of infection.

"Ai, Lady!" He hated himself at that moment. Slowly the encounter by the tree unwrapped itself from the heat of lust and he saw it more clearly. Perhaps the woman really had thought him handsome. Certainly, he had found her desirable. But she would never have thrown herself against him if he hadn't been Lavastine's heir. She had *wanted* something from him—a position for her brother in his retinue. This coin she had to offer in trade. Had he been simple Alain, foster son of Henri the merchant, he would have had nothing to give her in return. She would not have looked twice at him, just as the girls at Lavas Holding had never looked twice at him before this summer except that one time, on a dare. And this summer, under stern orders given by the count himself to Cook who had delivered those orders to all the servingwomen in Lavas Holding, none had dared approach him for fear of the count's wrath. The man who had made a bastard intended that illegitimate son to make none of his own.

"My lord, I beg you, forgive us." The three soldiers knelt before him. The stench of mead on their breath was almost enough to stagger Alain where he crouched beside the ravaged man. "But he made such claims! He said any boy could claim to be a bastard, that any noble lord might tumble a woman or two and think nothing of it—"

As he had been about to do, without thinking at all!

"—and so we said we'd see how well *he* did, claiming to be Lavastine's heir."

Alain let out a breath. "So you threw him into the kennel."

They didn't answer, nor did they need to.

Men from the stables came running up, and there was shoving and angry words. The man on the ground ceased his muttering and lapsed into quiet.

"You've killed him!"

"Bastard lovers! Our lord Geoffrey is a true nobleman!"

"You wouldn't know a noble lord if he bit you in the—"

"Quiet!" cried Alain, standing. He set a hand on the gate and shook it, and that shut every one of them up and brought Rage and Sorrow to the gate, panting to be let out. He opened it, chased the others back, and let Rage emerge. Sorrow whined at being left behind and thumped his tail against wood, barking once.

"Take this man and give him care. All who witnessed, come with me. This will be settled."

They followed like sheep, the handlers—some Lavastine's, some Geoffrey's—the three soldiers, and a pair of Geoffrey's men-at-arms who had been comrades to the injured man and who now admitted to having goaded him on. Except for the handlers, they were all drunk. Rage herded them to the doors which led into the hall. Alain stepped across the threshold and was assaulted at once with a haze of smoke. The annoying buzz of whispering voices made an undertone beneath the ringing tenor of the poet.

Lady and Lord Above! The poet was *still* going on. It was no wonder the Salian king had thrown him out to make his fortune elsewhere.

"*In the woods every manner of wild beast makes its lair. Through these glades the admirable hero, Taillefer, would often go hunting and give chase with hounds and spears and arrows. At the very dawn of day, when the sun first rises to spread its light upon the fields and the great city, a band of nobles waits at the threshold of the emperor's bedchamber, and with them wait the emperor's noble daughters. A clamor arises in the city, a roar lifts into the air, horse neighs to horse, and hound strains at its leash. At length all set out. The young men carry the thick hunting spears with sharp iron points, and the women carry linen nets fastened with square mesh. A throng encircles the emperor, and he and his daughters lead their black hounds with leashes round their necks, and in their excitement the hounds snap at any person who comes near them except for their master and his children, for even the dogs in their dumb loyalty bow before such bright nobility . . .*"

*   *   *

The poet was last to see and last—*finally*—to stop talking.

Lavastine rose from behind the long table at the far end of the hall. "What does this mean, Alain?"

Alain walked forward with Rage padding obediently at his side. Every soul in the hall shrank back from the hound who panted with mouth open, revealing her teeth. "There has been a fight outside. One of Lord Geoffrey's men-at-arms was thrown into the kennel and badly torn. He may yet die."

Geoffrey leaped to his feet. A moment later, Lady Aldegund rose together with her uncle. At a sign from her, Geoffrey sat down; the uncle did not. The girl set a hand briefly on his hand as if to remind herself that she had the weight of his arm to back her up.

"How did this happen?" she asked.

"I believe," replied Alain calmly, "that they had all drunk too much."

"It is *my* man who may die!" exploded Lord Geoffrey, jumping again to his feet.

"Sit down, cousin," said Lavastine in a cool voice. Geoffrey sat. Aldegund and her uncle did not.

"If he dies," said Aldegund, "there will be a price to pay."

"And so shall those men responsible pay it," said Alain, halting just before the table like a supplicant. Except that, with Rage at his side and, indeed, a growing anger in his heart, he did not feel one bit as if he had to beg anyone's pardon. "They will pay the proper fine to the man himself if he is crippled or to the man's kin if he dies. But the man, or his kin, must also pay a fine."

Geoffrey gasped. "Why is that?" demanded Aldegund.

This, here and now, was the test of wills—and of whether the illegitimate son deserved what he had been given.

"All of these men took part in the fight or witnessed the fight, and they will swear before your deacon and Count Lavastine's clerics that the man involved spoke words disloyal to Count Lavastine, lord of his lord."

At that even Lady Aldegund blushed, for every person there knew what sort of things a tongue loosened by too much mead might have said: not against the count himself—no one disputed Lavastine's deeds or prerogatives or virtues—but against the count's judgment.

There was a long silence.

At last Lady Aldegund inclined her head, acquiescing to Alain's judgment in the matter. Her uncle sat down and, after a moment, she did as well. Lavastine sat, too, and took the cup she offered him.

Alain bowed his head. Rage snuffled into his palm, smelling something of interest there—perhaps the lingering scent of the servingwoman. Ai, Lady; as if the thought made her appear, there she stood beside Lavastine, filling the count's cup. She glanced up, briefly, at Alain, and then away. She did not look at him again. The feast proceeded without incident, and the poet—whose diction and voice were decent enough—was encouraged to sing something more popular.

Only in the morning when they had ridden away from the holding and lost sight of it past hills and forest did Lavastine comment on the incident.

"I am pleased with your cleverness."

"But—"

Lavastine lifted a hand, which meant he had not finished and did not yet wish for Alain to reply. Dutifully, Alain waited. "But you must not be unwilling to boast of your accomplishments, Alain. To display prowess in battle is a fine thing for a man in your position. You must not boast immoderately, beyond what you deserve, but it is just as bad to claim false humility. Modesty is a virtue for churchmen, not for the son and heir of a count, one who will lead these same men and their younger brothers and cousins and *their* sons into battle. They must believe in you, and they must believe that your good fortune will lift them as well and keep them alive and prosperous. That the Lady of Battles, a saint, has given you her favor—that will weigh heavily with them. But you must not mire yourself in humility. You are not a monk, Alain."

"I was meant to be one," he murmured.

"Not any more! We will no longer speak of this, Alain. A good man remembers and honors his oaths. In time, when you are an old man and have an heir who is ready to take your place, then perhaps you can retire to a monastery and live out the rest of your years in peace. But that oath was made for you by others, before it was known who you were and what role you have to play. You never stood before the monastery gate and pledged yourself to the church. That you think of this obligation at all is to your credit. But it is not to be spoken of again. Do you understand?"

Alain understood. "Yes, Father," he replied. The hounds, on their leashes, padded obediently alongside.

Lavastine took in a deep breath of the autumn air. "No need to hasten to Osna Sound." He turned to survey his retinue. "We've heard no reports of Eika wintering there. I think we may take a few days to go hunting."

VI
THE CHILDREN OF GENT

1

SPADES stabbed into loose dirt. From where she stood, Anna caught flecks of soil on her cheek, spray thrown out as the gravediggers filled in the latest grave. They had buried twelve refugees in a mass grave this bitter cold morning, including a young mother and her newborn babe.

Anna had been on her way to the stream, but it was hard not to stop and stare. A few ragged onlookers huddled in the wind. Rain so cold it felt like droplets of ice spattered down, and she tugged her tattered cloak tighter about her shoulders. Here in the camp, corpses went naked into the grave since the living had need of the clothes off their backs.

198

A child no more than two or three winters old bawled
at the lip of the pit. It had straggly hair that might have
been blond once, a face matted with filth, a dirty tunic, and
nothing covering its feet. It also looked about to fall into
the pit with the dead folk. She set down her buckets and
hurried forward just as the child slipped and fell to its rump
on the crumbling slope.

"Here, now," she said, grabbing it by the arm and pulling
it back. "Don't fall in, child." Looking around, she hailed
one of the diggers. "Where's the child's kin?"

He pointed into the grave, where woman and infant lay
bound together by shreds of old cloth, all that the folk in
the camp could spare to make sure they weren't separated
in death. With a stab and a heave, he tossed another spade-
ful of earth onto the grave. A shower of dirt scattered
across the waxy faces of mother and child.

"Isn't there anyone here to look after it?"

"It was crying when we came to carry away the corpse,"
he said, "and it's crying still. Ach, child," he added, "perhaps it was a blessing that the children of Gent escaped
the city, but most of them are orphans now, as is this poor
babe. Who's to care for them when we can't even care for
our own?"

The child, safe away from the rim, had now fastened
onto her thigh and it snuffled there, smearing her tunic with
snot as it whimpered and coughed.

"Who, indeed?" asked Anna softly. With a finger she
touched the Circle of Unity that hung at her chest. "Come,
little one. What's your name?"

The child didn't seem to know its name, nor could it talk.
She pried its arms off her leg and finally, with some coaxing, got the child to drag one of the empty buckets. In this
way, with the baby toddling along beside her, they made it
to the stream, where they waited in line to dip their wooden
buckets into the water.

"Who's this?" asked one of the older girls, indicating the
child who stood fast at Anna's heels like a starving dog. "I
didn't know you had a little brother."

"I found him by the new grave."

"Ach, indeed," said an older boy. "That would be
Widow Artilde's older child."

"Widow?" asked Anna. "But she was so young." Then

she realized how stupid the comment sounded as the older children snickered.

"Her husband was a militia man in the city. I suppose he died when the Eika came."

"Then you know her?" Anna tried to draw the child out from behind her, but the child began to bawl again.

"She's dead," said the boy. "Had the baby, and they both of them caught sick and died."

"Doesn't anyone want this child?"

But having filled their buckets, the others were already walking away, hauling the precious water back to camp or to Steleshame. So she let the child follow her back to the shelter she and Matthias called home. Indeed, the child seemed unlikely to let her out of its sight.

"God forfend!" exclaimed Helvidius when she ushered the child into the shelter of the canvas awning. A fire burned brightly in a crude hearth built of stones, and the old poet sat on his stool watching over the pot in which they kept a constant hot stew made of anything edible they could scavenge. Today it smelled of mushroom and onion, flavored with the picked-over bones of a goose. The remains of yesterday's acorn gruel sat in their one bowl next to the fire. Anna handed spoon and bowl to the child. The spoon dropped unregarded from its hand and it used its dirty fingers to shovel down the lukewarm gruel.

"What's this creature?" demanded Helvidius.

"One more helpless than you!" Anna had taken the buckets of water around to the tanners in exchange for scraps of leather. "Can you help me make it something to wear on its feet?"

"You're not taking this brat in, are you? There's scarcely room for the three of us."

But Anna only laughed. The old poet was always grumpy, but she didn't fear him. "I'll let him sleep curled at your feet. It'll be like having a dog."

He grunted. The child had licked the bowl clean and now began to snivel again. "Dogs don't whine so," he said. "Does it have a name?"

"Its mother's dead, and no one else claimed it. You watch over it while I go haul more water."

She made four more trips down to the stream. At this time of year, with the winter slaughter underway, the tannery was busy with many new hides, so Matthias had seen to it that she could take his place hauling water and ash for the tanning pits or collecting bark from the forest. He had taken on more skilled work scraping or finishing skins which had cured over summer and autumn. She didn't mind the work. The activity kept her warm and gave them a certain security that many of the other refugees, dependent on what they could scavenge from the forest or on Mistress Gisela's charity, did not have.

Yet although the winter slaughter went on, and meat was salted or smoked against the season to come, little of that meat reached the refugees. Once a day a deacon distributed a coarse oat bread at the gate, but there was never enough to go around.

Now, when Anna returned to their shelter from her last trip to the stream, it was to find the child wailing, old Helvidius vainly singing some nonsense tune with all the enthusiasm of a woman proposing marriage to a dowerless man, and Matthias glowering over the stewpot.

"What's this?" Matthias demanded as she shoved the canvas awning aside. The canvas didn't really keep out the cold as much as it kept in some of the heat in the fire and their massed bodies. It did keep off rain tolerably well. Still, her toes and fingers ached from the chill and her nose was running. "Where did *this* come from?"

"It's a child, Matthias," she said.

"I can *see* it's a child!"

"It had nowhere else to go. I couldn't just leave it to die! Not after St. Kristine saved it from death at the hands of the Eika." The child sniffed and babbled something unintelligible but did not let go of the old man's knee.

"And it stinks!" added Matthias.

It certainly did. "Master Helvidius—"

"I didn't know it couldn't take care of such things itself!" the old man wailed. "I'm a poet, not a nursemaid."

"Well, you must learn how to watch over the child, since it will be under your care all day," she said tartly.

"Under my care all day!" he cried.

"You mean to *keep* it?" Matthias looked appalled.

There was a sudden silence.

"We must keep it," said Anna. "You know we must, Matthias."

He sighed, but when he did not reply, she knew she had won.

"Well, then," said Helvidius grudgingly, "if we keep it, we must name it. We could call it Achilleus or Alexandros, after the great princes of ancient Arethousa. Or Cornelius, the Dariyan general who destroyed proud Kartiako, or Teutus of Kallindoia, famous son of the warrior-queen Teuta."

She had coaxed the child over to her and, by the door flap, was now peeling off the soiled cloth that swaddled its bottom. She laughed suddenly. "You'd best find a girl's name, Master Helvidius. We'll call her Helen, for didn't Helen survive through many trials?"

"Helen," said the old poet, his tone softening as he regarded the child. "Fair-haired Helen, true of heart and steadfast in adversity."

Matthias snorted, disgusted, but he was careful as always to share out the stew equally between them as they each took turns spooning stew out of their shared bowl.

It was dusk outside, almost dark, when they heard shouts from the roadway. Anna thrust little Helen into Helvidius' arms and ran outside with Matthias. They heard a great commotion and hurried to where the southeast road ran alongside the tanning works in time to see an astonishing procession ride past—noble lords on horseback and more men-at-arms, marching behind them, than she could count.

Even in the twilight their arms and clothing had such a rich gleam that she could only gape at their finery. They laughed, proud, strong young lords, a handful of women riding in their ranks, and appeared not to notice the ragged line of people who had gathered to watch them arrive.

The gates of Steleshame had already opened and there, lit by torchlight, Anna saw the mistress of Steleshame and the mayor of Gent waiting to welcome their guests.

"Where are you from?" Matthias shouted, and a man-at-arms called back, "We've come from Osterburg, from Duchess Rotrudis."

When they returned to the shelter and gave their news, Helvidius was beside himself. "That would be one of the duchess' kinsmen," he said. "They'll want a poet at their feasting, and where there is feasting there are leftovers to be had!"

* * *

In the morning she rose with Matthias at the first light of dawn and in the cold dawn began her daily haul of water. The stream ran with a bitter ice flood over her bare fingers, but its chill was nothing to the cold fury that seized her upon returning to their little shelter.

Helvidius and Helen were gone and with them the old poet's stick and stool and her precious leather bag of dried herbs, onions, four shriveled turnips, and the last of the acorns. No sooner had she stuck her head under the canvas, searching to see what else the old man had taken, than a spear butt prodded her in the back and a harsh voice ordered her to come out.

"I thought we'd cleared this place," said a soldier to his companion, eyeing Anna with disgust. "These children are as filthy as rats, each and every one." She gaped at the two soldiers—well fed, well brushed, and warmly dressed—who confronted her. "Go on, then, girl—or are you a boy?"

"Go where?"

"We're clearing out the camp," he said. "You'll be marching east, where we can find homes for you orphans. Now go on, get your things or leave them behind."

"But my brother—"

This time when he jabbed her with the butt of his spear, his touch wasn't as gentle. "Take what you need, but only what you can carry. It's going to be a long march."

"Where—?"

"Move!" His companion walked on, poking a spear through hovels and the other pathetic shelters the refugees from Gent had put up beyond the tannery, but they were already empty. Indeed, the camp itself was far more quiet than usual, but now that she listened, she heard the nervous buzz of voices from down by the southeast road.

Though she had five knives tucked here and there inside her clothes, she knew it was pointless to resist. She scrambled back inside the canvas shelter, grabbed the pot and bowl, nesting the one inside the other, rolled up their blankets and tied them with a leather cord, and bound up her shawl to make a carry pack. She began to take down the canvas shelter.

"Here, now, leave that!"

"How can I leave that?" she demanded, turning on him. "What if it rains? We'll need to shelter under something!"

He considered this, hesitating. "We're to shelter at church estates, but there are so many of you . . . perhaps it's wisest to have some shelter of your own. If the weather turns colder, or there's snow . . ." He shrugged.

"Is everyone leaving?"

But he wouldn't answer more of her questions, and she sensed that time was short. The rolled-up canvas was an unwieldy burden, and together with buckets, blankets, and pot she could barely stagger along under the weight.

The sight of the refugees made her sick with terror. Herded into a ragged line along the road, she realized suddenly how very young they all were. For every twenty children there was, perhaps, a single adult—even counting the soldiers, all of them grim as they held spears to prevent any child from slipping out of line. The sheer amount of bawling and wailing was like an assault, a wave of fear spilling out from the children who had escaped Gent and now were being driven away even from the meager shelter they had made here at Steleshame.

Anna spotted Helvidius. He leaned heavily on his stick and little Helen, beside him, sat on the stool with the precious bag of food draped over her lap. She cried without sound, and yellow-green snot ran from her nose. The old poet's face brightened when he saw Anna.

"Where's Matthias?" she asked as she came up beside him.

"I don't know," said the old man. "I tried to tell them I'm a great poet, that the young lord will be angry at them for sending me away, but they drove me out and didn't listen! I think they mean to march these four hundred children to the marchlands. I suppose there's always a need for a pair of growing hands in the wilderness."

"But this isn't everyone."

"Nay, just those deemed useless and a burden. When we first got here from Gent last spring, some third of the children were taken away by farming folk who live west of here, for a strong child is always welcome as a help to work the land. And those who work now for Mistress Gisela, like the blacksmiths—they'll stay. And a few families who hope to go back to Gent in time, but only those which have an adult to care for the children. Nay, child, all the rest of us will be marched east to Osterburg and farther yet, past the Oder River and into the marchlands—"

"But how far is it?" Helen began to cry out loud, and Anna set down the pot and hoisted the little girl up onto her hip.

"A month or more, two months, three more like. Lady Above, how do they expect these children to walk so far, and how do they intend to feed them along the way?"

Three months. Anna could not really conceive of three months' time, especially not with winter coming on. "But I don't want to go," she said, beginning to cry, beginning to panic. "It's better to stay here, isn't it?"

Someone had managed to get a flock of goats together, and in truth the goats milled no more aimlessly than did the frightened children. Pinch-faced toddlers whined and wriggled in the arms of children no older than eight or twelve. An adolescent girl with a swelling belly and her worldly goods tied to her back held tightly onto two young siblings who could not have been more than five or six; they, too, carried bedrolls tied to their thin shoulders. Two boys of about Anna's age clung together. A girl tied cloth around the feet of a small child to protect it against frost and mud. A little red-haired boy sat alone on the cold ground and sobbed.

"Saved by a miracle," murmured Master Helvidius. "And now what will become of us?"

The young lord and his retinue waited beside the gate to Steleshame. They only watched, mounted on their fine horses, but the sick feeling in her chest curdled and turned sour. They only watched, but they would enforce this order. Any child who ran into the forest would be hunted down and brought back. Mistress Gisela stood beside them. Anna imagined she surveyed the chaos with satisfaction. Soon she would be rid of most of the refugees who had been such a burden on her, and if Helvidius was right, she would keep exactly those people who would do her the most good.

Ai, Lady. Where was Matthias?

"I have to go find Matthias!" she said to Helvidius. "Keep watch over—" She set Helen down and the little girl set up a howling.

"Don't leave me!" he gasped, suddenly white and leaning

on his stick as if he might fall the next instant. "If they go—
I don't believe I can walk so far alone, me and the child—"

"I won't leave you!" she promised.

"Anna!"

Matthias came running with one of the men from the
tannery. They conferred hastily with a sergeant, who
stepped back from the pungent smell that clung to their
clothes. Quickly enough, Anna, Helvidius, and little Helen
were called out of the line.

"Yes," said Matthias, "this is my grandfather and my
two sisters."

"You're to stay here, then," said the sergeant, and dismissed them by turning away to order his soldiers into formation, a group in the van and one at the end and some
to march single file on either side of the refugees. Anna
could not tell whether this was meant to protect the refugees or to keep them from escaping the line.

"Come on, then, lad," said the tanner with a frown,
glancing toward the mob of children and away as quickly,
as if he didn't like what he saw. "Let's get back to work."
He walked away.

Anna started after him. She had no desire to stay and
watch.

"Anna!" Matthias called her back. "We're to get a hut.
Give the canvas over to those poor souls, and the pot, too.
And you may as well give over the food as well, what poor
scraps there are. There's so few of us left here that we
won't want for so much, not until late in the winter, anyway, and those scraps will help them better than us."

She stared as the soldiers at the van started forward.
Slowly, like a lurching cart, the line of children moved forward, and the wailing and crying reached a sudden over-
whelming pitch. "I can't do it," she said, sobbing. "How
can you choose? You do it." She blindly thrust canvas, pot,
and food pouch into Matthias' arms and then grabbed
Helen up and ran as well as she could back toward the
tannery precincts. She could not bear to watch the others
march away into what danger and what uncertainty she
could not imagine, only dreaded to think of walking there
herself. Ai, Lady, what would they eat? Where would they
shelter? What if the cold autumn winds turned to the cruel
storms of winter? How many would even reach the distant

east, and what would become of them, saved from Gent
and yet driven away from this haven, such as it was, by the
greed of householder and duchess working in concert?

And yet perhaps it was too hard to shelter so many here
with no rescue for Gent in sight—for surely no one expected the young lord and his retinue to drive the Eika
away on their own.

Helen had stopped bawling and now clung to her in silence. She paused on the rise and stared back as the mob
of children, hundreds of them, started walking reluctantly,
resignedly, toddlers stumbling along in the wake of elder
children, thin legs bare to the cold, their pathetic belong-
ings strapped to backs already bowed under the weight.
They had so far to go.

Tears blinded her briefly as a glint of sun struck out from
a rent in the clouds and shone into the midst of the line of
children. She blinked back a blurring vision of a bright
figure walking among them, a woman robed in a white tunic
with blood dripping down her hands, and then the vision
vanished. Anna turned away to look toward the young lord
who surveyed this exodus with dispassion.

Master Helvidius hobbled up beside her, so exhausted
from the morning's excitement, his legs buckling under him,
that she and Matthias had to half carry him back to the
tannery. Little Helen walked beside them singing a tuneless
melody, and by the time Master Helvidius and Helen were
settled in the shelter of a lean-to set up against the tannery
fence, and Matthias sent back to work, and Anna gone out
again to the stream to haul water, the line of refugees had
vanished from sight.

Only the deserted camp remained.

2

ANNA had never seen a noble lord so close before. Nor had she ever imagined that a table could groan under the weight of so much food. She had never seen people eat and drink as much as these did: Lord Wichman, eldest son and second child of Duchess Rotrudis, his cousin Lord Henry—named after the king—and their retinue of young nobles and stalwart men-at-arms. The young nobles boasted about the battles they would fight with the Eika in the days to come. The men-at-arms, who drank as lustily as their noble masters, were wont to get into fistfights when their interest in Master Helvidius' lengthy and complicated court poems waned.

It had not taken long after the departure of the refugees for the mayor of Gent—desperate to find amusement for Mistress Gisela's noble guests—to remember that he had left a court poet out among the refugees and to wonder if the old man had remained behind.

"You'll go to his summons?" demanded Matthias that next afternoon, amazed and appalled, "after he deserted you here when he took the rest of his servants inside the palisade?"

"Pride hath no place among the starving," said Master Helvidius. So each evening he took Anna with him to carry his stool and help support him on the long walk up the rise that led to the inner court, and of course Helen had to tag along as well, for there was no one else to watch over her with Matthias working until last light each day. The tanners and smiths and foresters worked long hours and harder even than they had before, for they now had over seventy men and thirty horses to care for, feed, and keep in armor and weapons besides those they had brought with them.

Over the next many days Lord Wichman's force marched out every day, searching for Eika, fighting a skirmish here, burning a ship there, each feat of arms retold in great detail at the night's feast. Helvidius quickly became adept at turn-

ing the details of these expeditions into flattering paeans to
Lord Wichman's courage and prowess, which the young
Lord never grew tired of hearing.

Anna grew equally adept at grabbing half-eaten bones
off the floor before the lord's dogs could get them, or at
begging crusts of bread from drunken soldiers. Master Helvidius, fed at the high table, slipped her food from the
common platter, delicacies she had never before tasted:
baked grouse, black pudding, pork pie, and other savories.
Helen was content to sit sucking her thumb in a corner, by
the hearth, eating what was offered her; the rest Anna
saved in her pouch and took back to Matthias in the mornings—she, Helen, and the poet had to sleep in the hall
because once night fell, the gates to Steleshame remained
shut.

Sleeping on the floor of the newly built longhall in Steleshame was a more luxurious bed than any she had slept on
before. It was never bitter cold inside even as autumn eased
into winter and the days grew short and gray. Little Helen
got roundness back in her cheeks, and Master Helvidius'
legs got stronger, although he still needed his staff to walk.

"They've turned all the lands round Gent into pasture, I
swear," said Lord Henry, Wichman's father's sister's son.
He was a young man, not much older than a boy, with dark
hair, a fresh scar on his cheek which he wore as proudly
as his sword, and a boastful tongue. "There's enough cattle
out there trampling good fields to feed an army a thousand strong!"

"Why have none wandered back to us?" demanded
Gisela.

"They're tended by slaves and guarded by Eika."

"Do the Eika have so many soldiers still wintering
there?" asked the mayor nervously.

"We haven't ridden close enough to the town to count
them," said Lord Henry, glancing reproachfully toward his
elder cousin. "But we might still do so, *if* we dared more."

Young Wichman merely belched in reply to this appeal
and called for Mistress Gisela's pretty young niece to fetch
him another cup of wine. He had, as Master Helvidius said,
"an itch between his legs," though she didn't quite understand what that meant except that he pestered the young

woman in a way the niece didn't like, yet no one else
seemed inclined to prevent.

Helen had already fallen asleep. Anna curled up beside
her, smoke and warmth a haze around them, and closed
her eyes while Master Helvidius droned on, his slightly
nasal voice intoning the lay of Helen. Neither he nor the
young lord ever seemed to tire of the long poem—and what
the young lord wanted the young lord got.

". . . Now the servants removed the tables, and while the
second course was brought, as much talk sprang up among
the banqueters as echoed in the hall like the din of battle.
But King Sykaeus raised his cup and called silence to the
hall. Huge bowls were brought and filled to the brim with
wine, and out of these the king himself filled the first cup
and this he passed among the company.

"Thus he entreated Helen for the story of Ilios. 'Fair and
noble guest, tell us your tale from the beginning . . .' "

A dog nosed Anna awake, sniffing her face and licking
the dried juice of meat off her fingers. She could tell by
the somber gray of light within the hall that dawn was close
at hand. Helen lay fast asleep on a heap of dirty rushes,
her breath a liquid snore. Helvidius had fallen asleep still
sitting, head draped over the table; he would regret that
later, when his muscles stiffened.

She had to pee.

She got up and picked her way over the sleeping servants, tiptoed around the men-at-arms who reeked of ale
and piss and sweat. Outside, in the open dirt yard, she crept
around to where a line of privies had been dug up against
one palisade wall, well away from hall and longhouse. The
sky grayed toward twilight and the last stars shone faintly,
fading into the growing light of dawn.

The stone keep stood like a stolid, faithful servant, its
shadow blunt against the lightening sky. Outbuildings were
scattered about; she saw a flash of coals, bright red, from
one of the open huts. Smiths and tanners worked outside
the palisade wall now, so their stink wouldn't disturb the
sleep of the householder, her kin, the mayor of Gent and
his retinue, and their noble guest.

Here, by the privies, the noble guest was clearly disturbing Mistress Gisela's niece.

"I beg you, Lord Wichman," said the young woman, twisting away as she tried to hurry back to the safety of the hall, "I have much work to do."

"What better work than what I can give you, eh?"

"My lord." She tugged out of his grasp and slipped sideways, trying to escape into the gloom. "Forgive me, but I can't stay."

Angry, he grabbed at her cloak, jerking her up short. "I hear it said you thought yourself good enough for my bastard cousin Sanglant. Surely you're good enough for me!"

At first, Anna thought the slow hiss came from the niece, preface to an angry outburst. Then she saw a pale stream of light trailing above the distant treetops, undulating in languid curves. A great golden beast rose into the sky, and as the sun's rim pierced the bowl of the horizon, its roar shuddered the air.

The niece screamed and bolted. Young Lord Wichman, still groggy from a night of drinking, gaped at the sky, groping at his belt to draw his sword. He staggered back and Anna shrieked as the dragon, its golden scales more blinding than the sun, flew directly over the holding. Gouts of flame boiled upward into the clouds, the hiss of fire meeting ice. Anna had never seen anything so beautiful or so terrifying.

"Dragons!" shouted guards from the wallwalk.

Lord Wichman sheathed his sword and cursed. His bland face suddenly creased with delight, and he spun and ran toward the stables, shouting. "To arms! To arms!"

The alarm sounded, horn blasts piercing the quiet of dawn.

"Dragons! Dragons!" The cry lifted again as men-at-arms scrambled out of the hall and servants brought horses from the stables.

She had to get back to Master Helvidius and Helen. Ai, Lady, she had to get back to Matthias who, with the other tanners and laborers, slept outside the main palisade in little enclosures sheltered with mere fences, more to keep livestock out than to protect against fearsome beasts. But could anything protect against a dragon?

The huge creature rose sluggishly, each flap of its wings like a sheet of gold thrumming and throbbing in the air. Slowly it banked and turned for a second pass. Before she

knew what she meant to do, she ran for a ladder and
climbed up to the wallwalk to get a better look. It was
madness; ai, Lady, indeed, she was crazy and Matthias
would say as much, but even Matthias must be astonished
by the sight. This seemed more uncanny, more miraculous,
than the daimone chained in the cathedral. She had to get
a better look. And perhaps from this angle she could see
the tannery.

She had to hop and scramble up, hooking her arms over
the top of the palisade and brace herself on the logs, in
order to see over. What she saw caught her breath in her
throat.

The guards at the gate yelled again: "Dragons!"

But they were not pointing at the sky.

Through the deserted camp, strewn now with the remains
of hovels and shelters, littered with garbage and beaten to
dirt churned muddy by yesterday's rain and frozen by the
last night's frost, rode a hundred horsemen. Their helmets
gleamed, fitted with polished brass. Their gold tabards
shone as brightly as the dragon's scales, each one marked
with a menacing black dragon, miniature hatchlings that
rippled and moved as the Dragons approached.

As from far away she heard a man shout in a thin, hysterical voice: "Don't open the gates! Don't open the gates!"

Fire sparked from the hooves of the Dragons' horses as
they pounded through the empty camp. There, by the
stream, fire leaped into the scatter of buildings that marked
the tanning works. Anna screamed, pointing, but it was
useless. No one could hear her. No one would hear her.

They weren't Dragons at all. She saw now the gaping
holes in the tabards, the gleam of bone where ragged mail
parted to reveal a skeletal jaw or flesh scored deep from a
putrefying wound. Empty eyes stared from beneath nasals.
Skin peeled away from bone where the morning wind
whipped them clean. They made no sound.

Yet they came on.

Months ago she had seen them lying dead in the cathedral crypt at Gent. They were not Dragons at all, only the
remains of them, only the memory of that force that had
fought against the Eika. What terrible magic had raised
them from the dead?

The gates yawned open, and out from Steleshame rode

young Lord Wichman and his retinue. They shone as bright as their enemy, and they charged with abandon.

"Anna!"

She fell, caught herself on the lip of the walk, and half slid down the ladder.

"Anna!" Fright made Master Helvidius able to walk without his staff. "Child! Child! Come in! The Eika are attacking! Come to shelter!"

"Where's Helen?"

"In the hall. Still asleep." The old poet wept with fear. "Go get her and then come to the keep, but make haste, Anna! Hurry! There's not enough room—"

"Matthias—!"

"There's nothing we can do for him! Go!"

She ran across the yard. A spinning ball of flame hurtled past and smacked into the dirt: a torch cast from outside. It guttered and failed, but she heard more torches thunk onto the roofs. Most slid down the slope of roofs, plummeted to earth, and were stamped out, but a few caught and began to burn.

As she came to the great doors that opened into the long hall, she saw Mistress Gisela's niece slap a ladder against the side of the house. Climbing to the top, with another woman halfway up behind her, she took buckets of water drawn from the well and threw water onto the roof, wetting it down. To the left, half hidden by the bulk of the hall, Anna saw other people struggling to save the old longhouse whose thatch roof had caught fire.

She had to shove and elbow to get inside, for people ran every which way, some in, some out, some no place at all but frozen in terror or dithering in circles. A table had been knocked over; dogs gulped down the remains of food, lapped at puddles of ale.

Helen had retreated to a corner beyond the great hearth and there she sat, utterly silent, thumb stuck in her mouth. Anna hoisted her up to her hips. She was such a tiny thing that she was no burden.

But it was harder to get out than in. The mayor and certain of his servants crowded the door, seeking shelter, and Anna could not fight past them. Their press against her caused her to stumble and fall to one knee, and for a horrible instant she thought she and Helen would be trampled.

Smoke stung her nostrils, and suddenly the cry arose: "Fire! Fire!"

She found a wedge through which to shove herself, got herself to the wall, and hurried down the hall's length past the open hearth to the far wall where stood the single window, now shut against winter. She set Helen down, dragged a chest over and, getting up on it, pounded the shutters open. Tugging the little girl up behind her, she swung a leg over the sill, and dangled there. Together they dropped, hitting the ground hard just as a shower of embers floated down from above. The little girl began to cry. Anna scuttled backward, jumped up, and lifted Helen to her back.

In this way, with Helen fairly choking her with thin arms vised round her neck, Anna threaded her way through the chaos of the yard up the rise to the stone keep. Inside, the storerooms were pungent with barrels of salted meat, with ale and wine, with baskets of apples and unground oats and moldering rye. Master Helvidius cowered behind a chest, weeping softly. Anna thrust Helen onto his lap and climbed the ladder to the second level. There she found six grim-faced men laying arrows, point down, against the wall on either side of the six arrow slits.

"Here, child," said one, beckoning to her. "Stack these neatly." He left without ado, and she hurried to carefully place the arrows in a line, pausing once to lean into the slit and peer out.

Her view gave her a vantage of the ground just beyond the gates. There, in a melee more like the frenzy of market square on the busiest autumn day in Gent, Lord Wichman, Lord Henry, and their riders battled Eika, cutting about themselves, parrying ax blows. A line of men-at-arms struggled forward, shields held high against the press. Eika swarmed everywhere. The huge Eika dogs darted through the swirling fight, ripping and rending. Of the horrible Dragons there was no sign, nor any remains.

An ax hooked over Lord Wichman's shield, dragged, tugged, and there was a sudden titanic struggle as the young lord grappled with an Eika soldier braced at his horse's shoulder. Then—sliding, gripped, tugged—he fell from his horse and vanished under a hail of flailing arms.

Anna gasped out loud and jerked back, bumping into the careful rack of arrows. With a clatter, they fell, but the sound was drowned out by a howl sent up from outside— the young lord's riders had gone mad with fury.

Anna began to cry.

A man shoved her away roughly and began to set up arrows again. A woman called up from below.

"The longhouse is burning! We're getting a flood of people in here. What shall I do?"

"Squeeze in as many of the young and weak as you can!" shouted the man next to Anna. "But any who are able-bodied must take to the walls. It'll be slaughter if the Eika get through those gates. Anything they can fling down— anyone who can lift a hoe or spade or shoot a bow or stab with a spear—" He spun round. "Girl! Don't be ham-handed again. Now set these arrows upright for those who will need them later!"

He climbed down the ladder.

She did as she was told. Such a din of wailing and shouting had arisen from within the holding—the squawking of chickens, the barking of dogs, the screams of horses and men—that she could only stay moving by pretending nothing was happening, by hearing nothing at all. She concentrated on each arrow as she leaned it with fletching upright against the stone wall.

Smoke billowed in from outside, but she could not, dared not, look again out through the arrow slit. A hugely pregnant woman came up the ladder, blood streaming from a gash on her forehead. With a grunt, she heaved her ungainly bulk up over the lip, got to hands and knees, then with a shove from foot and hand got herself up. She stationed herself with a bow by one of the slits. The man whose place she took scrambled down, disappearing below.

Soon, other women and one adolescent boy had stationed themselves by the arrow slits, each with a bow. The boy played nervously with an arrow, rolling it through his fingers. More people clambered up the ladder and cowered, some weeping, some stunned, against the walls and then along the floor until there was scarcely room for anyone to move. And yet more tried to come up, and more yet. Such a noise swelled up from this mass of terror-stricken people and from the battle raging outside that Anna could only hunker down, clap hands over ears, and pray. The sting of burning timber and thatch made her eyes burn, and the fear made her heart thud hard in her chest. Her breath came in gasps.

"Come, child," said a woman's brusque voice. Anna looked up into the heat-seared face, blackened with soot, of Mistress Gisela's niece. Dozens of tiny burns and charred holes from flying embers pitted her clothing. "Hand me arrows as I shoot."

"Who are you shooting at?" she breathed. Horror rose in her throat until it choked the breath out of her and she thought she would fall and faint.

But the woman only took careful aim and loosed the arrow and, without thinking, Anna handed her another. She nocked and aimed and shot while screams pierced above the clamor of battle and fire roared and dogs howled and a horn blared long and high and distantly a man's voice shouted: "Form up to my left! Form up to my left!"

One by one Anna handed her the arrows, and as each one was nocked and loosed, the young woman's expression wavered not at all from blank concentration. Only once did she grunt with satisfaction, and once she whimpered, suddenly made afraid by some sight in the yard beyond. But she gulped down her fear as everyone had to, or die through being helpless. That was the way of war.

One by one, Anna handed up the arrows until they were all gone.

3

IN the end the Eika retreated, but by that time Steles-hame lay in shambles, a quarter of the palisade wall burning or battered down, the longhouse in flames and the outbuildings in ruins. Only the newly built hall still stood, though it was scorched. Some of the roof tiles had fallen in where the smoke hole opened and both doors had been wrenched off their hinges.

It was a miracle anything at all had survived. Of the Dragons there remained no sign, but everyone agreed they, like the flying dragon, had arisen from the Eika enchanter's magic, a false vision used to strike fear into their hearts and render them incapable of fighting.

It had not worked, not this time.

"That is the weakness of illusion," Master Helvidius said when the people hiding in the stone keep ventured out to the horrible scene opening before them in the yard. "Once you know it is illusion, it is easier to combat."

Anna held little Helen tightly on her hip as she picked her way through the rubble to the gate. She kept her eyes fixed on her feet, so she wouldn't have to see the dead bodies. There were a lot of dead, human and Eika alike. If she didn't look, then maybe it would be as if they weren't there.

Soldiers staggered through the gates, leading wounded horses, carrying their dead or injured comrades. Some of their number wandered the killing field, sticking Eika through the throat to make sure they would not rise again. A sudden shout rose from their midst as a figure armed in mail, his tabard rent and bloody, shoved himself up from the ground where he had been pinned down by a dead Eika.

It was Lord Wichman himself, by a miracle unharmed except for the battering his mail and helmet had taken. But he had not gotten far before he dropped to his knees and wept over the body of his young cousin, Henry, who had fallen by the gates. Mistress Gisela appeared beside him. Roused by her appearance, the lord rose and began directing the soldiers as they methodically looted the Eika corpses of weapons, shields, and whatever fine mail armor the creatures wore round their hips, mostly silver and gold wrought into delicate patterns.

Anna spied a knife lying in a pool of muck and blood. She knelt quickly, grabbed it, and tucked it into her leggings. Its blade pinched her calf, but she went on.

Beyond, both smithy and tannery burned. A few men had begun to cast dirt onto the fires.

"Here, now, child," said a soldier, coming up beside her. "Get back inside. You don't know how far the Eika have run. They might come back any moment."

"Were those truly Dragons? All dead and rotting?"

"Nay. They were Eika. They only looked like Dragons until they got close. Then we saw through the enchantment."

"Did we win?"

He snorted, waving a hand to indicate the destruction. "If this can be called winning. Ai, Lord, I don't know that we beat them. Rather, they got what they wanted and left."

"But what did they want?" she demanded. "My brother—" She faltered when she saw the flames that raged round the row of small huts abutting the tannery fence. She began to snivel and Helen, catching her fear, started to cry.

"They drove off the livestock." The soldier grimaced as he raised his left arm, and she saw a gash running up the boiled leather coat he wore, a slash running from waist to armpit. Underneath a thin stream of blood seeped through his quilted shirt, but he seemed otherwise unharmed except for a cut on his lip and a purpling bruise along his jaw. "I saw them myself. I'd guess they were raiding for cattle and slaves more than to kill my good Lord Henry, namesake of the king, bless them both." He drew the Circle of Unity at his breast and sighed deeply. "Come, child, go on in."

"But my brother worked at the tannery—"

He clucked softly and shook his head, then surveyed the scene. The old camp looked as if it had been flattened by a whirlwind. A single chicken scratched diligently beside a hovel. Two dogs cowered under the shelter of a single straggly bush. "Thank God the refugees had already left.

Come, then, we'll go down and see, but mind you, child, you'll go up again when I tell you."

By the time they got down to the stream the tannery fire was under control, though still burning. She saw a body, charred and blackened, over by the puering pit, but it was too large to be Matthias. This body alone remained; of the other inhabitants of the tannery, none could be found.

"There's nothing here, child," said the soldier. "Go on back where it's safe. I'll ask about. You say his name is Matthias?"

She nodded, unable to speak. Helen sucked her thumb vigorously.

With this weight on her, the walk back up the rise to the wrecked palisade seemed forbidding and it exhausted her. Helvidius found her sobbing just inside the gate, and he took her into the hall just as a cold drizzle began to fall.

He brought her heavily watered cider and made her drink, then fussed over Helen, complaining all the while. "The livestock stolen! Food stores trampled or spoiled or burned! What will we do? How will we get through the winter without even enough shelter for those left? What will we do? Without fodder, the young lord will ride back to his home, and then who will protect us? We should have gone with the others."

But by the hearth Mistress Gisela had called a council. A stout woman, she gripped an ax in one hand as if she had forgotten she held it. Blood stained her left shoulder, though it did not appear to be her own. Beyond, in the farthest corner of the hall, the pregnant woman who had been shooting from the keep leaned against the wall, panting, then got down on her hands and knees as several elderly women clustered around her. A boy carried in a pot of steaming water, and Gisela's niece hurried forward with a length of miraculously clean cloth.

"Lord Wichman! I beg you," Gisela was saying, "if there is not enough fodder for those of your horses which remain . . ."

But the young lord had a wild light in his eyes. With his helmet off and tucked under one arm, he warmed his free hand over the fire while a man-at-arms wiped the blood from his sword. He had a fine down of beard along his

chin, as fair as his pale hair. "Did you see the dragon?" he
demanded. "Was it a real thing, or another enchantment?"

Master Helvidius hobbled forward, Helen dragging on
his robes. "My lord, if I may speak—"

But the young lord went on, heedless. "Nay, Mistress, I
won't let the Eika drive me away! Are there no old wise-
folk here, who can braid a few spells of protection into
being? Give us those, Mistress, and we'll raid as the Eika
do, like a pack of dogs harrying their heels!"

"But we've lost full half our livestock, or more! And I
hear now from those who escaped into the trees that a
good half of my laborers were herded away to be slaves!"

"Or eaten by the dogs!" said a sergeant.

Mistress Gisela set down the ax and looked about for
support. "Is Mayor Werner not here? He will advise as I
do. How can I support my own people and yours as well,
Lord Wichman?"

"The mayor is dead, Mistress," said Wichman. "Or had
you not heard that news yet? How can you *not* support
me? I am all that stands between you and another Eika
raid. And let that be an end to it!" He handed his helmet
to the sergeant, stomped his boots hard to shake dirt off
them, and sat on a bench, beckoning to Gisela's niece to
serve him drink.

Anna began to shake. All of a sudden the cold struck
her, and she could not stop trembling. Helvidius limped
over and threw a bloodied cape, trimmed with fabulous
gold braid embroidery, over her shoulders. "Here," he said.
"Him as owned this before won't be wanting it now."

She began to cry. Matthias was gone.

In the far corner, the pregnant woman's grunting breaths,
coming in bursts, transmuted into a sudden hiss of relief.
The thin wail of a newborn baby pierced the noise and
chaos of the hall.

"It's a boy!" someone shouted, and at once Lord Wichman was applied to for his permission that the woman
might name her son Henry in honor of his dead cousin.

Ai, Lady. Matthias was gone.

He did not appear that day or the next among the dead
pulled from fallen buildings nor among the living who crept
out one by one from their hiding places. Amid such disaster, one boy's loss made little difference.

VII
BELOW THE MOON

1

BISCOP Antonia had a high regard for her own importance. Granddaughter of Queen Theodora (now deceased) of Karrone, youngest child of Duchess Ermoldia (now deceased) of Aquilegia, daughter of two fathers, Prince Pepin (now deceased) of Karrone who had sired her and Lord Gunther (now deceased) of Brixia who had raised her, most favored cleric of King Arnulf (now deceased), she had been ordained twenty years ago as biscop of Mainni when the previous biscop had suddenly died. Antonia did not like to be kept waiting.

She was being kept waiting now, and in the most unsightly hovel, a small shepherd's cottage with a bare plank floor, unwashed walls, no carpet, and one narrow bench. On that bench she sat while Heribert stood by the single window and peered out between the cracks in the barred shutters. There was not even a fire in the hearth, and it

was bitterly cold. Heribert shivered, thin shoulders shaking
under an ermine-lined cloak and two thick wool tunics.

"Come away from the window," she said.

He hesitated, and she frowned. "It's growing late," he
said. "Rain has started falling again. It looks as if it's more
ice than rain. If someone means to come, then they must
do so soon or we will be left here in this Lady-forsaken
place to face nightfall."

"Heribert!"

"Yes, Your Grace." Nervously, he touched the holy rel-
ics hanging in a pouch at his neck and backed away from
the shutters.

The roof was, thank the Lord, sound enough. No rain
leaked through to drip on the uneven plank floor. A single
lantern that hung from a hook by the hearth gave light to
the single room. Antonia had not failed to notice that it
had burned for hours now with no change in the level of
oil. So, she supposed, their mysterious confederate meant
to put them on notice that she—or he—had arts of magic
at her disposal. Someone not to be trifled with.

As they are trifling with me!

Antonia did not like to be trifled with. Only disobedience
in those sworn to obey her annoyed her more. She glanced
at Heribert, watched him pace back and forth before the
cold hearth, now rubbing his arms. He sneezed and wiped
his nose, and she hoped he was not getting sick. This frustration also nagged at her: Some of the magi knew arts by
which a sorcerer could bring heat or cold. These were not
arts she had mastered or even discovered the secrets of.
The irritating thing about hidden words was that they were
hidden, and difficult to dig out of whatever cave or ciphered
manuscript or reluctant, stubborn mind she found them in.

Wind shook the cottage and rain lashed the walls and
roof. Surely no one would venture out to this isolated hillside in such weather. Why had she responded to the summons? For weeks now they had been led through the
hinterlands of Karrone and northernmost Aosta like idiot
sheep. Lured by signs as elusive as sparrows, she found at
each turn that these mysterious messages fluttered away
just when she thought she might grab hold of them. But
she had nowhere else to go. She could not return to Mainni,
not yet, not now. The courts of King Henry of Wendar and

Varre and Queen Marozia (her aunt) of Karrone were closed to her; they would only detain her again and send her south to Darre to await trial before the skopos. Many lesser nobles might take her in for a month or two, not yet knowing of the accusations made against her, but she hated living on the sufferance of others.

If she could not clear herself, if the false and misguided testimony of others was to be used against her, then she would simply have to bide her time until she could rid herself of her enemies. Until that time, she followed such will-o'-the-wisps as had led her here, to this Lady-forsaken cottage on a windswept barren hillside on the southern slopes of the Alfar Mountains. They had only reached the spot with difficulty; poor Heribert had had to walk alongside her mule up the rugged path that led here. Technically, she supposed, this cottage rested in the queendom of Karrone or perhaps on the northern boundaries of one of the Aostan principalities. But it was so isolated that in truth no princely jurisdiction reigned here, only that of wind and rain and the distant mercy of God in Unity.

The latch snicked open. A gust of wind slammed the old door so hard against the wall that one of the door planks splintered. Heribert yelped out loud. He lifted a hand to point.

She rose slowly. Biscop Antonia, granddaughter and niece of queens, did not show fear. Even if she were afraid.

A *thing* loomed outside the door, not one of the dark spirits such as she had learned to compel but something *other,* something made of wind and light, shuddering as rain rippled its outlines and wind shredded its edges into tatters. It wore the form of an angel, of which humankind is but a pale wingless copy, and yet there was no holy Light in its eyes. By this means Antonia knew the creature was a daimone coerced down from a higher sphere to inhabit the mortal world for a brief measure of time.

If a human hand could control such as *this,* then certainly she could learn to compel such creatures. She gestured Heribert to silence, for he was mumbling frantic prayers under his breath as he clutched his holy amulet.

"What is it you want?" she demanded. "Whom do you serve?"

The *thing* stretched as if against a hidden mesh of fine

netting. *I serve none, but I am bound here until this deed is accomplished.*

It had no true mouth but only the simulacrum of a mouth, a *seeming,* as its corporeal body was obviously more seeming than physical matter. The rain, now waning, fell through it as through a sieve. Beyond it, *through* it, she saw the stunted trees and wild gorse as through thick glass, distorted by the curves and waves of its form. It was as restless as the wind, chafing in a confined space. Antonia was entranced. Into how small a space could such a creature be bound until it screamed with agony? Would fire cause it to burn? Would iron and the metals of earth dispel it or obliterate it entirely? Would water wash it away or only, like the rain, pour through it as a river pours through a fisherman's net?

"Do you not serve that person who has bound you?" she demanded.

I am not meant to be trapped here below the moon, it answered, but not with anger or frustration such as she understood. Such as humankind felt. It had no emotion in its voice she could comprehend.

"Ai, Lady," murmured Heribert behind her, his voice made delicate by terror.

"Hush," she said without turning to look at him. His sensitivity irritated her at times; this was one of them. Sometimes boys took too much of their nature from their father's transitory and fragile seed and not enough from their mother's generative blood. "It cannot hurt us. It does not belong to this sphere, as any idiot can see. Now come forward and stand beside me."

He obeyed. It had been a long time since he had failed to obey her. But he shook. Those pale, soft, perfectly manicured hands clutched at her cloak and then, sensing her displeasure, he merely sniveled and twisted the rings on his fingers as though the fine gems encrusted in gold—gems dug from the heavy earth—could protect him from this aery being.

"What is it you wish, daimone?" she asked the creature, and it swayed at the utterance of the word, "daimone," for any being, mortal or otherwise, is constrained by another's knowledge of its name and thus its essence.

I wish to be free of this place. It stretched again. The rain

had passed and the wind lulled, but still its shape was blown
and whipped by unseen and unfelt winds, perhaps not
earthly winds at all but a memory of its home in the upper
air, above the sphere of the moon. *Come. I will lead you
to the one who awaits you.*

"Dare we go with it?" whispered Heribert, nearly on his
knees with fright.

"Of course we dare!"

In this way she had been punished for the one sin, the
one occasion of weakness. She had been younger and not—
then—immune to the desires of the flesh, though she had
rid herself of such desires since that time some twenty-six
years ago. And to have succumbed to *his* blandishments,
of all people! His concupiscence was legendary. He simply
could not keep his hands off women, of any station. Someday that desire would be his downfall, she sincerely hoped.

The child gotten of the union she loved immoderately—
she recognized that—but she also despised him, because he
was weak. Yet he was hers, and she would take care of
him. She had in the past, and she would in the future.

"Come, son," she said sternly. Without more than a
squeak, Heribert followed her over the threshold. The sky
was clearing rapidly. The glowering front receded to the
east, tearing itself to shreds against the imposing heights of
the mountains. Behind it, ragged bands of high white clouds
striped the sky.

Like the storm, the daimone receded before her. It did
not walk; neither did it fly. Like the wind, it simply moved
across the land. Its humanlike shape bulged and shrank in
conformity to its own nature or to the weather in some far-
off clime. It moved up the hill on a muddy footpath, though
it left no imprint of its passage except the disturbance in
the air that was its presence. She followed, wondering what
had become of the mule and the old laborer who had led
her and Heribert up to this abandoned cottage. It was very
very cold, far too cold to stay in the heights overnight. The
laborer, cowed by her importance, had asked no questions
and had himself no answers to give her, though she had
compelled answers from him; he was as stupid as the beasts
he shepherded.

They walked until Heribert coughed as he labored upward and even Antonia felt winded. The daimone, of

course, showed no sign of strain; it could easily have out-
paced them, but did not. Antonia wondered if such creatures felt impatience. Was it without sin, as all humanfolk
were not? Or was it beyond salvation, soulless, as some in
the church claimed?

They crossed a field of rubble.

"It's an old fort," said Heribert, his words more breath
than voice; he coughed more frequently as they climbed
higher. But she heard spirit in his voice. Old buildings were
his passion; had she not forbidden it, he would have left
her to train as an architect and builder in the school at
Darre or traveled even as far as Kellai in Arethousa to
become an apprentice in the schools there. But if he went
so far away from her, then she could not watch over him.
Now, of course, he never questioned her at all.

He paused, leaning on dressed stone tumbled to the
ground, and surveyed the ruins. "It is an old Dariyan fort.
I recognize the pattern."

"Come," she said. The daimone had not waited; it
coursed ahead like a hound that has scented its prey.
"Come, Heribert." With a wrench, he pulled himself away
from this strange ruin, an old fort lost—or abandoned—in
such desolate country.

They climbed and, in the odd way of slopes in such country, ground that seemed level ahead proved to be the crest
of a hill. Coming over it, they saw in the vale below a ring
of standing stones.

"A crown!" breathed Heribert. He stared.

Antonia gazed with astonishment. Broken circles she had
seen aplenty; they were well known in the border duchy
of Arconia at whose westernmost border stood the city of
Mainni—across the river to the west of the cathedral lay
the kingdom of Salia. But this circle stood upright, as if it
had been built yesterday. It did indeed have a superficial
resemblance to a giant's crown half buried in the earth,
but that was peasant superstition, and Antonia despised the
credulity of the common folk.

The daimone surged down through bracken; bare twigs
whipped at its passing as if a gale had torn through them.
She sent Heribert to find a trail, and on this paltry track—
the poor lad had to beat back as much undergrowth as if
there had been no path at all—they descended into the

vale. Down in the bowl the wind slackened to silence, and the undergrowth gave way to a lawn of fine grass clipped as short as if sheep had grazed here recently.

The daimone circled the standing stones and paused before a narrow gateway made of two upright stones with a lintel placed over them. Air boiled where the creature stood, like a cloud of translucent insects swarming. Antonia halted just far enough away from it and looked in through the flat gateway toward the center of the stone circle. She felt, in her bones and as a throbbing in the soles of her feet, the power that hummed from the circle. The ground here was impossibly flat, as if it had been leveled by human labor—or some other force.

Heribert gazed at the sky, then at the circle, and whispered, "It's the eastern-facing doorway. Does that mean something?"

"Of course it means something," she said. "It means this doorway looks toward the rising sun, perhaps at midwinter or midsummer."

He shuddered. As the sun set behind the hills opposite them, west across the eerie architecture of stones, it threw long shadows out from the stones that made weird patterns, almost like writing, on the short grass. The rising moon, its pale face lifting above the distant mountains, heralded night.

Enter by this gate, said the daimone.

"Certainly," said Antonia graciously. "I will follow you."

I go no further. I cannot enter the halls of iron. My task is done once I have guided you here.

"If we choose not to go?"

It vanished. One moment its disturbance roiled the air, the next the sun slipped down below the hills and the moon breathed paler light across a landscape empty of wind or the pulsation of air that had marked the daimone's presence.

"What do we do?" whimpered Heribert, shivering harder. "We don't know what's in there. How could anyone drag such huge stones up these foothills?"

"We enter," said Antonia calmly. "We have no fire, no food, no shelter. We'll freeze out here. We have chosen to put ourselves at the mercy of our mysterious correspondent. We must go forward." *And take our revenge for this insulting treatment later,* she finished in her own thoughts. Such sentiments she could not share with poor, weak Heribert.

She did not wait for him to go first. They would be here all night while he gathered up his courage. "Take hold of my cloak," she said, "so that we can by no means become separated."

"But it's only a stone circle. We'll freeze—!"

When she walked under the threshold, the heavy stone lintel almost brushed her head; Heribert had to duck. But they did not come out into the empty center of the circle with the twilit sky above them and tattered clouds blowing past the rising moon.

Once under the circle, once circled by stone—below her feet, above her head, and on her right and left—they crossed into earth without any obvious transition. They walked into a darkness relieved only by a pale globe receding before them—the constant moon—and yet when she put her hands out to either side she pressed stone walls, ragged to her touch. Stone made a ceiling above them, and smooth paving led their feet forward into the hidden dark.

Heribert caught in his breath and tugged at her cloak. "We're in a tunnel!" he gasped.

"Come," she said, more impressed than afraid. "This is powerful magic. Let us see where it leads us."

2

THERE *are spirits burning in the air with wings of flame and eyes as brilliant as knives. They move on the winds that blow above the sphere of the moon, and now and again their gaze falls like the strike of lightning to the earth below, where it sears anything it touches. Their voices have the snap of fire and their bodies are the conjoining of fire and wind, the breath of the sun coalesced into mind and will.*

All this she sees inside the vision made by fire. Here she runs as would a mouse, silent and watchful, staying in the shadows. She braves the unknown passageways and the vast hidden halls where other creatures lurk. This skill alone—that of seeing through fire—Da did not strip from her, or perhaps the skill manifested only because Da died. It may be all that saves her, if she can learn to use it to spy on those who seek her out, to hide herself from whatever—whomever—murdered Da.

It may even be that someone who also can see within the vision made by fire can help her. Can save her.

Ai, Lady, no one can save her. Hugh *has returned, as he promised he would. How foolish she was to think she had escaped him. All this time she thought she had at last won free of him, but she cannot now and never will be free of him on the realm of earth where his power is vast and hers insignificant, only here, in the vision made by fire, where he cannot follow her. And in the vision made by fire, other things stalk her.*

She needs help so desperately and she does not know where to turn.

Through the endless twisting halls she seeks the gateway that will lead her to the old Aoi sorcerer.

There! *Seen in shadow, in a dark dry corridor walled in stone, she sees two people walking, searching as she is.*

There! *A boy sleeps with six companions, heads pillowed on stone, feet and knees covered by heaps of treasure, armbands of beaten gold, rings, gems, vessels poured out of the silver of moonlight, and smooth scarlet beads that are drag-on's blood turned to stone with exposure to the air.*

There! *Creatures move and crawl among the tunnels, mis-shapen knuckles tamping down soil clawed from the dank walls. Like the Eika, they seem fashioned more of metal and soil than of the higher elements, trapped forever by the weight of earth that courses through their blood and hardens their bones.*

When she at last finds the burning stone that marks the gateway to the old sorcerer, he no longer sits beside it rolling strands of flax into rope against his thigh. He has left that place, and she does not know where to find him. But she has to keep looking. Because he is one of the Lost Ones, he is not human and surely therefore not bound to human con-cerns, to human intrigues and jealousies, to human lusts for power and possession. He might know the answer. He might know the pattern of the paths she must unravel.

Perhaps Da left her a message here, secreted in the laby-rinth in such a way that she alone can find it. He must have prepared for this, knowing he might be gone and that she yet lived. Behind the locked door in her tower in her City of Memory there burns a fiery light; is it Da's magic, hidden away? Is it the living manifestation of the spell he cast over her? If she had the key, could she open the door? Did Da hide the key here, somewhere in these halls whose pathways she cannot trace unless she explores them?

And yet, what will happen if she does unlock the door?

A whisper of breath touches the back of her neck. She shudders. Her back stings as if, simply by closing in on her, the creature blisters her with its poisonous intent. Is this what Da felt? Some thing *always getting closer, always coming up behind him? Did he know it would kill him in the end?*

She begins to run through the halls seen in the vision made by fire, although on the realm of earth her body sits silent and still in front of a roaring campfire. But the creature is stronger than she is, here, in this place. It knows these paths, and it is looking for her.

"*Liath.*"

It knows her name. *She flees, but there is nowhere to go. Da used his magic to conceal her from their eyes on the realm of earth, but* here *she is vulnerable to their sight—*

and there, *where she is hidden from them, she is vulnerable to Hugh.*

Fear leaps and burns in her heart like wildfire. She is lost. Gasping, weeping, she forces herself to stop. She turns to face what stalks her, but she sees no thing, *no shadow, no creature or human form; yet she knows it has marked her and that it closes in. It wants her. The air itself carries the sound of her breathing, the simple heat of her being, to the ears of that which listens for her.*

This—one creature or many working in concert—killed Da.

She feels their breath like air stirred by an arrow, an arrow whose sharp point seeks her heart. In this place, she has no weapons.

Nay, she has one *weapon here: the gift given to her by the old Aoi sorcerer.*

"Ai, Lady," she breathes, a prayer for strength. Closing her hand around the gold feather, she escapes the maze.

3

SIDE paths fainter than the breath of a dying baby teased Antonia's vision, but she could catch only glimpses of what lay down their paths: halls piled with treasure; a sleeping boy; a young woman running in fear; the fading image of an old, old monk with one hand laid tenderly upon a book while the other lifts to ward off the clutching fingers of daimones whose insubstantial hands reach right inside his body for whatever secret he has hidden within his heart. A hound barked. An owl hooted and struck in the depths of night. A man—no man, but an elven prince armed in the style of the ancient Dariyans—fought to save a burning fort from the assault of the savage Bwrmen and their human allies. A dragon slept in enchanted sleep beneath a ridge of stone. A young man sat in sunlight and surveyed the quiet sea. Did she recognize him? The vision was too brief for her to look more closely.

Were these glimpses of the past or the future or the present?

She could not know. She was entirely lost; she knew that she existed only because her son dragged at her cloak. At least his terror was so great that he was mercifully silent rather than gibbering prayers and psalms.

God would see them to safety, or God would see them dead.

If the first, then certainly she would discover the secrets of this place and bind to herself the knowledge of how to coerce daimones down from the upper air and lead unsuspecting souls into a prison as torturous as this. She fully expected the Abyss to open at her feet at any moment and give her a gratifying vision of the punishment of the damned.

If the second, then she was content to know that her soul—and that of her son, of course—would ascend as did the souls of all the righteous to the Chamber of Light beyond the seven spheres.

Stairs opened before them. Wind brushed her face. The pale round moon wavered before her eyes, high above, and she realized with a start that she was looking up the stairs to the world above, to an actual night sky now shot through with stars. Behind her, Heribert moaned slightly as she had heard laboring women do when the child was, at long last, finally and safely birthed.

She shook him off brusquely and climbed the stairs. He came up so close behind that his boots clipped her heels but, this once, she did not berate him for his carelessness. She sensed that at long last they had come to the place where she would learn what she wanted to know.

The stairs brought them up out of the earth into the center of a small stone circle, seven stones placed equidistant from each other on a grassy sward. Beyond, like hulking beasts against the heavens, three mountains loomed. They had not returned to the first stone circle, that was obvious, but Antonia guessed they still walked among the Alfar Mountains.

Her second thought, unbidden and unwelcome, was that it was surely no longer late autumn. The air was clement, the night mellow and almost warm. But the moon remained full, much farther gone in the sky than it had been when they entered the first stone circle. They had walked beneath the earth, guided by the moon's distant light, for many hours—and it was nearing dawn.

The stone circle stood on a low hill. Beyond, down the slope and half hidden by trees, stood several buildings. The sinking moon still gave enough light that she could make out the rest of the little valley: a copse of lush trees, a few neat strips of cultivated field, a vineyard, squat boxes for bees, a chicken shed, and the leaning wall of a stable set into the steep side of a mountain. A single lantern burned by the gate that led into the enclosure. A stream whispered, murmuring, in the distance. High cliff walls enclosed them, shutting out half the night sky in which stars dazzled, uncloaked by any sign of cloud.

A hand brushed her cheek and she started. "Heribert."

He stood three steps behind her, too far away to have touched her. He seemed to have been struck dumb.

"Biscop Antonia." The speaker stepped out from behind one of the stones and made the gesture that in the sign language of the convent signified *Welcome*. She gave no obeisance. "I am glad you chose to follow my messenger."

"Who are you?" demanded Antonia, annoyed by her lack of deference. "Are you the one who has led us this far?" She had many more questions, but she knew better than to ask them all at once.

"I am the one who has brought you here, for I have seen your promise."

Promise! Antonia snorted, but held her tongue.

"You may call me *Caput Draconis*."

"The head of the dragon? A strange name, or title, to give oneself."

"A strange road has brought us all here, and we must tread stranger and more dangerous paths yet if we are to succeed. You are not trained as a mathematicus?" The question was, in fact, a statement, waiting on Antonia's acknowledgment.

"I know that the constellation known as the Dragon is the sixth House in the great circle of the zodiac, itself called the world dragon that binds the heavens." Antonia did not like to be toyed with in this manner. She did not like to be reminded that others might know things she did not.

"So it is. And it wields its own power. But the stars do not in their movements gather as much power as do the seven erratica, which we know as the planets: Moon, Erekes, Somorhas, Sun, Jedu, Mok, and Aturna. I speak of the ascending and descending nodes of the moon, where that vessel crosses the plane of the ecliptic. The ecliptic is the path on which the planets move, which we also call the world dragon that binds the heavens. South to north the moon ascends across the ecliptic, and that is the caput draconis, the head of the dragon. North to south she descends, and that is the cauda draconis, the tail. Every twenty-seven days, in the sphere above·us, the moon moves from caput to cauda and back again. In every movement we observe in the heavens, there is power to be taken and used."

"And these are the secrets hoarded by the mathematici? By such as you?"

The woman lifted her hands, palms up and open, empty, to reveal that she needed no weapon cast of brute metal or grown out of earth in order to triumph over her adversaries.

"The teachings of the mathematici are forbidden by the church," Antonia added.

"And you were being sent to Darre to stand trial before the skopos on the charge of maleficent sorceries whose use is *forbidden* by the church. I know of you, Antonia. I know your skills. I need them."

"I tire of this portentousness," said Antonia bluntly. "Did you compel the daimone? Can you teach me such power?"

"Indeed I can, and more besides. Your great talent is for coercion. I need that talent, for I only possess it in small measure."

"You have drawn down and trapped a daimone! Is that, to you, possessing only a 'small measure' of talent?"

"For compulsion, yes. With the others I can draw down such creatures, but our ability to coerce them is sorely limited. The one you met we could only command to a single task—to find you and guide you to the circle by whose path you then came here. But I cannot, as you evidently can, command spirits and beasts to kill—unless it is already their own desire to do so."

"Is that what you want? To kill someone?"

The other woman smiled slightly.

"At what do you wish to succeed, Caput Draconis?" Antonia said, curious now. She hated being curious. It put her at a disadvantage.

"I want only that we might all become closer to God," murmured the woman.

"A worthy goal," agreed Antonia. The moon set, and with its passing came the first glimmers of dawn. A bird sang. Stars had faded. Clouds massed now at the second of the three snow-covered peaks that guarded one side of the little valley. Thin streamers of mist rose from the ground and seemed to coalesce into shapes with human limbs and human hands and half-formed human faces. But that surely was only a trick of the light.

"But I must know if you have the strength and the will to aid us," continued the woman, looking past Antonia to what stood behind her. "Some offering. Some sacrifice . . ."

Antonia knew at once, and a small fire of anger bloomed inside her. Such presumption! "Not that," she said. "Not

him." She refused to show weakness by turning to make
sure Heribert was still in one piece.

Now there was enough light for Antonia to see the other
woman's face: pale of complexion, it had a certain distant
familiarity about it—but, as with the sparrows, she could
not grasp how she knew it. She could have been as old as
Antonia or as young as Heribert; no obvious sign of age,
or of youth, marked her. Her hair remained tucked away
in a scarf of gold linen. She wore a fine silk tunic dyed a
rich indigo and leather shoes trimmed with gold braid. At
her throat she wore the golden torque that signified royal
kinship in the realms of Wendar and Varre and Salia.
Though the granddaughter and niece of queens, Antonia
had no right to such a symbol of her royal kinship. Karrone
had been a principality allied to Salia not three generations
ago, in the time of Queen Berta the Cunning. Berta had
been the first of its rulers to style herself "Queen." Neither
did the petty princes of the many warring states of Aosta
wear the torque. They, too, could not trace their royal
blood back to the forebears of the legendary Emperor
Taillefer.

"Very well," said the woman. "Not him. But let that,
then, be your first lesson. That is why you are neither caput
nor cauda draconis but rather seventh and least of our
order. You can only take as much power as you are willing
to give of yourself."

Antonia did not agree, but she was too wise to say so
out loud. She gestured to Heribert, and he crept up beside
her. She noted with some approval that, though he was
silent and certainly quite frightened, he held himself
straight and with the pride of a man who will not bow
before fear. Or perhaps he *had* been stricken dumb by a
spell thrown on him by this woman. He was not, as was
his habit when nervous, murmuring a prayer.

"What do you want from me, then?" asked Antonia.

"I need a seventh. I need a person who has strong natural powers of compulsion, as you do. I am trying to find a
certain person and bring that person here, to me."

Antonia thought about power. Imagine how much *good*
she could do with greater powers, with the ability to compel
others to act as she knew they truly wanted to. She could
return order to the kingdom, return herself to her rightful

place as biscop and Sabella to the throne that was lawfully hers. She could go farther even than that: She could become skopos and restore the rule of God as it *ought* to be observed. "Let us imagine that I agree to join you. What happens then?"

"To come into our Order you must give something."

"What is that?"

"You would not give me the young man. So give me your name, the secret, true name your father whispered in your ear as is every father's right when a child is born of his begetting."

Antonia flushed, truly angry now. This was impertinence, even from a woman who wore the golden torque. Although by what right she wore that torque Antonia, who knew the royal lineages of five kingdoms as if they were her own names, could not guess. "My father is dead," said Antonia icily. "Both of my fathers. He who sired me died before I could walk or speak."

"But you know."

She knew.

And she wanted the power. She wanted the knowledge. She could do so much with it. So much that *needed* to be done.

She spoke it, finally. After all, Prince Pepin had not lived long afterward. His spite could not haunt her, for it had fallen with him into the pit.

"Venenia." Poison.

The woman inclined her head respectfully. "So shall you be called Venia, *kindness,* in memory of that naming and to honor a new beginning. Come, Sister Venia." She stepped outside the circle of stones. They followed her out onto grass moist with dew. Heribert gaped and knelt to touch, wonderingly, a violet.

"Come," repeated the woman as she set off along a well-worn path that wound down the gentle slope toward the buildings below. A man dressed simply in a tunic and drawers came out to the gate and snuffed the lantern. Goats left the shed and moved in a mass—herded by what manner of creature Antonia could not tell—up into the gorse and heather.

"It's so beautiful," breathed Heribert.

It *was* beautiful as the sun rose and light washed over

the little valley, all greens and rich browns, with a rushing
stream bubbling and boiling through pastureland. The
woman smiled at the young cleric, then continued down.
Heribert hurried after her. Antonia lingered, staring at the
peaks as the sun, rising in the east, set their proud heads
glaring, ice glinting fire. She recognized them now, those
three high peaks: Young Wife, Monk's Ridge, and Terror.
Just over the steep, impassable ridge on which the goats
grazed so peacefully rested the hostel run by the monks
of St. Servitius, hospitable souls making shelter for those
travelers who braved St. Barnaria Pass.

VIII
THE HARVEST

1

ALAIN sat on Dragonback Ridge, halfway down the spine of the Dragon's Tail, and watched the surge and fall of waves on the shore. Rage and Sorrow sat beside him, tongues out to catch the wind off the bay. Two men-at-arms loitered at a discreet distance. A seagull circled in the wind over the water; a tern took careful steps through the surf on the gravelly beach below. To the left, along the curve of the beach where it grew sandier, ships lay at their winter's rest, set up on logs. Out in the surge, dark heads bobbed in the swells: seals . . . or mermen.

He scanned the distant islands, studded like jewels along the horizon, where fishermen and merchants might take refuge in times of storm if they were out on the open sea. He had survived a storm, caught out on these heights. That storm had changed his life.

After hunting, Lavastine and his retinue had ridden to

the ruins of Dragon's Tail Monastery. Alain could not imagine what his father expected to find there. Surely the villagers had gleaned from the wreckage every last unscorched bench and table and scrap of cloth, beehives, paving stones, spoons, knives, bowls, lanterns, candle wax and candles, salt basins, pickaxes, spades, hatchets, sickles, pothooks, baskets, shingles, all the fine small tools of the scribe's trade, parchment leaves scattered from books whose jeweled covers had been ripped off and carried away by the Eika raiders. Anything that could be hauled would have been taken away and put to use, or shipped to Medemelacha for trade.

But the sight of the destroyed monastery had upset Alain so much that Lavastine had allowed him to go on ahead. Alain could have walked the long path along the rocky ridge all the way to Osna village but now, as he stared at the sleeping ships below, he knew he was afraid to meet the man he had called "Father" for most of his life.

He shut his eyes. The wash of late autumn sun was not warm enough to heat his fingers. The hounds whined; Sorrow stuck her moist nose into Alain's palm. He set that palm down on gritty rock. In the old story, a Dariyan emperor versed in magic had come to this land and turned a dragon into stone, into this very ridge that swelled from the head up across a great back and down to the tip of the tail—where lay the now-burned monastery. Was there a dragon lying in enchanted sleep beneath this rock? If he stayed still enough, could he feel the pulse of the dragon's heart—or only the fine grains of rock ground by wind, rain, and time into granules that crunched under a man's boot?

As a boy, he had climbed this ridge many times, seeking a sign of the dragon's presence. He had never found any, and Aunt Bel had told him more times than he could count that he dreamed so much he was as likely to stumble off the edge of the path and into the waters below as make his way safely through the world. *"The world is* here, *Alain" she would say, knocking on the tabletop with her knuckles, then doing the same, sharply, to his head, "not* here, *though I think sometimes this table and your head are made of the same thing." But she would smile to take the sting out of the words.*

But if he only had the hearing of Fifth Brother, the keen

hound sense of Rage and Sorrow, could he not hear the dragon's breath under the weight of earth? Sense the contour of its spine under rock, the texture of its scales under dirt? Touch its dreaming mind, so like to his own?

The earth shuddered and moved beneath him.

He jumped to his feet, shaken and frightened. Rage barked and Sorrow howled, as if baying at the absent moon. The two men-at-arms hurried forward.

"My lord Alain, are you well? What is it?" They kept well clear of the hounds, who snuffled at rock and dirt, ignoring the soldiers.

"Did you feel it?"

"Ah, yes." The men turned as the faint jingle of harness, the clop of hooves, and a murmur of jovial voices drifted up to them. "You've good hearing, my lord, as good as those hounds, I'd wager. There come my lord count and the others."

Count Lavastine and his company emerged from the winter forest and made their way up the path to the high ridge. Even after two months on the road fighting Eika and mopping up ragtag packs of bandits, and after a week of hunting in the dense forest a day's ride east of here, the count and his retinue still looked impressive with banners flying and dressed in tabards dyed bright blue and embroidered with two black hounds—the mark of the Lavas counts. Count Lavastine let none of his personal guard go into battle unarmed, and each man had at least a helmet decorated with blue ribands, a spear and a knife, and a padded coat under the tabard. Some, if they could afford it or had been lucky enough to glean such winnings from the field, had more armor: a boiled leather coat or a scale hauberk, a leather aventail, even leather bindings on their arms and legs. Like any good lord, Lavastine was generous with his winnings and always gave his men-at-arms their fair share of the spoils.

Alain mounted his horse and rode dutifully alongside his father. They crested the dragon's back and started down the slope of shoulders and neck. A jutting boulder at the base of the ridge, lifting the height of three men, was commonly called the dragon's head; it was crowned with a scraggly yew tree and the stubble of old climbing roses, planted years ago.

By this boulder the people of Osna village waited to greet Count Lavastine. Osna village was an emporium— a trading port—and as such it needed protection. Count Lavastine provided that protection . . . at a price levied in goods and services. And in any case, as Aunt Bel used to say, *"It's wisest to greet politely those as have better weapons than you do."*

Everyone stared at him. Embarrassed, he fixed his gaze on the reins twisted across his palm, but he still heard whispers, his name a mutter in the background.

They rode through the palisade gate and past the fields, halting in front of the church made proud and handsome by the contributions of Osna's wealthiest families. But their wealth was nothing compared to the wealth he had seen at Biscop Constance's palace and at the king's court, or to that he enjoyed every day as heir to a count.

The rough-hewn longhouses, built of undressed logs patched with mud and sticks, looked shabby compared to the palaces of the nobly born. Yet weren't they good houses built of good timber by the willing hands of good people? He had always thought himself well off when he lived here—though he had forgotten how strongly the village smelled of fish.

Was it pride that made him see modest Osna village differently now? Or only the experience of the wider world?

Deacon Miria declaimed a formal welcome. Count Lavastine dismounted, and Alain hurried to do the same, handing his reins to a groom but keeping a firm hold on the leashes of the hounds. He looked about him, then, and saw many familiar faces, people he had grown up with, people he knew well. . . .

But he saw not a single member of his family.

Not my family any longer.

Not one of them stood among the crowd.

"Come, my lord," said Deacon Miria. "I trust you will find the lodgings here in Osna village not beneath your notice." She led them away . . . to Mistress Garia's longhouse. The men-at-arms remained behind to be dispersed into other households.

Why were they not honoring Aunt Bel with their presence?

Their path gave him a view of the entrance to Aunt Bel's

longhouse. A woman stood in the threshold, a ladle in one
hand and the other holding a toddler on one hip. It was
not Aunt Bel.

Why was old Mistress Garia's daughter standing in the
entrance of Aunt Bel's house as if she lived there?

Afternoon eased into dusk. Garia and her daughters laid
out a feast at which her own sons and grandsons served
the count, his heir, and his most honored retainers.

Though a feast by Osna standards, it was poorer fare by
far than the feast celebrated at Lady Aldegund's manor.
The bread was dark, not white; besides the ubiquitous fish,
there were only two kinds of meat, pig and veal, and they
were spiced only with pepper and such herbs as could be
found locally; there were apples baked in honey but no
sweet custard to melt on his lips. He blushed, thinking of
the servingwoman and what she had wanted.

At a remove between courses, Mistress Garia came forward to offer Count Lavastine her eldest grandson as a
retainer, to serve the count as a permanent member of his
guard. "It is hard, indeed, my lord, to find places for all
my grandsons. Our Lady has blessed my line with many
healthy children, but the girls will inherit the workshop,
and we do not yet have the means, as some do—" For the
first time, her gaze darted to touch on Alain's face, then
away. "—to build another ship. Meanwhile, the boy is almost sixteen. I hope you will honor us with your notice."

Your notice.

At those innocuous words, every person present turned
to stare at Alain. "I—" he started to say.

Lavastine raised a hand. Alain fell silent. "In the spring,
I will know my requirements. I will send word with my
chatelaine, Mistress Dhuoda, when she comes around on
her usual progress."

Terror stood, baring his teeth, and Mistress Garia drew
back, frightened. Alain quieted the hound and got him to
lie down. Sorrow nudged up against him, sticking his head
under Alain's hand for a caress. The company returned
their attention, firmly, to the table.

After the main courses, instead of entertainment, Count
Lavastine questioned the townsfolk of Osna about the
Eika.

Two Eika ships had been sighted the summer after the monastery had been sacked, another three this past summer, but they had all sailed by Osna Sound, keeping out beyond the islands. No reports had come of villages nearby being burned; no one had heard any rumors of winter encampments. A forester—one of Garia's cousin's sons who ranged wide looking for game and exceptional stands of timber—had seen nothing along the coast for two days' walk in either direction, nor had he heard tales from those he met on his travels.

Lavastine questioned the merchants in greater detail, and from them he heard more varied stories. None had himself run afoul of Eika, but merchants traded not just goods but gossip. Four Eika ships poised along the coast just north of the rich emporium of Medemelacha had suddenly turned north and sailed away. A noble's castle in Salia had been the scene of a vicious attack; one city had held out two months against a siege; refugees from a monastery burned on the island kingdom of Alba had arrived in a skin boat in Medemelacha late in the summer with an awful tale of slaughter and looting.

Alain sat dutifully and listened, but what he most wanted to ask he dared not ask: Where was Henri? Why did he not sit among the Osna merchants? What had happened to his family?

Not my family any longer.

Mistress Garia's bed, the best in the house, was given to the count and his heir for the night. Their servants commandeered pallets or slept on the floor around them, and, in the warmth of the longhouse with a hearth burning throughout the cold late autumn's night, all were comfortable. The smell of old timber, the wreath of smoke curling along the roof beams, the smell of babies and sour milk nearby and of livestock crowded into the other end of the hall comforted Alain; they reminded him of his childhood. He had slept in such a house for many years, and his dreams had been good ones.

In the morning he drew Deacon Miria aside as the grooms saddled the horses and the soldiers made ready to leave. "Where are Bella and Henri? What has become of them and the family?"

"Alain!" Lavastine had already mounted and now gestured impatiently for Alain to join him.

"You're a good boy, Alain, to ask after them," she replied with a look compounded of sympathy, distaste, and amusement. Then she recalled to whom she was now speaking. "My lord."

"But where are they?"

"At the old steward's house. They come to Mass each week faithfully, but many of the others can't forgive them their good fortune."

"Alain!"

"Thank you!" He would have kissed the old deacon on the cheek but he was not sure, with so many folk standing about and staring, if the gesture was one he was now allowed to make. She inclined her head with formal dignity.

He mounted. As the count and his retinue rode out of the village, children trotted at a safe distance behind them, giggling and pointing and shouting.

"What did you ask?" demanded Lavastine.

They rode past the stink of pig sties and the winter shelters for the sheep and cows. They crossed through the southern palisade gate and skirted the stream which was bounded on its eastern shore by a small tannery and the village slaughterhouse—still busy with the butchering of the animals who couldn't be wintered over. Alain held a hand over his nose and mouth until they got downwind. If the stench bothered Lavastine, he did not show it; his attention remained focused on Alain.

"I asked about my foster family," said Alain at last, lowering his hand. "I found out where they've gone to."

"They've gone somewhere?" Lavastine said without much curiosity, although for an established family to pick up and move was unheard of.

"They've taken the steward's house. . . ." He hurried on since Lavastine clearly did not know what he meant. "It's a small manor house. It was built in Emperor Taillefer's reign for the steward who oversaw these lands then. That was before the port was established. An old man lived there. He was the grandson of the last steward, but he'd little to keep and no servants . . . the fields went fallow. And he'd no ship to send out, though there's a decent landing spot below the house."

"Make your point, son, if there is one you intend."

But the road made Alain's point for him: The packed-dirt way forked ahead. The wider left fork continued south, where it would eventually veer east to join the road that took the traveler to Lavas Holding.

"The path to the right leads to the steward's house, which lies down in a sheltered vale by the bay."

"And?"

But Alain knew he would never forgive himself if he did not see them. "I beg you, Father, may we go see them?"

Lavastine blinked. He looked, for an instant, the way a man might who has just been told that his wife has given birth not to a child but to a puppy. But he pulled up his horse just before the fork in the road, and his soldiers, obedient, halted behind him.

Alain's breath ran shallow as he tried desperately to hold back further words, but could not. "I beg you," he burst out. "Just this one time."

Alain knew of no window into Lavastine's soul and thoughts. His curt speech, his brusque gestures, his impatience and his efficiency, all melded into a whole so seamless that Alain could only suppose, as the church taught, that the outer man mirrors the inner. Only Frater Agius had taught differently: that an outer seeming might mask the inner heart—just as pious Agius had, until the end, concealed his belief in the heretical doctrine of the flaying knife and the death and redemption of the blessed Daisan.

"Very well," said Lavastine crisply. Whether he approved this course or disliked it Alain could not have said, nor did he really wish to know. He had to see Aunt Bel and Stancy and Julien and little Agnes and the baby, if it still lived. He had to speak with Henri, to be sure that he didn't—

Didn't what?

Didn't condemn him as an oath breaker for not entering the church?

He took in a breath and started forward. His mare, a meek creature at the best of times, picked her way through the litter of leaves shrouding the trail. Lavastine let him lead their little cavalcade down the narrow path that wound through oak and silvery birch, maple and beech. He saw the outline of buildings past bare branches, a small estate

with a house, stables, cookhouse, and outbuildings set
around an open court that could also serve as corral. They
passed out of the forest and into the scrub surrounding the
estate, stumps not yet burned and dug out, brushy undergrowth and new seedlings struggling up toward the light,
strips of field cut out of the brush, wisps of winter wheat
growing in neat green rows along soil ridges.

It took him a moment to recognize the young man standing in unmown grass at one end of a long log set up on
sawbucks. Stripped of bark and being planed down to an
even curved round, the log had the lean supple strength
necessary for a mast. At the far end of the log, scraping,
stood Henri, his back to the road; Alain knew him instantly.
The young man at the near end had the broad shoulders
of a soldier, but when he turned to stare, Alain realized
this was his cousin Julien, filled out to a man's stature now
and half a head taller than he had been two winters ago.

Julien saw the cavalcade and cried out so loudly that first
two children and then Aunt Bel came to the door of the
house; several laborers Alain did not recognize emerged
from the workshop. Henri looked up once and with a deliberate shrug went back to his work. But the others flooded
out, all of them, Aunt Bel and Stancy, and little Agnes
looking more like a woman than the girl Alain remembered. Even the baby toddled out, curly fair hair wound
down around thin shoulders. Stancy had a new baby in a
sling at her hips. A woman in the robes of a cleric hurried
forward to stand next to Aunt Bel. A small child Alain
did not recognize stood, mouth open and stick upraised,
forgetting the geese she had been set to watch over. The
birds strayed into the woods, but only Alain noticed because everyone else was staring at *him*.

Aunt Bel walked forward to place herself between her
family and the count's entourage. She folded her hands
respectfully before her and inclined her head in the same
manner, not quite as an equal but neither as a servant.
"My lord count, I give you and your company greetings to
this house."

"Mistress Bella," said Lavastine in acknowledgment, a
fine mark of notice since Alain hadn't imagined the count
remembered her name.

The cleric murmured a blessing upon them all.

The geese were wandering unnoticed back in among the trees while the child gawped at the soldiers in their blue tabards and at the banners that fluttered in the breeze.

"The geese!" Alain blurted as the first one vanished from his sight. There was a sudden flurry in the crowd. The goosegirl began to sob, frozen in place. Julien ran toward the wood, but that only startled the geese and sent some flapping every which way while the others hissed and snapped; one bit a laborer hard on the fingers.

Alain dismounted and flung his reins to a groom. "Move back," he said to the laborer and the few children who had pressed forward. "Down," he called to the hounds, who had started to bark and strain against their leashes. They stilled obediently. "Julien!" he scolded, coming up beside his cousin, "you know that's no way to bring in geese."

"Yes, my lord," mumbled Julien, red in the face.

Alain blushed. Had he sounded so proud? But the geese were scattering and the goosegirl had now hunkered down on her haunches and started bawling outright. He squatted beside her. "Hush, child." He reached out to touch her dirty chin. "This will not bring them back. Now you go stand there, by the gate to the pen, and you shut it tight once they've all gone in."

His fine clothing and his clean face and hands overawed her; he saw that by her expression and the way her gaze darted from hands to face to tunic and back again. Her bawling ceased and, though tears still ran down her cheeks, she obeyed him. He went a few steps into the forest and began the onerous job of coaxing the flustered and annoyed geese back out of the trees and into the pen. But he spoke softly and moved slowly, and in time they came, suspicious and ill-tempered but not, at this moment, intent on inflicting bodily harm. Long necks arching, still hissing at the audience of family and soldiers, they followed Alain to the pen and went inside as meekly as geese were able. At the gate, one gander hissed and retreated. Alain circled him carefully, crouched, and snaked out a hand to grab the feet from behind, sweeping the bird up while he took a firm grip on its neck with his other hand. He deposited the squawking, furious bird in the pen, jumped back, and let the goosegirl slam the gate shut. The geese subsided with a hissing and flapping of wings.

He looked back in time to see Aunt Bel trying not to laugh, the soldiers and laborers staring in outright astonishment, and his father watching with his thinnest smile—the one always linked with his disapproval.

"I see you haven't forgotten everything you learned here," said a voice at his side. Alain turned to confront his father—not his *father,* but his foster father. Henri.

Aunt Bel raised her voice. "My lord count, I hope you and yours will take a meal with us. My own daughters will prepare it."

Lavastine nodded curtly. He could scarcely refuse. It was practically a sin to scorn hospitality. But after he dismounted, he gestured to Alain to attend him.

"If you will allow me, my lord," Aunt Bel continued while Stancy and Agnes and the other women hurried inside and the laborers retreated to stand at a respectful distance. Julien followed Henri back to their work on the mast. "Rather than wait inside, perhaps I may show you around the manor. It was your largesse that made it possible for us to improve upon our circumstances and settle here."

"Indeed."

Aunt Bel kept a careful distance from the hounds, who growled at her while a padded handler staked them out away from the house. While the soldiers took the horses to graze and water, she conducted Lavastine and Alain on a tour; the cleric attended Aunt Bel much as if Bel were herself a noble lady. It was a fine grand house, although not of course nearly as grand as Lavastine's fortress, and included a good stretch of ground with fields, two workshops, pastureland and woodland, and a broad path leading down to a sheltered beach where the family's ship had been drawn up onto logs and covered with a thatch roof for the winter.

"My brother Henri is a merchant, my lord, and we have for some years shipped both cloth and quernstones south to Medemalacha. There is a quarry near here in the hills where we get our stone. With the generous payment we received from you, my lord, we have been able to expand our business in addition to moving to this manor. I have hired laborers to carve soapstone into vessels for cooking and storage. We will ship them to Medemalacha also. In time Henri hopes to sail north as far as Gent, although there is more risk of Eika attacks in that direction, and next year he intends to attempt his first trip northwest to Alba, to the port of Hefenfelthe on the Temes River."

Lavastine began to look interested. A good husbandman, he was wealthy in large part because of his careful stewardship of his lands and possessions. "One ship cannot sail to three places."

Aunt Bel smiled. "We are building a second ship this winter. My third son Bruno we have apprenticed to Gilles Fisher, a local man who builds most of the ships hereabouts. In return the shipbuilder will aid my brother with those parts of the ship Henri does not know the secrets of."

Lavastine surveyed the work that continued on the mast. Henri, sweating even in the chill, seemed oblivious to the visit of the great lord. "But is it not also true, as my clerics have read to me from the commentaries on the Holy Verses, that 'the farmer must save some of the grain when he makes bread, else there will be nothing for sowing'?"

" 'And in the days to come not pride nor greed will fill his stomach,' " finished the cleric. She was a young woman, not much older than Alain himself, with crooked teeth, a pockmarked face, and a cheerful expression. "Your attention to the words of Our Lady and Lord marks you with favor, my lord."

"Indeed," said Lavastine. "So have They shown me Their favor." He glanced at Alain. Bel, miraculously, appeared not to notice the aside. She moved away toward the other workshop, which was attached by a covered causeway to the main house.

"Three ships we may hope for in time, my lord," she said, "but for now the seaways north are closed to us by the Eika. As you say, we must move slowly as we expand lest we overreach. In this room my daughters and I weave. In time we'll expand to four looms. In time we hope also to hire more laborers and expand the farm as well. We have betrothed my daughter Agnes to a merchant's son in Medemelacha. He's an experienced sailor. In time he'll take over the third boat, should Our Lord and Lady shower their favor upon our enterprise."

"But Agnes is too young to be married!" said Alain, shocked.

Lavastine swatted away a fly and stepped back from the door into the weaving shop, held open by the cleric so that he could look inside. "How old is this daughter?"

"She is twelve, my lord. Her betrothed will come to live with us next year, but they won't wed until she is fifteen or sixteen. If you will come this way." It began to irritate Alain that she addressed all her conversation to Count Lavastine and none to *him*, as if *he* were a stranger. Yet certain small expressions familiar to him came and went on her face like so many private signals to him alone of her thoughts and of unspoken comments too personal to share with someone who did not know her intimately, the arched eyebrow that betrayed amusement, the dimple that hid annoyance, the pursed lips with which she swallowed any sign of satisfaction she considered unseemly. "We have bought more cows and will export cheese as well. We hope, in time, to bring a blacksmith here. As you can see, we have hired the Osna smith to come in twice a week and do work for us." They crossed into the house itself, the long hall busy with women and girls setting out cups and bringing in platters of food from the cookhouse. Beside the threshold Alain saw an unpainted wooden shield, a helmet, and a spear. "We are are sending my eldest son Julien to the new duchess of Varingia as a man-at-arms, because we can afford to outfit him now."

They had promised *him* to the church when he had wanted nothing more than to be a soldier! Stung with jealousy, he flushed in shame—but no one remarked on it. No one even paid attention to him. Of course it would be different for Julien. Julien was Aunt Bel's legitimate child, her eldest son, and of course she would want to give him such an opportunity now that they had the means. They had done their best by him; it wasn't their fault they hadn't known who he really was . . . was it?

Aunt Bel went on, discussing various potential marriage alliances for her children and relations. To Alain's consternation and utter confoundment, Count Lavastine appeared to relish these discussions; he asked questions and gave advice. Indeed, he treated Aunt Bel with the same distant familiarity as he did his own chatelaine, Dhuoda, a woman whose ability to run his household he respected enough to leave her alone to do her job.

"—and now that we have more business, we have brought in Sister Corinthia of Salia to write and read letters and do our accounts. We also hope to put Julien's daughter, Blanche, into the church with a dowry. Sister Corinthia will teach her so that she isn't unlettered when she goes."

Julien's daughter, the baby, was illegitimate, although Julien and his sweetheart had proclaimed publicly their intent to marry before the young woman's death in childbed.

"You have done well," said Count Lavastine. He was—perhaps—impressed. Alain was vastly irritated. He felt *used*, as if his family had only wanted him for what they could get from him, the count's generous reward for his fosterage.

Aunt Bel glanced at Alain, then away. Her features were stern now. "It is nothing we looked for or expected, my lord," she said as if she had heard Alain's thoughts spoken out loud. Perhaps she had, seeing his expression. She knew him that well. He was ashamed. "But is it not said in the Holy Verses that 'you shall eat the fruit of your own labors'?"

" 'You shall be happy and you shall prosper,' " quoted the young cleric, evidently eager to show off her knowledge of the Holy Verses, " 'and your daughters shall be like the fruitful vines and your sons like the rich stands of wheat. For the hearth-holder who lights each day a candle from the hearth in memory of the Chamber of Light, this shall be the blessing in store for her: She may share the prosperity of Saïs all the days of her life and live to see her children's children!' "

"Please, my lord count." Aunt Bel gestured to the single chair at the table. Everyone else would sit on benches. "If you will be seated." Now she turned to Alain as well and made the same respectful gesture. "And you, my lord."

"Aunt Bel," he began, hating this formality.

"No, my lord." He knew better than to argue with *her*. "You're a count's son now and must be treated as one. 'God maketh poor and maketh rich; They bringeth low and lifteth up.' "

"So said the prophet Hannah," added the cleric.

Aunt Bel turned back to Lavastine. "I will send one of my children to bring your company in to table, my lord."

"I'll go," said Alain, though it was not his place. He

should not offer, not without asking his father's permission. But he knew, suddenly, that he would have no opportunity to speak to Henri, that Henri would not eat with them. None of the family would eat with them; they would serve their guests. That was all.

The soldiers began to stamp in, a flurry of activity by the door.

Lavastine said, "Alain!"

Alain made his escape.

Outside, Julien and Henri were still working on the mast. When Henri saw Alain coming, he straightened and waved Julien away. Then he bent back to his task.

Alain halted beside the older man. Out here, outside the confines of Osna village, it smelled different. There the ever-present smell of drying fish and salted fish and smoked fish pervaded streets and common and even the Ladysday service. In the longhouse, fish and smoke and sweat and the dust of stones and wet wool and drying herbs and sour milk and rancid oil and candlewax all blended into a rich, familiar aroma. At the manor house there was no such ripe blend, for here there was room to store foodstuffs in the shed beside the cookhouse, to grind stone in a separate workshop, to weave in a room set aside for that purpose. Although perhaps thirty people lived on this farm, they were not crowded together except on winter nights when they would all sleep in the main hall.

He smelled the sea foam and heard the cries of gulls. The animal sheds stank, of course, but the smell of earth and wind and the late chill of autumn dying into winter overrode anything else, made all else into a fragrant herbal, the scent of life. The smell of land and opportunity, even though it was only an old steward's house from the time of the Emperor Taillefer.

"You've done well with the payment Count Lavastine gave you," said Alain, not meaning to say anything of the kind.

Henri smoothed the sides of the log into an even curve. "As have you," he said without looking up from the steady rhythm of his work. The words, spoken so bluntly, cut into Alain's heart.

"I didn't ask for this!"

"How then did it come about?"

"You don't think I—!" His voice gave out as he struggled with indignation.

"What am I to think? I promised the deacon at Lavas Holding to put you in the monastery when you came to your majority at sixteen, and she did not say me 'nay.' Had she known who you were, do you think she would have offered you up so easily?"

"She didn't know Count Lavastine wouldn't marry again! She couldn't have known that seventeen years ago. You think I somehow cozened him, cheated him, made up a story—! Just to get out of the church!"

"What am I to think?" asked Henri. He had not once raised his voice. "You made it clear enough you didn't want to enter the church, though the promise was made at the same time you were given into the Circle as a newborn babe."

"Made by others," retorted Alain furiously. "I couldn't even speak. I was a baby."

"And then," Henri went on as quietly, "after the monastery burned, you went to serve a year at Lavas Holding and we hear nothing more of you until this *payment* comes, and you are suddenly named heir to the count. I counseled Bel to send it back."

"To send the payment back!" Henri might as well slap him in the face as say such words. "You would have sent it *back?*" His voice broke like a stripling's.

" 'Accursed thirst for gold, to what fell crimes dost thou not force men's hearts?' The cleric, a fine educated woman I can tell you and a very Godly one as well, has been reciting to us the lay of Helen, which they call the *Heleniad*. Those words I took to my heart and I said them to Bel."

"You don't think Aunt Bel is greedy!"

"Nay," admitted Henri. "Nor has she acted in any way except for the family. Indeed, we will be the better for her stewardship. But we should never have accepted that which came to us through false pretenses. The Lord and Lady do not smile on those who lie to advance themselves."

Now he had said it baldly. Alain was stunned. When he spoke, all his hard loud words had vanished and he could only whisper. "You don't think I'm Lavastine's son."

"Nay," said Henri as calmly as if he had been asked to predict the next day's weather. But for the first time he stopped from his work and straightened, scraper dangling from one hand, to inspect Alain. His quiet gaze was devastating. "And why should I?"

Rage and Sorrow barked and whined where they stood tugging at their leashes, which were staked to the ground. Furious, Alain spun and ran, too angry to think, too angry to do anything but jerk the stake out of the ground and pull the leashes free.

"Go!" he shouted, and they leaped forward, growling, toward the man who had made their master so angry.

Lavastine appeared, crossing the threshold of the house. "Alain!" he shouted.

Rage and Sorrow ran flat out and bounded over grass and shavings while Henri stood and stared them down, although Alain saw him shaking, scraper raised as if to protect himself. Nothing would protect him from the hounds. Nothing except the voice of an heir of Lavas.

"Halt!" Alain cried, and the hounds, an arm's length from Henri, stopped dead. "Heel." He whistled. They growled once, longingly, at the other man, then, obedient, they slewed their great heads round and trotted back to Alain. Shaking, his hands trembling so hard he could scarcely hold the leashes, he staked them back down.

By that time Lavastine had reached him. "What means this?" The count glanced toward Henri, who had not gone back to his work but stood slackly by the mast and who, as a tree leans under the wind, moved now to rest a hand and then his weight on the log, bent over like an old, old man.

"N-nothing," whispered Alain. He wanted to weep. He dared not.

"Indeed," said Lavastine. "If it is nothing, you must come inside. You should not have run out in that way. It is a great honor to this family that we eat at their table and allow them to serve us." He signed to one of his servingmen. "Get my cup."

Alain followed him inside. He could not look to his right or left. He could not look at all, not to meet anyone's eyes. Lavastine took from the hand of his servingman his fine walnut cup which he used when he traveled. Four golden rivers had been carved into the wood, and the fine grain was polished until it gleamed. This cup he graciously gave to Aunt Bel, who had Stancy fill it with wine and returned it to him to drink first. Only after the count had drunk from it did she agree to sit at his right and take food herself, though the rest of her family served.

"This cup I hope you will accept," said Lavastine, "in memory of your hospitality toward myself and my son this day."

"You do us honor, my lord," said Aunt Bel, and she drank.

The meal was not as fancy as that served by Mistress Garia, who had, after all, had several day's notice of Lavastine's arrival. But there was veal and good bread and wine and apples, and several chickens had been freshly killed and cooked, spiced with coriander and mustard. Most importantly, the meal was served with dignity and pride, and there was more than enough for all.

Henri did not come inside.

To Alain, silent in the midst of his old family's newfound plenty, it all tasted like ashes and dust.

2

THEY sail at dawn into the fjord. Cliffs surround them, glittering with ice and snow and cold gray-black stone, the stone of the Mothers. Waves beat on the prow, spraying the rowers with bitter cold water, so cold that a human drenched in it will die. Not his kind, of course. His kind are RockChildren, the children of earth and fire, and the only thing they fear is the venom of the ice-wyrms. All other fates lead merely to death, and against death they are strongest of all. Iron can kill them, if wielded with sufficient strength. They can drown. But heat and cold alike melt off their beautiful skin, for are they not marked with the rich colors of the hidden earth, melded as if in the forge from the very metals with which they adorn themselves?

He hefts his spear in his right hand as the ship slides in past islands of ice and prepares to jump as it grinds up onto the rocky beach. This valley, this tribe, is unprepared for his coming. They will rue that. But they will bare their throats before him.

The hull scrapes on stone. He leaps out of the ship, hitting ground hard, then splashes forward through the surf while his dogs jump out after him, followed by his war band. His feet grip ice, slick on pebbles, while the dogs flounder behind him and regain their footing. He races up the shore and runs on snow. Behind, he hears the ragged panting of the dogs and the intent breathing of his warband. They believe in him, now. This is their fourth tribe this season. Winter is a good time for killing.

Too late the Watchers at water's edge raise the alarm. Too late the smoke fire rises to alert those living farther up along the paths which lead to the high slopes and the fjall. He hears the sudden bleat of the OldMother waking from her trance to danger. The SwiftDaughters run from the long hall carrying baskets, the nests of unhatched eggs. He sets the dogs on them. SwiftDaughters are not sacred, although the OldMother is. The dogs scatter them and baskets drop and eggs fall to the cold earth, to be lost in snow or splintered by ice, claw, tooth, or wind. Those that are strongest will survive. The others deserve to perish.

Now the warriors of Hakonin fjord gather their weapons and rush like a herd of furious goats down into the fray. He is proud of his people. He has never seen one of them turn and run. And on this day they have his cunning as well as courage to aid them. His second and third boats have beached farther down the strand and his soldiers have raced up from behind, so that the Hakonin RockChildren are already encircled. Death already sweeps down on them, as dragons and eagles take their prey from the skies. Only they do not know it yet. But as the battle is joined and they realize their plight, they fight the harder. They are strong and fearless, and because of that he calls his soldiers off sooner than he would have otherwise, leaving perhaps half of the Hakonin warriors still in the fjall of the living rather than sending them to the cold stone pathways of the dead.

He gives them a choice.

Proud warriors, each one that is left, and properly raised. They do not throw down their weapons but neither do they fight on when all is hopeless. They do not surrender. They pledge their death, or their life, to the will of their OldMother and her knife of decision.

Now, and at last, when all is lost, she emerges from the long hall. She is stout and as gray and strong as rock, which she much resembles. Her movements are as stiff as those of trees unbent in storm. It is the peculiar beauty of the Old-Mothers that, like the mountains and the cliffs and the jutting ridges of stone that scar the fields and pastures, they are glimpses of the bones of earth that lace all land together and give strength and solidity to the world. The SwiftDaughters left to her hoist baskets and gather up those eggs, fallen among the detritus of their sisters, which remain unbroken. These they collect together to form new nests, but there are few, many fewer than a tribe needs to survive.

In the pens behind the long hall the human slaves wail and moan; their noise is appalling and irritating, but he restrains himself from killing them outright just to silence that awful mewling. He gestures. His own soldiers part, forming a path down which his human slaves can come forward. These slaves he has gathered to himself as the SwiftDaugh-

ters gather the unbroken eggs. At Valdarnin fjord he set these slaves to watch over warriors and dogs alike as humiliation, for the Valdarnin warriors fought weakly and some even surrendered before they knew their OldMother's will. But he will not humiliate the Hakonin; instead, he lets his human soldiers, such as they are and armed only with weapons of wood, stand watch over the penned slaves. They have served him well this season of fighting. He is pleased to have thought of using them, the strong ones, the ones that aren't afraid to look him in the eye, to wish to defy him, and who are yet intelligent enough to know that defiance is useless.

"Who are you?" asks Hakonin OldMother. She waits at the threshold. It is gesture enough that she has emerged into the ragged winter sunlight, torn by clouds and a few drifting curls of snow.

"I am of Rikin fjord, fifth son of the fifth litter of Rikin OldMother. I am son of Bloodheart, and it is to his teeth you will now bare your throats."

"To what purpose?" she asks, her voice like the grinding of pebbles on the shore beneath the hull of his ship.

None of the other OldMothers have asked this question, only his own, Rikin's Mother, before he set off for the winter's hunt.

"The many can accomplish what the few cannot," he replies.

"You serve Bloodheart," she says.

"I do," he replies.

"Someday, as does all that is mixed with air and water, he will die," she says.

"He will," he replies, "for only the Mothers who are un-mixed with any element save that of fire and earth may re-main untouched by time for as long as the embers burn and smolder beneath their skin."

"You arm the Soft Ones." She does not look toward the human slaves. They are beneath her notice, and like the icy waters her touch is dangerous to them.

"I use what weapons I can gather," he replies.

"You wear their sigil at your heart," she says, and now her sons and brothers murmur, seeing that it is true, noting the wooden circle that hangs by a new-forged iron chain around his neck.

"It signifies my understanding of their ways," he replies. *"I can walk through their dreams."*

"You are one who has spoken with the WiseMothers," she says. *"I hear it in your voice and I see with their vision for they have shared this vision all along the fjalls. They have shared this vision with the bones of the earth. That you have the patience to find wisdom, and that you think strong thoughts. But you have no name. Bloodheart is a powerful enchanter. He has taken a name, as only enchanters may."*

He bows his head respectfully. He knows better than to contest the old laws that govern RockChildren. He is nameless, as is fitting, and yet did Alain Henrisson not give him a name? Did the human not call him *"Fifth Son,"* thinking this was a name? He will remain patient. Patience is the strength of the WiseMothers, as it is the strength of the earth.

From the pouch of skin at her thigh, Hakonin OldMother draws the knife of decision. *"If my sons and brothers fight with you,"* she says, *"if we let our dogs run with your army and our slaves labor for Bloodheart's purposes, what will you give me in return?"*

"I have defeated you," he replies.

"With this knife I crack the eggs." OldMother lifts the knife so that sun glints off its black blade, a sliver of obsidian so smooth it is depthless and so sharp it can cut both bone and the stone-sheathing of eggs. *"With this knife I winnow the weak from the strong, as do all my sisters to the north and to the south. This knife is the choosing of death or life, and you cannot defeat death, for you are mortal. What will you give me in return?"*

"What do you want?" he asks, curious now.

"I have birthed my daughters," she says, *"and one begins to harden now. Her ribs are stiffening and soon her time will come. These nests that are my laying you have scattered, and she will have few brothers to tend her fields and her pastures and to fight for Hakonin hall. I will lay no more eggs, but she has not yet begun. Promise me that when she has birthed her daughters and it comes time for her to breed her nests, of which she must have many in order to harvest a strong clan, I can send for you and you will perform the ritual with her. The Hakonin nests will be of your making."*

"Only a male who is named may perform the ritual with a YoungMother," he replies carefully. But he feels the course

of excitement in his blood. These words, this pledge, once spoken, cannot be taken away. It is dangerous to take for himself what is the prerogative of Bloodheart and the other, the very few, named males. But this OldMother knows as he knows that he intends to be one of them, in time. He must only be patient and ruthless.

"Many seasons will pass," says Hakonin WiseMother, "before I must begin my walk to the fjall and before she will take the knife from me and seat herself in my chair. Promise me this, and we will seal our bargain: your breeding for our nests, our sons and brothers for your army."

"I make this promise," he replies. "I seal it with the blood of my brother." He whistles one of the dogs to him, curses it as it snaps at his arm, and grabs its collar to wrestle it close. Its breath, weeping with the broken eggs it has feasted on, hits his face like the breath of fetid summer wind. He cuts its throat and its blood pours out onto the earth in offering. When it sags, dead, he drops it to the ground, into its own blood, some of which has spattered him, mottling his chest and the delicate faience and gold and silver links of his long metal girdle, a thousand tiny linked rings flowing like water around his hips and thighs.

The OldMother bids one of her SwiftDaughters kneel before her. Then she takes in her hand the wealth of the daughter's deep gold hair and cuts it off with a single efficient motion. "With this token I seal our bargain. Spin this and smith this and wear it when I summon you."

He nods, accepting her bargain. Her sons and brothers lift their throats and the chill winter sun glints on smooth metal skin, copper, bronze, gold, and silver, and iron-gray. In response, he grins, baring his teeth and the jewels studded there. Tonight he will add another. For as it is said among his people, jewels are like boasts, hard to keep once they are displayed.

The SwiftDaughter carries her shorn hair across the forecourt to him, stepping carefully over her dead sisters and the broken shells of eggs, her never-to-be-born brothers. She lays the hair in his waiting arms, and he is careful not to stagger under its weight. No gold as pure exists anywhere, not even in the mines dug deep into the earth by the goblin-kin. With this gold, spun and beaten, he will fashion a new

*girdle, one of his own making, not one granted him by his
father's strength.*

"Alain!" his father said, and he woke from the web of
dream and struggled to free himself of its coils.

He sat up to see light pouring in through the open shutters of the sleeping chamber he shared with his father and
the hounds. Another lord might sleep with many servants
in his chamber; the counts of Lavas could not.

"You were dreaming," said Lavastine, standing now and
crossing back to close the shutters. It was bitter cold outside; three braziers, a sinful luxury, burned in the room. As
soon as the shutters closed, darkening the chamber, Alain
rubbed his arms and shook off sleep. He rose and began
to dress. Rage scratched at the door, whining.

"You were dreaming," repeated Lavastine.

"I was." Alain bound his calves with linen bands and
then pulled on an undertunic of wool over his shirt, and
his thick winter tunic, lined with marten fur, over all.

"The Eika again." Lavastine always wanted news of
the Eika.

Alain laughed suddenly, a short, sharp laugh, much like
his father's. Much like Lavastine's.

The memory of his last glimpse of Henri still hurt, but
not as much, not after two months. He was too busy here
at Lavas Holding. Life went on at the fortress at a more
sluggish pace in wintertime, but it went on nonetheless. He
trained at arms, though he knew himself a coward. *Next
time it will be different. Next time I won't fail in battle.* He
sat with his father as Lavastine spoke with his chatelaine,
with his stewards, with his clerics, and with those few winter
travelers who lingered a day or two in the warm hall of
Lavas fortress before continuing their journey. Alain
learned what it meant to be a great lord, what gestures to
make, what polite phrases to utter, how to judge a visitor
and greet him according to his station.

"The Eika," said Alain. "Fifth Son. I think he's going to
get married. But not in any way we understand."

Lavastine regarded him without answering until Alain
grew uncomfortable, as if he had said something wrong or
made a comment more fitting to a farmer than a count's
heir.

"Father?" he asked, not liking the count's silence. Henri had been silent in that way.

But Lavastine quirked his lips finally, upward, signifying approval. "It is a portent. We have spoken of this before, but it has come time to act on it. We will send my cousin Geoffrey to the court of King Henry."

Speaking of Geoffrey, whose open dislike of Alain still crawled fresh along his skin, made the young man nervous.

"Come," he said to the hounds. He tied leashes around the necks of Rage and Sorrow and old Terror and Bliss, the four favored to sleep at night in the tower chamber with their masters. He tied the ends of the leashes to a hook set into the wall and then rapped on the door with a staff. It opened at once, servants entering—not without their usual nervous glance toward the hounds—with two pitchers of steaming water scented with mint, basins and cloth for bathing his face, and a clean covered chamberpot.

"It is time for you to be betrothed, Alain."

"Betrothed!" He let the servants wipe his face. The water heated his face, a touch of summer, and every least curve of skin on his hands was washed until his hands smelled of the herb garden. The scent of warmth and summer made him think of Tallia, and he bent over the table to shield himself, lest he betray his feeling to anyone, even to Lavastine.

"When Geoffrey asks King Henry for a marriage alliance between you and Lady Tallia, it will remind Geoffrey of the order of things in Lavas now. As he needs reminding."

Any discomforting memories of the visit to Aldegund's manor vanished with the mention of Tallia's name. "Tallia," Alain breathed. "But—she's the daughter of a duke and of Henry's own sister."

"Half sister. Alain, my son, you must understand this about marriage. Henry must marry the girl to some lordling or else put her in the convent. As long as she is in the convent, there is always the chance some lord will abduct her and marry her against Henry's will. The king does not want to marry her to a lord whose power is already too great, or to a lord or lady's son he does not trust. He needs me, and you, because the counts of Lavas bow to no duke or margrave, and yet we are not as powerful as some of the great families of Wendar and Varre. Nor as weak as others. He would be wise to grant us this alliance. Especially since we saved his army, his kingdom, and his life at Kassel. Lady Tallia is a small price to pay, I think."

"Just as the gold and silver you gave to my foster family was a small price for you to pay," said Alain, suddenly bitter again.

"For their fostering of you? A small price, indeed, Alain. Never begrudge the seed you sow in good soil, for it is the harvest that comes from that sowing that will determine whether you live or die the next spring. Think not only for this day, but for the one that is to come. In this way, Lavas has prospered and it will continue to do so under your stewardship."

"Yes," whispered Alain, promising it, determined to make it true. He did not want to fail Lavastine, now or ever. How keenly he felt, suddenly, that need to have Tallia beside him. It was more than liking, more than advantage. It was simpler than that. Perhaps it was not altogether pure. "Tallia," he said, trying her name out on his tongue. Wondering how he would speak to her once they were married, once they were alone in the intimacy of the bridal chamber. He flushed and looked up in time to see Lavastine smile, so quick he might not have glimpsed it.

"And sooner," said Lavastine casually, "rather than later." Alain's face burned. Was the sin of lust emblazoned on his face? "It is vital you secure the succession as soon as possible." The count turned to the servants and signed to them to open the door. Sorrow barked. Bliss whined, tail whipping against tapestried wall, as the door was opened and the servants braced themselves well back from the path that would be taken by the hounds.

Alain let the servants help him with his boots, and then he unhooked the hounds and led them down the curving staircase to the outside where they could run—under his supervision, of course.

He sat on a bench. The snow of last week had melted, though it was still cold. The cloudy sky had the look of porridge. He chafed his hands to warm them. A servant, seeing him, ran into the hall and emerged soon after with gloves. Soft rabbit fur caressed his hands as he slipped them on.

He had, in these moments when the hounds ran, a brief

time to himself. Everyone kept well away and Lavastine
was already about his business, business Alain would join
as soon as he put the hounds into the kennel. He closed
his eyes and drew a picture of Tallia in his mind's eye, all
wheat, like the harvest, frail, bending under the weight of
the wind, of her mother's ambition and her father's ancestry, and yet always whipping back. She seemed so . . .
unreachable. So clean. So pure and holy, she who scarcely
ate a crust of dry bread when riches sat on her plate.

That night when he lay down on the bed beside his father, he closed his eyes and thought of her again. She had
never been far from his thoughts all day. The idea that he
might actually marry her was so incredible that he might
as well dream of being a fatherless bastard child raised
by commoners suddenly elevated to the rank of heir to a
powerful count.

God bringeth low and lifteth up.

With this comforting thought and the vision of Tallia as
close as his own cloudy breath in the chill air, he slept.

*Rain edged with slivers of ice batters the canvas tents of
their camp. His warriors do not need the tents to sit out the
storm, though it makes the wait more comfortable. But the
human slaves do. Another war-leader would let the slaves
sit in the freezing rain and half of them would die. So are
the weak winnowed from the strong. But he is not like the
others.*

*He touches the Circle at his breast, circles his finger
around its smooth grain in memory of the gesture made by
the child—seen but not forgotten—at the door of the crypt
in the cathedral at Gent. That child he had let go free, because she had reminded him of Alain.*

*The slaves sit in the warm billow of smoke and heat from
the fire he has allowed them to start, up against a rock face
beneath the canvas tent. One man stares at him, then looks
quickly away when he realizes he has attracted his master's
attention.*

*"Why do you stare?" he asks. In his dreams he has
learned the language of the Soft Ones.*

*The slave does not reply. The other slaves look away
quickly, hunching their shoulders, their way of trying to*

*avoid notice, of pretending to be invisible as the spirits of
air and wind and fire are invisible to all but enchanters.*

"Tell me," he commands. Wind stings his neck and tines
of ice shatter on his back where he crouches at the open end
of the shelter.

"I beg your pardon, master," says the slave without looking up again, but even so he cannot keep the hate out of
his voice.

"You saw something." The long winter's night shrouds
them, blanketed by the ice storm and serenaded by the howling wind. By the red sullen light of fire he watches the slaves
stare at their knees and their hands, even this one, the one
who spoke. The one whom he caught looking. "I will
know."

"You wear the Circle of Unity, master," says the slave at
last, knowing that to disobey is to die. "But you do not
worship God."

He touches the Circle, drawing his finger round its curve
with that same remembered gesture. "I do not hide the
Circle."

"It is the way you touch it, master." The man's voice
gains strength, of a kind. "It reminded me of . . . someone
I once knew."

Someone this man does not wish to speak of. Bored by
the storm, irritated by the delay, since no ship can brave the
seas in such conditions, he forces the slave to go on. "Do
you have a family as, I think, is common among your
kind?"

"No, master." Here, finally, the slave lost his fear and let
his hate take wing. "Your people murdered them, all of my
kin: my wife, my sisters, even my poor innocent children."

"Yet you serve me." This human interests him. He has
fire, perhaps even some stubborn strength of earth in him.
The penned slaves who have lived among the RockChildren
for many generations are more like dogs than people, but
these new slaves to whom he has given sticks for weapons,
better food, and decent clothing all come from the southern
lands, and they think before they bark. That is why he believes they will be useful.

"I have no choice but to serve you," replies the slave.

"You have the choice to die."

The slave shakes his head. "You wear the Circle, but you

do not know God. The Lady weaves and the Lord cuts the thread when our time has come. It is not for us to choose to die. Death comes to us by Their will."

He examines the other slaves, who hunker down. One, at the limit of the canvas, shaking in the raw wind, turns and turns about until another slave, closer in, sees her plight and changes places with her, there at the edge of the shelter where the fire's warmth scarcely reaches and the wind's breath bites with killing cold. After a bit, yet a third slave takes the worst place. They help each other live. Is this the mercy that Alain Henrisson spoke of?

"Do you have a name?" he asks.

The slave hesitates. He does not want to offer his name. The other slaves stare, watching, surprised out of their pretense of mute stupidity. None of these, to whom he has given favor, are mute or stupid; he has studied his slaves carefully, just as he studies his livestock.

Still the slave does not speak.

He lifts a hand and unsheathes his claws.

"My name is Otto," the slave says at last and reluctantly.

The others whisper and then silence themselves. He can smell their nervousness beneath the hot pitch smoke of the fire and the cold blast of the storm.

"Do you all have names?" he asks.

To his surprise, they do all have names. They speak them, one by one, a sound drawn out of each one as an arrow is pulled from a wound, carefully, with respect.

Are they all enchanters, then? No, he reminds himself, they are merely different. They are not RockChildren. They are weak, and yet, in their weakness, they survive by helping each other.

He sheathes his claws and shifts backward far enough that he can stand outside the shelter of the canvas awning roped down and angled to give them shelter at the cliff face. The canvas flaps and moans in the tearing wind.

He steps out from its sheltering angle into the full fury of the storm. The icy wind drives into his face, its touch like that of thousands upon thousands of knives flung from the wind's hand into the wild air.

He listens as the wind pounds him and the ice stings his face. Dimly he can see the ships drawn up on a rocky beach, five ships now, since two new ships came with him out of

Hakonin's fleet. He sees his soldiers hunkered down, waiting out the storm with the patience of stone, and the dogs lying in jumbled heaps like fallen boulders.

He listens. It is said among his people that on this far western shore in the wintertide, when storm wracks sea and land, one can hear the keening of dragons—the FirstMothers—who in ancient days bred with the living spirits of earth and gave birth to his kind.

But all he hears is the wind.

PART THREE

THE ORNAMENT OF WISDOM

IX
THE WINTER SKY

1

ON bitterly clear nights he saw stars through certain sections of unpainted glass window whose patterns themselves formed the shapes of stars, some with five and some with six points. On this night he watched the moon's light ease across the gulf of darkness that was night in the cathedral, its glow a wavering dim light as illusive as a will-o'-the-wisp.

There came to him in an instant the searing memory of Count Hildegard and her retinue fleeing to the gates. It had all been a trick, an illusion. He had seen what he wanted to see, what *Bloodheart* wanted them all to see, the count and her ragged army in flight, when in fact Bloodheart had cast a glamour over his own Eika troops to make them appear human. In that way the Eika had gained entry into the city, and stalemate had turned to slaughter.

Only Liath had been clear-sighted enough to see through

the illusion. If only he had such sight as that, he could make out a way to escape his captivity. But his gifts from his mother did not include sight beyond that common to humankind. And in any case the chains, and the dogs, were no illusion.

Here in the bitter cold of the winter cathedral, tears stung at his eyes, but he blinked them back, fighting them. Only men were allowed to weep, but never dogs. Men might weep honorably in grief, in anger, or in joy. He no longer deserved such distinction.

With the tears came the cloud, a gray haze covering his vision, a roaring in his ears as clamorous as a thousand Eika howling, as maddening as a swarm of bees, as seductive as the din of battle to one confined. But that cloud was madness. He must fight the madness.

Slowly, struggling with each breath, he formed an image in his mind like to the images he saw on the windows, painted scenes from the Life of the blessed Daisan to uplift and illuminate the worshipers. He formed no holy image but rather a common one, a scene he had been struggling to build for days now, or weeks, or months; he didn't know how long it had been, only that it was winter and once, long ago, when he was a free man and captain of the King's Dragons, it had been spring.

He built in his mind's eye a manor house such as his Dragons often lodged at as they rode here and there in the kingdom, defending King Henry and his sovereignty. In this season, in winter, fields would be stripped clean of their harvest, some few budding with winter wheat. The vines and orchards would be bare; barrels of apples would line the cellars; cider would be brewed. The extra animals would have already been killed and their meat smoked or salted away against winter's barrenness and the quiet hunger of spring.

This manor house he built was no lodging place. He constructed it, in his mind, as his own, his refuge—*his* land, not another's. He had nothing of his own save his status as the king's son, his sword and spear, his shield and armor, his clothing and tent and, over the course of years, a number of horses. All else he received because of obligations owed to the king or, now and again, certain gifts from certain women. But he was careful in his affairs as in all else, obedient to his father's wish that he choose wisely and discreetly and never ever indulge himself where his interest might cause trouble farther down the road.

None of this he had now, of course, not even the gold torque he had once worn around his neck, symbol of his royal lineage. That torque now adorned Bloodheart's arm, symbol of his victory, and Sanglant wore an iron collar such as all of Bloodheart's dogs wore.

He must not think of his humiliation. He must think of other things or else he would fall into madness. He walked, in his mind, across fields and forest and pastureland. *His* lands. Through these lands he would walk, no longer outfitted for war, no longer dressed in a Dragon's tabard and armor, no longer wearing the Dragon helm that marked him as captain.

No longer a Dragon.

In this place, he was outfitted like any other noble lord, with a retinue, with servants and field hands. The outbuildings would include a stable, of course, for his horses, a byre, beehives, a forge, a weaving house.

Like any other noble lord, he would be married. This was more difficult to imagine. All his life he had been told, repeatedly, that the king's bastard son *could* not marry. Only legitimate children married. For an illegitimate one to do so might set in motion endless intrigues whose fruit would be as sour as discord. Indeed, no one had expected him to live long enough to chafe against the prohibition; he had already served as captain of the King's Dragons longer than any other man before him except wily old Conrad the Dragon.

But the lord of a manor must wed, and must beget children to inherit from him and his lady. He had always been an obedient son. Now, among the dogs, wreathed by iron and no longer by gold, he need not be.

What woman in Henry's progress, what daughter of a noble lady, might be suitable? Whom would he choose? Who would choose him?

But when he skirted the kitchens where servants prepared the evening's feast, when he passed through the broad-beamed hall, striped with afternoon's light through the narrow windows, when he crossed under the threshold and out into the garden where a lord might find his lady-wife picking herbs for healing simples or dictating a letter to her cleric, he saw no noblewoman from the king's progress waiting for him. No count's or duchess' daughter smiled up at him, greeting him with affection.

When he opened the door that led into the bedchamber, the woman who waited inside, half surprised but obviously pleased by his appearance, was the young Eagle. *Liath.*

2

IT was bitter cold, and out here by the dying fire the wind cut and burned Liath until she shuddered under its bite. But she dared not go inside where the nobles sat at table, carousing long into the night in observance of the Feast of Saint Edana of the Bonfires, whose saint's day was celebrated with much drink and good cheer. Hathui had returned from Quedlinhame, and *she* could attend the king. Better for Liath to remain outside, as far away as possible, even shivering in the breath of coming winter.

Out here the stars shone with brilliant clarity. The waning crescent moon had not yet risen. This sky was perhaps her favorite, winter's sky. The Child and the Sisters, second and third Houses of the zodiac, rode high in the heavens; the Crown of Stars, just outside the grasp of the Child, stood almost at zenith. Below, the Hunter guarded them from the *Guivre,* whose yellowish eye gleamed directly overhead. But it was not the Hunter who was fated to vanquish the dreadful *Guivre* but rather his unseen companion, the Huntress, valiant Artemē. In Andalla one could just see her where she rested among the southern stars, and Liath had even once glimpsed her golden boot, known to the Jinna as the star Suhel, the handsome one. Here in the north only her Bow and its fire-tipped Arrow star, blue-white Seirios, could be seen above the horizon.

She searched for the planets and found three. Wise Aturna, eldest and slowest of the wandering stars, moved through the Sisters, the third House, and stately Mok through the Lion. Red Jedu, the Angel of War, shone in sullen grandeur in the Penitent. A baleful influence, according to the astrologi. But Da scorned the astrologi. He called them street merchants and ignorant tinkerers and claimed they knew nothing of the *true* knowledge of the heavens. That knowledge hadn't saved him.

She shivered again in the wind's chill and put more sticks on the fire, building it until flame licked and popped up a lattice of branches. Smoke stung her nose and eyes. She chafed her hands to warm them and tugged her cloak more tightly about herself, prepared to wait out the night. The stables were close by, but even there among the horses and servants she could not feel safe. In any enclosed place *he* might corner her. Only out here, under the winter sky, did she have room to run.

The debate entertained Rosvita and to some extent surprised her. The subject was well worn, of course: *Is it better to be useful or to be good?* From his earliest days as sovereign, King Henry had encouraged such debates; his younger sister Constance, now Biscop of Autun, had excelled at them during her time at court.

No, indeed, this time it was the participants who surprised her. For once, Princess Sapientia showed wisdom and kept her mouth shut, letting others argue while she sat in the chair of honor at her father's right side and basked in the attention of the courtiers. Her younger sister Theophanu sat beside Rosvita in silence, her expression as smooth as cream; she, too, kept quiet, although she never spoke recklessly under any circumstances. Henry's youngest child, Ekkehard, actually listened to the debate, mouth half open. Like his elder sister Sapientia, he stared wide-eyed and worshipfully at the younger of the two debaters. Ekkehard had been seized with one of his admirations and this time Rosvita could not deplore his choice.

Three years ago she would have, had Ekkehard stared in this way at this particular man. But Hugh, abbot of Firsebarg and the bastard son of Margrave Judith, had altered so greatly in the five years he had been absent from the king's progress that it was only by his lineaments, his actual face and hair, that she knew him.

"The Rule of Saint Benedicta commands abbot and abbess to do good rather than to govern," said Hugh in response to Cleric Monica—she had for many years now taught all the young folk in the king's schola, where he had once been a pupil.

"But if our stewardship is given us for the profit of many,

then must we not learn to govern in order to benefit our subjects most usefully?" A vigorous elderly woman who had disliked Hugh when he was her student, Monica was softening as the debate wore on. Rosvita recognized the gleam in her eye and the quirk of her lips with which she favored only her most exemplary students. Hugh had been brilliant, but he had also known he was brilliant and wished others to acknowledge it, and that sort of arrogance had never been tolerated by a teacher such as Monica.

Now, however, Hugh smiled gently. "But of course," he said mildly, "I must bow before the wisdom of my preceptor. Is it not true that the teacher is an artist who molds her students as clay is fashioned into vessels of glory? A good student will imitate his teacher's example and strive to become her image in excellent and sublime qualities. We learn to govern, and the first person we learn to govern is ourselves. Then virtue without creates virtue within, and thus we become both good and useful."

How had Hugh, as brilliant and handsome and arrogant as he had once been, become so gracious, witty, and charming, if no less beautiful in form? His voice was moderate, his gestures composed, his manners amiable and elegant. Only this morning, when the king's progress had left the manor house at which the king had rested overnight, Hugh had distributed bread with his own hands to a family of beggars standing alongside the road. By no sign did he betray that he had any interest in Princess Sapientia except that of a well-mannered courtier privileged to ride with the king's progress.

" 'Virtues alone make one blessed.' " Monica smiled sweetly on him and began to quote at length from the *Commentary on the Dream of Cornelia* by Eustacia.

"Good and useful, indeed," whispered Theophanu suddenly to Rosvita. "I observe that my sister is now pregnant by him, so we must presume he has learned both lessons well enough."

"Theophanu!" breathed Rosvita, shocked. Belatedly, she added, "Your Highness."

Theophanu said nothing else.

Monica declaimed at length on the virtues as written in the *Commentary*. " 'Thus do the virtues come in four types, and these types are distinguished each from the other in regard to the passions. For the passions are these, Fears and Desires, Griefs and Joys, Anger, and Envy. The political virtues of prudence, temperance, courage, and justice mitigate the passions. The cleansing virtues put the passions aside. The purified and serene mind has forgotten the passions, and to the divine Mind whose virtues are exemplary, the passions are anathema.' "

Torches and candles flickered; the hearth fire burned steadily, stoked by servants. King Henry smiled softly on the two debaters, although these past months at odd moments he could be found staring off into nothing, attention lost to the matters at hand. Now he yawned, finally, and signed to his servants that his bed should be made ready. Rosvita, finishing her wine, toyed with the cup. The others made ready for sleep; Theophanu did not move.

"You do not like him," said Rosvita at last.

"You did not, before he left."

"I did not," agreed Rosvita. "But he is much changed." She watched as Father Hugh retired discreetly to the back of the hall while Sapientia waited for her camp bed to be set up behind a screen next to her father. Hugh's movements were decorous and graceful, and if it were true that virtue radiated more brightly in beauty of form, then he was virtuous, indeed. "Ai, Lady," she murmured to herself, catching herself looking at him. She had thought herself long past such half-formed yearnings, but perhaps her mind was not as serene as she hoped.

"He's very handsome," said Theophanu suddenly, standing. "Does the Psalm not say, 'The Lady desireth your beauty'?" Then she walked away to her own camp bed, modestly placed behind a curtain away from her sister.

"This bodes ill, I fear," said Rosvita to herself as she set down her winecup. She rose. Did clever Theophanu dislike Father Hugh, or was she envious at her sister's good fortune in finding such a courtier? In finding, to be blunt, such a lover? Indeed, how could Sapientia have resisted him, even though she knew he was a churchman and that it was wrong of her to desire him and wrong of him to accede to such a seduction? She was a royal princess, after all, and it was necessary for her to get with child in order to prove she was worthy of the throne. One might say, as had Theophanu, that he was only doing his duty and being useful.

One by one, torches were extinguished as nobles and servants found sleeping space in the hall of the hunting lodge where they had arrived this afternoon.

Tomorrow, the king would ride out after deer.

Tonight, some slept more restfully than others.

Liath pulled off her gloves and, her fingers clumsy with cold, found the gold feather in her pouch. Instinct had warned her not to pick up the white feather she had found beside Da's body the night he was murdered. Now she had seen what manner of creature shed such feathers. But this gold feather, plucked from the ashes of a dying fire through which she had seen a vision of the old Aoi sorcerer, had a different texture, one of promise, not pain or fear.

Drawing the feather gently through her fingers, she stared into the fire, thinking of Hanna, forming Hanna's face and expression in her mind's eye, the curve of her shoulders, the twist of her braided hair, the seal ring of the Eagles on her right middle finger. On one other occasion this past summer she had formed Hanna so in her mind, and within the gateway made by fire she had seen shadows of a narrow pass winding through mountains whipped by storm, of a landslide that had obliterated a road. Was it only her fear, imagining such a scene, or had she truly visioned Hanna in the mountains, threatened by an unseasonable storm?

Where was Hanna now? As she concentrated, spinning the feather through her fingers, she saw movement within the flames, images seen through a veil of fire.

A standing stone in the midst of a clearing burns with a fire born of no natural kindling, for it burns without fuel and gives off no heat. No one sits on the flat rock where once the old Aoi sorcerer sat and spoke to her. Sinewy plant stalks lie in a heap at the foot of the rock, awaiting his return. A rope the length of her arm lies draped over the rock. Where did he go? When will he return?

But the burning stone is itself a window, shutters opening through which she can look onto another place.

Hanna rides with three ragged Lions at her side across a

plain populated more by grass than by trees. The rising sun glints off her brass Eagle's badge. They are leaving a village, a cluster of sod huts thatched with grass; some of the roofs are scorched. The wooden palisade is also scored with fire and the scars of battle. Fresh graves lie outside the palisade and beyond them stretch empty fields dusted with fresh snow.

Ice rimes Hanna's eyebrows. In her gloved left hand she holds a broken arrow tipped with an iron point and fletched with iron-gray feathers that resemble those of no bird Liath has seen or heard tell of. The Lions, grim of face, sing as they walk; Liath cannot hear the words, but it is not a happy song. Villagers cluster at the palisade gate to call out fare-wells. One lad breaks away, bundle thrown across his back, and hurries after them. His mother weeps, but she lets him go. The Lions make room for him among their number. Hanna stares straight ahead, eyes to the west, where their path leads.

Why is Wolfhere not with Hanna? The feather brushes Liath's palm, and fire snaps and wavers. Now she sees a lofty hall illuminated by the winter sky seen through huge glass windows and by what seem a thousand candles burning in imitation of the stars. A man steps humbly forward in the way of a person brought before a regnant, and as he bows before an unseen figure, Liath recognizes him: It is Wolfhere. On the walls behind him she sees bold frescoes depicting the martyrdoms of the seven disciplas: Thecla, Peter, Matthias, Mark, Johanna, Lucia, and Marian. Is this the audience chamber of the skopos in Darre?

He straightens up, and his eyes lift to take in a dimly-seen person sitting in great state on a gilded chair. His nostrils flare in surprise. He murmurs a name under his breath.

"Liath."

Liath started back, remembering all at once that there was also danger within the vision made by fire. *They* were looking for her, and they could see her when she wandered in the flames.

But it was too late.

Their touch came, fingers laid lightly on her shoulders.

Ai, Lady. Not *their* fingers.

His.

"Liath, my beauty." His hand closed over her shoulder and with that grip he forced her to rise and turn away from the fire to face him. The wind was not more cold than his expression. "So at last I find you alone." He smiled.

She jerked away, but he held on to her, not letting go. She caught back a whimper. Ai, Lady, she dared not let him know how scared she was. Clutching the feather behind her back, she stared at the fine brocade on his tunic and willed herself to become as hard as stone.

"You look well, my beauty. And perhaps it is best I have looked but little upon you these past six days since I came to the king's progress, or I should have been dreadfully tempted."

She said nothing, but she knew he was still smiling. She felt, though his left hand did not touch her, that hand close and then open, flexing. His right hand burned her shoulder as if ice pressed against her skin.

"Do you have nothing to say to me, Liath?"

She said nothing. She moved not at all. She was stone, heavy, insensible.

"I am not happy that you left me," he said in his most gentle voice. "Indeed, I am disappointed. But I forgive you. You didn't know what you were doing. And it matters not. What happened that day means nothing to us. You are still my precious slave."

"No!" She wrenched away from him, almost falling into the fire as her heel scattered coals and burning brands. Heedless, she stooped to grab the end of a burning stick and held it out like a sword. "I am free of you. Wolfhere set me free!"

He laughed, delighted. "This is the Liath I remember and the one that the court will see beside me, in the fullness of time, when I can display you as you are meant to be displayed. But no one can see us now." He touched a finger to his lips to enjoin her to silence. His handsome face looked no less beautiful in the firelight, adorned by shifting light and shadow. "Look you, Liath." He lifted his left hand, two fingers raised, and murmured a word. The burning stick extinguished as if a sudden gust of wind had blown it out.

Her voice caught in her, and all that came out was a fragile whisper of sound, more breath than word.

"A child's trick," he said modestly, "but we must all begin somewhere." He carefully drew the stick out of her hand and tossed it away. "Wolfhere did not set you free. He stole you from me. I have not yet laid my grievance against Wolfhere before King Henry, who will pass judgment. Be assured I will—although, alas, I must wait until Sapientia has the child and it lives and is healthy. After that blessed event my position at court will be unassailable. But until then, Liath, do not think you have escaped me. We will ride together and speak together, sing together and feast together, and you shall be near me every hour of every day."

"I am not your slave," she repeated stubbornly, hand smarting from the sting of the brand. "Wolfhere freed me."

He shook his head as a wise father considers his child's foolishness. "Wolfhere? Wolfhere wants you for his own reasons. Don't think Wolfhere took you except to use you himself."

"Not in *that* way." Then, horrified she had spoken of such a thing when they were alone, she tried again to bolt.

He was too fast for her, and his grip was strong as he took hold of her arms and pulled her against him. "In what way, Liath? No, not in *that* way. He and his kind have other plans for you, no doubt."

"What do you know of Wolfhere and his kind?" Ai, Lady, what if Hugh truly knew something and could tell her? How much would she be willing to give him in return?

But he only sighed deeply and kissed her on the forehead. She shuddered, paralyzed by the sick, helpless fear in her belly. He did not let go of her. "I will be honest with you, Liath, as I have always been honest with you. I only suspect Wolfhere works in league with other unknown people. He was thrown out of court for *something,* some act, some opinion, and it is well known he has mastered the art of seeing through fire and stone. Surely he must have other skills, or be in league with those who do. I know your father was murdered, and I know he was trying to hide you, his most precious treasure. Therefore, someone else must be looking for you. Does that not follow? If they are willing to murder your father, how can you expect kindness from them? You will wish most devoutly, my beauty, that you were back in my bed if they get hold of you, as they will, if you don't come back to me. I can protect you."

"I don't want your protection." Twisting, she tried to

spin out of his grasp, but he was too strong. And she was too weak.

"You are bound to me," he whispered. "You will always be bound to me. No matter where you run, I will always find you. You will always come back to me."

She glimpsed a figure in the gloom, a servingman out in the night, perhaps walking to the privies. "I beg you, friend!" she called out to him, her voice ragged with fear.

Hugh wrenched her arm tightly up against her back, trapping her. The servingman turned, his face indistinguishable in the darkness—but her position was silhouetted plainly by the fire.

"How fare you, friend?" the man asked. "Need you help?"

"Please—" Liath began, but Hugh pressed his free hand to her throat and suddenly she *could not speak.*

"Nay, brother," answered Hugh sternly. "We need no help here. You may move on."

Whether because he recognized the voice of a nobleman, the robes of a churchman, or was simply obedient to a tone in Hugh's voice which he could not resist, the man turned away and vanished on his errand, abandoning her.

"No," she whispered, finding her voice again when Hugh lowered his hand.

"Yes." Hugh smiled. "You are mine, Liath. You will love me in the end."

"I love someone else," she said hoarsely. The feather, still hidden, burned like a hot coal against her free hand. "I love another man."

She only knew how gentle he had been before because he now went white with rage and shook her viciously. "Who? *Who is it?*"

Unable to help herself, she began to weep. "Ai, Lady, he's dead."

"Any man you love will die, for I proclaim it so. I will make it so. Love no one, love only me, and you will be safe."

"I will never love you. I *hate* you."

"Hate is only the other face of love, my beauty. You cannot hate what you cannot also love. My beautiful Liath. How I love the sound of your name on my lips."

She believed him. That was the worst of it. He spoke so

persuasively, and his voice was so soft—except she knew what he was, she had seen that glimpse of it when she made him angry.

"I will always treat you well," he said as if he had heard her thoughts, "as long as you obey me."

She began again to cry. Seeing her reduced to weeping in front of him, her fear and weakness revealed utterly, he let go of her. Like a rabbit miraculously released from the clutches of a hawk, she ran.

"Where will you go?" he called after her, mocking her as she ran. "You will never escape me, Liath. Never."

She ran to the stables where so many animals and stablehands crammed in together that breath and sweat made the air almost warm. But she would never be warm again.

3

ANNA shivered as wind wailed through the trees. Snowflakes spun down; a thin dusting made the ground bright, and the wind shuddered branches of trees and shook snow from them in sudden waterfalls of white.

It was so cold.

Here in the shelter of a fir tree, she had at least some respite from the constant cut of wind. But there was never any respite from fear or from the pit of hunger that yawned in her belly like the dreaded Abyss. Two horses also sheltered under the cave made by the fir's branches; with reins wrapped loosely around a crook in one thick branch, they snuffled at the forest litter, trying to graze. *"Watch the horses,"* two of Lord Wichman's soldiers had ordered her after finding her foraging in the woods. *"Pull the reins free and flee if the Eika approach."*

She hadn't known she was so close to Eika. She stayed within the cover of trees on her daily foraging expeditions into the forest, but every day she had to search farther away from the battered holding of Steleshame to find any pittance to add to the shared pot. In this way, with the young lord growing bored of Master Helvidius' poetry and Mistress Gisela eager to exclude anyone who didn't "earn their keep," Anna staved off the cold knife of starvation. It would not have been like this if Matthias hadn't died.

She shuddered. She could not bear to think about Matthias. Maybe it would have been better to have died with him, it hurt so much to be without him. But the old poet and the child relied on her as well; she had to go on.

She rubbed her hands and listened. She had been told to stay on the lee of the hill, to save the horses should things go awry. Yet, there *was* grass atop the hill, yellowed and dry under the winter sky and high enough to hide her. If she could watch the raid, wouldn't she be better able to protect herself and the horses she had been put in charge of? What if the soldiers' blades couldn't penetrate Eika hides? What if Lord Wichman and his men were all killed and the Eika came searching for her and she didn't know they were coming? What if she were unable to flee, or the reins wouldn't unwrap from the tree limb? What if she fell from the horse? She didn't know how to ride.

Maybe it would be better to wait here by the horses, to wait for the soldiers to return, driving captured cattle before them, but she couldn't bear to wait as if she were blind and crippled.

And anyway, there was nothing she could see on this day that would be worse than what she had already seen in this past year.

She crept up the slope on hands and knees. Grass rustled under her weight and she froze, then slowly crawled to the crest, checking always to assure herself that the foxtails waved above her head. At the top of the hill lay a large gray rock with dry orange lichen clinging to it as if to a scaly hide. From behind this screen she dared to peer down into the vale.

A single ragged byre stood at the far end of the vale. Cattle grazed in their dull fashion, watched over by three slaves dressed in far less than what Anna wore. They leaned heavily on staves. Occasionally a cow lifted its head from the grass to low nervously. Goats strayed over one rise beyond which Anna could see copses of trees and the suggestion of floodplain; if she moved *just* enough she might be able to see the towers of Gent in the distance. A woman so weak that she frequently stumbled hurried after the straying goats and herded them back. Anna could not count very high, but there were plenty of cattle and goats just in this one sheltered vale where grass still covered the hillside. No doubt these livestock had been stolen from Steleshame or some other unfortunate village. According to the reports brought in by the mounted soldiers, many such herds grazed the lands around Gent now, good cropland which had gone to seed under the stewardship of the Eika.

Lord Wichman and his soldiers weren't raiding, not really; they were just getting back what the Eika had stolen.

A few trees stood in this pasture, which by the patchwork of grass, some long and dying, some short and new, had perhaps once been a series of long, narrow fields. But cattle, grass, and slaves did not hold her attention for long. Other objects stood in the vale, and these she could not help but stare at with a grim, hungry fear pulling at her gut.

Rising above the grass, occasionally under a tree yet most often atop a gentle rise, stood a number of standing stones the same hue as the stone she lay beside but tall and monolithic rather than low and rugged. No Eika with gleaming skin and ice-white hair, with jewel-studded teeth and fierce spear point, stood guard over the slaves and the precious livestock. Nothing stood here except those dozen stones, yet the slaves did not run in the face of such freedom.

Of Lord Wichman and his soldiers she saw no sign.

She knew these stones, they were somehow familiar to her, each alike, each . . . a threat.

The stone nearest to her stood at the base of the slope at whose height she knelt. Its pitted surface lay a bit more than a long bow-shot away. Hadn't it been farther away when she first peeked out? Why would stones stand out here in the middle of this vale, in no discernible pattern? Why did they look different from the boulder she hid behind? Why did no lichen grow on them?

She stared at the stone, frightened. Something was not right here. What was it Master Helvidius had said about illusion?

But it was only a stone.

Her pouch dug into her thigh, the scant reward for her hours of foraging. She had found a few handfuls of acorns which could be leached and ground up into gruel, withered nettle and parsley to flavor soup, and a dead squirrel.

Her thoughts wandered to those happy days when Matthias had labored in the tannery and Helvidius had sung for the lordling every night, when she had begged scraps of food from the soldiers and they had eaten every day. Now they were always so terribly hungry, and little Helen had barely strength to cry. Maybe it would have been more merciful to have left her to die with her mother and infant sibling.

Slowly, while she stared without truly seeing, the stone took shape as illusion toys with the form of things: a spear point, a head, eyes peering up at her, seeing her . . . it was not a standing stone at all but an Eika soldier creeping one cautious step at a time toward her, easing up the low rise.

Terror seized her heart. Goose prickles rose on her arms and neck. She wanted to scream, yet no sound rose out of her throat.

"They find you if you scream," Matthias had said when *they lay in the stinking tanning pit while Eika and their dogs prowled the deserted tanning grounds. "Lie still without a noise."*

Yet would a scream turn it back into stone? Would a scream wake her up and free her from this nightmare? Would the two soldiers come running to save her? They were still out there somewhere, hiding, searching for the Eika guards. . . .

Or had the Eika already slain them?

Did the soldiers see only stones and fail to strike? Had they been cut down unaware that they already faced their foe in the guise of unmoving rock?

Movement stirred in the dark entrance to the byre, a figure ducking out from under the low roof. Smaller than the others, this one had a bad limp and a familiar tilt to his head.

At last the scream rose out of her throat, loud and piercing.

"Matthias!" She could not help herself. She leaped to her feet. "Matthias!"

His name carried upon the breeze and across the vale. Most of the cattle lifted their heads, dull wits responding at last to this unknown sound.

The Eika stalking her froze in its tracks, as if trying to turn itself again to stone, but it was too late. The waning rays of the sun silhouetted every detail of form—no dream at all, but illusion shrouding it: the obsidian leaf-shaped spear; the jut of its lips and the gleam of teeth beneath; the smooth sheen of gold-tinted scales that were its skin. All showed plainly now, illusion banished. A dozen Eika stood frozen in the vale, like statues, and not until the first of the soldiers sprang from his hiding place in the grass and struck a fierce blow did the Eika realize their illusion was shattered.

They moved, dashing to fight, but the trick had worked against them. As a half dozen soldiers rushed in and the pound of hooves alerted Anna to the arrival of Lord Wichman, the Eika ran here and there, almost at random as if, separated, they were confused.

The Eika below her took two great strides up the hill, then, hesitating, turned back toward the vale. From the far slope ten horsemen crested the hill, Lord Wichman at their head, and raced down the gentle slope at a full gallop. Swords held high, they bore down in pairs upon their scattered foes. Another six soldiers appeared from the grass with spears.

An Eika with a large stone ax rushed a spearman. The huge form of the Eika eclipsed the warrior so Anna could see only the Eika as the two met. The point of the spear pushed through the Eika's back; the two fighters twisted around, both now visible. As he was forced to the ground, the spearman's spear shaft bowed as the man attempted to shift the Eika aside to avoid a blow from the creature's ax. The haft snapped and the ax fell hard upon the warrior's leg. A sound reached Anna; she did not know whether it was that of the broken spear or of splintering bone. Still from the ground, first with the splintered shaft of wood and then with a dagger the man rained thrusts and blows upon the face and neck of the Eika until it at last lay still. All over the field Eika fell, most in silence, some in flight.

Matthias dashed back into the shelter of the byre. Of the other slaves, one followed him into the ragged shelter while the other two ran for freedom.

"Matthias!" she shrieked. He had to run *now*. What if the others retreated and some of the Eika were left alive?

The Eika at the base of her hill turned at the sound of her voice and raced up the hill—whether to flee the fight or to catch her she did not know. But it made no difference. A knife in the hand of a starving girl was no match for a spear wielded by an Eika warrior.

Anna bolted. She scrambled, half sliding, half leaping, down the slope, back to the safety of the tree where she should have remained all along. Distantly, she heard the shouts of Lord Wichman and his men.

If she could only reach the horses, she would have the safety promised her by his soldiers.

But the Eika was far swifter, and quickly he closed to within a few paces. She heard his breath behind her, felt his presence; his long shadow reached out to encompass, to blot out, her slight shadow that danced across the ground as she ran. But though it was useless, she could not stop running.

Another sound drowned out the heavy stamp of the Eika feet—the pound of hooves. A taller shadow, a man upon a horse, overtook them both and a trilling war cry shattered the air. She dove and rolled. The long thin line of a sword leaped ahead of the mesh of shadows upon the grass and then it cut down into the darkness. There was a thud behind her. The horseman passed her, slowing and then bringing his mount around. She stuck out her hands and knees and stopped herself, rose up, hands and face scratched and just beginning to bleed softly. Her breath came in such gulping gasps that she thought she couldn't get any air in. She twisted around.

The Eika lay behind her sprawled on its belly, cleaved from shoulder to spine. Its ugly head was twisted up to the left, almost all of the way around. Life drained rapidly from its eyes. It wore no wooden Circle on a thong around its neck. It had sworn no allegiance to the kin of humankind. Ai, Lady, it—and its brothers—had killed so many of her people and probably Papa Otto, too. It would have killed Matthias, given the chance.

She stood, bent, and spit in its face, but it was already dead.

"Ai, there, child!" The horseman reined up beside her. He unhooked his helm and pulled it off. She stared up, astonished, at Lord Wichman himself. He had a crazed look in his eyes and a wild grin on his lips. "You're the one my men found foraging in the woods. Why didn't you go with the refugees we sent off months ago, to the marchlands? You're a cursed nuisance, almost ruining our raid like that."

He had the full cheeks of a man who doesn't want for food, even in hard times. Terrified, she did not know how to address him. No lord had ever even noticed her before.

At last, stammering, she found her voice. "Master Helvidius is my grandfather, my lord." The lie came conveniently to her lips. "I had to stay with him, and he was too ill to walk so far when the others left."

He grunted, sheathing his sword. "He'll have a victorious tale to sing tonight. A good sixty cattle and as many goats we've claimed back today." His grin was fierce and sure, and he looked ready to ride out this minute on another raid. "Go on, then." He gestured to the west. Snow blew and skittered round him, white flakes spinning in the wind. "It's a long walk back to Steleshame."

Then he turned and rode away to meet a half dozen of his mounted soldiers. They headed east. Anna ran for the top of the hill and there—

All the breath slammed out of her as if she had been struck in the stomach. *There!* At last she found breath to shout.

"Matthias!"

With the other slaves, rescued now, he had formed up to help the remaining soldiers herd cattle and goats back to Steleshame. Hearing her voice, he started away, cast about, then saw her and limped up the slope.

She burst into tears and ran down to meet him. Ai, Lady, he was all bone with only a layer of skin holding him together.

"You're so thin," he said, hugging her tightly. "Oh, Anna! I thought I'd never see you again."

She couldn't speak she was sobbing so hard.

"Hush, now," he said. "It's over and done with."

"It's not done with! It's never done with! They'll never go away. They'll always be here, hunting us, won't they?"

"Hush, Anna," he said more sternly. Because she had learned to obey him, she choked down her sobs and quieted. "I just thought of Papa Otto," he continued. "I thought if Papa Otto could survive even after he lost everyone in his family, then I could, too, knowing you still lived."

"But you didn't know I still lived—you saw them attack—"

"I had to believe it!"

That silenced her.

"Come now." He took her hand. The herd had begun to creep sluggishly westward. "Other Eika will come when this group don't report back to the main camp. We've got to be long gone. Lord Above, Anna, why were you with them? Are there so few of you left at Steleshame that they're taking children out to fight?"

Like the Eika made by illusion into stone, he appeared to her different than what she had known before. Still familiar, he was no longer the same Matthias. He was not a boy any longer.

"There aren't any dogs here," she said softly, to say something, finally beginning to tremble with reaction. Her feet hurt, and her nose was cold.

They fell in line with the others. Matthias used his stave to nudge back a straying goat. "The dogs kill the cows, and the Eika would have to spend more time guarding the cows against the dogs than the cows against—well—a raid like this. Out here with the livestock we don't see many dogs."

"What's wrong with your leg?" she asked.

But he only shook his head and would not answer.

It took them the rest of the day to walk back to Steleshame. Matthias' limp got progressively worse, and finally one of the soldiers took pity on him and let him ride behind him.

Mistress Gisela fell into ecstasies, seeing what a great number of livestock had been rescued from the Eika. At once, she ordered her servants to prepare a thanksgiving feast.

Anna led Matthias out to a hovel in the courtyard where she, Helvidius, and Helen made their home, such as it was. Stuck cheek by jowl with a number of other hovels constructed after the attack, the tiny hut had at least the benefit of lying within the newly reconstructed palisade wall. No one slept outside the palisade now; of course, Steleshame was no longer as crowded as it had once been.

Master Helvidius sent Anna to sit with Helen while he tended to Matthias' leg, grumbling all the while about Mistress Gisela and her airs of nobility: "Feasting when there isn't enough to feed the weakest! The biscop of Gent would have fed the poor, bless her memory!"

Matthias was feverish, too restless to sleep, too nauseated to eat much more than a sip of ale and a crust of bread, but at last he fell asleep on their single pallet, little Helen curled up at his chest. Anna heaped all three blankets over him and resigned herself to shivering out the night.

"Nay," said Helvidius. "You'll come with me into the hall. No use your getting sick when you have both of them to tend for. And there'll be roasted cow, I'll wager. You can grab a bone before the dogs get to it." Thus coaxed, Anna reluctantly left Matthias and the little girl.

But later that night as Anna sat half-dozing by the hearth, after Lord Wichman had returned from his scouting expedition, after he and his men had feasted and the fortunate servants been allowed to wolf down their scraps, after Helvidius had serenaded the young lord endlessly with his exploits, a sudden cold undercurrent chilled the girl like a wordless cry for help.

Quite drunk now, soldiers sang a bawdy tune as Mistress Gisela retired to the shadowy end of the hall. Anna heard angry words hushed as though under a blanket. But at last the householder returned bearing the prize which Lord Wichman had so far not obtained.

Gisela's niece, as pretty a woman as Anna had ever seen, was led forward, decked out in whatever fine garb had survived unscathed from the autumn attack on the holding. The young woman's expression wore no emotion at all; she seemed, like the Eika, more statue than living being. But Lord Wichman smiled broadly and toasted her beauty with one more cup of wine. Then he took her hand and she went, unresisting, to his curtained bed while his soldiers cheered and laughed.

A servant went outside with a bucket of slops for the pigs. As the door opened, the night's wind cast a sudden cold glamour over the hall like the breath of the winter sky, turning the ground to frost.

Then the door shut and, as with a collective breath, the soldiers began to drink and sing again.

Much later, when even the most stalwart fellow snored and Helvidius slept with his head pillowed on his arm, she heard the sound of a woman weeping softly.

4

IT was a symptom of the remarkable persistence of lust-fulness in humankind that no matter how cold and dreary the weather outside and how cramped the conditions inside, folk did find ways to carry on more—or less—discreet affairs. Certain of Rosvita's younger clerics had the habit, both annoying and amusing, of keeping track of who was sleeping with whom.

"—and Villam has a new concubine, which I grant you is nothing unusual, but I swear to you I saw her sharing her favors, such as they are, with Lord Amalfred." Brother Fortunatus was one of the many sons of the robust and prolific Countess of Hesbaye as well as by far the worst gossip among the clerics.

"Perhaps when Lord Amalfred returns to Salia, he will take the concubine with him and spare poor Villam the pain of her duplicity," said Sister Amabilia.

"Ah, well, Villam no doubt has his eye on more succulent prey. I swear I saw him eyeing the young Eagle."

"Our friend the hawk?" asked quiet Sister Odila, astonished.

"Of course not! The dark one. But you know how Eagles are and the code they swear to. Eagles don't indulge themselves in such a way, except among their own number. But I have observed some new developments in other places—hands meeting and petting in the bowl at table, if you take my meaning.

Sister Amabilia sighed profoundly, and Brother Fortunatus looked downcast that his hint provoked no greater reaction than this. "Even so," Amabilia said in a weary voice, "it isn't half as interesting now as when Prince Sanglant was alive."

"I beg you," said Rosvita sternly. "Do not speak disrespectfully of the dead."

Brother Constantine looked up from his muller where he ground vermilion to form the base of red ink. "I never saw Prince Sanglant. He was gone before I arrived here."

"Ai, well," said Sister Amabilia. "Court was much livelier when Prince Sanglant graced it."

"I will thank you," said Rosvita, setting down her quill pen, "not to mention his name within the king's hearing." She tested the point of the pen on her finger, sighed, and picked up her penknife to recut the tip of the quill.

"But he was only a fighter," said Brother Constantine. "Surely he could not have cut such a fine figure, so elegant and charming in manners, so affable and benevolent, so even-tempered, so *learned,* as Father Hugh."

Amabilia sniffed. "Father Hugh ought to be tending to his monastery rather than playing the courtier. But I have been with the king's progress for eight years, Constantine—"

"As you are ever reminding me," muttered the young cleric.

"—and I recall Frater Hugh when he was at the schola here. A bird's feathers may change in color, but it's the same duck inside!"

"And you will be at your task another eight years, Sister," Rosvita said gently, "if you do not set yourself to work."

For all of Amabilia's tart character, she had a remarkably sweet smile, which she used now to good effect. She had also the finest hand Rosvita had ever seen, master of the *Litteras Gallica* and *Tulay-tilah* as well as knowing the antique *Scripta Actuaria.* For this reason, though she was not of the highest nobility, she had become a fixture in the king's chapel; she also taught writing to the most promising students in the king's schola. "I beg your pardon, Sister Rosvita. You are right to reproach me for my unseemly attachment to the amusements the world affords."

"To the amusements *people* afford," said Constantine reprovingly. He really was too serious given how very young he was, not above fifteen.

"God gave us eyes so that we could observe and a tongue with which to speak our minds!"

"And humility teaches us to cast our eyes to the ground and to keep silence!"

"My children," said Rosvita without raising her voice. "Attend to your tasks."

Constantine flushed and bent back to the muller, now

mixing white of egg and a bit of gum arabic into the vermilion powder. Amabilia did not look chastened; for all that she had a wicked eye for human foibles, she was at peace with herself. She sharpened her quill and returned to her work: making a copy of the precious *Vita of Saint Radegundis* for the library at Quedlinhame. The other clerics, some listening, some not, worked on in pleasant silence. Rosvita bent back to her *History*.

She read over what she had most recently accomplished: the crowning of the first Henry, Duke of Saony, as King of Wendar and of his wife, Lucienna, Count of Attomar, as queen; his speech before the nobles and their acclamation of his rule; certain small rebellions and battles as well as armed struggle with the Varren queen, Gisela. With red ink she wrote in the initial line to a new chapter, then changed to black.

> "To Henry and his most renowned wife Lucienna were born these children, the first called Arnulf, beloved by all the world, the second, brave and industrious, called Otto, while the third, Kunigunde, Mother of Quedlinhame Convent, was a woman of singular wisdom and authority. Henry had also another daughter, named Haduidis, who married Immed, Margrave of Eastfall. Lucienna had another child, a son named Reginbern. This son rode as captain of the Dragons. He fought against the Eika who were at the time laying waste to Saony, and so ruthlessly waged war against them that they were driven away and feared even to sail within sight of the Wendish coast for many years.

> "When all these wars ceased, there came into the east country of Saony an army of Quman horsemen, burning cities and towns and monasteries. They worked such slaughter that it is better to pass over this destruction in silence rather than set it all down again in words. However, it happened that one of the Quman princes was captured. Margrave Immed brought him to the king, but he was so esteemed by his kin that the Quman offered to King Henry as much gold and silver as ten wagons could carry for the prince's ransom. But the king despised their gold and demanded peace, which they gave him in return for the prisoner and certain other gifts."

From outside she heard the return of the hunters and the clamor of horses, hounds, and voices in the forecourt. She rose, needing an excuse to stretch her back, and crossed to the door. In the yard beyond, King Henry laughed at a comment by his trusted companion, Margrave Helmut Villam, while Father Hugh dismounted and turned to help Princess Sapientia dismount. Behind, courtiers crowded around; farther back, servants carried in a number of deer, several brace of partridge, an auroch, and a boar.

Sapientia hurried away toward the necessarium and, as smoothly as a silk robe slips down over a body, Hugh turned to assist Princess Theophanu in dismounting—though, as good a horseman as she was and with a servant already prepared to take her foot in his hands, she scarcely needed such aid. But Hugh offered kindnesses to every person, regardless of rank. Did Theophanu's hand linger longer in his than was necessary? Was that blush in her cheeks from the wind, or his touch? Turning away from the door, moving back to make room for the king's entrance, Rosvita wondered what Brother Fortunatus might say had he witnessed that little scene and was then irritated with herself for even thinking such a thing.

The courtfolk flooded into the hall, brash with their success at the hunt. Ekkehard followed at Hugh's heels like a love-smitten puppy. King Henry seated himself in his chair. Servants brought water and linen and wiped his hands clean of dirt and blood. Luckily, this hall—the third at which they had stopped—was the largest of the royal hunting lodges in Thurin Forest; though the crowd of people entering was large, it did not overwhelm the gabled hall. Sapientia entered and shed her cloak, then seated herself in the place of honor beside her father. Now poor folk who had walked a half day from the forest's edge were let in to receive alms from the king. As they left through a side door, Hugh assisted Ekkehard in dispensing bread to them while Sapientia, from across the hall, watched with greedy eyes.

Theophanu came, as she always did, to sit beside Rosvita. Her cheeks were still flushed.

"I hope you have not taken a fever," said Rosvita, setting aside her work.

Theophanu flashed her a startled glance, then, as quickly, composed herself. "I trust I have caught no fever from

which I cannot recover." She played with the fabric of her
riding tunic, rolling the cloth up between thumb and
forefinger.

Amabilia looked up from her copying on the other side
of the long table but, mercifully, did not speak.

"Where is my most valued cleric?" asked the king after
all the alms seekers had been led back outside. "Rosvita."
She rose obediently. "Read to us, I pray you. Something
eloquent and pleasant to the ear that may yet educate us."

Rosvita signed to Amabilia and the younger woman set
aside her pen so that Rosvita could take up the *Vita.* "Shall
I continue to read from the *Life of Saint Radegundis,* Your
Majesty?" she asked.

He nodded.

Ekkehard, settling himself at his father's feet, piped up.
"Let Father Hugh read. He has such a fine voice. I am sure
I learn more than I might otherwise just from listening to
his cadences as he reads."

Theophanu's cheeks burned. The king looked startled.
Sapientia gloated.

Hugh stood over by the door next to the young Eagle,
Liath; he was wiping crumbs from his hands but he looked
up and smiled gently, giving the cloth into the care of a
servant before walking forward. "Your notice would flatter
any man, Your Highness," he said to Ekkehard, "but I am
unworthy of such praise. Our esteemed Sister Rosvita has
by so far outshone me in every branch of knowledge and
in good manners that I know only too well how poorly I
compare to her. 'To one desiring to know by what path
blessedness is reached, the reply is, "Know thyself." ' " He
bowed respectfully toward Cleric Monica, who was seated
on a bench near a shuttered window, close by the hearth
and yet out of the worst of the smoke. But Rosvita thought
for one instant that his gaze skipped to and halted on the
figure of the young Eagle, Liath, hovering by the door as
if she wanted to escape outside.

Interestingly, the Eagle's expression seemed composed
of equal parts loathing, fear, and humiliation, though she
struggled to maintain a blank facade. No one else was looking at her, and by now Hugh's gaze had traveled on. Only
Rosvita kept half an eye on her, still curious about that
book—*Had* she stolen it?—and her ability to read.

"Your humility is a good example for the others, Father Hugh," said Cleric Monica.

"Do please read to us," said Ekkehard.

Rosvita was too wise to protest. She presented the book to Hugh. "I, too, hope that you will read to us, Father Hugh."

"You are too generous," he said, but he took the book.

"Indeed," muttered Sister Amabilia.

Rosvita sat down again. Theophanu, restless, was still playing with her gown, her gaze fixed on her elder sister's face.

Henry gestured to the seat beside him, opposite Sapientia. If he was taken aback at this change, he showed no sign on his face; he seemed as pleased by Hugh's presence as he would have been at Rosvita's—which unpleasant thought she berated herself for immediately.

Hugh opened the book, cleared his throat softly, and began to read.

"Here begins the Life. The most blessed Radegundis was born into a family of the highest earthly rank. She came of the royal bloodline in the barbarian nation of the Athamanni, youngest daughter of King Bassir and niece of Queen Hermingard, for it was the custom of that country to set brother and sister to rule together. But the Enemy works as cunningly as any burglar who wishes to divine the treasures most worth stealing out of a house, yet work in utter darkness. This the burglar accomplishes by tossing a fine sand into each corner of the room so that she may deduce the value of the object by the sound the sand makes when it strikes that object. So, too, do the creatures of the Enemy toss a fine sand of evil suggestion among the treasures of the human heart and by this means divine what they may steal.

"In this way Queen Hermingard suddenly lost her natural feeling of kinship for her brother. Inviting him and his guests to a banquet, she had them all murdered. It happened that among his guests were several Salian lords, and when news of this treachery got back to Salia, their kin were so outraged that they gathered together a host and descended upon the Athamanni and wiped them out. Only some few of the children survived, among them the saintly

*Radegundis. It was her lot to be quarreled over by certain
lords as part of the plunder, each of them desiring her to
come into his grasp. When news of her terrible plight
reached the great emperor Taillefer, he had her removed
from their keeping and placed under the care of guardians
at his royal villa in Baralcha.*

*"Here she was taught her letters and became familiar
with the treatises on agriculture by Palladius and Columel-
lina, and learned to maintain inventories, and other things
suitable to a lady who will manage an estate. She would
often converse with other children being raised at the villa
about her desire to become a martyr. She herself brought
the scraps left from table to the poor assembled outside,
and with her own hands she washed the head and hands
of each poor beggar child. Often she would polish the
pavement by the Hearth with her own dress, and the dust
that drifts around the altar she would collect in a napkin
and place reverently outside the door rather than sweep
it away."*

Abruptly Sapientia choked down a giggle, then blurted out,
"God help us. She sounds much like Lady Tallia. Do you
suppose Radegundis is Tallia's great-great-grandmother?"

Henry, frowning, turned to his daughter. "Do not speak
so lightly of a blessed saint, Sapientia. No child came of
the marriage between her and the emperor, and after his
death she cloistered herself in the convent for full fifty
years. It is unseemly to suggest she might have lapsed from
her vows."

There was a sudden profound silence while everyone
in the hall attempted *not* to look at Father Hugh, whose
lapse so prominently showed in the swell of Sapientia's
belly. Brother Fortunatus squeaked and snorted, stifling
a laugh.

Theophanu stood up and went forward. "I will read now,
if you will," she said, and for this rescue was rewarded with
a charming smile from Hugh.

"Showing off your accomplishments?" said Sapientia.

The book had not yet touched Theophanu's hand, but
her cheeks flushed as if her sister had slapped her. "At
least I have some!"

"Children," said Henry sharply. He took the book from

Hugh, closed it with gentle care for the binding, and beckoned to Rosvita. "If you will, Sister, read to us."

"I don't *want* to hear any more of that story." Sapientia smoothed a hand over her abdomen, then rose restlessly and wandered over to the fire. Lords and ladies parted to let her through; a few of the wiser souls had slipped out the door, escaping the heat, but most remained. A public quarrel between the royal sisters would enliven any long winter's evening.

A plague on all of them, thought Rosvita grimly as she went forward to take the book, and then berated herself for her ill temper. But as winter chilled the air outside, so did it chill the mind and heart, and quarrels always surfaced under the winter sky that had been lulled to sleep by summer's warmth and cheer. Yet, in almost nineteen years Rosvita had never seen Theophanu lose her temper, not even as a small child. What had caused her to do so now, and at such small provocation?

"I have nothing to do here," said Sapientia, striding back to her father's chair. "If you made me Margrave of Eastfall, as you promised, then I would have lands of my own to administer until—" She broke off, had the grace to flush.

"Sit," said Henry. He did not glance at his courtiers, but he knew they were all listening. "I do not wish you to leave my side until you are safely brought to childbed."

Sapientia fidgeted, glanced toward the other end of the hall where servants prepared tables for the night's feast, and set her mouth in a sulky frown.

"I will ask our clerics," said Henry, setting a hand on her arm placatingly, "what copies we have of these agricultural treatises, perhaps even the ones mentioned in the *Life of Saint Radegundis.* You may have them read to you."

Sapientia considered this. She sighed. "It's a fair idea, Father. But I want an Eagle or two for myself as well, so that I may have people to send at my own beck and call. It is only what is due my new consequence, isn't it?"

"It would be fitting," he agreed, aware, as he always was, that every soul in the hall waited on his judgment. He glanced toward Hathui, newly returned from her errand to Quedlinhame, then around the room. Four Eagles were in attendance on him right now, many more out on some errand or another, such as Wolfhere and his young compan-

ion who had journeyed south to Aosta with the renegade
biscop, Antonia.

Theophanu had retreated in silence and during the exchange had gotten all the way to the door unremarked.
Now, looking about, Henry saw her just as she stepped
outside into a soft rain. Liath still stood, obedient, beside
the door.

"There is one I would be willing to part with," said
Henry. Hathui looked up sharply. Hugh did not look at all.
"She is young and strong, and she has proved herself at
Gent. I have also heard it said that she is very accomplished
for a common Eagle. My clerics say she can read."

Sapientia grimaced. "I don't want one who can read so
that everyone will remember that I can't and Theophanu
can. And anyway, she's too pretty. I don't like her. What
about this one, Father?" She gestured toward Hathui.

Reading the simple upward quirk of an eyebrow, Rosvita
deduced that Henry had had enough—either of Sapientia
betraying her lack of wisdom and patience before the assembled court or of himself for allowing it to go on. "You
may take the one offered you, daughter—or none at all."

"Princess Sapientia," interposed Hugh gently, "is it not
true that one Eagle is as like to another as are the field
mice to our eyes?"

"But she's educated. They all say so. It was all the clerics
were talking about when we arrived. Don't you remember?"

"Do they really speak so much about a common Eagle?"
he asked, and his tone was the very model of a reproof
disguised as quiet amazement.

She shrugged, recalling her dignity and position.

"Let me discover if it is true that she is educated," said
Hugh. "I will question her." He inclined his head toward
the king. "With your permission, Your Majesty."

Henry signed, and the young Eagle came and knelt before him. She looked to Rosvita rather like a field mouse
forced into the clutches of an owl. The prospect of such
entertainment excited the interest of the court almost as
much as did the quarrel—now denied them—between the
royal sisters. Those who had slipped away to warm themselves by the other hearth or to try to claim beds for the
night in one of the sidechambers now returned.

"Let me see." Hugh tapped fingers together as he considered. Liath kept her gaze fixed on the king's boots. "You can read Dariyan, can you not, child?" he asked kindly.

"Y—yes," she murmured, keeping her eyes lowered.

"Yes?"

"Yes, Father Hugh."

"Do you consider yourself well educated?"

Now she hesitated.

"Come now," said the king. "You need not fear any word you speak plainly and honestly in front of me."

"So my da told me," she said finally, still staring at the king's boots.

"Is that a yes?" asked Hugh, evidently puzzled by this answer—or wanting her to state it plainly.

"Yes." And though she said it softly, Rosvita detected—perhaps—no small amount of pride.

"Ah. Well. To what work of the ancients might I be referring? 'As had been noted, there are roots and shrubs that have many powers affecting not only living bodies but also bodies without life.' "

Again she hesitated. Courtiers leaned forward. Was there something of reluctance in her expression? Was she afraid to reveal her knowledge? Where *had* she gotten that book, and what did it contain?

"'You would not wish to lie before the king, I hope," said Hugh mildly.

"It is from the *Inquiry Into Plants* by Theophrastus," she replied finally, her voice scarcely audible.

A murmur rose from the crowd, and there passed among them a certain amount of nudging and winking and a few sly glances toward Helmut Villam. Rosvita wondered if it was true that Villam had propositioned the handsome young Eagle. Indeed, the old margrave was gazing with rapt attention at the young woman.

"From whence does this come? 'To one desiring to know by what path blessedness is reached the reply is, "Know thyself." '?"

Startled, she looked up. "I don't know," she admitted.

He nodded, expecting this answer. "So writes Eustacia, repeating the words of the oracle at Talfi: 'Gnosi seaton.' But of course you do not know Arethousan, do you?"

"The one who taught me knows how much Arethousan

I know," she said with such an odd inflection that Rosvita
wondered who *had* taught her Arethousan—and *why*.

Hugh lifted a hand in a graceful gesture that suggested
there was more like this to come. "You have some knowledge of Dariyan. Does the word 'Ciconia' mean anything
to you?"

"It means 'stork,' " she said instantly as if, bested once,
she meant to defeat him now.

"Nay, child, I refer to Tullia Marcia Ciconia, the great
orator of ancient Dariya. Which works of hers have you
read?"

"Which works of hers?"

"*De officiis? De amicitia?* Can you speak to me some of
the wisdom contained in her words?"

"I—I don't know those works. I mean to say, I've heard
of them, but—" She faltered.

He nodded gently and glanced toward Sapientia as if to
say, 'Shall we stop this now?' but he went on. "Surely you
have instructed yourself in the writings of the church
mothers?"

"I know the *Acts of Saint Thecla*," she said defiantly.

"That is proper. Your Highness," he nodded toward Sapientia, "you are familiar with the *Acts* as well, are you
not?"

"Isn't every child?" demanded Sapientia, looking
affronted.

"The *Acts,* like *The Shepherd of Hermas,* is a work both
noble and common folk may hear for their edification. But
what of the writings with which the educated cleric instructs
herself? Macrina of Nyssa's *The Catechetical Orations* and
her *Life of Gregory?* These fine works you have read, of
course?"

She shook her head. A few of the courtfolk whispered
among themselves. Some snickered.

"*The City of God* by Saint Augustina? Or her *De Doc-
trina Daisanitia?* Jerome's *Life of Saint Paulina the Hermit?*
Justin Martyr's *Dialogue with Zurhai the Jinna?*"

Numbly, she shook her head and, just as King Henry
raised a hand, growing bored with this display of ignorance,
Hugh stood up. His audience quieted expectantly. The poor
Eagle ducked her head, as any shamed creature would, to
stare at the floor.

"Is it not said," Hugh asked of Sapientia and the assembled clerics and layfolk together, as a teacher addresses his students, "that the emperor of all Jinna keeps a bird which he has taught to speak human words? Have you ever seen entertainers make dogs to walk upon two legs? Such learning makes neither bird nor dog educated, however. A child trained early enough can learn the meanings of words written upon a page, and speak them out loud, but that does not mean her understanding is equally trained. I believe we have before us a curiosity." He smiled wryly but with a touch of gentle amusement such as an adult shows before an incredulous child's outrageous claims. "*Not* a prodigy. Is it not so, Your Highness? How do you judge this case?"

Thus appealed to, Sapientia nodded sternly. "Of course what you say must be true, Father Hugh. It might be a mercy, then, to take this poor creature under my wing."

Henry rose, and quickly any seated man or woman rose as well, young Brother Constantine almost spilling his red ink in his haste not to show discourtesy toward the king. "Let that be a lesson, daughter, that we are well served by wise counselors."

"And some more than others," murmured Villam so softly that only Rosvita and the king could hear.

Henry's lips quirked, and he signed to his servants. There was a sudden flurry of activity at the other end of the hall. Two servants picked up his chair and carried it over to the central place. "I think we may now sit down to table," Henry observed. He led the way.

Rosvita lingered, bitten by curiosity. The young Eagle remained kneeling. A few tears streaked her cheeks, but she made no sound, moved not at all even to wipe them away. She simply stared fixedly at the cold stone floor.

"Eagle!" called Sapientia from her seat at the central table. "Attend me!"

She rose and, silent, attended her new mistress.

X
A DEER IN THE FOREST

1

"I still don't like her," said Sapientia to her companion, Lady Brigida, whose status as Sapientia's current favorite gave her the privilege of combing the princess' hair in the evening before bed. "That skin of hers. It's so . . . so . . ."

"Dirty? She might wash more."

"It isn't dirt. It doesn't come off. I rubbed at it yesterday." The princess giggled. "Perhaps she's the lost sister of Conrad the Black, or his by-blow."

"Hmm. She's too old to be his by-blow . . . but perhaps not, if he bedded some girl when he was young Brother Constantine's age. Perhaps she's a Jinna slave girl who escaped her master."

"Then how would she know how to speak our language?" demanded Sapientia.

"Duke Conrad's mother didn't enter the convent after the elder Conrad died, did she? Perhaps this is her *second child* by another man." Lady Brigida had the unfortunate habit of snorting when she giggled, and she giggled a great deal, possessing ample inheritance in lands but little in wit or sense. "You wouldn't think she would have had to hide the child unless there was something *wrong* with the lover she had taken."

"I believe she lives quite retired. Still, there's something in what you say, Brigida, that she must have Jinna blood in her, for they're all brown like that. But I still say she must have some Wendish blood in her, or she'd not be able to speak our language."

"Didn't Father Hugh say any bird can be taught human speech?"

Liath endured this without flinching. Their idiocy and arrogance bothered her not one whit. At this moment, Hugh was not in the room, and after three days as Sapientia's Eagle that was the only mercy she lived for.

"Keep brushing," said Sapientia. "Whom should I marry, Brigida?"

"Lord Amalfred," said Brigida instantly. "He's very handsome and he killed a bear last week with his own hand, as you saw, as well as a dozen deer or more. I should like a husband like that. When I inherit from my mother, I'll expand her lands eastward, and I'll need a strong fighting man at my side."

"He's only the son of a Salian duchess. I must marry a man with royal connections."

"Isn't King Henry going to send for an Arethousan prince for you to marry, since your mother was an eastern princess?"

Sapientia sighed sharply and tossed her head, disturbing the smooth flow of black hair that Lady Brigida had been stroking with the comb. "Even my Eagle knows better than that, Brigida. Isn't that so, Eagle? Why can I not marry an Arethousan prince?"

In three days Liath had learned that Sapientia liked her to be stupid. "I don't know, Your Highness."

Although, in this case, she did know. But the humiliation at Hugh's hands still stung bitterly, not least because he had been right as well as wrong. It was true she read well and that Da had taught her a great deal—but when Hugh had paraded her ignorance publicly, to torture her, she had suddenly realized that Da had taught her narrowly. She knew far more than Hugh and probably any person at court of the knowledge hoarded by the mathematici, and yet how could she judge how much Da had truly known?

She *was* young, and she had been educated on the run and in the way of arrowshots toward a hidden foe—scattered far and wide and toward no set target. There was so much she did *not* know that any person educated in the king's schola or a cathedral school, in the convents and monasteries, would know and would be expected to know in order to be considered educated. Yet, if truth be told, she had no interest in Macrina's *The Catechetical Orations* or in the *Lives* of the early saints. The wisdom of the ancients drew her—as long as it concerned the heavens, sorcery, or natural history and the workings of the physical world. That Da had taught her to construct her city of memory, and thus she had many facts available to her stored away in that city—such as Arethousan inheritance practices—did not mean she was educated as anyone else understood the term.

"Poor thing," said the princess. "The Arethousan princes are never allowed to leave the palace, you see, my dear Brigida, because they are such barbarians that only a male can become emperor among them, and only one among the sons and nephews and cousins of the reigning emperor can become emperor after him. So if any of them get away, then they might have a claim to the throne and come back to the palace with their own army and cause a civil war. That is why there are never any civil wars in Arethousa, because once the new emperor is chosen, all of the royal princes of his generation are poisoned by his mother."

The temptation washed over Liath to correct Princess Sapientia, for if partly correct her account was so jumbled as to be absurd: The Arethousans did indeed only allow a male to be titled "Emperor," but it was the infidel Jinna *khshāyathiya* who had his mother poison all those relatives who might contest his claim to the throne.

"Is that what you mean to do to Theophanu?" asked Brigida lightly.

The chill hit Liath's throat and spine at the same instant,

and her hands tightened on her belt. She could not help but look toward the door, which stood half open; smoke leaked in from torches stuck in sconces in the corridor beyond. *He* came with his attendants. The torchlight made a halo around him, gilding his fine golden hair. He wore long hose, an azure tunic embroidered with sunbursts, and a cloak thrown back over one shoulder, clasped by a handsome gold-and-jeweled brooch in the shape of a panther. He looked like a noble lord just in from the hunt; only by his shaven chin could one tell he was a churchman.

Both noblewomen and all the other attendants in the chamber looked up at the same instant. Sapientia glowed. Brigida simpered.

"I beg your pardon," said Hugh smoothly. "I did not mean to interrupt you." Sapientia gestured at once and a chair was unfolded for him so he could sit beside her. Servants brought linen and water for him to refresh himself. He did not look at Liath. He didn't need to.

"We were speaking of nothing important," said Sapientia too quickly.

"No, indeed, Father Hugh," said Lady Brigida. "I heard that next we go to my uncle Duke Burchard's palace in Augensburg, and then to the royal palace at Echstatt. There's lots of good hunting."

"And a host of soldiers," added Sapientia, who always grew excited speaking of battle, "to be gathered for the attack on Gent."

"I am glad to hear it," said Hugh.

In this way they readied themselves for bed. In this guest room there were four actual beds and four additional camp beds. In every room at this time, Liath knew, an elaborate dance went on, just as it did when it came time to seat for dinner, testing rank against rank, establishing the order for who would sleep where and next to what person, so that all might know who was most privileged and who less so. Sapientia took the bed that held pride of place, centered in the room, and Hugh the one next to her. His proximity to her caused no comment—not any more. Brigida slept on the other side of Sapientia, lesser ladies by degrees farther away on the other beds and the favored and most noble of the clerics on the remaining camp beds. Liath retreated to the door, hoping for the chance to escape out to sleep in the stables or at least, as she had the last two nights, in the corridor.

"It is a bitter chill night," said Hugh, "and some few of my attendants have gone out to help warm the stables. All of your people may sleep herein with us, Your Highness, so that none must suffer the cold."

"Of course!" said Sapientia, always wishing to appear magnanimous, and disposition was made.

"Here, Eagle," he continued casually, "there is a place here." Hugh indicated an open space on the floor beside his bed.

She dared not object. She wrapped herself tightly in her cloak and lay down. Soon the torches were extinguished and in blackness she lay, catching now and again the wink of a gold buckle where belts or ornaments had been hung from the bed frames to wait until morning. She could not sleep, not even after the restless settling down of the twelve or fourteen people in the room had ceased and most every breath gentled into soft snoring or the long cadences of sleep. His presence and the faint murmur of his voice in a prayerlike monotone wore on her as painfully as if she lay on a thousand prickling needles. Her chest felt tight, but she could not resist peeking up at him. The shadow that was his form sat upright in bed, curved over his hands— and threads gleamed between his fingers. He seemed to be *weaving*.

As if he sensed her scrutiny, he moved, hiding his hands. "Your Highness," he whispered. "You are not yet asleep."

Sapientia yawned. "There are so many things that trouble my mind, my love. Whom shall I marry? Why can it not be you?"

"You know that is impossible, though it is my fondest wish. Were I not illegitimate—"

"Not in my heart!"

"Hush. Do not wake the others."

"What do I care if they hear me? They know my heart as well as you do, and so shall all the court, even my husband, whatever poor sorry fool he may be. I love you more than anyone—"

"Your Highness." He broke in gently. "It is your fate as Heir to marry, and mine as bastard and churchman to remain unwed. What God has granted us, we must endure gladly. You shall find affection and good will toward your husband in time—"

"Never!"

"—for it is the will of Our Lady and Lord that woman cleave to man, and man to woman, all but those who cleave instead to God and turn away from the vanities and temptations and empty pleasures of the world."

"Is that all I am to you—!"

"Your Highness. I pray you, speak no harsh word to me, for I could not bear it. Now, what else troubles you?"

Liath dared not move, though a stone pinched her thigh. All the others breathed the even breaths of sweet dreaming.

"Theophanu."

"You need not fear Theophanu."

"That is all very well for you to say, but—"

"Your Highness. You need not fear Theophanu."

Something in his tone made Liath shiver, and as if the slight shift of her wool cloak on the hard stone floor alerted the princess, her voice changed.

"Are you sure all of them sleep?" she hissed.

"No one can hear us whom you need fear, Your Highness." He shifted on the bed, and Liath heard the muffled sighing sound of two people kissing passionately.

"Ah," gasped Sapientia at last, "how I long for the day when I am rid of this burden—live and healthy, God grant—so that we may again—"

"Hush." He moved away from her and again, hidden from all but Liath, began to wind the gleaming threads, as faint as spider's silk, between his fingers. "Sleep now, Your Highness."

Her breathing gentled and slowed, and she slept. Liath lay as still as stone, but he shifted on the bed, rolling back until he lay above her as a boulder poised on the edge of a cliff shades the delicate plants beneath in its shadow. She held her breath.

"I know you are not asleep, Liath. Have you forgotten that I had many nights to study you, where you lay beside me, to study your face in repose, or when you were only pretending to sleep? I know when you sleep, and when you do not. And you are not sleeping now, my beauty. All the others sleep, but not you. And not me."

He could only speak in this way if he was sure everyone else slept, and how could he know that? Or perhaps he did not care. Why should he? He was the abbot of a large institution, the son of a powerful margrave, an educated churchman out of the king's schola. She was nothing compared to that, a King's Eagle, a kinless fugitive whose parents had both been murdered.

"Tell me, Liath," he continued in that same soft, persuasive, beautiful voice, "why do you torment me so? It is wrong of you to do so. I cannot understand what power lies in you that eats at me so constantly. You must be doing it on purpose, you must have some scheme, some end, in mind. What is it? Is it this?"

He shifted. She would have screamed, but she could not, she could only lie in mute dread, and then his fingers brushed her cheek, probing for her lips, explored them softly before tracing down over her chin to her vulnerable throat. Bile rose, burning her tongue.

"Come up here," he whispered, fingers drawing a pattern on her throat.

If she went to him now, perhaps he would stop tormenting her. If she only made him happy, if she obeyed him, he would be kind to her.

As quickly, the thought washed off her as water slides down a roof. She rolled away from him, bumping up against a sleeping servant. Sapientia murmured, half waking, and a man laughed in the corridor outside.

"Damn," muttered Hugh. She cringed, waiting for the blow, but he only shifted away from her and at last she heard his breathing slow and deepen. All the others slept on, so gently, so peacefully. Only she did not sleep.

2

MORNING came none too soon, and she crept
out as soon as there was any least graying of darkness
toward light through the cracks in the shutters. A few
torches burned by the entrance to the kitchens as servants
began to prepare for the afternoon's feast. Mist wreathed
the palisade and twined around corners, covering the courtyard in a dense blanket of cold. Drops of icy rain stung
her cheeks.

The gates were already propped open, but no one had
yet ventured out to the privies beyond. Most servants were
not yet up, and any of the noble folk would use their cham-
berpots rather than venture out so early. But Liath could
see perfectly well in the morning gloom, and she wanted a
moment of freedom. She relieved herself and started back,
but when the gates loomed before her out of the trailing
mist, she was seized with such horror that she could not move
except to sink down to her knees. The ground was bitter cold;
wet soaked up through the fabric of her leggings.

They did not see her, but she saw them: concealed from
the sight of any in the courtyard within, Hugh paused in
the lee of the gate to meet Princess Theophanu. The princess was hesitant, drawn but reluctant, as a half wild but
starving creature shies forward, then away, then forward
again to sniff at food laid out by alien hands, suspicious of
a trap but desperate to slake its hunger.

He touched her hand in an intimate manner, twining fingers through hers but in no other way touching her. He
spoke. She replied. Then he slipped something into her
hands. It winked as sun cut through a gap in the trees,
dispelling an arm of mist that shadowed the gate: his panther brooch.

Furtively, Theophanu hurried back inside. He lingered,
looking about, looking for *her,* but she was still hidden by
mist and the flash of the rising sun. He turned and walked
out toward the privies.

Liath jumped up and bolted inside the gates—and ran into Helmut Villam. He caught her in a strong grasp as she jerked back and stumbled. The sleeve hung empty below the elbow of his other arm, the wound he had received at the Battle of Kassel when he had defended King Henry against the false claims of Henry's half sister, Sabella.

"I beg your pardon, Lord Villam," Liath gasped.

"You are well, I trust, or in a hurry about the princess' business?"

"I was only out—I beg your pardon, my lord."

"No need to beg anything of me," he said without releasing her, a certain spark in his eyes as he looked her over. He was at least fifteen years older than King Henry but still robust in every way, as everyone on the progress continually joked. "It is I who should beg comfort of you, for it is cold these nights and I have been, alas, abandoned to shiver alone."

At any moment Hugh would come back through the gates and find her. "I beg you, my lord, you are too kind, but I wear the badge of an Eagle."

He sighed. "An Eagle. It is true, is it not?" He released her and clapped his hand to his chest. "My heart is broken. If ever you choose to heal it . . ."

"I am sensible to the honor you do me, my lord," she said quickly, retreating, "but I am sworn."

"And I am sorry!" He laughed. "You are well spoken as well as beautiful. You are wasted as an Eagle, I swear to you!" But he let her go.

She could not bring herself to return to the confinement of Sapientia's supervision. And she had one other thing to check on. She went in search of her comrade.

She found Hathui sitting on a log bench outside the stables, polishing harness for the day's hunt. Her gear lay at her feet, and she looked up, smiled wryly at Liath, and beckoned for her to sit down beside her. "There is plenty for you to do." She gestured toward a pile of mud-splattered harness. The light had changed, spare and silver now although the sun had not yet cleared the surrounding trees. Hathui's hands, gloveless, were chapped red with cold.

"I must return," said Liath. "Her Highness will be looking for me when she wakes. I just wanted to—"

"I know." Hathui glanced to her right where saddlebags lay heaped. "Still in my possession."

"You are a good comrade," said Liath.

"I am your comrade in the Eagles!" Hathui snorted. "And I will expect no less of you, Liath, when I must ask for your aid. Here, now. Will you trim my hair again?" Her hair, shorn short, had gotten ragged at the ends.

Liath took out her knife, tested it on a strand of hair, and then began carefully to trim the ends. "Your hair is so fine, Hathui," she said. "Not coarse, like mine. It's so soft, like the touch of a beautiful cloth."

"So my mother always said." Hathui spit into a cloth and used it to rub a shine into her bridle. "That is one reason I dedicated my hair to St. Perpetua when I swore myself to her blessed service."

"Should I cut my hair?" Liath asked suddenly, remembering Villam.

"What does *that* mean?"

"I only . . . it's just . . . oh, Hathui, on my way back from the privies the margrave asked me if . . . if, you know—"

"Did he tell you the sad story of how his paramour has gone over to Lord Amalfred and he is most cold at night?"

Liath snorted and then, unable to stop herself, laughed. "Did he proposition you, too, Hathui?"

"No, indeed, for I wear my hair shorn, as you say. But he did once, some years ago when I first came to the Eagles and spent time at court. Wolfhere told me that Villam is one of those men afflicted with lust or perhaps certain tiny fire daimones have taken up residence in his loins and dance there night and day. He is notorious for having a taste for very young women and a new one frequently. It is no surprise to me that he has gone through four wives, or is he on his fifth now?"

"But if he has so many concubines and lovers—?"

"I don't mean he wears his wives out with his physical attentions, but with grief, for he's always straying, and though he is a good man, a cunning general, and a wise counselor in other matters, King Henry at least knows better than to emulate him in this."

"How can I avoid him?"

"It is impossible to avoid anyone on the king's progress. But Villam is a good man, more so than most, and if you

are modest and respectful when you are around him, so
that he knows you mean to keep to your Eagle's vows, he
won't bother you again. What do you have in the bag,
Liath?"

She almost nicked the other Eagle's neck. "Nothing.
Something. It's a book."

"I *know* it's a book. We saw it at Heart's Rest. What
sort of book is it that you hide as if you'd stolen some of
the king's treasure and mean to keep it hidden for fear of
losing your life if you were found out?"

"It's mine! It was Da's. I can't tell you, Hathui, you or
anyone. Some words aren't meant to be spoken out loud
or they attract—some words must be kept in silence."

"Sorcery," said Hathui, and then, "ouch!"

"I beg your pardon." Liath staunched the wound with
the end of her tunic. "It isn't bleeding much."

"Was that to punish me for my curiosity?" But Hathui
sounded more like she was about to laugh than to get
angry.

"You just startled me."

"Liath." Hathui sighed, set down her bridle, and turned
'round. Over her shoulder Liath could see the walls of the
hunting lodge still wreathed in mist. Servants led horses out
from the stable doors. Men and woman came and went
from the privies. Smoke boiled up from the kitchens as the
roasting for the afternoon's feast was begun, and servants
grimy with smoke and soot hauled buckets and kettles up
from the river beyond the palisade gates. "Every village in
the marchlands has its wisewoman or conjureman. We listen to what they say, because it's always wise to hear the
words of the elder folk, what few of them there are. Some
of them only tell stories from the old days, before the Circle
of Unity came to the outlanders and the Wendish tribes.
Aye, those tales are so dreadful and exciting that I fear for
my soul when I hear them. Sometimes I still dream of those
tales, though their heroes and fighting women are all heathens. Ha!" She clapped her hands to chase off a thin little
dog that had sidled over to sniff at her gear. "Anyway,
certain of the old ones have powers no one speaks of out
loud. But anyone who lives on the edge of the wilderness
knows that if you call out the true name of the creatures
that live beyond the walls and fields, you might attract their

notice and then they would *come*. Where I come from, we call that sorcery."

"Ai, Lady," said Liath, not needing to turn round to know who was approaching her.

"Ai, Lady, indeed." Hathui's eyes narrowed as she looked past Liath. She rose, inclining her head. "Father Hugh."

"Princess Sapientia requires the services of her Eagle," he said crisply. He said nothing else but did not move until Liath put away her knife and turned to follow him.

"Does *she* have the book?" he asked in a low voice as they crossed the courtyard. "Eagles are notoriously faithful each to the other. One would scarcely think common folk capable of such loyalty. But how can you trust her, a mere freewoman, and not trust me, Liath?"

She did not need to answer because Sapientia was already waiting, impatient to be out on the hunt. She busied herself with duties beneath an Eagle, for Sapientia had servants aplenty, but keeping busy kept her away from Hugh. At last they rode out, a great cavalcade of noble riders, their servants on foot, the hounds and their handlers, and the king's foresters who lived year round in the tiny village beside the royal lodge. Amid the noise and shouting and hubbub, Liath noticed a sudden and disturbing detail: Theophanu had clasped her hip-length riding cloak with a gold panther brooch. No one else appeared to notice, not even Sapientia.

3

AT first, the forest around the lodge lay fairly open.
Trees grew back at shoulder height where they had been
cut for firewood for the king's hearth; half-wild pigs raced
away into the shelter of brush and young trees. But soon
the foresters led them into the older, deeper, uncut woods.
The hounds were released, and the hunt was on.

Their course led them down a ravine and up a steep
slope where half the riders had to dismount and lead their
horses. Burrs caught on their cloaks. A gap formed between a forward group of the hardiest—and most reckless—riders, and a more cautious group. The unmounted
servants lagged behind. Liath could barely keep up with
Sapientia, who even halfway through her pregnancy was
determined to ride at the head of the host.

Oak and beech had lost most of their leaves, though a
scattering of pale gold and dull red leaves still clung to the
branches of the trees. Here and there evergreens stood in
clumps, shafts of dense green. Ghosts of morning mist wove
around the boles of trees and settled in hollows or near
pools of standing water. A light rain fell intermittently.

The progress of the hunters sounded a steady din
through the litter and deadwood on the forest floor. Breaking through a dense growth of bracken, they flushed a
covey of partridges. The king's huntsmen laid about themselves and clubbed some down, dragging the dogs still with
the company out of reach of the birds. Ahead, braches
belled.

"Deer!" cried a forester. The chase was on.

Now the forward group itself split into two groups, King
Henry and the older nobles falling behind to leave pride
of chase to the younger adults. Sapientia rode to the fore,
Liath laboring after her on a gelding more hardy than agile.
Lord Amalfred, Lady Brigida, young lords and ladies shout-
ing and whooping in their excitement, all pressed forward.
Theophanu came up beside Liath, face intent. The panther

clasp sparked in a flash of sunlight through the branches. She glanced back over her shoulder and, reflexively, Liath did as well. Hugh was behind them, but his presence was curiously lost to Liath as if for once he was not aware of her at all. His head was bent over his saddle and his lips moved soundlessly. With his left hand he clasped a tiny gold reliquary hung on a golden chain around his neck.

Sapientia disappeared into bracken. Lord Amalfred's horse shied back, refusing to cross through the heavy growth of fern, and he kicked it forward, angry.

"Your Highness!" A forester called out to Theophanu. "A path! This way!"

Faced with a wall of bracken or a clear, if narrow, path, Liath chose to ride after Theophanu, but the princess' horse was superior to hers in these woods, fearless and sure-footed. Theophanu forged ahead as if she meant to catch up and pass her royal sister. As if she meant to have for herself what her sister wanted to possess.

"Out of the way! Out of the way!" cried a man behind her, and Liath just got her gelding aside before a group of some dozen young nobles including Lord Amalfred pounded past on the track. "I see the deer!"

"A deer! A deer!" The others took up the cry.

Liath saw it, too, a handsome doe springing away before them, bolting through the trees. Amalfred and the others pulled up, taking aim.

Except it wasn't a deer. It was Theophanu, riding farther ahead of them into trees still wreathed with morning mist. It was an illusion. The memory of Gent hit her so like a blow that her hands went lax on the reins and she gasped aloud. An illusion that only *she* could see through. Even Sanglant, who wanted to believe, had not dared to.

She screamed. "Halt! Don't shoot!" She yelled as loudly as she was able. "Your Highness! Say something! Pull up your horse!"

Did her warning reach that far?

Theophanu slowed her horse and began to turn, as if she had heard. . . .

"Ai, Lady!" cried one of the noblemen. "It's slowed. Now's your chance!" He turned to wave a new rider forward. "Princess Sapientia. Come forward."

But Lord Amalfred had already drawn down. "This one is mine!"

"Stop!" cried Liath, but Hugh rode up beside her and set his hand on her arm. Her voice vanished.

Theophanu was still turned, raising a hand in acknowledgment; there was an instant when her face registered the tableau behind her. Her expression froze in horror.

Amalfred shot. Another lord shot. The arrows sped toward their target.

She would not be powerless this time! She wrenched her arm out of Hugh's grasp. Please God let her bring fire through her eyes alone. Let the fire in the vision of the burning stone pass through her as through a doorway, as though a daimone of the fiery sphere above had reached down below the moon and pressed its blazing touch onto the speeding wood of the arrows.

Both arrows ignited in midair. Theophanu threw herself off her horse. The wailing and shouting that deafened Liath now was its own conflagration.

"My God, the princess!"

"A miracle! A miracle!"

"Lord Amalfred, what meant you by this?"

"But I saw a deer. These others—!"

As all protested that they, too, had seen a deer, Sapientia began to sob noisily. Liath threw her reins over the horse's head, dismounted, and ran forward; she stubbed her toes on a log, jumped over another only to have her boots sink into the dense litter of fallen and rotting leaves in her haste to reach Theophanu.

The princess' hair lay in disarray, braids fallen loose, her riding tunic twisted at her hips, her gold-braided leggings ripped at the knees, her face scraped and stained with dirt. She shoved herself up and reached for her knife as Liath dropped down beside her. "Have you come to finish the job at her bidding?"

Liath threw up her hands to show she was empty-handed. "Your Highness! Are you hurt?"

"Your voice." Theophanu's eyes flared with astonishment. "Your voice is the one I heard warning me. What treachery is this?"

"They saw a deer where you rode, Your Highness."

"I am no deer to be hunted and slain. Was this an accident, Eagle?"

But now a forester had come up, and the crowd like a mindless writhing creature moved across the wood to engulf them. Back on the path, Hugh comforted a weeping Sapientia.

By now the king had come up to the others, and in their babble of voices Liath heard repeated over and over that all dozen or so there and even in addition the foresters had seen not Theophanu but a deer.

"Witchcraft," someone said.

"A miracle," said another.

"Too many damn fool young hotheads hunting for prizes and seeing visions in the mist," said Villam with disgust.

"This day's hunt ends now," said King Henry. A groom helped him dismount. He came up to his daughter and extended a hand. She took it, and he raised her up off the ground. "You are unhurt?" he asked. Villam by now had forced order into the milling mob behind them, pressing them back from the frightened horse. Far away, hounds bayed wildly. Henry released Theophanu's hand and beckoned a huntsman forward. "Follow the hounds," he said, "and bring back to the lodge whatever meat you take."

The man nodded. Soon, foresters and huntsmen went on alone, though some of the young nobles clearly wished to go with them.

"May I have a moment alone to collect my wits, Father," Theophanu asked, "before I ride again?"

He gestured to his attendants to back off and himself moved away. Liath began to retreat, but Theophanu signed to her, and Liath hesitated, afraid to be seen with her, afraid not to obey.

"Was it an accident?" the princess repeated, her gaze hard, her mouth a thin line. "Did my sister devise this treachery?"

The thought of Sapientia concocting any kind of intrigue made Liath's mouth drop open in amazed disbelief. "Your *sister?* No! But it was not an accident—" Then she broke off. She had revealed too much.

Theophanu said nothing for a long while. Slowly, one scratched and bleeding hand came up to touch the panther brooch that held her cloak closed. "Was it sorcery? And from whose hand?"

"I can prove nothing, Your Highness. I know only what I saw."

"Or did *not* see." She looked up at a sight behind Liath's back, and away quickly, as if she was ashamed. "Am I any better than those who saw a deer in the forest, which is only what they wished to see?" With a jerk and a sudden grimace, she ripped the panther brooch off her cloak and flung it behind her into the leaves. "I am in your debt, Eagle. What reward can I give you?"

She blurted it out, not meaning to say it, but it was more impassioned for its rash honesty. "Get me away from him, I beg you."

" 'The meekness of the dove with the cunning of the serpent,' " Theophanu muttered. "But I need proof." Still pale, she groped through the leaves until she found the brooch again. Gingerly, as though it were poison, she tucked it in between belt and tunic. "I will do what I can. Go now. It is not wise that you be seen with me, if what I suspect is true. Say nothing to anyone until I give you leave."

4

HENRY was furious. The hunt came clattering back early in an uproar to upset the quiet tenor of a day that Rosvita had hoped would be a productive one for her clerics. But the stories she heard, from so many different sources, were alarming enough that she was relieved when Princess Theophanu rode in unharmed. Strangely, for all that her dress was in disarray, her hair disordered, and her skin scratched and stained with loam and dirt, the princess was herself perfectly composed.

"So eastern," muttered Brother Fortunatus. "You know these Arethousans are inscrutable."

"Spare us these false wisdoms," said Sister Amabilia. "Poor Theophanu! To be mistaken for a deer!"

The king was not to be mollified by the testimony of all who had been present. Everyone, even the foresters and huntsmen who had raced ahead with Sapientia's party, had seen a deer in place of a princess.

"The rain confused our eyes." "The mist confused our eyes." "It was the shape of the branches above her head." On they went, all of them grievously shocked at the accident.

"Or there was a deer behind her in the woods and in your rashness you shot without looking closely! Lord Amalfred. Lord Grimoald. You are no longer welcome at this court. You will be gone by nightfall. We will all of us leave this ill-omened place tomorrow. One of my children I have already lost. I do not intend to lose any more."

No protest, even by Sapientia, could mitigate the king's judgment. The two young lords left the hall in disgrace. Henry spent the rest of the day at Mass led by Father Hugh. In particular, the king prayed and gave thanksgiving to St. Valeria, whose day this was and whose miraculous intervention had spared his daughter worse harm than the fall she had taken. Before the feast he handed out bread with his own hands to the usual supplicants who had gath-

ered outside the palisade. Hearing of the king's arrival at
this southernmost of his royal hunting lodges, they had
come from villages at the forest's edge. Some of them had
walked several days on rag-clad feet hoping for food or
a blessing.

At the feast, Theophanu begged a boon of her father. "I
pray you, Your Majesty, let me undertake a pilgrimage to
the Convent of St. Valeria to offer a proper thanksgiving
for my deliverance from harm. Surely her hand lay over
me this day."

He was reluctant to let her leave after such an incident,
but the miracle had been attested by a dozen or more
persons.

"I will take an Eagle," she said, "and thus any message
can be sent quickly from my hand to yours."

"As a sign of my favor," he said, "you may take my
faithful Hathui, daughter of Elseva, as long as you and she
return in one piece to my progress by the end of the year.
It should take you no more than two or three months to
complete the journey."

"I would not take such a loyal servant from you, Your
Majesty," she replied, as calm as if no arrows had sped
toward her head and breast that morning. "But if I could
take another Eagle—" Here her gaze came to rest on the
young Eagle who stood several paces behind Sapientia's
chair.

Sapientia leaped to her feet, the gesture of anger made
ungainly because of her increasing girth. "You just want
what is mine!"

"Sit down," said the king.

Sapientia sat.

"It is true," said Henry, "that Sapientia has an Eagle,
one whose service I gave into her hands, which I will not
now take from her. But it is only right, Theophanu, that
you be given an Eagle as well. Since you are going on a
journey, two would be better. Hathui will choose among
those who attend me now, at your pleasure."

The feast went on. But the damage had been done to
Rosvita's peace of mind, for she suddenly recalled that Sapientia enjoyed the novelty of having an Eagle in constant
attendance. Liath had been on that hunt and, surely, had
seen the whole; someone had mentioned seeing her go to

the princess after the fall. But no one had called her to testify when even the king's foresters and huntsmen had given testimony after the noblefolk had finished speaking. How could such a lapse be possible? Why did the young Eagle not come forward on her own?

Why should Theophanu, inscrutable Theophanu, notice her now and, even, attempt to take her into her own retinue? *Only* to provoke her sister?

For that matter, why should Theophanu undertake a pilgrimage across the winter landscape when she could as easily send servants with gifts of gold and silver and an altar cloth to grace the convent's church and treasury?

Two arrows bursting into flame in midair. Any soul would agree that it was a miracle wrought by the hand of a saint. But Rosvita did not believe in coincidence.

"*In the guise of scholars and magi,*" Brother Fidelis had said to her last spring, "*tempting me with knowledge.*" Why did his words come back to her now?

Theophanu knew as well as any why the Convent of St. Valeria was renowned: Its Mother Abbesses were known for their study of the forbidden art of sorcery.

5

IT was raining, again. Rain made Sapientia irritable; she was only happy when she was active

"Fetch me wine, Eagle," she said, although she had servants to fetch her wine. "And milk. I want milk." Leaving the Thurin Forest had made Sapientia irritable. Riding south into the duchy of Avaria had made Sapientia irritable. Being pregnant made Sapientia irritable. "Read to me, Hugh. I am so bored. It isn't right I'm not allowed to ride out to the hunt just because I have a little fever." She yawned. "I am so tired always."

Hugh turned away from the great hearth of the king's hall in the palace of Augensburg. More restless than usual, for he was usually as smooth as cream resting in an untouched bowl, he had been shredding leaves and tossing them into the blazing fire. He did not look toward Liath nor even appear to notice her. He did not need to.

"I rather like Lord Geoffrey," Sapientia continued, rattling on despite her protestations of being tired. "He's a good hunter and he has very good manners. Father likes him so much he asked him to ride beside him on today's hunt. Poor Brigida. I suppose you wish he wasn't already married!"

"He's from Varre," retorted Brigida. "I don't know if my uncle Burchard would *want* me to marry a Varrish lord, not after what happened to my cousin Agius. And I don't know what kind of inheritance Geoffrey would bring as his dowry."

"Poor man. He lost his inheritance to a bastard!" The princess giggled.

Hugh looked up abruptly. "Isn't Lord Geoffrey heir to the Lavas count?"

"Indeed not!" Sapientia smiled with the satisfaction of a slow child who has, at long last, won a footrace against its rivals. "But you weren't at court then. Father pardoned Count Lavastine for his treachery and allowed him to name his illegitimate son as his heir."

"His *heir*," murmured Hugh with such an odd inflection that Liath actually paused to stare at him.

He knelt beside a clay bowl filled with dried herbs. A strip of linen marked with a writing she could not read lay over his thighs, and as Liath watched, his hands tied the linen strip into a complex knot.

Binding.

The word leaped unbidden into her thoughts. A fragment of *The Book of Secrets*—which she had herself copied out of a penitential from a monastic library in Salia—rose up from the city of memory and stirred on her tongue. She murmured it under her breath.

" 'Hast thou observed the traditions of the mathematici, that thou shouldst have power through the binding and loosing made by that woven fabric formed out of the courses of the moon and the sun and the erratica and the stars, each in relationship to the others? These are the arts known to the daimones of the upper air, and it is written, "Whatsoever ye do in word or in work, do all in the name of Our Lord and Lady." If thou hast done this, thou shalt be judged before the skopos herself.' "

But there had been more, which she had not written down because it did not concern the astronomical arts. "*Hast thou made knots, and incantations . . .*"

Hugh looked up at her as if he could sense her thoughts, and she flushed, afraid, when a smile touched his lips. He had not addressed a single word to her since the incident in the forest, and that was worse than anything that had come before . . . because she knew, and he knew, that he was only biding his time.

"That Ungrian ambassador is so uncouth." The princess continued on obliviously, just as all the others seemed oblivious to Hugh's actions by the fire—as if he had shielded himself from their curiosity. "The way he picks at his food as if it isn't fit for him to eat! You don't suppose Father means to marry the son of the Ungrian king to me, do you?"

"I think not, Your Highness." Hugh dumped the last of the herbs into the fire and stepped away, dusting white ash from his otherwise spotless tunic. The linen strip had vanished. "The Ungrian king is newly converted to the Faith of the Unities, praise God, and I believe he wishes for a woman of Wendish kin to settle there so that she may bring her knowledge of the Circle of Unity and the example of her faith to his people."

"That might be a useful occupation for Theophanu when she returns from her pilgrimage. Where is my milk?"

A steward fetched wine and milk. Hugh left the hall for the guest rooms beyond. With the shutters closed, it was dim and smoky within the hall. The tapestries carried on the progress by King Henry had been hung over the frescoed walls for warmth, creating an odd mosaic of images, painted and woven, all jumbled up together. Freshly cut rushes smothered the floor. Three hearthfires burned, and lamps glowed on the far table where a dozen clerics worked. The rest, even Sister Rosvita, had gone out on the hunt.

Candles sat in clay bowls on all the mantelpieces; lit this morning, they would burn all day and through the night. It was the first day of the month of Decial, called Candlemass: the shortest day of the year, the winter solstice. The heathens called it Dhearc, the dark of the sun, and on this day it was traditional to go hunting no matter what the weather was like, because on this day the sun and light, in the person of the regnant, at last defeated darkness and disorder, in the body of the wild game which would be killed and feasted upon. St. Peter the Discipla, whose feast day this was, had been martyred by being burned alive by unbelievers.

In *The Book of Secrets,* Da had written: "*When the sun stands still, certain pathways otherwise hidden become clear and certain weavings otherwise too tangled to unravel become straight. Thereby with what power you can bind a small spell into life on other days, you can bind your wish into life in an altogether greater manner at the hinges of the year. Therefore, be cautious.*"

Bind your wish. Therefore, be cautious. She crouched by the fire. Two stone posts framed the hearth, carved with the forelegs and heads of griffins, and she touched the one nearest her, tracing its lion's claws. Tiny singed fragments of flowers lay scattered at the base and on the bricks; she rolled them between thumb and finger and sniffed. Lavender. A single apple seed lay on the flagstones. The scent from the fire was heady and thick, and she had to step back to let her head clear.

Was Hugh working magic? Ai, Lady, she could not regret saving Theophanu's life, but what if Hugh suspected—what if the others discovered—that *she* had made those arrows catch fire? Would she be taken before the skopos to stand trial? And yet the thought gnawed at her, like a nagging pain: *If you can bring flame and see visions through fire, then why not other magics? Why did Da lie?*

She was not deaf to magic. She was protected against it: against the magic of others and, perhaps, against her own. But she had no way to discover the truth, she had no one to confide in, no one to teach her. Suddenly Wolfhere's hints and gentle suggestions, his attempts to convince her to trust him, seemed both more sinister and more welcome. If only he were here now.

Hugh returned, carrying a book. She recognized Polyxene's *History of Dariya* at once. The binding was almost as familiar to her as her own skin. He had stolen it from her as he had stolen so much else. He seated himself beside Princess Sapientia, and two servants stood over him with lamps. The dozen clerics at the other end of the hall set down their pens, turning as flowers toward the sun, eager to hear him read.

"I shall read today from Polyxene," he began.

"What should I care about such an old history, and written about heathens, at that?" asked Sapientia.

He raised one eyebrow. "Your Highness. Surely you are aware that the *Dariyans*, who were said to be half of humankind and half of elvish kin, conquered and ruled the largest empire the world has ever known. Only in the myths and tales of the ancient Arethousans do we hear of older and greater empires, that of Saïs which was swallowed by the waves, or of the wise and ancient Gyptos peoples across the middle sea. After the destruction of the Dariyan Empire the many lands they had once held together in greatness became the haunts of savages, and uncivilized heathens fought over the spoils. It was only a hundred years ago that the great Salian Emperor Taillefer restored the empire, by the grace of Our Lord and Lady, God of Unities. He had himself crowned Holy Dariyan Emperor, but at his death his empire was lost to the feuding of his successors."

Sapientia's expression cleared, and she looked oddly

thoughtful. "Father believes that it is the destiny of our family to restore the Holy Empire of Dariya."

"And so your family shall," murmured Hugh, "and be crowned in Darre before the skopos, as was Taillefer."

Liath shivered. Was this why Hugh had tried to murder Theophanu? So Sapientia would have no rival for the imperial throne, not just for the throne of the kingdom of Wendar and Varre?

He cleared his throat, took a sip of wine, and began to read out loud in his beautiful, almost hypnotic voice. " 'The fact is that we can obtain only an impression of a whole from a part, and certainly neither a thorough knowledge or an accurate understanding. It is only by combining and comparing certain parts of the whole with one another and taking note of their resemblances and their differences that we shall arrive at a comprehensive view.' "

Was that what Da was doing all along in the first part of *The Book of Secrets?* In that first part he had written down so many snippets from so many different sources, compiling them so that he could better understand the knowledge hidden in the heavens. She yawned, feeling a sudden sense of numbing lassitude, then shook herself back awake.

" 'By what means and in what time the people we know now as the Dariyans first came to Aosta rests outside my consideration. Instead, I shall take as my starting point the first occasion on which the Dariyans left Aosta, crossing the sea to the island of Nakria.' "

Sapientia snored softly. She had fallen asleep, as had two of her servingwomen; her other servants, seated around her, also nodded off. Liath had a sudden desperate fear that if she did not get up and get outside this instant, she, too, would fall asleep.

The youngest cleric spoke up from the other end of the room. "I beg you, Father Hugh, read to us of the seige of Kartiako."

The distraction gave her cover. She crept out the door but took a wrong turn and at once was confused. The Augensburg palace boasted two reception halls, a solarium, courtyards, barracks, guest rooms, chambers for the regnant and for the duke of Avaria, a safe room for the king's treasury, and a dozen cottages for envoys and servants. All this was built out of timber felled from the surrounding forest. Only the bathing complex and the chapel were built of stone.

Liath had left her saddlebags in the barracks, but Sapientia held her on such a tight leash that she'd had no time to commit the palace layout to memory. She retraced her steps. In the hall, everyone was asleep—and Hugh was nowhere to be seen. Backing out of the room, she tried again to find the barracks by cutting through a side corridor, but it only let her out through a tiny fountain courtyard where an old gardener sat dozing in the cold air on the lip of a frost-encrusted fountain. No water ran.

The reception room opened before her. Frescoes gleamed on the walls, splashes of color in the dim chamber. Great wooden beams spanned the ceiling. A languor hung over the hall. Two servants, brooms in hand, snored on the steps that led up to the dais and the regnant's throne, itself carved cunningly with lions as the four legs, the back as the wings of an eagle, and the arms as the sinuous necks and heads of dragons. A woman had fallen asleep by the hearth fire while mending a seat cover; she had pricked herself with her needle, and a tiny drop of blood welled on her skin.

Suddenly uneasy, Liath climbed spiraling wooden stairs to a long corridor. Built above the north block of buildings, the corridor was reserved for the king, his family, and his messengers; it provided a way for him to proceed from one quarter of the complex to another without walking through the common rooms below or setting foot in the muddy alleyways. She hurried down the narrow corridor, not wider than the width of her arms outstretched. Now she remembered; the barracks lay in the northeast corner of the palace complex.

She became consumed with the fear that something was following her. She felt breathing on her neck, spun around. The far end of the corridor, down which she had just come, lay blanketed in darkness except where spines of light shone through cracks in the wooden shutters. A footstep scraped on the stair.

"Liath," he said, his voice muted by the distance and the narrow walls. "Why are you still awake?"

She bolted.

She ran down the length of the corridor, scrambled, half

falling, down the other stairs, banging her knee, wrenching a finger as she gripped a smooth square railing and shoved herself forward. It was dark in the palace, all the shutters closed against winter's chill. Most of the nobles were out on the hunt. In every room she came to, every corridor she escaped down, those who had stayed behind slept.

Even in the barracks the soldiers rested, snoring, on straw mattresses on the floor. Her friend Thiadbold and a comrade slumped in chairs over a dice game and cooling mugs of cider. Beyond them, a ladder led up to the attic loft where she and the other Eagles slept. But as cold seeped in through the timber walls and the single hearth fire burned low and flickered out, she could not bring herself to go up the ladder. Once she climbed that ladder, she would be trapped.

She ran to Thiadbold. His Lion's tunic folded at odd angles, creased by the twist of his body in the chair and the way his right arm was flung back over the chair back. His head lolled to one side, mouth open. She shook him.

"Please, I beg you, comrade. Thiadbold! Wake up!"

"Nothing you do will wake them, Liath," he said behind her. He stood in the doorway, perhaps twenty paces away. He held a lamp in one hand. Its soft light gilded him, as gold does a painting or the favor of the king does a virtuous man.

"I'm very angry with you, Liath," he added kindly, without raising his voice. "You lied to me." Indeed, he sounded more hurt than angry. "You said you knew nothing about sorcery, and yet . . ." He lifted his free hand in a gesture of puzzlement. ". . . what am I to think now? Arrows bursting into flame in mid-flight. You are not asleep with the others."

"Why do you want to kill Theophanu?" she demanded.

"I don't want to kill Theophanu," he said, as if disappointed she would think he did. He took a step forward.

There was another door at the far end of the barracks. But if she ran out now, he would get the book. Surely the book was what he had wanted all along.

"Liath! Stop!"

She did not stop, but when she reached the ladder, she scrambled up it, panting, heart so frozen with fear that her chest felt as if it were in the grip of some great beast.

Heaving herself up over the top, she turned on her knees, grabbed the legs of the ladder, and yanked up.

And was jerked forward almost falling back down through the opening as Hugh caught the ladder from below and dragged it back down.

"Don't fight me, Liath. You know it makes me angry."

She fought him anyway, but though she was physically strong, he had the advantage, braced on the floor. It was a losing battle. It had always been a losing battle. And once he fought the legs back into their braces and settled his full weight on the bottom rung, it made no difference. The opening was too small for her to cast the ladder off and drop it away.

She scrambled back, scraping palms against the rough-hewn plank floors, rising and bumping her head against the low pitch of the ceiling. Her feet got tangled in gear, but she knew her own gear, knew it as well as the feel of Da's hand holding hers when she woke at night from a bad dream. She grabbed the leather saddlebags, draped them over a shoulder. Her quiver caught on a beam above, and she stumbled.

"Liath." He had no lamp, but she needed no lamp to see his shadow emerge into the loft and swing onto the floor.

Bent over, breathing in gasps more like whimpers, she drew her short sword.

"Now we shall have this out. And you will put away your sword, my beauty." He walked forward two steps, one hand held out. "I have no doubt you can thrust that blade through me, but what will you tell them when they find me dead? You will be condemned for murder, and executed. Is that what you want? Give me the sword, Liath."

"I'll tell them you used sorcery to spell everyone to sleep and then tried to rape me."

He laughed. "Why would anyone believe you? Can you imagine such a story coming to my mother's ears and what she would say about it? A mere Eagle accusing a margrave's son?"

Theophanu would believe her, but Theophanu had charged her to keep silence on the matter of sorcery. Theophanu had her own plans and, to a royal princess, an Eagle was simply another servant.

"I am right, as you know," he added, his tone coaxing. "Put down the sword."

"Get away from me," she whispered. "Why can't you leave me alone?"

"That is the choice given you after your da died. Be mine, or be dead. Which will it be?" He stopped, shifted, then fumbled with something unseen. A moment later he unlatched the shutter and opened it. The dull light of winter's sky flooded into the loft, searing her eyes. And when she had done blinking and had finally, truly, to look upon him, he smiled. Cold air boiled in past him, a wind of ice drawn in to this, her prison, for her prison was any place where she was confined with him. The cold was itself the shackles, binding her as it curled around her, freezing her heart.

"Hush, my beauty," he murmured softly. "Do not be scared of me. I won't hurt you. I found a book at the monastery at Firsebarg, locked away in a chest which only the father abbot is allowed to open. I learned much from that book, as you see. 'Lavender, for sleep.' How did you make those arrows burst into flame? Do you even know? I can teach you what it means to have power, to know what is within yourself that you can use. I want only what is best for you. For you and for myself."

The hilt of her sword felt like ice in her hand. He crossed the low attic to her, ducking his head, and took the sword out of her lax hand. His touch was warm, but his eyes were cold.

At last, she recognized that peculiar deep tone in his voice; she had learned well what it presaged, in the depths of winter in Heart's Rest.

"I can't wait any longer, Liath. And there is no one here to witness."

"I'll give you the book," she whispered, voice half caught in her throat. Ai, Lady, she was begging. She was offering the only and most precious thing she had left to her, but losing that would be better than *this* again.

He shook his head impatiently. "You already gave me the book, and your submission, last spring, before Wolfhere stole them from me. I have been waiting a long time to get them back."

She was too numb to resist when he gently stripped her

of bow and quiver and saddlebag, when he lay her down on the hard plank floor. But when he kissed her, when his hand sought and found her belt, loosening it, she remembered finally through terror and numbing weakness one thing.

Wood burns.

6

THE road back to the king's progress had proved so miserable and so full of hardships, appalling detours, and frustrations that Hanna had begun to wonder if Wolfhere might have gotten back with the news about Biscop Antonia before her. She had never seen the palace at Augensburg, of course, but two of her three remaining Lions had slept in the barracks there only two years ago while attending the king.

Now, with clouds sweeping in low over hills glazed with a thin crust of snow and with the last forest crossing behind them, they could see in the distance the market village and sprawling palace complex of Augensburg.

"That," said Ingo, the most senior of the Lions, "is a lot of smoke. Even for Candlemass."

"Lady's Blood!" swore Leo. "Fire!"

Hanna had been walking in order to spare her horse. Now she mounted and left the Lions behind. Soon she came upon traffic that slowed her down as people rushed out away from Augensburg and others—farmers and foresters—rushed in, coming to aid the king against an implacable foe. They made way for her as best they could in the crush, but despite this she was forced to pull up just inside the low outer wall. Here she stared past river and market village, which lay to her left, and up at the palace, which lay on a low rise protected by its own inner palisade and the steep bluff on its other side. Her horse laid its ears back, trying to back up. The stench of burning was caustic as she breathed in.

Hanna had seen fire before, but never anything like this. The fire *roared*. The hot wind streaking off the flames baked her where she stood, though the day was cold and beyond town a thin blanket of snow covered field and forest. Half the palace was on fire, sheets of flame rising into the heavens, a second wall that mirrored the wooden wall of the palisade. In the town, ash rained down on women loading their valuables into carts, on children carrying infants out of houses, on men and women hauling buckets of water up the rise toward the burning palace. Gaping, she sucked in ash; the sharp bite in her throat made her hack.

"Too little water!" shouted Folquin, the fastest runner among the Lions. Panting hard, he came up beside her and leaned, coughing, on his spear. "They'll never put that out! Pray to the Lady it doesn't catch the roofs in town."

Hanna dismounted and thrust reins into the Lion's hands. "Let young Stephen take the horse and hold it for us," she said. "Then you and Ingo and Leo follow me up. We must aid those we can."

"I pray the king is not inside—" he said, but she gave him a look, and he drew the Circle of Unity at his breast and shut up.

She ran up the hill, easily outpacing people burdened with buckets. A ragged procession filed past her down the hill, some with empty buckets, some with handcarts heaped with furniture and books and chests and every kind of item salvaged from the fire. A cleric clutched an ancient parchment codex to her chest; her face was streaked with ash and she had a weeping red welt on her right arm where her cleric's robe was ripped open. Other clerics followed behind her, each holding something precious. One man had pressed unbound parchment sheets against him, hands struggling to keep them all together. A woman held her robe out as a basket, full of quills and inkpots, stands and styluses and tablets all jumbled together, ink leaking through the fine gold fabric of her rich vestment. The youngest of them stumbled behind, looking stunned, carrying a magnificent eagle's feather quill and a little pot of red ink that, tipping, had stained his fingers. A child cried. Servants staggered under loads of bedding salvaged from the blaze.

"Make way!" cried a man in Lion's tabard. "Make way for the princess!"

Hanna stepped aside as Princess Sapientia was carried past reclining on a camp bed. She looked only half conscious, but both of her hands clasped her swollen abdomen and she moaned as she passed Hanna. Behind her, sobbing or gabbling like panicked geese, more servants hauled chests, tapestries that kept coming unrolled, even the splen-

did chair carved with lions and dragons and an eagle's
wings that Hanna recognized as belonging to King Henry.

At the palace gate, grim-faced guards forced back the
curious and only admitted those persons carrying water—
as though such a trifle could stem the inferno. The wind
off the fire singed her skin, and her eyes stung with heat
and burning ash.

"Make way!" she cried, pushing forward to the guards.
"Where is the king?"

"Out on the hunt, thank God!" shouted the one nearest
her. He had no helmet; part of one ear was missing—but
it was an old scar. His red hair was stained with ash. "There
were few enough therein, by Our Lord's Mercy, but surely
some have perished."

"Is there anything I can do?" she yelled. She had to yell
to be heard above the roar of flames. Already her voice
was hoarse from heat and ash.

"Nay, friend. This is one foe we can't fight. Ah!" he
exclaimed, a gasp of relief. "There's one of your comrades
who's run mad. Can you calm her?"

Shifting to look past him, she saw a crowd of some
twenty people, a handful of men in Lion tabards, servants,
and one man in noble garb who directed the others. He
had golden hair, and as she watched he reached to help
two figures struggling out of the smoke: a dark-haired
young woman in an Eagle's scarlet-trimmed cloak who half-
dragged and half-led a man in a singed and dirty Lion's
tabard.

"Liath!" Hanna bolted toward the fire.

A sudden *pop* sounded, followed by a low thundering
gasp of air, a thousand breaths drawn in. People stumbled
back from the courtyard, crying out, as the roof of the back
portion of the palace collapsed in a huge unfolding bloom
of flame and smoke and stinging red hot ash. Four men
grabbed the harness shaft of a wagon loaded to bursting
with iron-bound chests: the king's treasure.

"Liath!" shouted the golden-haired nobleman as Liath
turned and vanished back into the boiling smoke, back into
the burning palace. He started after her. Three soldiers
broke forward, grabbed him, and dragged him away from
the raging fire.

"Liath!" Hanna cried, running forward. She hopped awkwardly sideways to avoid being run over by the wagon, which had now gathered speed as the men at the shaft got momentum. One small chest jolted, bounced, and fell out, splitting open at Hanna's feet to spill delicate cloissoné clasps and buckles onto the cracking mud.

"My lord! There is nothing you can do! You must come away, my lord!" So the Lions shouted at the nobleman, and he cursed them once, without feeling, and then began to weep.

Ai, Lady. Surprise brought her to a jarring halt while fire blistered the timber walls of the palace and parched her lips. It was Hugh. He dropped to his knees as if he meant to pray, and only when the Lions hoisted him up bodily could he be persuaded to move back to safety as the fire scorched the peaked roof, spit, leaped the chasm of an alley between buildings, and kindled a new fire on the roof of the fourth quarter of the palace—the only quarter as yet untouched. Everything would go. Everything.

"Lady forgive me," said Hugh as he stared into the blaze. "Forgive me my presumption in believing I had mastered the arts you gave into my hands. Forgive me for those innocent souls who have died needlessly." He looked up, saw Hanna, and blinked, for an instant examining her as if he recognized her.

She almost staggered under the weight of his stare. She had actually forgotten how glorious he was.

Then he shook his head to dismiss her and spoke to himself—as if to convince himself. "Had I only known more, it would not have happened this way. But I cannot let her go. . . ."

"Come, my lord," said a servant, but Hugh shook him off.

"Father Hugh!" A new man had come running up; he was clearly terrified to stand so close to the blaze. "Princess Sapientia calls for you, my lord."

Torn, he wavered. Rising, he could not bring himself to follow the servant.

"She is having pains—"

Clenching a hand, he glared at the raging fire, cursed under his breath and then, with a last—beseeching?—glance at Hanna, spun and followed the servant.

Liath had gone back inside the inferno.

"Keep your wits, Hanna," she muttered to herself, recalling the first Lion's words: "*Your comrade has run mad.*" Pulling her cloak tight over her mouth and nose, she pressed forward into the blaze.

"Come back!" they shouted, those Lions who remained. "Eagle!"

Her skin was aflame, but no flame touched her. She crossed into a great hall ragged with smoke and blowing ash. Heat boiled out. She saw nothing, no one, no figure struggling through the smoke. The thick beams supporting the ceiling above smoldered, not yet in open flame. A far wall cracked, splintering, burst by heat.

She heard the scream. It was Liath.

"Help me! God save us, wake up, man!"

Hanna could not take a deep breath, for courage or for air. But she ran forward anyway into the fire. Ash rained on her head. The boom and surge of fire raged around her as harshly as the tempest of battle. Smoke burned her eyes and the air tasted acrid.

She found Liath in the corridor behind, dragging a man so big and so burdened with armor that it was a miracle Liath had managed to get him this far.

"Hanna!" That she had breath to talk was astounding. "Oh, God, Hanna, help me get him free. There's two more, but the beams have fallen—" She was weeping, although how could she weep when the heat should have wicked all moisture away?

Hanna did not think, she merely grabbed the Lion's legs and together they tugged him out of the corridor while the fire blazed closer. They had dragged him halfway across the hall when beams began to fall and the far walls to crack and disintegrate.

Just out the door her three faithful Lions were waiting, together with the red-haired Lion; Ingo and Leo grabbed their limp comrade and yanked him free as Liath turned and started inside again.

"Stop her!" screamed Hanna. Folquin wrapped his arms around the young Eagle and lifted her as she kicked and pleaded and wept, trying to get free—but he was a brawny, farm-bred lad and as strong as an ox.

"Liath!" Hanna shouted.

But there was no time to reason with her. They retreated

in awkward haste as the great roof beams collapsed in the hall. The gates remained open but stood now deserted, and they paused outside the gates to look behind. Everyone had fled to safer ground. Townsfolk carried their buckets of water to the houses closest to the palace wall, dousing their roofs with water to stop the flaming ash from setting a new blaze. The market village was all there was left to save.

On the wind, a faint counterpoint to the blaze, she heard a hunting horn.

"Let me go back! Let me go back! There are two more—at least two more—" Liath struggled and fought and even tried to bite poor Folquin, whose leather armor had protected him from worse attacks.

"Hush, friend," said the red-haired Lion sternly. "This one is dead, though you tried valiantly to save him. I doubt not the others have already died. No use risking yourself to drag out their bodies. May God have mercy on their souls, and may they come in peace to the Chamber of Light." He bowed his head.

Gingerly, Folquin set Liath down, glanced at Hanna and, with a nod from her, let Liath go. Liath collapsed to her knees but simply sat trembling as the palace burned and ash drifted down like a light rain of snow upon them. Despite her forays into the raging fire, she had nary a mark or burn on her.

"We are still too close," said Ingo.

There was a commotion on the road below. Hanna turned to see Hugh striding up toward them. Seeing Liath, he stopped dead. Such an expression transformed his face that it chilled her to her bones and yet made her want to weep in compassion for his pain. But he said nothing. He only looked. Perhaps that was worse. Then, wincing at a pain in his shoulder, he turned to limp away along the path. Servants and townsfolk and clerics swarmed him. Someone brought a chair on which to carry him, but he waved it away. Closer now, the hunting horn sounded again, high and imperative.

Liath broke into gulping sobs, so racked by them she could hardly breathe. Hanna gestured to her Lions to step back, and they ranged out, helping other Lions and guards pick up any detritus that could be saved without venturing too close: items lost from wagons or thrown down from the wallwalk; swords, shields, spears; clothing, saddlebags, scattered jewelry; a browned and blistered book, two carved stools, a sandal, a trail of ivory chess pieces. The fire burned on, but already the flames seemed less furious— or perhaps she had become accustomed to the heat searing her face. Her hands were red with it, her lips so dry that licking them made them bleed.

"Liath." She crouched down beside her friend. "Liath, it's me. It's Hanna. You must stop this. Liath! There was nothing you could do to save them. You tried—"

"Ai, Lady. Hanna! Hanna! Why weren't you here before? Why didn't you come? Oh, God. Oh, God. I lost everything. Where is he? Please, Hanna, please get me away from him. You don't understand. I did it. *I caused it.* Why did Da lie to me?" On she went, more sobbing than words and all of them incoherent.

The horn blasted close at hand, and Hanna looked over her shoulder to see the magnificent train of the king and his hunting party emerge from the forest west of the blaze with the setting sun at their backs.

On Dhearc, the shortest day of the year, light triumphed at last over the advance of night. Candles were lit to aid in that battle. Some fallen candle, surely, had kindled this fire; the bitter irony did not escape her. But Hanna could only sniff back tears, feeling the heat of fire blazing on her cheek as she held Liath and tried to get her to stop shaking and babbling and crying, but Liath could only go on and on about fire and rape and ice and power and sleep as if she had truly lost her mind.

"Liath," said Hanna sharply, "you must stop this! The king has arrived."

"The king," whispered Liath. She sucked air in between clenched teeth. She struggled more fiercely than she had against Folquin's hold, but in the end she fought herself out of hysteria and into something resembling control. "Stay by me, Hanna. Don't leave me."

"I won't." Hanna looked up as she tasted a new scent on the wind. "Is it raining?" But there were only a few clouds. "Look at the fire. It's as if all the timber's gone." Indeed, the fire was ebbing, although it was as yet far too hot to venture close.

"Don't leave me, Hanna," Liath repeated. "Don't ever leave me alone with him, I beg you."

"Ai, Lady," murmured Hanna, suddenly afraid. "He didn't—"

"No." Her voice dropped to a whisper, barely audible. Her hands gripped Hanna's so tightly it hurt. "No, he didn't have time to—" Her hands convulsed, her whole body jerking at some horrible memory. "I called, I *reached* for fire—" Shaking again, she could not go on. The wind had come up, fanning the flames. Beyond, king and retinue approached. Already a small entourage had gone out to meet him and give him the terrible news, although surely he could divine the worst from any distance. The air stank of burning.

"Hanna, don't desert me," Liath breathed. "I need you." She rested her head on Hanna's arms. Her hair was caked with soot, as were her arms and hands, every part of her. She was so grimy that anything she touched came away streaky with soot. "I didn't know—I didn't know what Da was protecting me from."

"What was he protecting you from?" Hanna asked, mystified.

Liath looked up at her, and her bleak expression cut Hanna to the core. "From myself."

7

SISTER Amabilia had saved the *Vita of St. Radegundis.*

This single thought kept leaping back so insistently into Rosvita's mind that it became hard for her to attend to the council at hand. Brother Fortunatus sat at her feet, hands still gripping the loose pages of her *History,* which he had grabbed instead of the cartulary he had been working on. She had thanked him profusely, as he deserved, poor child. But though it would have been a blow to lose the *History,* she could write it again from memory.

Sister Amabilia had saved the *Vita.* Had it burned, it could never have been restored. Brother Fidelis was dead. Only this copy remained, except for the partial, also saved by Amabilia, which the young woman had herself been copying from the original.

Rosvita felt sick to her stomach just thinking about it. What if the *Vita* had been lost? Gone up in smoke to join its creator, Fidelis, where he rested in blessed peace in the Chamber of Light?

"But it did not," she murmured.

Her clerics glanced at her, surprised to hear her comment while the king was speaking. She smiled wryly at them and made the gesture for *Silence* just as Amabilia opened her mouth to reply.

". . . to the efforts of my faithful clerics who rescued my treasury and much of the business of the court, and mostly to Father Hugh. He stayed to the end until all who could be brought out of the fire were saved. He risked his own life with no thought for himself. Where is Father Hugh?"

"He is still with Princess Sapientia, Your Majesty," said Helmut Villam.

They stood or sat, all in disorder, in the hall of a well-to-do merchant. Even so, most of the court could not crowd in. They had slept out in the fields and forest last night, in barns and hayricks and under such shelter as could be

found, safely away from the fire. Rosvita had been glad of
straw for bedding; most of the court and the townsfolk
rousted from their homes had been glad simply to have a
roof of some kind over their heads. It had rained half the
night. Now, in the morning, with the palace smoldering and
a light rain still falling, Henry had felt it safe enough to
venture back into town and take shelter there while he
held council.

Burchard, Duke of Avaria, and his duchess, Ida of Ro-
vencia, sat beside the king. Burchard had the look of a man
who has touched Death but not yet realized it; Ida looked
stern, tired, and very old, as befit a woman who has seen
her two eldest sons die untimely.

The king himself looked tired. Though his tent had been
salvaged from the fire, he had not passed a restful night.
Last to sleep, sitting by his pregnant daughter's bed, he had
been first to wake and with a number of attendants had
walked to the palace to investigate the remains.

It was still too hot to enter. A few pillars stood, the
remaining roof sloped precariously, about to cave in, and
the stone chapel was scorched but otherwise intact. All the
chapel valuables—a reliquary containing the dust of the
thighbone of St. Paulina, the gold vessels for holy water,
and the embroidered altar cloth—had been saved.

"What of the cause?" asked the king now.

A palace steward came forward. He had obviously slept
in his clothing and himself risked his life in the fire, for his
sleeves were ripped and stained with soot and the hood of
his cape was singed and blackened. "No one knows, Your
Majesty. All the Candlemass candles were carefully watched.
We always set them in clay bowls so if they spill there
won't be danger of fire. Alas, the Lions have testified that
some among their number fell asleep while gaming in the
barracks. Perhaps they knocked over a lamp."

Henry sighed. "I see no point in casting blame, not when
a dozen souls lost their lives, may God grant them peace.
Let us consider this as a sign that we take our leisure at
our peril, as long as Gent remains in the hands of the Eika.
Thus does our sport blind us to our duty. Let greater care
be taken in the future."

Sister Amabilia had saved the *Vita of St. Radegundis*
from the fire.

The book lay on Rosvita's lap, swaddled in a lamb's wool blanket, the softest cradle Rosvita had found for it. She had slept with it clasped to her breast last night, though its presence had triggered strange dreams, and she would not let it out of her grasp today.

Was this obsession unseemly? Perhaps it would be best to give the original to the monastery at Quedlinhame and keep only Amabilia's copy for herself, to keep herself free of the sin of esurience—that greedy hunger she had for the knowledge that had died with Brother Fidelis: *his* knowledge, some of which was retained in the *Life* he had written.

Henry sat forward suddenly, his expression lightening. "Here is Father Hugh. What news?"

Hugh knelt before the king. He looked ragged and unkempt. Possibly he had not slept at all. Yet his lack of concern for his appearance, under these circumstances, could only reflect well on him. He alone of all the nobles had remained behind beside the conflagration; he had directed the rescue efforts; he had made sure all who could be brought safely out of the palace were gotten free.

Perhaps it had been a wise choice when Margrave Judith had sent Princess Sapientia on her way, directing her to visit first with the young abbot of Firsebarg, Judith's bastard son. Poor Sapientia, whose name meant *wisdom,* had never shown much of that quality; perhaps, with such a name, she had been bound to become sensitive to comparisons to her clever younger sister. But she had chosen wisely when it came to Hugh.

Truly it could be said, as the court wits said now, that he was the ornament of "wisdom." Even in such a state as this.

"Princess Sapientia sleeps, Your Majesty," he said, his voice as calm and well-modulated as ever. "Her pains have gone away, but she still feels poorly. With your permission, I will send a message to my mother. Her physician—"

"Yes, I am acquainted with Margrave Judith's physician." The king gestured toward Villam. "The man saved my good companion Villam's life, if not his arm. Very well, send for her—or for the Arethousan, if her business keeps her in the marchlands."

"What business?" whispered Sister Odila.

"Oh, come," muttered Brother Fortunatus, "don't you recall? Judith had to return to Olsatia because she is to marry again."

"Again?" squeaked young Brother Constantine.

"Hush," hissed Sister Amabilia, but a moment later she, too, could not contain herself. "I thought she meant to celebrate the marriage here on the king's progress."

"Indeed," said Fortunatus smugly, certain of his sources of information and pleased to have knowledge Amabilia lacked. "But the young bridegroom never showed up. His family made peculiar excuses, so the margrave journeyed back to find out for herself."

"Hush, children," said Rosvita.

". . . Sapientia has become fond of her Eagle," Hugh was saying, "and I fear it would upset her at this delicate time to send the young woman away. If another Eagle could be found to ride . . ." He smiled gently.

The king's Eagle, Hathui, now leaned forward. "Your Majesty. You have not gotten a report from the Eagle who rode in yesterday."

The king nodded. Hathui gestured and a young woman walked forward from the back of the hall to kneel before the king.

"Give your report," said Hathui to her.

The young Eagle bowed her head respectfully. "Your Majesty, I am Hanna, daughter of Birta and Hansal, out of Heart's Rest."

Heart's Rest! Rosvita stared at the young woman but could see no resemblance to any person she recalled from her childhood; it had been so many years since she had visited her home and her father's hall. Perhaps her brother Ivar knew the family—but it was unlikely unless Count Harl had himself brought the young woman to the notice of the Eagles.

"You sent me south with Wolfhere, escorting Biscop Antonia, late last spring after the battle of Kassel."

"I remember."

"I bring grave news, Your Majesty. While in the Alfar Mountains, a storm hit St. Servitius' Monastery, where we took shelter for the night." She described a rockfall and the destruction of the monastery infirmary. "Wolfhere believes it was no natural storm. He believes Antonia and her cleric escaped."

"He found no bodies?"

"None could be found, Your Majesty. The rocks were too unstable to move."

"Where is Wolfhere now?"

"He went on to Darre to bring the charges against Biscop Antonia before the skopos. He does not believe she is dead, Your Majesty."

"So you have said."

At this, she looked up directly at him. "And so I will say again, Your Majesty, and again, until you believe me."

He smiled suddenly, the first smile Rosvita had seen since their return from the hunt yesterday into the chaos attendant on the disastrous fire. "You believe Wolfhere is correct?"

She hesitated, bit her lip, then went on. "I myself witnessed such sights that night . . . I saw *things,* Your Majesty, creatures in the storm such as I have never seen before and hope never to see again! They were not any creatures that walk on earth unless called from—other places, dark places."

Now he leaned forward. She had caught his interest. "Sorcery?"

"What else could it be? We saw the *guivre,* such as only a magi could capture and control. But these were not even creatures of flesh and blood. Wolfhere called them *galla.*"

Every person in the hall shuddered reflexively when the word came out of her mouth. Rosvita had never heard of such a thing, and yet some tone, some intonation, made her flinch instinctively. But as she glanced round the room she saw Father Hugh look up sharply, eyes widening—with interest? Or with distaste?

"I have no reason," said the king wryly, "to distrust Wolfhere in such matters. Well, then, Eagle, if this happened while crossing the Alfar Mountains in the summer, why has it taken you until winter to reach me?"

She lifted a hand. "If I may, Your Majesty?"

Curious, he assented.

She gestured behind, and three Lions walked forward and knelt beside her, heads bowed. They, too, looked travel-worn, tabards and armor much mended; one had a newly healed cut on his left cheek. "These Lions were my escort, and they will witness that all that I say is true. When we turned back from the monastery, we found the pass was closed, blocked by another avalanche. Therefore we had to keep going south into the borderlands of Karrone until we could link up with the road that led back north through the Julier Pass. But here, too, we could not get through."

"Another storm?" demanded Villam, and Father Hugh leaned forward as if he feared the Eagle's answer would be too faint for him to hear.

"No, my lord. Duke Conrad closed the pass."

Henry stood up, and immediately any persons in the hall who were sitting scrambled to their feet as well, including poor Brother Fortunatus, who had sprained his knee in the conflagration yesterday. "Duke Conrad has *closed* the pass? On whose authority?"

"I do not know the particulars, Your Majesty, only what I could learn from the border guards. It seems there is a dispute about borders between Queen Marozia and Duke Conrad, and neither will back down. So to spite her, Duke Conrad refused to let any traffic through the pass."

"To spite himself," muttered Villam. "That pass links the duchy of Wayland to Karrone *and* to Aosta." He shook his head, looking disgusted.

"Nevertheless," she replied, still sounding offended at the memory of the incident, "we were not let through although I carry an Eagle's ring and badge, the seals of your authority."

There was a silence while Henry considered this news. A few whispers hissed through the hall, then hushed. Abruptly, he sat down. Rosvita could not read his expression. "What then?" he asked, his voice level.

"We had to ride farther east until we came to the Brinne Pass, and farther east still, once we had crossed over the mountains. We came into the marchlands of Westfall where Margrave Werinhar fed us most handsomely and gave me a new horse and all of us generous supplies. But so many of the paths and roads had been washed out by heavy rains that we had to go even farther east into the marchland of Eastfall before we could find a good road leading west." Again she hesitated and looked toward Hathui, as for courage. The older Eagle merely nodded crisply, and the

younger went on. "Every person there sent word by me,
Your Majesty. They beg you to set a margrave over them
for protection. The Quman raids have been more fierce this
year than in any year since your great-grandfather the first
Henry fought and defeated the Quman princes at the River
Eldar." She turned and signed to the Lion, eldest of her
companions—the one with the scarred cheek.

He presented a broken arrow to the king.

Fletched with iron-gray feathers, the arrow had an iron
point; it looked innocuous enough for a tool meant for
killing, and yet a kind of miasma hung about it as if it had
a rank smell or some kind of repelling spell laid on it.
Those feathers resembled none of any bird she had ever
seen.

But in the eastern wilderness, griffins hunted. Or so
books said and report gave out. But Rosvita rarely trusted
the reports of credulous folk who might see one thing and
believe it was another—as had the lords and ladies out
hunting, seeing a deer instead of Theophanu. It was stuffy
in the small hall with so many people crammed in, even
with the high windows thrown open. A restlessness plagued
them all at the sight of the arrow. A few slipped out the
door, but even as they left, others shouldered in to take
their place.

Henry took the arrow from the Lion's hand and at once
cut a finger on the hard edge of the fletching. He grunted
in pain and stuck his finger in his mouth, sucking on it.
Immediately, the Lion took the arrow out of Henry's hand.

"Let me hold this for you, Your Majesty," said the man.
"I beg you."

"Where did you get this arrow?" asked the king as he
pressed on the finger with his thumb to stop the bleeding.

"At a village called Felsig," continued the Eagle. "We
arrived hours after dawn, when they had repulsed an attack
of Quman raiders. We helped fight off the last of them,
some of their foot soldiers who I swear to you are so unsightly that they could be born of no human mother, though
they are nothing like the Eika. Our comrade Artur died of
wounds taken there. We brought with us a lad, named Stephen, who fought bravely in that skirmish. He wishes to
swear himself to the service of the Lions."

"And I, as senior among us, deemed him fit to serve," added Ingo.

"Do as you see fit," said Henry. "Such a brave fighter is welcome in my Lions."

"Whom will you nominate as margrave of Eastfall?" asked Lady Brigida from the crowd. As niece of Duke Burchard and Duchess Ida, she might expect to be named.

Several voices spoke. "Princess Theophanu. Prince Ekkehard."

Henry raised a hand for silence. "I will think on it. It is not a decision to be made rashly. Duke Burchard." He turned to the old duke. "Can you send a force into the marchlands from Avaria?"

The duke coughed before he spoke, and his voice was weak. "I have no sons of an age to lead such an expedition," he said slowly and pointedly—thus reminding all listeners that his second son Frederic had died fighting in the marchlands and his eldest son, Agius, just last spring, had sacrificed himself to save the king from the dreadful *guivre.* "It is my experience that the Quman riders must be met by cavalry. Foot soldiers cannot defeat them. You must reform the Dragons, Your Majesty."

"I have no sons of such an age either," said Henry harshly, not even looking toward poor Ekkehard who sat unnoticed in the corner behind Helmut Villam. "Not any more. Nor any soldiers as brave as those who died at Gent."

No one spoke or ventured an opinion, for Duke Burchard had thrown the meat among the dogs and everyone waited to see how ugly the fight would be for the spoils. But no one dared contradict the king, not even Burchard.

"What other news do you bring for me, Eagle?" Henry demanded, turning his attention back to the young woman kneeling before him. "There has been enough of bad news. Pray you, tell me nothing more that I do not want to hear."

She had been pale before. Now she blanched. "There is another piece of news," she began, almost stuttering. "I heard it when we halted at the Thurin Forest, where we had come searching for you. They had it there from Quedlinhame." Then she broke off.

"Go on!" said the king impatiently.

"N-news from Gent."

"Gent!" The king stood again.

"Ai, Lady," muttered Brother Fortunatus, wincing as he got up.

"*What news?*"

"Only this: that two children escaped from the city. The children said that a daimone imprisoned by Bloodheart showed them the way out through the crypt, but there was no trace of such a tunnel when the foresters thereabouts went later to look."

"Such a tunnel," said Villam, "as the other refugees from Gent claimed to have used to flee to safety?"

"I don't know," said Hanna, "but Liath—"

"Liath?" asked the king.

"My comrade in the Eagles. She would know. She was there."

"Of course," said the king. "I will question her later. Go on." His interest was keen and his attention, on the young Eagle, utterly focused.

"There is little else to report. The Eika still infest the city. They have brought in slaves who work the smithies and armories and in the tanneries, so the children reported. They saw—" She made a kind of hiccuping sound, then got the words out. "According to the report I heard, they saw the bodies of fighting men in the crypt below the cathedral. Tabards sewn with the sigil of a dragon."

"That is enough." The king signed her to silence. She looked relieved to be free of his notice. "I am weary. Today my stewards will organize the train. Tomorrow we ride toward Echstatt. Duke Burchard, you will give me fifty soldiers to send to Eastfall. Young Rodulf of Varingia and ten companions attend me. He can prove himself loyal to me and cleanse his family honor of the stain laid there by his father the late duke by fighting well and bravely in the east. Let them be called Dragons." The words came hard, but he spoke them. "In time, others will be added to their number."

He shut his eyes a moment, seemed to be praying silently; then he shook himself free of memory and went on. "God guide us in this hour of loss." He touched a hand to his chest where, Rosvita knew, he kept an old bloodstained rag—the birthcloth of his bastard son Sanglant—nestled against his skin. "Now we must consider Gent. We have recovered from our losses at Kassel. There has been time to get the harvest in, and by the mercy and grace of Our Lord and Lady, the crop has been good. Sabella remains safely in the custody of Biscop Constance. I need only an army sufficient to attack Gent."

Many people in the hall, mostly young and male, clamored at once. "I will go! Let me ride, Your Majesty! The honor of my kin—!"

The newest arrival at court, pleasant and able Lord Geoffrey, shouldered his way to the front. "Grant me this honor, Your Majesty," he said, kneeling.

Henry raised a hand to cut short the outcry. "Winter is a poor season for Eagles to ride, but ride they must for my purposes. Hathui. Send one hardy soul to Margrave Judith, to inquire if she will lend her physician for the care of my daughter until she gives birth to the child. Send one with the expedition to Eastfall. Send another to Duke Conrad in Wayland with these words: 'Attend me on my progress to explain your conduct toward my Eagle at Julier Pass.' And choose a fourth carefully, to send to Count Lavastine, in Varre."

Lord Geoffrey glanced up, surprised.

"You, my young friend," said Henry to him, "I will keep by my side for a few more hunts at least. Let the Eagle ride now to your kinsman. You can return there later."

"Why to Count Lavastine?" asked Burchard querulously.

Villam, who had been listening carefully to the king, smiled softly as at a joke only he understood.

"He has gained a son. I have lost one. Let Lavastine prove his loyalty to me by meeting me with an army at Gent. If God grant us victory over the Eika and restore the city to our hands, then I will grant him the reward he seeks."

8

IN the end it had mattered not. And she had, besides, brought death to a dozen or more people. Could God ever forgive her? Could she forgive herself?

"Please, Da," she prayed, hands clasped tight before her lips, "please tell me what to do. Why didn't you teach me, Da?"

"I will teach you, Liath."

She jerked away just before he could set his clean, white hand on her shoulder. Stumbling up to her feet, she jumped out of his reach. Mist curled around them, a low-lying fog that shrouded trees and the market village, just out of sight of the king's encampment. Hugh had worked some terrible magic on Sapientia's mind, such that the princess would not let Liath out of her sight, as if she were a talisman for the safety of the unborn child. So Liath had risen early and come outside to relieve herself, and afterward lingered in the bitter cold of a fog-bound winter dawn, hoping to have one moment of solitude, of respite.

But Hugh could not let her be. He would never let her be. He had known long before she had what Da was protecting. And he wanted it for himself.

"Have you learned your lesson, Liath?" Hugh continued. "So many dead." He shook his head, clicking his tongue with disapproval. "So many dead."

"If you hadn't spelled them to sleep—" she cried.

"It's true," he said, amazing her. She broke off. "I thought too well of what little I had learned. I will pray to God for wisdom." His lips curled up. He seemed, for an instant, to be laughing at himself; then the moment passed and, as quick as an owl strikes, he grabbed Liath's wrist. "Don't be a fool. The longer you ignore it, the less able you will be to control it. Is that what you want?" He gestured toward the rise where the blackened hulk of the palace scarred its height. "Liath, whom else can you trust?"

"I'll tell the king I set the fire—"

He laughed curtly. "Imagine what the king and his counselors will say when they discover they have harbored a maleficus in their midst. Only the skopos can judge such as you—a monster!"

"I'll go to Wolfhere—"

"Wolfhere! We have had this discussion before. Trust Wolfhere, if you will. But I have *The Book of Secrets* now. I have seen what you can do, and I do not hate you for it. I love you for it, Liath. Who else will love or trust you once they know what you are? *I* have the trust of the king, and Wolfhere does not. I can protect you from the king's wrath, and the church's suspicion. And when Sapientia gives birth to our child, I will be guaranteed the place of her closest adviser for as long as she reigns."

"Not if she miscarries—"

He hit her, hard, on the cheek with an open hand.

"I carried your child," she gasped, jerking away, but she could not get free. "Ai, Lady, I am glad you beat it out of me."

He hit her again, and then again, harder, and the fourth time she staggered and fell to her knees—but this time she drew her knife.

"I'll kill you," she whispered hoarsely. Tears stung her eyes and blood dripped from her nose.

He laughed, as if her resistance delighted him.

"My lord Father!" A servingman ran out of the mist, leaping between her knife and Hugh's body. He jumped in to grapple with her, but she flung the knife away before he could touch her. What use was a knife against Hugh's magic—if it even were magic? Hugh wielded his earthly power as effectively as any magic.

"My lord Father, are you unhurt?" Numb, she listened as the servingman fawned over Hugh. "God Above! That an Eagle should threaten you so! I'll take her into custody until the king—"

"Nay, brother." Hugh broke in with a gentle smile. "Her mind is disordered by the minions of the Enemy. I thank you for your watchfulness, but God are with me and I need not fear her, for I intend to heal her instead. You may go on, but be sure I shall remember you in my prayers." He nodded toward Liath. "As you must pray for her soul."

The servingman bowed. "As you wish, my lord." He

shook his head. "You are all that is generous." Clucking softly under his breath as if with veiled disapproval, he walked away.

Hugh's gentle demeanor vanished as soon as the man was out of earshot. "Don't provoke me, Liath, and don't mock God." His tone was as hard as the rocks digging into her knees. He picked up the knife and used the point to lift her chin so that she had to look at him. "Now go in. The princess wants to see you." Then, in an action meant to flaunt his power and her weakness, he flipped over the knife and handed it to her, hilt first.

Still numb, she sheathed it. Her nose still bled. She pressed one nostril with a hand, to stem the blood, and walked stiffly back to the princess' tent; Hugh walked right behind her. Her eyes stung and her head pounded, but her heart was frozen. Nothing she could do mattered. She had no recourse. Perhaps it was true that she could stop him physically should he try again to rape her . . . but he was still her jailer, and she was in every other way his prisoner.

Sapientia did not even notice Liath; she was gossiping with Lady Brigida about who might be named as the next Margrave of Eastfall. But Sister Rosvita was there, attending the princess.

"Good child," she exclaimed as she noticed Liath. "What happened to your face?"

"I tripped on a stump. I beg your pardon, Sister."

"No need to beg my pardon, Eagle. Your Highness, your father has sent me to get news of your health."

"I'm feeling better," said Sapientia. "I can ride today."

"Perhaps not today," said Rosvita gently, glancing curiously over at Liath again. "Your father wishes you to remain here resting another week before you attempt the journey to Echstatt."

"I don't want—!"

"Your Highness," said Hugh softly.

Sapientia stopped dead, looked up at Hugh with a most disgustingly exultant expression, and smiled. "What do you advise, Father Hugh?"

"Heed the king's advice, Your Highness. You must conserve all your energy to bring this child safely to term."

"Yes." She nodded soberly. "Yes, I must." She turned

back to the cleric. "Tell my father I will abide by his wishes."

"I will. There is one other thing. King Henry wishes to interview your Eagle about Gent."

Liath waited stupidly, stripped of purpose, until Sapientia gave permission for her to go. Hugh begged leave to attend the king. Together, Liath, Rosvita, and Hugh left and crossed to the king's tent. Not even in such a small way would Hugh leave her alone. Henry was awake, seated in his chair while his servants packed what remained of his possessions into chests for the journey.

"There is the Eagle," said the king as he looked up from a consultation with a steward about the outfitting of the new Dragons. He indicated Hathui, who stood over to one side of the tent with Hanna and a redheaded Eagle named, of course, Rufus. "You will give your report to your comrades. One of them will be riding to Count Lavastine. Father Hugh! How may I aid you?"

Hailed by the king, Hugh could hardly follow her over to the others.

"What happened to your face!" exclaimed Hanna.

"I beg you, Hathui," pleaded Liath in a whisper, grasping Hathui's hands. "I beg you, if you have any influence with the king, let me ride with Hanna, get me out of here."

"I'm sorry, Liath. It's already been decided."

"But if you all go today, if you leave me alone—" She was suddenly so nauseated, head pounding, eyesight blurring, that she knew she was going to be sick.

"This way," said Hathui briskly, and hustled her outside.

She retched, heaving up mostly spume for she had taken nothing to eat or drink since last night's sparse dinner, and hacked and shuddered until she thought she might as well die now and be rid of this misery.

"Child!" Rosvita appeared out of the mist and touched her gently on the shoulder. "What ails you?"

Hysterical with fear, she no longer cared what she said or did. She could not endure this any longer. She flung herself down and clasped Rosvita's knees like a supplicant. "I pray you, Sister. You have influence with the king! I beg you, ask him to send me away, anywhere, to take any message, anywhere, only away from here. I beg you, Sister."

"You are from Heart's Rest," said Rosvita suddenly, in

a tone of surprise. Liath looked up, but the cleric was examining Hanna, not her.

"I am."

"And this one, too," said Rosvita slowly, looking from
Hanna to Liath and then back to Hanna. "Is it possible,
Eagle, that you also know my brother Ivar?"

Hanna blinked, then dropped like a stone to kneel before
the cleric. "My lady! I beg your pardon for not knowing—"

"Never mind it," said Rosvita. "Answer my question."

"Ivar is my milk brother. He and I nursed from the same
breast—my mother's. My lady, I beg you." Coming from
Hanna's lips, the pleading sounded freakish. Hanna never
begged. Hanna could always handle any emergency that
came her way. Hanna was so calm. "It is presumptuous of
me to claim kinship with you, my lady, but I beg you by
that bond of kinship I hold with your brother, that if you
can help her, please do."

Liath gulped down a sob, she was so desperate, so hope-
ful, so stripped of hope.

"But why are you so eager to leave the king?" Clearly
Rosvita was groping for answers and having trouble finding
any. "You were with Wolfhere in Gent. Has he poisoned
your mind somehow against Henry? Any dispute Wolfhere
had with Henry was not of Henry's making."

"No," gasped Liath, "it was nothing Wolfhere said. He
never said anything against King Henry."

"True-spoken words," muttered Hathui.

"It isn't the king at all." Ai, Lady, how much could she
say? How much dared she say?

"Come, now, daughter, take hold of yourself." Rosvita
set a hand, like a benediction, on Liath's forehead. "If it is
the service of Princess Sapientia you chafe under—"

"Yes!" Liath leaped at this. "Yes. I don't—I can't—We
don't suit, I—"

"An Eagle serves where the king commands," said Rosvita sternly.

Having freed himself from the king, Hugh came out of
the tent. Liath began to sob. She had lost.

But Rosvita took her by the hand and lifted her up.
"Come, daughter, dry your eyes and sit yourself down here,
where there is shelter. It has begun to rain."

Indeed, it had begun to rain. Liath only noticed it be-

cause the sleeting rain slid under the neck of her cloak and
straight down her spine.

"I will take her back to Princess Sapientia's tent," said
Hugh softly. "I fear the fall she took earlier has disordered
her mind."

"Let her rest here a moment," said Rosvita. For a miracle, Hugh did not press the issue while Rosvita left Liath's
side and went into the king's tent. Hathui followed the
cleric in, leaving Hanna and a confounded Rufus to stand
beside her. She swallowed tears and, through the fabric of
the tent, heard Rosvita speaking to the king.

"Would it not be wisest, Your Majesty," she asked, "to
send the Eagle who has come from Gent to Count Lavastine, so that he may question her directly?"

"There is wisdom in your words, Sister," said the king.
"But my daughter is fond of the Eagle, and I wish to keep
her spirits up."

"I trust Father Hugh and her other companions can keep
her spirits up, Your Majesty. But Count Lavastine will need
the best intelligence if he is to have any hope of retaking
Gent, surely, and you cannot afford to leave Gent in the
hands of the Eika. Not when it comes time for them to
raid again, and they have control of the river."

"It is true," spoke up Hathui, "that Liath led the refugees through the hidden tunnel so many have spoken of.
If any can find it again, she can."

Liath heard no reply from the king. Beside her, Hugh
cursed softly under his breath. "Eagles," he said curtly.
"Withdraw." Rufus did at once, but Hanna hesitated.
"Go!" She backed away. "Look at me." She kept her head
down. "Liath!" he hissed, but she would not look. Let him
strike her where everyone could see, even his noble peers.
Let her at least have that satisfaction, even if it would make
no difference in the end.

From inside the tent the king spoke. "It is good advice,
Sister. Hathui, see that the young Eagle who came from
Gent rides with the message to Lavastine. You may dispose
of the others as you see fit."

"Do not think you have escaped me," said Hugh in a
reasonable tone. "I will go in now and tell the king which
Eagle Sapientia wishes to replace you. You know which
Eagle I will choose. . . ."

She could not look up. He had won again.

He smiled. "Your friend will be my hostage until you return. She, and the book. Remember that, Liath. You are still mine." He turned and walked into the tent. So, with his honey-sweet words, did he convince the king.

"Liath." Hanna laid a hand on her arm. "Stand up."

"I've betrayed you."

"You've betrayed no one. I am an *Eagle*. That means something. He can't harm me—"

"But Theophanu in the forest—"

"*What* are you talking about? Liath, stop it! He doesn't care about me, he only cares about you. As long as I behave myself, he won't notice me. Lady and Lord, Liath, I have survived Antonia, an avalanche, creatures made of no flesh or blood, two mountain crossings, a Quman attack, flooded rivers, and your bawling. I think I can survive this!"

"Promise me you will!"

Hanna rolled her eyes. "Spare us this!" she said with disgust. "Now go collect your things."

Liath winced, remembering. "Burned," she whispered. "Everything burned in the attic."

"Then tell Hathui and she'll see new gear is issued to you. Oh, Liath—did you—did you lose the book, after everything?"

"No." She shut her eyes, heard the soft flow of words from inside the tent, heard Hugh laugh at a jest made by the king, heard Rosvita answer with a witty reply. "Hugh got the book."

"Well, then," said Hanna sharply, "it's just as well I stay behind to keep an eye on it, isn't it? Wasn't it I who got it away from him at Heart's Rest?"

Liath wiped her nose with the back of a hand and sniffed, hard. "Oh, Hanna, you must be sick of me. I'm sick of myself."

"You'll have no time to get sick of yourself when you're traveling all day and just trying to keep alive! That's what you need! Now go on. The king wants his Eagles sent out as soon as they can get horses saddled."

Liath hugged her and went to find Hathui.

But in the end, when she left the king's encampment, the road swung back by the market village and, curious, she

took a quick detour up to the rise to see the burned palace.
Hathui had found no bow to replace the one lost, and there
were no swords to spare with so many having been lost in
the burned barracks. She had a spear, a spare woolen tunic,
a water pouch and hardtack for the road, and a flint to
make fire. She had not told Hathui she needed no tools to
make fire.

She could not help herself. She dismounted at the
charred gates and led her horse into the ruined complex.
Already human scavengers tested the blackened timbers
nearest the edge of the fire, those that had cooled; they
searched for anything that could be salvaged. Liath threw
the reins over the horse's head and left it to stand. She
trudged through wreckage, boots collecting soot, her nose
stinging from the stink. A sticky trail of blood from her
nose tickled her lip, and she licked it away and sniffed hard,
hoping the bleeding would finally stop.

She knew where the barracks stood. Though confused
about the palace's layout in her first days at Augensburg,
she now knew the route well because of the fire, when she
had plunged in more times than she could count in her vain
attempt to drag all the sleeping Lions to safety.

There, at that spot, in that courtyard, she and Hugh had
jumped to safety. He had had the presence of mind to grab
her saddlebags before he jumped. That he still limped from
a twisted ankle gave her some pleasure, but not enough.

She had been too horrified to think. The flames had come
so fast, so fierce, and she had not meant them to come into
being at all. They had come to her as fire leaps to any dry
thing within its reach. She had scrambled to safety after
him, and only then had she remembered all the people
lying asleep in the palace.

*I will not blame myself. He sent them to sleep. He drove
me to the act, whose consequences I could not imagine.*

But that was no excuse.

Da had been right to protect her. But he should have
taught her, too. She had to find some way to teach herself.
She had to find a way to keep Hugh away from her.

Light winked, a jewel flash among ash and fallen timbers.
She stepped forward over the crumbled threshold into the
main portion of what had once been the barracks. Everything had caved in and she could not tell which planks

came from the walls, which from the attic floor, and which
from the roof. Her boot broke through a plank and she
fell, foot hitting the ground a hand's breadth beneath. She
tugged her boot out of the hole and gingerly stepped over
two fallen beams, skirted a litter of swords and spear points
and shield bosses, all chary and still glowing, and stopped
where three planks composed more of charcoal than of
wood lay in perfect alignment, one, two, three in a row like
the lid to a chest. She nudged one aside with her boot.

There, lying amidst cinders and ash and blackened wood,
rested her bow in its case, untouched, unharmed except for
a thin layer of soot streaking it. Amazed, she lifted it off
the ground to find her good friend, Lucian's sword, beneath
it, still sound, as if together they had weathered the
firestorm.

"*Liath.*"

She started back, grabbing bowcase and sword to her,
and spun, stumbling over a fallen beam and the detritus of
the blaze.

But there was no one there.

XI
THE SOULS OF
THE DEAD

1

ANTONIA had become heartily sick of staring
into fire. The smoke stung her eyes and chapped her
cheeks. But she knew better than to complain. At this moment, as the heat chafed her skin, she watched with her
five companions. She had not yet mastered the art of opening such a window, a vision drawn through fire, but she
could *see* with the others. In her first days in the valley she
could not even do that, and Heribert, who had tried many
times, still could not see through fire or stone.

She saw shapes as insubstantial as flames, but the others
had assured her that these shapes were the shadows of real
forms, real people, real buildings; they had assured her that
every incident they saw through the window made by fire

occurred somewhere in the world beyond their little valley. By this means, through their power, they could see what transpired in the world beyond—although there were limits to their ability to see.

Right now, in a distant place whose outlines were limned by the hearth fire, a young noblewoman and her retinue arrived at the gates of a convent and requested admittance to pray and offer gifts.

"That is Princess Theophanu," said Antonia, amazed.

"Hush, Sister Venia," said she who sat first among them, caput draconis. "Let us listen to their words as she speaks to the gatekeeper."

Antonia did not want to admit she heard nothing. She never heard anything through the flames, only saw shapes and people as they moved and spoke in a kind of dumb show. The conversation within the fire went on and on as the elderly gatekeeper questioned the princess at length.

Antonia examined her companions.

She disliked their habit of addressing each other in the clerical way: Sister and Brother. It suggested they were equals. And yet, in truth, she had to admit that Brother Severus was an educated man of obvious noble blood and proud bearing; his name reflected his severe manner and ascetic ways. Sister Zoë spoke with the accent of the educated clergy of the kingdom of Salia, precise and clean. A lush beauty with evident charms that had, alas, attracted Heribert's notice, she looked more like a courtesan than a cleric. Brother Marcus was older than Zoë but younger than Severus; small, tidy, and arrogant, he had unfortunately encouraged Heribert in his obsession with building and had soon involved Heribert in a complicated scheme to rebuild the admittedly dilapidated cluster of buildings that housed their little community. Sister Meriam looked more like a Jinna heathen than a good Daisanite woman; old and tiny, with slender bones that looked as fragile as dry sticks, she nevertheless carried herself with a fierce dignity that even Antonia respected.

None of these names were true names, of course. Like Antonia, they had all taken other names when they came to the valley. She did not know what they had once been called or who their kin were, although any fool could see that Sister Meriam came from the infidel east. They did not volunteer such information, nor did they ask her about herself. That was not their purpose here.

The vision in fire faded to the orange-blue blur of flames crackling and the snap of wood. Antonia blinked smoke out of her eyes, and sneezed.

"Bless you, Sister," said Brother Marcus. He turned to the others. "Can this be true, that Princess Theophanu was mistaken for a deer? Does the princess suspect a sorcerer walks unseen in the king's court? Could it be she suspects our brother who walks in the world?"

She who named herself Caput Draconis answered. "She came to St. Valeria Convent because she suspects sorcery. But that she suspects our brother—I doubt it, just as I doubt Mother Rothgard suspects that her faithful gate-keeper is in fact our ally. We are not known, Brother Marcus. Do not trouble yourself on that score."

He bent his head in submission to her words. "As you say, Caput Draconis. What of this suspected sorcerer, then, whom Princess Theophanu wishes to make known to Mother Rothgard?"

"She is precipitate, this princess," said the caput draconis. "How can we be sure that the young folk in question did not simply see what they wished in their eagerness and mistake branches for antlers and mist for the flash of a deer's body? That is what the king suggested, is it not?"

"What of the burning arrows?" asked Sister Zoë. "Taken separately, I would put little credence in either incident. Taken together, I become suspicious."

It was dusk, but not chill, for it was never chilly here in this valley. The gold torque worn by the caput draconis winked and dazzled in the firelight. The woman's face remained calm; she alone Antonia could not put an age to. This difficulty puzzled her and made her fret at odd moments, waking at night, wondering, as she did about so many other things.

Above, the sun sank behind the mountains and the night stars emerged, brilliant fires burning beyond the seventh sphere, lamps lighting the way to the Chamber of Light. The stars and constellations had names and attributes. Like any educated cleric, she knew a bit of the astrologus' knowledge, but if she had learned one thing in the last six months, it was this: She knew nothing about the knowledge

of the stars compared to her new companions. She and
Heribert had come to rest in a nest of mathematici, the
most dangerous of sorcerers. Antonia had learned more
about the stars and the heavens in the last six months than
she had ever before imagined existed.

She had thought to teach *them,* for had not the caput
draconis admitted that she—Antonia—had a natural gift
for compulsion? But her early demonstrations had not impressed her audience. Hers had been a study of magics used
to bring people into her power, magics born from the earth,
from ancient and fell creatures that waited, hidden, in the
earth or in the deep crevices of the soul or of the land
itself. Such creatures and spirits were eager to serve, if commanded boldly and given the right payment, usually in
blood.

"Anyone can spill blood," Brother Severus had said con-
temptuously, "or read bones, like a savage." After that she
had confined her study of such magics to times when she
was alone.

Though she resented him for speaking such words out
loud, even she had to admit—grudgingly—that he was right.
Another power arched above all this, and her companions
had studied long and fruitfully to master a sorcery which
she had only now taken the first and tiniest steps toward
understanding.

Why was it that spring lay always in the air here in this
valley while winter's sky wheeled above them? How old,
truly, was the caput draconis, who carried herself with the
gravity of a woman of great wisdom and age and yet to
judge by her face and hair might be any age between
twenty and forty?

"The burning arrows," mused the caput draconis. "Our
Brother Lupus brought the one we seek closer to us but
not into our hands, as we had hoped. We have been patient
so far, but this news of burning arrows makes me wonder
if it is time to act."

"Act in what way, Sister?" Brother Severus raised an
eyebrow in muted surprise. Even at night, he wore only the
one thin robe, and he never wore shoes. His bare feet reminded Antonia at times of poor Brother Agius, whose
heretical notions had led him in the end to the unfortunate
death that had proved most inconvenient for *her.* But God,

no doubt, would forgive him his error. God were merciful to the weak.

"It is time to investigate," said their leader. "There are gentler ways of persuasion, now that no obstacle but distance lies between us and that which we seek. Brother Marcus, you will journey to Darre to be our eyes and ears in the presbyters' palace once our brother must leave to return north. Meanwhile, I, too, must venture out into the world to see what I can learn there."

"Is that safe?" demanded Antonia.

"Why should it not be safe, Sister Venia?" asked Sister Meriam, speaking at last.

A good question, it was one Antonia could not answer.

"I do not suggest *you* go, Sister," continued the caput draconis. "You must not leave here yet. But I am under no such constraints. I can walk in anonymity, as I have pledged to do."

"A prince is no prince without a retinue," said Antonia snappishly, indicating the gold torque the other woman wore.

But the other woman only smiled, her expression almost like pity. "I have a retinue." Lifting a hand, she indicated the darkened valley beyond them where uncanny lights winked into existence, burning without flame, and stray breezes wove their unsteady way through trees and flowers blooming in unseasonable splendor. "And my retinue is more powerful than any that exists in *this* world. Let us go, Sisters and Brothers. Let us bend our backs to this task."

They rose together, clasped hands in a brief prayer, and left the hearth.

Irritated, Antonia had to acknowledge the truth of what their caput draconis had said. No human servants lived in this valley, only beasts, goats and cows for milk, sheep for wool, chickens and geese for eggs and quills. No, indeed, their little community was not attended by *human* servants.

She left the small chapel behind Brother Marcus and crossed to the site of the new long hall. Though it was growing dark quickly, Heribert was still out measuring and hammering, aided by certain of the more robust of the servants. Strangely, he had gotten used to the servants more quickly than she had, perhaps because he worked beside them every day as he designed and constructed his projects.

She still was not used to them. At times, she could barely bring herself to look at them.

It was one thing to use the abominations nurtured in the bosom of the Enemy to punish the wicked. It was one thing to harness the power of ancient creatures which had crawled out of the pit in the days before the advent of the blessed Daisan to frighten the weak into obedience.

It was quite another to treat them as honorable servants, to use them as allies, no matter how fair some of them appeared.

At her appearance beside the construction site, they fluttered away, or sank like tar into the ground, or folded in that odd way some had into themselves, vanishing from her sight. One, the most loyal of Heribert's helpers, simply wound itself into the planks which were set tongue to groove along the north wall of the long hall. It now appeared as a knotlike growth along the wood.

"Heribert," she said disapprovingly. "Your work finishes with sunset."

"Yes, yes," he said impatiently, but he was not paying attention. He was setting a tongued plank into a grooved plank, clucking with displeasure at the poor fit, and planing the narrow edge carefully down.

"Heribert! How many times have I told you that it is not right that you dirty your hands in this way. That is the laborer's job, not that of an educated and noble cleric."

He set down board and plane, looked up at her, but said nothing. No longer as thin and delicate as he had once been—an ornament to wisdom, as the saying went, rather than to gross bodily vigor—he had grown thicker through the shoulders in the past months. His hands were work-roughened, callused, and scarred with small cuts and healed blisters. He got splinters aplenty now, every day, and could pull them out himself without whimpering.

She did not like the way he was looking at her. In a young child, she would have called it defiance.

"You will come in now and eat," she added.

"When I am finished, Mother," he said, and then he smiled, because he knew it irritated her when he called her by that title. As a good churchwoman, she should not have succumbed to the baser temptations, and in time she would have her revenge on the man who had tempted her.

"You would never have spoken to me so disrespectfully before we came here!"

A whispering came on the breeze, and he cocked his head, listening. Was he hearing something? Did the abominations speak to him? And if so, why could she not hear or understand their speech?

He bowed his head. "I beg your pardon, Your Grace." But she no longer trusted his docility.

Had the caput draconis lied to her? Misled her? Did they mean to take Heribert from her—not by any rough and violent means but simply by allowing certain dishonorable thoughts to fester in his mind, such as the idea that he could turn his back on his duty to his elders, his kin, his own mother who had borne him in much pain and blood and who had bent her considerable power to protecting him against anything that might harm him? Would he disobey her wishes simply to indulge himself in the selfish and earthly desire to partake of such menial tasks as building and architecture? Was this the price she would have to pay: the loss of her son? Not his physical loss, but the loss of his obedience to her wishes? Would she have to stand by and watch his transformation into a mere artisan—a builder, for God's sake! She would not stand by idly while they worked their magics on him, even if they were the trivial magics of flattery and false interest in his unworthy obsessions. They were using him for their own gain, of course, since certainly the buildings they lived in were not fit for persons of their consequence. It was infuriating to watch as those who were supposed to be her companions in work and learning encouraged the young man in these inappropriate labors as if he were a mere artisan's child.

But she was wise, and patient. She bided her time. Her companions were also powerful, and it would not do to offend them as long as they knew more than she did about sorcery.

She bided her time, and watched, and listened, and learned.

Heribert stored his tools in a chest, ran a hand lovingly down the partially finished north wall, and with no further insolence walked away to the old stone tower where they now took their common meal.

Antonia waited until the door opened onto light and

closed behind him. She lingered in the pleasant evening
breeze, staring up at the sky. This knowledge did not come
easily but, like all things in life, one had only to grasp and
squeeze firmly enough to choke obedience out of that—
human or otherwise—which was recalcitrant.

On this night high in the mountains whose breeze was
that of spring, certain constellations shone high in the sky,
betraying the proper season: winter.

"Name them for me, Sister Venia," said Brother Severus,
coming suddenly out of the gloom to stand beside her.

"Very well," she said. She would not be intimidated by
his solemn tone and dour expression. "At this season, the
Penitent, twelfth House in the zodiac, rides high in the
sky—" She pointed overhead. "—while the tenth House,
the Unicorn, sets with the sun and the Sisters, the third
House, rise at nightfall. The Guivre stalks the heavens and
the Eagle swoops down upon its back. The Hunter begins
his climb from the east as the Queen sets in the west and
her Sword, her Crown, and her Staff ride low on the horizon, symbol of her waning power."

"That is good," said Severus, "but you have listened in
your youth to too many astrologi. The Hunter, the Queen,
the Eagle: These are only names we give to the stars, drawing familiar pictures on the face of the heavens. In heaven
itself, they have their own designations whose names are a
mystery to those of us who live here beneath the sphere of
the ever-dying moon. But by naming them, even in such a
primitive way, seeing our own wishes and fears among them
as the young hunters saw Princess Theophanu as a running
deer, we gain knowledge enough to see the lines of power
that bind them together. With knowledge, we can harness
the power that courses between them through that geometry which exists between all the stars. Each alignment offers
new opportunities or new obstacles, each unique."

He raised a hand, pointing. "See there, Sister. How many
of the planets do you see, and where are they?"

Her eyesight was not what it had been in her youth, but
she squinted up. "I see Somorhas, of course, the Evening
Star, lying in the Penitent. Jedu, Angel of War, entered the
Falcon ten days ago. And Mok, mistress of wisdom and
plenty, must still be in the Lion, although we can't see
her now."

Whatever pride she felt in this observation he punctured with his next words. "There also find Aturna, who moves in retrograde through the Child, his lines of influence opposite the others. There—see you?—almost invisible unless you know where to look, lies fleet Erekes, just entering the Penitent. The Moon is not yet risen this night. The Sun, of course, has set. Yet within twenty days Mok and Jedu will also move into retrograde, so that only Somorhas and Erekes move forward. Thus the planets on this night as on every night form a new alignment in relationship to the great stars of the heavens. There you see the Guivre's Eye, and there Vulneris and Rijil, the Hunter's shoulder and foot. There are the three jewels, sapphire, diamond, and citrine, which are the chief stars in the Cup, the Sword, and the Staff. The Child's Torque rises toward the zenith, as does the Crown of Stars. Tomorrow we will send our companion on her way, aiding her swift travel through the halls of iron by such power as we can draw down to us through these alignments. Only with knowledge can we use the power of the heavens. Do not think it is fit knowledge for any common mortal soul who walks the earth. Only a few can truly comprehend it and act rightly."

"That is why God through the hand of Their skopos ordained biscops and presbyters, Brother, is it not? To guide and to shepherd?"

He considered this comment in silence while he studied the stars above, looking for something, some sign, some portent, perhaps. As she waited, she became lost in contemplation of the River of Heaven, the track of sparkling dust like a great serpent circling the sky, each faint light a soul streaming toward the Chamber of Light.

At last Severus spoke, slowly now and as if to himself as much as to her. "You are accustomed to power, Sister Venia. But you must forget all you have learned in the world. You must leave it behind, cut yourself off from it, as we did. That is the only way to learn what we have to teach you."

"How can we let go of the world when God have given us as our task the means to guide the mistaken back to the righteous way, to chastise the weak, and to punish the wicked?"

"Is that what God have asked us to do?"

"Is it not?"

"We are all tainted with the darkness which is the touch of the Enemy, Sister Venia. It is arrogance to believe we can see through the darkness that veils us and understand God's will better than any other mortal soul. Only there—" He gestured toward the River of Heaven, streaming above them. "—will we be cleansed of that darkness and shine only as light." He lowered his hand. "Shall we go in to dinner?"

2

"THE River of Heaven," Da always said, "was called the Great Serpent by the heathen tribes who lived here before the Holy Word came to these lands."

"Why is the zodiac called the world dragon, Da?" she would ask, "when it's actually twelve constellations and not one creature at all? And if that's a dragon, then why is the River of Heaven called a serpent?"

"We have many names for things," he would answer. "It is the habit of humankind to name things so that we may then have power over them. The Jinna call the River of Heaven by another name: the Fire God's Breath. In the annals of the Babaharshan magicians it was called the Ever-Bright Bridge Which Spans the Chasm. The ancient Dariyan sages called it the Road of Lady Fortune, for where She sets her foot, gems bloom."

"What do you think it is, Da?"

"It is the souls of the dead, Liath, you know that. That is the path by which they stream onward into the Chamber of Light."

"But then why don't we see it moving—I mean really moving, flowing, not just moving as the stars all do, rising in the east and setting in the west? Rivers flow. Water is always moving."

"That is not water, daughter, but the light of divine souls. And in any case, the aether does not follow the same laws as the elements bound to this earth, nor should it."

"Then is there fire in our souls, that they should light up like that once they reach the heavens?"

But at the mention of fire, he would get upset and change the subject.

Now she wondered. "Hindsight is a marvelous thing," Da would always say. "Every person sees perfectly with hindsight." She had done brushing down her horse and lingered outside the door, staring up at a winter sky unblemished with clouds. It was bitter cold, this night; snow had fallen yesterday, delicate flakes like the shedding of down from angel's wings, but there had not been enough to make more than a thin crust on the road today.

"Then is there fire in our souls?"

She built the City of Memory in her mind as she stood, arms crossed and gloved hands tucked under armpits for warmth, staring up at the sky. The city lies on an island, and the island is itself a small mountain. Seven walls ring the mountain, each one higher up on the slope, each one named by a different gate: Rose, Sword, Cup, Ring, Throne, Scepter, and Crown. Beyond the Crown gate, at the flat crown of the hill, stands a plaza, and on this plaza stand five buildings. Of the five buildings, one stands at each of the cardinal directions: north, south, east, and west. The fifth building, a tower, stands in the very center, the navel of the universe, as Da sometimes said jokingly.

But perhaps he had not meant it as a joke. Inside the topmost chamber of the tower stand four doors, one opening to each of the cardinal directions. But in the center of that chamber stands a fifth door, which neither opens nor closes because it is locked; because, standing impossibly in the center of the room, it leads to nothing.

Except there *was* something beyond it. If she, in her mind's eye, knelt and peered through the keyhole, she saw fire.

Da had locked the door and not given her the key. He had meant to teach her—she was sure of that—but poor Da, always running, always suspicious, always afraid of what might be walking up from behind, could never decide quite when the time was right. So the time had never come.

Some things cannot be locked away.

"I miss you, Da," she whispered to the night air, her breath a cloud of steam. Glancing up, her attention was caught by the River of Heaven, and she suddenly wondered if it, too, was a cloud of steam, warm breath on the cold celestial sphere of the fixed stars far above her. Like the zodiac, it was a circle banding the heavens, but it crossed the zodiac obliquely, cutting across at the foot of the Sisters and again, one hundred and eighty degrees round the circle, at the bow carried by the Archer.

Suddenly, with this vision of the sky bright above her, she realized that she had known all along which Eustacia

Hugh had quoted from when he humilated her in front of the court. Of course she knew the *Commentary on the Dream of Cornelia*. But she had always skimmed over the bits about philosophy and virtue and the proper government for humankind. Those chapters didn't interest her. She had memorized the chapters in which Eustacia commented upon the nature of the stars.

Where was it stored? She searched, in her mind's eye, in the city, found the level, the building, the chamber, where Eustacia's chapters resided, those she had copied out years ago at the biscop's library in Autun.

"Concerning the River of Heaven, many writers have offered explanations for its existence, but we shall discuss only those that seem essential to its nature. Theophrastus called it the Via Lactea, the Milky Way, and said it was a seam where the two hemispheres of the celestial sphere were joined together. Democrita explained that countless small stars had been compressed by their narrow confines into a mass and that by being thus close-set, they scatter light in all directions and so give the appearance of a continuous beam of light. But Posidonos' definition is most widely accepted: Because the sun never passes beyond the boundaries of the zodiac, the remaining portion of the heavens gets no share in its heat; therefore the purpose of the River of Heaven, lying obliquely to the zodiac as it does, is to bring a stream of stellar heat to temper the rest of the universe with its warmth."

"Eagle! No need to stand outside. There's a fire and supper within!"

She shook herself free of musing and went back inside. A long-house with stables at one end and living quarters at the other, it was as warm and welcoming as its mistress.

"I admit to you, Mistress Godesti, that I have not always met with as warm a hospitality as you grant me, now that I ride on King Henry's business here in Varre." Her family had been at their meal at dusk when Liath had ridden in to this hamlet, but they had saved a generous portion for her.

The woman grunted and gestured to the children of her household to go back to their beds. A single lantern and the hearth lit them, all they could spare on a winter's night.

Her elder daughter hovered by the fire, pushing sparks and
coals back within the brick circle; another girl ladled out
stew. "Many resent the rule of King Henry, here in Varre,"
she replied in a low voice.

"You do not?"

A son set down the bowl of stew and mug of warm cider
before Liath as his mother spoke. "I fear war if the great
lords fight among themselves. So do we all. But I fear a
bad harvest more. And I fear the invisible arrows of the
shades of the Lost Ones, those who lingered behind when
their living cousins left this world. They plague us with
illness and festering."

"The shades of the Lost Ones?" Liath asked. This hamlet
lay on the edge of forest, and everyone knew that many
strange and ancient creatures preferred the shelter of trees.

"Go on, eat now. I would be a poor host if I were to
make you talk instead of fill yourself up. We have nothing
to complain of. This has been a good year for us, ever since
our new master took control of these lands."

"Who is your master?"

"We tithe to the abbey of Firsebarg."

Liath choked on her cider, coughed, and set down the cup
hastily. "I beg your pardon. It was hotter than I expected."

"Nay, I beg your pardon, Eagle. Careful of the stew."

Liath recovered her breathing and, now, blew on the
stew, anything to distract herself. Would she *never* be free
of reminders of Hugh? "Firsebarg is many days' journey
north of here, isn't it?"

"It is, indeed. It happened in my grandmother's time that
these lands were given into the care of the monks by a
grieving lady, in memory of her only daughter. For the
same reason my brother gives an extra tithe in memory of
his dead wife so that the monks will pray for her during
Holy Week. As for the rest of us, we pay what is due twice
a year, without fail, and the abbot has always been merciful
when crops were bad."

"And this year?"

"Nay, this year was no trouble at all with our new lord
abbot. They say he's a good Father, for all that he's Wendish.
He's generous to the poor, feeds seven families every Ladysday in honor of the disciplas of the blessed Daisan, and lay
hands on any who are sick. His rule is strict, but kind, they

say. The harvest was very good this year, for the weather was perfect—the proper portion of sun and rain, and no bad storms though we heard hailstorms wiped out the barley crop west of here. It must be God's favor, don't you think?"

Or weather magic. But Liath didn't say that aloud. Instead, she changed the subject. *Just as Da always did,* she thought wryly and with no little disgust. How many such little habits had she learned from Da, both for good and for ill? "Is there any resentment here, Mistress, that King Henry defeated Lady Sabella?"

"Defeated her? We heard no such tidings. When did he fight her?"

"She led a rebellion . . ." They listened with rapt attention as she told them the tale.

"What does the king look like?" asked the daughter from her station by the hearth. With her hair bound back and a shawl over her head, she looked modest and quiet, but her voice was bold. "Is he very grand and terrifying?"

"He is a man of good height, noble in bearing. He is merciful in his judgments, but his anger is as fierce as that fire you tend." Then, because she saw many pairs of eyes glinting from the alcoves, child and adult alike, she went on to tell of the king's progress and the noble lords and ladies who rode with him. She told them of the places she had passed through on her way here, places they would never see and had never heard of: Augensburg; the elaborate palace at Echstatt; Wendish villages much like this one; the Sachsen Forest; Doardas Abbey; Korvei Convent; the market towns of Gerenrode and Grona; the city of Kassel, where Duchess Liutgard herself had interviewed her about the proposed expedition to Gent to drive out the Eika.

"I've heard of demons called Eika." Godesti's brother had just come from checking on the animals. He hunkered down by the fire to listen. A small child crept from her bed and slunk into the shelter of his arms. "But I thought they was just stories."

"Nay," she said, "I've seen them with my own eyes. I saw—" Here she faltered.

"What did you see?" demanded the son, creeping up beside her, face alight with interest.

So she told them about the fall of Gent, and somehow, telling it to these simple farming folk whose farthest journey was to the market town two days' walk from here, it became more like a tale of ancient and noble deeds told a hundred times on a winter's night. Somehow, telling the tale drew the pain out of it.

"Ai, the prince sounds so brave and handsome," breathed the sister by the hearth.

Her young brother snorted. "That would be a cold lover for you, Mistress Snotty Nose, too good for your suitors."

"Now, you!" said Mistress Godesti sharply, chucking the boy under the chin. "Hush. Don't speak ill of the dead. His shade might hear you."

"But all souls ascend to the Chamber of Light," began Liath, then stopped, hearing a whispering from the alcove and seeing a certain furtive look pass among them all.

Mistress Godesti drew the Circle at her breast. "So they do, Eagle. Will you have more cider to sooth your throat? This food is scarcely fit payment for such tales as you have told us this night."

Liath accepted the cider and drank it down, its bite a fire in her chest. After eating a second helping of stew, she rolled herself up in her cloak near the fire on a heap of straw filthy with fleas. The house cat, as dainty a creature as ever prowled a longhouse for mice, curled up against her stomach, liking the warmth of her body. Waking on and off, restless, she saw one or another person kneeling beside the hearth, a chargirl, an old man, a woman dressed even more poorly than the others, each taking a turn tending the fire through the long winter's night.

In the morning, in a light fall of snow so insubstantial that little seemed to touch ground, she rode on. Mistress Godesti's brother walked with her a good hour or more beyond the hamlet into the forest, though she tried to dissuade him because he had no boots, only sandals with cloth tucked in to warm his feet. But when they reached the spot where the autumn rains had washed out the path as it twisted down a thickly wooded slope, she was grateful for his guidance. He showed her where the new cut lay, a detour that switchbacked down a ridge and back to the old road. This far out, there was deadwood aplenty and no felled trees marking where folk from the village came out to get firewood. He made polite farewells.

"Not all in Varre have been so friendly," she said, thanking him.

"Aid the traveler as you would wish to be aided were you in their place, that's what our grandmother taught us." He hesitated, looking troubled. "I hope you know my sister meant nothing by her mention of the dark shades walking abroad."

"I carry messages for the king, friend. I do not report to the biscops."

He flushed. "You know how women are. If the old ways were good enough for our grandmother, then—" He restlessly hoisted his threadbare tunic up higher through his rope belt.

"You live close by the forest. Why shouldn't you see the old gods of your people still at work here?"

This startled him. "Believe you in the Tree and the Hanged God?"

"No," she admitted. "But I traveled to many strange places with my da and—" She broke off.

"And?" Did he look curious or merely tired and worn out? By the age of his children she guessed he was only about ten years older than herself, yet he looked as old as Da had at the end, aged by constant work and worry and by grief at the death of his wife. "Godesti says that if my dear Adela had given gifts to the Green Lady at the old stone altar, then she wouldn't have died, for the Green Lady helps women through their labor. Is it because she did as the deacon from Sorres village commanded and turned her heart away from the old ways? She prayed to St. Helena when her birth pains came on her, but maybe the Green Lady was angry for not receiving any gifts. Is that why she died?"

"I don't know your Green Lady. But I lived in Andalla once, with my da. The Jinna women there didn't pray to Our Lord and Lady, they prayed to the Fire God Astereos, yet they survived and bore healthy children—many of them, at any rate. I'm sorry about your wife. I'll pray for her soul. Maybe it had nothing to do with God—except that God watch over us all," she added quickly. "Maybe the child didn't move right within her. Maybe it was breech and couldn't come out. Maybe some sickness got into her blood and made her weak. It might be any of those things, or something else, and nothing to do with God at all, just as"—she gestured at the path behind them—"this track was washed away by a combination of rain and rockslides, not because the creatures of the Enemy made mischief here to bedevil you—"

"I pray you!" He drew the Circle at his breast hastily, and then another sign, something she didn't recognize but which was clearly pagan. "The shades might be listening."

"The shades?"

"The souls of dead people too restless to board the ship of night and sail to the underworld. Or worse . . ." He hefted his walking staff, twirled it once, dropping his voice to a whisper. ". . . the shadows of dead elves. Their souls are confined in a dark fog. They have no body, but they weren't released from the earth either. They aren't allowed into the Chamber of Light, but they have nowhere else to go if they were killed on this earth. They haunt the deep forest. Surely you know that, you who have traveled so much."

"The shades of dead elves . . ." She stared at the forest around her: leafless winter trees stood dark against the gray-white sky with undergrowth of all shades of brown and dull green and the pale yellow of decay interwoven beneath; evergreens skirted the edge of open areas. All of it was dense with growth and fallen limbs and the tangle of a wild land untouched by human hands. Had that been Sanglant's fate? To wander the earth as a shade, because he could not ascend through the seven spheres to the River of Heaven and thence stream with the other souls into the Chamber of Light? Was he near her now?

Then she shook herself roughly, and her horse stamped and shook its head as if in sympathy. "Nay, friend," she continued. "The blessed Daisan taught that the Aoi were made of the same substance as humankind. Some of the ancient Dariyan lords converted to the faith of the Unities. So why should the blessed Daisan turn elvish kin away from heaven if they served God faithfully? And even if they do live here, why should they concern themselves with us?" Suddenly, Liath realized she didn't believe the souls of dead people lurked in the forest. And she wasn't afraid of the shades of dead elves. Of course, many other things might lurk in the forest, wolves and bears least among them. *"To be fearless is to be foolhardy and likely dead,"*

Da always said. But away from Hugh, fear did not ride constantly on her shoulder.

"Who knows what lingers in this forest." The man looked around nervously, afraid even in a morning light that painted the gray-limbed trees and stubborn clouds of morning with the burnished light of pearls. "Near the ford there may be bandits. But by dusk tomorrow you'll come to a big town called Laar."

They parted. He seemed relieved, but whether to be returning to the safety of his village or to be rid of her and her uncomfortable views Liath could not be sure. She did not mean disrespect to the old gods or the saints. But it was not God or the shades of dead elves or the half-formed creatures who served the Enemy who had caused her to miscarry last winter. No, indeed. It was the very abbot whom these villagers praised.

Snow drifted down between the bare branches of trees. She walked most of the day to keep warm and to spare her horse. The road was good, considering what little use it must get. Two wagon ruts wide, it remained clear of undergrowth, and puddles hidden beneath a film of ice were the worst of its treacheries.

Was there really any point to being in a hurry? It had taken Hanna months to reach the king. No one would know why she had herself been delayed, and in any case, Count Lavastine would be unlikely to muster an army before summer. Spring, with sowing and swollen rivers and muddy roads, was not the time for an army to march. The Eika surely could make no attack down the Veser River in the full flood of springtide.

Yet she owed it to the people of Gent to make sure the message arrived as soon as it could. She owed it to Sanglant's memory, so that his death could be avenged.

Late in the day, snow turned to sleeting rain and she escaped the downpour by sheltering under a huge fir tree; its limbs made a kind of cave where they arched to the ground. She tied up her gelding and piled twigs and sticks on the cold ground, surrounding them with a firewall of stones. Then, biting her lip, she reached through the window of fire that she could see in her mind's eye and called flame.

Flames shot up from the little heap of twigs, stinging the

branches above. She jumped back. The horse snorted, kicked, snapped a rein, and bolted out of their shelter.

"Damn!" she swore. She ran after the horse. Luckily, it calmed quickly and waited for her. Wet and shivering, she led it back to the overhang. The fire had settled down, and now, half ashamed, she fed it in the normal manner. The horse ate such leavings as she could glean from the nearby undergrowth and she chewed on a hard end of bread and a sour handful of cheese.

It was cold, that night, but the fire burned steadily. Fir needles rained down on her at erratic intervals. Though she slept fitfully, this rough shelter with fir needles sticking through her cloak and the breath of winter wind chafing her neck and chilling her fingers was far better than any fine, warm, elegant chamber shared with Hugh. If winter harmed her, it would not be because it wished to but because of its indifference to her fate. Somehow, that vast and incomprehensible indifference comforted her. The stars wheeled on their round whether she died or lived, suffered or laughed. Against the eternity of the celestial sphere and the great harmony sung in the heavens, she was the merest flash, so brief in its passing that perhaps the daimones coursing in the aether above could no more comprehend her existence than she could comprehend theirs. After all those years running with Da, after what she had endured with Hugh, it was a great relief to be unworthy of notice.

Yet she was still not free. She so desperately needed a preceptor—a teacher.

Could Wolfhere see her through the fire? Was Hanna well? Coals glowed, and it was the work of a moment to feed sticks to the fire. Flames leaped up, bright yellow, and she pulled out the gold feather.

"Hanna," she whispered as she spun the feather's tip between thumb and forefinger, spinning the faint breath of air stirred by that turning into the licking flames of fire and twisting out of those flames a gateway through which she could see. . . .

Sapientia sits restless in a chair, obviously unwell. Of all her attendants the only one whom she tolerates for more than a moment is Hanna, who speaks soothingly to her and gets her to drink from a silver cup. Of Hugh there is no sign.

The feather brushes Liath's palm, and fire snaps and wa-

vers. Now she sees a dim loft carpeted with straw. A man
stirs, and in his unquiet sleep she recognizes him. It is Wolfhere. He murmurs a name in his dream and, that suddenly,
as if a voice called to him, he wakes, opening his eyes.

"Your Highness."

Liath's sight blurs and sharpens, and she sees a pallet on
which a woman lies in a desperate fever, clothes soaked in
sweat. She is no longer in the loft. Here a trio of women
stand over the patient, tending her. By their clothing Liath
recognizes them as a servingwoman, an elderly nun, and the
Mother Abbess of a convent.

"Your Highness? It is I, Mother Rothgard. Can you
hear me?"

Mother Rothgard wrings out a cloth and turns the sufferer
over to press the damp cloth to her forehead. As the lax face
rolls into view, Liath recognizes Princess Theophanu, but so
changed, all vitality burned out of her, leached away by
fever. Mother Rothgard frowns and speaks to the servingwoman, who hurries out. She unfastens the princess' tunic
and eases it open to examine the young woman's chest:
Beads of sweat pearl on her nipples; moisture runs down
the slope of her shoulder to vanish into her armpits. The
thunder of Theophanu's heartbeat, frantic, irregular, seems
to resound in the small chamber. She wears two necklaces;
one is a gold Circle of Unity, and the other—a panther
brooch hung from a silver chain.

This brooch Mother Rothgard lays in her palm and examines. Turning it over with a finger, she traces writing too
faint for Liath to see. The abbess has a clever face made
stern by perpetual frowning.

"Sorcery," she says to her attendant. "Sister Anne, fetch
me the altar copy of the Holy Verses, and the basket of
herbs sanctified under the Hearth. Speak of this to no one.
If this ligatura comes from the court—even if Princess Theophanu survives—we cannot know who are our allies and
who our enemies. This bespeaks an educated hand."

Mother Rothgard speaks a blessing and Theophanu
grunts, and the vision smears into the dull glow of fading
coals.

The rain had slowed to a shushing patter, and as Liath
replaced the gold feather against her chest and clasped her

knees for warmth, the twilight faded into the chill expectation of dawn.

Sorcery. How powerful had Hugh become? Was she herself no longer immune to his magic? Had she ever been?

With this disquieting thought like a burden weighing on her, she saddled her horse and made ready to leave. As she took its reins to lead it out from under the shelter of the overhang, a stabbing pain burned at her breast. She pressed a hand to the pain . . . where the gold Aoi feather lay between tunic and skin.

In that pause, standing motionless and still half-hidden by the hanging evergreen branches, she heard a twig snap. Mounting, she drew her bow and an arrow out of its quiver. She laid the bow across her thighs and started west on the forest road, one hand on the bow, one on the reins.

A covey of partridges took wing, a sudden flurry, startled out of their hiding place. She stared into the undergrowth but saw nothing. But the crawling sensation grew: Someone—or something—watched her from the shelter of the trees.

She urged her horse forward as fast as she dared. With the next town so far ahead, she couldn't risk exhausting her horse, and anyway the road was cut here and there with gashes, holes of a size to trap a horse's hoof. Nothing appeared on the forest road behind her, nothing ahead. In the forest, all she saw was a tangle of trees and little sprays of snow where wind rattled branches.

Abruptly, dim figures appeared in the shadows of the forest, darting around the trees like wolves following a scent.

A *whoosh* like the hiss of angry breath brushed her ear, and she jerked to one side. Her horse faltered. An arrow buried itself into the trunk of a nearby tree. As delicate as a needle, it had no fletching. Pale winter light glinted off its silver shaft. Then, in the space of time it takes to blink, it dissolved into mist and vanished.

The scream came out of nowhere and seemingly from all directions: a ululating tremor, more war cry than cry for help. It shuddered through the trees like the coursing of a wild wind.

Maybe sometimes it *was* better to run than to stand and fight.

Galloping down the forest road, she hit the opening in the trees before she was aware that trees had been hacked back from either side of a wide stream. At the ford, a dilapidated bridge crossed the sluggish waters.

A party of men blocked the bridge and its approach. They raised their weapons when they saw her. She pulled up her horse and while it minced nervously under her, she glanced behind, then ahead, not sure what threatened her most. The men looked ill kempt, as desperate as bandits—which they surely were. Most of them wore only rags wrapped around their feet. A few wore scraps of armor, padded coats sewn with squares of leather. Only the leader had a helmet, a boiled and molded leather cap tied under his scraggly beard. But they stood in front of her, surly and looking prepared to run; they were tangible, real. She had no idea what had let loose with that scream.

"I am a King's Eagle! I ride on the king's business. Let me pass."

By now they had guessed that she rode alone.

"Wendar's king," said the foremost, spitting on the ground. "You're in Varre now. He's no king of ours."

"Henry is king over Varre."

"Henry is the usurper. We're loyal to Duchess Sabella."

"Sabella is no longer a duchess. She no longer rules over Arconia."

The man spit again, hefting his spear with more confidence. He cast a glance at his comrades, who were armed with clubs fashioned from stout sticks. Two came off the bridge and began to circle around on either side to flank her. "What the false king says of Duchess Sabella don't mean anything here. It's his mistake to send his people here and think his word protects them. We'll treat you better, woman, if you give up without a fight."

"I've nothing worth anything to you," she said as she raised her bow, but they only laughed.

"Good boots, warm cloak, and a pretty face," said their leader. "Not to mention the horse and the weapons. That's all worth something to us."

Nocking the arrow, she drew down on the leader. "Tell your men to pull back. Or I'll kill you."

"First rights," said the leader, "to the man who drags the rider off the horse."

The two men charged. The one to her right made the mistake of reaching her first. She kicked him, hard under the chin, and as he reeled back she turned just as the other man reached her. Her string drawn back, she held her arrowhead almost against his face as he grabbed for her boot. And loosed the string.

The arrow drove through his mouth. He staggered and dropped.

No time to think. They had no bows. She could outrun them.

As she pulled her mount around, she saw shadows in the forest. They moved like hunters and yet at once she knew they weren't men, no kin of these bandits come to aid them. They carried bows as slender and light as if they had been woven from spider's silk twisted and folded together a thousandfold to make them as strong as wood.

Caught between the one and the other. She had no reason to trust either side.

The man she had kicked struggled back, grunting, and jumped for her.

Living wood in damp winter cold burns poorly . . . she reached for fire and called it down on the old bridge.

The logs and planks caught fire with a burst, a snap and *whuff* of flame. The men on the bridge screamed, jumping to safety into the river's cold waters, floundering there or leaping for the shore. Her horse screamed and bolted. A thin silver arrow gashed its flank and fell to the ground. The man coming after her yelled in terror, then crumpled as he groped at a silver needle embedded in his own throat.

She rode for the river. Men scrambled away, fleeing from her—or from what pursued her, half hidden in the forest behind. The cold water came as a shock, coursing past her thighs as she urged her horse across the stream. The animal needed no pressing; it, too, was smart enough to run. The water flooded its rump and washed away the thin stream of blood that ran from the cut made by the arrow. For a moment, Liath felt the horse lose its footing; then they were struggling up the far bank, breaking through the film of ice that rimed the shoreline.

From behind she heard screaming; she did not pause to look. In the center of the road, stunned into immobility, stood one of the bandits. He stared in horror at the burning bridge and at his comrades falling on the other side or thrashing their way down the cold stream.

"Do you think King Henry leaves his Eagles unprotected?" she cried. He bolted into the woods, running from her—or from what lay behind her. She turned.

The burning bridge flared like a beacon. No shadows emerged from the forest, and the bandits had scattered. The bridge would be ruined. As she stared, she realized she could not put the fire out—she did not know how. She tried reaching, imagined a fire dying to embers and embers dying to dead coals, but the bridge burned on with the glee of a raging fire. It terrified her. She had no way to control it.

Then *they* came out of the forest. They had bodies formed in human shape, even the suggestion of ancient armor, hammered breastplates decorated with vulture-headed women and spotted lions without manes. But she could see the trees through them. They were more like a dense smoky fog forced into an alien shape, humanlike and yet not human at all—and they were coming after her. One raised its bow and shot at her, but the silver arrow, a wink against the sun, vanished in the flames. They came to the stream's bank, well away from the scorching flames that devoured the old bridge, but they did not attempt to cross the water.

She turned her horse and fled.

She rode, walked beside her horse, rode again, then trotted again alongside her tired mount. But though a winter's day was short, this one seemed to drag on and on. The forest would never end.

At dusk, at last and amazingly, it gave into scrub and overcut woods. Pigs scattered away from her. Fields which cut into stands of trees like gaping scars lightened her way. She was still shaking with reaction when she reached the town of Laar as the waxing gibbous moon rose behind her.

At the closed gates she called out. "I beg you. I am a King's Eagle riding on the king's business. Give me shelter!"

The gate creaked open, and they let her in. Good Varren villagers, they were not sympathetic to Henry, but she was a lass riding alone and, when it came down to it, they were eager to hear what news she had.

The village deacon led the 'horse away at once and applied a salve of holy water, dock, and stitchwort to the elfshot gash while singing psalms over the wounded beast. "It is clear you have been at your prayers, daughter," said the deacon, "for surely the intervention of St. Herodia—whose feast day this is—saved you from harm this day."

Liath left the horse in the deacon's care and let herself be escorted to a longhouse where the whole village gathered to watch her eat a cold supper. The villagers knew of the bandits and were glad to be rid of them, and it was clear that Laar's townsfolk had long ago resigned themselves to the depredations of the nameless creatures who lurked in the forest.

"Do you know what they are?" Liath demanded.

"The shades of dead elves," said the householder who had taken her in.

"They are doomed to wander the earth," said a village elder, "because they cannot ascend to the Chamber of Light."

"My wise aunt told me the Lost Ones ruled here once," added the householder. "Their shades can't bear to leave the scene of their great glory. So they haunt us and try to drive us away so that their kin can come back and rule again."

One tale led to another, and of course they wanted to know what message she took to Count Lavastine, whom they had heard tell of; his southernmost holdings lay not ten days' ride from here. A few of the villagers had even seen the count and his army when they had returned this way last summer after the battle at Kassel.

"He had his heir with him," said the householder. "A good-looking boy, tall and noble. What does the king want with Count Lavastine? Him being Varrish, and all, and the king Wendish. Maybe the king don't like Varrish counts."

So she told them about Gent.

"Ai, the Dragons!" said one old woman. "I saw the Dragons years ago! Very glorious, they was."

That night, lying rolled in her cloak before the hearth fire, she dreamed of the Eika dogs.

XII
READING THE
BONES

1

AS winter dragged on and the Eika left in Gent grew bored, Sanglant began to lose his dogs. Like his Dragons, they fought for him when he was attacked. Like his Dragons, they died. He did what he could to save them, but it was never enough.

Eika needed to fight and the combats they arranged against slaves were terrible to watch. The few combats they arranged against *him*, they lost. It was beneath their dignity to fight him many against one or with a weapon while he stood unarmed, and he had honed his skills so well over the months that none of them, however stout or bold, could best him.

That some Eika still raided he knew when one of the

restless princeling sons brought in a few pathetic slaves or a handful of baubles to parade in front of Bloodheart, but the pickings in the region around Gent were pitifully thin by now after three seasons of raiding. Others hosted gatherings during which one or another of the savages would tell a tale of butchery in their harsh language that sometimes included horrible reenactments with living slaves, poor doomed souls.

Such shows impressed Bloodheart not at all. He, too, was restless. He played his bone flutes. He played with his powers, such as they were—Sanglant had little experience with sorcery and did not know how to measure what he saw: webs of light caging the cathedral with brightness; keening dragons that filled the vast nave with slashing tails and searing fire before they dissolved into mist; glowing swarms of mitelike bees that tormented Sanglant, stinging him until his hands and face swelled—only, all at once, to vanish together with the swelling when Bloodheart grew tired of the game and put down his flutes.

When the madness threatened to descend, he took refuge in his manor house, built as painstakingly over the winter as if he had sawed the logs and raised the roof with his own hands. The vision of the manor house saved him from the black cloud more times than he could count.

But it was never enough.

He smelled smoke on the wind, fires burning in the city, and then the acrid stench of charred wood. He heard the Eika play their game, day in and day out, in the square that fronted the cathedral. Always the winning team howled and laughed as they threw their trophy, the sack containing its gruesome burden, down in front of Bloodheart. Perhaps they moved more sluggishly in the cold, but neither heat nor cold, not the bitter hard wind or the silence of a dense snow, not the lash of freezing rain or the dull ache of a cold that chills down to the bones affected them adversely, no more than it did a rock.

As winter eked its way toward spring and the days grew longer, he noticed a change in their appearance. More of them now wore leather armor cut from the tanneries of Gent or carried spears and axes and iron-pointed arrows forged in Gent's smithies. The cries of the slaves came to his ears day and night, but there was nothing he could do to help them.

There was nothing he could do but watch, and think. Spring was coming. The river would soon flow at floodtide. Few ships would sail upstream until late spring. But Bloodheart was mustering an army. Any fool, even a mad fool, could see that. Daily, Eika came and went. Some—for Sanglant could now tell certain ones apart from the rest—did not return, as if they had died on their errand or, perhaps, gone a much longer way away. Surely not even Eika dared to cross the northern seas in winter, but who could know? They were savages, and savages might try anything.

Chained here as he was, he could only watch. If he could keep the madness at bay, like the dogs, he could think. He could try to plan.

Bloodheart must not muster an army out of Gent. The Veser River ran deep into Wendish lands and with enough ships and a clear road past Gent, Bloodheart and his Eika army could wreak havoc on Henry's lands.

Even Bloodheart must have a weakness. He needed only to be clear-sighted, like Liath, to find it out.

Certain things he observed.

A small gallery—the choir—ran above the nave along one side of the cathedral, but no Eika ever walked here or crowded above to stare down at their brothers.

The dogs never had puppies, nor did they ever seem to mate.

Just as he was tethered to the altar stone by his chains, so the Eika priest seemed tethered to Bloodheart. If Bloodheart sat on his throne, the priest did not venture out of doors. If Bloodheart left the cathedral as he did four times a day, then the priest left as well, dogging the chieftain's heels.

The Eika showed no sexual interest in their slaves, none that he had ever seen; perhaps their contempt for their human enemies ran too deep for such intercourse.

Wooden chest and leather pouch never left the priest's care. From the pouch he drew the bones which he read to prophesy the future. The chest he never opened.

However many Eika crowded the nave, they never stank. Humans stank; Sanglant knew that well enough because he had lived so long among them. The king's progress reeked with the smell of many humans jostled together. Villages and estates had each their own aroma of sweat and mold and damp wool, cesspits and rotting meat, women's holy blood, manure, all the lingering smells of human activity in the smithies and tanneries, the butcheries and the bakeries rolled into a fetid whole. He suspected the Eika thought *he* stank, even though he was only half of human kin. But it had been months since he had washed; even the dogs were cleaner than he was.

Ai, Lady, he was no better than a wild animal rolling in the forest loam, matted with filth—though he took what care he could of himself. But it was never enough.

When would King Henry come? Sanglant understood now that he could not die here among the dogs. His mother's geas was also a curse, for death would have been a blessing; it had been one for his faithful Dragons whose bones rotted in the crypt or, smoothed and bored, made music for Bloodheart's pleasure. That some other event had prevented Henry from marching last autumn on Gent Sanglant believed. Not for Sanglant's sake: Revenge was a luxury. But Henry had to retake Gent.

And someone had to stop Bloodheart.

If one only looked clearly at what lay in plain sight, the answer was obvious. He was amazed that it had taken him this long to realize it. He knew how to kill Bloodheart, if only he could get close enough.

2

IVAR was of such little importance to Mother Scholastica that she allowed Master Pursed-Lips to deliver the message, which might as well have been a death blow.

"I'll hear no more complaining from *you*, feckless creature!" scolded the schoolmaster. He did not exactly smile, but he clearly felt an unpleasant glee in the words which followed. "Your lord father has replied at last to your unseemly request to be released from your vows. Of course you are to stay in the monastery. You will offer up your prayers in the service of your kin—those living and those now dead. *Now*." He rapped Ivar hard on the knuckles with his switch. "Get back to your labors!"

What choice did he have? The daily round at Quedlinhame was, in its own monotonous way, soothing to his bruised heart. Trapped forever. Even Liath had rejected him, and that after everything he had promised to do for her.

Only once a day did this monotony lift, did he feel one iota stirred from the numbness that afflicted his heart and soul. And even this event was attended by obstacles.

"The problem," said Baldwin, "is that we can't get close enough to her. It's all very well to listen to what she preaches, but there is a fence between us."

"What matters a mere fence?" demanded Ermanrich. "How can you even doubt her, Baldwin? Can't you hear the truth in each word she utters?"

"How can we truly see how sincere she is if we can't see her face except through a knothole? What if she has been set here as a test for us?"

"A test, indeed," murmured Sigfrid, voice muffled by his clenched hands pressed against his lips. Head bent, he had his eyes shut tight and seemed to be grimacing.

Ever since Tallia had come to Quedlinhame, ever since she began speaking in her monotonously fervid voice about the *Redemptio* of the blessed Daisan, of his death and rebirth, poor Sigfrid seemed engaged in an inner struggle which caused him much pain.

The four boys were not her only audience. Each afternoon just after the office of Vespers she walked barefoot out from under the colonnade to the fence that separated the girls' side of the novitiary from the boys' half. Each day for the last three months, no matter how awful the weather, she knelt, covered only by her novice's drab brown robe, and prayed. Only a few prayed with her *every* day. One of these was Ermanrich, who knelt on the opposite side of the fence, shivering in snow, in sleet, in gusty winds, in the heavy chill of winter's hard breath, to hear her speak. Some of the female novices did as well, among them Ermanrich's cousin, Hathumod.

Baldwin and Ivar came to listen on those days when it wasn't too much of a hardship. Many of the female novices collected on those pleasanter days as well, or so the boys assumed by the weighty sense of many breaths drawn and released in time to Lady Tallia's testimony, by the rustling and murmuring of coarse robes, by the whispers of light voices and, now and again, a giggle. But the giggling was never directed toward Tallia's words. No one ever laughed at Lady Tallia or her heretical preaching.

Lady Tallia never raised her voice. She never traded on her high position, unlike Duchess Rotrudis' son Reginar, nor did she expect to be deferred to or made much of. Quite the contrary.

Her privations had become legendary among the novices. She never wore shoes, not even in the winter. Her diet consisted wholly of barley bread and beans. She never drank wine, not even on feast days. She never allowed a stovepot by her bed, no matter how cold it became, and she allowed no servant to wait upon her, as the other noble girls did, but rather insisted—when her aunt Scholastica allowed it—on serving the servants as if *she* were the commoner born and *they* the noble.

There even circulated a rumor that she had worn a hairshirt under her robe until Mother Scholastica forbade her to indulge herself in such a prideful display of humility.

"Hsst!" said Baldwin. On his knees, face pressed up against the knothole, he peered through onto that which was forbidden them. "Here she comes."

Ivar sank to his knees. The cold ground burned a chill into his skin through the fabric of his robe, and he wondered if he should go back inside. But inside sat Master Pursed-Lips, snoring by the stovepot, or Lord Reginar and his dogs, hoping to make life miserable for anyone who disturbed them while they diced. The second-year novices, led by Reginar, always diced just before Vespers, the only time during the day when novices were allowed a short period without occupation.

Only at this time did Tallia have opportunity—and privacy—to speak.

"Then why is it," whispered Baldwin, turning away from the fence to let Ermanrich press nose and eye up against the knothole, "—if she speaks the truth—that she doesn't testify in front of Mother Scholastica?" Like most handsome and favored children, Baldwin nurtured a blithe assurance that the adults in charge would bow before any reasonable, or passionately felt, request.

"Why didn't you just tell your parents you had no liking for the noblewoman who wanted to marry you instead of claiming you had a vocation to the church?" said Ivar.

Baldwin's beautiful eyes flared. "That wouldn't have mattered! You know as well as I that *liking* matters not when it comes time for one family to ally itself with another. Especially for the family which seeks advantage in the match."

"You're too skeptical, Baldwin," said Ermanrich.

"About marriage or Lady Tallia?" Baldwin retorted.

Sigfrid took his turn. As the female novices on the other side settled down with a rustling of cloth and several coughs and sniffles, he leaned back to speak. "Of course she would be condemned by Mother Scholastica and the other authorities if they heard her speaking such heresy!"

"Hush," said Ermanrich. "I can't hear her."

Sigfrid moved aside and let Ivar take his turn at the knothole. Ivar squinted, seeing first a wash of faces and fabric blended together as his sight adjusted. Like the twelve virtues, virgins all, in *The Shepherd of Hermas,* the female novices and even the meek schoolmistress had gathered around Tallia to listen. Ivar matched faces with virtues. Tallia for Faith, of course; Hathumod for Simplicity; the elderly and mild schoolmistress for Concordia. The rest—unremarkable girls with their hair covered by shawls and with noses red, or white, from cold and their pale hands clasped devoutly before them—would do for Abstinence, Patience, Magnanimity, Innocence, Charity, Discipline, Truth, and Prudence. Of them all, only Tallia had a truly interesting face, drawn to a fine pallor by her austerities. But perhaps it was only her tinge of fanaticism that lent attraction to her. She had nothing of Liath's warm beauty, but she was the only truly enticing object Ivar had seen at Quedlinhame since Liath had departed with the king's progress.

"Death is the cause of life," she was saying now. "By sacrificing the blessed Daisan in that ritual by which the Dariyans flayed the skin from the body of a living man, the empress relieved Him of His earthly clothing. So was He freed forever from His body, which He would not need in the Chamber of Light."

"But why did he have to be killed like that?" demanded one of the girls. "Didn't he suffer?"

"He already suffered by the measure of our sins." Tallia lifted her hands and turned them palms up to display to her audience. "This is mere skin, molded from clay, nothing more than that. Like all else outside the Chamber of Light, it is tainted with darkness. We do not return to God in the flesh but rather in the spirit. It is our soul that ascends through the spheres to the Chamber of Light."

"But then how could the blessed Daisan have come back to the earth and walked among his disciplas again, as you say, if he didn't have a body?"

"Is there any power God does not have? She gave us birth. She gave birth to the universe—Ah!" Tallia gasped, swaying, and Hathumod, as stout a young woman as her cousin was a young man, held her up so she did not fall. "Lady bless!" said Tallia in an altered voice, high and breathless and yet somehow piercing. "I see a light like the blinding glance of angels. It penetrates the haze of mist that envelops the dull earth." Head lolling back, Tallia appeared to faint.

Ivar jerked back from the fence to find Baldwin, Ermanrich, and Sigfrid clustered at his shoulder, pressing him back into the rough wood.

"What happened?" demanded Ermanrich.

The bells rang for Vespers and the four young men scrambled up guiltily to take their place in line.

Ivar braved Master Pursed-Lip's willow switch to get a good look at the line of female novices as they proceeded into the church, but he did not see Lady Tallia among their number . . . and she never, ever, missed a chance to pray.

Nor did she appear before Vespers at her usual place the next day.

It took two days for Ermanrich to arrange a private rendezvous with his cousin, and then the news he had to report hit all four boys with horror.

"Hathumod says Tallia has been stricken with a paralysis."

"Devils have inhabited her because of her heretical words!" said Sigfrid, biting at his nails. "She's been possessed by the Enemy!"

"Don't say such a thing!" Ermanrich's ability to defer to the wishes of another—in this case his lady mother—without resentment had allowed him to enter Quedlinhame with a resigned heart and a peaceful spirit. He looked anything but peaceful now. "She lies as if dead, Hathumod says, with only the faintest blush of red in her cheeks to show she still lives. It is God who afflicts her, to test her faith with infirmity!"

"If it's true she eats so little, she probably fainted from hunger," observed Baldwin, whose appetite was as certain as the promise of the sun's rising each morning. "My aunt said that's a sure sign of starvation, when farmers are too weak to sow. The biscop enjoins us to sow charity and distribute grain in lean times for the good of our souls, but my aunt says we'd best do it for the good of our holdings."

"Baldwin!" Poor Sigfrid looked deeply affronted. "How can you say such a thing, and in God's house, may They forgive you for your disrespect."

"It's no disrespect to speak the truth!"

"Quiet!" said Ivar. "It won't help us if we quarrel like princes." But a sudden fear gnawed at him, and he did not know why.

He did not know why, but he and the others knelt every day at the usual time beside the fence, hoping for news.

And news came in the most startling fashion four days later when Tallia herself, leaning on Hathumod, made her slow way out to her accustomed place. There she knelt on fresh snow as though it were spring flowers, brought her hands together at her chest, and prayed.

She had no color in her lips. Her hands were curled up like claws, nails tucked into her palms. Although she was frail in body, her voice was strong.

"God be praised! By the blessing given by the Holy Mother and Her blessed Son we have all been granted eternal life if only we shall testify to the Holy Word of the sacrifice and redemption. I was overcome by light, and while my body was laid low by God's hand, a vision enveloped me."

Her face had so fine and delicate a pallor that she appeared almost aethereal, as if her body had leached away and all that held her together in this world was the strength of her immortal soul. The very fragility revealed in her flesh, woven with the fierce glamour of her gaze, gave her a beauty she had not possessed before—or so Ivar thought, staring raptly until Ermanrich poked him hard between the shoulder blades and demanded his chance to look.

Though they shouldn't have been looking.

"My soul was led by a spirit of fire to the resting place of the angels. There I was granted a vision of the rewards God prepares for those who love Her, in which infidels and those who heed the False Word of the Unities put no faith." She lifted her fists. With great effort, face straining against obvious pain, she uncurled her swollen fingers.

Ivar gasped out loud, as did every female novice clustered on the other side of the fence.

Her palms bled, each one marked by a single shallow scarlet line down the center—just as if a knife had begun the first cuts to flay her skin from her body. Blood dripped from her palms to color the snow crimson.

Ivar staggered back, clapping his hands over his eyes.

Ermanrich pressed his face against the fence. "A miracle!" he breathed.

Sigfrid, after peering through the knothole, was too overcome to speak.

Baldwin only grunted.

*   *   *

But not a month later, when the snow had finally melted and the first violets bloomed, a climbing rose grew from the very spot where Tallia's blood had stained the earth. On the Feast Day of St. Johanna, the Messenger, a single bud unfolded into a crimson flower.

"It's a sign," murmured Sigfrid, and this time Baldwin made no objection.

It had been almost a year since Ivar had knelt outside the gates and pledged himself as a novice. For the first time since that day, he walked into the great church at Quedlinhame with no thought for his own grievances. His heart was too full with mystery and awe.

3

ALAIN saw her from a distance. He stopped, calling
the hounds to heel, and made them sit in a semicircle
around him.

"Go," he said while his escort, his usual retinue of padded dog handlers, a half dozen men-at-arms, and a cleric
who had been brought into the household to read aloud to
Alain various practical treatises on husbandry and agriculture, stared down the long open slope at the unusual sight
of an Eagle walking instead of riding. "Ulric and Robert,
go down and escort her to me."

It was always safer to escort a new person to him; if he
approached them with the hounds, anything might happen.

The thin sheen of snow turned the winter landscape a
glittering white, muddied by the dark line of the southern
roadway and the skeletal orchard that stretched along it on
either side. From this vantage he could see the tower of
Lavas keep behind him but nothing of the town except
trails of smoke rising into the clear sky. On this, St. Oya's
Day and the first day of Fevrua (so the cleric had informed
him this morning), the weather remained mild and bright.
It was a good omen for those girls who had come to their
first bleeding in the past year; they would now sit on the
women's benches at church and those whose families were
well-to-do enough might think of betrothing them to a suitable man. In thirty days would come the first day of the
month of Yanu, the new year and the first day of spring.

In that new year, if God willed, *he* would be betrothed.

"Lady Above!" swore the cleric, and the remaining men
in his retinue murmured, likewise, in amazement. Alain,
too, stared, as the Eagle met the two guards and walked
with them up the slope. He had never seen an Eagle arrive
except on horseback—for of course Eagles must move
swiftly and how better to do that than by riding? But that
was not the only strange thing about her.

Young, she had the most astonishing complexion, as

brown as if she had just stepped through into winter's pale
daylight from a land where summer's sun burned night and
day in all seasons. She wore quiver and bow on her back,
had a sword strapped to her side and leather bag of provisions slung from one shoulder, and strode along as easily as
any foot soldier. But there was yet another quality, something he could not name. She had a certain brightness about
her, a warmth . . . it made no sense and yet struck him as
one sees the shadow of the mother in her child's face.

"Autun!" he said suddenly, out loud. "She was one of
the Eagles who came to Autun after the battle at Kassel.
She brought the news of Gent's fall."

The hounds began to whine.

They cowered, heads down, whimpering away from her
as she approached. First Good Cheer, then Fear, then the
others tried to slink away, as meek as puppies frightened
by thunder; only Sorrow and Rage remained, though they,
too, stirred restlessly. "Sit!" he commanded and, reluctantly, the other hounds sat. But as the Eagle walked up
to him, old Terror flopped down, rolled over, and exposed
his throat.

"What a sweet old dog," the Eagle exclaimed. "I love
dogs." She reached down to pet him.

Terror snapped at her hand, terrified, rolled and scrambled back to his feet, and at once all the hounds were up
and barking wildly at her. She leaped back. His retinue did
the same reflexively.

"Sit!" commanded Alain. "Sit, you!" He tugged down
Sorrow and Rage. "Terror!" He jerked the old hound down
by his collar, calmed the others. But even so, when they
had subsided, they whined and growled and kept Alain between her and them.

"My lord!" She stared at the hounds, aghast. Alain had
never seen eyes as blue as hers, as bright as fiery Seirios,
the flaming point of the Huntress' bow in the night sky. "I
beg your pardon—"

"Nay, think nothing of it." But he was puzzled by the
hounds' reaction. "You have a message for my father?"

"For Count Lavastine, yes."

"I am his son."

She was surprised. "I do not mean to interrupt your

walk, my lord. If one of your men will show me to the count—"

"I will do so myself."

"But, my lord—"

He waved aside the cleric's objections. They had as their object this morning the little abbey of Soisins, founded by his great-grandfather after the death of his first wife in childbirth and added onto by his great-grandfather's second wife after his own death in battle. "This is more important." No one argued with him. "Come." He said it more to the hounds than to the others: where he and the hounds went, the rest followed. "Walk beside me," he said to the Eagle.

She glanced toward the hounds. "I'm sorry to have startled them. They don't seem very . . . welcoming."

Alain heard the men-at-arms muttering behind him, and he could just imagine what they were saying. "Sometimes they surprise even me, but they won't harm anyone as long as I'm with them." With only a slight hesitation she moved up beside him. At once, still growling low in their throats, the hounds flowed to his opposite side, a mass of black coats and legs scrunched together. So intent were they on avoiding her that they scarcely noticed the handlers and men-at-arms hurriedly sidestepping to make room for them.

"What happened to your horse?" he asked.

"Ai, Lady!" She glanced behind herself as if wondering if someone followed besides his guards. "Elfshot, my lord."

"Elfshot!"

"Fifteen days south of here. I've almost lost track of the days." She told a jumbled story of bandits and shadowy figures in the deep forest. "One of their arrows struck my horse's flank, just a scratch, but even though the deacon at Laar blessed it, the poor creature sickened and died."

"But you're a King's Eagle! Surely you could have commandeered another horse."

"So I could have, had I been in Wendar. But no one here would give me a fresh mount in exchange for a sick one."

"And this in my father's lands?" He was appalled. "That isn't how we serve the king's messengers! I will see the deacons hereabouts are reminded of our duty."

"Do you support King Henry, my lord?" she asked, clearly surprised.

He could only imagine the reception a Wendish rider—though she scarcely appeared Wendish, with that complexion—had received in this part of Varre. "I do what is right," he said firmly, "and I hope my aunt—I hope my elders will never be disappointed in me by hearing I have stinted in hospitality to a stranger."

She smiled, a brief flash on her face that he wished, at once, to see again. "You are kind, my lord."

"Didn't the blessed Daisan say, 'If you love only those who love you, what reward can you expect?' "

That did make her smile again. "In truth, my lord, many of the folk who offered me shelter and food these last fifteen days had no horse to give in exchange. It was the ones who did who were least hospitable."

"That will change," he promised her. "What is your name, Eagle?"

Startled, she took a stutter step, stumbling to catch up as he paused to look at her. "I beg your pardon, my lord. It's just not—few noble folk ask—"

Of course. Eagles hatched from common stock. No nobly born lord or lady would ever think of asking one's name. He had betrayed his upbringing, and yet, why should he be ashamed of simple courtesy? "I am called Alain," he said, to reassure her. "I meant nothing by it. It's just hard to address you as 'Eagle' all the time."

She ducked her head as she thought over this answer. She had a fine profile, limned now by the morning sun to the east. But for all her obvious physical vitality, she wore under that vigor a mantle of fragility, as if she might break apart at any moment. *She is afraid.* The revelation came to him with such force that he knew it to be true, yet he could hardly say so aloud. *She lives in fear.*

"I am called Liath," she whispered, and sounded amazed to hear her own voice.

"Liath!" This name had meaning for him. He remembered it. "Liathano," he said in a low voice as he took a step forward.

The weight of memory drowned him.

He stands in the old ruins, midsummer's stars rising above him as bright as jewels thrown into the heavens. The Serpent's red eye glares above. A shade detaches itself from the

*far wall, entering the avenue of stone. Fitted in a cuirass,
armed with a lance, he carries a white cloak draped over
one arm. Behind him, flames roar as the outpost burns under
the assault of barbarians. He is looking for someone, but he
sees Alain instead.*

"Where has Liathano gone?" the shade asks.

Liathano. *Surprised, Alain speaks.* "I don't know," he
*says, but in answer he only hears the pound of horses gallop-
ing past, a haze of distant shouting, a faint horn caught on
the wind.*

His foot came down.

"What did you say?" asked the Eagle.

He shook himself, and Sorrow and Rage, trotting alongside, slewed their great heads round to look at him. Rage
yipped once. Sorrow butted him on the thigh with his shoulder, and he staggered and laughed and rubbed Sorrow affectionately on the head with his knuckles.

"I don't know," he said, blinking into sunlight that
seemed abruptly twice as bright. "Just that I've heard that
name before."

For an instant, he thought she would bolt and run. Instead she stopped dead, stared at him as he, too, halted,
the hounds sitting obediently beyond. Bliss whimpered
softly. His retinue eddied to a halt around him, keeping
well away from both Eagle and hounds.

"No," she said at last, more to herself than to him, her
voice so soft only he and the hounds heard her. She seemed
more perplexed than anything. "I can't make myself feel
afraid of you."

Poor creature. Did she think she had to be afraid of
everyone? "Come," he said gently, showing her the way.
"You must be hungry and tired. You will find a place to
rest in my father's hall. Nothing will hurt you there."

And with that, she burst into tears.

Nothing will hurt you there.

The young lord made sure she had something to eat and
wine to drink before he took her upstairs to his father. She

was too bewildered, too confused, and too embarrassed by
her sudden storm of weeping on the road beyond Lavas
stronghold to know what to say to him, so she kept quiet.

With the count, she felt on surer ground.

"What brings you to my lands, Eagle?" he asked. He did
not, of course, ask her to sit down, nor did he ask her name.

"This message I bring to you from King Henry. 'The city
of Gent still lies under the hand of the Eika. Its defenders
lie dead. The count of that region and her nearest kin are
dead as well and her army scattered. The lands all round
the city lie as wasteland. It is time to take it back before
the Eika can do worse damage. You were rewarded with a
son for your honesty before me in Autun, after the Battle
of Kassel. But I could not then ride to Gent's aid because
of Sabella's treachery, which you once supported. Prove
your loyalty to me by taking on this task. Meet me at Gent
with an army before Luciasmass at midsummer. If you restore Gent to my sovereignty, with or without my aid, you
will receive a just reward as well as my favor.' "

Lavastine smiled slightly. His smile had no warmth in it;
neither, like Hugh's, was it cold, merely practical, as at the
sight of a good harvest. "Gent," he mused. "Come, come,
Alain. Sit down. Don't stand there like a servant."

Mercifully, the hounds had been kenneled, all but two.
These padded obediently after the young lord, who sat himself in a fine carved chair to the right of his father. One of
the hounds draped itself over the boots of the count. The
other yawned mightily and flopped down near one of the
three braziers that heated the room. After two months of
traveling through the winter countryside, Liath appreciated
how very warm it was in this room, as long as you kept
out of the drafts. Tapestries smothered the walls. Rugs lay
three deep on the floor. She was so warm she wanted to
take off her cloak and outer tunic but feared it would
look disrespectful.

"Gent," repeated Lavastine. "A long march from these
lands. Yet the reward may be a rich one." He glanced up
at his captain, who stood with his other intimate servants
here and there about the chamber. Liath recognized a soldier when she saw one; like the count, this man had a
brisk competency about him and a squared strength to his
shoulders that reminded her—briefly and painfully—of

Sanglant. "How many men-at-arms can we muster after the sowing?"

"I beg your pardon, my lord count," said Liath. Surprised, he looked at her, raised a hand to show she might continue. "King Henry also sends this message. 'From my kin you may ask for aid. Constance, Biscop of Autun and Duchess of Arconia, will provide troops. Rotrudis, Duchess of Saony and Attomar, will provide troops. Liutgard, Duchess of Fesse, will provide troops. I ride the southlands now to gather an army for the coming battle and I will meet you at Gent unless events in the south or east prevent me. Only a strong army can defeat the Eika.' "

"Ah," said Lavastine. "Captain, what do you say to this?"

"It is a long march to Gent," said the captain. "I don't rightly know how far, but it lies a good way into Wendish lands, up along the north coast. We heard many stories, at Autun, that the Eika chieftain was an enchanter, that he had brought a hundred ships to Gent together with a thousand Eika savages."

"You were at Gent," said the young lord suddenly. *Alain.* That was his name. He had offered her his name in the way of equals. She could not stop sneaking looks at him. Tall, broad-shouldered but slender, with dark hair and the thinnest down of pale beard on his face so that it almost appeared as if he had not yet grown a beard, he looked nothing like his father. Ai, Lady. He had spoken so gently to her, in the same way one coaxed a wounded animal into shelter.

"You were at Gent?" demanded Lavastine, suddenly interested in her. Before, she had only been, like a parchment letter, a medium through which words reached him.

"I was there at the end."

So *again* she had to tell the whole awful story of the fall of Gent. And yet, telling it at almost every hamlet she had slept at these past two months had softened the pain. Told again and again, it could hardly be otherwise. "*If you pound your head against the wall enough times,*" Da would say with a bitter smile when she was furious with herself for making a mistake, "*it will finally stop hurting.*"

Lavastine questioned her closely about the lay of the city, the land thereabouts, the approaches from the west, from the north and south, which she knew little about, and from the east, which she had never seen. He asked her about the river, how close the city lay to the river's mouth, how the island on which the city lay was situated, how the bridges gapped the water and in what manner the gates and walls stood in reference to roadway and shoreline.

"This tunnel," he said. "The farmer claimed the cave ended in a wall."

"So he did, my lord count. I have no reason to disbelieve him. It was a miracle that anyone survived or that the tunnel appeared."

"But a tunnel did appear," said Lavastine.

"And you survived," said the young lord, and blushed.

His father glanced sharply at him, frowned, and then played absently with the ears of the hound that lounged at his feet. "Dhuoda," he said to the woman seated to his left, the only other person so honored in the chamber. "Can you be without so many men for another summer's season? If we leave after sowing, I don't know if we can return by harvest."

"Much depends on the weather," she said. "But despite everything, last year's harvest was decent and this winter has been mild. It could be done if you muster after the Feast of St. Sormas . . . *if* you think it worthwhile."

"The king's favor and a just reward." Both he and the noblewoman looked at the young man. "Eagle, where is Lord Geoffrey?"

"Lord Geoffrey remained behind to hunt with the king. He will follow later and will meet you here by the time you muster your troops."

"Was the king so certain I would agree?"

"He said, my lord count, that he would grant you the reward you asked for."

The young Lord had the propensity to blush a fierce red. He did so now. Liath could not imagine why. But at this moment she did not much care about the embarrassments of the nobly born. She only wanted to stand in this room, to shelter in this safe hall, for the rest of her life.

"Tallia!" said Lavastine in the tone of a man who has scented victory. "He will give us Tallia." He stood. "Let it be done. Eagle, you will return to the king to let him know that I hereby pledge to free Gent from the Eika."

4

HE climbs upward on the old path through a forest of spruce, pine, and birch. Soon the forest fades to birch only and at last even these stunted trees fall away as he emerges onto the fjall, the high plateau, home of the WiseMothers. The wind blows fiercely at this height, whipping his ice-white hair. A rime of frost covers the ground.

The OldMother, who is both his mother and his aunt, sent him here. "Speak to them, restless one," she said. "Their words are wiser than mine."

He finds the youngest of the WiseMothers still on the trail, her great bulk easing upward toward her place with the others. He sees them now in the distance like stout pillars surrounding a hollow burnished to a bright glare by the glittering threads that mark the spawning net of ice-wyrms. But he does not mean to brave the ice-wyrms' venomous sting this day.

Instead he stops beside the youngest of them, who has not yet reached their council ground. Although she passed the knife of decision to his OldMother before his hatching, it has taken her these many years to get as far as a morning's hard walk for him. But she, like her mothers and mothers' mothers before her, grew from that same substance that carves the bones of the earth. She has no reason to move swiftly in the world: She will see many more seasons than he can ever hope to, and long after her bones have hardened completely, her thoughts will still walk the paths of earth until, at last, she departs utterly to the fjall of the heavens.

He kneels before her, brings her in offering nothing durable or hard, only those things made precious by their fragility and transience: a tiny flower once sheltered in the lee of a rock; a lock of downy hair from one of the Soft Ones' infants which just died last night; the remains of an eggshell from Hakonin fjord; the delicate bone of a small bird such as a priest would carve marks into and with its fellows scatter onto stone to read the footprints of the future.

"WiseMother," he says. "Hear my words. Give me an

answer to my question." Having spoken, he waits. One must have patience to converse with the WiseMothers and not just because of the ice-wyrms.

Her progress up the path is so slow he cannot actually see her forward movement, but were he to come in another week, the lichen-striped boulder that lies beside the tread of her great hooves would be a finger's span behind. In that same way they hear and they speak to a measure of years far longer than his own. Perhaps, indeed, once they are no longer bound to the world of the tribe by the knife, it is actually hard for them to understand the words of their grandsons who speak and move so swiftly and live so short a time, not more than forty circuits of the sun.

Her voice rumbles so low, like the lowest pitch in the distant fall of an avalanche, that he must strain to hear her. "Speak. Child."

"OldMother heard from the southlands. Bloodheart calls an army together, all the RockChildren who will come to him, to campaign against the Soft Ones. If I take such ships as I have gathered and sail south when the wind turns, will I still be in disgrace? Is it better to remain here, risking little, or sail there, risking much?"

The wind blusters along the rocky plateau. Rocks adorn the land, the only ornament needed to make of it a fitting chamber for the wisdom of the eldest Mothers—all but the FirstMothers, who vanished long ago. Below, trees shush and murmur, a host of voices in the constant wind. It begins, gently, to snow. With the thaw will come spring rains, and then the way will lie open to sail south.

Her voice resonates even through the earth beneath his knees, though it is faint to his ears. "Let. Be. Your. Guide. That. Which. Appears. First. To. Your. Eyes."

His copper-skinned hand still lies over her rough one. He feels a sharp tingling, like lightning striking nearby, and withdraws his hand at once. The offerings he has laid upon her upturned hand melt and soak into her skin as honey seeps into sodden earth, slowly but inexorably. The audience is over.

He rises obediently. She has answered, so there is no need to walk the rest of the way up the fjall, into the teeth of the wind, to kneel before the others by the hollow where all come to rest in the fullness of time.

He turns his back on the wind and walks down through the sullen green and white of the winter forest. Below the trees he walks through pastureland, the steadings of his brothers and oldest uncles, the pens of their slaves. All this is familiar to his eyes; he has seen it many times before: the sheep and goats huddling in the winter cold, scraping beneath the snow to find fodder; cows crowded into the byres, fenced away from the dogs; the pigs scurrying away to the shelter of trees; the slaves in their miserable pens.

But as he comes up behind his own steading, newly built from sod and timber, he sees a strange procession wind away into the trees. Silent, he follows. It is a small group of slaves, six of them; one carries a tiny bundle wrapped in precious cloth. They are hard to tell apart, but two he can recognize even from a distance: the male named Otto and the female-priest named Ursuline. These two have become like chieftain and OldMother to the other Soft Ones he keeps as slaves; over the winter he has observed their actions among the others, forming them into a tribe, and it interests him. As this interests him.

A clearing lies in the trees. Certain markers of stone, crudely carved, are set upright into the soil. It is a slave place, and he leaves it alone as do all the RockChildren. Slaves have their customs, however useless they may be. Now, he sees what they are about. They have dug a hole in the ground and into the earth they place the body of the infant that died in the night. The female-priest sings in her thin voice while the others weep. He has tasted the tears of the Soft Ones: They are salt, like the ocean waters. Is it possible that their Circle god has taught them something of the true life of the universe? Why else would they cover their dead ones in earth even as they leak water onto the dirt? Is this what they give in offering? He does not know.

But he watches. Is this event the one he must use as his guide? What does the funeral presage? His own death if he returns to his father's army? Or the death of the Soft Ones whom Bloodheart will attack?

Risk much or risk little.

In the end, staring through the branches at the small mourning party, he knows he always knew the answer to his question. He is too restless to stay. Death is only a change in existence; it is neither ending nor beginning, no matter

*what these Soft Ones may think. He will return to Hundse,
to Gent.*

*The mourners file past him on the narrow track. One of
them, a young female with hollow eyes and a body frailer
than most, still cries her salt tears though the others attempt
to soothe her. Did the infant come from her body? And if
so, how was it planted there? Are they the same as the beasts,
who also plant their young in and feed them out of the
mother's body? But though the Soft Ones resemble brute
animals, he thinks it cannot be completely true. They speak,
as people do. They gaze above themselves into the fjall of
the heavens and wonder what has brought them to walk on
the earth. This, also, true people do. And they do something
he has seen no other creature, not RockChildren, not animal,
not the small cousins of the earth nor the fell beasts of the
ocean water, do.*

They weep.

Alain woke to the profound silence of Lavas stronghold
asleep in the dark and cold of a late winter's night. But a
tickle nagged at him, like a hound scratching at the door.
Rage slumbered on. As he rose, Sorrow whuffed softly and
clattered to his feet, following him. The other hounds lay
curled here and there on the carpet or near the bed. Terror
lay atop Lavastine's feet, the two of them snoring softly
together, in concert. Alain slipped on a tunic. He had heard
something, or perhaps it was only the residue of his dream.

He latched the door carefully behind him and placed a
hand on Sorrow's muzzle. It was cold in the hall and cold
on the stairs. A draft leaked up the stone stairwell, a breath
of warmth from the hall. He followed its scent and at last,
beneath the breathing silence of hall and stone, heard what
he was listening for: the sound of weeping.

It was so soft that he only found its source when he was
halfway into the hall, attracted by the red glow of hearth
fire. In the alcoves, servants and men-at-arms slept; others
would have returned to their own huts outside the palisade
or down in the village. But a single heaped shape more like
a forgotten bundle of laundry lay by the fire, shuddering.

The Eagle wept alone on her rough pallet by the fire.

Sorrow whined nervously.

"Sit!" Alain whispered, leaving the hound sitting in the

middle of the floor with his tail thumping in the rushes. He approached the Eagle.

She did not notice him until he was almost upon her. Then, gasping aloud, she choked on a sob, started up, and reached for a stick in the fire.

"Hush," he said. "Don't be scared. It's only me. Alain. Don't burn yourself."

"Oh, God," she murmured, but she drew her hand away from the fire and used it to wipe her nose instead. He could not make out much of her face, but he could smell the salt of her tears in the smoky air.

"Why are you crying?" he asked.

"Ai, Lady," she whispered. "It wasn't so bad, riding away. But now I must go back."

"Go back where?"

She shook her head, trying now to dry her tears, but they still came despite her wish. "It doesn't matter."

"Of course it matters!"

She was silent for so long that he began to think he would have to speak, or that he had somehow offended her.

"Why should it matter to you?" she asked at last, haltingly.

"It should matter to every one of us when we see one of our kinsfolk lost in sorrow."

"We are not kin, you and I." The words came choked from her mouth. "I have no kin."

"We are all the sons and daughters of God. Isn't that kinship enough?"

"I—I don't know." She stirred restlessly and held out her hands toward the coals to warm them. Reflexively, he fetched some sticks from the woodpile just inside the door and fed the fire. She watched him, still silent.

"You don't want to go back," he said, settling beside her and pulling his knees up to his chest. Sorrow whined softly but kept his distance. "I saw you," he added, "when you rode in from Gent, when the king was in Autun. You and the other Eagle. I don't know his name."

"Wolfhere."

"Aren't Eagles your kin?"

"In a way."

"You've really no one at all?"

"My mother died about ten years ago. And Da is dead." How bitter this admission came he could hear in the tight

rein she held on her voice. "Ai, Lady, almost two years
ago now. He was all I had."

"And I was granted a wealth of fathers," he said, suddenly struck by how great his good fortune had been.

"How can you have a wealth of fathers? How can you
have more than one?"

He hung his head, shamed to think with what anger he
had left Merchant Henri at their last meeting, how badly
he had behaved. Would Henri ever forgive him for that
pride and anger? "I was fostered to one, a good man, and
grew up calling him 'Father.' I came lately to the second."

"Oh, yes." She turned toward him, expression almost visible in the darkness. "King Henry granted Count Lavastine
the right to name you as his heir. Isn't that right?"

"And I only a bastard before," he said lightly, but even
so, and even though Lavastine's soldiers and servants had
now accepted him, the memory of their visit to the manor
of Lady Aldegund and Lord Geoffrey still stung.

"Who was your mother?" she asked, then said, embarrassed, "I beg your pardon, my lord. I've no right to ask
such a thing."

"No, no, I asked *you* questions. You may ask me questions in my turn. She was a servingwoman here, gotten with
child by my father and put aside when he married."

"That story has been told before," she said sharply.
"Noble lords never ask if their attentions are welcome.
That is the last thing they think of." Then, while he was
still so astonished by this accusation that he could only
blink, eyes tearing from the smoke, she huddled away from
him, cowering as if she expected to be hit. "I beg your
pardon. I meant no such thing. Forgive me."

But he could only gape, struck so hard by this new and
unwelcome notion that it was only when a flea crawled up
his ankle from the rushes matting the floor that he came
to himself, scratching it off. "It never occurred to me,"
he said, ashamed now. "Perhaps she loved him, too—it's
possible—or wanted something from him. But maybe she
never cared for him at all and had no choice—" Hard on
this thought, another flashed before him in all its brilliance.
"Is there a noble lord on the progress who torments you
in this way? Isn't there anything the king or the other Eagles can do to stop it?"

"Ai, Lady," she whispered, and because she began to cry again, he knew his guess was right. "There's nothing Eagles can do. And nothing the king will do, for *he's* cleverer than the king and all the lords and ladies at court. They can't see *him* but only what he lays before them to see. There is no one to aid me in any case. He is the son of a margrave. I have no one to protect me!"

"I will protect you," said Alain. "I am heir to the county of Lavas, after all. That counts for something."

Suddenly she clutched his hands. Though the air was cold, her skin was hot. "I pray you, my lord, if you can do anything, if you can make it possible for me to stay here—to send someone else in my place back to the king's progress. . . ."

"Then what?" asked Alain, amazed by the intensity in her voice. "Is this noble lord so loathsome to you?"

She let go of him at once. "You don't understand," she said fiercely. "I have no kin, only the Eagles. Even if I had any fondness for this man—which I do not!—if I became his concubine I would be cast out of the Eagles. Then where would I be if he tired of me? I wouldn't even have the protection of the Eagles. God help me, it doesn't matter. He'll never tire of me. He'll never let me alone."

He was afraid she was going to start weeping again. The confident Eagle he had seen on the road this morning seemed a distant memory now. She was all tears and fear. "What you're saying doesn't make sense! First you say you fear he will cast you off, and then you say you fear he'll never do so. It must be one or the other, surely, and in truth, my friend, I think you are right to fear the first more. If he favors you for a few years until he finds another younger, prettier woman, then you are kinless and without support when he puts you aside. If he never puts you aside, then surely you will live in good circumstances for the rest of your life, and any children you have by him will be well provided for."

At that, she began half to cry and half to snort with laughter. Had she gone mad? "You sound like Mistress Birta. Always calculating what is most practical."

"That's what my Aunt Bel—the woman who raised me—taught me. No use worrying about the fox stealing the chickens when the henhouse is safely locked and it's your house that's burning down."

Her sobs and laughter subsided into hiccuping chuckles. "That sounds like something Da would say. But you don't understand. You can't understand. I'm sorry. I'm sorry to have disturbed your rest this night."

"I want to understand!" he said, angry that she would think he *didn't* care. He sought and found her hands where she had wrapped them in an end of her cloak. "There is so much fear in you, Liath. What are you running from?" He leaned forward without thinking and kissed her on the forehead. A few stray ends of her hair tickled his nose. Her entire body stiffened and at once he dropped her hands and leaned back. Sorrow, behind them, growled softly and scrabbled forward, but not too much, not too close.

"I beg your pardon!" said Alain. What had come over him? Yet what he felt now was nothing like the sinful, intense yearning that engulfed him when he thought of Tallia. He simply knew he must find some way to shelter Liath, just as he had known he had to save the Eika prince that awful night when Lackling was sacrificed in place of the Eika.

By now his eyes had adjusted well enough to the gloom that he could see her fairly well, sitting stiff and straight, her cloak draped in folds down to the floor, her single braid tucked away inside the hood. When she turned her head to stare at the fire, her eyes glinted with a spark of blue.

She only needed encouragement.

Haltingly, hoping to encourage her by his own open-heartedness, he told his story. It came out all in a jumble as he skipped from one thing to the next, watching her face by firelight to see how she responded. He told her of Fifth Son and the hounds, of Lackling's murder by Biscop Antonia, of the *guivre* and Agius' death. Of the vision he had seen in the old Dariyan ruins, the shade who spoke the name "Liathano" and then vanished in a maelstrom of fire and smoke and battle. Of the dreams he still had, his link to the Eika prince.

When he stumbled to a close, she held a hand out to warm it over the coals. "Artemisia describes five types of dreams: the enigmatic dream, the prophetic vision, the oracular dream, the nightmare, and the apparition. It's hard to judge what you experienced. 'Enigmatic' because the meaning of your dreams is concealed with strange shapes and veils—"

"But they don't seem like dreams at all. It's as if I see through his eyes, as if I *am* him."

"The Eika are not like us," she said softly. "They wield magics we have no knowledge of."

The comment surprised him into blurting out a careless thought. "Do you have knowledge of magic?"

Their silence drew out until it became like a living thing which, hiding in the shadows, does not know whether to bolt into the nether darkness or advance into the clear, clean light. Abruptly, in a low, almost monotone voice and in short bursts punctuated by silences, she began to talk.

She told him of a childhood faintly remembered, of the sudden flight she and her da had made from that pleasant home after the death of her mother. She told him of many years wandering in distant lands, and though she spoke as one who has lived every day in fear, he ached to hear her speak so matter-of-factly about all the far and curious places he had ever dreamed of visiting. It seemed, strangely, that inside her words he heard her wish for a safe haven, like the walls of a monastery, to which she could retire, while she had lived the very adventure he had always hoped for and known would be denied him. She had seen Darre and the wild coast of eastern Aosta. She had sailed to Nakria and roamed the ruins of dead Kartiako. She had explored the fabulous palace of the ruler of Qurtubah in the Jinna kingdom of Andalla and wandered the market stalls of busy Medemelacha in Salia. She had seen with her own eyes creatures and wonders he had never heard tell of, not even from the merchants of Osna village, the most traveled people he knew.

But for this she had paid a price. She had lost her father, murdered at night by sorcery with no mark left on his body. Even now, fell creatures stalked her—some of them inhuman and one all too human. Seeking sorcerous knowledge from *The Book of Secrets* as well as what secrets he was sure she held hidden inside her, a holy man of the church had made her his slave—and worse.

After such misery as made Alain wince to hear it, she had been rescued by Eagles. Yet she could not trust even them, certainly not Wolfhere. She couldn't trust anyone except an Eagle named Hanna who was now, somehow, Father Hugh's prisoner. Except Prince Sanglant, whom she had met in Gent—and he was dead. Except perhaps an Aoi sorcerer seen through fire, and she had no idea where he was. In the end, tormented again by Father Hugh, she had discovered the most terrifying knowledge of all: She held locked inside her a sorcerous power trapped in her bones or in her blood over which she had no control.

"I don't know what to do with it. I don't know what it means or what it is, how much Da locked away and how much he never knew of. I only know he was trying to protect me. What if I go back to the king's progress? Hugh is holding Hanna as a hostage to make me come back. And if I don't go back, then what becomes of her? Ai, Lady, I don't know what to do! I don't know what's going to become of Hanna. But if I go back to the king's progress, Hugh will imprison me again. There's nowhere to run any more. I'm so afraid."

"Then maybe you have to stop running," he said reasonably.

Her laughter was sharp in reply. "And let them find me? Let Hugh trap me?"

"Find yourself." The answer didn't come cleanly; answers rarely did. But he sensed that they groped closer to the question now, and only when they could discover the question could they search out the path that would lead her to the answer she sought.

"*Gnosi seaton,*" she murmured. " 'Know thyself.' That's what the prophetesses of the ancient gods said at the temple of Talfi."

His hand. The memory from his dream engulfed him so abruptly that he had to cover his eyes. " 'Let be your guide that which first appears to your eyes.' It wasn't the funeral at all. It was his own *hand.* That's what she meant."

"What funeral?"

He shook himself free of the windings of forgotten sleep. "My dream of Fifth Son, the one I had this night."

"I only have nightmares," said Liath, her voice so quiet that even the snap of twigs and roll of burning logs drowned it. "I've never had a true vision, except through fire—and that isn't truly a vision but a gateway."

Before he knew what he was about, he had pulled the leather thong up from around his neck and opened the little cloth pouch. He laid the delicate red rose on his palm for her to see. It gleamed uncannily in the firelight.

She stared. "The Rose of Healing," she whispered. Her voice caught, broke, and she sniffed back tears. She did not attempt to touch it.

The petals burned on his palm. Quickly he replaced it in the pouch. Then, trembling slightly, he took another log and set it on the hot coals. It smoldered, caught, and blazed, flames dancing along its length.

She wiped her nose again with the back of a hand and looked up at him. She reached, hesitated, then laid a hand on his arm. The touch was so light it might not have been there at all, and yet in that simple act Alain understood that, as with the hounds, he had won her trust forever.

5

HE crept back upstairs when the first stirrings of dawn reached him. She had fallen asleep hours ago. Yet he could not bear to leave and instead had sat watch over her and the fire for the rest of the night.

Upstairs, his father was awake and waiting for him.

"Alain." He nudged Terror out of his way and swung his legs out of bed, rose, stretched, and then turned to examine his son with a frown. "Open the shutters."

Alain obeyed. The sting of cold air chased along his skin like so many gnats.

"Close it again," said Lavastine after examining him. "Have we not spoken of this? You of all people must be more careful than most."

"Careful of what?"

"I hope you are not about to say you went out to the pits to relieve yourself when we have a perfectly good chamber pot here, and a servant to carry it away in the morning?" Alain flushed, having finally realized where his father thought he had been for most of the night. "Where *have* you been?"

"Down in the hall, talking with—"

"*Talking* with?"

"That's all!"

"Perhaps it isn't fair to expect so much from you. It's a rare man who in his youth can resist a fair morsel set before him. Had God wanted us to remain as pure as the angels, They could have molded us differently, I suppose."

"But I didn't—"

"Is it the Eagle? You know they swear oaths. They aren't allowed congress of that nature with any but their own kind, on pain of being thrown out of their Order. But you're a good-looking boy, and fair spoken, and she's a long way from the king. We each of us have our weaknesses."

"But we didn't—!"

"So it was the Eagle."

"I *talked* to her. You know I've always told the truth, Father! I heard her crying and I went to see—I comforted her, that's all. Can't you send another messenger in her place?"

"Why shouldn't she return to court? That is her duty."

"She has an enemy at court."

"An *Eagle* has an enemy at court? Why should anyone at court even notice such an Eagle, unless she has brought the king's displeasure down on herself?"

"It isn't that at all. There's a nobleman at court, an abbot, who wants to force her to become his concubine."

"Indeed." Lavastine walked over to the shutters and opened them again, framing himself in the full blast of cold air. He stared outside, examining some sight in the courtyard below. No one could ever doubt Lavastine ruled here. He did not have the height or bulk of King Henry or of his own cousin Geoffrey, but even standing in his bare feet, dressed only in a linen undershift as a robe against the chill, he had authority, that absolute assurance that all he surveyed lay under his command. Some gray colored his sand-pale hair; no longer a young man, neither was he old in the way of men entering their decline. Alain wished *he* could feel so sure of himself, could in the simple act of opening a shutter proclaim his fitness to stand in his ordained place in the world. Aunt Bel had that assurance; so had his foster father, Henri. "Perhaps it's even understandable, if the nobleman is insistent enough. If she becomes his concubine, she'll lose her position as an Eagle. Then, should he tire of her, she would have no recourse except to return to her kin—if they would take her in."

"She has no kin."

"Then it is doubly wise of her to resist such an arrangement. I admire her pragmatism. She is better off in the Eagles." He shut and latched one shutter, leaving a draft of cold air to spill into the room while he called over Terror, Ardent, Fear, and Bliss and leashed them to a ring set into the wall. "But I remain puzzled. Why did she confide in *you?*"

Alain hesitated. For an instant, he wanted to say, "Because she's a wild creature, like the hounds, and she trusts me," but the notion was so outrageous that he knew he could speak no such thing aloud. "I don't know."

Lavastine had marked the hesitation. "If you have conceived some fondness for the Eagle . . . you understand why nothing must happen, Alain. You of all people must be more careful—"

As he hadn't been when the servingwoman at Lady Aldegund's manor had accosted him. Only the savagery of the hounds had saved him from giving in to base desire! Hadn't he learned anything from that? "I wouldn't—if I'm to marry Lady Tallia—" But this was too much. He sat down heavily on the bench and buried his face in Sorrow's flank. The thick smell of dog drove all impure thoughts out of his mind—or most of them, anyway, though he could not banish the image of Tallia. And why should such thoughts be impure? Wasn't it true that desire came from the Lady and Lord, that They had granted it to humankind so that woman and man could create children between them?

"What wouldn't you do since you're to marry Tallia?" asked Lavastine, sounding more curious than anything.

"She's so holy, so pure. It wouldn't be right if I didn't come to her as . . . pure as she will come to me."

"A Godly sentiment, Alain, and I am proud of you for it. It is just as well that the Eagle leaves today. If you have conceived a *fondness* for her, it might prove hard to keep your pledge to your future bride."

It took Alain a moment to sort through this. Then he jerked his head up. The untied hounds swarmed over to him, licking his hands. "Go away!" he said, irritated at their attention. "But I wouldn't—I wouldn't think of—" He stammered to a halt. With the window open, he could see his father's expression clearly and read what it meant: Not that *Alain* was tempted by the young Eagle, but that *Lavastine* was.

Was *this* how Alain had been conceived? By a young man who, seeing a young woman, determined to have her in his bed no matter what *she* wanted? "Isn't it written down by the church mothers that *we* must all come cleanly to the marriage bed?" he demanded, horrified to see Lavastine in this unflattering light. No word of scandal had ever touched Henri the Merchant.

Lavastine bowed his head and looked away. "So I am justly reminded of my own faults."

"I beg your pardon, Father." How had he come to blurt out such an appalling statement—even if it was true?

But Lavastine only smiled wryly and crossed the chamber to touch Alain's hair as a praying man might touch a reliquary. "Never beg pardon for telling what is only the truth. Be assured I have learned my lesson in such matters. I have learned to confine myself to whores and married women, such as may be approached discreetly."

"Father! But the church mothers enjoin us to—"

The count laughed sharply and called Steadfast over to him. She had become more restless of late; most likely she was going into heat. Already the males had begun to grow more irritable than usual. "I am not that strong, son. We must all learn the measure of our strength. Otherwise we exhaust ourselves striving for that which we can never gain." He tied Steadfast up away from the others and frowned at her, then whistled for Sorrow and Rage. Good Cheer was, as usual, hiding under the bed. "Let the servants in, Alain," he added curtly, motioning toward the door.

"But, Father, what about the Eagle?"

Lavastine was down on his knees now. Grabbing Good Cheer by the forelegs, he dragged her bodily out from her hiding place while she whined and attempted to lick him into leniency. He grunted, heaved her up, and wrestled her over to the wall while she leaned heavily against him, anything to impede his progress. "Cursed stubborn hound." He patted her affectionately on the shoulder. Then he turned round.

"Well, then, boy, we shall keep the Eagle here with us, which is the only practical choice, is it not? She knows the lay of the land by Gent. She has walked in the city and remembers its streets and walls. She traversed this hidden tunnel. What use to us is her knowledge of Gent if she is with King Henry when we attack?" He lifted a hand, forefinger raised as the deacon did when she meant to scold her congregation. "But there will be no—"

"I never even thought of it!"

Lavastine smiled thinly. "Perhaps you did not. Not yet, at any rate."

"Then you must make the same promise!" Alain retorted, still waiting at the door.

Steadfast barked, and all at once all the hounds began yipping and barking. "Hush! Stop that noise, you miserable creatures!" snapped the count, but he was not truly angry with them. He could not be. Just as, Alain saw suddenly, he was not angry at what Alain had said. Having been granted the heir he so long desired and despaired of ever having, he could not bring himself to chastise him. Nor, perhaps, did he even want to, though the demand had been impertinent.

"Very well. She will stay with us . . . untouched. We march to Gent after the Feast of St. Sormas. Once we have retaken the city, we will collect Tallia and return home."

Collect Tallia. It made her sound like a chest of gold or a jeweled cup, a valuable treasure held by the king to be given out as a prize. Wasn't that what she was, now that her parents had been disgraced and shorn of their position? But their disgrace did not strip from her the inheritance she received through her mother nor the royal bloodlines that tied her to both the ruling house of Wendar and the princely house that had once ruled Varre.

A servant scratched lightly on the door.

"What if we fail to take Gent?" asked Alain.

Lavastine simply looked at him as if he had uttered words in a language the count did not know. "They are savages, Alain! *We* are civilized people. The city of Gent fell because it was unprepared and overwhelmed. The same will not happen to us. Come now. We have spent far too long talking about a common Eagle who is no doubt more useful to us when she flies as is her nature than when she is left bound to a post for us to admire her beauty. Let us get on with our day."

6

HE had not spoken words in a long time except to respond to taunts or to call down the dogs. Indeed, it took him a long time—hours, perhaps days—to find the words that would say what he meant them to.

But he struggled, piecing them together. Never let it be said he did not fight until his last breath. He would not let Bloodheart and the dogs defeat him.

"Bloodheart."

Was that his voice? Rasping and hoarse, he sounded brutish compared to the light, fluid tones of the Eika, who for all their ugly metal-hard bodies had voices as soft as the flutes Bloodheart played.

Bloodheart stirred on his throne, coming to life. "Is this my prince of dogs who addresses me? I thought you had forgotten how to speak! What boon do you ask?"

"You won't kill me, Bloodheart. Nor will your dogs."

Bloodheart didn't reply, only fingered the ax laid across his thighs and the smooth bone flutes tucked into his girdle of glistening silver-and-gold chain links. Perhaps he looked irritated.

"Teach me your language. Let your priest teach me to read the bones, as he does."

"Why?" demanded Bloodheart, but he might have been amused. He might have been angry. "Why should I? You are only a dog. Why should you want to?"

"Even dogs bark, and gnaw at bones for sport," said Sanglant.

At that, Bloodheart laughed uproariously. He did not answer. Indeed, he left soon after to tour the armories and tanneries of Gent, to take his daily excursion down to the river.

But the next day the priest settled down just outside the limit of Sanglant's chains and began to teach him the language of the Eika, to teach him how to roll and interpret the finely carved bones he carried in his pouch. And every

day, lulled by Sanglant's muted voice and intent interest—
for what else did the prince have to be interested in?—the
priest edged a little closer.

Even a dog could be patient.

PART FOUR

SEEKER
OF
HEARTS

XIII
A GLIMPSE BEYOND
THE VEIL

1

BECAUSE of the rugged terrain and the lay of the mountains, no roads fit for the king's progress led between the duchy of Avaria and that of Wayland. An Eagle had ridden straight west from the palace at Echstatt along tracks impassable for the heavy wagons that made up the train of the king's entourage. So after several weeks at Echstatt, the court itself moved north along the Old Avarian Road toward the city and biscophric at Wertburg. Although not as well traveled a road as the Hellweg—the Clear Way—that ran through the heartland of Saony and Fesse, the road accommodated king and retinue without too much hardship for the royal party, though they moved slowly.

Old fortresses, royal manors, and estates under the rule

of convents or monasteries provided lodging and food.
Common folk lined the way to watch the king and his entourage ride by. According to Ingo, the king had not ridden
this way for some five years, accounting for their enthusias-
tic welcome. To Hanna, their welcome resembled all the
others she had witnessed, just as this land looked much like
any other land with hills, vast forest, and the friendly sight
of fields and villages, churches and estates. But the hills
were steep and high while in Heart's Rest the wilderness
gave way to heath; beech and fir dominated in open fields
where she was used to a dense canopy of oak and elm and
lime; and the village folk spoke in a dialect that was hard
for her to understand.

Each day on the king's progress brought new fascinations
for Hanna. Heralds rode ahead to shout the news of the
king's adventus—his arrival at the next stopping place. A
levy of soldiers and servants forged ahead of the main party
to clear the road of snow and debris. At the forefront of the
main procession rode the king and his noble companions in
full glory. After them came the swelling ranks of an army,
growing with each day as nobles joined Henry or sent soldiers in their place. The horde of servants followed them,
and farther back, wagons rolled, lumbering and jolting over
the rutted road, skidding on ice, getting stuck in drifts. A
century of Lions marched at the rear.

But of course there were always stragglers, beggars trailing behind, women and men hoping to hire themselves out
as laborers. Peddlers, prostitutes, homeless servants, persons with grievances to bring before the king, and anonymous young men hoping to find employment or loot in the
aftermath of battle, all of these followed in the track of the
king's progress, some joining as others dropped out.

"Is it always like this?" Hanna asked Hathui. Fifteen
days ago they had left Echstatt. Now she and the other
Eagle pulled up their horses on a rise that looked down to
the north over the episcopal city of Wertburg and down to
the south over the road that wound away through the stubble of fields and lines of hedges before it lost itself in forest.
Riding at the front, they had a good view of the king's
train, a long and colorful procession strung across the landscape below. The line of stragglers still emerged from forest. Below them, the king ascended the hill. The hugely

pregnant Sapientia rode beside him, mounted on a gentle mare, with Helmut Villam, Sister Rosvita, and Father Hugh in close attendance. At the Wertburg city gates, a large party led by the biscop and the local count had already begun its own procession out to meet the king.

"We'll be in Mainni by the thaw," said Hathui. "There are several royal palaces where we will sit out the floods. It's hard work traveling in the spring. How do you fare, Hanna?"

Hanna considered the question seriously; she knew very well what Hathui was asking. "I fare well enough. There's nothing wrong with Princess Sapientia that wise companions and fields of her own to plow won't cure, as my mother used to say."

"Are you her champion now?"

"It's true she's rash and proud and thoughtless, but from what I hear she lived for a long time in the shadow of her brother, Prince Sanglant—"

"True enough," observed Hathui.

"—and if she has many companions now, I fear it's mostly because they expect King Henry to name her as Heir—not for herself. So it's no wonder she's—well, as my mother would say, if you bring up a child on table scraps, then it will surely gorge to sickness when you finally sit it down to a feast."

"A wise woman, your mother," said Hathui with a grim smile. "But I didn't mean to inquire about the princess. What of Father Hugh?"

"I am of no concern to him," Hanna said at last, but she knew she was blushing. "He pays no attention to me." Why, then, knowing what she did about him, did she sometimes still wish he did?

"If I did not have Liath's testimony, it would be hard for me to believe the things she has accused him of."

"Perhaps he's changed."

Hathui shot her a sharp glance. "Do you think so?"

"He's so . . . kind and gentle, so soft-spoken. So clever and industrious. You've seen him yourself, laying hands on the sick, giving out alms to the poor. He attends Princess Sapientia faithfully and advises her with care."

"As well he might!"

Hanna had to grin. "If it's a child of his own begetting,

then it's no wonder he attends her so closely. But he doesn't seem . . . the same person as he was in Heart's Rest."

"He's with his own people now."

"That's true enough. We were only common folk in Heart's Rest, far beneath his notice."

"Except for Liath."

"Except for Liath," Hanna echoed.

"Did you ever think she might be lying?" asked Hathui casually. Ahead, the biscop's procession had unfurled banners and the bright standards representing the city and the local count. Behind, riders in the king's procession began to sing.

Clouds covered the heavens this day, and it was cold, yet surely no soul could be gloomy observing such pageantry. Hanna turned her face into the breeze and stared, the lick of the wind on her lips. Even in gloves her hands were cold, but she would have been no other place in the world than this one as the king and his party ascended the hill, reaching the crest behind them. Their song carried fitfully on the breeze.

"She's not lying, Hathui. I saw her carried in that day, when she miscarried. I know what he did to her. And he stole her book."

"Some would say the book became his when he bought off her father's debts. She *was* his slave."

"And many's the man or woman who uses a slave as they see fit, and no one would ever fault them for it. It still doesn't seem right to me. She never welcomed his attentions. Is it right that she be forced to accept him just because he's a margrave's son and she has no kin to protect her?" Her tone came out more bitter than she intended.

"Some would say it is," remarked Hathui. "You and I would not. But you and I do not rule this kingdom."

There was more Hanna wanted to say, but she was ashamed to say it out loud: Hugh was a selfish, arrogant lord with the faultless manners of a cleric and a voice like that of an angel—but sometimes beautiful flowers are the most poisonous. "Yet we can't help admiring them," she murmured.

"What?" Hathui looked at her sidewise, then mercifully turned her horse aside. "Come, here is the king."

They made way, letting the king's standard bearers and then the king himself pass before them, and fell in behind, singing.

King and court celebrated the Feast of St. Herodia at Wertburg, with the biscop of Wertburg presiding. After a week eating from the biscop's table, they continued north for three days to Hammelberg, on the Malnin River, where they sheltered at a monastic estate. From here they cut across overland by the Helfenstene Way, a journey of four days, until they rejoined the Malnin Road at Aschfenstene. Turning northwest, they followed the river for five days until they reached the city of Mainni, where the Brixian tongue of the kingdom of Salia bordered the duchy of Arconia and lapped up against the duchy of Fesse. Once Biscop Antonia had presided over Mainni. Now, upon arriving, King Henry installed Sister Odila, a relative of the local count, as biscop.

Their arrival in the city coincided with the feast day celebrating the conversion of St. Thais. She had been a prostitute before embracing the God of Unities and walling herself up in a cell—from which she did not emerge for ten years, and then only to die. Hanna heard more than one cleric comment that Henry had offered the biscophric first to Sister Rosvita, but that the cleric had remarked that she was not yet ready to wall herself up when there were many more places she needed to visit for her *History*. She had suggested Sister Odila as a suitable candidate, and Henry had taken her advice in this as in so many other things. The appointment, of course, was contingent on the approval of the skopos, though as yet they had no news from Darre about the case brought against Antonia.

"I wonder how Wolfhere fares," Hanna asked Hathui many nights later after the feast celebrating the miracle of St. Rose a'lee; the saint, a limner in a humble village outside the city of Darre, had painted a set of murals depicting the life of the blessed Daisan that had so pleased the Lord and Lady that a holy light had shone on the images ever after.

"Wolfhere fares well enough, I have found." Hathui heaped the dwindling winter fodder in the biscop's stables into a plush heap, over which she threw her cloak, bundling herself up in her blanket. With so many animals stabled

below, the loft was a warm, if pungent, resting place. "I
wonder how Liath fares. It's almost the end of the year
and we've had no word from Count Lavastine."

"You don't think the count will refuse to march on
Gent?"

"I think it unlikely. The question is whether the king will
be able to meet him there." Hathui settled herself comfortably in the straw. "From Mainni, we can follow the road
north to Gent—or the road south to Wayland."

"Why would the king want to go to Wayland?"

"Answer that yourself, Hanna!"

"Duke Conrad's soldiers turned me back from the Julier
Pass. Is that a grave enough offense that the king would
march against the duke?"

"Picking a fight—without the king's permission—with the
Queen and King of Karrone? Remember, the King of Karrone is Henry's younger brother. And Duke Conrad also
wears the golden torque that marks him as born of the
royal line. His great-grandfather was the younger brother
of the first Henry."

"Do you think he means to rebel, as Sabella did? Surely
any claim he might have to the throne isn't nearly as strong
as hers."

"I don't know what the noble folk intend. Their concerns
are different from those I grew up with. I hope," she added,
"that King Henry finds a good margrave for Eastfall, a
woman or man who can stop the Quman raids and protect
the freeholders. A person who is not concerned with the
intrigues of the court."

"Aren't all the nobles concerned with the intrigues of
the court?"

Hathui only grinned. "I haven't asked them all. Nor
would they answer me if I did. Hush now, chatterer. I want
to sleep."

In the morning a messenger arrived from Count Lavastine—a messenger who was not Liath. Sapientia reclined
on a couch while her attendants fluttered around her and
her new physician—on loan from Margrave Judith and
newly arrived—tested her pulse by means of pressing two
fingers to her skin just under her jawline. Hanna had observed that the princess liked commotion, as if the amount
of talking and movement eddying around her reflected her

importance. Behind the couch Hugh paced, more like a caged animal than an amiable and wise courtier. He held Liath's book tucked under his arm. In the two and a half months since the disaster at Augensburg, Hanna had rarely seen him without the book in his hands; if not there, then he stowed it in a small locked chest which a servant carried.

"Why did she not return?" he demanded of no one in particular. Looking up, he saw Hanna.

Hanna froze. She could not bring herself to move, not knowing whether to bask in his notice or fear it.

Sapientia yawned as she rubbed a hand reflexively over her huge abdomen. "Really, Father Hugh, I prefer my Hanna. Her voice is so very calming. The other one was too skittish. She serves Gent better riding with Count Lavastine than with us."

Hugh frowned at Hanna a moment longer. Then, with a palpable effort, he turned his attention to the princess. "Wise advice to your own counselor, Your Highness," he said in an altered tone.

Sapientia smiled, looking pleased. "More fruitful to wonder if we will ride south to Wayland and Duke Conrad, or north to meet Lavastine at Gent. And what is keeping my dear Theophanu? Perhaps she has turned nun at St. Valeria Convent." Her favorites, surrounding her, giggled. Hugh did not laugh, but when the gossip turned to the latest news—which was none—about Duke Conrad, he joined in with his usual elegance of manner, gently chiding those who were mean-spirited and encouraging those who supposed King Henry would find a peaceful solution to any misunderstanding which might arise.

"It is true," he remarked, "that force is sometimes necessary to win what is rightfully yours, but God also gave us equal parts of eloquence and cunning which we rightly point to as the mark of the wise counselor. We are better off hoarding our substance in order to fight off the incursions of the Quman and the Eika than wasting it among ourselves."

With this judgment King Henry evidently agreed. The court did not move south toward Wayland. But as the early spring rains began and the rivers swelled with the thaw, his advisers deemed the journey north toward Gent as yet too difficult to attempt. While they waited for the roads to open, they visited the small royal estates that lay in a wide ring—each about three days' ride from the last—around Mainni. The court celebrated Mariansmass and the new year at Salfurt, fasted for Holy Week at Alsheim, and moved north to celebrate the feasts of St. Eirik and St. Barbara at Ebshausen. On the road from Ebshausen to the palace at Thersa, Sapientia felt her first birth pangs.

"But Thersa is so comfortable," she complained, looking both disgruntled and frightened when the king declared that they would go instead to the nearby convent of St. Hippolyte for the lying-in. "I want to go to Thersa!"

"No," said Henry with that look that any observant soul would know at once meant he could not be swayed. "The prayers of the holy sisters will aid you."

"But they can pray for me wherever I am!"

Hugh took Sapientia's hand in his and faced the king. "Your Majesty, it is true that the palace at Thersa is a grander place by far, more fitting for a royal lying-in—"

"No! The matter is settled!"

Sapientia began to snivel, gripping her belly—and the king seemed ready to lose his temper. Hanna moved forward and leaned to whisper in Sapientia's ear. "Your Highness. What matters it what bed you lie in as long as God favor you? The prayers of the holy nuns will strengthen you, and your obedience now will give you favor in your father's eyes."

Sapientia's sniveling ceased and, once a birth pang had passed, she grasped the king's hands in her own. "Of course you are right, Father. We will go to St. Hippolyte. With a patron saint like Hippolyte, the child is sure to grow strong and large and of stout courage, suitable for a soldier."

Henry brightened noticeably and, for the rest of the damp ride to the convent, fussed over his daughter, who put up a brave face as her pains worsened.

Sapientia was taken inside the walls of the convent with only two attendants and Sister Rosvita to act as witnesses, as well as the physician who, being a eunuch, was considered as good as a woman. Everyone else waited in the hall, what remained of an old palace from the time of Taillefer, now under the management of the convent sisters. Henry paced. Hugh sat in a corner and idly leafed through the book.

"She's small in the hips," said Hanna nervously, remembering births attended by her mother. Not all had happy outcomes.

"Look here." Hathui examined the carvings that ran along the beams in the hall. Blackened with layers of soot, cracked from the weight of years of damp and dryness, they depicted the trials of St. Hippolyte whose strength and martial courage had brought the Holy Word of God to the heathen tribes who had lived in these woodlands a hundred years before. "A good omen indeed for the child who will prove Sapientia's fitness to rule and also ride as captain of the Dragons when he grows up."

Hanna surveyed the old hall. Servants swept moldering rushes out the door. Ash heaped the two hearths and had to be carried away by the bucket load before a fresh fire could be started. Even with all the people packing into the hall, the cold numbed her. At a time like this, the stables provided better shelter. She could still hear, like an echo, the soft cries of the sister cellarer of the convent bemoaning the loss of so many scant provisions—it took a vast amount of food and drink to satisfy the king and his company.

"Why didn't the king want Princess Sapientia brought to bed at Thersa? Everyone is saying that Thersa is a grander place by far, and the steward there more able to supply the court."

"Look here." Hathui took a few steps away from the younger clerics who, clustered nearby, were muttering among themselves. She wet her fingers and reached up to brush away grime and dust from one carving. Deep in the wood a scene unfolded down the length of the old beam. A figure draped in robes advanced, spear in one hand, the other raised, palm out, to confront the tribespeople retreating before her: a stylized flame burned just beyond her hand. Behind her walked many grotesque creatures, obviously not of human kin, but it wasn't clear whether they stalked the saint or trod in her holy footsteps, seeking her blessing.

As the clerics moved away, Hathui dropped her voice. "It's better not to speak out loud of these matters. Henry's bastard son Sanglant was born at Thersa. So Wolfhere told me. The elvish woman who was the prince's mother was so sick after the birth that some feared she would die. The court couldn't move for two months, but when she did rise at last from her bed, she walked away never to be seen again. They say she vanished from this earth completely."

"But where could she have gone?" demanded Hanna. "Where else is there to go, for a creature such as that? To the island of Alba?"

"It's only what I heard. That doesn't mean it's true."

"That doesn't mean it's not true," replied Hanna thoughtfully, examining the next carving. The same figure—she recognized the robes and the mark of fire before the saint's hand—approached an archway out of which emerged a man-sized creature with a circle of stylized feathers behind it that appeared to be wings; it also wore a belt of skulls. Following to the next scene, Hanna saw the same archway, made small now, standing among a circle of standing stones which were, apparently, in the act of falling to the ground, their power banished by the saint's holy courage.

"How was St. Hippolyte martyred?" Hanna asked.

Hathui smiled grimly. "Crushed by rock, as you see here." She indicated the last carving. They stood now at the far end of the hall. At the other end, fire flared, and Villam at last entreated Henry to sit down and take some wine.

The princess labored long into the night. At dawn on the next day, the Feast of St. Sormas, thirteenth day of the month of Avril, she bore a healthy girl child.

And there was great rejoicing.

Henry called Hugh before him. "You have proved yourself a good adviser to my daughter," he said, presenting him with a fine gold cup out of his treasury. "I have hopes now for her ability to reign after me."

"God has blessed your house and bloodline, Your Majesty," replied Hugh, and though the compliments came many over the rest of the day, by no act or word did he display any unseemly pride in an event he had helped bring about. Nor did he appear conscious of the new status this safe birth brought him.

That evening, at the urging of Sister Rosvita, he read aloud from the *Vita of St. Radegundis,* the happy tale—somewhat startling to find in a saint's life—of how the saintly young woman, so determined in her vow to remain chaste and thus closer to heavenly purity, was overcome by the great nobility of Emperor Taillefer. Wooing her, he overcame her reluctance. Her love for his great virtues and imperial honor melted her heart, and they were married as soon as she came of age.

"It is time to think of marriage for Sapientia," said Henry when the reading was finished. "The king of Salia has many sons."

"It might be well," suggested Villam, "to send Princess Sapientia to Eastfall once she has regained her strength. Then she would gain some experience in ruling."

"It is better to keep her beside me as we travel," said Henry in the tone which meant he intended no argument to sway him. "But Eastfall needs a margrave. Perhaps I should send Theophanu to Eastfall . . ." With the king musing in this way, the happy feast passed swiftly. For the first time in months, for the first time, really, since he had heard the terrible news of Sanglant's death, Henry looked cheerful.

The court feasted for three days, for it took a feast of such magnificence to properly thank God for Their blessings upon the royal house. Sapientia was as yet too weak to appear, and in any case it was traditional for a woman to lie abed for a week in seclusion before receiving visitors. That way she might not be contaminated by any taint brought from the outside or any unholy thoughts at this blessed time.

Hanna was astounded yet again at the sheer amount of food and drink the court consumed. She could only imagine what her mother would say, but then, her mother might well say that as the king prospers, so does the kingdom.

Ai, Lady, at this time last year she and Liath had just left Heart's Rest behind, riding out with Wolfhere, Hathui, and poor brave Manfred. She touched her Eagle's badge. Where was Liath now?

2

LIATH hunkered down, arms hooked around her knees. The ground was too wet to sit on, and everything was damp. Mud layered wagon wheels and dropped in clumps from the undersides when they jolted over the roads. Every branch scattered moisture on any fool sorry enough to touch it. The grass wept water, and the trees dripped all day even when it wasn't raining.

Though they had waited until the first day of the month of Sormas to leave, it was still a wet time to be marching to war. But that deterred no one—not with such a prize within reach.

"Can you do it?" whispered Alain. He kept a cautious three steps back from her. Sorrow and Rage sat panting a stone's throw away.

She did not reply. That the hounds would still not come near her only made her wonder if they sensed the awful power trapped inside her. *Wood burns.* She shuddered. Would she ever learn to control it? She had to try.

"We don't have much time," he said. "They'll come looking for me soon."

"Hush." She lifted a hand, and he shuffled another step back. Behind, the hounds whined. In wood lies the propensity to burn, the memory of flame. Perhaps, as Dèmocrita said, tiny indivisible building blocks, hooked and barbed so that they could fasten together, made up all things in the universe; in wood some of these must be formed of the element of fire. If she could only reach through the window of fire and call fire to them, they would remember flame—

And burn.

Wood ignited with a roar. Fire shot upward to lick the branches of the nearest tree. Liath stumbled away from the searing heat. The hounds yelped and slunk backward, growling.

"Lord Above!" swore Alain. He took another step away from her and drew the sign of the Circle at his breast—as if for protection.

Falling to one knee, Liath stared at the fire. Gouts of flame boiled up into the sky. Branches hissed. Grass within the ring of penetrating heat sizzled and blackened. Only when it was this wet dared she attempt to call fire; only when it was this wet was it safe to attempt an act whose consequences she could not control.

A light rain began to fall. Alain pulled his hood up over his head and took a hesitant step toward her. Liath stared into fire and in her mind twisted the leaping flames into an archway that would let her see into another part of the world.

"Hanna," she whispered. *There.* The sight was more of a whisper than a scene unfolding before her. *Hanna stands beside Hathui; all else is shadow.* But Liath could see by the set of Hanna's shoulders, the sudden grin she flashed at a comment made by the older Eagle, that she was well. Hugh hadn't harmed her.

Reaching inside her cloak, she drew out the gold feather. It glinted fire, bright sparks, a reflection of the blaze. Alain murmured an oath. The hounds growled.

"Like to like," she murmured. "Let this be a link between us, old one."

As a curtain draws aside, revealing the chamber behind, so the fire's roar without abating shifted and changed in pitch. A low rumble like distant thunder shivered around her. The veil parted and within it, beyond it, she saw the Aoi sorcerer.

Startled, he looks up. Flax half twisted into rope dangles from his hand. "What is this?" he asks. "You are the one I have seen before."

She sees through the fire burning before her, which is fed by wood, but sees also through fire burning an upright pillar of stone. This mystery attracts her notice. She must speak, even if it might attract those who are looking for her. But her first words are not those she had intended. "How do you make the stone burn?" she demands.

"Rashly spoken," he replies. With that, he begins to roll flax into rope against his thigh. But he appears to be thinking. He regards her unsmiling through the veil of fire, but he is not unfriendly. "You are of the human kin," he says. "How have you come here? Yet I see my gift reached you."

She grasps the gold feather tightly, mirror to those trimming his leather gauntlets. "You have touched that which I have touched. I do not know how to read these omens."

"I beg you," she says. "I need help. I made fire—"

"Made it?" His smile is brief and sharp. "Fire exists in most things. It is not made."

"No, no." She speaks quickly because she does not know how long she has before she and Alain are interrupted, and this man—no man—this Aoi sorcerer is the only creature she can ask. "I called it. It's as if the element of fire lies quiescent within the wood, and remembers its power suddenly and comes to life."

"Fire is never quiescent. Fire rests within most objects, in some more deeply than in others."

"Then in stone it rests more deeply than I can touch. Why can that stone burn?"

He pauses, flax rope draped over his thigh. "Why do you ask questions, child?"

"Because I need answers, old one. I need a teacher."

He lifts the rope and twirls it through his fingers. The white shells on his waist-length cloak clack together as softly as the whisper of leaves on the forest floor. He turns, glancing once behind him, then back at her. "Are you asking me to teach you?"

"Who else will teach me? Will you?" The fire does not burn more fiercely than the hope which leaps up in her heart.

He considers. Shells, stones, and beads wink and dazzle in the firelight. He wears a round jade spool in each ear. His hair, bound simply into a topknot, is as black as the veil of night, and he has no beard. His dark eyes regard her, unblinking. "Find me, and I will."

At first she cannot find her voice, as if it has been torn from her. Then, struggling, panicking, she gasps out words. "How do I find you?"

He lifts a hand, displaying the rope, gesturing toward the burning stone. "Step through. The gateway already exists."

She rises, takes a step forward, but the heat is too strong. She can't move any closer.

"I can't," she says, half weeping. "I can't. How do I get there?"

"One strand of flax has no strength." He twines a single unwound thread of flax around a finger. Straining, he snaps

it through. Then he wraps the finished rope around a hand. "Twined together, they make a strong rope. But it takes time to make rope, just as it takes time to twine strands of knowledge together to make wisdom."

Abruptly he stands, glancing around as if he has heard something. "They are coming."

In that instant she sees beyond him down a path which snakes oddly through the trees. A short procession winds its way along the path, rather like King Henry's progress but in smaller numbers. Bright colors so overwhelm her sight that she can make no sense of what walks there. One thing she sees: a round standard carried on a pole, a circular sheet of gold trimmed with iridescent green plumes as broad across as a man's arms outstretched. It spins, like a turning wheel. Its brilliance staggers her.

"You must go," says the sorcerer firmly. He licks a finger and reaches forward with it into fire as though to douse a wick. Moisture sizzles and snaps, popping into her face. She jerks back, blinks, then with a gasp leans forward again. But the veil has closed.

She saw nothing but raging fire and the mist of water rising as steam into the cool spring air.

"Liath!" A hand closed on her elbow, but it was only Alain, kneeling beside her. "I thought you were going to walk right into the fire."

She licked her finger, reached out toward the fire as if to extinguish it—but nothing happened. "If only I could have."

"Now, there," he began, meaning to soothe her while behind him the hounds growled at the flames.

She shook out of his grasp and stepped back. The skin on her face felt baked; when she touched it, it smarted. "I saw the Aoi sorcerer. He said he'd teach me, if I could find a way to get to where he is."

He glanced at the fire suspiciously. "Can you trust a Lost One? They don't even believe in the God of Unities!"

"Maybe that's why," she said slowly, trying to understand it herself. "I'm a curiosity to him, that's all. He doesn't *want* anything from me—unlike the others."

"But why can you see him through fire?"

"I don't know."

"It is a mystery, like my dreams," he agreed, mercifully letting the unanswerable question drop. He raised a hand in front of his face, absorbing some of the heat. "How it burns!" he exclaimed, and she hung her head, ashamed, thinking he would realize what a monstrous thing she had done and be repelled by her now that he knew what she was: sorcerer's child, untrained, ignorant, and uncontrollable. "Only think of what you could do with such fire!"

"Haven't I already done enough?" she asked bitterly, thinking of the Lions she had killed.

"We are none of us without sin," he pointed out. "But if you could learn to do something useful with it . . ."

"Call it down on the Eika," she replied caustically. "Burn Gent and all the poor dead bodies rotting there!"

"Nay, don't say that! If you could only scare them with it, enough to make them run—"

"Ai, Alain! You've fought the Eika. Fire won't scare them."

"And there are slaves in the city, or so it has been reported. If the city burned, they would burn, too." He frowned, then looked at her. "We must tell my father."

"No!" This she had no doubts about. "If the king knew I had burned down the palace at Augensburg, if the biscops knew, what do you think they'd do with me?"

Troubled, he busied himself with flicking ashy flakes of wood off his cloak. "They'd condemn you as a maleficus and send you to stand trial before the skopos," he said reluctantly. "But *I* would speak up for you! *I* trust you."

"They'd only accuse me of binding you with charms. Nay, they'd never trust a maleficus who can call fire. And why should they believe I can't control it? Only that I don't want to—or that I'm more dangerous for being flawed."

"You can't control it?" He glanced nervously toward the raging fire.

"I can't even put it out," she said with disgust. "I can only make it light."

"But I must tell my father, Liath. He won't condemn you. He has too much on his own conscience to cast stones at others."

"But he might order me to call fire onto Gent, wouldn't he? If he did, and if I could do it, how many innocent slaves will die in the conflagration?"

He hesitated. By his expression he clearly feared she was right, that Count Lavastine would sacrifice a few slaves, even if they had once been honest freeholders, for the sake of taking Gent. For the sake of getting a noble bride for his heir.

Out of mist and rain and steam, they heard a shout. "They've discovered I'm gone," Alain said. "You cut around the back. Then they won't know you've been gone. If they find this fire, they won't associate it with you."

"Yes, my lord." She was not sure whether to be grateful or amused by his high-handedness. He had nothing of the nobleman's arrogance but, like Da, he had an inexplicable dignity about him that made it impossible to do anything but respect him.

Darting forward, he grabbed a brand in each hand out of the fire and jumped back. "No use letting the poor soldiers shiver in this rain. We can start other fires with this. Go on!"

"How will you explain that?" she demanded, but he only smiled, mocking himself more than her.

"I am the count's heir. No one will question me except my father, and there's no reason he need ever hear about it. Now go on. I will say nothing of what I've seen today." He dashed off into the woods in the direction of the shouting. The hounds loped behind him.

She lingered by the fire, but she knew that if she looked within it now, no veil would part, no gateway would open. With a sigh, she started by a roundabout way back to camp. Ai, Lady. Her knee was sopping wet; the baggy cloth of her leggings alternately stuck to her skin and, as she walked, peeled off only to slap back again, cold and slimy.

But such discomfort mattered little against the offer the Aoi sorcerer had made to her: "*Find me.*"

3

ROSVITA thought she recognized the book Father Hugh now carried with him. But he had such an elegant way of keeping it close against him or tucked away in the carved chest that one of his servants carried along behind him, of closing it softly, as if without thinking, or laying his hand over the binding to half conceal it, that she could never get a good look. She wasn't *quite* sure that it was, in fact, the same book she had seen Liath carrying last autumn on the very day Princess Sapientia had returned to the king's progress.

Rosvita hated being curious, but she had come to accept the fault and, perhaps, embrace it a little too heartily.

After seven days, the infant girl was anointed with holy water and perfume and given the name suggested by her father: Hippolyte, after the blessed saint. A robust child, she wailed heartily, indignant at the cold touch of water on her skin, and flushed a bright red from head to toe. Sapientia left seclusion and pleaded with Henry to let the court travel the four days to Thersa, whose accommodations were far more pleasant than these.

King Henry's good humor could hardly be improved upon. But Rosvita had observed that a man or woman who held their own child's child felt a certain triumph, as at a victory over the fragility of life on this mortal earth. Without argument, he relented. The entire court bundled itself and its possessions up yet again and headed off. God were gracious: The weather for the short journey was mild and sunny. At Thersa they settled in for a three-week stay so that the new mother and child could gain strength before continuing north to Gent.

"Perhaps it is time to lay his memory to rest," said Henry in a low voice one evening, and Rosvita merely murmured encouragement.

So it was arranged. A small party rode out the next morning, consisting of King Henry, Helmut Villam, Rosvita

and three clerics, Father Hugh, and a company of Lions
with an Eagle in attendance. A track led through greening
fields to a village whose residents hurried to greet them.
Father Hugh passed out sceattas to the householders; King
Henry blessed the little children, held up for him by their
mothers and fathers so he could set a hand on each dirty
head. A little-used path led to a stream's edge. Here,
clumps of grass waved in the rush of high water. The steep
banks had overflowed slightly, but only the Lions got wet;
the ford proved passable for the riders.

The ruins lay in a jumbled heap along the slope of land
before them, crowned by a ring of standing stones. Once,
buildings had stood here. Had they been built by the same
people who raised the circle of stones, or was this a later
fortress, built here to guard—or guard against—the influence of the crown of stones? With the nearby stream and
cultivatable land, it made a good homestead, as the persistence of the villagers showed: Few people would willingly
live within sight of a ring of stones unless they had a compelling reason to remain there.

Henry dismounted and, with Villam beside him, made
his way up through the ruins alone.

"Now there's two men still mourning the loss of sons,"
said Brother Fortunatus, looking around the scene with interest. "Is this where the Aoi woman vanished?"

"Up in the ring of stones, I should think," said Sister
Amabilia. "And poor Villam lost his son in a ring of stones."

"He did?" demanded Brother Constantine. "I never
heard that story."

"That was before you came to us," said Amabilia
sweetly, never loath to remind the solemn young man that
he was not only young but the son of a Varren lady sympathetic to Sabella. "Young Berthold was a fine young man,
a true scholar, I think, though it's a shame he was being
kept out of the church so that he could be married."

"But what happened to him?"

Brother Fortunatus wheeled around, excited by the prospect of gossip. "He took a group of his retainers up to
explore the ring of stones above the monastery of
Hersfeld . . ." He paused, relishing Constantine's wide-eyed
stare, and dropped his voice to a dramatic whisper.
". . . *and they were never seen again.*"

"Hush!" said Rosvita, surprised at her own snappishness. "Berthold was a good boy. It isn't right to make a game of his loss and his father's grief. Come now." She saw Hugh seat himself on an old wall somewhat away from everyone else and open his book. "You may look around, as you wish. Brother Constantine, you may wish to discover if there are any Dariyan inscriptions on the stones and whether you can read them. Do not approach the king unless he requests your company." Together with Villam, the king had vanished into the circle of stones, a half dozen Lions and his favorite Eagle hard on his heels. "Go on." They scattered like bees out to search for honey. Rosvita composed herself, then strolled casually across the ruins, picking her way over fallen stone and mounds of earth, until she reached Hugh.

"Father Hugh." She greeted him as she seated herself on a smooth stretch of wall. "You must be pleased at your mother's loyalty, sending her physician so far away from her lands in order to attend Princess Sapientia."

As he turned to smile at her, he gently closed the book; she gained only a glimpse of a bold hand scrawled in uneven columns down the page. "Indeed, Sister. But I believe my mother intends to return to the king's progress as soon as she has completed her business in Austra."

"Ah, yes, her marriage. Have you had any recent news?" Since any recent news would have spread to her clerics the instant it came in, this was pure gambit, and she knew it. Perhaps he did as well, but he was hard for her to read, never being anything less than polite and well-mannered.

"None, alas. But perhaps," and now he smiled with a sudden and winning shrewdness, "Brother Fortunatus has heard that which we are not yet privy to."

That made her laugh. Hugh had much the look of his father about him. The Alban slave Margrave Judith kept as concubine had still been a fixture at court when Rosvita arrived in the last years of King Arnulf. No young woman, even one pledged to the church, could have failed to notice him, although upon closer examination he had proved to be stupid and vain. But in the end he had died in a hunting accident and the boy child who had come some years previously of this begetting had been given to the church. Hugh did not have the sheer breathtaking beauty of his father, but he was handsome enough that it was no wonder Sapientia had seduced him. If, indeed, the seduction had been one-sided, which Rosvita doubted. For all his arrogance, Hugh had always been noted as a dutiful son to his mother; by becoming Sapientia's favorite and adviser, he enhanced his mother's strength among the great princes of the realm.

"It is a fine day, is it not, Father Hugh?" She lifted her face to the sun.

"I am only sorry the king should find sadness on such a favored day." He indicated the ring of stones above. Henry and Villam could be seen moving slowly among the stones. Henry had an old rag pressed to his face, dabbing now and again at his eyes.

"He must lay the prince to rest in his own heart," she said, forgetting her own purpose for a moment, "before the prince can go to his rest above." She gestured toward the sky.

"Can he?" asked Hugh suddenly. "He is half of elvish kin, and it is said they wander as dark shades on this earth after they die."

"Only God can answer that question. You and Sanglant were of an age, weren't you?"

"Oh, yes," he said, the words clipped short.

"But you attended the king's schola, and he did not."

Hugh looked away, up toward the stones. He was tall, though not as tall as Sanglant had been, and fair-haired where Sanglant had been dark. As a churchman he went beardless, and in this way he might be said to resemble the dead prince; in all other ways they were utterly unlike. Indeed, Rosvita knew very well that Sanglant had been a favorite at court in his youth; Hugh, while tolerated, envied, and sometimes grudgingly admired, had never inspired liking—not until now. "There is no virtue in speaking unkindly of the dead," he said at last. His hand shifted on the book he held, bringing it back to her notice.

"True words, Father Hugh," she said, seeing her opening. "What book is that you carry?"

He blinked. Then he glanced at the book, tucked his fingers more tightly around its cracked leather binding, and returned his gaze to her. "It is a book I have been studying for some time."

"How curious. I could swear that I saw that book before Princess Sapientia returned to the king's progress. Before you came back to us with her. Yes." She pretended to consider, then carefully looked away, surveying the ruins and the fine view of trees and stream and distant village as if the book was of only passing interest. After a while of basking in pleasant silence in the spring sun, as if she had just that instant recalled their conversation, she turned back to him. "I must be mistaken. I saw a book like to this in the possession of one of the Eagles. What was her name? These Eagles all run one into the next."

He raised his eyes to look at her but said nothing. She found a cluster of white flowers growing out from a crevice within the stones that was filled in with dirt. Plucking them, she pressed the rustic bouquet to her nose.

"Liath," he said finally, so baldly that she was startled, and showed it.

"Ah, yes, Liath," she managed, lowering the flowers. "A curious name, Arethousan in origin, I believe." He did not reply. "Didn't you serve as frater in the north, Father Hugh?"

"I did indeed, in that region called Heart's Rest, just south of the emporia of Freelas."

"Now there is a strange coincidence. The Eagle, Liath, and her comrade, Hanna—who is now Sapientia's Eagle—both came from Heart's Rest."

"That is where you come from as well, is it not, Sister?"

"So it is."

"You are the second child of Count Harl, I believe."

"Of course you would be acquainted with my father and family, if you resided there."

"I have met them," he said with a hint of condescension—something he normally never showed toward her, the favored cleric among Henry's intimate advisers, his elder in the church, and a woman.

"Did you bring the two young women to the notice of the King's Eagles, then? It was a generous act."

His pleasant expression did not waver—by much—but a certain hard glint came into his eyes. "I did not. I had nothing to do with that."

Had lightning struck, she could not have been more surprised by revelation. The memory of their visit to Quedlinhame last autumn jolted her so hard she lost her grip on the flowers, and they fell to scatter over her robe, the stones, and the soil.

Ivar, talking to Liath in the dark sanctuary of a back room in the convent library. Liath had said, "I love another man." And that had made Ivar angry. Whose name had he spoken?

"Hugh."

Liath had not denied it, only said that *he* was dead. Now, with Hugh regarding her as innocently as a dove, she was angry with herself for not questioning Ivar closely about the incident.

"I am confused, then, and I beg your pardon, Father Hugh," she said at last. "I had thought you must have known the young women, as well as my brother, Ivar, when you were in Heart's Rest. Thus my curiosity about the book, which resembles one I saw Liath carrying."

He toyed with the book, tucked it more firmly against his thigh, and sighed deeply as at an unpalatable decision. "She stole it from me. But now, as you see, I have gotten it back."

"*Stole* it from you!" That she had suspected as much—that Liath had stolen the book from somewhere—did not make the fact any more pleasant to hear. "How did she steal it? Why?"

He closed his eyes a moment. It was difficult for Rosvita to imagine what thoughts might be going through his mind. Like the book, like a veil drawn to hide the chamber behind, he was closed against her. He had completely given up abbot's robes and now dressed like any fine lord in embroidered tunic, a short cloak with a gold brooch, silver-banded leggings, and a sword; one knew he was a churchman only by his lack of beard and his eloquent speech.

"I do not speak easily of this," he said finally. "It pains me deeply. The young woman's father died in severe debt. I paid it off because it was the charitable thing to do, as you can imagine, being a Godly churchwoman yourself, Sister. By that price, she became my slave. She had no kin and thus, really, no prospects, so I kept her by me to protect her."

"Indeed," murmured Rosvita, thinking of Ivar's protestations of love. Of course a count's son could never marry a kinless girl who was also another man's slave! He should never even have considered it. "She is a beautiful girl, many have noticed that, and has an awkward smattering of education. Enough to attract the wrong kind of notice."

"Indeed. That she repaid me in this manner . . ." Here he broke off.

"How then did she come into the Eagles?"

He hesitated, clearly reluctant to go on.

"Wolfhere," she said, and knew she had made a hit when his lips tightened perceptibly.

"Wolfhere," he agreed. "He took what was not his to have."

"But only free women and men may enter into the Eagles."

Elegant, confident Hugh looked, for an instant, like a man stricken with a debilitating sorrow. "My hand was forced."

"Why do you not tell the king? Surely he will listen to your grievance?"

"I will not accuse a man if he is not beside me to answer in his turn," said Hugh reasonably. "Then I would be taking the same advantage of Wolfhere that he took of me, in a sense, when he claimed the young woman in question for the king's service without letting the king judge the matter for himself. Nor do I wish to be seen as one who takes unseemly advantage of my—" He smiled with that same shrewd glint. "Let us be blunt, Sister Rosvita. Of my intimate association with Princess Sapientia."

"No one would fault you if you brought the matter before the king now. It is generally agreed that your wise counsel has improved her disposition."

But he merely bowed his head modestly. "I would fault myself."

4

THEY gathered an army and, helpless, he watched them do so. By the angle of light that shone through the cathedral windows and the sullen warmth that crept in through the vast stone walls during the day when the doors were thrown open to admit sunlight, he guessed that spring had come at last. With the spring thaw running low, the winds would give the Eika good sailing out of the north.

From the north they came, droves of them, collecting at the foot of Bloodheart's throne like so much flotsam cast up by the tide.

That day, when the rebellious son returned, he knew he had to act. When even rebellious sons return to the fold, it means great movements are afoot, even so great as to attract back those who once were condemned to leave. Even the priest, crouching just out of range of Sanglant's chains while he taught him to read the bones, turned to stare at the unexpected sight of the young Eika princeling who wore a wooden Circle around his neck.

"Why have you come back?" roared Bloodheart in the human tongue, confronting the slender Eika who stood, proud and unflinching, before him.

"I bring eight ships," said the son, gesturing to certain Eika who stood behind him, representative, perhaps, of soldiers who remained outside. There were by now in Gent too many Eika to all crowd into the cathedral. He could smell them; their metallic scent permeated the air. "These two, from Hakonin, these two, from Skanin, and this one, from Valdarnin. Three more sailed with me from Rikin. These will swell the number of your army."

"Why should I take you in, when it was my voice and my command which sent you home without honor?"

Sanglant measured the distance between himself and the priest, then patted the rags draped over him that had once been clothing. He slid a hand under cloth and pulled out the brass Eagle's badge. With a flick of the wrist, he tossed it at one of his dogs, to his left. The sudden growling movement of two dogs leaping to growl over the badge startled the priest enough that he jumped sideways.

With that jump, the priest came for an instant within reach of Sanglant.

He sprang. As his hand closed on the Eika priest's bony arm, he jerked the knife out from under his tunic. Yanking the priest around hard, he dropped his grip on the creature's arm and snatched the little wooden chest out of the crook of its elbow.

Then he leaped back into the protection of his dogs—barking and raging wildly now—as a roar of fury broke from Bloodheart's throat and all the Eika in the hall began shrieking and howling at once, their dogs echoing them until Sanglant was deafened. He had only moments to act before he would be overwhelmed.

There was no time for finesse, but then, there rarely was in a pitched fight.

He hacked violently at the hasp of the chest. The knife, little used, still bore a good edge. The hasp snapped and wood splintered as he struck down and again, with all his strength, then wrenched the lid open and dumped the contents out on the floor.

He didn't know what an Eika heart would look like. But where else would Bloodheart keep his heart if not close by him? Why else would the priest carry a chest night and day, never letting it leave its side?

But all that spilled onto the floor was a bundle of down feathers and a white hairless creature smaller than his hand. With rudimentary ears and eyes, a nub of a tail, and four limbs, it looked like the premature spawn of an unholy mother, a ghastly colorless thing without defined features and with no recognizable parentage. It fell with a sickening plop onto the flagstone floor and lay there, limp, unmoving.

Dead.

Never trust the appearance of death.

He raised his knife.

A spear haft hit him broadside and then, as he spun, he felt a second spear pierce him in the back, just below the ribs. He jerked forward, brought the knife down as his dogs swarmed forward to attack his attackers. But his vision had gone awry; the world spun and staggered before him.

A shift of sunlight spilled over the stone floor, its golden touch illuminating the tiny corpse. With a shudder, the embryonic creature stirred, curled.

Came alive.

It darted away just as the point of his knife stabbed and skidded on the stone floor where it had lain.

Bloodheart screamed in rage.

The spear point was yanked out of his flesh and he staggered forward to keep himself upright; his neck snapped back when, at the limit of his chains, the iron slave collar brought him up short. The priest yipped wildly, scurrying after the slender dead-white creature now scrambling away between the feet of the Eika soldiers who had dashed forward to mob him.

Bloodheart, still roaring, his own dogs at his heels, slapped his howling soldiers aside as he shoved his way through. Blood streamed down Sanglant's back, coursing over his buttocks and down his thighs. He faltered and fell to his knees, knife raised before him.

"Dog! Son of dogs! The heart you seek with that blow lies far away from here, hidden among the stones of Rikin fjall. For *this* sacrilege you will pay the price in blood."

Bloodheart struck, but Sanglant was faster. He jumped up and sank the knife into the Eika chieftain's shoulder and hung there as two packs of dogs swarmed forward. At once he and Bloodheart were surrounded by a maelstrom, all teeth and tails and claws.

In this whirlpool Bloodheart grabbed Sanglant by the iron collar at his neck and hoisted him into the air. With his other hand, he took Sanglant's wrist, where he still held the knife, and twisted it hard.

The snap of bone and the wash of hot pain almost made him pass out. But he did not let go of the knife, not until Bloodheart ripped it out of his own shoulder and shook it free of Sanglant's grip. He tossed Sanglant back, flipped the knife to hold it, jeweled hilt in his huge scaled hand, and struck furiously to either side at the ravening dogs, then leaped in among them.

Sanglant groped, found the brass Eagle's badge, and hauled himself to his feet. This tiny shield he held before him, like a talisman, but it was useless. Bloodheart's fury had passed the point of thought. The Eika stabbed the knife again and again into Sanglant's chest.

Sometimes the remains of his chain mail turned the point, but at the ragged ends it could not protect him. The knife pierced him repeatedly, tearing him inside, shattering him, until his dogs leaped howling and biting and Bloodheart was forced to defend himself against them. He let go of Sanglant, who could not stand, could not even kneel, could only fall to the floor as his dogs drove back the mob that had come howling to watch him die. He could only watch as spears and axes fell on his dogs and the other dogs indiscriminately, splitting them open, spattering viscera and green-tinted blood and the wet matter of brain over him, over the floor, over everything. He could only feel the press of bodies and the sting of their whipcord tails as the last of his dogs pressed in around him, defending him even until the bitter end—as had his Dragons.

He would have wept at their loyalty, but he had no tears.

Bloodheart was still howling in rage, shouting at his priest, calling the Eika to silence, to stillness, so that they could hunt for the hideous creature that had escaped from the shattered chest. The mob stilled, broke, and parted.

In this way, abandoned for more important prey, Sanglant was left alone. Pain washed like water over him, the flood tide swelling to its height as black hazed his vision and he struggled to remain conscious, then ebbing to reveal every point of scalding pain in his body.

He heard the breath of the dogs, those panting out their last breaths and those few which still remained upright. The last six stood around him in a protective circle to face their common enemy. Surrounded by this fortification of dogs, he lay there breathing shallowly and waited for the blinding pain to end.

5

HE could not quite manage to open his eyes. But he knew he was surrounded by bodies strewn about him like so much refuse. Some few of the dogs were still alive, and they growled when any movement sifted near him. It was so hard to wake up and perhaps better not to. Perhaps it was better to slide unresisting into oblivion.

Ai, Lady. Would he be admitted to the Chamber of Light? Or was he, because of his mother's blood, condemned to wander the world forever as a bodiless shade?

In the distance or in a dream, he heard the flutelike voices of the Eika speaking in Wendish, two voices accompanied by the mocking, harsh counterpoint of Eika calling and crying out in their own rough tongue. Some few of the words he now knew. In his dream he recognized more than he ever had before, but that was the nature of dreams, was it not?

"I have seen this army in my dreams." This in fluent Wendish.

"No better than dog, why dare you speak so before the great one?" This in the Eika speech.

"My dreams are more honest than your boasting, brother! Do not toss aside the gifts the WiseMothers give you just because they are not made of iron or gold."

"How can I believe your dreams are true dreams, weak one?" This from Bloodheart.

"I am stronger than I look, and my dreams are not just true dreams, they are the waking life of one of the humankind. He marches with this army, and as he marches, I march with him, seeing through his eyes."

One of the dogs nudged him, testing for life, and he gasped so loud the echo of it split his skull with pain, but no sound came out of his mouth. Blackness fell. For an endless time he drowned in a black haze of unrelenting pain that spun and sparkled like the knife which had been driven countless times into his body. Finally the darkness lightened to an early morning gray. Glints of light burst here and there in the limitless mist.

The veil parted.

The woman appears young and is certainly beautiful. She wears a fringed skirt sewn of leather so thin and supple that it moves around her with her movements like a second skin. A double stripe of red paint runs from the back of her left hand up around the curve of her elbow, all the way to her shoulder. Her hair has a pale cast, though her complexion is as bronze-dark as his own; drawn back from her face, it is bound behind her head with painted leather strips nested with beads, trailing a long elegant green plume. A wreath of gold and turquoise and jade bead necklaces drapes down her chest almost to her waist. She wears no shirt or cloak, only the necklaces, concealing and revealing her breasts as she shifts.

But for all her beauty and fine grace, she works patiently toward a brutal goal: with a curved bone tool, she is shaving stout lengths of wood into spear hafts. Obsidian points lie on a reed mat nearby with rope heaped beside them.

Does he make a noise? She looks up as if she has heard him and in that instant as a sudden lance of sun cuts down through trees to pierce across her shoulders, flashing on her necklaces, she sees him.

"Sharatanga protect me!" she exclaims. "The child!" She flinches away from the sight, drops wood haft and bone tool, and gropes for the stone points lying on the mat.

"It is not yet time for him to die," she mutters to herself, although he can hear every word clearly in a language he ought not to know yet understands perfectly. Grabbing one of the thin blades, she lifts it and raises it high above her and cries in a clear, strong voice. "Take this offering, She-Who-Will-Not-Have-A-Husband. Give life back into his limbs."

She drags the blade across her palm. Blood wells, dripping down the length of the cut to spill into the air and she shakes the hand out, blood spitting toward him. Behind her, a voice calls a sudden frantic question. A touch of moisture spatters his lips, dissolving there, and as the harsh taste spreads to the back of his throat, the veil closes in a swirling pattern of grays and sparkling stars.

"I know you," he whispers.

But his voice was lost in the snuffling of dogs, and the touch of familiarity drifted away on the last tendril of mist.

Stillness hung like the weight of stone in the vast nave of the cathedral.

Terror hit with sudden force. Had he died? Had he seen, beyond the veil of the living, one of his own kinfolk or only a soulless shade caught forever in the memory of life?

He had always thought his mother's curse protected him from death. Ai, Lord, it wasn't true. It had never been true. He had only been lucky.

If this could be called luck.

He strained, listening, but heard nothing except the dogs. Had everyone gone away? Had they deserted the city, leaving to raid downriver into the heart of Wendar? How long had he lain here, dying and living again?

The footsteps that neared him came as soft as a breeze sliding through dead leaves scattered on the forest floor.

Never let it be said that he did not fight until his last breath.

He twitched but could not move his hands. His dogs growled, menacing their visitor. The smell of rancid meat hit him hard, gagging him, and he swallowed convulsively. He heard the damp slap of meat thrown to the floor and suddenly all the dogs skittered off, nails scraping the floor, and they fought over the remains. The footsteps eased closer. He lay there, paralyzed and unprotected, working his throat as if the movement would spread to his numb hands and allow him to defend himself.

He managed to open his eyes just as the slender Eika princeling who wore the wooden Circle crouched beside him. The Eika's movements had the easy arrogance of a creature who has the confidence of perfect health.

"Are you going to kill me now?" asked Sanglant. He was surprised to hear his voice, faint and hoarse. He struggled to lift a hand, to shift his shoulders beneath him, and felt the merest tick in his neck. One hand flicked up, the one with the unbroken wrist.

But the Eika princeling only blinked. His copper-melded face wore no human expression. He had eyes as sharp as obsidian blades, thin nostrils, and a narrow chin. His ice-white hair was itself as bright as the sun that glanced in through the cathedral windows. His thin lips remained set, considering. "No. You are my father's challenge, not mine. I only want to know why you are still alive. You are not like the other Soft Ones. They would be dead by now of such wounds. Why aren't you dead?"

Sanglant grunted. The pain was bitter and would remain with him for some time, but he was used to pain. He got an elbow to move and, with a second grunt, heaved himself up onto the elbow. He stared down the Eika, who merely appeared . . . curious? Sanglant was himself curious.

"What was it?" he whispered. "The thing in the chest."

The Eika glanced toward the dogs, but they still munched on the bones. One raised its head to growl at him, but as no violence seemed imminent, it turned its attention back to scrounging for the last scraps of meat. "Don't all the leaders of your people carry the trophy of their first kill with them?" He lifted a copper-scaled hand, turning it slowly to display the tufts of bone claw, filed and sharpened to points, that sprouted from his knuckles. "That is the mark of the strength of their hands."

"*That* was his first kill?" Disgust swamped him, and he briefly forgot the pain under a spasm of nausea.

"So it is with all of us. Those destined to mature into men must prove their manhood by killing one of their nest-brothers. Don't you do the same?"

"It wasn't dead. It ran."

The Eika flashed a sudden and startling grin, white sharp teeth glinting with bright jewels. "What is dead may be animated by sorcery. So Bloodheart protects himself against his sons and any others who might attempt to kill him."

Sensation had returned to his legs and he got one heel to move, sliding under him. His broken wrist was stiff but whole. "Protects himself? How?"

"It is the curse we all fear, even the greatest chieftain."

"A curse on you all," muttered Sanglant under his breath. He jerked over, fist swinging.

But the Eika laughed and nimbly leaped out of the way as the dogs, alerted, bolted away from their food and rushed the princeling.

"Stop," said Sanglant and the dogs sat, yipped irritably, and returned to the scraps. "Did you come to strip me of what little I have left?" He could move enough now to indicate his tattered clothing.

The Eika recoiled. "No Eika would want such things so

foul. Here." He kicked at something on the floor and the brass Eagle's badge skidded across the stone and lodged against Sanglant's thigh. Dried blood caked his skin—or at least, the dirt that grimed his skin. He was all dirt and stink except where the dogs had tried to lick him clean. The tatters of his undertunic were translucent, almost crystalline, because they were soaked with months of sweat. What remained of his tabard had so much dried blood and fluid on it that flakes fell off with each least movement and the cloth itself was stiff with grime.

The Eika princeling stared, then shook his head as he stepped away. "You were the pride of the human king's army?" he demanded. "If you are their greatest soldier, then no army they bring can be strong enough to defeat us."

"No army," murmured Sanglant, the words bitter to his ears.

"Even the one that has now camped in the hills toward the sunset horizon cannot possibly be strong enough to defeat us."

"Is it true? Has King Henry come to Gent with an army?"

"*Henri*," mused the Eika, naming the king in the Salian way. Without answering, he walked away.

"Ai, Lady," murmured Sanglant, crawling to his hands and knees. "How long has it been? Lord, have mercy upon me. I am not an animal to roll in my own filth. Spare me this humiliation. I have always been Your faithful servant." He tried to get to his feet but did not have the strength. One of the dogs wandered back and, seeing his weakness, nipped at him. He barely had strength to slap it back, and it whined and slunk away, snapping at the other dogs who came to trouble it for its own sign of weakness.

What had he done wrong? He had been so sure that Bloodheart kept his heart in the wooden chest; it was the obvious place. It was the only place. But Bloodheart had said: "*The heart you seek lies hidden among the stones of Rikin fjall.*"

Ai, Lady, he was only grateful that the cathedral was empty, that the Eika had left. That way they could not see him humbled. That way they could not see him weep with pain as he struggled to stand upright like a man.

XIV
A SWIRL OF
DANGEROUS
CURRENTS

1

LORD Wichman's deacon sang Mass every morning, and that morning she closed with her usual prayer: "From the fury of the Eika, God deliver us."

That morning after Mass, Anna paused beside the tannery to catch a glimpse of Matthias, as she did every morning to remind herself he really was still alive.

Not *well,* perhaps, but alive. He spoke no word of complaint; he never once said that his leg ached him although he could scarcely put weight on it. How he had broken the calf bone she never knew. He wouldn't speak of his captivity among the Eika. He had suffered terribly from fever and swelling after his rescue, but in the end he had recovered although the leg had healed crookedly, with an unnatural skew to it, ugly and discolored. Now he limped like an old man, leaning heavily on a stout stick, and had to brace himself on his good leg and prop his weight on a stool while he scraped hair and the residue of flesh from skins draped over a beam of wood. He had a delicate hand at this labor and could do it quickly, and for that reason had been allowed back at the rebuilt tannery despite his crippling injury. For his work he was fed twice a day.

Anna slipped away before he saw her; he didn't like her to forage in the forest, but with her gleanings and the scraps given Master Helvidius for his songs and poetry, they had survived through winter and early spring. Now, as spring ripened into summer, the first berries could be harvested, mushrooms gleaned from damp hollows, and all kinds of plants collected in glades and meadows and in the shade of trees. Certain bugs were edible, too—and, Anna had discovered, if you were hungry enough, they could be quite tasty.

Little Helen had grown but never uttered an intelligible word. Master Helvidius complained incessantly but, with a steady if sparse diet and a rough bed to sleep in every night, he had grown stronger and had less need of a stick in order to walk than did Matthias.

It was Matthias who worried Anna the most. "That I survived is a blessing from God." That was all he would say on the matter.

Outside the palisade she hurried down paths that led west through fields where men and women labored in the hot sun. Many of them—male and female alike—had stripped down to breechclouts for comfort's sake; there was little place for Godly modesty under the sweltering sun. Anna would gladly have shucked her tunic, but in the forest she needed its protection against burrs and bugs. The heat and recent rains, though, meant that nature's bounty prospered, and indeed Lady Fortune smiled on her this day. She found sweet berries and a trove of mushrooms. She collected fennel, parsley, and onion grass as well as moss for bedding. By midday her wandering brought her to the westward road.

The wide track lay quiet at this hour, pleasant and bright.

Little traffic moved in and out of Steleshame these days although Mistress Gisela often talked of the great days of Steleshame, before the Eika had come to Gent, and how nobles had sheltered in her longhouse and merchants haggled over the fine cloth woven by her women. No one, seeing Steleshame now, would be reminded of these past glories. Anna herself was not sure if Mistress Gisela was telling the truth or only a story, as Master Helvidius told stories. But Master Helvidius' stories were all true, or so he claimed; it was only that they had happened so very long ago.

Anna stood in the sunlight. Such moments of peace came rarely and were to be savored as long as the threat of the Eika hung like a sword over them all. Anna supposed that eventually the Eika would mass an army and wipe out Steleshame completely, for the Eika were as numberless as flies supping on carrion. Lord Wichman rode out each day to harry the Eika, but he had lost perhaps a third of the men he had come with, and while young men from distant villages had joined him in the hope of sharing in the spoils, he could not hope to hold off the Eika forever—not when he was a mortal man and his foe not only a savage but an enchanter into the bargain.

But what point in dwelling on such horror? She sighed and opened her eyes to survey the roadside with pleasure.

No one had gleaned here along the verge of track and wood. She found tansy growing in abundance, and this she pulled and bundled, for it could be mixed with the rushes strewn on the hall floor to drive away fleas. She found nettles densely packed along a ditch, their feet sodden in standing water. Swathing a hand in cloth, she plucked as many leaves as she could stuff into her bursting shawl. Then she bundled up her skirt, tucking it under her belt, and picked dandelion leaves and bistort. These, and delicate clover, she heaped into the folds made of her skirt.

Humming tunelessly, she did not at first hear what she ought to have listened for. She felt it first through the soles of her feet where they pressed against the pleasantly coarse dirt: the thrum of an army, marching. Too late she heard them, the creak of armor, the hum of voices, horses blowing and the sudden warning bark of dogs. The Eika had circled

all the way around Steleshame and now approached from
the unprotected west.

Clutching her treasures to her, she bolted for the shelter
of the trees.

"Hai! There! Child!"

The voice called, a human voice, and she hesitated, glancing back over her shoulder.

"*Never hesitate,*" Matthias always said.

But for once, Matthias was wrong.

She lurched to a stop, spilling a few stalks of tansy,
and stared.

"How far to Steleshame, girl?" asked the voice, but it
was no phantom but a real flesh-and-blood man outfitted
in a leather vest and a thick leather cap. He carried shield
and spear. There were many more with him. She was too
astonished to reply.

Soldiers. Led by a noble lord who was mounted on a fine
gray horse, they advanced without fear and only the lead
file even noticed her as they marched past where she stood,
balanced on the lip of the ditch of nettles. Three banners
flew before them: two black hounds on a silver field; a red
eagle; a gray tower surmounted by a black raven.

An army had come at last.

That night neither she, Matthias, nor Helen could get
into the hall to observe the great nobles, for such a press
of folk stood there, some of them soldiers newly marched
in, others residents of Steleshame who wanted to catch a
glimpse of the noble lord and his son, that they had to go
stand by the corner of the great hall and listen through the
gaps in the wall to the gathering within.

Amid the buzz of a feast, Anna could hear Helvidius
intoning the now-familiar phrases from the *Heleniad*.

"Now the guests of King Sykaeus fell silent, and each
one turned to face Helen. In this way they waited intently
for her to speak, to tell the tale of her sufferings and of
the fall of Ilios."

"Look," whispered Matthias.

A young woman emerged from the hall. In the darkness
her complexion had a strange shade, as if she had rubbed
her skin with soot. She wore a gray cloak trimmed with

scarlet and clasped with a badge marked with the likeness of an eagle.

"A King's Eagle!" murmured Matthias, his tone breathless with admiration. "She's a messenger for the king himself! So would I become, given the chance." His tone turned sour. "If I wasn't crippled now."

Escaping from the crush, the Eagle pushed her way past the crowd and came to rest in the open a few steps from Mistress Gisela's niece, who had also come outside.

"Ai, Lady," swore the Eagle. "He's mangling Virgilia again!"

"Who is that you speak of?" asked the niece, wiping a speck of dirt from her eye and turning to regard the other woman.

"The old poet. But I oughtn't to complain of him, I suppose. It's a miracle and a mercy he survived Gent."

The niece eyed the young Eagle with regret and hesitation before, at last, she spoke. "You were there at the end."

The Eagle got a still, sudden look on her face, like the Eika statues, like the niece when she had been handed to Wichman as his prize. "So I was, alas. The prince died bravely."

"Of course," replied the niece. She bit at her lip, then reached out to touch the delicate embroidery that trimmed the cloak.

"It's excellent work," said the Eagle. "Things have changed, here at Steleshame."

"So they have." The niece looked first one way, then the other and, seeing only the three children within earshot, leaned forward. "Ai, Lady. If you know of a way that I can attach myself to the army and march with them, out of here—" She broke off, leaving the rest of the question unasked.

The Eagle raised an eyebrow, astonished at this request. "Count Lavastine has allowed no camp followers, no stragglers, nothing that could impede the progress of the march or that might make him vulnerable when we come to meet the Eika on the field."

"I can shoot a bow, wash clothes, cook for twenty men, repair torn cloth—"

"What is it?"

The blunt question shocked the niece into silence. Then

tears flooded her eyes and coursed down her cheeks. "My aunt has given me to Lord Wichman, to do with as he wills," she said on a hoarse whisper. "Eagle, I beg you, free me from this if you can!"

The Eagle stood as if she had been struck dumb, but in a moment she shook herself free of her paralysis.

"I will see you free of him before we leave on the morrow."

The niece sagged forward, resting a hand on her abdomen. "Ai, Lord, I carry his child. What will become of it?"

"Fear not," said the Eagle sternly. She set a hand over the other woman's, her fingers clasped over the niece's faded skirts. "I will speak with Lord Alain. If you wish, the child will be promised to the church. I am sure Lord Wichman's mother will give a dowry for it, knowing it is of her son's begetting."

"It would be a great honor," murmured the niece, but her shoulders remained bowed although she untangled her hand from that of the Eagle. "And a better future for the child than what I can give it or can expect for myself. Ai, Lady. What's to become of me?"

"He made no gift to you?"

"A morning gift, do you mean. If we are not to be wed, then why would he gift me with anything?"

"A noble lord or lady might well gift a concubine with some mark of their favor, isn't that so?"

"Their attentions are not mark enough?" The niece laughed harshly, bending as at a sudden pain in her side. "Nay, friend Eagle, I was the gift—to him. A nobleman of his kind would only gift his bride in that way, celebrating the consummation of the marriage. Not even the prince made such a gift to me—" Here she faltered and could not for a moment go on.

The Eagle shut her eyes.

"But kindness and a sweet temper are their own gifts," finished the niece softly. Then Mistress Gisela's voice could be heard, shouting her niece's name from the crowded hall. "I thank you," she added, her voice heavy with tears. She hastened back into the hall.

The Eagle leaned back against the wall, eyes still shut. Dusk had fallen and, seeing her half caught in that attitude, a shape pressed against the wall that was more shadow than

woman, Anna could imagine the Eagle as much a part of
the wall as the wood itself. Then, suddenly, the young
woman stirred, came to life, and pushed away. She squared
her shoulders under the cloak, took in a breath, and
pressed back into the crowd, who parted to let her through
into the packed hall.

At first she thought they were alone in the pavilion, and in
that instant a sudden wave compounded more of adrenaline
than fear washed through her. What did he want of her?
It was very late. The feast had just ended.

The hounds ranged around his chair growled and slunk
back to keep their distance from her, and she saw how he
raised his eyebrows, surprised at their behavior. Then his
captain stepped out from the shadows to attend his lord.

"My lord count," she said. "I have come, as your steward
directed me." Still rumpled from being woken out of sleep!
She did not add that thought, knowing he would judge it
as impertinence. He did not tolerate impertinence.

"Sit, Terror," he said. The old hound, a handsome creature despite its fearsome size and disposition, sat obediently. He called the others to order as well, firmly but
without cruelty or roughness. From his tone she could tell
he regarded them not with the loving care one bestows on
a beloved child but with the absolute unthinking consideration one has for one's own limbs.

Two lanterns illuminated the tent, just enough for her to
see a wide pallet in one corner of the tent, draped with a
gauzy veil, a camp table with pitcher and basin atop it, and
his mail shirt glittering faintly where it draped from a
wooden post and cross post in another corner. A servant
hustled in through the entryway, bearing a candle that
flashed and flamed in her eyes. The count lifted a hand and
at once the servant licked two fingers and pressed them to
the wick, dousing the flame. The servant took up the
pitcher and retreated outside.

The count looked up at her then. His expression discon-
certed her. She had come to recognize that look in a man's
eyes, the one that betrayed his interest in her as a woman,

but it flashed and faded as quickly as the candle had been extinguished. This was not a man who acted upon impulse, or who let his desires or obsessions get the better of him. She had never met anyone quite like him. Had Da had such qualities, perhaps they could have stayed in Qurtubah instead of being forced to flee because of his folly; perhaps his temper would not have gotten them into so much trouble in Autun that they had been driven out; perhaps he could have covered his tracks better, seen the assassin coming, and saved himself—and her—in Heart's Rest.

At once she felt miserable for thinking such traitorous thoughts toward Da. Da was who he was. He had done the best he could. He had protected her for as long as he was able.

And if all had not happened as Lord Fate and Lady Fortune and God Themselves willed, then she would never have met Prince Sanglant—however brief that time had been.

"Eagle." The count beckoned her to step closer. "What do you want from my son?"

Too startled to take a step forward, she gaped at him. "I want nothing from your son, my Lord."

"But it is clear to me that he has put you under his protection." Now the count leaned forward, gaze hard. "I do not want his situation complicated by a bastard of his making!"

A fish might have bubbled so, mouth popped open.

One of the hounds yipped. "Hush, Ardent," he commanded. He turned his gaze back on her. "My servants report that he gave you coin earlier."

"It isn't for me!"

He lifted a hand, as if to say: *Then for whom?*

She flushed. "It is for Mistress Gisela's niece."

"She is Lord Wichman's lover, is she not?"

"Not by her own choice!"

Terror growled, and the count set a stilling hand on the hound's white mantle. "Ah," said the count, enlightenment dawning. "It reminded you of your own situation at the king's court."

Shame made her angry, and reckless. "Your son is as honest a person as I have ever met. You shouldn't suspect him of concealing from you what you have already forbidden him. You have nothing to fear from me in that regard. I have long since pledged my heart to a man who is now dead. *And* I have sworn the oaths of an Eagle."

"That will do," he said with an edge on his voice so quiet that she almost didn't hear it. But she understood its intent and inclined her head to show she meant to speak no further—on that subject, at least.

"We haven't much time." He looked toward his captain. "Alain will return soon, and we must finish before he comes back. This tunnel, into Gent—" He beckoned the captain forward. The soldier had certain small blocks of wood in his hands. He knelt before his lord and arranged them: here two towers to represent a city; a strip of leather cord stood in for the river.

"Now, Eagle, come forward and place the tunnel where it would lie in relation to the city, as far as you remember. Lord Wichman says there is a line of bluffs here—" The captain set down sticks in a ragged line to demark the bluffs. "And the river's mouth, *so,* with two channels but only one of them navigable and perhaps vulnerable . . ."

She must have made a noise in her throat, or a soft grunt.

He looked up with an impatient grimace. "Do you have a question? Speak it!"

"I beg your pardon, my lord." She glanced around the pavilion, but she, the count, his hounds, and his captain were the only occupants. "Oughtn't we to wait for Lord Alain to return before we speak of such plans?"

Irritation flared in his expression, but instead of speaking, he took wood chips from the captain's hand and placed them, "below" the bluffs and within sight of the city, in the shape of an oval rampart, like unto a fort. After all, *he* did not have to explain his actions to *her.* With a moment's thought she knew the answer anyway. Alain shared dreams with an Eika prince. If the one could dream the other's life, why shouldn't the opposite be true? Lavastine could not risk betraying his thoughts to Bloodheart, even if it meant deceiving his son in such a way as this. "Eagle!" He handed her a stiff length of thread. "Can you see this in your mind and make a picture of it?"

She took the thread and squatted to consider the landscape before her. "I've seen maps at the kalif's palace in Qurtubah. I know how to read them."

"Qurtubah!" But the count's exclamation was voiced so softly that she deemed it better not to respond. She was not sure how much Alain had told his father, and she did not want to risk betraying to the count that, in one matter at least, Alain had concealed *her* secrets from his father.

After a long pause, she set one end of the thread between the two block towers representing Gent and lay it down stretching westward, its other end coming to rest beyond the sticks that marked the uplands above the river plain. Then she frowned and moved the line of sticks back a bit. "The river plain is broader here. Lord Wichman must know the lay of the ground better than I, since he's been raiding through this area for months."

"Lord Wichman is brave but foolish. I will use him as I judge fit." The count examined the little map, then moved the placement of the fort so that it rested on the plain but up against the uplands, near the place where the tunnel supposedly had its end. "River's mouth," he said, touching that place and having evidently forgotten—or dismissed—young Lord Wichman. "Gent. A fortified camp. A secret tunnel. The Eika have ships, foot soldiers, and herds. Wichman's last scout brought in news that there are forty-seven ships beached near Gent. I know from my own experience that each ship can carry about thirty Eika. With Lord Wichman joining me I have about seven hundred soldiers, a third of whom are cavalry."

"But that means they have twice as many soldiers as we do! Shouldn't we wait here at Steleshame for King Henry?"

"Who knows when King Henry will arrive?" asked the captain. "Or if some other conflict distracts him? Nay, lass, we can't wait on an army that may never come. And certainly not in a place like this holding, where there aren't supplies enough to keep us fed and with the Eika raiding at their will, should they wish to harass us here. You can be sure they have scouts in these woods, watching us just as our scouts have gone ahead to watch them."

"We will leave a messenger here to tell Henry where we are, *if* he arrives," added the count. An odd light of excitement glinted in Lavastine's expression, a man who has seen his heart's desire and at last knows which path will lead him to it. "Bloodheart may have numbers," he said, "but *I* have a plan."

"Did you see how Count Lavastine praised my singing last night!" It was morning, and Master Helvidius could not contain his excitement. "The counts of Lavas are great landholders in Varre, practically dukes given the power they can wield. Of course, they have no blood connection to the royal line. Still, a lord of his consequence will wish to have a poet of my gifts in his retinue."

Anna stood stunned. "You'd leave us?"

"Mistress Gisela doesn't appreciate my verse. And she's lost most of her wealth with this war. I'd be better off attaching myself to a new household." He hesitated.

The salad leaves picked yesterday lay in a chipped soapstone bowl, itself gleaned from the ruins of the tannery after the Eika attack. Anna had traded the tansy for a cup of barley from last season's scant harvest, and now Helen chewed happily on a little cake of spring pudding: barley mixed with chopped bistort, dandelion leaves, and nettle tops, boiled in a bag, then fried in lard on a battered tin sheet over the fire.

"Of course, you could come with me," he finished, but reluctance dragged on his words.

"But Matthias can't walk, not to follow a lord like that. I don't even know where Varre is. Poor little Helen probably can't walk so far either, and I can't imagine they'd give such as us a place in a wagon."

Helvidius grunted, irritated now, and bit at his nails. He always had clean hands, which Anna admired. "Eh, what matter? They'll likely all die fighting the Eika at Gent. But perhaps I can sing to them tonight. I suppose they'll march on in the morning."

After all she and Matthias had done for him, how could Master Helvidius even think of leaving them? How could she forage if there was no one to watch over Helen during the day? But she did not voice these thoughts out loud. Instead, she took three of the little cakes and two handfuls of the fresh greens, wrapped them in the corner of her shawl, and walked over to the corner of Steleshame that stank of the tannery.

Crowded already, the large inner yard of Steleshame was

now packed with Count Lavastine's army. They had biv-
ouacked anywhere they could find room, making themselves free with the well—and not even the whole of the
army had encamped inside. Many remained outside to dig
a ditch around the palisades as a first line of defense in
case the Eika raided again.

But none of Lavastine's soldiers paid any attention to
her except to avoid bumping into her as she wove her way
through their ranks or pressed past those of the Steleshame
people who had come forward to offer berries or bread in
exchange for news. At the tannery, she found Matthias sitting on his stool. She paused to watch him. His face was
as pale as the bleached winter sky, but he worked vigorously. She waited until he had finished scraping the hair
side of the skin pegged out before him, then spoke his
name.

He turned, smiled, then frowned when she opened her
shawl and offered him the food. "There'll be bread tonight
and a porridge. You should eat that yourself."

"I've had plenty," she said, and for once it was true.
"You're never given enough. You know it's true, Matthias.
Now don't argue with me."

He was tired enough and hungry enough that this time
he didn't argue, only ate. He had barely finished the scant
meal when, looking over her shoulder, his eyes widened
and he grabbed his stick and heaved himself to his feet.

"Matthias!" she exclaimed, but he made a sign with his
hand and dipped his head. She spun.

Ai, Lady! She touched her Circle, traced her finger
around it, and gaped. Lord Wichman might be the son of
a duchess, but he was nowhere near as fine as this noble
lord and his son, who even fresh off the march looked as
grand as Anna supposed the king might. The noble lord
was not as tall or robust as Lord Wichman, who walked
beside him, but he had the same kind of brisk and effortless
pride which she had noticed in the master currier back in
Gent, when Matthias first apprenticed in the tanning works:
Such a man—or woman—knew their domain, and that they
commanded it absolutely. No doubt the master currier was
dead now; she had never seen him among the refugees at
Steleshame and supposed he had stayed behind during the
final attack to defend his beloved demesne.

This lord had hair as colorless as the sand, a narrow face, pale blue eyes, and a keen gaze. He paused to speak to one of the workmen, indicating some leather which lay over a beam, and asked if the tannery had any leather cured and finished enough that his soldiers might use it to repair their armor. Lord Wichman fidgeted, having no patience for this sort of practical talk, and turned to speak to the lordling who stood at Count Lavastine's side.

"Don't stare!" whispered Matthias, nudging her with his free hand.

Master Helvidius had said that the count traveled with his son. Yet this young man was half a head taller than the count and had black hair rather than pale. He wore a padded coat worked with silver-and-gold thread in the outline of a hound, and, indeed, two huge black fierce-looking hounds walked meekly at his heels. He and his father were also attended by the Eagle. In the daylight Anna could see that her skin had not the tone of soot at all but rather that of a certain honey-colored soft leather prized by rich merchants for gloves.

A messenger from the king; a noble lord and his son; even Lord Wichman, who after so many months engaged in constant skirmishing looked ill-kempt beside his noble comrades. The assembly quite took Anna's breath away, but not nearly as much as when the young lordling turned as if aware of her stare and looked right at her.

She cringed, knowing she ought not to stare. "Anna!" But Matthias' muttered warning came too late.

The young lord crossed over to her, the hounds right behind him, and bent to touch a finger to her wooden Circle. "Poor child," he said kindly. "I saw you at the roadside, I think, when we were marching in. Did you come from Gent?"

She could only nod.

"Are you one of the children who escaped through the tunnel?"

"Yes, my lord," said Matthias gamely, having a voice. Anna had lost hers. The black hounds panted, tongues lolling, so near to her that she expected them to suddenly bolt past their lord and tear her to pieces. But they made no movement, nor did they growl or bark. They simply sat, watching their lord with eyes the color of melted honey.

The young lord lifted the Circle from her chest and regarded it quizzically. "I once wore a Circle fashioned such as this, but I have it no longer."

"What became of it?" asked Lord Wichman who, more restless than the hounds, had come up beside the young lord. He glanced incuriously at Anna; he did not recognize her as the girl he had chastised on that winter raid months ago.

The young lord's mouth quirked into a smile as fleeting as Wichman's attention. "I gave it to an Eika prince." He let go of the Circle and Anna, gaping, staggered slightly as if having lost the touch of his hand she was no longer anchored to the earth.

To an Eika prince.

It could not be. She wanted to ask but dared not. She *ought* to ask but was afraid to.

The young lord had already looked past her to Matthias. "Lady Above," he said softly. "You have some injury, I think?"

Matthias bobbed his head respectfully, fighting to balance himself on his crutch. "I was taken as a slave for a time among the Eika, my lord." His voice was amazingly steady. "Lord Wichman freed me on one of his raids, my lord," he added, knowing it wise to flatter as many lords as were within earshot.

"You took the wound then, among the Eika?" asked the young lord. He had dark eyes and an expressive face, filled now with pity as he laid a hand on Matthias' filthy and matted hair. "Poor child. I wish you may have the healing you deserve."

"I'm a man now!" retorted Matthias suddenly.

Anna winced.

Lord Wichman snorted and gave a stiff, sharp laugh.

But the young lord only nodded. "So you are, come young to it through hardship. What is your name, friend?"

This was too much even for Matthias, who lost his boldness. "M-m-matthias, my lord."

"And this is your sister?" The lord took his hand from Matthias' head and smiled at Anna.

"My sister, Anna. It's short for Johanna, my lord, the blessed Daisan's discipla."

"So it is. How came you to remain here when we have

heard from the mistress of this place that most of the refugees—the children—were sent south?"

"Our grandfather was too feeble to make the journey,
so we stayed on here after the others left."

"Then I pray Our Lord and Lady watch over you."

Only after he moved on, did Anna begin to cry, her tears
as silent as the slip of rain down a wall.

"Anna!" Matthias set a hand on her shoulder. "Anna!
What is it? Did they scare you? The hounds were big,
weren't they, fierce-looking, but they're nothing like the
Eika dogs. You don't need to cry."

Struck dumb.

She opened her mouth to speak but could not form
words or make them whole in the air. There was something
she ought to have asked but had not asked, something she
ought to have done but did not do, something she was
meant to accomplish but had turned her gaze away from
as the well-fed merchant turns her gaze away from a starving beggar, not wanting to see him.

"Anna!" Matthias clutched her shoulders, his weight sagging onto her as, frightened, he shook her. "Anna! What
is it? Ai, Lady, it was the hounds, wasn't it?" He pulled
her tight against him in an embrace. The noble lords moved
out of sight, heading back to the hall.

It wasn't the hounds. But she could not speak words to
tell him so.

Terrified now, he grabbed his stick and hobbled back to
their hut with her in tow, but Helvidius and Helen were
gone. "Anna! Say something to me!"

Unlike the Eagle last night, faced with a heartfelt plea,
she had not spoken. She had not acted. Like a fish tossed
from water to dirt, she could only thrash helplessly. She
was bitterly ashamed, and scared—so scared.

"Lord protect us!" whispered Matthias. "I must take you
to the herbwife. A devil has gotten into your throat and
stolen your voice."

She grabbed his hand and gripped it until he winced. She
shook her head fiercely, so that he would understand. She
had been struck dumb by God's hand, not that of the
Enemy or such of its minions as skittered through the world
hoping to make mischief.

But Matthias had always been stubborn.

In the morning, Count Lavastine and his army marched out, the count and his son at their head—and Lord Wichman and his unruly retinue with them. Gisela's niece stood in the shadows and counted through a pouch filled with silver sceattas.

After the army vanished down the forest road, Matthias took Anna to see the herbwife. The old woman listened to their troubles and took a knife in exchange for her treatment: a noxious-smelling salve which she applied to Anna's throat and a more palatable tea brewed of waybroad and spear-root which Matthias insisted on trying first. Anna gulped the remainder down dutifully, but the day passed with no change in her condition.

That evening, Matthias led Anna to Lord Wichman's deacon, who had remained behind rather than ride into battle. A woman of noble birth, she eyed them with misgiving, as well she might considering their filthy condition and obvious look of common-born children seeking a boon.

"She can't speak, good deacon," said Matthias as he thrust Anna forward.

"Many's the child too weak or slow-witted to speak," said the deacon patiently. "Or has caught a sickness, although that's more common in wintertime. Or she may have taken a blow to the head in one of the skirmishes."

"Nay, good deacon." Matthias was nothing if not persistent. Otherwise, they would never have survived Gent. "She spoke as good as me until yesterday."

"Go see the herbwife, then."

"We've done so already."

"Then it's in God's hands." A mute child among so many who were injured in countless ways was of little concern to the deacon, good woman though she was. She prayed over Anna, touched her on the head, and indicated she should move on.

"Do not go yet, child," she said to Matthias, who had moved away with Anna. "I remember you. You were sore wounded by the Eika, were you not? I came to pray last rites over you some months ago, but you survived by God's mercy, and indeed I thought you must live out the rest of your days as a cripple. I see that God have healed you in the meantime. It is a blessing we must all be thankful for, that some have escaped this terrible time with whole bodies and strong minds."

Anna had been so terrified at losing her voice that she had scarcely had time to notice Matthias. He had been so busy fussing over her that he had taken no notice of himself. But like the sun rising, the light dawned on her now: Matthias wasn't limping.

Hastily he unwrapped the much worn and stained leggings from his calf, and there they stood, both of them gaping while the deacon looked on mildly, unaware of how remarkable—indeed, how impossible—the sight of his leg was now to their eyes.

No festering wound discolored the skin; no horrible, unnatural bend skewed his calf where the bone had broken and healed all wrong. The leg was straight, smooth, and strong.

He was a cripple no longer.

But even so, there was yet one more wondrous event in store for them.

Four days later the shout came from far down the west road.

"The king! The king rides to Steleshame!"

Anna and Matthias, like every last soul in and around Steleshame, ran to line the road for the adventus of King Henry as he and his retinue, armed for war, rode in to the battered holding.

The magnificence of his host would have struck any soul speechless. The king did not notice her, of course. She was only another dirty common child standing barefoot in the dirt beside the road.

What a fine handsome man he was, upright and proud, strong and stern! He dressed much like the other lords, no richer than they, but no one could have mistaken him for anyone but the king.

Surely someday her voice would return to her. Surely someday, if she lived to be an old grandmother, she could tell this story to a host of children gathered at her feet and astonished to hear that a soul as humble as her own had been privileged to see the king himself.

2

"IT will be the ruin of me! I have already depleted my foodstuffs sending provisions with Count Lavastine. Now I must feed this host, and give up the rest of my stores as well?"

The mistress of Steleshame was overwrought and Rosvita had, alas, been given the task of calming her nerves. Outside, within palisade and ditch, the army set up camp for the night. Obviously, with Count Lavastine and his army ahead of them and the householder in hysterics, they could not expect to stay in Steleshame for more than one night. Rosvita had to admit that she was getting tired of the saddle.

After Sapientia's recovery from childbed, they had ridden north at a steady but unrelenting pace, wagons lurching behind, the army swelling its ranks with new recruits at every lady's holding at which they sheltered and feasted.

"And with Lord Wichman gone now," continued Mistress Gisela while her pretty niece stood behind her and listened to this rant with the calm face of a woman who has learned to survive by being pliant, "who will protect us against the Eika?"

"I should think," said Rosvita, "that with two armies sent against the Eika and with Margrave Judith and Duchess Rotrudis likely to arrive at any day now from the southeast, you need not fear the incursions of the Eika, good mistress."

But the householder only wailed and clutched at her niece's arm. "Ai, Lord! But the count and his force are days ahead of you, Sister! It takes four days to ride to Gent with the main road so neglected and dangerous. By now the Eika could have slaughtered them all and be eating their bones as their evening's feast!"

"Then it is one feast you will not have to provide," said the niece tartly, twisting her arm out of her aunt's grip.

Sister Amabilia and Brother Fortunatus, hovering at

Rosvita's back, both made sudden piglike noises and Rosvita turned to see them covering their mouths with the
sleeves of their robes. Fortunatus began to cough. Amabilia
snorted unsuccessfully in an attempt to stop laughing and
then, luckily, young Brother Constantine came forward to
remonstrate with the young woman for making a joke out
of what was no joking matter.

"I beg you, Brother," interposed Rosvita swiftly, "let us
soothe the fears of good Mistress Gisela. We need only a
simple supper, I should think, since the good mistress is no
noble chatelaine of a large estate to lay a fine table—"

But this was too much for the householder. Goaded into
action by this assault on her dignity and wealth, she turned
on her niece and ordered fifty cattle slaughtered at once,
as well as one hundred chickens and . . .

Rosvita and her clerics beat a hasty retreat to the table
within the hall set aside for their use.

"It sounds as if she means to kill every chicken in the
holding," said Sister Amabilia. "I wonder if there will be
any left for the poor souls who bide here."

"There will be no poor souls left at all," retorted Brother
Fortunatus, "if King Henry does not drive the Eika out
of Gent."

Rosvita left them to their squabbling and walked outside.

There she found Villam sitting on a bench, watching
while the inner yard was raked so that the king's pavilion
might be set up where no refuse littered the ground. His
hand rested quietly on a thigh. The empty sleeve of his lost
arm was pinned up to the shoulder so that it wouldn't flap.
He smiled and indicated the bench beside him. She sat.

"You are serious today, Lord Villam," she said, noting
his frown.

He merely shrugged. "It is hard for a man, even one as
old as I, to watch as a battle approaches while knowing he
cannot fight in it—and has no son to send out in his place."

"True enough." She did not glance at his missing arm,
lost in the battle of Kassel, but surely he did not regret the
loss of the arm as much as he did the loss of his son,
Berthold, all those months ago—more than a year!—in the
hills above the monastery at Hersfeld. Then she followed
his gaze and could not contain a gasp. "Surely she doesn't
mean to ride into battle so soon after giving birth?"

Under an awning Princess Sapientia sat in a camp chair, attended by Father Hugh, her favorites, her Eagle, and the servants and wet nurse who took care of baby Hippolyte. A vigorous child, the infant was even now wailing heartily as an armorer measured a stiff coat of leather against Sapientia's frame, stouter now after her pregnancy.

"It has been almost two months since the birth," said Villam.

"Almost two months!" Rosvita shook dust off the hem of her robes and resettled them. "I do not like it, I admit, although she has gained remarkably in strength." Since Sapientia had almost nothing to do with the infant, she had adjusted quickly to her new state: that of uncrowned heir.

Villam nodded. "It isn't enough, truly, that she has proved her worthiness for the throne by right of fertility. She must still show she has the ability to command and to lead, and this is as good a test as any."

"And easy to hand." Rosvita smiled wryly.

It was true: Henry had neither crowned nor anointed Sapientia, but she was seen everywhere with him, she rode beside him on their progress, sat beside him at feast and at council, and was given leave to speak when it came time to exhort the ladies and lords of Wendar to spare troops for the assault on Gent. The infant, who was pleasant to look upon as well as strong, was noted and remarked on everywhere they went, and Sapientia kept it by her at all times—except at night—as if to remind everyone of her accomplishment . . . and of her new position as heir by that same right of fertility.

"I think we need not fear, Sister," added Villam, reading her silence with his usual sagacity. "She has grown steadier in the past months. And Father Hugh is wise enough to counsel her."

"Is he?"

"Do you doubt him?" he asked, genuinely surprised. "He is much changed."

"I suppose he is," she agreed, but absently, for looking at Hugh where he stood in perfect humble attendance on his princess, she could not help but wonder—again—about the book.

Ai, Lady, the thought of the book nagged at her. It worried at her, this mouse's hunger, day and night and even,

that evening, while she sat in the war council held beneath
the broad ceiling of the king's pavilion. The small and ill-
fitted hall at Steleshame had been deemed suitable for a
householder but certainly not for a king and his retinue of
nobles, so they had adjourned to the pavilion, now cramped
with bodies all wedged together.

Sapientia sat on Henry's left, Villam stood to his right.
Around them stood those nobles important enough to demand or beg entrance to the nightly war council, chief among
them young Duchess Liutgard of Fesse, who had joined up
with them northeast of Kassel several weeks ago; Father
Hugh; Villam's daughter's husband, Lord Gebhard of Weller
Gass; the latest Count of Hesbaye, a stocky, placid man rumored to be a doughty fighter; Lady Ida of Vestrimark, who,
as cousin to the late Countess Hildegard, was eager to per-
sonally avenge her cousin's death as well as lay claim to
her lands; and any number of sons or husbands or nephews
of prominent landholding noblewomen who had sent their
male kinfolk as their representatives.

Sapientia alone of Henry's children now rode with the
king. Theophanu had not yet returned from the convent of
St. Valeria, nor had they heard any word from her—although she might well be looking for them in Wayland if
she had missed the messenger sent to the convent with
news of their march on Gent. Ekkehard had been left with
the rest of the children in the schola at the palace of Weraushausen, in the keeping of the monks of Eben, some ten
days' ride southwest of Steleshame. The boy had begged
to be allowed to attend the march; he was almost of age,
after all, and the experience would in truth help temper
him, but Henry had left him behind with the others—for
safekeeping.

A servant brought wine and passed the cup among the
restless nobles.

"We're only four days behind Count Lavastine!" exclaimed Duchess Liutgard in her usual impetuous manner.
"I say we march on tonight!"

"And arrive there completely exhausted?" asked Villam.

"Better than arriving there to find the count dead and
his army cut to pieces! We can see well enough to march
at night—the moon is nearly full!"

"But our road lies through the forest," said Henry, thus

ending the discussion. "I, too, see the need for haste, but not the need to be reckless. I have sent outriders ahead to alert Count Lavastine. We will follow at a steady march without depleting ourselves."

Too restless to remain, with her mind wandering in such an irritable fashion, Rosvita rose and went outside. Just beyond the awning stood the king's Eagle, Hathui, her head upturned to examine the heavens.

It was a drastic step, but Rosvita took it nevertheless: She glanced around to make sure they could speak without being overheard and then asked the woman what she knew of the matter.

"The book?" said the Eagle, obviously startled. "Indeed, I know of the book. Liath always carried it with her, and as far as I ever knew it belonged to her. I suppose it's true she might have stolen it from Father Hugh."

"But you don't think she did?"

"Wolfhere didn't believe she stole it, though she kept it hidden even from him. We all knew she had it, but Wolfhere never demanded she show it to us. He said once to me that it was her right to conceal it from the rest of us, as she wished."

Wolfhere. It seemed to Rosvita that far too much of this mystery revolved around a simple Eagle—although by all accounts Wolfhere was by no means simple. "You were traveling through Heart's Rest when you came upon Liath and Hanna? The king always wants for Eagles, it's true, and I suppose Wolfhere might have found them likely candidates."

"Nay, Sister. Wolfhere was looking for Liath. Both Manfred and I had been sent out by him to look for a girl answering to her description, but it was only when we joined up again that he told us he'd discovered her. That was when we rode to Heart's Rest together."

"Manfred?"

Rosvita could not read the expression on the Eagle's face, but the marchlander made a shrugging motion with one shoulder, as at a nagging pain. "Our comrade. He was killed at Gent."

So did God remind even the strong that life is short, and grief long-lasting. "I will add his name to my prayers."

"Thank you, Sister!" For a moment Rosvita thought the

Eagle meant actually to clasp her hand as she would a comrade's, but she hooked her fingers under her belt instead and with her other hand brushed something out of her eyes. "So may he be remembered on earth and sung into the Chamber of Light."

But the fate of an anonymous Eagle, however tragic, did not lodge for long in Rosvita's thoughts. She had already begun to rearrange the evidence in her mind. Did it begin to form a new and perhaps more interesting picture? "Wolfhere went to Heart's Rest to *find* Liath. He knew her?"

"That I don't know, Sister."

"Father Hugh tells me she stole the book from him while she was his slave," said Rosvita, more irritated than ever. Hugh's story was easy, and convenient, to believe—and not entirely at odds with what the Eagle had told her—and he *was* the son of a margrave. But Hathui's account of events had an Eagle's eye behind it, and a certain ring of bald truth. "Why should I believe you, a common-born woman, over the son of a margrave?"

Hathui smiled wryly. "God makes the sun to rise on noblewoman and commoner alike. The Lord and Lady love us all equally in Their hearts, my lady."

"Yet Our Lord and Lady follow Their own will in parceling out to individuals whatever They wish. To some They give more, and to others, less. Could we not also argue that we merit what we each receive? That They confer on the elect these gifts of grace that set them apart from others?"

But the Eagle shrugged, her expression untroubled. "All gifts are given to us by God. Without such gifts, no matter how noble, we are dust. So we are all equal before God— and the honorable word of a common-born woman no different than that of a nobly born man."

It was startling to hear a commoner speak so bluntly, but Rosvita could not gainsay the truth in her words. "There is wisdom in what you say, Eagle."

Hathui touched a finger to her lips as though to force words back before she blurted out something unseemly. The wind lifted dust from ground already stirred up by the passage of so many feet and so much activity. Soon, all too soon, the night would be alive with Eika—and many of those who marched in this army would die. Rosvita shuddered, although it wasn't cold.

"I would say one thing more, if you will, Sister."

"You have my permission."

"What benefit to me to lie about this?"

"Your own vows, to protect your sister Eagle."

"True-spoken. I admit freely to being a woman who holds to her vows. Ask yourself this: What benefit to Father Hugh to lie about the book?"

"That would depend on what is in the book. Do you know?"

"I do not. I cannot read, and Liath never showed the book to anyone, except perhaps to Hanna."

Hanna. Ivar had nursed at the same breast as Hanna, making him and the young woman milk siblings. To some extent, then, Hanna was kin to Rosvita even if the young Eagle was a common-born woman and Rosvita born out of an old and noble lineage.

Hanna might know. But to speak with the Eagle, Hanna, she would have to pry the young woman out of Princess Sapientia's tight grasp, for Sapientia held all her creatures close against her as if she feared that, given too much room to run, they would dash for freedom—or for someone more worthy.

But there *was* no one else—no one else more worthy to become Henry's heir. Sapientia *had* steadied in recent months. Perhaps Father Hugh's counsel was guiding her toward the "wisdom" she was named for. She might yet grow into a queen.

Thoughtful, Rosvita returned to the council in time to hear Henry announce that which they all knew was preordained:

"We will ride on in the morning, battle ready. Should we be set upon as we march, we will take up at once what positions we can along the road. Duchess Liutgard will command the vanguard, which will take up the left flank. Her Highness Princess Sapientia will command that portion of the ranks which will form the right flank. I will ride in the center, commanding the center, and Margrave Villam will command the rear guard, with the reserve."

So was it decided. There came from the assembled nobles a taut hiss of breath, a gathering of resolve. Soon, and at long last, they would face the Eika.

3

COUNT Lavastine sent a contingent of infantry northeast, ahead of the rest of his army. Commanded by Sergeant Fell and reinforced by a levy of light cavalry from Autun, they guarded four wagons which contained certain pieces from a siege engine as well as sections of a huge chain forged by blacksmiths at Lavas Holding in the spring.

"The Eagle as well," the count had said, "so that she may report back to me the success of your efforts."

They marched hard for three days, seeing nothing except the desolation of farming lands gone wild, then set up camp on the lee of a bluff overlooking the western channel of the Veser River. This was the channel all ship traffic used since the eastern channel—split off from the western by a spur of rocky land, was too shallow, spreading out into marsh before it reached the sea.

Artisans from the city of Autun quickly set to work felling trees and constructing two engines, called ballistae by the ancient Dariyans. They also began work on a small catapult that used a stout young tree, stripped of leaves, branches, and bark, as its arm.

The work proceeded quickly. By the time Liath and the other mounted soldiers had checked out the area, finding nothing but a few burned villages, swathes of heavily grazed fields with no cattle in evidence, and a fallen keep built by some ancient race that had guarded the river in another age, the engines were taking form.

All the next day the engineers worked on their machines. It was so hot that they stripped down to breechclouts as they worked, men and women alike sweating under the sun. Meanwhile Sergeant Fell and a few of his men who had fought the Eika along the north coast of Varre scouted the river as the tide ebbed. Near midday, at low tide, the river ran shallow near the mouth, glistening tidal flats scored by deeper channels coursing seaward.

Late that night, under the light of the gibbous moon, the

work parties set out as the tide ebbed again. On the last lip of solid land, they stripped and began the long trudge across exposed sand and rocks, towing logs sharpened at one end. The day's heat had spilled over into night's air, making it so heavy and warm that Liath was grateful for the pull of cool water against her skin as they headed into the river's main bed. Pebbles rolled smooth by their passage downriver slipped under her feet. She smelled the salt of the sea. The waters streamed past, brown with silt, and sang in their murmuring chorus of the long journey from their original home in the mountains far to the south. A branch grazed her thigh and swirled on.

On the flats, where the water flowed no more than knee-deep at low tide, it was an easy matter to drive in beams for piles, though the current was strong enough that a fair bit of wrestling was required to get the angle right. Like the stakes set leaning forward to stop a charge of heavy cavalry, this line of piles was to be angled and fastened so that the bow of a ship might only drive it deeper. With the piles protruding half an arm's length above the water at the low, so Sergeant Fell said, then an Eika ship could not pass even at high tide.

"Here, comrade!" called a woman to her. As she plunged forward, the water rose along her thighs and she shivered as the cold current dragged at her, coursing around her hips and tugging her seaward as she waded farther out. A man, seeing her struggle against the pull of river, linked arms with her and together they got out to a raft anchored against the current by a section of the heavy chain. She helped five laborers as they wrestled a log as big around as her waist into the deep water and turned it up. Others hauled out rocks from the shore and used these to weight the log on the seaward side while a burly man with a blacksmith's thick arms hammered the log into place. Still more rocks were brought until Liath, standing on this foundation, could touch the top of the log, the water only up around her waist, submerged rocks slick under her bare feet.

From this vantage, the moon's light cast a glamour over the scene; its light washed the waters with a silver gleam that winked ceaselessly as the river rushed forward to the sea. Overhead, many of the stars had been bleached to nothing by the moon's waxing light, but at a glance she could identify the three jewels of the summer sky shining high above her, diamond, sapphire, and citrine. The River of Heaven, unlike the earthly river that coursed round her now, was only a faint mist. On a moonless night it would have stretched like a shimmering beacon right across the zenith, dropping down into the coils of the Serpent in the southern sky. The Penitent and the Eagle, its wings unfolded, rose to the east; in the west, the Dragon set. She shut her eyes. The current dragged against her like the pull of grief.

"That'll hold," said Sergeant Fell, startling her back to earth. He had waded out to test their handiwork. "Go on, then. There's more to set in, all the way across. The tide's well turned, so we've only a few hours before it'll be too high to do the job Count Lavastine's set us to do. We can't sink piles into the deep channels, so these here'll have to hold strong for the weight they must bear."

At last, with the tide rising around them and the river's mouth a swirl of dangerous currents, they finished the line across the entire mouth of the river, all but the deepest channels whose current was too strong and too deep for driving in such stakes. Then all of them gathered like so many hairless seals, soaking wet from their labors and by now shivering from the cold, and with their full complement and many grunts and groans, dragged the chain across the river and fastened it to the piles.

With dawn the work was done and the engines put in place, well hidden along the bluff by palisades of bush, log, and rock but within easy range of the channel. Exhausted, Liath toweled herself dry with her tunic, dressed, and curled up in the sun behind the ballistae, head pillowed on her hands. She fell asleep at once.

And was woken even sooner by a hand shaking her shoulder. She staggered to her feet, clutching for her sword, but Sergeant Fell touched his fingers to his lips for silence and waved her forward.

"Stand ready," he said to her before going on to the next man, his voice as low as if he feared the Eika might hear him on the summer breeze. "We'll see how the trap works."

She stood full up and squinted into a setting sun. Opposite, the moon rose over the eastern bluffs.

Liath readied her horse, then slung on her quiver and got down on her belly to sidle up the bluff and watch the Eika ship approach. It was running with the tide but against the wind. A dozen oars on each side stroked at a leisurely pace toward the now-submerged posts. Sunlight ran golden over the water like streaks of fire.

"Easy, lads," said Fell from below, speaking to the engineers at the ballistae. "Be patient. Wait. Wait. She's in the sweet spot and . . . Ho!" Fell's call to fire rang out like a smith's hammer.

The air reverberated with the ballista's release as a great iron-tipped javelin shot through the air. All froze. The ship's bow ceased moving forward as it hit the chain, and its stern swung wide, yawing under the pull of the current. The javelin hit the water and vanished; at once Fell made adjustments as the second ballista's shot splashed and subsided, this time closer to the helpless ship. The first crew ratchetted back their machine for a second shot. This javelin struck midship, passing through an oarsman and disappearing into the ship. The sound of cracking wood and Eika shouts reached the shore as the fourth javelin hit the ship at an angle, glancing off the wooden planks. She heard the catapult set loose at last, and she gasped. It seemed the sun itself had loosed a burning brand, an arrow cast gleaming from the fiery heights fletched with billowing smoke . . . but it was no arrow from the sun but rather a ball of burning pitch launched from the catapult. Falling on the ship, it splashed flame on Eika oarsmen and ship timbers alike.

Fell guided the adjustment of the second ballista as the crew re-loaded and the ship foundered. Another javelin followed by another ball of burning pitch struck the ship. Sail, folded on the deck, caught fire. The Eika abandoned ship. Leaping into the waters, they swam toward the shore, floundering in the tide. Sergeant Fell broke away from the crews above and slid down the bluff to the soldiers waiting below. Liath ran down to her horse, mounted, and followed a dozen riders down to the shore. There she found Fell waiting with six spearmen and five archers.

The first Eika righted himself in hip-deep water as an archer took careful aim and, at no more than a stone's toss, put an arrow through the Eika's eye as the savage blinked into the blinding western sun. A trio of dogs blundered up out of the river, growling and yelping, and at once the spearmen set upon them, jabbing and thrusting until the creatures howled and thrashed and, finally, lay still.

"To the left!" shouted a rider. Liath cut out away from the others and found two Eika emerging from the water just downriver. She quickly nocked an arrow and shot as she rode, striking one Eika through the heart. The second charged after her with ax poised to chop her down. She kicked her horse into a gallop as the frustrated Eika howled and struggled to keep up. Within moments the Eika, hampered by the pull of the water, slowed to look for other prey. Liath turned in the saddle and nocked another arrow, easing her horse to a walk. It was an easy shot. She took it.

Behind her, a dozen corpses littered the waterline, water streaming past and around them as though around flotsam wedged into the sand. Sergeant Fell chased down what appeared to be the last living Eika—this one unarmed. Ax raised, Fell whooped as he bore down on the confused Eika. The sight was almost humorous. Fell's men shouted encouragement, but no one stepped in to help. Tough-skinned the Eika might be; Fell's ax cleaved its skull and it, too, dropped to the ground with a hideous scream.

Across the river, under the light of the setting sun, Liath watched as a few Eika stumbled up onto the eastern shore only to be met by the patrol left there last night. As for the rest, and their dogs . . . they burned with the ship or drowned.

Around her and above she heard the cheers of artisans, smiths, and soldiers alike. The ebb tide slammed the Eika ship repeatedly against chain and piles until it splintered and began to break up, flames spitting and failing as water swamped the deck. Below, on the shore, a half dozen of Fell's soldiers stripped again and dragged the Eika bodies to the seaward side of the barricade where they rolled them into the water. The dead sank like stone.

4

DUCHESS Liutgard led the vanguard at a grueling pace and by the first evening out of Steleshame the train had fallen behind, its wagons bogged down where the road twisted through a muddy swale. Men from Villam's reserve hurried forward to help them dig out, and while Rosvita waited on a patch of higher and drier ground she saw a familiar Eagle ride past.

"I beg you, Eagle!" she called. "What news?"

The young woman reined her horse aside. "The vanguard has set camp for the night, my lady. The king has decreed that the army must not get separated lest the Eika attack us in pieces." She glanced nervously back the way she had come. "I'm riding a message for Princess Sapientia, my lady."

"I won't keep you long." She could see by the Eagle's expression that she wanted to ride on but dared not disobey. "A few moments of your time won't harm your errand, I trust. Hanna, is it not?" The young woman nodded. She had a clean, strong face and wonderfully pale hair the color of old straw. "I recall your comrade, Liath, once had a book—"

Hanna blanched. "The book!" She glanced around like an animal seeking a safe path out of a burning forest. The horse minced under her, and she reined it back with the studied if somewhat awkward determination of a woman who has come late to riding and means to master it.

"I see you know of which book I speak. Did she steal it from Father Hugh?"

"Never!" No one Rosvita knew could feign this kind of passion, and surety. "It was never his. *He* stole it from *her,* just as he stole her freedom from her when she was helpless."

"Helpless?"

"Her da died leaving debts, and then—"

"That can scarcely be called helpless, if she was of an

age to take on the debts as his heir. But that is not my question, Eagle."

"Always the book," muttered Hanna. *The book* clearly had a long and interesting history, and Hanna's reaction only made Rosvita more determined to discover the truth. "I swear to you by Our Lord and Lady and by the honor and virtue of the blessed Daisan that the book is Liath's, not Father Hugh's. It belonged to her da before her, and he gave it to her."

It was an impressive oath. "But if Liath was Father Hugh's slave because he bought out her debt price, then anything she had became his."

"She didn't have it when he bought her. It wasn't included in the tally of debts and holdings. I hid it for her. Ai, Lady!" She cursed, words learned from the soldiers, no doubt, and then flushed. "I beg your pardon, my lady."

"You must address me as Sister Rosvita, my child."

"Yes, my lady. May I ask you a question, my lady?"

Rosvita almost laughed out loud. *May I ask you a question?* Yet at the same time she refused to acknowledge the rightness of the law. How could anyone possibly argue that Father Hugh had *stolen* Liath's freedom if he had paid the debt price legally?

"Why do you care about—" And then, shuttering suddenly, her expression closed down and she looked away. "May I go on with my errand, my lady?"

Rosvita sighed. "You may go." Of course she had been about to ask why Rosvita cared about the book; but evidently she believed she already knew the answer.

Had an injustice been done? Yet the tale Father Hugh told was different in no particular except that of justice. Who was in the right? Whose claim would God defend?

Brother Fortunatus struggled up from the mired wagons, his robes sloppy with mud. "Here is a stool, Sister Rosvita."

"You surprise me, Brother! For all your gossip, you have a kind heart within." But she sat gratefully, and he only chuckled and went back to oversee the soldiers trying to unstick the wagons.

After a time the wagons lurched on, all but the one which was hopelessly bogged down, sunk to the axles in muck. Its contents were divided between other wagons or given to servants to carry on their backs. By dusk they had caught up with the main group.

Sentries riddled the forest on either side of the road. Trees had been chopped down to form barriers in case of a raid, but beyond that Rosvita could see little of the disposition of the camp. She and the other clerics were shown to the king's pavilion, which lay snug in the center of the sprawling camp, but although Princess Sapientia attended her father, talking excitedly about the coming battle, Father Hugh did not. It took no effort for Rosvita to ease herself away from the group gathered there, to gain directions to that part of the camp where those soldiers under Sapientia's command had staked out a position. By this time it was dark, but she had a single attendant with a torch and, as well, the moon was almost full, now rising over the treetops. Its light streamed through the trees onto a broad clearing where Sapientia's servants had set up her traveling tent.

Father Hugh knelt below the awning, unattended except by a few distant guards who chatted around a campfire. Here it was calm and quiet.

Hugh knelt on a carpet, lush grass crushed beneath its edges. He was praying.

Where was the book?

Hidden in the darkness, she remained anonymous. Any lady or captain went attended by servant and torch in such a place as this and, in addition, she took care to stand just outside the flame's corona so he couldn't recognize her cleric's robes. She watched and searched . . . And found it thrust under his left knee, almost hidden by a fold in his robes.

He finished his prayers, sat back, and slid the book forward into the light cast by twin lanterns. The distant croaking of frogs in an unseen pool scored the night with a chatter no less intense than that of hundreds of soldiers whispering of the battle to come and the fury of the Eika.

He opened it delicately.

Something lay within there, something she was not meant to see. She knew it in her bones. Did Liath steal the book from Hugh, or Hugh from Liath? Should she believe the testimony of the Eagles, or that of a margrave's son now sworn to the church?

Suddenly he twitched, closed the book, sat back, and looked out into the darkness toward her.

An eddy in the breeze swirled around her as suddenly as a roiling current turns a boat in the water. The sensation that Hugh could see her, that he knew *she,* Rosvita, was there when by no possible natural means he ought to be able to, struck her so forcibly that without meaning to she brushed her attendant on the arm and retreated.

That fast.

Only when she was back at the king's tent, when the first sip of ale cooled her throat, did she wonder why she had fled, and if it had been her own choice to do so.

5

IVAR hooked his feet under the bench and yawned. If he slid his feet forward in his sandals, he could rub his toes along the grain of the wood floor. Sweat prickled on his neck where the heat of the sun washed his back. At the front of the room, the schoolmaster droned on about the *Homilies* of the illustrious skopos, Gregoria, called "The Great."

The slow haze of summer heat smothered the room. Behind, the new first-year novices sat very quiet indeed; maybe they had fallen asleep. Ivar didn't dare turn to look because that would attract Master Pursed-Lip's attention. On the benches in front, Lord Reginar and his pack bent to their task diligently.

Their numbers had been reduced by one this spring when the unfortunate death of one lad's two elder sisters in a Quman road had left him as his mother's only remaining heir. Lord Reginar had railed bitterly against the fate that had deposited him in the cloister while leaving his elder brothers free to fight the barbarians, a tirade that had for the first time given Ivar some sympathy for the arrogant young lord. But his complaints had only precipitated a private interview with his aunt, Mother Scholastica, after which he had emerged chastened and so obediently humble that Ivar and his comrades wondered if the Mother Abbess had actually worked magic on him.

Ivar yawned again. Heat sapped all energy from his limbs, and the schoolmaster's voice grated on him as annoyingly as the ever-present tickling of flies. From outside he heard the barking of dogs and the neigh of a horse. The monastery kept few horses, so perhaps visitors had come to stay in the guest house, either to worship in the church or merely to spend a night before traveling on. But he couldn't bring himself to fret, as he once would have, at the idea that those unseen people beyond had leave to go out into the world at will.

"What is the world," Tallia had asked, *"compared to the sacrifice made by the blessed Daisan? How little do our small jealousies and selfish desires mean next to his agony, suffered on our behalf!"*

A distant if familiar voice—his own self of a year ago—nagged at him sometimes. *What about Liath? What about his promise to Liath?* But there was nothing he could do about Liath, no court of higher appeal he could make than to his father's authority; his mother had died years before and any inheritance she might have passed on to him had been confiscated soon after her death by her siblings.

Like Ermanrich, he had become resigned to his fate.

He glanced sidelong at his comrades.

Baldwin sat with chin cupped on hand and stared attentively at the schoolmaster although Ivar knew him well enough by now to recognize that look as one of daydreaming. Ermanrich sneezed, then wiped his nose on his sleeve and resumed fiddling with his stylus. Even Sigfrid was restless; he had a habit of playing with the tip of his ear with his left hand when he was thinking about something other than what went on in front of him.

Ai, Lady. Ivar knew what they were thinking about. He knew *who* they were thinking about, all of them.

The door to the schoolroom creaked open. As the schoolmaster faltered, every head canted up to see who had interrupted. Brother Methodius came into the room, his expression so dour that Ivar had a sudden horrible fear that the old queen, whose illness had taken a turn for the worse, had actually died.

Methodius called the schoolmaster aside. A low conversation ensued. Ivar stretched his shoulders and then regarded the words inscribed in the tablet before him: *docet, docuit, docebit.* Thinking of Tallia, he wrote, *nos in veritate docuerat.* "She had instructed us in the truth."

Baldwin kicked his foot. Ivar started and looked up to see Brother Methodius signing to them: *Come, in silence.*

He stood obediently and followed the others out of the room and down the stair, but it became immediately apparent that only he, Baldwin, Sigfrid, and Ermanrich had been singled out. Perhaps Sigfrid knew why, or Ermanrich had heard something from his cousin, but Ivar dared not ask,

not when Brother Methodius had already enjoined them
to silence.

But quickly enough he began to fear the worst: Methodius led them to Mother Scholastica's study and ushered
them inside, then took up a station beside the door as a
jailer bars an escape route from his prisoners. No one else
was in the room.

Both shutters in the room stood wide, and dust motes
trailed through the sunlight. Outside, a nun worked in the
herb garden. From this angle Ivar could not tell if she was
weeding or harvesting, only see the curve of her back and
the stately, measured movements of a soul at peace with
her place in the world and her understanding of God.

Ivar was not at peace.

Baldwin tugged surreptitiously at Ivar's robe and angled
his head, a slight jerk to the right. There, through an open
door, another room could be seen with the base of a simple
bed in view. There the old queen lay, failing fast—or so
rumor had it. A robed figure, shawl cast over her head,
knelt at the foot of the bed with her hands clasped in
prayer. Ivar made a noise in his throat, surprised. Even
with the shawl covering her wheat-colored hair, he knew
her posture in prayer intimately by now; he dreamed of it
at night.

Suddenly Mother Scholastica stepped into view, concealing Tallia as she crossed the threshold and closed the door
behind her. The latch fell into place with an audible click.
All four novices dropped at once to their knees in an attitude of humility. Ivar heard her walk across the room and
settle into her chair. Crickets drowsed outside, their lazy
rhythms punctuated by a sudden burst of song from a wren.

"Heresy," said Mother Scholastica.

They all four, as one, looked up guiltily at her. But she
said nothing more, and her face remained as still as if it
were graven in stone as she regarded them in silence. Behind her, a blackbird flitted to perch on the windowsill. He
wore his black plumage as boldly as any proud soldier wore
his tabard, marked by a bright orange bill and an orange
ring around his keen eye. He hopped along the sill as they
stared. Ermanrich coughed, and the bird took wing, fluttering away into the garden.

"You have all been contaminated by the words of a girl

who is not even sworn to the church. Is this not so? Will you swear before me that you have not been tainted by her false preaching? Will you swear that her false vision of the blessed Daisan has not tempted you?"

Each word rang like the iron-shod hooves of a warhorse charging to battle. Ivar cowered under the weight of her outrage. Ermanrich sniveled. With his hands clasped before him and his head bowed modestly, Baldwin looked the very picture of a saintly penitent—his goodness made manifest in his beauty—praying before God to be forgiven his sins, of which there were few and all of them trivial.

But not one of them—not even her favored young scholar, Sigfrid, promised at age six to a life of learning within the arms of the church—crept forward to swear what she asked.

They could not.

They had heard Tallia speak of her visions. They had seen with their own eyes the marks of flaying on her skin, the stigmata that mimicked the wounds borne by the blessed Daisan in His trial of agony.

They had witnessed the miracle of the rose.

Mother Scholastica rose from her chair like the very angel of God rising to strike down the wicked. "Do not tell me that you *believe* what she has told you? That you profess this heresy yourself? Lady and Lord preserve us!"

"I–I pray you, Mother," began Sigfrid, stuttering slightly. His voice was hesitant, and he was pale. "If you only listened to what Lady Tallia teaches, if you had seen the miracle as we did. . . . Surely the good biscops at the Synod of Addai understood the matter wrongly when they passed judgment on this matter. It was over three hundred years ago. They were misled by—"

"Silence!"

Even Baldwin flinched back.

"Children." Thus did she set them in their place. "Do you not understand that the punishment for heresy is death?"

But Sigfrid had a stubborn streak in him, hard to see beneath his unfeigned modesty. He moved through the world with eyes for nothing but books and learning, but once fastened to an idea, he did not let go of it. "It is better to speak the truth and die than to keep silence and live."

"A miracle!" said Brother Methodius suddenly, and with deep disdain, although Mother Scholastica had not given him leave to speak. "Roses grew in that courtyard before we moved them to make way for the fence. Which has not done its duty!"

"Nay, Brother, do not blame the fence. It has served God and its purpose well enough until now, and will continue to do so. It is the taint of heresy that has planted its seed in the ranks of these novices. But now that we know how far it has spread, we can uproot it. These four alone among the young men are stained. They are to enter seclusion. Brother, you will watch over them, see that they speak to no one else, until they are sent away."

"Indeed, I will," said Brother Methodius with such emphasis that Ivar felt a cold tremor of doom in his heart. Brother Methodius, a small man of middle years whose scholarship was greatly respected although he was only a man, and whose calm steadiness in the face of emergency was legend, could be counted on to fulfill his promises.

"Sent away?" asked Baldwin, saintly posture crumbling. "You're sending us home? I beg you, Mother—"

"The time for obedience came and went," was her sharp retort, cutting off his pleading.

Ermanrich grunted, hiding his thoughts. Sigfrid had his head bowed so deeply that Ivar couldn't see his face.

Ivar thought of home, but it meant nothing to him now. What would he do there? Go hunting? Fight the Eika? Marry an heiress? Seek an estate of his own in the marchlands?

After hearing Tallia's words, after seeing the miracle, these occupations seemed so . . . trivial. No matter what Brother Methodius said about the rosebushes, Ivar knew a miracle when he saw one. And he *had* seen one. Of course Mother Scholastica and Brother Methodius did not want this miracle to be true, because it would overturn everything their faith was based on.

They believed in the Ekstasis, when the blessed Daisan had fasted and prayed for seven days seeking redemption for all humanity and the Lord and Lady in Their mercy had conveyed him directly to heaven. They did not want to believe that the blessed Daisan had suffered and died on this Earth and been redeemed by the Lady's power because he alone of all things on Earth was untainted by darkness, because he was the Son of God, She who is Mother of all life.

"You will not be sent home," said Mother Scholastica without any softening in tone or expression. "Each one will be sent to a different place. This taint is a disease that has affected all of you together. A flock of sheep is more easily brought to ruin when there is one foolish and reckless creature among them ready to leap off the cliff while the others follow. What you feel now is only a passing fancy. With enough hard labor, seclusion, and prayer you will find your way back to the truth. Be assured that the Fathers of those establishments to which we will commend you will be warned of the taint you carry with you. They will watch you carefully, and compassionately, to see that you do not spread the disease to others and that you are freed from it in the end."

Ermanrich had started sniveling again. "What about my cousin, Hathumod?" His nose had flushed bright red.

"She has her own destination. It is not for you to know." She nodded toward Methodius, who lifted a hand for silence. Ermanrich choked down his sniffles, sneezed, and wiped his eyes. Baldwin was trembling. Ivar felt nothing except a tingling in his knees; one side of his left foot had gone numb.

"Ermanrich will journey to the abbey of Firsebarg. Baldwin will become one of the brothers at St. Galle." Baldwin caught the barest exhalation, like relief, in his throat. "Ivar will be dedicated to the monastery founded in the name of St. Walaricus the Martyr."

Ermanrich gasped. "But that's all the way east, in the marchlands."

"Nay," murmured Baldwin, "farther even than that. It lies in Rederii territory, outside of the kingdom."

"Hush," said Mother Scholastica, her tone more of a threat for its softness. "You have not been given leave to speak.

"Sigfrid," continued Brother Methodius in the same cool voice, "will remain here at Quedlinhame, under our guidance."

Cast to the four winds: Ermanrich to the west, all the way into Varingia, Baldwin south to the mountains of Wayland, and himself east beyond the marchlands into barbarian country, a dangerous place in the best of times.

"But what of Tallia?" asked Sigfrid. Lifting his gaze from his hands, he wore a resolute expression. Of them all, Sigfrid had remained most skeptical, and most torn, and yet his belief, once won, was probably unshakable. Ai, Lady, thought Ivar with a stab of foreboding, what would become of poor Sigfrid without his three comrades to look after him?

But at this moment Mother Scholastica looked kindly upon her favorite novice, even one who had disobeyed her order for silence. However severely she looked upon the others with her hair covered and her robes sweeping to the floor in all their white splendor, with her golden torque at her neck to remind them all of her earthly power and the abbess' ring on her finger as a mark of God's favor and authority, even her stern face softened when she looked upon Sigfrid. "Her fate is no business of yours, child. She has no place within these walls. The king may deal with her as he sees fit."

Sigfrid cast his eyes dutifully to the ground again and said nothing more.

Ivar did not know what to think. He tried to think of Liath, but she slipped away. She had slipped away long ago, but Tallia had remained. Tallia had wanted to remain and Liath had not; she had not even been willing to escape with him. She had not had faith. When he thought of her, he remembered keenly the mystery of her, for she was not beautiful in an expected way but rather she was like no woman he had ever seen before. He remembered the way she had a warmth about her that drew the eye and held it; he knew he still loved her. But did not the blessed Daisan say that lust was a kind of false love and that it was only true love whose peace lasted until the end of days? It was not Tallia's *body* he dreamed of at night but the zealous fierceness of her passion. He wanted to hold on to so fierce a love.

The murmur of voices sounded beyond the door. It cracked, swaying open, and Brother Methodius stepped outside. A moment later he returned together with the sister guest-master, a normally unflappable woman who now looked flustered.

"I pray your pardon for this interruption, Mother," said the sister guest-master, glancing at the novices with a frown.

"You would not come if you had no reason to. What is it?"

"You know of our guests, who sent a servant ahead this morning to warn of their coming?"

Mother Scholastica nodded. She took up her owl feather quill and set it to lie parallel to the parchment leaves on which she had been writing. "All was ready for them, as befit their rank?"

"Of course, Mother!"

The abbess glanced up, evidently startled by this evidence that the guest-master was so shaken by the turmoil that had driven her here, to this study, that she could not respond with humor to this mild sally. "Rest easy, Sister. I have no doubt they, and their mistress, return to the king's progress. Indeed!" She looked at Brother Methodius and as one mind with two bodies they looked together toward the closed door that let onto the sickroom of the old queen. "She can take Tallia back with her."

"And Ivar as well," added Methodius, "since she will eventually return east. Then we can charge her with the lad's safety, and her own people will make sure he reaches St. Walaricus safely."

"Yes. I will warn her myself of the heresy, and she will know to watch out for it and to keep them isolated from those weak of heart who might be tempted."

Still Ivar heard voices outside, one louder than the rest, impatient and startlingly loud in the quiet of the cloistered grounds where silence and humility reigned.

The sister guest-master gestured helplessly toward the door, even now swaying open again. "But she waits outside, Mother. *Now.* I could not dissuade her though I told her you were in the midst of a conference of grave importance. Though no other would be so brash . . ." Here she faltered, recalling prudence and the strictures of a woman sworn to the church. "She claims to have other business—*urgent business*—with you."

"With me?" It was so rare to see Mother Scholastica surprised that Ivar forgot for an instant his own troubles and his own desires. Urgent business?

The door was flung open. *She* had not waited outside.

Ai, Lady, had *she* no respect for the authority of the church at all?

She came in at the head of a troop of servants, lords, ladies, and richly dressed stewards, a veritable herd of them. All laughed and chattered and then, belatedly, recalled the respect due to a formidable abbess who was also the sister of the king. All bowed in some manner, or knelt as need be. All but *her*. Ivar stared, mouth agape.

Oh, God," whispered Baldwin beside him, his voice barely audible. "God, I pray You, spare me this."

She was a great lady of middle years, a fine noblewoman dressed in great state, almost as if she were a king's sister herself. She had height, strength, vigor, and much silver in her hair; no doubt she had children older than the young men kneeling on the floor, and perhaps a grandchild besides. She was not unhandsome, and she wore the arrogance of a great prince of the realm as easily as she wore a light summer cloak, trimmed with a cunning embroidery of birds and flowers, over her riding tunic and gold-braided leggings, but she did not look particularly likable. No doubt she cared little whether she was liked; nobles such as she demanded respect and the honor due to their position, nothing more, nothing less.

"Who is it?" hissed Ermanrich from Ivar's other side.

"Margrave Judith," said Mother Scholastica curtly. She did not incline her head in greeting. Margrave Judith made no obeisance.

Baldwin made a soft choking noise, as though a bone had caught in his throat. He had gone pale—although in Baldwin not even fear could dim his unfortunate beauty.

"I greet you," continued Mother Scholastica in the same crisp fashion, "and offer you the hospitality of Quedlinhame. You are here on your way to King Henry's progress? I fear Queen Mathilda is too ill to receive visitors."

"I am grieved to hear it and I will pray for her quick recovery." Margrave Judith spoke with the tone of a woman who always gets what she wants, when she wants it. "But I have other business at Quedlinhame. Indeed, a matter dear to my heart for I am certainly now old enough and powerful enough and with heirs enough to suit myself in such a matter."

Hugh's mother. Ivar could see nothing of the son in her

except in height and in the almost contemptuous imperious-
ness with which she regarded the abbess.

Baldwin stirred beside him like a leaf shaken in a
strong wind.

Mother Scholastica lifted a hand, palm up, to encourage
the margrave to go on, but instead the margrave turned
and, as a basilisk fixes its prey with a fateful gaze before it
strikes, she looked directly at Baldwin.

"I have come," she said, "for my bridegroom."

Baldwin burst into tears.

6

LAVASTINE had chosen to camp on a low hill about a league from Gent. He stood with a hand on Alain's shoulder as they looked out over fields long since gone to riot with half-grown wheat and barley struggling to lift their heads above weeds and grass. Herds of cattle and sheep could be seen in the distance, but all had been moved a good way from Lavastine's position. The Eika knew they were here.

"Do you think the Eika will let us wait?"

Lavastine did not reply at once. Below, the soldiers had started digging a trench about halfway up the hill. The ring of axes sounded from above them where, at the level height of the hill, a copse of trees was being chopped down.

"Look there." Lavastine indicated the lay of fields before them and the distant herds. "They've been grazed extensively. The Eika have turned all this good farmland into pasture. Strange, that they are like to us in many ways and yet so unlike." The eastern shore lay gray-blue, with clouds streaking the horizon and tendrils of mist streaming up along the river's bank especially around the distant city walls and the square cathedral tower. "Come."

"Father, is it wise for me to attend a war council? What if the Eika prince sees my life in his dreams just as I see his in the hours when I sleep?"

Behind Lavastine the sun sank toward the horizon, demarked here by the tops of trees ranged along the ridgetops that signaled the start of hilly country lying above the river plain. Fires burned, smoke curling up into the sky, a clear beacon of their presence. Alain smelled meat cooking and with that sudden sharp dislocation of his senses, he could hear the hiss of the fire and taste the juices dripping down to snap and sizzle on wood burned down into red-hot coals. Flies swarmed over offal from the slaughter of cattle, and he twitched and tried to brush them off his arms before he stopped himself; the trash heap was well out of sight of the

count's pavilion. Fifth Brother had given him the gift of
preternaturally keen senses—just as he had, with that exchange of blood so many months ago, given Alain the ability to dream snatches of his life.

Lavastine had been staring eastward, examining the city,
which was now almost lost in a haze made of equal parts
river mist and twilight. His smile was as thin as the gleam
of the distant river. "You will attend the council as befits
a young lord who will one day hold great responsibility as
the Count of Lavas." When he used this tone, Alain knew
better than to argue.

They walked together back to the pavilion, where the
captains of his army waited for him under the awning. Lavastine sat and motioned to Alain to sit in the camp chair
at his right. Everyone else remained standing, even Lord
Geoffrey, whose bland gaze made Alain nervous.

Alain studied the men and one woman ranged before
them. Lavastine's captain stood steady at the count's left
side, of course, a trustworthy man and a good soldier. Lord
Geoffrey had acquitted himself honorably at his cousin's
side two years ago when they turned back the Eika threat
on the northwest coast; surely he would do as much now,
when the stakes were so high. Lord Wichman had months
of experience fighting these Eika, but he was reckless and
arrogant and chafed under Lavastine's rule—and yet under
Lavastine's rule he remained. Biscop Constance's captain,
sent in her place, was a son of the Countess of Autun; Lord
Dedi was a man near to Lavastine's age, weary-looking,
laconic, and with a sure hand over his soldiers. Duchess
Liutgard of Fesse had sent a distant cousin with a troop of
mounted cavalry; this young woman had a glance like the
edge of a sword and had gotten in at least three fist-fights
on the way here, once breaking the nose of a drunken
young lord—one of Wichman's retainers—who had asked
her why she fought instead of bred. Alain suspected that
Lord Wichman admired her, although of course he could
not importune a noblewoman with as little thought for the
consequences as he could a freeholder's daughter.

Several sergeants who commanded units of *milites*, freeholders massed as infantry, stood in the background. One
slapped at a fly.

Lavastine whistled, and the great black hounds padded

forward. Old Terror draped himself over the count's feet while Ardent, Bliss, Fear, and Steadfast thrust their muzzles into his hands seeking a pat on the head before they finally settled down. Sorrow and Rage sat on either side of Alain, and Good Cheer lay down heavily on Alain's boots. Arrayed so, they presented a formidable entourage.

The count glanced at Alain, then set his hands on his mail-clad knees, silent for a moment as he met the gaze of each of the captains standing in his council. Stout-hearted, or at least foolhardy, none of them flinched from that gaze . . . only Alain.

Ai, Lady, *was* it wise for him to sit in on this council and hear Lavastine's plans? But he dared not go against his father's wishes—even if it meant that Fifth Son might use what he learned here against Lavastine and his army. Even if it meant that the Eika prince would see the count's even, intelligent gaze in his dreams tonight.

Having taken the measure of his captains, Lavastine went on. "We know a score of Eika clans hold the city under the leadership of their chieftain, Bloodheart. Given all we have heard from Lord Wichman, who has fought them bravely these past months—" He paused here to indicate the young lord, who preened at this mention and looked sidelong at Lady Amalia to make sure she had heard. "—and from the testimony of the refugees and of our own scouts, we must assume the Eika force outnumbers our own. We must also assume Bloodheart knows this as well."

"We haven't seen any Eika scouts," protested Lady Amalia. "For I would have ridden them down and stuck them like the dogs they are had I seen any."

Wichman snorted. "You haven't met the Eika—or their dogs. That we see no Eika doesn't mean they aren't there."

"Magic and illusion! I haven't seen such, nor do I believe it exists. Savages can't control magic."

"You'll see it soon enough, Lady Doubtful—!"

Lavastine lifted a hand and gained their silence, although Wichman shifted restively, only half listening now as he brooded over the bold and prideful Lady Amalia, who did not deign to look at him. Her attention was reserved for the count. "Bloodheart also knows that we wait for the host of His Majesty, King Henry, who will arrive soon by swift march, Lord willing. I think Bloodheart will not withdraw his army while he still believes he can bleed these lands, and for all of these reasons we must be vigilant and expect that great deeds await us."

He regarded his captains, then looked past them to the sergeants standing quietly at their backs. "Through the night we must dig a stockade. I want all those fitted to the work to labor in shifts through the night until we have an earth palisade and a good deep ditch to protect us against an Eika attack. Those who are not working must rest. Our victory will come about through stout hearts and strong arms, and by the blessing of God, may They smile on this enterprise and grant us triumph in this place." With that, Lavastine rose as a sign of dismissal. "Go to your places. I shall speak again with each of you before the night is gone."

Lord Geoffrey hesitated as the others left. "Is this course of action wise? We should attack while surprise is with us, or withdraw and await King Henry. That would be prudent."

The count waited in disapproving silence until Geoffrey began to look uncomfortable. "Do you acknowledge my leadership, cousin, or reject it?" he demanded suddenly.

Flushed, Geoffrey knelt. "I ride with you, my lord."

"Then follow where I lead."

Geoffrey nodded in acquiescence and, with a final glance toward Alain, took himself off. Only Lavastine, his captain, and Alain remained.

The captain approached the count carefully, one eye on the hounds—but they only growled softly at him and did not move. "You know, my lord, that when I speak my mind it is from an honest heart."

"That is why I trust your advice," replied Lavastine, and the merest quirk lifted his mouth, as close as he ever came to showing amusement. "Go on."

"I advise that we withdraw back to Steleshame and wait there for the king and his army. Then, if we unite our forces, the Eika will not be able to stand against us."

Lavastine and the captain were of a height, although the captain had broader shoulders and the stocky build of a man who has marched much and hewn a great deal of wood. Old Terror moved up beside him, sniffing at the captain's hand, and Alain knew then how brave the captain truly was, for he did not flinch.

"Sit, Terror," said Lavastine. "I think you for your council. I have great respect for your knowledge of war, good captain, but we do not know how far behind us King Henry rides or if he can ride to Gent at all. I have prayed that by some miracle we may welcome the king on the field here, but since that is not to be, we must hold out here until he comes—or until we triumph through our own strength. I have given my word to take Gent."

"My lord." The captain coughed, looking uncomfortable, perhaps because the hounds waited so close by. He glanced toward Alain, then seemed to flush and look away. Good Cheer whined and thumped her tail. "My lord, I pray that it is not your head that greets the king from the walls of Gent. A vow may be broken if life and land are at stake."

"Nay." Lavastine turned to look out over the river plain. It was too dark now to see the glint of river or the distant city walls, but the moon rose, full, gleaming in the mist that swaddled the east. "The value of an oath is far greater than the worldly gifts of life and land. We'll speak more before the dawn. See now to your camp, and have faith."

To this the captain inclined his head obediently. "My lord count," he said to Lavastine, and then, with a half turn, "My lord Alain." Without further words, he left.

Was it truly wise to sit here and wait for the king with uncounted Eika nesting in Gent? The captain's advice seemed prudent as dusk lowered over them and the evening's wind rose off the river. A corner of the pavilion came loose and began to flap, and a servant hurried forward to bind it down.

But the count seemed to know what he was doing. Then again, he always did. He had the gift of a clear conscience and absolute conviction in his own judgment and, in most things, he proved himself right.

Lavastine turned to Alain as if he had completely forgotten the previous exchange. "Alain, I want you to oversee the defenses here at the central portion of the camp. From the top of the hill my banner can be seen by all the troops under my command. All shall rally here should the day go ill for us."

"Go *ill* for us? But I thought you intended for us to wait here until King Henry arrives."

"So I do." Lavastine's expression was shrouded as he

glanced into the evening mist. The huge moon had crested the low-lying mist and now washed the eastern sky with its light. Alain could only pick out a few bright stars. "But the Eika know we are here, and they are not lacking in battle sense. We must be ready in case they attack us. If I fall, then our soldiers must follow you."

"If you *fall!*"

Lavastine seemed not to have heard him. "If the center is hit and the rampart and ditch breached, then form the infantry into a wall of shields, spears, and axes. Against such a wall the Eika will break in the same way surf breaks on a cliff. Should the shield wall breach—are you listening, Alain?"

"Y–yes, Father." He was listening, but with horror more than anything.

"Are you afraid, son?" the count asked, more gently.

"Y–yes, Father. I wouldn't lie to you, even about that."

The count reached out and with an odd, awkward gesture touched Alain on the cheek, a brush more than a caress, almost as he would pat one of his beloved hounds. "There's no shame in being afraid, Alain. There's only shame if you let your fear cloud your good judgment. Now then, listen carefully. You, and the men here in the center, will protect the banner. Lady willing, you will know I am with you throughout. I will leave you Graymane as a mount. I will ride the roan gelding."

"But where will you be?" Alain demanded, confused and troubled by these orders.

"I go now to inspect the camps and the work on the ditch and rampart."

Torches flamed below in a ring midway around the hill that rose like a bubble from the fields below. Men worked diligently there in a silence punctuated by brief orders or sudden laughter, and an occasional grunt as stones were hacked at, uncovered, and moved up to reinforce the growing rampart of earth. Alain heard, as distantly as the flies, the stab of shovels into the dirt, the spray of earth flung up onto the earthen rampart that would be their first bulwark against an Eika attack.

"Ditch and wall will protect us," murmured Lavastine, setting one hand on Alain's shoulder and the other on Terror's great head, "but it is our hearts and our determination and our wits that will see us to victory. Remember that, Alain."

Leaving Alain with the hounds, he called his servants to him and went to inspect his army.

Alain called the hounds over and staked them out in a ring around the pavilion, all but Sorrow and Rage, who sat placidly beside him. Then he stood for a while, gazing at the full moon. Were those ragged shadows to the east the outline of Gent's walls and towers? He would see the city again if he slept. What would Fifth Son learn from him? What had Lavastine told him that Bloodheart would wish to know?

"I beg pardon, my lord Alain." Lavastine's captain appeared before him, inclining his head respectfully. "The men will work in shifts all night. We should have rampart and fosse finished by dawn, though I'm not sure we can have much faith in it. You've seen them Eika, my lord. Fought them, too, and killed your share." He grinned, remembering the skirmish last autumn, and his praise warmed Alain's heart and gave him courage. The captain hadn't stayed so long at Lavastine's side because he handed away praise to curry favor for himself. Lavastine did not tolerate fools and sycophants; they did him no good. "Though I pray to Our Lord that no such thing will be the case, I'm still betting that the Eika will swarm that wall like mice into a granary. Ai, well, your father the count knows what he's doing." He said it not to reassure himself but with complete confidence. "We'll leave three gates for the mounted troops, each blocked by wagons. All's proceeding as planned. I'd advise you to get some rest, my lord. When battle comes, you most of all will need your head clear."

Alain nodded. "Very good, Captain," he said, but the words sounded lame. He felt helpless and, what was worse, useless. Many of these men were veterans of numerous campaigns against the Eika. Here, after a single battle in which he had killed a *guivre* that was already wounded and probably dying and one skirmish in which he'd been unable to strike a blow and yet been praised for his killing, he was second in command—albeit watched over by an old veteran.

Like the mail shirt he wore, the weight of this responsi-

bility weighed heavy on his shoulders. But he had no one
he could confide in, only the Eagle, and Lavastine had sent
her and a small contingent back to search for King Henry.
Ai, Lady, he could not even protect poor Liath.

"Come now, my lord," said the captain, who had not yet
moved away. "I remember when I was a lad. There's no
use in worrying about the tide coming in, as it'll come
whether you wish it to or no. Just get off the beach, that's
what my old dad always told me."

Alain could not help but smile. "Spoken like my aunt—"
He broke off, for it was still painful to speak of Aunt Bel—
his aunt no longer—but the soldier only nodded and indicated to Alain that the entrance to the pavilion lay open
and servants waited to attend him.

He had this responsibility now. He was Lavastine's son
and heir, and this night and in the days to come, whether
the Eika attacked or waited, he had his duty.

Dismissing the captain, he went inside with Sorrow and
Rage at his heels. He lay down on a pallet, still in mail and
tabard, with his helmet, sword, and shield beside him. Behind the pavilion he heard horses snuffling, that group of
riders under the command of the captain who would remain
with him here on the hill. His hand, drifting over the side,
came to rest on Sorrow's head. Rage whined, turned a few
tight circles, and settled down.

Perhaps there would be no battle. Perhaps if Henry arrived in time, then peace might be forged between Henry
and Bloodheart. Perhaps Fifth Son dreamed of peace as
well.

But peace did not come to his dreams.

Battered and still weakened by loss of blood, he sat as
silent as stone in his chains and listened as the Eika held
a war council. His six dogs ringed him. They scratched at
the flagstone floor, sensing the excitement. Blood and
death: At times like this Sanglant wondered how much the
dogs understood, how intelligent they really were. Voiceless
they might be, but they did not act mindlessly—yet neither
had they the cunning of men, or of their Eika masters.

Bloodheart conferred with his son, the one in disgrace.

"One army," said Bloodheart.

"Many fewer in number than our own people, if my dreams are true dreams, and I believe they are."

"So you believe," said Bloodheart. "What standard flies at the head of this army? That of the king?" He leaned forward, claws extended, his great, scarred face a gleam of iron and shadow. The scent of his anticipation lay sodden over the assembly of Eika soldiers.

"Black hounds on a silver field," said the son. "A red eagle. A tower attended by ravens."

Sanglant shut his eyes, fighting back the pain. If he shifted on the floor to find a more comfortable position, stone scraped his flesh raw. His wounds had healed, licked clean by his dogs, but the touch of Aoi magic had somehow scoured his senses so every touch of his skin on stone or on the harsh coat of the dogs or on the coarse metal of his chains flamed like fire through his body, every smell—even and especially his own—made him reel, every taste of such food as he could glean from the garbage tossed aside by Bloodheart and his sons nauseated him.

Black hounds on a silver field. That would be the Count of Lavas. This much he dredged from his memory. A red eagle: Fesse. A tower attended by ravens: his aunt, Constance, if indeed she still presided as biscop in Autun.

But not King Henry.

He shifted his shoulders to try their strength. The dogs, sensing his movement, growled softly.

Bloodheart sighed and sat back. "So my scouts report also. The chieftain of this army is not the king, then. Well enough. The king is coming, or so you report. And I sense him, likewise, like a rot breathing in my bones." When he grinned, his jewel-studded teeth flashed in the light that lanced in low through the western windows. He looked toward his prisoner. "But he won't arrive in time. A little army, this first one that troubles us." He fingered the bone flute at his belt, tugged it out, and lifted it to his lips. "I'll chew up each little army piecemeal, as it comes to me, and let the dogs fight over what remains.

"All but *you.*" Abruptly he jabbed at the son, who danced back and then had to slap away the sudden assault of growling dogs—Bloodheart's pack, those who hadn't transferred their allegiance to Sanglant.

The Eika prince's own dogs bolted forward, teeth bared, but he kicked them back and, slowly, all the dogs settled down while Bloodheart watched their interplay with unholy glee.

"*You!* You returned here without my permission, and so you will taste no blood in the coming battle. So will *you* remain behind, still in disgrace, to watch while your nest-brothers run forth to the glory of slaughter."

The son did not protest this judgment, but an unfathomable expression flashed across his sharp face before he retreated to the accompaniment of his brothers' howls and jeers.

Bloodheart laughed, settling himself deep in his throne. He lifted his flute and began to play while beyond, in the vast nave, the scrape and ring and grunt of Eika preparing for battle filled the vault with reverberations as complex as those of a congregation singing a hymn.

Outside, like a pulsing echo, drums began to beat.

7

LIATH and ten lightly armed riders bearing spear and shield started south at dawn the morning after the destruction of the Eika ship at the river's mouth. They rode through woods and fallow fields, many grazed, some growing wild after last year's burning. Beside a stream that drained downslope toward the Veser River they stopped to water and graze the horses, and to eat.

Soon they cut inland to avoid Eika patrols. The rough country above the river plain made for hard going. They rode too deep in the woods, sundered now from the river bottoms by the bluffs, to see the river or any indication that they neared Gent.

When they stopped at nightfall, the cavalry captain took her aside. "How far to Gent?" he asked.

"I don't know. A day or two from the river's mouth—that's what Mistress Gisela told us—but none survived in Steleshame who'd made the journey themselves and I'm thinking now that the day's trip they mentioned from Gent to the sea was by boat, running with the current."

These skirmishers had come from the county outside Autun, and swore allegiance to Biscop Constance. Now, smiling wryly, Captain Ulric indicated the full moon rising through a gap in the trees. "If we can make our trail where there's light enough to see, then perhaps we can ride farther tonight. I don't like riding out here alone. God know the Eika might leap out from behind any tree."

So, after a rest, they went on, nervous and watchful.

It was a long night.

In the predawn stillness, with the moon sliding below the trees, they groped their way along an overgrown trail and came out to a burned farmstead.

"I recognize this place," said Liath, breath hissing between her teeth. She led them into a meadow beyond the sad remains of buildings and there, in the clearing, she had light enough to discern the landscape.

"This is the cave's mouth!" she exclaimed. "Look there!" The light on the eastern horizon rimmed the bluff with a dim glow but its rocky slope lay still in darkness. "From the height you can see the city. Who will follow me into the cave? I'll need a torch once we get inside." .

None of the men seemed eager to follow her into the cave, but Captain Ulric picked out a volunteer, left six men with the horses, and took another two to climb the bluff with him.

"Come now, Erkanwulf," she said to her companion, a slender young man with pale hair, "I can't believe you'd be afraid of the dark."

"Ai, well, mistress," he said politely but with a slight tremor in his voice, "I'm not feared of the dark. But my good mother did tell me that the old gods fled to the caves when the deacons and fraters came to our country and drove them out of the villages and crossroads and stone circles. How do I know that wasn't true in this land as well?"

"I didn't see you flinch at fighting the Eika, friend. You dispatched one yourself, at the river's shore."

"So I did, but they're savages, aren't they? And they can die just like you and me can, so there's no reason to be feared of what is mortal." She sensed him grin by his tone; it was too dark to see. "Unless it has an ax and you don't, I suppose." He chuckled, perhaps recalling Sergeant Fell. But he followed Liath gamely enough as she thrust through bushes and found the mouth of the cave.

· Setting flint to rock, Erkanwulf caught a spark and lit the pitch-soaked torch just as he stepped inside. She sucked in breath, seeing the flame spit into existence. Could she have lit it with the touch of her hand? It was still too dangerous for her to try.

The young man had already gone forward, made bold by fire. "See here," he called back over his shoulder, his shadow writhing over the walls as he moved into the back of the cave. "There's no outlet. This must be the wrong cave."

"No." She shook herself free of this fruitless worrying; she couldn't unravel the mystery of her own magic until she found a teacher. As Da always said: "*Harvest the wheat that's ripe instead of watching the shoots grow.*" "I know this is the right place." Coming up behind him, she stopped short. It was all rock, a rough wall of stone that curved back above them, sealing them in . . .

. . . and yet, wasn't there a kind of vibration to the wall, a disturbance in the barrier of rock?

"No," she said as it dissolved before her. "See, there, you can see the break in the wall," she stepped forward as Erkanwulf gasped.

"You'll walk right into the wall—!"

She found the first step with her foot, poised there with the touch of air swirling up against her like an echo of the river's currents where the Veser met the sea. She smelled the dank passages of stone, the dry scent of old earth, the holy remains of the dead who lay in the cathedral crypt and, surely, the rank presence of the Eika in the cathedral itself and the blood of all those who had died.

Sanglant. And poor Manfred, and all the others who had fallen together with Gent.

Erkanwulf gasped again. The torch's heat flamed against her back, and she shifted sideways as he came up beside her. "By our Lord! It's as you said! I'd never have seen it with the shadows so deep here. Lady Above! Do you think the old spirits were hiding it from us?"

She turned back in time to see him retreat, face golden under the torch's light. He looked all about himself as if he expected a peevish sprite to swoop down upon him with elfshot nocked and ready to let fly. She laughed. "Nay, friend Erkanwulf. Remember, I saw the vision of St. Kristine with my own two eyes, and I'll never forget it, so long as I live. I think she hid the entrance so that only those in need could find it. Come on, then. We've news to take to Count Lavastine—"

"And his army yet to find," countered the young man as he followed her out. He snuffed the torch, tossed it to his waiting fellows, and climbed the bluff after her. She could hear him puffing and grunting as he scrambled, slipping on loose scree. Was that pounding his heavy tread?

As she reached the top, it hit her as the sound swirled around her like a breath of distant wind off the river. It was not thunder or the pound of feet but rather the sound of Eika drums. How could she hear them from this distance—unless the battle had already been joined?

Captain Ulric and his two companions knelt on the ridge, looking eastward, all of them in identical postures: hands flung up to shade their eyes from the glare of the rising sun. At their feet, the hill dropped away precipitously to the river plain. Eastward, bright as a string of jewels, lay the river, but although Liath knew where Gent must lie, the blinding glance of the sun concealed it.

"Look, there," said Erkanwulf, pointing southeast. "Do you see that hill?"

That hill: It lay somewhat south of their position and a short way out on the river plain. It looked from this height more like a tumulus than a hill, treeless and bare at the height except for banners and a handful of bright pavilions.

"That's the Lavas banner, and the tower of Autun," said Erkanwulf.

"You're sure?" demanded Ulric, rising now.

"Who else could it be? I've keen sight, you know that, Captain."

"Thank God, then," breathed the captain.

The hill lay close enough that although the figures swarming round it looked small, she could clearly see the earthworks, like a fallen coronet, that ringed it halfway down the slope. Lavastine's camp lay a good league west-southwest of Gent. Now, as the sun rose higher, she could see the city itself and the river winding past it, tiny boats like children's toys beached along the eastern shore.

"Thank God that they're still here," she asked, "or that they're here at all?" Liath shaded her eyes. The drums pounded in her ears like distant surf threatening storm, like the beat of the army's heart.

Ulric chuckled. "Thank God that Lavastine hasn't taken the city without us. Else he'd get all the glory, and the city's taxes for a tithe as his reward, no doubt."

Erkanwulf let out a sigh. "I'd feared worse. I thought we'd be as like to see the army lying dead on the—"

"Hush, boy," broke in Ulric, drawing the Circle at his breast. "It's ill luck to speak of such things."

"It's a peaceful day, at least," retorted Erkanwulf. "You can't have expected that."

"The quiet before the storm," said Ulrich ominously.

"More like the thunder before the storm!" said Liath.

No one said anything more. They all looked at her, puzzled, and then at the clear sky above.

"You don't hear it," she said suddenly.

"Hear what?"

"The drums!"

"Drums?"

None of them heard and none of them saw: In distant Gent, a league away, ants swarmed out of the gates of the city. Except those weren't ants.

In that moment she shut her eyes, swept by such a sickening tide of foreboding that she staggered under its flood. Erkanwulf caught her by the elbow, and she opened her eyes, shook him off, and spoke fiercely to the captain.

"By my Eagle's sight, I swear to you, Captain, that I see what you cannot. The Eika are marching out of their city even now to attack Lavastine's army. We must ride to warn the count. *Now!*"

Perhaps it was her tone of voice. Perhaps it was the stories they had heard at Steleshame of the horrific illusions that had marched alongside the Eika soldiers when the savages had attacked the holding. Perhaps they had heard her own story of the fall of Gent, retold endless times.

No one argued, though Erkanwulf stared and stared eastward trying to see what she saw until Ulric grabbed him by the arm and yanked him back.

"Come, boy! You heard the Eagle!"

No one heard the drums. No one saw the Eika coming. No one but her. She was the only one who could warn Lavastine—and make him believe.

XV
THE FURY OF
THE EIKA

1

ALAIN woke at dawn and scrambled outside to find his father sitting at his ease under the awning, sipping wine. The count had unchained Terror, and the old hound rested his head on Lavastine's knee and gazed adoringly at his master.

"Did you rest well?" Lavastine offered Alain the cup.

"Well enough." The wine hit Alain's stomach with a bracing flood of warmth. Rage whined, scenting eastward.

"Did you dream?"

"Just nightmares of the Eika arming. Like locusts, swarming everywhere. But Fifth Son did not leave the cathedral."

"It seems the Eika intend no attack, then. Not this morning, at least. All lies at peace."

"My lord!" The captain hurried up. "A band of some dozen horsemen has been sighted, riding hard from the north."

Lavastine jumped up and strode to the north corner of the hill. Alain thrust the cup into the hand of a servant and hurried after him. He scrambled up onto the rough platform and from there could clearly see the earthworks laid out below, ringing the hill, and—to the north—a dozen or more riders galloping toward their position. As this group enveloped a pair of waiting outriders, one rider slowed to pass on their news. At once the scouts turned and followed the rest toward the hill.

"They ride with some urgency," observed Lavastine calmly. He beckoned to a servant. "My arms. And another glass of wine." Like Alain, he already wore sword and mail.

"That's Liath!" Alain saw scarlet flash in her Eagle's cloak.

Lavastine leaned down toward his captain. "Bring the Eagle to me as soon as she enters camp. Let the other captains assemble." When he turned back to Alain, he regarded the young man with a seriousness that made Alain flush with more than wine—with a dreadful anticipation, a fluttering in his stomach. "No matter what is said, or left unsaid, you must trust me, Alain. Your part is to defend this hill." His gaze shifted to encompass the expanse of fields stretching eastward toward the river and Gent, which lay silent and peaceful under the new sun. "How quiet it is this morning," he added softly.

Voices swelled below, a hubbub of excited speech and shouting. The captain rode up the hill, Liath right behind him. Her horse was foundering and, as soon as she dismounted, a servant led it away.

"My lord count!"

He lifted a hand for silence and counted his captains: Lord Geoffrey, Lord Wichman, Lady Amalia, Lord Dedi of Autun. The sergeants had already assembled. "Eagle, give us your report."

Out it spilled so quickly that Alain could scarcely make sense of it: an illusion that appeared as *no* illusion? the Eika attacking now? With each phrase she glanced east, her expression so transparent that Alain thought he could read each least slight grimace or widening of eyes. She was not as afraid of what she claimed to see as of how her news would be received by her listeners.

They all looked. They could not help it, her gaze drew their own so strongly toward the plain lying bright and empty between their position and the distant city of Gent.

There was nothing there, no army racing toward them, no drums beating to sound the advance.

Nothing but the quiet land under the morning sun.

"Ai, Lady," she burst out at last, seeing their skeptical expressions.

Alain stepped forward.

Seeing him, she reached toward him like a supplicant. Sorrow and Rage, growling softly, retreated behind him, and old Terror whined and slunk back behind Lavastine. "Lord Alain! You *must* believe me. They're halfway across the plains. They'll overwhelm us if we aren't ready for them—if they don't overwhelm us with sheer numbers!" She grabbed Alain's arm. Rage snapped at her just as Lavastine began to protest this liberty, but Alain called Rage down and, with a look at his father, gained silence. "Don't you *see?*" she cried, gesturing toward the east.

He murmured under his breath. "I pray you, Lady of Battles, let me see with her sight. Let me see with the inner heart, not the outer seeming."

In the late summer heat, waves of heat often rippled off the fields and rocks. It was like that now, a distortion over the fields, an image of peace blurring and changing, dust rising in a haze to cloud the sun—

There! Jogging at a ground-eating pace came the war bands of the Eika, drums pounding at their backs, their shields a blur of blue and yellow. They had already covered three quarters of the distance from city to camp; the haze of dust marked their passage. In all there were a dozen or more units, each one marked out by spears decorated with feathers, bones, and tattered strips of cloth braided into streamers. Each unit contained many more than a hundred Eika—and all had dogs loping beside them.

"Lord have mercy!" exclaimed Alain. "There are at least three times as many of them as of us!"

"There's no one there at all!" scoffed Lady Amalia.

"And no illusion to see through," added Lord Wichman.

"*That* is the illusion," said Liath, her tone ragged as she stared at Alain with hope flaring in her eyes.

Wichman snorted. "Ai, I've had experience with these Eika," he began, "and there was always some fearsome sight to be seen—" He faltered as Count Lavastine moved up beside Alain.

"What do you see, son? Like the others, I see nothing."

Alain could only whisper. "It's true. What she says is true."

"This is not what I had planned for," said the count, as if to himself. Then, with no change of expression, he turned to his captain. "To arms! Sound the horn!" The captain signaled, and at once the blare of the horn lifted, a high note caught in faint echoes off the distant bluffs. The camp came alive with movement as soldiers prepared for battle and manned both outer rampart at the base of the hill and the inner one near the top which used the slope to best effect.

Then, and only then, did the count's eyes widen with astonishment as he stared eastward. His expression hardened as he examined the tide of Eika. He set a hand on Alain's shoulder, and for the space of three breaths they stood thus, together, as the Eika flooded toward them over the fields. Finally he turned even as the captains uttered oaths or caught in gasps, at last seeing through the illusion. By now they could hear the howling of the Eika dogs and the ululations of the screaming Eika. The drums shuddered like thunder through the air.

"My captains!" Lavastine caught their attention and held it with his gaze and his posture. A servant ran up beside the platform and handed his helmet and a cup of wine up to him. This cup he passed among those assembled before him.

"There are more Eika than I hoped, but all is not lost. Our plan remains the same. Alain, stay on the hill. You, and the bulk of our army, which holds the hill, are the anvil. I, with the cavalry, will be the hammer. Had we more warning, we would have had more chance to strike them unawares from the rear—but nevertheless our only hope is to use our cavalry to destroy them on the field. Assemble your riders." Each took a drink from the cup, pledging their courage and strength, and left. Only Lavastine's captain and the Eagle remained, together with Lavastine's personal servants, themselves armed and ready with shields hitched across their backs and spears in hand.

"Alain." He touched the cup to his own lips and then handed it to Alain. "I will return to you through the Eika host and meet you here. God's grace upon you, son. Trust our captain, who will remain beside you. Trust your own instincts. You are a born soldier."

He leaned forward and kissed Alain on the forehead. Stunned, Alain could only drop to his knees before the count and grab his hand, to kiss it.

"Do not kneel before me," said the count irritably, lifting him up. "You are my heir and need kneel before no one but God."

"I will not fail you, Father," said Alain, surprised he could speak at all.

"Of course you won't! Eagle, attend me."

Liath cast a glance over her shoulder, but only one, as she hurried after the count. The hounds, barking, tails whipping with excitement, clustered around Alain as he watched them go.

The cavalry assembled on the western side of the hill, hidden from the Eika assault—or so Liath prayed. She tried to estimate their numbers, perhaps three hundred in all. Behind, the infantry who had dug into the hill numbered at most twice that many. As she moved down the hill with the count, he inquired of the other business she had been about.

"The river's mouth is chained. One Eika ship already has been destroyed. We found the tunnel."

Lavastine watched as the units formed up under their banners: the black hounds of Lavas behind him, the red eagle of Fesse behind Lady Amalia, Lord Wichman and his men at the head of the gold lion of Saony, Lord Dedi with the raven tower of Autun and the *guivre* of Arconia. "How far from here to the tunnel?"

"I saw the Eika leave the gates of Gent and yet I arrived here before them." She heard, nearing their position, the beat of drums and a low shuddering roar. "It lies just beyond that bluff," she lifted her hand to point, "beyond the small wood."

"You've done well, Eagle."

Now he lifted a hand, seeing his cavalry in place.

Ai, Lady. If only the count had waited in Steleshame, perhaps Henry would have come. But he had had a plan, and yet, as plans often do, it had come to naught. He had planned to meet the Eika in battle in the field, forcing their hand by moving siege engines into place and then meeting their sally with his cavalry as his infantry used the tunnel to enter the city, but now the opposite was true. His foot soldiers were pinned; to abandon his horses and lead his cavalry soldiers, on foot, through the tunnel into Gent would condemn those on the hill to annihilation. Yet surely the city had been emptied of Eika. A surprise attack from within could take the city and probably hold it against an Eika army stuck outside the gates—but by then that army would have done their gruesome work at Lavastine's camp, a camp commanded by his only child.

His people watched, expectant, as he paused before riding forth. They waited, three hundred strong, horses shifting, spears waving against sky and the looming hill behind them.

He lowered his hand and, in silence except for the rumble of hooves, they moved out, swinging wide to give themselves as much space as possible to maneuver. Above them, from the hill, a roar of shouts followed by the clash of arms rolled across the valley like thunder.

The roar of the Eika host overwhelmed even the maddened beating of their drums as they closed the distance. Alain stood at the top of the hill so that he could see his entire force.

"What is that?" he gasped, squinting toward Gent. It seemed to him a dome of fire arched over and concealed the city, but surely no such thing could exist; it must be the sun shining in his eyes.

From below came the call to shoot, but the first volley

of arrows had little effect against the huge round shields or the tough hides of the Eika. Only a few dropped, among them a handful of dogs. Arrows lodged in their arms or necks or quivered in their glittering mail girdles, the metal "skirts" woven of hundreds of interlinked rings of brass or iron—but still they came on.

In answer they sent a volley of spears, axes, and stones from their back ranks even as the foremost Eika units swarmed onto the ramparts. Men braced behind earth and shield.

The lead Eika leaped over the ditch onto the earthern walls and hacked at the palisade stakes. A few of his comrades tried to slip between those stakes, turning shields sideways, but spears thrust up through their armpits or stomachs and they died straddling the earthern wall. To the left, a clot of Eika pressed hard against the wooden stakes, iron-tipped spears forcing the shieldmen back from the rampart. Men-at-arms with spears dueled back, and a small band of archers gathered behind the men-at-arms and riddled the Eika with arrows.

Other Eika bands swarmed on all sides, trying to swamp the rampart from every direction. Because the south slope of the hill was steep, the Eika had trouble maneuvering up to the wall. From his platform, out of reach of arrow and spear, Alain saw the men there tossing rocks and rolling logs into the Eika ranks. The north slope had a more gentle pitch and here the Eika pressed hard against the north "gate," made of wagons rolled up against a gap in the rampart. An Eika armed with a stone-bladed club leaped in a great bound onto the wagon that sealed the gate and struck a man with such force the blow shattered the man's shield and slammed him down to his knees. Already two arrows protruded from the chest of the Eika. A dozen spears and swords wounded him. The creature leaped again, arms outspread as if flying. A soldier thrust his spear upward, and the weight of the Eika's fall drove the spear clean through its chest as the spearman collapsed underneath its dead weight. More Eika clambered after him, screaming and howling.

"There!" Alain cried as a hole opened in the eastern defense, but the captain was already in motion sending reserves in to plug the gap. Was there nothing he could do? Only watch as others fought, and bled, and died?

Along the north wall, held by what remained of Lord Wichman's infantry, an able sergeant with a long spear stayed close to the gate. His standard bearer leaped to and fro shouting encouraging words of scripture and at one point dropped the standard over the face of an Eika to confuse it as others set upon it with axes and swords.

It seemed an eternity that Alain sat there, restraining himself. His father had told him to wait until the time was right. If he acted too soon, there would be no reserve for when it was truly needed. It was worse to stand and watch. If these men who were dying in order to protect him knew that he could not strike a blow in battle and that in war he was a coward, would they so willingly lay down their lives under his banner? Did he deserve their respect and confidence?

From the east rampart the sound of splintering wood signaled the breaking of the stockade wall. Many logs, weakened by strokes of ax and sword or pulled up by Eika, split or gave way as the weight of the Eika charge pushed into camp. On the south the line still held, but on the north slope the wagons blocking the gate had been shattered. A pack of Eika dogs bounded through the breach and over those men who now formed a shield wall as they attempted to close the gap.

Two dogs charged the gold lion banner of Saony. The standard bearer dropped the standard to make a spear of it, and with a mace in his right hand he countercharged, but one dog dodged nimbly aside and bowled the man over while the other grabbed the standard in its teeth and shook it viciously. Still the man refused to yield the standard. Splayed with his left hand gripping the banner-pole and the right arm fending off attack, he lay helpless.

"Lord Alain." The captain jumped up to the platform. Alain's horse—his father's favorite gray gelding Graymane—waited patiently beside. "Take your men to the north gate. I'll drive them off the east."

At last a decision had been made. Alain mounted and raised a hand, the only way to communicate over the roar of battle surrounding them. He charged, two dozen men and seven hounds behind him.

At the north gate the weight of the Eika broke the line
of shields. Men stumbled back to leave a wide gap thick
with Eika and their dogs. There came an Eika, grinning up
at Alain in a battle fury, his teeth studded with gems and
his bone-white hair braided into a thick rope. Alain leveled
his lance and rode in, but it was like play, like a dream
with no fury, no fire; he charged for the sake of his men
who died holding back the Eika, nothing more, nothing
less.

The Eika stood its ground and at the last instant batted
the lance aside and drove in toward the gelding's neck with
its stone-tipped spear.

Alain reined sharply aside and the spearpoint passed
through Graymane's mane, striking Alain's mailed right
shoulder. The shaft of the spear splintered. The shock sent
Alain tumbling, his shield slapping into the Eika's face as
he fell. He struck earth with a slam, air driven from his
lungs. A pack of dogs leaped on him, biting, ripping at his
shield, clawing and jumping over him. Only his mail saved
him. He tried to reach for his sword, but it lay twisted
beneath him. He tried to roll, but a huge slavering dog
landed on his chest, slamming him back down, and lunged
for his throat.

Sorrow arrived first. His weight at full run slammed the
Eika dog sideways, and Sorrow pressed on, biting and clawing, heedless of a gash opened on his great black head.
Then Rage swept in, silent and deadly, and the Eika dog
fell to lie twitching, hide opened in a dozen places, its life
bleeding away onto the dirt.

Sorrow had already clamped down on the throat of another dog, twisting his massive neck back and forth until
the Eika dog died with a spasm.

Then the other hounds charged in, a mass of black fur
and fierce fighting that clouded Alain's vision. He struggled
up to his feet, drawing his sword. Tears streaked his face
beneath his helmet.

"Lady of Battles, forsake me not, I beg you."

He had never been so afraid in his life. Terror barked
an alarm and Alain barely turned, rising from his knees, in
time to catch a blow from an Eika ax upon his shield—but
it drove him back down to his knees. A spear stabbed past
him, from behind, thrusting in the Eika's face, shattering

its gem-studded teeth. They came, his guard, forming up around him, crying out to each other, calling Alain back. With an ax-blow one of the men severed an Eika's hand at the wrist, and though the creature tried to retreat, howling in pain, the press of his shield brothers forced him forward straight into Alain.

Alain struck feebly at him, more reflex, more for his own defense. Ai, Lady, the savage was helpless, disarmed now with foul greenish blood pumping from the wound. The spearman struck again, catching the Eika at the throat and finishing him. As he fell, blood gushing at Alain's feet, two more pushed forward. Alain could only fend off blows, hold hard against the rush of Eika while his men with spears and axes did damage around him.

"Back, Lord Alain!" they cried. "Back behind us!"

Weeping with shame, he stumbled backward, the hounds following in among the legs of his guard. The shield wall parted to let him into their ranks.

All along the north face the line at the rampart gave in toward the center, and throughout the camp Lavastine's troops gave way from the wall to stand shoulder to shoulder against the Eika tide.

Alain prayed that his father would arrive soon.

2

THE heavy cavalry formed up in three open ranks, twenty paces between, with Lavastine and his banner in the center of the lead rank. A line nearly a hundred horsemen wide swung around the hill. Liath rode behind Lavastine. At first they advanced around the north side of the hill at a trot. As the enemy came into full view, the first rank broke into a charge followed by the second and third ranks.

The banner of Lavas drove all the way into the back ranks of the Eika. The lances struck high, hitting shields and heads, breaking through the Eika line in a hundred places. Lavastine himself at the front bore onward, the steel of his sword winking in the morning sun as he raised it between strokes. The second and third ranks thundered through behind him, slaying the now disorganized Eika who had received the first charge. Liath followed Lavastine and his guard and, as his charge slowed, she sheathed her sword and drew her bow. Few of the horsemen fell at first, but as their charge slowed, the Eika began to mass around any horseman who had become separated from his companions in the press, and these poor souls were dragged off their mounts to disappear into the claws of the howling Eika.

Lord Wichman forged ahead, having learned this lesson from the Eika. Small pockets of his men, under the banner of Saony, pressed on ever forward until they came around the east side of the hill. Lady Amalia and her standard bearer had also pushed on deep into the Eika forces, but as the troops from Fesse ground to a halt against stiff resistance, she and her standard pressed on until they struggled alone, an island amidst a sea of Eika.

There, Liath saw them, the red eagle banner of Fesse with a small knot of soldiers surrounding Lady Amalia, all striking furiously around themselves as, one by one, their horses staggered and collapsed or they themselves were dragged from their mounts. Her black horse raised and kicked at Eika and dog alike, Lady Amalia seated firmly on its back. She had lost both lance and shield and now cut so fiercely to either side with her sword that her attack itself was her shield.

The red eagle banner faltered and crumpled, drowned by the flood, and a great roar of triumph rose from the Eika host. Beyond, the gold lion of Saony was never still as Wichman and his men broke through the small openings between the Eika bands, slaying as they rode, and then turned and charged again into their midst to rescue the red eagle.

Lavastine had brought his riders through and now they regrouped. Behind them, Lord Dedi, in a black tabard and beneath the standard of the raven tower, led a charge through the ranks of those Eika who struggled to form back up, faltering as the weight of the horses drove them again into disorder.

Lacking armor, Liath stayed out of the thick of the fight. A few Eika charged her, perhaps thinking an archer easy prey, but all fell pierced through the chest.

To the east Gent sat silent. Its gates stood closed, shut tight, and she felt from within the watchful eye, the gloating trimphant heart, of Bloodheart. The Eika standards that bobbed upon the field were not his; he did not walk this bloody ground. She knew it. He waited, and watched through his magic, while his Eika fought for him. What need had he to test his strength on the field? He had already killed Prince Sanglant, the best among them. These were but nuisances, rats to smash beneath his heel while he waited for his real prey to arrive: the king.

A movement flashed to her right. She shook off these disheartening thoughts and quickly nocked, drew, and shot a charging Eika. Was this more of his magic, to dishearten his foes as they felt him gloating over his imminent triumph? Wasn't that all illusion was, the power to project your own will upon others, to make them see what you wished them to see?

Upon the hill the host of Eika massed thickest. She saw no trace of Alain or his guard except the infantry standard which still commanded the height of the hill. Ai, Lord! Eika swarmed the ramparts. The cavalry had not broken the back of the Eika charge, only stemmed it in places. Even as Lavastine gave the signal to charge back through, she

knew the impetus of their attack had gone, that no help
could be given to those trapped on the hill.

The charge lumbered forward, gained speed, and Liath
hunkered down as they thundered through the back ranks.
Ahead, a countercharge by Lord Dedi had cleared an opening, and for this opening Lavastine rode with his cousin at
his side and his men hard behind him.

The banner of Fesse had vanished beneath the churning
sea of Eika. Beyond, the gold lion of Saony regrouped and
charged again only to withdraw swiftly, regroup and change
position, and charge again, slowly working ever eastward
until the banner stood between the Eika and the city.

The standard of Lavas together with Lord Geoffrey and
Liath and most of the men finally reached the open ground,
but as Liath turned to look behind she gasped. Lavastine,
perhaps unwilling, perhaps trapped by the press, remained
behind with a half dozen of his men, striking wildly about
himself. Lord Geoffrey called out to him, but his voice
made no more sound amidst the tumult than the pouring
of water from a cup against the booming reverberation of
a waterfall.

An Eika dog charged under Lavastine's mount, ripping
at its underbelly, and the horse leaped into the air only to
be struck by three spears in its chest. Lavastine sank beneath the waves.

Without hesitation Geoffrey and his men charged headlong into the Eika, their onslaught so irresistible that the
outermost rank of Eika were trampled beneath them. The
Eika surrounding Lavastine, intent on their prey, went
down under a furious wave of cuts and jabs.

Liath stared with an arrow loose in her hand as Geoffrey
caught his cousin up behind him and rode back to safety.
Lavastine's helmet bore two deep dents. Lavastine slid off
the back of the horse, struggled with his helm, then yanked
it from his head and threw it with disgust to the ground.
He coughed, sucking in air. On the left side of his face,
where his mail coif covered his cheek, rivulets of blood ran
and the metal rings had crushed into his skin from the heat
of a blow.

A soldier brought a riderless mount, and the count
swung on.

Lord Dedi, already regrouped, rode up. "Count Lavastine! Lord have mercy, I thought they had you."

Two troops of Eika formed into units under their dreadful banners and set out at a trot after the retreating horsemen.

Lavastine's gaze swept the field. "Where is Bloodheart?" he demanded. Anger flared in his expression, then damped down to furious concentration as he surveyed the chaos beyond. Of the cavalry, only the two groups with him now and the distant standard of Saony still rode. "Ai, Lord," he breathed. "Does my banner yet fly upon the hill?"

All of them, Liath, Lord Geoffrey, Lord Dedi, the men surrounding them, and last of all Lavastine, wiping blood from his eyes, turned. High up on the height of the hill, the banner pole above his pavilion snapped at that moment and fell amid an Eika assault.

Lord Geoffrey leaned forward. "Cousin, the day belongs to Bloodheart. Let us gather our forces and retreat to join with Henry. We can prevent a rout of the men who yet remain on the hill and screen their westward retreat if we move in on the western side."

"Where is Bloodheart?" demanded Lavastine again, and he looked at Liath.

She pointed to Gent.

"That the day is lost is an illusion," he said hoarsely. "An illusion cast by Bloodheart, who is an enchanter." Blood streamed from his head, matting his hair, and one of his hands was streaked with blood trickling from a wound on his arm. "We must have faith."

"Faith!" Geoffrey cried. "Prudence would have served us better! If only we had waited for the king at Steleshame!"

"For how long? With what provisions? Our supplies run low, and this land is exhausted by war and neglect. Nay, Geoffrey, I took the course that seemed wisest to me then. Now we must take the only course open to us. We must strike from behind or all is lost, including that which is most precious to me." He glanced again at the hill, where the fighting ran thick and the standard was lost, then deliberately away as if to shut it out of his thoughts. Only by that small gesture could Liath see how much his son meant to him. Lord Geoffrey flinched back as at a rebuke.

"Lord Dedi," continued Lavastine. His voice had the

brisk confidence of a man without a care in the world—and no time to waste. "Take your men and ride 'round to join with Saony. Do not allow the Eika to return to the gates of Gent. Geoffrey, take half the men of Lavas, the standard, and those of Fesse that you can muster and join Lord Dedi. The rest, with me." His gaze, taut, like a bowstring strung tight, met Liath's. "Eagle, how long must they keep the Eika at bay for us to take the gates from within?"

She glanced at the sky, judging the height of the sun. "To midday, at least."

"So be it. Watch for us at the gates. If we do not appear, then save those you can and join with Henry. God be with you."

The sound of the riders shifting to their new order rushed around her like the flow of the river that night on the Veser.

"Eagle," said Lavastine. Blood mottled his face and hair. Bruises stood out on the sharp plane of his cheek. Behind, the pound of the drums throbbed over the field while the clash of arms and the wail and shout of men and Eika alike rose like an unholy, intangible wraith off the battleground. The count lifted a hand to ready his troops, those splitting off with him, but he did not take his gaze from Liath. "Lead on, Eagle. To your sight we now entrust our victory."

3

SOON after midday a message eddied down through the column that was Henry's army, and in its trail ran an audible buzz of excitement and fear.

"Hai! Hai!" shouted the messenger, none other than Henry's favored Eagle, Hathui, as she pulled up her mount beside the wagon that held the clerical paraphernalia. She had a strong voice that carried easily over the train of wagons now shuddering to a halt as their drivers slowed oxen and horses and bent to listen. Rosvita's servingman stopped walking and set a hand to the nose of the mule she rode. The other clerics, mounted on donkeys or walking beside her, also came to a halt.

"Word has come from an outrider that battle has been joined outside Gent. The train is to travel on as far as it can before dusk while the army marches ahead."

"Eagle!" Rosvita caught her attention before she could ride on. "How far are we from Gent?"

The Eagle's sharp gaze measured the cleric, and then suddenly the marchland woman grinned grimly. "Too far, I fear. The scout who rode in had taken a horse from her comrade, so that she could switch from one to the other and make better time. Even so, both horses foundered when she reached us. The battle was joined about the hour of Terce, she guesses, and it has taken her since then—with two horses—to reach us." The Eagle glanced reflexively up at the sky. Rosvita squinted, wincing at the high glare of the sun. Sext had passed, though they had not halted to sing the proper psalms. "Over three hours ago," she murmured; and the daylight hours in summer were long.

"I wielded a wicked staff when I was a girl!" said Sister Amabilia suddenly. She twirled her walking stick in her hands quite convincingly for a woman who had spent the last ten years as a studious cleric.

"Then it's well you'll remain behind with the train," said the Eagle, already looking ahead, trying to sight the reserve that marched behind the halted wagons. "If by some evil chance the Eika escape our net and swing wide to attack those of you left behind the main army, the infant Hippolyte will need stout defenders. I must go, Sister." She nodded to Rosvita and rode on.

All was in an uproar as drivers, servants, and guard talked at once. But eventually the line got going again. Soon the Eagle came thundering back toward the head of the line. After her rode Villam and the cavalry reserve. He paused as he came alongside Rosvita, and once again her servant stilled her mule so that she could speak with the margrave.

"My infantry, about one hundred men, I leave behind to guard you. Pull your wagons into a circle if you haven't reached Gent by dusk. Then move on in the morning. Under no account keep traveling in disorder. Princess Hippolyte will be placed under your care."

"Go with God, Lord Villam," said Rosvita, making the sign of the Unities to bless him and his soldiers. "May we see victory before the sun sets."

"May we get there before the sun sets," muttered Villam. He signed to his captain who called out the order to advance. Soon Villam and his cavalry, too, vanished into the forest ahead as the wagons trundled on. The reserve infantry jogged up and their captain deployed them around the wagon train much as Rosvita imagined stock-drovers might surround a large herd of cattle in the wild lands, protecting them from wolves.

Soon the solitude grew eerie and disturbing. In two days of travel beyond Steleshame, she had stopped hearing the distant sounds of the host ahead and the reserve behind. Now, when she could no longer hear the distant sounds of their passage before and behind, she noticed their lack.

"Ho!" A shout carried from the forward scouts. "Party ahead!"

An anxious group of servants waited for them alongside the track. By this means Rosvita could see how far ahead Duchess Liutgard and Princess Sapientia had pushed their groups even in the course of the regular march. The men and women clustered here greeted them with relief and explained that they consisted of those noncombatants who had for one reason or another ridden ahead with the main army. Most importantly, they included Sapientia's personal servants with her traveling pavilion and her baby, the precious child whose existence conferred on Sapientia the right to rule after Henry.

Father Hugh was not among them.

Rosvita found one of his servingmen at once, a monk called Brother Simplicus who had come with him from Firsebarg Abbey. He leaned against a tree a bit away from the others and combed a hand nervously through his thinning hair. A beautifully carved chest rested on the ground at his feet with a stone wedged under one corner so he could grip one side easily when it came time to pick it up.

"Brother," she called, indicating that he should come over to her. He started, surprised at her notice, and hefted the chest. It took some effort for him to lumber over to her; not a big man, he had also the rabbity eyes of a man made nervous by small worries.

"Where is Father Hugh?" she asked kindly.

With a grunt he set down the chest again, grimacing as he tipped it up on one foot. "He rode out with the army." His nose was running. He glanced around, then wiped it on his sleeve and twitched nervously under her gaze. "I begged him not to, good Sister. I am well aware that a man of the church ought to walk in peace and . . ." Here he faltered, evidently coming to the conclusion that she did not mean to rebuke him for his failure to keep his noble superior from doing what the man had clearly already determined to do. "B-but he armed himself in mail and helm and with sword strapped over his back rode out beside the princess."

"No doubt Father Hugh has training at arms," she said, meaning to comfort him. With some difficulty she kept her gaze off the chest. "Even in battle his presence may provide ballast for the princess, should she need counsel. Many a good churchman or woman has fought when desperate need arose." But her thoughts were not on battle, not right now. For some odd reason Sister Amabilia's comment, made months ago, popped into her head: "*A bird's feathers may change in color, but it's the same duck inside!*"

And she smiled. "Brother Simplicus, bide with us as we travel. Set your chest in the wagon so that you may walk more lightly. It looks to be a heavy burden."

Ah, he was tempted. She recognized the look. He glanced at the chest and winced as it shifted more heavily onto his foot, the other end pressing deeply into the loamy ground. First he ran a hand through his thin hair, then scratched at his shaven chin nervously as he swept the woods with a wary gaze, and finally toyed with the two thin gold chains at his neck.

"I wonder," commented Rosvita casually, "if those trees conceal Eika scouts. Alas, I fear they might spring out from the woods upon us at any moment."

He started, almost comical in his fear; not, she chided herself, that he didn't have good reason to feel afraid. "Nay, I dare not, Sister," he said at last. "Father Hugh charged me not to let it out of my grasp."

"Well, then," she said, and signaled to the captain. The train lurched forward.

But of course he tired after a while. He didn't look to be a strong man, pampered perhaps by the light service set on him as Hugh's personal servingman. Finally, as he staggered along with his eyes darting from one side to the other and his face blazoned with an understandable fear that if he lagged, he might simply be left behind to suffer a terrible death at the hands of Eika or bandits or such creatures as lurk in the woods at night, she coaxed him to set the chest into the wagon. There he walked close beside with one hand always clutching the rim, sometimes to test that the chest had not vanished, sometimes to rest his weight and gain some respite as he puffed along. She did not offer to let him ride in the wagon or on one of the ponies, although there were a few ponies to spare for riding.

On they went, at a steady pace, but the track was neglected and narrow and, after all, wagons cannot move as quickly as soldiers and horses.

Dusk came, and the captain found a decent clearing. He supervised the wagons as the drivers brought them into a circle, making a rough fortress of them. The livestock were driven inside and in these cramped quarters rank with the smell of ox and horse manure and crowded with drivers and grooms and servants terrified at being left this far behind and yet relieved at being in a relative vale of peace, they set up a spartan camp. Rosvita led the clerics in Vespers.

Princess Sapientia's servants worked efficiently and quickly to set up her pavilion. In this shelter they installed the baby. In the brief interlude between Vespers and Compline, Rosvita went in to pay her respects.

Little Hippolyte rested in the arms of her wet nurse with perfect equanimity. She had a bright gaze for such a young baby, dark hair like her mother, and eyes as blue as her father's. She had a happy gurgle compounded half of fat contentment and half of spit-up. In particular, she liked to grasp things: fingers, jewelry, rolls of cloth, the hafts of spoons and, once, that of a knife—quickly taken away but not before she could wave it lustily about while her wet nurse squealed, her servingwomen crowed with laughter, and Rosvita finally and gently pried the dangerous knife from her chubby little fingers.

"Aye, she'll fight off the Eika for us!" chuckled the servants.

"Let us pray for her safety," said Rosvita sternly, which made them frown and grow serious. They were glad enough to kneel with her as she sang a brief Compline service over the baby to give it the protection of God's blessing for the night.

Then she excused herself and retired to find that her own orders had been carried out and her small traveling tent had been erected. A servant had lit a lantern and hung it from the central pole where its light cast distorted shadows over the cloth walls and the carpet pressed down over the meadow grass. Sister Amabilia had already lain down on her pallet and was now snoring softly. The other clerics, sitting outside the tent reserved for the men among their number, sat or stood around the wagon while they chatted softly—and not without an edge of nervousness in their voices.

Rosvita made her way to the healers and begged an infusion of one of the herbwomen, something to calm nerves and bring sleep. It took only a few words to coax Brother Simplicus into drinking it, and there was even some left over for Brother Fortunatus. She regretted the deception of Brother Fortunatus but, unlike Amabilia and Constantine, he was not a sound sleeper.

She returned to her tent and knelt before her pallet for a long time while she prayed to God to forgive her for what she was about to do.

When at last she emerged from the tent, the camp lay as quiet as any camp could be around her and the bright moon rode high above in the night sky.

Brother Simplicus had chosen to sleep outside next to the wagon, lying on his mantle on the ground. It was a warm night and pleasant. Gingerly she knelt beside him and teased out his two necklaces: One was a fine silver Circle of Unity, the other a tiny cloth pouch tied with a sprig of elder and smelling of licorice and a spice whose fragrance bit at Rosvita's nose but whose name did not come to mind. Why would a monk in the Daisanite church be wearing a heathen amulet? She tucked both objects back under his robe.

There was no key. Hugh had kept the key himself.

The chest was indeed heavy, but Rosvita was a robust woman still even if her back was no longer as supple and strong as it once had been. She lugged it inside her tent and half-dropped it down on her pallet; the thick batting absorbed the thunk of a heavy weight hitting the ground.

She glanced behind her. Sister Amabilia snored on. Then she tested the haft. It was locked, of course, but she had expected that.

Under the light of the lantern she wedged her knife between haft and lock. It didn't budge. With a grimace, she examined the keyhole. A sprig of juniper had been thrust into it, like a key. She scrabbled at it with her fingers, getting a grip on the slick needles, and pulled it out. Its touch stung her fingers and she dropped it with a soft curse and touched her smarting fingers to her lips, licking them until the pain subsided.

She undid the brooch from her cloak and probed into the lock with the pin. She was patient and at last found the right point to put pressure on. It unlocked with a soft *pop*. At once she glanced back, but Amabilia slept on, not even stirring. Rosvita lifted the lid.

The book.

Nested in a cowl of undyed linen, it lay on top of the rest of the chest's contents: a man's fine embroidered tunic and a woman's pale gold silk overdress—a curious item for a churchman to carry with him—as well as two other books.

But she did not have time to puzzle out their titles in the dim light afforded her by the lantern. At this moment, in this place, she could not afford to be curious. She lifted the book out and turned it so the lettering on the spine glinted in the lantern light: *The Book of Secrets*.

Amabilia snorted and shifted in her sleep. Rosvita jerked back, startled. With a grimace, she wrapped the book in the linen cloth and thrust it under her pallet, then closed the chest and slipped a glove over her hand before she picked up the sprig of juniper and crammed it back into the keyhole.

Was it magic, hastily performed? She knew something of magic and of herbs but not enough to know if Father Hugh employed their power. God have mercy if he had.

Then she chastised herself for thinking such a thing of a good churchman like Hugh. He had proved himself, if not chaste, then at least a good adviser. He was learned and well-spoken.

And he had stolen a *Book of Secrets*.

"No better a soul than mine," she murmured. She braced herself, legs bent, and grunted slightly as she picked up the chest and staggered outside. For some reason it seemed heavier now.

She replaced it in the wagon, brushed her hand over lock and wood to make sure there were no obvious signs of entry—such as Brother Simplicus might think to look for—and then retreated back to her tent.

Of guards she saw none, but they would be set out along the perimeter. The camp lay silent, brushed by the noises that attend any forest at night: the sigh of wind through the trees, the chirping of crickets, the eerie hoot of an owl.

The moon alone witnessed her sin.

When Rosvita reentered the tent, Sister Amabilia blinked up at her and rubbed bleary eyes as if to clear them. "What are you about, Sister?"

"I am merely restless," said Rosvita. "And with a full bladder now emptied. Go back to sleep. We'll need our strength tomorrow."

Amabilia yawned, groped to find her walking staff laid

on the ground beside her, and then, reassured by its presence, she went back to sleep.

Merely restless. Merely a liar.

Merely a thief.

She had spent more than half her life in the church and served faithfully and well, only to find herself now shaking in the shadow of a lantern, in a tent in the wilds of a forest night. Was it only her imagination or could she hear the howls of Eika and the screams of dying men on the wind that fluttered the tent flaps and twined round the tent poles?

"Sister Amabilia?" she whispered; but there was no reply.

She eased the book from under the pallet and opened it on the blanket, just where the light streamed with its honey glow. It was hard to see, especially with eyes no longer young and sharp as they once had been, but with her hands, leafing through the book, she discovered at once that the binding contained not one book but three, bound together. The third and last book was written in the infidel way, on paper, and in the language of the Jinna—which she could not read. The second book, bound into the heart of the volume, was of such brittle papyrus that she hesitated to touch it for fear it would crumble under her fingers. It, too, was composed in a language she could not read, but in this case she did not even recognize the *letters*. "Hide this" was written in Arethousan at the top of the first page of the middle manuscript, and there seemed to be other glosses, also in Arethousan, but the ink was unreadable in this light.

She turned back to the very first page of the first book, a good quality parchment leaf—and written in Dariyan, she noted even before she noted the substance of the words or the strange handwriting. Whoever had written this had been church-educated, certainly, for the lettering paraded down the page with a trace of Aostan formalism. But the "q"s curled strangely, and the "s"s had a Salian bent, while the "t"s and "th"s had the stiff, strong backs of a cleric trained in a Wendish institution. With most calligraphy she could read in the script where the scribe had gotten her training; this person wrote in such a hodgepodge of styles that she—or he—might have come from anywhere, or everywhere.

It was very strange.

But nothing like as strange, and disturbing, as the words themselves.

With mounting horror, she mouthed the first sentence.

"Through the art of the mathematici we read the alignment of the heavens and draw down the power of the ever-moving spheres to work our will on the earth. I will now set down everything I know of this art. Beware, you who read this, lest you become trapped as I have in the snares of those who seek to use me for their own ends. Beware the Seven Sleepers."

A twig snapped outside and she started violently, slapping the book shut and shoving it under the blanket. God have mercy. She trembled like a sinner afflicted through God's just judgment with a palsy.

The art of the mathematici.

The most forbidden of sorceries.

4

THEY left the horses with a half dozen of Captain
Ulric's men, the light cavalry from Autun. A few of the
light cavalry had torches among their equipment; Lavastine
ordered other branches collected from the brush, enough
that each man carried two stout sticks.

Liath stepped into the cave mouth and took hold of a
torch. There was no longer time to agonize over the gift
she held within her, that Da had protected her against.
Alain's life—if he even still lived—hung in the balance.

Wood burns. The torch flared to life, flames licking and
smoking with a resiny smell. Lavastine had come in behind
her, and now she turned to see him staring at her.

"It's a trick," she said quickly. "An Eagle's trick."

"Not one I have heard tell of before now," he replied,
but he merely called to the forty soldiers who followed him,
mostly light cavalry pulled off the field, and every fourth
man lit torch or stick from the one she carried.

She set foot on the stairs. Lavastine followed directly
behind her, then some of his men and, last, young Erkanwulf and the other Autun soldiers. Captain Ulric brought
up the rear. With each step downward the light of day
faded, dimmed, grayed into oblivion. The rough stone
gripped her boots though now and again a trickle of water
slipped under her feet, welling up from some untraceable
crack of moisture dripping through a seam in the rock. She
kept the torch thrust forward to see the steps below her.
They were so evenly spaced that she had to stop herself
from trotting down them, from gaining too much speed. Ai,
Lady, was Alain alive yet on the hill or were he and his
troops destroyed by the fury of the Eika assault? Once she
heard a man stumble and cry out behind her, and she
slowed down, waiting, as did Lavastine, who matched her
step for step. Tension coiled on him like a second skin, and
he hissed between his teeth with impatience but said nothing as the man behind caught up and they descended again.

But after a hundred or more of such evenly placed steps even the most cautious man became bolder and their pace increased as they descended down and ever down.

They came to the base of the stairs, and the tunnel forged forward into a blackness so profound that it seemed alive. She walked out far enough to give them room to assemble behind her, forming up into twos. There was some jostling and whispering, and after a moment Erkanwulf appeared, wan in the light of her torch.

"I've been given leave to walk scout beside you," he said, "since it's well known I have keen eyesight."

"I thank you."

"Ai, Lord, but I can't see a thing in front of us! Are you sure there're no ditches or abysses to swallow us up?"

"There were none before. But that's not to say none could have opened up since."

He snorted. "I thank *you,* Eagle, for setting my heart at peace."

"Forward," said Lavastine behind her. "Let our pace be swift. Keep some distance between you—but not too much—so if we are attacked, we are not caught up the one upon the other."

She went cautiously at first, but the way lay silent and pitch-black before her, a weight of still air stirred and lightened by their passing but by no other breath of life. All lay around her in the flickering gaze of the torches as she recalled it: the smooth walls, the beaten earth floor as though thousands had passed this way in some long ago time, the ceiling a hand's reach above. Now and again she heard the scrape of a metal spear point on the rock, and a low curse from its bearer, shifting it down. Her bow and quiver rode easily on her back. She held the torch in her left hand and her good friend Lucien's sword in her right. The torch burned without flagging, as did all the others. Erkanwulf walked on her left so the torch illuminated the way evenly between them. But after a while she began to forge ahead of him, sure of her path. Behind her, Lavastine strode swiftly, and his troops kept up by sheer force of his will if nothing else.

"Ai, Lord," whispered Erkanwulf. "It's sorely dark down here, Eagle. What if all that rock caves in on us?"

But she smelled only the metallic tang of earth, a distant

whiff of the forge, and the dank moisture of a place long
hidden from the sun. "Why should it fall now? If it's lain
here for so long?"

"The torches burn so strongly," added Erkanwulf. "It's
uncanny, it is."

"Hush," said Lavastine from behind, although the tramp
of so many armed men through the tunnel could not be
hidden—or at least not by any gift she possessed.

They walked steadily and, like the torches, without flagging. She realized now that the journey out of Gent had
taken so long for the most part because they had gone so
slowly, and because the refugees had been mostly frightened children or the weak and the wounded. With forty
robust soldiers behind her, she could lead at a brisk pace.

"What's there?" muttered Erkanwulf even as she realized that in the far distance ahead she could see a dull
lightening cast of fire. And as they neared she saw that,
indeed, it was fire: A wall of it stretched from floor to
ceiling, wall to wall, leaping and burning in the tunnel with
all the frenzy of a gleeful pack of fire daimones at their
dance.

"Defended!" said Lavastine angrily.

Liath stared. Defended. But why, then, had the Eika not
used the tunnel as a way to ambush Lavastine's army when
it first arrived?

"Stay back," she said to Erkanwulf. She strode forward
with her torch outthrust to make a barrier, but as she
neared the wall of flame, it faded in her sight to become a
whisper, a haze, a memory of fire, nothing more.

"Eagle!" She felt Erkanwulf dart forward to grab at her
as she stepped into the blaze. He screamed. She stopped
and turned round to order him back only to see the look
on their faces, as much as she could see expressions in the
torchlight. Only Lavastine watched impassively. Erkanwulf
staggered back, a hand thrown up to shield his face from
the heat. The rest murmured or cried out, or covered their
eyes to hide them from the horrible sight of a young
woman burned alive.

"It's an illusion," she said.

Erkanwulf fell to his knees, gasping and coughing.

Lavastine stepped up beside him. What courage it took
him to do so she could not imagine. Would she do the

same, if she had only another's word to go by? Around her, the ghost fire shimmered and leaped, burning rock no less than air.

"If Bloodheart has guarded this tunnel with illusion," asked the count, "doesn't that mean he must know of it?"

"Perhaps. But then why wouldn't he have used it for an ambush? Nay, Count Lavastine, I think there is fire above, on the plain, and his illusion is all of one seam. Have you ever seen an orrery? A model of the heavenly spheres?"

"Go on," said Lavastine curtly.

"As above, so below. His illusion may be one seamless part, and thus exists below the ground as well as above it. It's possible that these illusions would be seen by anyone attempting to approach the city, that Bloodheart cast them without knowing they would extend here, too."

"Or perhaps his soldiers wait for us, beyond."

In answer, she stepped through. A man shrieked, was brusquely ordered to be silent. Beyond the wall of fire lay the silent tunnel, dark and quiet. She turned and could not see the fire from this direction at all, only a misty haze and the men waiting on the other side.

"Nothing," she said. "Unless Bloodheart ordered his men to wait for us on the stairs. It would be very hard to fight up those stairs and win."

"Making it a better place to set an ambush, then," said Lavastine. "But what choice do we have but to go forward?" He nudged poor frightened Erkanwulf with the toe of a boot. "Come. She has the true sight. We must trust in her."

"We must trust in St. Kristine," she said suddenly, "for without her intercession we would never have found the tunnel. The heat will not burn you."

"I can't go through," sobbed Erkanwulf, still with a hand flung up to protect his eyes.

"Nay, boy!" said Ulric from the back of the group. "Think of Lord Wichman and his stories. They saw illusions at Steleshame, but that was all they were."

"I will lead." Lavastine gripped his sword more tightly and walked forward into the fire.

Even so, Liath felt him trembling slightly as he halted beside her. One by one, with increasing confidence, his troops came along after. Only a few shut their eyes as they passed through the illusion.

They went on.

After a time, she stumbled on a bottomless abyss, too wide across to jump. But even as she stared, the gulf of air solidified into the rock floor, littered with pebbles and scored by old footprints unstirred for months by the passage of wind or any other traffic, even the tiny creatures of the dark, over them.

This time, when she moved forward across the gaping abyss, Lavastine walked right beside her—though when he took the first step out over the yawning chasm, she noticed that he shut his eyes.

She called back over her shoulder. "Shut your eyes! Shut your eyes and walk forward. Your feet will not lie to you."

In this way the soldiers followed, shuffling behind until the chasm lay behind them. With mounting confidence they went on. The torches burned steadily without consuming themselves.

"Are you a mage?" asked Lavastine softly, beside her. "Why do you possess this power to see through illusion? Where comes it from?"

How can I use it to my advantage? He did not say the last words aloud, but she heard such calculation in his tone.

"My father laid a—a mage's working on me," she said, hoping that she spoke the truth nearly enough that God would forgive her for lying.

Lavastine made no reply. She could not even imagine what he was thinking; she understood him less than any person she had ever met.

They went on, pressing into the darkness that would lead them to the crypt—and to the Eika. And to Bloodheart.

Liath led them and did not look back.

5

PRESSED back and back, Alain held his place in the second rank of shields, keeping low so that the spearmen behind him could thrust over him. He braced hard with his feet to shore up those in the front rank who bore the brunt of the Eika assault. His strength was all he had, for surely it must be obvious to all by now that he could not fight.

The Eika sagged back, and in the brief lull, he surveyed the hill. The west and south lines still held at the wall, but to the east, facing Gent, and at the north gate where Alain had thrown in his reserves, the army had fallen back and now presented a wall of flesh and steel instead of earthen ramparts to face the Eika stone. Alain hoped that someone would take his place in the ranks so he could gain a vantage point to observe the field below and the progress of his father, but those with shields were already at the fore and none stepped up to relieve him.

The Eika gathered their strength. They, too, presented a line of shields, rounds painted with cunning blue or yellow serpents twined into interwoven spirals. Twenty paces separated the two lines. Aside from an occasional arrow or thrown stone, or the Eika stooping to stab some poor wounded man left behind in the retreat, or the dogs feeding hideously on corpses, the Eika remained still.

Lord have mercy. One black hound sprawled in an awkward heap and, even as he stared in horror, dogs leaped upon it to savage its corpse. Which one it was he did not know. He felt the press of the other hounds around him, but he dared not take his eyes off the enemy to count their number. Eika drummers had moved up to the second rank of their line and they beat a rhythm like a slow heartbeat. It quickened, and the Eika became restless, just as hounds would, scenting their prey but still held on a tight leash. The beating of the drums boomed louder and faster and then, like thunder, it broke with deafening claps as the Eika charged.

The soldiers around Alain braced themselves with wide stances. Spearmen shouldered up beside Alain, wedging spears in between the foremost shields, a line of points to impale the charging Eika on their own momentum.

The Eika hit. Alain staggered, caught himself, and sank back. He reinforced his shield with the pommel of his sword, but even so he, with the others, gave ground at a slow grind. Round Eika shields pressed into the fray, first overlapping him to his left, then to his right. He struggled as he caught an Eika shield with the corner of his own. If he could only draw the strength of the earth up through his legs . . . a hound leaned against him, adding its strength, but despite everything, his boots skidded on the dirt as he was forced back. The hound scrabbled and whined and retreated.

Over his head axes and spears did their work, but the huge shields of the Eika served them well. The line gave back, back toward the center of camp, back until the banner of black hounds on silver, placed near the top of the hill, vanished in the press.

Now the Eika overran the edge of camp and strangely this gave them some respite, since a number of the Eika would simply stop and pull back from the fighting to loot through chest and bag.

The east and north lines met and melded, and out of the din Alain suddenly heard the captain's voice as he shouted orders. The captain carried the standard, now that the banner was lost, and he rallied the troops with it by raising it high wherever the fighting was fiercest and the cause seemed lost.

"Hold the line!" Alain cried, but only those men right round him could hear, and surely they were already conducting themselves as best they could to keep their lord alive.

At last the standard signaled the captain's approach. "Lord Alain!" he cried. "Let him back, let him back! Now close it up, lads. Form up to the right—" As Alain staggered out of the press into the dusty reserve ground—what little remained—the captain turned on him. "I lost track of you! Ai, Lord, what your father the count would say to me—"

"Where's my father?" Alain shouted.

The captain waved vaguely to the east. "Out there. I saw Lord Wichman's banner, but a host of Eika ran between them and the hill and the sun shines so as to hide the land. We must trust to our swords and to the Lady."

From this vantage, Alain looked out over the plain. Eika swarmed like flies across the land. Off to the right a small band of horsemen carrying the raven tower of Autun formed up—or made ready to retreat. Of Lord Wichman and the gold lion of Saony, of the Lavas banner, he saw no sign.

An unearthly dome of fire concealed Gent, as bright now as the sun that rode high above them. Already it had passed midday while they struggled on the hill, and the sun had begun its steady descent toward the western horizon. But a long afternoon and an endless high summer twilight stretched before them.

He whistled and even over the din of battle the hounds heard him and came to huddle at his feet: Sorrow and Rage, both cut and bleeding but whole, thumped their tails into his legs; Fear strained forward, barking wildly while blood streamed from a cut on his hindquarters; Bliss had an ugly gash on his back and one of his ears had been ripped to shreds; Ardent limped, old Terror's jaw dripped with the greenish-tinted blood that belonged to the Eika. Oddly, Steadfast had not a mark on her. But Good Cheer was missing. And Graymane was gone.

There was no time to mourn.

He gave them all a quick pat, and they licked him vigorously. Who was reassuring whom? As he straightened, he tried to make sense of the field.

The east and north lines were gone and those ramparts given up to the Eika advance. For the moment only flurries of fighting raged to the south and west, where the Eika had had little luck up to now. Here, down off the top of the hill, Alain and his company waited and watched as Eika looted Lavastine's camp. Where the night before the commanders had discussed strategy, the enemy now reveled. Alain could pick out individuals, Eika somewhat larger than the rest and clad in glittering gold and silver mail girdles that draped from hip to knee, flashing and glinting in the sunlight. Each of these—and there were not many—walked through the carnage with an easy lilting step. Each had a standard beside him, a grotesque pole festooned with feathers and bones and skins and other unknowable things. These were princelings like Fifth Son: Bloodheart's many sons.

They howled and the slow roll of the drums quickened. The Eika gave up their looting, the dogs were kicked and slapped into obedience, and they formed up again.

With a howl, they attacked. A huge Eika princeling hefted his obsidian-edged club and sprang forward at their head. Lavastine's captain bolted forward to brace the line for the impact, but it was no use. The line of men split asunder as two shieldmen were bowled over by the massive Eika. The captain thrust with the banner pole and stuck the Eika princeling in the brow, the point lodging in the scaly forehead. The creature flailed and smashed its club into the banner pole, breaking it, then grasped the splintered end, tugged, and heaved the captain bodily forward and struck him to the ground. With the point of the pole still thrust out from its forehead and the Lavas banner drapped over its shoulders like a cloak, the Eika plunged on, roaring.

Men screamed and retreated and the line dissolved into chaos. But Alain stepped up to meet him with a blow swung with all of his strength. The Eika caught it with his bare hand, the sword's point splitting the skin but doing no more damage than that, and then wrenched Alain forward, and down, and lifted his club for the death blow.

Alain tried to shift his shield, but it was too late. It was too little. More Eika swarmed past toward the crumbling troops. The hounds had vanished into the maelstrom.

I am with you Alain. You have kept your promise to me.

The club arced down, but he was a shadow and she the life that lived within the light. She was there, a thing of effortless and terrible beauty as she wielded the sword that is both war and death.

She rolled and the princeling's killing blow struck earth, spitting clods into the air, into Alain's teeth. She cut to the back of the Eika's leg, hamstringing it, and the Eika fell. It seemed no more than a dance as she rolled up to her feet, and with a second blow, as fast as the lightning strikes to herald the coming of thunder, she beheaded the savage.

With her, Alain retreated, but only to form up the line

around him—around *her*. Where the shields parted, where the line buckled or men's spirits wavered, he had only to go, the shadow to her light, and she would go there as well. In her wake men's spirits lifted, and they fought with renewed ferocity, shouting his name: "Lord Alain! Lord Alain!"

For where she stood, where Alain was, no charge could succeed. But even the Lady of Battles could not succeed against the thousands, the endless onslaught of savage Eika and their ravening dogs.

The Eika surged forward. Drums pounded until he could hear nothing above them, not even the clash of shield and sword, not even the screams of the wounded or the howling of dogs. He could not be everywhere at once, and where he was not, the line gave way.

The Eika came on and on up the hill from all sides, and soon all sides were hard-pressed. The drums boomed. With a sudden shift of rhythm, the force of their reverberation deafened him, and the very hill beneath trembled as the shield wall failed in a dozen places and the battle no longer had order.

It became a melee as men clumped together fighting desperately just to stay alive. Eika flowed in from all sides. Fear clutched at Alain's throat as he realized how few were still afoot—and those who fell had no chance against the dogs.

Even the Lady stilled, staring. The hounds boiled up to him then, yipping. Sorrow took his tattered tabard in his teeth and dragged him westward and in this way, with the Lady at the point and Alain right behind her, they drove westward step by agonizing step down the hill toward the distant shelter of the western forest. Men fell in beside him and behind him, seeking shelter, seeking safety in what numbers they had left to them, a wedge of men thrusting through the Eika onslaught. With each step they struggled as Eika raged forward. They had no choice but to escape to the woods, for their hill and their camp—and the day—was lost.

All was lost.

He could no longer see the plain, only the horde of Eika surrounding them.

At the point of their wedge, the Lady cut a path westward until they were at the west "gate," its wagons smashed and dead bodies littering the gap. The drumbeat increased, and with each beat the determination of the Eika to stop them from retreat grew. There, at the ruined gate, their wedge ground to a halt. The sun beat down with the hammer blow of heat.

With a great breath, like a beast so immense that its voice was that of a thousand and more mouths, the Eika shifted, steadied, and howled until the roar of it drove men to their knees under the merciless bright eye of the sun.

Only the Lady blazed bright in answer. And only Alain could see her as, behind her, he lifted his sword in desperation.

"Hold fast!" he cried. "God is with us!"

But no one could hear him.

6

SHE did not count the stairs, only cursed each clank and rustle and whisper from the men behind her. But no Eika waited for them where the stone steps curved upward and opened into the crypt. She stumbled on a gravestone and fell to one knee as the rest came up behind her, emerging one by one into black silence.

Erkanwulf helped her up.

Each least movement or murmured comment fell heavily, weighted by the dampening earth and magnified by the stillness of the waiting dead.

"Hush," said Lavastine. "Listen."

They listened but heard nothing but their own breathing.

"Now." He did not need to speak loudly. In the dim light afforded by torches, ears became keen of hearing. "We must open the gates of Gent. And we must kill Bloodheart, if we are able. My experience of the Eika tells me that they follow a war chief and will fight like dogs among themselves if that leader is dead."

The tombs lay in dense silence around them. Torchlight made a haze of the air. In the curve of shadow beyond the smoky glow Liath saw a glint of white, recognizable but indistinct.

"Captain Ulric, you will take fifteen men. I will take fifteen men. We must take separate routes for the western gates of Gent. Eagle." She nodded. "These seven men I leave under your command. As the old stories say: Send a mage to kill a mage."

"My lord count—!" she protested.

He lifted a hand to silence her. "It is your job to hunt down and kill Bloodheart."

"Yes, my lord count," she said obediently. At that instant a torchbearer turned and the glow of the torch spread wings and illuminated the far doorway of this vaulted corner.

Bones. Not safely interred in the sanctity of a tomb but scattered like leaves on the forest floor, the bones littered the far vaults of the crypt, all tumbled together. As she moved cautiously into the next chamber, she knew they were the bones of Dragons. The smell of lime stung her nostrils. The Eika knew to cast lime over the remains. Little putrefaction remained because of clay soil and moisture . . . and because it had been over a year since the fall of Gent. Skulls grinned at her; open eyes bled pools of blackness. Ribs showed white under tattered tabards and padded gambesons chewed to pieces by rats. Skeleton fingers clutched at her boots and a thighbone rolled under her so she slipped and almost fell.

"Lord have mercy!" breathed Erkanwulf beside her. "Look! The badge of the King's Dragons!"

Reason enough to kill Bloodheart.

They picked their way through the terrible remains of the king's elite cavalry. At least the Eika, for unfathomable reasons of their own, had dragged them down to decay among the holy dead.

She dared not look too closely for fear she would see the dragon helmet that marked the remains of Sanglant. Her memory of him was so clean, so strong, of his living face watching her in the silence of the crypt, his chin as smooth as a woman's under her fingers; of him standing proud and confident in the midst of the crowd that had threatened to mob the palace; of his last dash into the fight, when all had seemed lost. She could not bear to see his beauty reduced to dust. So she stopped looking at the remains around her except to place her feet with care so that she did not step on too many of them, poor dead souls.

With each step, purpose weighed more heavily on her: She could become the instrument of vengeance for what had been done to him and to his Dragons. It gave her heart as she neared the steps that led up to the cathedral.

When her boots nudged the bottom stair and she peered upward where spiderwebs wreathed the canted wall and glittered like a silvery net of moonlight above her torch, she turned back. "Let me scout ahead," she whispered.

"Your group will file up behind you," said Lavastine. "We dare not be caught here."

"Let me just scout first alone," she said. "Should I be caught, and if they guess where I have come from, then you are on an equal footing. Eika see in the dark no better than a human man—" Although not as well as she did, but she could not say so out loud. "—and you will have a better chance of fending them off . . . and of escape back through the tunnel."

"What of the dogs?" whispered Erkanwulf. "What if they smell us?"

"Then again you are safer to remain here, where the smell of lime and damp will somewhat cover your trail."

"And if they don't know of the tunnel," said Lavastine quietly, "then they would have no reason to look down here. If they discover you, they'd be as likely to look else-where and thus give us time to get out and move for the gates." He nodded curtly. "Go on."

Go on. So coolly he considered her death and resolved that it might benefit him.

But Liath only smiled grimly, gave her torch to Erkan-wulf, and set off up the stairs.

The curve soon took her out of sight of the soldiers wait-ing below, but even the memory of torchlight was enough to light her way. She heard the delicate tread of men com-ing up after her. Soon a thin line of light limned the door that led out onto the nave, but she passed it by and crept on up a narrower set of stone steps that led to the choir.

Here, in a cramped landing, she set her hand on a thick door ring and rested her ear against the rough planks. What she heard from beyond was faint, a teasing melody as light as air. Dust coated the iron ring, slick under her fingers. She gave a nudge with her shoulder. The door cracked open. Daylight blinded her and she had to stand for the count of twenty until her eyes adjusted even to the thin line of light that now edged the stone column around which the stairwell wound. From the nave she heard the sound of flutes.

She tucked her sword against her and eased open the door. The choir walk ran empty, a balcony no wider than an arm outstretched, all the way to the opposite end of the nave. A layer of dust blanketed the floor. Tapestries whose brightly woven stories were muted by dust hung on the walls beneath the huge second tier of windows through which the sun shone, motes of dust everywhere streaming and dancing in the light. Where a few of the tapestries brushed the floor, sagging or half fallen, their bases had been nibbled into ragged ends by rats or mice.

She set a foot forward and eased herself into the quiet walk. A dart of movement startled her, and she froze. But it was only a mouse, bold enough enough to prowl the choir in broad daylight. The sight of it gave her courage. If mice skittered about so freely, then it was not likely anyone lurked up here.

She stepped farther out, hugging the wall, and eased the door closed until it stood with only a crack. Each step left a distinct print behind as she crept forward.

She crouched and made her way along the solid railing. Above, the ceiling vaulted high to span the nave. Flute music echoed below and beside and beyond her. She dared not look at the windows for fear one glimpse of sunlight would ruin her eyes when she needed to look below. Her quiver brushed the rail, and she rose slightly to peer over.

And there, in a shaft of sunlight streaming in through the western windows, sat Bloodheart on his throne.

He played music on flutes crafted of bone, and she shuddered to hear him as the music wafted into the air and twined and curled around as if it were a living thing. And she knew, then: He wove with his flute, wove the very illusions that protected him.

Next to him, almost in his shadow, crouched the skinny Eika priest she remembered. Naked except for a loincloth, he rocked back and forth on his heels in time to the melody. A wooden chest sat tucked against his feet, and one of his clawed hands rested protectively on its painted lid.

And there were dogs, packs of dogs all here and there, panting, lying in heaps, tongues lolling and saliva dripping onto the flagstone floor. Beside the holy altar Bloodheart had let a midden grow, a low mound of garbage, rags and trash and bones and old rusting chains piled up against the most sanctified place in the cathedral. She winced to see the holy Hearth defiled in such a fashion, but no doubt Bloodheart pleased himself by desecrating the blessed Hearth of the Lady.

She knelt, laid her sword down on the dusty walk, and with her heart afire with fear and with an implacable burning determination, she slipped out Seeker of Hearts. In a moment she had an arrow free and loosely nocked to the string.

Light streamed down all around her, the blessed Daisan walking through his seven miracles, each one outlined in glass. Light splintered everywhere, rainbows dancing in the air of the nave, yet if she shifted slightly they would vanish only to reappear if she leaned back. She rose again from her crouch, as silent as the breath of morning—or of fate's unyielding hand.

The memory of the beauty of the cathedral hit her with doubled force. *There* the biscop had led Mass. *There* the congregation had gathered, standing, to sing. *There* Sanglant and his Dragons had knelt, before the altar, that morning in their last brief moments of life before they rode to their deaths.

Voices. She froze, canting her head back to listen. Let Lavastine and his men not come out yet!

Into the cold emptiness of the nave, below, an Eika strode into her line of sight. He wore the distinguishing marks of a princeling, a skirt of mail fashioned of gold and silver links that draped from hips to knees, winking in and out of the light as he walked the floor between shafts of sunlight, and a torso painted with an elaboration of the same swirling cross pattern that graced Bloodheart's chest. Strangely, he wore a wooden Circle of Unity around his neck.

Alain's prince! Could it be?

In her surprise, she must have scuffed her boot on the floor.

The Eika princeling faltered, and for that instant she panicked, not moving and yet with her mind shut like a door, blank and empty. But he only faltered because he stared at the heap of garbage beside the altar, which now stirred, woken by that scuff or by the perfume of her secrecy or by the music of the flutes, to reveal dogs and some kind of ghastly creature, surely not human, heavily chained and clothed in the tattered remains of a tabard marked with a black dragon. Yet it had substance and weight, unlike a daimone; it had unkempt black hair as tangled and ratted as that of a filthy ascetic who has sworn off the trivial clothing of human grooming. It had arms and legs, hands and feet, very humanlike, and a cast of skin made dark by grime. It was a hideous thing, so matted and foul that it might as easily have been a grotesque illusion born out of Bloodheart's vile magic. Or so she hoped. Then it swung round, shoulders bracing as against an attack, and she saw its face.

"God have mercy," she whispered, the sound forced from her by a shock so profound that she forgot everything, everyone, and even her purpose for being here: The Eika chieftain who sat, unwitting, below her, an easy target. "Sanglant."

He uncurled completely from the midden and in that instant with his head flung up like that of a hound tasting a scent on the air, she knew he had heard her.

She knew he recognized her voice.

Lady and Lord have mercy. Trapped. Bloodheart's prisoner for over a year.

He looked more like an animal than a man.

Her throat burned, and she thought she was going to be sick.

She rose.

"No!" he cried, lunging forward to the limit of his chains, lunging toward Bloodheart, or toward the priest, she couldn't tell. The priest grabbed the chest and hopped backward just as Sanglant was brought up short by the chains, jerked back painfully by the force of his lunge. His dogs growled and leaped forward into the nave. *They* were not chained.

Bloodheart lowered his flutes and barked out a command in his harsh language. Several Eika soldiers jogged toward the prince, howling and jeering with their inhuman voices.

She lifted Seeker of Hearts and drew down on Bloodheart, string drawn tight, her eye sighted along the arrow to the swirling cross of paint that marked his chest over his heart.

One shot was all she had.

From behind and below she heard the eruption of shouts and pounding feet, the clang of steel and a man screaming, then the howling of Eika calling to battle.

Lavastine had not waited for her—or perhaps he had heard Sanglant's shout. It no longer mattered.

One shot. She poised, made ready to release, a perfect target, a perfect kill there at his heart—

The bow tugged leftward.

For that instant in which a breath is drawn and released by a person panting under the threat of danger, she resisted.

And then she gave in to it.

"Seeker of Hearts, guide my hand," she murmured. She let it pull her aim as it willed, and she sighted again as the point of the arrow slid away from Bloodheart, past the little wooden chest resting on the priest's knees, and rose slightly to fix on the left center of his wizened, scaly torso.

There.

She loosed the arrow.

The point buried itself in flesh. The priest clapped both hands to his chest and tumbled backward as the wooden chest on his knees spun forward and cracked on the stone floor.

With a great, ear-shattering roar, Bloodheart lurched out of his throne, staggered, and stumbled to his knees. His bone flutes scattered around him. One splintered and broke.

"Priest! Traitor!" He roared again, a cry of pain and fury that echoed and hammered in the nave, resounding and rebounding off the vault. One window cracked and shattered, and shards of glass rained down from on high.

"Nestbrother!" he cried. A greenish fluid trickled from his mouth as he fell forward and crawled, trying to reach the wooden chest—or the old priest, both of which now lay within the limits of the prince's chains. But Sanglant reached them first only to have the old priest stagger to his feet, snap off the haft of the arrow embedded in his chest, and scramble out of reach of prince and enchanter alike. Sanglant kicked the wooden chest out away from Bloodheart's groping hands.

"Nestbrother!" The Eika chieftain's voice was ragged now with a liquid lilt as though blood drowned him in his unmarked chest. Dogs bolted in to nip and bite at him, sensing his weakness, but he slapped them away and jerked up to his feet as bubbles of blood frothed on his chin. "By the bond between us I call on you to avenge me. Let your curse fall on the one—"

He clawed at his throat, staggered forward again while the old priest scuttled backward and made some kind of averting sign with his hand as he spoke words Liath couldn't hear. Dust swirled on the choir floor, caught up in a sudden whirlwind, and a swarm of unseen creatures like stinging gnats spun around her, then sheared away as though wind had blown them off. Flailing blindly, Blood-heart made one last desperate lunge—

Only to drop, dead, at Sanglant's feet.

And there on the westward flank of the hill, as the Eika horde took breath to make their final charge and annihilate the last of Lavastine's infantry, the drums clapped once.

And not again.

XVI
THE UNSEEN
CHAIN

1

"CAPTAIN Ulric, to the gate!" shouted Lavastine above the sudden outbreak of howling and keening that shattered the silence made by Bloodheart's death. At once, the sound of fighting reverberated through the nave as Lavastine and his men bolted out of their hiding place.

She drew another arrow in time to see Lavastine himself cutting frantically, shield raised, as a trio of enraged Eika bore him backward. A soldier fell beside him, struck down. Lavastine was next, battered to his knees by their attack.

Sanglant lunged forward at the sight of the nobleman trapped and struggling. Liath winced, bracing herself for the jerk when he hit the limit of his chains, then gaped.

There were no chains. All but the iron collar rattled to

the ground, lay crumbling there as if they were a hundred years old and turning to dust. Dust they became, sagging in heaps around Bloodheart's corpse.

She nocked the arrow, but Sanglant and a half dozen Eika dogs hit the melee before she could get a shot off. He had nothing, only his hands, to fight with. Without thinking, she swung a leg over the railing, meaning to drop down, to save him—

His attack was as swift and as brutal as that of the Eika dogs. He had laid two Eika out flat and ripped one's throat out with his own teeth while she gaped in horror. An Eika swung hard at him, but a dog leaped between them and took the cut meant for the prince while the rest of the pack swarmed the would-be killer, bearing him down to the flagstones. The other Eika retreated. The dogs gorged on the corpses—three Eika, one human. Lavastine jumped to his feet and he and Sanglant vanished from her line of sight as they ran toward the great doors. She swung her leg back and stood, panting, half in shock, trying to steady herself.

"Eagle!" Erkanwulf called to her from the door. "You must run! We're sore outnumbered, and we're to retreat through the tunnel!"

"Down!" she screamed as she drew—Erkanwulf dropped to his hands and knees—and shot the Eika who loomed behind the lad. The Eika fell with a surprised grunt and tumbled backward down the stairs. She ran, tugged Erkanwulf to his feet, and drew her sword, keeping Seeker of Hearts in her left hand.

"After me," she said. They had to clamber over the dead Eika soldier to get down the curve of the stairs. She did not know what awaited them below, but as they came around the last curve before the door that let onto the nave her nose caught a whiff of it.

Just beyond the open door, Lavastine and his men had formed up. A line of Eika waited beyond among the litter that carpeted the vast nave, but no one moved. They made a broad curve to cut off access to the cathedral doors as well as leaving Lavastine and his men no room to maneuver out in the expanse of the nave itself.

Next to the door the creature that was Sanglant beat back five dogs, cuffing them until they lay down, whining, and bared their throats to him. Blood from their gorging dripped from their muzzles.

The prince stank. There was no kinder way to put it; the reek hit her like a tangible substance, something you could put your hands into. He started back at her appearance in the door. Blood rimed his lips. His clothes, or what remained of them, hung in tatters on him, cloth pressed into mail, stiff with grime; she had seen poor folk and beggars aplenty in her travels but never anyone as wretched as this. It was hard to believe he was a man, still, or to recall that he had ever been one. He was so foul that she had to look away, but even so she caught a glimpse of his expression. Whatever he was, now, he was ashamed of it.

"God have mercy," whispered Erkanwulf, behind her. "What is it?"

"Hush." She slipped out the door.

The dogs growled at her but kept their distance, nipping at Erkanwulf as he dodged past. Sanglant slapped them down but said nothing. Could he even speak?

"We retreat," said Lavastine. "There are a hundred or more of them beyond the door. But Captain Ulric and his group got out ahead of me. We must hope they win through to the gates."

"Bloodheart is dead," said Liath.

Lavastine only nodded curtly. "Make ready to move," he said to his men. Already she noticed three faces missing, but she could not see beyond the Eika line to count them among those who had fallen in the initial skirmish. "Prince Sanglant, you must go first, with the Eagle. We must get you to safety."

The Eika line stirred and parted to reveal the Eika princeling who wore the Circle. In the harsh tongue of the Eika, he barked an order and the line faded back by several steps as the princeling stepped forward into the gap.

Erkanwulf handed Liath another arrow from her quiver and she drew on the princeling, sighting at his heart.

He spoke again, still in the Eika language, and the Eika soldiers began an orderly withdrawal from the cathedral. Liath stared, utterly bewildered.

Slowly, cautiously, Lavastine took one step forward.

"Both of you I have seen in Alain's dreams," said the

princeling in perfect Wendish, pointing with the tip of his spear first at Lavastine and then at Liath.

"Fifth Son!" breathed Lavastine.

"*You* captured me once—but *he* freed me. For that reason, I spare your life now." He set the butt of the spear on the flagstones and canted his head arrogantly, or as at a sudden and compelling thought. Compared to Sanglant, he was a glorious beast, not handsome—for Liath supposed she would never be able to find beauty in their sharp, metal-bright faces—but striking. His eyes had the clarity of obsidian. Gold armbands curled around his arms like snakes. He grinned at them, jewels winking in his teeth, and with each least shifting of his weight the mail girdle he wore made a faint shimmering like distant high bells whispering secrets. "Tell me, Count of Lavas. Did Alain lie to me? King Henry did not come, nor did you intend to wait for him as you told him you meant to."

Lavastine hesitated, but he did, after all, owe the Eika princeling something in return for their lives. "Visions can't lie. I did not tell him everything I intended."

"Ah." Fifth Son whistled and his dogs bounded over to crowd at his heels. They, too, had been feasting on the corpses, perhaps even on Bloodheart. Scraps of clothing stuck to their tongues, and the saliva dripping from their jaws had an ocherous tint. Most of his soldiers had cleared the cathedral, leaving it empty except for the ravaged corpses. "You're a wise foe, Count of Lavas. Alas for you that Henry's army did not come sooner."

He did not turn to leave; he did not trust them that much. He edged sideways while never letting his gaze leave them until he was at the great doors, awash in sunlight. Then he was gone.

Sanglant bolted. Lavastine started after him, but the prince ran not after the fleeing princeling but rather to the altar where lay Bloodheart's corpse. The old priest had vanished; only the broken arrow haft remained. Sanglant upended the wooden chest and a downy spill of feathers wafted into the air as a cloudy haze. What in God's Names was he about? He coughed and pawed through the clot of feathers desperately, finding nothing, then gave up and knelt instead beside Bloodheart's body. With a howl, he wrenched the gold torque of royal kinship from the dead enchanter's arm.

The five dogs, crowded at his heels and sniffing and scrabbling at the corpse, raised their heads and howled wildly in answer.

"We had best be gone," said Lavastine. "We will head for the gates."

"Is that . . . *creature* . . . truly Prince Sanglant?" asked Erkanwulf, and several other men muttered likewise.

"Quiet!" snapped Lavastine, and then they hushed of their own accord because the prince now walked toward them with his retinue of dogs nipping and barking at his heels. He now held a spear and a short sword, gleaned from the corpses. Liath could not bear to look at him, and yet she kept looking at him. She could not believe he was alive, and yet, even if he was, could that . . . *thing* . . . truly be the man who had fallen at Gent over a year ago?

He broke away before he reached Lavastine and his men, as if he didn't want to get too close, and came to the huge, open doors of the cathedral. There, he stopped short as if chains had brought him up. As if he dared to go no farther.

"Come," said Lavastine to the prince as he led his party up beside—but not too close to—the dogs. A few of the men held their hands up over their noses, those who could reach them under the nasals of their helms. The count crossed out onto the steps that fronted the cathedral. The square beyond lay empty under the hazy afternoon sunlight. "We must make haste. My son—"

But he broke off, unable to speak further. In the far distance, Liath heard the sound of horns and the frenzied shouting of Eika.

That Sanglant had stepped out from the shelter of the cathedral she knew without looking, because of the stench. But now he spoke. His voice was hoarse, as if it had grown rusty from disuse—but then, his voice had always sounded like that.

"The horns," he said, head flung back to listen. "They belong to the king."

2

STROKE after stroke felled the Eika. As the Lady
cleaved through them, some looked into Alain's eyes, sensing the doom that came upon them, and others simply
dropped their weapons and fled. Even their savage fury
could not stand long before the Lady's wrath—and surely
not without the throbbing beat of the drums, now silent.

But there were yet more of them, even in disorder, than
remained of Alain's contingent. When an Eika princeling
rallied his forces and drove his soldiers back into the remaining wedge of infantry, *she* pursued that princeling
through the thick of fighting and slew him. His forces faltered and broke and ran from her while Alain's men
howled in glee and set back to their work, but even so,
Eika kept coming on, and on. There were so many, and
their scaly skin so tough to penetrate.

We can't hope to win through.

Then the call came, resounding from the last rank higher
up upon the hill.

"Fesse! the banner of Fesse!"

And then they heard the horns and the thunder of
cavalry.

"Henry!" cried another man, and they let out a great
cheer: "The king! The king!"

With new spirit they pressed forward, cleaving and hacking at the Eika. Eika banners wavered and retreated—or
fell. Eika soldiers hesitated. Some withdrew in an orderly
fashion, some fought on, but slowly the hill cleared of them,
and Alain struggled free of the press and got to higher
ground.

It was true! There, sweeping across the field, came the
banner of Fesse and the personal standard of Duchess Liutgard herself. Farther, a line of cavalry under the standard
of Princess Sapientia cut wide toward the east, retreating
toward the river's shore pursued by those Eika who fled to
their ships. Long shadows from the afternoon sun hatched

the western road. Yet another mass of soldiers emerged
from the forest under King Henry's banner.

Alain's legs gave out from under him and he staggered,
dropped, and was only caught by the sudden flurry of
hounds that pressed against him, licking him, whining. He
slipped on a clod of dirt and fell hard on his rump.

"My lord Alain." A soldier gripped his arm and bent
with concern over him. "My lord! Here, here! Water for
our lord!"

They swarmed around him and for once the hounds sat
quiet and allowed the soldiers to bring Alain water, to slide
his helm off and wipe his face in cool liquid.

"I never saw a man fight so fiercely!" cried one of his
soldiers.

"Aye, we would have been dead if not for you, my lord.
You shone with the battle lust, you did!"

He winced and thrust himself up.

"A victory!" they cried, celebrating around him with
their cheers. Alain squinted, but most of the fighting was
now out of his view. The Eika were routed.

And the Lady of Battles had vanished.

"Come," he said to the hounds. He began the hike to
the top.

"Victory!" sang his soldiers as the horns sounded distantly to announce the king's arrival on the field.

Eika corpses littered the hillside, but for every Eika who
lay dead, one of his own men did, too.

Some few lived, some stirred, groaning, and some few
would be dead soon enough, not having been granted the
mercy of a quick passage out of life. His hounds pressed
round him, Sorrow, Rage, Terror, Steadfast, Ardent, Bliss,
and Fear; battered and bloody, they yet lived when so many
others had perished, including poor Good Cheer.

He gained the height of the hill at last to find the camp
in utter carnage, tents torn down and ripped by the passage
of feet and the swell and ebb of uncaring battle, chests
burst open, bags whose contents lay strewn across corpses
and churned-up ground alike. Nothing remained of Lavastine's pavilion. Of the rough wooden observing platform,
constructed so hastily yesterday, only a few logs still stood.
Alain clambered up on them.

From this vantage place at the top of the hill, Alain could

see the banners of Henry's armies, but none from among those which had marched out beside Lavastine at dawn.

"I pray you, come down from there, my lord!" called one of the soldiers. "There are still Eika lurking, and they have bows."

As Alain jumped down he stumbled on a spear haft. He caught himself, grabbed for purchase and gripped the cloth of a tabard. A dead man rolled limply into view. It was Lavastine's captain. The Lavas standard lay trampled by his side.

Alain pried it out of the dirt and hoisted it high into the air, but as his men cheered around him, he could only weep.

3

THEY rode like demons, but the vanguard commanded by Duchess Liutgard stayed ahead of them and thus had the honor of thundering onto the battlefield first.

But Princess Sapientia was not to be deterred from her fair share of the glory. After their first awful pass through the battlefield when it seemed that every Eika fell beneath their horses' hooves with no resistance, Sapientia reined her horse around and for a mercy took an instant to catch her breath and survey the chaos.

For chaos was all that met Hanna's eyes. She had never seen so many people in one place at one time, nor heard such a din of screaming and howling melded together with the clash of weapons. Sticking tight to Sapientia's side, she could at least consider herself well protected. Father Hugh as well as certain oath-bound retainers kept close to the princess' side in a ring meant to protect her from death.

Hanna was not sure at that moment whether it was worse to witness the gruesome work of a battle from afar or to be thrown into its swirling, deadly currents. She would have gladly forgone both and risked another avalanche in the Alfar Mountains instead.

"The ships!" cried Sapientia suddenly and with a sudden gloating triumph in her voice. "To the ships! We shall stop them there!"

And off they went, pounding across the battlefield again. Distant banners marked the line of other units, some faltering, some pressing forward, but Sapientia paid no heed to the rest of the battle. She wanted to stop the Eika from reaching their ships. And, indeed, as they came up alongside the river they waited well out of the main fighting, which flurried round a distant hill and the flat stretch of plain beyond it, and had only isolated groups of fleeing Eika to contend with. These they slaughtered easily.

Ships lay beached on both the eastern and western shore, but it was the western shore—the one they guarded—which concerned them now. Eight ships were already launched into the water, steadying for the flight downstream. A half dozen bodies floated downstream in their wake.

"Send men to burn any ships they can reach!" ordered the princess, gesturing toward one of her captains.

"Your Highness!" shouted Father Hugh. "Is it wise to break up our formation? And we must not let the horses get pinned up against the river. We'll lose our mobility."

"But they are all so disordered," retorted Sapientia. "What matters it, as long as we outnumber them?" It was done as she commanded. Mclees broke out around the ships and, soon after, smoke rose from a handful, fire scorching up the masts.

A warning, the touch of a horn to lips, sounded from the outer ranks. Hanna stood in her stirrups to get a look, but what she saw chilled her and she shuddered despite the heat of the sun over the battleground.

Eika did indeed flee the battle now in disorderly groups—but not all of them, not those who were wounded, dead, or dying, not those who had kept their wits about them in the face of disaster. Pressing briskly and with purpose toward the river's bank marched a host of Eika, several hundred, in good order and with several standards borne before them. With shields raised in a tight wall and the gaps between them bristling with spears, they held off the human soldiers who harried them from behind. Were those bones swaying from the standards? Mercifully, from this distance, she could not tell for sure.

"Form up!" cried Sapientia, but it was too late; in her overconfidence she had allowed her troops to scatter.

"Send the Eagle for help!" shouted Hugh. "If they can be struck from behind while we charge from this side—"

"Nay!" cried the princess, glancing back over her shoulder to see how many riders remained with her. Others hastily mounted and galloped back from the shoreline. One man took an arrow from the ships and fell tumbling down from his horse. "I won't have it said I begged for help at the first sign of trouble. May St. Perpetua be with us this day! Who is with me?" With sword raised she spurred her horse forward straight toward the Eika line. Battle-trained, it did not shy away from the glittering ranks of spears and stone axes.

"Damn!" swore Hugh as her retainers followed her. He caught Hanna by the arm before she could ride after them. "Go to the king!" Then, sword drawn, he raced after the princess into the thick of the fight.

Already the Eika line had swung north along the river, cutting off Hanna's escape in that direction. Princess Sapientia vanished into a maelstrom of battle as the Eika host swallowed her troops. Some riders fled the skirmish, abandoning her; others bore down after her into the Eika tide, both sides caught in a desperate struggle—one for life, one for honor. In a moment Hanna, too, would be trapped by the flood tide of the battle as it reached the river's bank.

She kicked her horse to the south, down along the shoreline toward the ruins of Gent, and as she rode, her spear scraping up and down along her thigh, she began to pray.

4

SANGLANT led them through the streets at a
steady jog. Fifth Son had withdrawn his troops, but other
Eika scurried through Gent, fleeing the battle now that the
drums were silent and Bloodheart, and his illusions, dead.

Under the unsparing eye of the sun, the prince appeared
perhaps more pathetic than appalling. Yet he was a shock-
ing enough sight with the five monstrous dogs in attendance
as if they were all that remained of his proud Dragons.
King's Dragon he had once been. Now, except for his shape
and the princely authority of his bearing, he was scarcely
different from those dogs.

But he had not forgotten how to kill.

Their skirmishes were brief, and though Lavastine had
lost three men in the fight within the cathedral, he lost
none now, not with Sanglant at their head. Eika were as
like to run from them, seeing the prince in his madness, as
join the fray.

The gates lay open and they found Ulric and most of his
party on the bridge, staring at the river plain beyond where
the battle still raged. Clouds of dust as well as the lay of
the land obscured the fighting.

"My lord count!" cried Captain Ulric when he recognized their group.

"Beware!" shouted one of his men. A volley of arrows
showered into them. Two soldiers dropped, one with a hand
clasped to his thigh, another pierced in the throat.

Sanglant growled and leaped, dogs after him, into a stand
of brush that moments later Liath saw contained four
skulking Eika. She made ready to shoot. . . .

But there was no need. Sanglant struck down two even
as his dogs bowled over and rended the others, although
one of the dogs was slashed so badly that its fellows immediately turned on it and bit through its throat.

"There!" shouted Lavastine. Liath wrenched her gaze
away from Sanglant to see a troop of horsemen riding out

of the dusty murk that was the battleground. At once men shouted and waved, and within moments Lord Geoffrey reined up. He had but twenty men remaining as well as some extra horses following along.

"Cousin!" he cried, and he flung himself off his horse to clap Lavastine vigorously on the shoulder. "Ai, Lord! I thought you dead, surely."

"Any news of those who remained behind on the hill?"

Lord Geoffrey could only shrug. Then, eyes widening, he stared at the apparition that, silent but all the more frightening because of that silence, now commandeered one of the riderless horses and swung up onto it. "Lady have mercy!" he breathed. "What is it?"

The prince flung away the spear and galloped northwest toward the thickest cloud of dust.

"Eagle! Take a horse and ride after him. The king will have my head if he gets himself killed. I doubt he is in his right mind." With this cool assessment, Lavastine turned back to his cousin. "Has the king arrived?"

"I know not, cousin. It is madness out there, and most of our people long since lost."

"You've done well to survive this long." But Lavastine did not seem to mean the words as praise, any more than he meant his earlier comment, calling Sanglant out of his right mind, as censure. "Eagle!" His gaze tripped over her where she still stood, gawping, frozen, unable to act. "Go!"

It was easier to obey than to think. She took the mount offered her and left them just as a party of Eika came running and a new skirmish was joined.

Chaos.

Through the streaming battle she rode on the trail of Sanglant, who was himself all movement. Eika fled in confusion or retreated in disciplined groups, and cavalry charged through and reformed and charged back, scattering them, cutting down those who ran and pounding again and again those who held steady.

Sanglant drove his horse wherever the fight was thickest. Certainly he was brave; perhaps he was also insane. After he rallied a group of horsemen who had gotten cut off from their captain, she heard his name called out above the riot of noise like a talisman. *She* tried merely to keep away from Eika, for in this tempest she had few clear shots and plenty of chances to get hacked down from behind, though most Eika seemed to be running for their lives. It was all she could do to keep Sanglant in her sight.

Through the haze of dust she caught a glimpse of Fesse's banner. Then it vanished, whipping against the wind as its bearer galloped away in another direction with Fesse's duchess and troops.

They had come so far over the ground that she did not know where she was. Her eyes streamed from the dust kicked up and the glare of the westering sun. Ahead, a soldier leaned from his horse and struck down one of the dogs following Sanglant and rode on, spear ready to pierce the next which, loping after the prince, was unaware of the threat to its back.

But Sanglant was not unaware. He reined his horse hard around and brought the flat of his sword down against the soldier's padded shoulder. The man tumbled to the ground and the dogs leaped forward, only to be brought up short. Liath could not hear what the prince shouted, only saw the terrified soldier scramble back onto his horse.

Then, horns. "To the princess! She's surrounded!"

"To me! Form up!" the prince cried, his hoarse tenor ringing out over chaos. Shining with the heat of battle on him, he was not as frightful a sight as he had first appeared when he was Bloodheart's prisoner, a wild, chained beast. Men came riding to form up around him, and as his company gathered, they shouted jubilantly, sure of victory. Where Princess Sapientia's banner had gotten trapped in a strong current of Eika battling their way to the river, Sanglant and the newly regrouped cavalry drove in and scattered the enemy before them.

"The king! King Henry comes!"

Liath could not see the princess, for the entire flank had crumbled. But as the Eika line dissolved into rout, she saw Sanglant struggle free of the crush and ride northwest out beyond the fighting to where neglected fields lay drowsy under the afternoon sun. She fought her way out of the press and galloped after him.

He rode on, not looking back. Three Eika dogs pursued him as he left the battle behind, and she was too far away to shout a warning. At her back she heard horsemen, and she glanced behind to see a dozen or so men wearing the tabards of those he had rallied on the field.

Ahead, a line of trees and scrub marked the course of a tributary. There she lost sight of him as he crashed in among the trees. When she found his abandoned horse, she dismounted and prudently waited until her pursuit came up beside her.

"My God, Eagle!" said the man, a captain by his bearing and armor. "Was that Prince Sanglant? We thought him dead!"

"Taken captive," she said.

"And survived a year." Around him, his men murmured. She heard in their voices the melody of awe, composing now the beginning, she supposed, of another story of Sanglant's courage and cunning and strength. "But where's he gone?"

They followed his track, made manifest by a litter of filthy shreds of tabard and tunic and leggings, things that had once been clothing but now were only foul rags. He had dropped the sword and the gold torque by the water's edge. The current still bore sticks and grass and, once, a bloodied glove quickly carried along the far bank, but where a bend in the stream and a fallen tree made somewhat of a pool he had gone headlong into the water.

When they reached him, he was methodically tearing off every last piece of clothing that still hung on him, some of it adhered to his skin. The three Eika dogs had thrashed out after him and now ferociously worried at the odorous remains, such as they could grab in their jaws before it swirled downstream.

"My lord prince!" The captain strode forward, and at his exclamation the dogs howled and made for shore.

Sanglant barked at them. There was no other word for it; it was not a spoken command. They obeyed nonetheless and contented themselves with sitting half in and half out of water on a bank more pebble than sand, growling at any who came too near while the prince took handfuls of sand and scoured his skin and then his hair as if he meant to scrape himself raw.

"Lady bless us," murmured one of the soldiers as if for all of them, "he's so thin."

But as if in the coarse river sand lay the property of

truth, something emerged from the scouring, something recognizable: the man she remembered, although he was
clothed only in water and that only up to his waist.

"*I will never love any man but him.*"

Said so long ago, spoken so recklessly, what had she
bound herself to when she made that declaration before
Wolfhere?

He turned. If he saw her among those who waited for
him, he gave no sign of it. He extended a hand. "A knife."

But the captain stripped off his own armor and his own
tunic, and with tunic and knife he advanced cautiously. The
dogs nipped at him, but Sanglant waded out of the deeper
water and called them away.

Liath could not help but look. Now that he was somewhat clean she could see that although his hair was long
and tangled, he still had no beard even after a year without
any means to shave it clean. He had no hair on his chest,
either, but lower down he resembled his human kinsmen
in every respect. She looked away quickly, for this was not
like the work she and Fell's soldiers had done at the river's
mouth, all of them equals in labor and none of them having
the leisure to be shy about what needed to be done. He
was not a curiosity to be stared at, or at least ought not
to be.

When she looked up again he had the tunic on, a plain
garment of good, strong weave and stained with sweat
along the neck and under the arms, but compared to what
he had worn before it looked fitting for a prince. It hung
loosely around his frame, though it was a little short: He
stood half a head taller than the robust captain, and despite
his thinness he was still a big man. Now, taking the knife,
he began to hack at his hair.

"I beg you, my lord prince," said the captain. He had a
kind of weeping plaint to his voice as if he were about to
burst into tears out of pity. "Let me cut it for you."

Sanglant paused. "No," he said. Then, and finally, as if
only when he had scrubbed himself clean of the breath of
his captivity dared he acknowledge her, he looked up to
where she stood half hidden among the rest. He had known
she was there all along. "Liath."

How could she not come forward? The knife had a good

sharp edge and she had trimmed Da's hair many a time, although this was utterly different.

He knelt suddenly and with a sharp sigh. A tang of the old smell, the reek of his imprisonment, still clung to him and no doubt would for some time, but standing this close was no punishment. Ai, Lady, his hair was coarse and too matted to be truly clean yet, but when sometimes she had to shift him to get a better angle for cutting, she touched his skin and would bite her lip to stop herself from trembling, and go on.

"What is this?" She scraped the back of her hand on the rough iron collar that ringed his neck. Under it, the skin had been rubbed raw countless times and even now began to leak blood.

"Leave it."

She left it. No one dared go forward to pick up sword and torque, not with the dogs guarding these treasures.

The long rays of the sun splintered into glitters on the rippling current of the stream. Black mats of hair littered the ground as she cut. Made cautious by the noise and the thrashing in the water, the birds had fallen silent, all but a warbler among the reeds who sang vigorously to complain about the disturbance. Far away, a horn lifted its voice and fell silent. Horses shifted and snorted. A man whispered. Another peed, though she could only hear him, not see, for he had faced into the trees to do his business.

"His heart," Sanglant whispered suddenly. "How did you know he had hidden his heart in the priest's body? Whose heart lies hidden in Rikin fjall, then? It must be the priest's."

"I don't understand." But perhaps she was beginning to. She said it more to keep him talking, to hear his voice. She had thought never to hear that voice again.

"He couldn't be killed because he didn't have a heart. He hid it. He—" Then he halted as suddenly as if he had lost his power of speech between one word and the next.

"It's done," she said quickly, to say something, anything, torn as she was between the promise of this intimacy he had thrust upon her and her complete ignorance of what manner of man he now was and how much he might have changed from the man she had fallen in love with in besieged Gent. "It will have to do, unless you'd like me to

comb it out, for I hope I still have my comb in my pouch."
Then she flushed, cursing her rash words; only mothers,
wives, or servants combed a man's hair if he did not do
it himself.

Instead of replying he stood and turned—but not to look
at her. Belatedly she turned as well when she heard the
crashing in the trees. Another party approached.

The soldiers were already kneeling. She was too stupid,
too astounded, to do so, and only at the very last moment,
when the king broke from the trees, did she drop down as
was fitting.

The king strode forward and stopped dead some ten
paces from the prince. There was silence except for the
rushing mutter of the stream and the gurgle of water tumbling over the fallen log—and an echoing whisper from the
king's retinue, who followed him out from the trees and
stood staring at the scene before them.

The sun eased below the highest trees. All lay bathed in
the mellow glow of midsummer's late afternoon, the opening hour of the long twilight. As the silence drew out, the
warbler quieted but now other birds, made bold by the
quiet, began to call and sing: a thin "zee-zee-zee" among
the treetops and the monotonous "chiff-chaff" song in the
scrub. A woodpecker fluttered away, rising and swooping
down and rising again, yellow rump a flash against the
green foliage. Liath still held the knife in one hand and a
last hank of Sanglant's hair in the other.

At last the king spoke. "My son." It had a harsh sound,
startlingly so, but when she saw the tears start from his
eyes and course down his cheeks, she understood that the
harshness stemmed from the depth of his remembered an-
guish and the fresh bloom of joy.

He said nothing more, but he removed his finely embroidered short cloak from his own back, unfastening the gold-
and-sapphire brooch, and wrapped it around Sanglant's
shoulders with his own hands, like a servant. This close,
Liath could see his hands shaking under the weight of such
a powerful emotion: the incredible and almost overpower-
ing pain of seeing alive the beloved son he had thought
dead.

Sanglant dropped abruptly to his knees, exhausted or
overcome by emotion, and laid his damp head against his

father's hands in the way of a sinner seeking absolution or a child seeking comfort.

"Come, son, rise," said the king raggedly. Then he laughed softly. "I have already heard many stories about your courage on the field and how you rallied troops who had fallen into disarray."

The prince did not look up, but when he spoke, there welled up from him so much enmity that the force of his emotion alone might have felled an entire company of Eika. "I would have killed more of them if I could."

"May God have mercy on us all," murmured Henry. He took Sanglant by the elbow and helped him rise. "How did you survive?"

As if in answer—the only answer he knew how to give—Sanglant turned his head to look at Liath.

5

THE hounds smelled him coming first. They broke away from Alain—all of them, even Sorrow and Rage—to bound down the hill with happy barks, their tails whipped into a blur. Beyond, a company of mounted soldiers approached the ruined camp. Alain picked his way down through the dead and dying to meet Count Lavastine.

Along the ramparts where Eika dead lay in heaps and the few survivors dug among the corpses to find any wounded who might yet have a hope of living, Alain handed the ragged standard to Lavastine. "I thought you must be dead," he said, then burst into tears.

Lavastine raised one eyebrow. "Did I not say I would return to you through the Eika host and meet you here? Come now, son." He took him by the arm and led him down, away from the terrible work yet to be done, stripping and then burning the dead Eika and giving a decent burial to the hundreds who had fallen. The river plain beyond held a scene just as dismaying to look upon: as if high waters had overtaken the fields and ditches, washing in a flood tide of corpses and depositing them in eddies or along invisible streams where strong currents had once flowed.

"Good Cheer is dead." Alain choked back tears in order to have breath to confess his weakness. "And the good captain besides. I lost Graymane. We were overtaken by Eika. So few are left—"

"That any are left is astonishing. Now, Alain, do not speak so. We will settle the captain's widow very richly, I assure you, and mourn him as he deserves. And you see, Graymane was found on the field and returned to me unharmed. As for Good Cheer—" He busied himself patting the hounds, rubbing his knuckles into their great heads, and letting them lick him as they jumped around and, finally, settled down around him. Was there a tear in his eye? But a wind had picked up from the river and the spark of moisture vanished—or was only a trick of the light.

Now those who remained of Lavastine's infantry came forward to praise Alain and speak of his great feats in driving back the Eika when all was lost, how he had single-handedly struck down a huge Eika princeling, how he had shone in battle with an unearthly light, surely granted to him by the Lord's Hand.

Alain was ashamed to listen, but Lavastine nodded gravely and set a hand possessively on his son's shoulder. Only Lord Geoffrey fidgeted, for he had also dismounted and now attended his cousin.

"We must ride to where the king sets up camp," said Lavastine. "We have much to accomplish."

"Isn't this work enough?" Alain gestured about them.

"That we killed Bloodheart and routed the Eika? It was what I hoped for, and indeed all has fallen out as I wished."

"As you *wished,* cousin!" Lord Geoffrey stepped forward. The remnants of Lavastine's cavalry, some hundred and fifty men when they had marched onto the river plain two days ago, loitered behind him. Alain counted not more than thirty men as blood-spattered and dirty as was Lord Geoffrey himself.

Lavastine's face was smeared with dust and on one cheek ragged circular cuts and a ring of tiny bruises tore the skin where his mail coif had been crushed into his face. He found an empty helmet on the ground and set a boot up on it. The wind skirled through his hair and made the Lavas standard rustle and rise briefly, as if the black hounds embroidered there had taken a scent. He picked a twig out of his light beard and with an expression of distaste tossed it to the ground. With the wind came the scent of blood and death. In the air carrion crows circled, but there were too many soldiers still roaming the field seeking out wounded or stripping Eika of their mail skirts for the birds to land and feast.

"Not my good soldiers," said the count, musing. "Their lives I regret, as I always do. But we took Gent without Henry's aid. Thus it will be my privilege to present Gent like a gift to Henry when we meet."

"What ambition is this?" demanded Geoffrey.

"Not ambition for myself. For my *son.*"

No one would have missed Geoffrey's blanch, but he made no reply.

"*My* army took Gent," continued Lavastine. "That gives me a claim to it."

"But surely the children of Countess Hildegard will inherit these lands," protested Alain.

"If she has children. If they have survived the winter with the Eika raiding in their lands. If her kin are strong enough to sway the king in his judgment. But if Henry is beholden to me, Alain, then why not take Gent—which you will recall lies within his purview—and grant it to Tallia as dower? Thus it will come into our hands, as part of the marriage settlement —or the morning gift, should she make one to you. Remember, Alain, as the daughter of a duchess it is her right to gift you, as the son of a mere count—" Here any waking soul could hear the irony. "—with a morning gift. Although you may, of course, gift her with some smaller token as well. Is that not so, Geoffrey?"

Geoffrey simply gave a curt bow in acknowledgment, since his wife Aldegund's lands and inheritances were of a higher degree than any he could expect to receive—unless he inherited, as he had once hoped to do, the county of Lavas from Lavastine.

"Many a blood feud has started when a bride and groom of equal rank tried to outdo each other in an elaborate morning gift. It can be considered an insult for a noble of lesser degree to make a richer gift to his newly-wedded spouse than that which she gifts him, if her position and kin are superior to his. That is why we will not ask for Gent outright. But through Tallia we can still make a claim on these lands and on our rights to a portion of the tariffs taken from the merchants and the port."

They made a ragged procession, thirty riders, perhaps sixty infantry, but a proud one. In this way in the long lingering twilight of midsummer they picked their way across the battlefield to the place where the king had set up camp. The royal banner snapped in the evening breeze from atop the king's pavilion.

In front, tables had been set up and on them a victory feast laid out—such as it was: mostly mutton and beef from some among the many herds of cattle and sheep which under the protection of the Eika had flourished on farmlands gone to pasture in the past year. But there was also bread, not too stale, brought from Steleshame, and a few other delicacies preserved for such a moment. A king must reward his followers, especially on the field after such a triumph.

With Alain at his side, Lavastine knelt before the king and brashly, even presumptuously, offered Gent into the king's hands—Lavastine's to offer because his troops had won through at the gates. But Henry had anticipated Lavastine. The chair to the king's right sat empty, and it was to this chair that Henry waved the count, giving him pride of place.

An unfamiliar man with a thin, haunted face and bronzish skin sat to the king's left. He was dressed as richly as any noble there, and Alain heard the servingfolk whisper that this was the king's lost son. Instead of the gold torque marking royal kinship, he wore a rough iron slave collar around his neck. He did not speak.

To Alain was given the signal honor of standing at the king's right shoulder and pouring him wine. From his place, Alain could see—and hear—the nobles arguing among themselves, made irritable by hunger and the relief of a battle won at great cost.

From her place to the right of Lavastine, thrust out from her usual seat of honor, Princess Sapientia complained to her distant cousin, Duchess Liutgard. "*He* stole my glory!"

"That's not how I heard the tale! I heard your entire flank crumbled . . . and that *he* arrived in time to rally your forces when you could not!"

Of Sapientia's adviser and Liath's tormentor, Father Hugh, there was no sign. Liath stood in the shadows next to one of her fellow Eagles, a tough-looking woman who came forward, now and again, to whisper messages received from scouts into the king's ear. Liath had an arm draped around the shoulders of a straw-haired young Eagle Alain recalled from the battle at Kassel. She and her companion surveyed the assembly as if to see who was missing.

Henry's army had taken light casualties, all but the flank commanded by Princess Sapientia which had apparently had the misfortune to hit a ferociously vicious Eika attack when they had come between a retreating princeling and his ships.

Besides Lavastine and his cousin, there were few noble survivors of the army Lavastine had brought to Gent. Lord

Dedi was slain; Lady Amalia's body had not yet been found. Lord Wichman had been pulled, alive, from a veritable maelstrom of corpses, the detritus of his final stand, but he lay sorely wounded in a tent and it was not known if he would live. Captain Ulric, of Autun, had won through with most of his company of light cavalry intact.

But it was the fate of the common men, nameless and unmentioned in this assembly, which gnawed at Alain. Raised in a village, he knew what grief would come to their homes in the wake of this news, all invisible to the sight of the great lords who marked it as a victory. Who would till their fields? Who would marry their sweethearts now? What son could take the place of the one who had fallen, never to return?

There was still light to see as platters were brought and set before king and company, but in the background the first torches were lit. The moon had risen in the east above the ruins of Gent, and now as dusk settled over the land, the moon spilled its sullen light over the distant fields where the nameless dead lay, men and Eika alike.

A platter was set down before the king and his lost son.

Without warning, the prince bolted down the food as if he were a starving dog let free with the scraps. Gasps came, and giggling—quickly stifled—from the assembly. From behind, dogs began to bark and howl furiously, and in answer the Lavas hounds, which had been staked out some way off, growled and barked in challenge.

At once, the prince leaped up. Grease dripped from his lips. The king placed a hand, firmly, on his sleeve. Alain felt such a terrible surge of pity for the prince that he moved between Henry and Sanglant and made much of pouring more wine so as to draw attention to himself and away from them.

That was all it took. With an effort made the more obvious by the way his hands shook, the prince commenced eating again, only very, very slowly and with such painstaking care that anyone would know he could barely stop himself from gobbling down his food like a savage.

"Your Majesty," said Lavastine, catching Alain's eye and indicating with the tilt of his head that the young man could now move back. His ploy had served its purpose. "With great cost to myself and my people, I have freed Gent from the Eika and killed the creature who held your son prisoner for so long."

"So you have," said the king, with some difficulty turning away from his son to regard the count.

"We have spoken of a match between my son and Lady Tallia."

"You are frank with me, Count Lavastine."

"I always will be, Your Majesty. You know what I want and what I have paid to gain it."

"But do you know what I want," responded the king, "and what I need from you in order to achieve it?"

"Nay, Your Majesty, I do not know, but I am willing to listen. . . ."

The king glanced up at Alain. "A good-looking lad. I have heard great praise of his courage and skill at arms this day. That he held that small hill against such a tide of Eika is incredible. I have no objection to a marriage between him and my niece Tallia . . . *if* it is accompanied on your part by an oath that you and your heir will support me faithfully in all my undertakings."

Before Lavastine could reply, the prince stumbled up from his chair and fled into the darkness. The king made to rise.

"Nay, Your Majesty," said Alain, who had a sudden idea of what was wrong. "I'll go after him, if you permit."

The king nodded. Alain followed.

He had not gone six steps when Liath appeared beside him.

"What happened?" she whispered, as anxious as a hound in a thunderstorm.

"It's nothing serious," he said quietly, gentling her with a touch on the arm. "It's best if I go alone. Do you think he would want you to see him when he's not well?" Here he trailed off.

After a moment she nodded and returned to her post.

Alain and a few men-at-arms found the prince just beyond the edge of camp, vomiting. When he had done, he began to shake, resting on his hands. "Ai, God," he muttered as if to himself. "Don't let them see me."

Alain ventured forward and laid a hand on his shoulder. At once the prince started up, growling, just like a dog.

"Hush, now," said Alain firmly, as he would to his own

hounds, and the prince shook himself and seemed to come
to his senses. "If you've been starved, then you can't put
rich food in your stomach all at once, or at least, that's
what my Aunt Bel would say." He still winced when he
said the name. "She who used to be my aunt," he added
to no one except his smarting conscience.

"Who are you?" said the prince. He had an oddly hoarse
voice which made him seem stricken with grief when in
fact he was likely only exhausted and ill. But he had calmed
enough now to wipe at his mouth with the back of a hand.

"I am Lavastine's son."

Dogs began to bark again, and the prince lifted his head
to scent, then started back and became a man again. "God
have mercy on me," he muttered. "Will I never be rid of
the chains Bloodheart bound me with?"

"It is the collar." Why he spoke so freely Alain did not
know, only that—unlike the king—this half wild prince did
not awe him. "As long as you wear it at your neck, then
surely you will not be free of Bloodheart's hand on you."

"As long as I wear it, I am reminded of what he did to
me. I am reminded of what I was and what he called me."
His voice was so bitter. Alain ached for him, and what he
had suffered.

But even Alain was not immune from curiosity. "What
did he call you?"

The prince only shook his head. "I'll go back now. I
won't forget this kindness you've shown me."

They returned to where the king sat sipping at his wine
and the company ate with the self-conscious assiduousness
of people who chafe with curiosity but know that their regnant will not tolerate questions. The prince sat with exaggerated care and with even more exaggerated care sipped
sparingly at the wine and ate the merest scrap of meat and
bread. But sometimes his nostrils would flare, and he would
lift his head and search into the assembly as if he had heard
a whispered comment that angered him. The rest of the
feast passed without incident. They ate lustily and drank
without stinting on what was left of the wine.

"You acquitted yourself well, son," said Lavastine afterward when they had retired to a tent commandeered from
lesser nobles in Henry's train. "I am proud of you. Ai,

Lord, Prince Sanglant is more like to one of the hounds than to a human man. But I suppose it is his mother's blood which stains him." He scratched Terror's ears and the old hound grunted ecstatically. Alain tended the gash that had opened up Fear's hindquarters. He had already bound up Ardent's leg and washed the cuts on Sorrow and Rage. Steadfast was asleep, while Bliss waited patiently for his turn under Alain's hands.

Now that Lavastine's wounds had been tended to, Alain and Lavastine and the hounds were alone in the tent. From outside he heard the low rumble of activity as wounded were carried in, scouts came and went, men looted and burned the Eika dead under the moon's light, and sentries called out challenges.

"He must have suffered terribly," said Alain, scratching Fear under his jaw.

"But he is alive. They say he came attended by Eika dogs, as faithful to him as his Dragons once were. What do you think of that?"

Alain laughed. "Ought I to think something of it when I sit here with these faithful beasts?"

Lavastine grunted. "True enough." He stretched, wincing. "When I was your age, I would have felt no ache in my bones, even after a day such as this. What a strange creature the Eika princeling was, to let us go like that in the cathedral when he could have killed us all. How foresighted of you to free him, Alain."

"Even if meant sacrificing Lackling in his place?" The old shame still burned.

"Who is Lackling?" Lavastine yawned, stretched again, and tied up the hounds, then called for a servingman to take off his boots. "What happened to the Eagle, do you know?"

Alain saw there was no point in reminding his father about Lackling. "She went back to her duties."

"You were wise to gain her loyalty, son. It seems to me that when you marry, Lady Tallia's consequence will allow you to count Eagles in your retinue. You must ask for that one. There is some power at work within her. It would be well to have it for our use, if we can."

Marry Tallia. All else that Lavastine said swirled round

him like the night's breeze and faded into nothing. *Marry Tallia.*

Lavastine went on to discuss Henry's plans to send for Tallia and have her brought to his progress, but the words passed in a haze. When the hounds were settled and a rough pallet was set in place, Alain lay down beside his father and closed his eyes to see the terrible images of battle bursting like fire against his eyes. The rose burned at his chest like a hot coal. But slowly the pain faded. With the snoring of the hounds beside him and his father's even breath on his ear, the awful images faded into a vision of Tallia, her wheatpale hair unbound and her solemn face turned toward *him. His* wife. Bound to *him* by their mutual oaths sworn before witnesses and blessed by a biscop.

He slept, and he dreamed.

Both current and wind aid him this night. He can smell the sea and the estuary before he gets too close. He beaches his eight ships on the western shore and sends scouts westward to guard against an incursion of the Soft Ones' soldiers, should they have sent any in this direction to seek out the fleeing RockChildren. No doubt they are too busy killing those who fled in disorder. No doubt they are too busy burying their own kind, for they are distractible in their grief.

The disaster brought on by Bloodheart's death will hurt the RockChildren, certainly, but only a fool would not find advantage in it. No one of Bloodheart's ambitious sons could have killed the enchanter without bringing down on himself Bloodheart's vengeance. Now that fate is reserved for another.

Now, after the rout, how many of Bloodheart's sons survive? How many had taken their followers to raid eastward and did not fight at Gent at all? All this he must consider before he knows how and when to act.

The old priest sits in the belly of the boat and sings nonsense as he wipes blood from the oozing wound in his chest and licks it off his fingers.

"How did you do it?" he asks the old wizened creature. "Why did you do it?"

"Why are you curious?" asks the old priest, who talks mostly in questions.

"Bloodheart found your heart hidden in Rikin fjall. He

forced the bargain on you, to hide his heart in place of your own."

"Will anyone ever find my heart now?" cackles the priest.

No doubt he is half mad. His kind usually are; it is the price they pay for their power. "What happened to your heart?" he asks again. "How did you manage to hide Bloodheart's heart in your own chest when it was meant to be hidden in the fjall?"

"Did he think he was cleverer than I?" The old priest snorts, and for an instant cunning sparks in his rheumy eyes. The creature is very old, the oldest male he has ever seen. *"Did he think I would take my old heart to where there might be battle? I could have been killed!"*

"Do you fear death, then? The curse of the nestbrother—"

"The curse! The curse! Do I look like a hatchling? I turned the curse. I stole Bloodheart's voice and finished the speaking for him. Hai! Hai!" He begins to sing, but the song has an unsettling flow, like a river running uphill. *" 'Let this curse fall on the one whose hand commands the blade that pierced his heart.' Ailailai!"*

There is no more sense to be gotten from the old creature, so he only tests the chains with which he had bound the old priest before giving orders to his soldiers. Of those cousins remaining to him, he leaves half to guard the ships. The other half he takes with him as he trots north just above the bluffs to the very mouth of the river.

Fifth son of the fifth litter, he knows how to make use of a lesson: He was captured once by this male named Count Lavastine when his ship got bottled up at the mouth of the Vennu River. It will not happen again. If a trap lies in wait at the mouth of this river, he will be ready for it.

He smells human soldiers long before he sees the telltale lines of a small fort set upon a bluff and somewhat hidden by a cunning layer of branches and scrub. Some of the plants woven into the log ramparts still live though he can taste the brittle decay of the others on his tongue when he licks the air.

His cousins stir and growl restlessly behind him, for they were granted no leave to fight when they fled Gent. He can taste their dissatisfaction, but they have not learned patience. They will learn it from him tonight, or they will die.

He lifts a hand and gestures to them to fan out. The

ground slips beneath his feet, sand and coarse grass and such plants as can stand the ever-present blast of the wind. He bangs spear on shield and from the depths of the fort he hears the frantic rustling of men struggling to ready themselves for battle.

"Hear me!" he calls. "Send your leader to talk, for my force outnumbers yours." He tastes the air, scenting for their essences. "You have but some thirty of your kind, and I have over one hundred of mine. I give you this choice: Fight us and die, this night, or retreat from your fort south and west to the camp of your kin, and live."

"How can we trust you?" shouts one of them, appearing only as a dark shadow of helm against the sky and a certain tang of stubborn resilience in the air.

"I am the one whom Lord Alain freed at Lavas Holding. By the honor of that lord, I swear I will do you no harm . . . as long as you retreat at once and leave this place to me."

The man spits, though the spray cannot travel so far. "You, an Eika, swearing by our good Lord Alain's honor!"

Stubborn creature! He has no time to waste. Soon the other ships will come.

"Then if you have a brave man among you, send him out and I will stand hostage under his knife while the rest leave. When they are well away, he may follow unmolested. But you must act now, or we will attack."

They confer. He can't hear them, but their fear is a bracing scent on the breeze, pungent on his tongue. By now they must know they are surrounded and outnumbered.

In the end, of course, they agree. They have no other choice except to die, and Soft Ones always struggle to live even when they must live like dogs to do so. Like the old priest, they fear death and the passage to the fjall of the heavens, and that fear can be used against them.

One of them emerges. He goes forward and lets the man stand with knife poised at his throat while the others march in a swift but orderly fashion into a night made gray by the lowering moon. His own soldiers storm the fort after them and circle down to the strand. They bark to him. There are machines within the fort, and with some impatience he stares at the man before him, who at last withdraws the knife and retreats slowly.

"I remember you," says the man, and then turns and runs

as if expecting an arrow in the back. At once, one of his cousins raises his bow and nocks an arrow for the easy shot. He springs forward and bats bow and arrow down.

The rash cousin swears. "You are weak to let them run!"

It takes only a moment to kill him for his disrespect. Then he turns on the others. "Question me if you must, but do not disobey me. I intend to accomplish what Bloodheart could not accomplish because he was not willing to use the lessons of the WiseMothers to guide him."

He waits as blood leaks onto his feet and the fire that animated the cousin spills onto the earth and soaks into the ground. No one speaks.

"Then, go," he orders, for he has already seen what the count set in place here. A cunning man, the count, a worthy foe.

Soon the other ships begin to come, fleeing the death of Bloodheart and the collapse of his army and his authority. He watches dispassionately as they founder on the black tide.

Soon the mouth of the Veser is awash in wreckage as some swim free of the chain and the piles to cast up on the western shore. Those who will not bare their throats before him his soldiers kill.

Soon he will have to dismantle the chain so he can sail through safely himself and return to Rikin fjord with his prize, but for this night, at least, he will destroy as many of his rivals as he can.

There will not be many survivors from those who gathered at Gent—and those who survive will belong to him.

His followers do their work well, and efficiently. He climbs to the little fort and from this vantage point he watches as the heart of Old-Man, the moon, sinks into the west and the stars, the eyes of the most ancient Mothers, stare with their luminous indifference upon the streaming waters and the silent earth. In the fjall of the heavens, the vale of black ice, only the cold holds sway and their whispering conversations take lifetimes to complete. But they are nonetheless beautiful.

6

IT was night, but Liath could not sleep.

She had sent Hathui to sleep and offered to stand middle night watch, as one Eagle always did, over the king's pavilion together with the guards.

With the moon one day past full, only the brightest stars were visible. But she could not even concentrate enough to watch those stars and read their secret turnings in the language Da taught her, the language of the mathematici.

Sanglant was alive.

Alive.

Yet so changed.

Yet not changed at all.

"Eagle."

The whisper came out of the shadows, twisted from the steady breath of the night breeze on the many pavilions staked out around her. She stiffened and turned to seek out the voice.

Two guards with torches appeared out of the gloom. A third man led a mule, and there, on the mule's back, sat a woman in the robes of a cleric. But she did not venture in far enough that the guards beside the king's tent could see her face.

Cautiously, Liath walked out to meet her.

It was Sister Rosvita, looking drawn and anxious.

"Aren't you with the train?"

Rosvita allowed her servant to help her dismount and then waved him and her guards away. They retreated and stood a few paces off. "I was, but I had to leave and come here, and the moon gave enough light for the journey."

"But some Eika may still haunt the woods!"

"It was not as far as I feared it would be. We saw no Eika. I must speak to you, Eagle. It is by the Lady's grace that my path brought me directly to you."

To Liath's amazement, the cleric took a bundle wrapped in linen from a bag tied to the mule's saddle and held it up before her. Liath knew immediately what it was.

"How did you?" she whispered, scarcely able to force the words out.

"Do you know what is in here? Nay, do not trouble yourself to answer. I see that you do. I know you can read Dariyan . . ." The cleric spoke in a rush, clearly agitated though Liath had never seen her anything but calm before. "Why should I give this back to you?"

She was half the cleric's age. She could easily snatch the book from her and run. But she did not, though neither could she compose an eloquent or compelling reply. "It's all I have left of my da!"

"Was your da a mathematicus?"

There was no use in lying. Rosvita had obviously read in the book. "Yes."

"And what are *you*, Eagle?" the cleric demanded.

"Kinless," she said flatly. "All I have are the Eagles. I pray you, Sister, I am no threat to anyone."

Rosvita glanced up at the stars as though to ask them if this was truth, or a cunning dissemblance. But the stars only spoke to those who knew their language, so she did not. "I dare not keep this," she said in a low voice.

"How did you get it?"

"That does not matter."

"Can you—how much did you—?" But she was afraid to ask. She shifted. Beyond, the three servants who had escorted the cleric huddled close, sharing something from a leather bottle. She thought she smelled mead, but there were so many smells mingling and unraveling in the air around them that she could not be sure if it was honey's fermented sweetness or the aftertaste of drying blood.

"I cannot read Jinna, although you can." It was not a question. "And the fourth language is unknown to me. I had only a moment to look at the Arethousan and the Dariyan, but I needed no more than that to recognize what I was seeing. Lady protect you, child! Why are you riding as a common Eagle?"

"It is what was offered me."

"By Wolfhere."

"He saved me from Hugh."

The moonlight bleached Rosvita's face of expression, but she shook her head and then simply offered the book to Liath.

Liath grabbed it and clutched it against her chest.

"I think it properly belongs to you," said Rosvita softly, hesitantly. "Pray God I am right in this. But you must come speak to me, Eagle, of this matter. Your immortal soul is at risk. Who are the Seven Sleepers?"

"The Seven Sleepers," Liath murmured, memory stirring. "*Beware the Seven Sleepers.*" Or so Da had written. "I only know what he wrote in the book."

"You've never heard the story as related in Eusebē's *Ecclesiastical History?*"

"Nay, I've not read Eusebē."

"In the time of the persecution of Daisanites by the Emperor Tianothano, seven young people in the holy city of Saïs took refuge in a cave to gain strength before they presented themselves for martyrdom. But the cave miraculously sealed over, and there they were left to sleep."

"Until when?"

"Eusebē doesn't say. But that is not the only place I have heard that name. Do you know of a Brother Fidelis, at Hersford Monastery?"

"I do not."

" 'Devils visit me in the guise of scholars and magi,' " quoted Rosvita, recalling the conversation vividly, " 'tempting me with knowledge if only I would tell them what I knew of the secrets of the Seven Sleepers.' "

"Were they the ones—?" Liath broke off. Wind rustled the canvas of tents, and she was suddenly reminded of the daimone who had stalked her on the empty road. She shuddered. "I don't know what to do," she murmured, afraid again. Da always said: "*The worst foe is the one you can't see.*"

Rosvita extended a hand in the fashion of her kind, a deacon about to offer a blessing. "There are others better able to advise you than I. You must think seriously about making your way to the convent of St. Valeria."

"How can I?" Liath whispered, remembering her vision of stern Mother Rothgard. "The arts of the mathematici are forbidden."

"Forbidden *and* condemned. But it would be foolish of the church not to understand such sorcery nevertheless. Mother Rothgard at St. Valeria is not a preceptor I would wish to study under. She has little patience and less of a kind heart. But I have never heard it whispered that she is tempted by her knowledge. If you cannot bring yourself to trust me, then go there, I beg you." She glanced behind toward her servants. "I must return to the train, or they will wonder why I am missing. Morning comes soon."

She paused only to stare at Liath, as if hoping to read into her soul. Then she left.

Liath was too stunned to move. Her arms ached where they clasped the book, and one corner of the book pinched her stomach, digging into her ribs. She stood there breathing in and out with the breath of the night. A flash of white startled her and she spun to see a huge owl come noiselessly to rest on the torn-up ground just beyond the nimbus of lantern light that illuminated the awning of King Henry's pavilion. It stared at her with great golden eyes, then, as suddenly, launched itself skyward and vanished into the night.

"Liath."

Of course he knew.

She didn't turn to face him. She couldn't bear to.

"You've stolen the book," he said, astonishment more than accusation in his voice. "I left the field as soon as it was clear we'd won the battle and rode all the way back to the train, only to find it missing. How did you manage it? What magic did you employ?"

She would not turn to face him, nor would she answer him, so he grabbed her by the shoulder and spun her round to slap her so hard that guards looked up from their station by the awning.

But they knew the silhouette of a noble lord by his bearing and his clothes, and they knew she was only a common Eagle. With a few coughs, they looked away again. It was none of their business.

Furious, he took her by the elbow to drag her away, but her feet were rooted to the earth. She could not struggle, she could not fight, she could not flee. Her cheek stung.

Ai, Lady, was he using sorcery on her? But then what had Da protected her from, if not against this? He had protected her against other forms of magic. Why had he never protected her against Hugh?

"Damn you, Liath," he said, sliding down that slippery slope to anger. "It is *my* book and you are *my* slave. Tell me so. Repeat it back to me, Liath. 'I am your slave, Hugh.' You will never escape me."

Had Hugh plumbed her soul far enough down, had he imprisoned her heart so tightly in the frozen tower, that he could control the rest of her at his will?

She was helpless. She would never break free.

As his grip tightened, her boots shifted on the ground, failing, falling; she began to slide into the darkness.

"Say it, Liath."

Too stupified by fear even to weep, she whispered the only word that she could force out of her throat: "Sanglant."

7

THE rats came out at night to gnaw on the bones. The whispering scrape of their claws on stone brought him instantly out of his doze.

But he did not want to open his eyes. Why did God torment him in this way, giving him such dreams? Why had his mother cursed him with life? It was better to die than to dream that Bloodheart was dead and he was free. In this way, Bloodheart chained him more heavily, weighted with despair.

The dogs whined nearby, tails thumping against the ground. One growled.

"Hush, son," said a voice like his father's. A hand touched his hair, stroking it gently as his father had done years ago when he was a child and delirious with grief at the loss of his nursemaid, the woman who had nursed him and helped raise him. She had died of a virulent fever, and though he had sat at her bedside for days despite her whispered pleas and the commands of his father that he must leave her or risk catching his death, he had not left—and he had not gotten sick.

" '*No disease known to you will touch him.*' "

The hand stroking his hair now had weight and warmth.

He bolted upright, growling, and then flinched back from what he saw: not the cold nave of the cathedral but the interior of a pavilion, its contours softened by the warm glow of a lantern. His father sat in a camp chair beside the pallet on which he had been sleeping. Two servingmen slept on the ground; otherwise they were alone.

The king did not withdraw his hand but held it extended and brushed a stinging end of hair out of Sanglant's eye. "Hush, child," he said softly. "Go back to sleep."

"I can't sleep," he whispered. "They'll kill me if I sleep."

Henry shook his head slightly, a tiny gesture in the gloom. "Who will kill you?"

"The dogs."

Now the king sighed deeply and set a hand determinedly and firmly on Sanglant's shoulder. "You are Bloodheart's prisoner no longer, my son."

Sanglant did not reply, but his hand touched the iron collar. Henry took hold of that hand and drew it away from the harsh touch of the slave collar.

"Nay, nay, child. We'll have it taken off." He wet a clean strip of pale linen with his own spit and dabbed at the raw scrapes along the curve of Sanglant's neck where the collar rubbed and pinched. At his own neck the gold torque he wore glinted as he bent closer and then faded into the darkness at the curve of his neck as he leaned away, examining his son. But it flashed in Sanglant's eyes like a blinding stroke of lightning: symbol of the royal kinship that had given Henry the right to try for the throne, just as Sanglant's person, his actual safe delivery into the world, had given Henry the right to rule after his father, the younger Arnulf.

"Come, then," said Henry. "If you can't sleep, then eat a little bit. I had food brought in—"

"That I might feed in private and not embarrass myself?" But he hadn't meant to snap in the way of dogs nipping one at the other. He groaned and sank head in hands.

But Henry only laughed quietly. "Sometimes you weren't so different from this as a child, Sanglant. It isn't so bad, after all, to be as alert as a hound. Sometimes I think the princes are no better than those dogs who followed you out of Gent, fighting among themselves. They'd tear my throat out, some of them, if they thought they had the chance or if I showed any least sign of weakness before them."

"A fine lord with his handsome retinue," said Sanglant bitterly, remembering Bloodheart's taunt.

"Although we might as well cut their throats now that they're safely chained down—"

"No!" He started up. At his full height, he towered above his father. "They were faithful to me. Like my Dragons."

"Sit!" commanded Henry. Sanglant staggered, still exhausted, still disoriented, and sank down in the other chair. A small table stood at his elbow with a basket of bread and a bowl of berries, freshly picked. "But we won't kill them, for if we can keep them chained—they chew through leather, so my servants tell me—then they can serve as a reminder to you."

Sanglant picked up the bowl and brought it to his nose, but the lush fragrance of the berries made his stomach clench. He set down the bowl and tore off a hank of bread. Ai, Lord, he was so hungry, but he must not gorge. He must take small portions at first and teach his stomach how to eat again. "Remind me of what?" he asked, to stop himself from bolting the hank of bread.

"Of the princes and nobles of the realm."

"Why should I want to be reminded of them?" Still he twirled the bread through his fingers. It fascinated him: the sight of food that was his to take or leave as he wished.

Henry leaned forward and dropped his voice for all the world like a conspirator. Sanglant stilled, bread caught halfway to his mouth. "We must move slowly and plan each step with great care if we are to make you king after me."

Sanglant set down the bread. "Why would I want to be king?"

Henry began to reply, but the wind brought a different and more distracting sound with it: Liath's voice, her fear, her desperation. She was calling for him.

He started up so violently that the chair tipped and overbalanced. He was outside before he heard it, like the echo of his passing, thud on the ground. The guards jumped aside, startled, but he knew where he was going.

Some noble lord had laid hands on her.

Sanglant had grabbed his arm and ripped him off her before, at her gasp, he took hold of himself and stopped to see who it was.

It had been years, but he would never forget that face. "Hugh." He opened his hand, and the other man shook him off and took a hasty step backward. He was furious; Sanglant could smell his rage.

"I beg your pardon, my lord prince. This Eagle serves Princess Sapientia, and I was just escorting her back."

"By dragging her against her will?"

The other man's voice changed, gentled, soothed, but the tone only raised Sanglant's hackles. "No, she wants to come with me. Doesn't she? Doesn't she, Liath?"

In answer she slid sidewise to nudge up against Sanglant's chest. The bundle she carried pressed painfully against his lower ribs.

"Liath!" said Hugh, a command. But then, even in the old days in the king's schola, young Lord Hugh had expected obedience and resented those who would not, or did not have to, give it to him. "Liath, you will come to me!" She made a sound in her throat more like a whimper than a plea and turned her face into Sanglant's chest.

He could not help himself. It rose in his throat and was echoed from the three dogs who remained to him, back behind the king's pavilion: a low growl.

Hugh, startled, took another step back, but then he caught himself and smiled sweetly. "You know what they call you now, some of them, don't you? The prince of dogs."

"Stay away from her," said Sanglant.

But Hugh merely measured him and arched one eyebrow sardonically. " 'Do not give what is holy to the dogs.' " He turned with an arrogant shrug and walked away.

She did not move. Without thinking he set a hand on her shoulder, drawing her closer into him. Startled, she looked up.

He had endured hunger for a long time. He had dreamed of her, but she had been a shade, a remembered shadow given brightness by his own despair and need. Now he touched her on the cheek, as she had once touched him in the silence of the crypt. She did not respond, she did not draw back, but he felt the rhythm of her breathing. His was not so steady.

"Marry me, Liath," he said, because it was now the only thing he knew to say to her. Hadn't she cut his hair, back there by the stream? Hadn't she freed him from Bloodheart's chains? Hadn't his memory of her been all that kept him from drowning in madness?

The entrance flap to the pavilion stirred and the king emerged into a night suddenly shadowed with the first intimations of dawn: a whistling bird, a tree edged gray instead of black against the night sky, the lost moon and the fading stars.

Henry halted just as Liath saw him and started back, taking a big step away from Sanglant.

"Your Majesty!" she said in the tone of a thief caught with her hand in the royal treasure chest.

His face froze into a mask of stone. But his voice was clear, calm, and commanding. "Eagle, it is time to notify my son Ekkehard and those of the king's schola left behind at my palace at Weraushausen that we are safe and Gent retaken. You may leave now."

"My lord king," began Sanglant.

But she stirred and took yet another step away. "It's my duty. I must go."

He let her go. He would not hold her against her will, not when he had been a prisoner for so long. He hated himself fiercely at that moment for what he had become. Prince of dogs: that was what they were calling him now, that was what Bloodheart had called him. Why should she remember anything she had felt before, or what he supposed she had felt, when they had first met in Gent?

He had always been an obedient son.

She hesitated still, glancing once nervously toward the king, and with a sudden impulsive lunge she thrust the bundle she carried into his arms.

"Keep it safe for me, I beg you," she whispered so only he could hear. Then she turned and walked into the dawn twilight.

He stared after her. She lifted a hand to flip her braid back over her shoulder and there it swayed along her back, so sinuous and attractive a movement he could not keep his eyes from it.

"Come back inside, son," said Henry, an order and yet also a plea. There was a tone in his father's voice he could not at first interpret, but slowly old memories and old confrontations surfaced to put a name to it.

Jealousy.

"No," he said. "I can't go back inside. I've been inside for so long—" How long had it been since he had heard the fluting and piping of birds at dawn? Seen the brightest of stars fade into the sleepy gray dawn? Smelled fresh air, even if this was tinged with the distant aroma of burning and death?

Just before she passed out of sight beyond the distant tents, she paused and turned to look back at him, then vanished into the awakening bustle of the camp.

"I've forgotten how bright the sun is," he said without taking his gaze from where he had last seen her. "How sweet the air tastes."

"What is that she gave you?" demanded Henry.

A promise. But he did not say it out loud.

EPILOGUE

THEY came not just from Steleshame but from farther afield, folk who saw an opportunity to rebuild in Gent or farm the empty fields that lay around it. They began to trickle along the roads as soon as word spread that the Eika enchanter was dead and his army defeated. And when victory—and the chance to make one's fortune—was the rumor, word seemed able to spread as quickly as a bird could fly, trilling its message to all and sundry.

"We'll go back," said Matthias. "They'll need workers in the tannery. Lord and Lady Above, I don't know what we're to do with you and Helen! Two mutes!" Then he hugged her to show he wasn't angry about it. He was scared; Anna knew that, just as she knew he was right. They had to go back to Gent. They had to find Papa Otto who had saved them so long ago.

"Master Helvidius will speak for you, won't you, Master?" continued the young man. "It won't matter that you can't talk."

But the old poet fidgeted.

They sat on a log—the ruins of an outbuilding half burned and left to rot after the Eika raid on the holding last autumn—and watched the traffic on the road. Men dragging carts, women burdened by heavy packs, two ragged deacons, laden donkeys, and now and again a rich woman with oxen drawing her wagon and a small retinue of servants following behind. Now indeed Mistress Gisela's claim that Steleshame had once been a bustling holding along a main road seemed like truth and not an exaggeration built upon her own thwarted desire for status and wealth.

Their own small bundles leaned against the log to their right, but Matthias, for all his eagerness, could not quite make the first step onto the road, and Master Helvidius had not even removed his meager possessions from their hut.

"The army will march back by," said Helvidius. "There

are many noble lords and ladies among them who heard me declaim not four days ago. Surely they'll wish for a poet of my skills in their retinue."

"You'd leave us! You won't come with us!"

Anna set a hand on Matthias' tattered sleeve.

"What ever will I do in Gent?" whined Helvidius. "The mayor and his kin are dead. I don't know what lady will demand the right to collect the tolls there, or if the king keeps them for himself. I heard it said that the king intends to found a royal monastery there and dedicate it to St. Perpetua, the Lady of Battles, in thanks for the deliverance of his son. Monks won't wish to hear me sing of Waltharia or proud Helen!" He pried Helen's grubby fingers off his knee and transferred her to Anna, but she lost interest and squatted in the dirt to rescue a ladybug about to be crushed by the old poet's wandering sandals. "Nay, Gent won't be the same place. I must seek my fortune elsewhere."

"And what about us!" demanded Matthias, jumping to his feet. "You would have died over the winter if we hadn't taken you in!"

Anna grabbed his hand and made a sign with her free hand. *No.* One of the lowly clerics in the retinue of Lord Wichman had seen her plight and taught her a few simple hand signs, those used among the monastics, with which to communicate.

Matthias grunted and sat back down, looking sulky.

They heard a new voice. "Go, then! After all I have done for you, raised you when your dear mother died, taught you all I know of spinning and weaving, fed you with my own—!"

"Whored me out when it suited your purpose!"

The scene by the gates of Steleshame had all the volume, and drama, that was lacking when Helvidius sang *The Gold of the Hevelli* before an ill-attentive and drunken audience.

"I will no longer claim kinship with you, ungrateful child! Expect no hospitality in this hall! Stealing from me!"

"I have taken no more than what my mother's inheritance brought me." With those words, Gisela's niece turned her back on her aunt and started down the hill. She carried a rolled-up bundle of cloth and clothing on her back and she, unlike most of the travelers, commanded an entourage: three women whom Anna knew came from the weaving hall and a young man who had recently married one of them. The young man hauled a cart laden with a dye vat, sheepskins, beams for a loom, and a number of smaller items tucked away in pouches, pots, and small baskets; the women carried, variously, an infant, some of the small parts of the loom, and rolled fleeces.

"You'll starve!" Gisela shouted ungraciously after them.

Anna had a sudden instinct that now was the time to leave. She got up, grabbed her bundle, and beckoned to Matthias to do the same. He was so strong now that it was no trouble for him to carry a bundle as well as little Helen, who for all her cheerful smiles and gangling limbs still weighed next to nothing. Perhaps, somehow, Anna thought, she'd given her voice in trade for his crippled leg; it wasn't such a bad exchange.

Helvidius did not follow them. Helen began to cry.

The little girl's cry brought the niece's attention, who walked a short way ahead of them. She halted her group and turned, surveying the children.

"I recognize you," she said. "You were the last to escape from Gent. Come, walk with us." She addressed Matthias. "Perhaps you know Gent well enough to advise me."

"Advise you in what?" Matthias asked cautiously.

"I mean to set up a weaving hall. There are good sheep-farming lands east of the city, so it will be easy enough to trade for wool. And ships have always sailed in and out of Gent, trading to other ports."

Matthias considered. "I could help you," he said at last, "but you'd have to give some kind of employment to my sister, Anna, and let our little one, Helen, free with the other children in the hall." Here he gestured toward the sleeping infant, cradled in swaddling bands and tied to its mother's back.

Anna tugged furiously on Matthias' arm, but he paid no attention to her.

But the niece only smiled. "And yourself, Master Bargainer? No, I recall now: You work in the tannery."

"So I do."

"Very well, then. I think we can make a fair bargain that will benefit each of us. Will you walk with us?" She smiled so winningly at Anna that Anna could not help but smile back. She was certainly a pretty woman, but she had something more than that inside, a certain iron gleam in her eyes that suggested a woman who would make a way for herself despite what obstacles the world threw into her path.

Matthias glanced, questioningly, at his sister. Anna merely signed a *Yes*.

But she could not stop her tears as they walked away from Steleshame. Despite everything, she was sad to leave Master Helvidius and his stories behind.

On the second day as they trudged along the forest road, they heard a song rising from the east.

> *"It is good to give thanks to God.*
> *Their love endures forever.*
> *When I was in distress I called on the Lady,*
> *Her answer was to set me free.*
> *When I rode into battle I called upon the Lord,*
> *and though the enemy surrounded me like bees*
> *to honey,*
> *though they attacked me as fire attacks wood,*
> *with the Lord's name I drove them away."*

Ahead, travelers hastened to get off the road. Their party did so quickly as well, huddling along the verge. Anna appraised the plants along the forest's edge but what could be gleaned had already been taken, either by the folk ahead of them or by the two armies which had so recently passed this way. She could go farther into the forest while they waited, find berries and mushrooms, but even as she stepped back to do so, a glimmer of color flashed in the trees, and she hesitated as the great procession rounded a corner. The sight of such grandeur stopped her, and she could only stare helplessly with the others.

> *"Open to me the gates of victory.*
> *I will praise God,*
> *for They have become my deliverer.*
> *It is good to give thanks to God,*
> *for Their love endures forever."*

Six standards were borne before the main procession. They fluttered sporadically and she caught only glimpses of startling and disturbing creatures embroidered on their rich fabric: a black dragon, a red eagle, a gold lion, a hawk, a horse, and another beast whose fierce profile she did not recognize. Behind them rode a man carrying a silver banner marked with twin black hounds.

Anna had never imagined she might see the king *twice!* The weight of the cavalcade thrummed through the ground and up into the soles of her feet. She gaped in awe as the king himself, attended by his fine noble companions, rode past. Beside the king rode the young lord who had spoken to them at Steleshame. Although the others laughed and spoke joyfully, Lord Alain looked somber—but at least no harm had come to him. He leaned sideways and for an instant she thought he would see her, but he was only speaking to the thin, dark man beside him.

"*Sawn-glawnt!*" breathed Gisela's niece, the phrase more oath than word. She pulled a corner of her scarf up to conceal her face, hiding herself, but Anna did not see see Lord Wichman among the king's attendants. She could make out none but the king and Lord Alain as individuals; they were too many and too bright to her eyes in their fine clothes and rich trappings.

After the king came soldiers, and after them the long train of wagons bumping along the rutted road. She swallowed dirt chipped up by their wheels and shielded her mouth from dust. After the passage of such an army, though, the road beyond was easier to tread and they made good time, coming to Gent in the late afternoon of the fourth day.

It was odd to cross the bridge *into* Gent when she had never crossed it going in the other direction to leave. Once within the walls, Gent had changed so completely from those months when they had lived in hiding that it was as if none of that nightmare had ever happened. Few people walked the streets compared to the many who had once lived here, but already the ring of hammers reverberated off the city walls. Carpenters and masons labored to rebuild; lads hauled away trash. Women washed moldering tapestries or hung yellowing linen and moth-eaten clothes out on lines to air. Children dragged furniture out of abandoned houses while the goats they had been set to watch over foraged in overgrown vegetable plots.

Gent smelled of life, and summer, and the sweat of labor.

They went to the tannery first, but it was deserted as was the nearby armory except for a handful of men sorting through the slag for usable weapons. They complained that the king's forces had looted the armory for spear points and mail and axheads. A few dead Eika dogs lay here and there with flies crawling over them. Their eyes had already been pecked out by the crows.

Matthias found the shed where the slaves had slept, but though he overturned rough pallets and examined every scrap of cloth left behind, he found no trace of Papa Otto. They heard voices outside and hurried out to find Gisela's niece talking to an ill-kempt man with the telltale stains of leatherwork on his fingers.

"I suppose some of the dead householders may have kin who'll come to claim an inheritance," he was saying to her. "Ach, but who's to say if they're telling the truth? Or if anything can be known about what was left behind?"

"That's why I thought it worth the risk," she replied, eyeing him with interest. Through the dirt Anna saw he was a young man, broad through the shoulders and without the dreary hopeless expression she had seen in so many of the slaves. "I can take a house here in town without worrying I'll be thrown out for my pains. I saw how few escaped from Gent. Ah." She saw Matthias and Anna and beckoned them over. Helen clung to Anna's skirts and sucked on her dirty little finger. "These are the children I spoke of."

He clucked his tongue and made an almost comical expression of amazement. "You hid here, in this tannery? Ach, now there's a miracle that you survived and escaped. There were very few of us here at the end. . . ."

"You worked here?" demanded Matthias. "As a slave to the Eika?"

The man spit. "So I did. Savages. I hid when the battle started. The rest of them fled, I suppose. But I've nothing to go back to." He glanced at Gisela's niece and shifted his shoulders somewhat self-consciously under his threadbare and dirt-stained tunic. "I thought I'd start fresh, here, at the tannery. So, lad, you know the craft?"

"Did you ever—" Matthias stammered while Anna

pinched him to make him go on. "Did you know of a slave named Otto?"

"Nay, child, I never heard of such a one, but I only came recently. That's why I lived."

Matthias sighed and picked Helen up, hugging the little girl tightly against him as he hid his tears against her grimy shift.

But Anna only set her mouth firmly, determined not to lose hope. That didn't mean that Papa Otto was dead. He might have fled, he might have been taken elsewhere. . . .

"Come now," said Gisela's niece briskly. "You knew it was a slim hope to find him, poor man. But we'd best be moving on." Here she glanced at their new acquaintance. "Though we'll be back with Matthias. He's a good worker, and very clever. But there's so many folk coming back. We'd best stake out a claim before the best workshops are taken."

Just behind the mayor's palace, abreast of the old open market-place, they found a good-sized workshop with a sizable courtyard, a well, and access to the main avenue. Here the servingwomen began to sweep and wash out the interior while the servingman went to haul mud and lime to patch the walls. Anna drew water up from the well and filled the big dye vat while Gisela's niece ventured out to see what kinds of pots and utensils she could scrounge from the palace kitchens.

"Come on," said Matthias into Anna's ear. He had been raking the courtyard with a rake unearthed from a jumble of forgotten and rusty implements, but he now set down the rake and tugged on her sleeve. "I just want to go see if the daimone is still there, or if we can find the tunnel. We'll come right back."

She thought about it. Everyone else was busy. No one would miss them, and what was it to the others, anyway, if they went to the cathedral to pray for the soul of Papa Otto, who had saved their lives?

It was a short walk to the cathedral, much quicker than the roundabout way they had taken months ago, that night when they had fled Gent. Now they could mount the stone steps in daylight. The long twilight lent a hazy glamour to the scene. The cathedral tower draped its blunt, elongated shadow sidewise over the steps as they climbed to the great doors. Beside the doors lay a heap of fresh garbage and when they ventured cautiously inside, they saw two deacons patiently sweeping away the litter that had made of the nave a kind of forest floor of loam and debris. Of the daimone there was no sign, and it was too dark to go down into the crypt. Anna discovered she didn't want to go at all, and Helen began to snivel, faced with the gaping black stairwell.

"Maybe it's for the best," muttered Matthias. "Come, let's go back. Hey, there!" Helen, having backed away from the crypt door, now ran outside, and Anna and Matthias ran after her only to find her pawing through a gauzy cloud of down feathers that had surfaced in one of the piles of debris.

"She'll take some teaching, poor thing," said Matthias. "You may be mute, Anna, but at least you have your full kettle of wits. I fear our Helen does not." He scooped her up and started down the steps while the little girl crowed an incoherent protest.

Something rested within the downy bundle. Anna nudged it with her toe and all at once the bundle of feathers tipped, rolled, and spilled open. A hairless creature the size of her hand plopped onto a lower step.

It was not a rat, not even a malformed rat. It lay there, the kind of dead white of things that never warm under the sun's touch, its grotesque little limbs splayed in all directions. It didn't have recognizable eyes, only nubs where eyes had tried to grow.

But at least it was dead.

Sun and shadow shifted and the rich golden glow of the westering sun touched the ghastly little corpse.

It shuddered. Stirred. Curled. And came to life.

Anna shrieked.

As if the sound startled it or gave it impetus, it darted away. She blinked and in that instant lost sight of it.

Matthias turned, ten steps down, and looked up at her. Helen quieted in his arms. "What is it, Anna?"

But she couldn't speak to tell him.

BIBLIOGRAPHIC NOTE

I have, to say the least, taken liberties with history as we know it—but then again that's half the fun of fantasy. However, I'd like here to acknowledge a very few of the sources, without which the landscape of *Crown of Stars* would be much poorer.

Passages quoted or adapted from the Bible have been taken from *The New English Bible* (Oxford University Press, 1976). Some of the sayings of the blessed Daisan have been taken from the New Testament, others from *The Book of the Laws of Countries: Dialogue on Fate of Bardaisan of Edessa* (Van Gorcum & Co., 1965), translated by H. J. W. Drijvers. In addition, Drijvers' *Bardaisan of Edessa* (Van Gorcum & Co., 1966) has been of immeasurable aid in my construction of the church of the Unities.

For Rosvita's *History* I have drawn on Widukind of Corvey's *History of the Saxons,* made accessible to me via a translation by Raymund F. Wood (UCLA dissertation, 1949).

The life of the real St. Radegund, a Merovingian queen, is translated in *Sainted Women of the Dark Ages,* edited and translated by Jo Ann McNamara and John E. Halborg with E. Gordon Whatley (Duke University Press, 1992).

I have also been inspired by the writings of Macrobius, *Commentary on the Dream of Scipio,* translated by William Harris Stahl (Columbia University Press, 1952); Virgil, *The Aeneid,* translation by W. F. Jackson Knight (Penguin Books, 1958); Polybius, *The Rise of the Roman Empire,* translation by Ian Scott-Kilvert (Penguin Books, 1979); and the unknown author, possibly Einhard, of *Karolus Magnus et Leo Papa,* translated by Peter Godman in *Poetry of the*

613

Carolingian Renaissance (University of Oklahoma Press, 1985). *Medieval Handbooks of Penance,* by John T. McNeill and Helena M. Gamer (Columbia University Press, 1938) and Salvatore Paterno's *The Liturgical Context of Early European Drama* (Scripta Humanistica, 1989) provided me with further glimpses of source material from the early medieval church and society.

I must also mention Valerie J. J. Flint's *The Rise of Magic in Early Medieval Europe* (Princeton University Press, 1991) and Karen Louise Jolly's *Popular Religion in Late Saxon England* (The University of North Carolina Press, 1996), from which I derived a great deal of information on magic and its uses, and Alison Goddard Elliott's *Roads to Paradise: Reading the Lives of the Early Saints* (University Press of New England, 1987), with its fascinating analysis of late antique and early medieval saints' lives. C. Stephen Jaeger's *The Origins of Courtliness* (University of Pennsylvania Press, 1985) and *The Envy of Angels* (University of Pennsylvania Press, 1994) gave me, I hope, some insight into the court and clerical culture of the Ottonian period, which I of course adapted to my own lurid purposes.

Last, I must mention the work of Karl Leyser, in particular his wonderful *Rule and Conflict in an Early Medieval Society* (Basil Blackwell, 1989), itself a treasure-house of inspiration for a fantasist.

APPENDIX

The Months of the Year:
Yanu
Avril
Sormas
Quadrii
Cintre
Aogoste
Setentre
Octumbre
Novarian
Decial
Askulavre
Fevrua

The Days of the Week:
Mansday
Secunday
Ladysday
Sonsday
Jedday
Lordsday
Hefensday

The Canonical Hours:
Vigils (circa 3:00 a.m.)
Lauds (first light)
Prime (sunrise)
Terce (3rd hour, circa 9:00 a.m.)
Sext (6th hour, circa noon)
Nones (9th hour, circa 3:00 p.m.)
Vespers (evening song)
Compline (sunset)

The Houses of Night (the zodiac):
the Falcon
the Child

the Sisters
the Hound
the Lion
the Dragon
the Scales
the Serpent
the Archer
the Unicorn
the Healer
the Penitent

THE GREAT PRINCES OF THE REALM OF WENDAR AND VARRE:

Duchies in Wendar:
  Saony
  Fesse
  Avaria
Duchies in Varre:
  Arconia
  Varingia
  Wayland
Margraviates of the Eastern Territories:
  the March of the Villams
  Olsatia and Austra
  Westfall
  Eastfall

OTHER KINGDOMS KNOWN TO THE WENDISH:

  Salia
  Aosta
  Karrone
  Alba
  Arethousan Empire
  Andalla (heathen)
  Jinna Empire (heathen)
  Polenie (pagan)
  Ungria (pagan)

IMPORTANT CHURCH COUNCILS

77 *Council of Darre:* The biscop of Dariya (later called Darre) is named presiding biscop, or skopos, of the Daisanite Church.

243 *Council of Nisibia:* Outlaws adoption for inheritance purposes.

285 *Second Council of Nisibia:* Against determined opposition, presbyters are named as equal in honor to the biscops. Skopos Johanna II denies that her insistence on this matter has anything to do with a young presbyter, rumored to be her illegitimate son, whose career in the church she has championed.

327 *Council of Kellai:* Under the direction of the Skopos Mary Jehanna, the gathered biscops and presbyters proclaim that the Lord and Lady do not prohibit what is needful, and that therefore sorcery can lie within the provenance of the church, as long as it is supervised by the church. Only sorcery pertaining to fate, and knowledge of the future, is condemned and outlawed.

407 *Great Council of Addai:* The belief in the Redemptio— the martyrdom of the blessed Daisan in expiation for the sins of humankind followed by his ascension to heaven—is declared a heresy together with the revelation that he is the true Son, both Divine and Human, of the Lady. In strong language, the Skopos Gregoria (called "The Great") declares that the only right belief is that of the Penitire, that the blessed Daisan fasted for six days and that on the seventh, having reached the Ekstasis—the state of complete communion with God—he was lifted bodily up to the Chamber of Light (the Translatus), and that the blessed Daisan himself claimed no greater maternity than that of any other human: a divine soul made up of pure light trapped in a mortal body admixed with darkness.

499 *Council of Arethousa:* The Emperor of Arethousa refuses to accept the primacy of the Skopos Leah I in Darre. A nephew of the emperor is installed as Patriarch. They adhere to the greater of the Addaian heresies, that accepting the semi-Divinity of Daisan, although they do not acknowledge his martyrdom.

626 *Council of Narvone:* Presided over by the Skopos Leah III, whose predecesor Leah II had in the year 600 crowned the Salian king Taillefer as emperor of the reconstituted Holy Dariyan Empire, the Narvone synod confirms the ruling of the Council of Kellai but, in a deliberate repudiation of Taillefer's powerful daughters, specifically condemns the arts of the mathematici, tempestari, augures, haroli, sortelegi, and the malefici, as well as any sorcery performed outside the auspices of the church.

HE had run this far without being caught, but he knew his Quman master still followed him. Convulsive shudders shook him where he huddled in the brush that crowded a stream. His robes were still damp. Yesterday he had eluded them by swimming a river where the bluffs were too steep for them to get their horses down to the water, but he knew they hadn't given up. Prince Bulkezu would never allow a slave to taunt him publicly and then run free.

At last he calmed himself enough to listen to the lazy flow of water and to the wind rustling through leaves. Across the stream a pair of thrush with spotted breasts stepped into view, plump and assertive. Ai, God, he was starving.

The birds fluttered away as if they had gleaned his thoughts instead of insects. He dipped his hand in the water, sipped; then, seduced by its cold bite, he gulped down handfuls of it until the front of his threadbare robe was spotted with drops. By his knee a mat of dead leaves made a hummock. He turned it up and with the economy of long practice scooped up a mass of grubs and popped them in his mouth. Briefly he felt their writhing, but he had learned to swallow fast.

He coughed, hacking, wanting to vomit. He was a savage, to eat so. But what had the Quman left him? They had mocked him for his preaching, and therefore had taken his book and his freedom. They had mocked him for his robes, his clean-shaven chin, and his proud defense of Lady and Lord and the Circle of Unity between female and male, and therefore treated him as they did their own female slaves or any man they considered sheath instead of sword—with such indignity that he winced to recall it now. And they had done worse, far worse, and laughed as they did it; it had been sport to them, to make a man into a woman in truth, an act they considered the second worst insult that could be given to a man. Ai, God! It had not been insult but pain and infection that had almost caused him to die.

But that was all over now. He had run before they took away his tongue, which truly mattered more to him than the other.

Water eddied along the bank. A hawk's piercing cry made him start. He had rested long enough. Cautiously he eased free of the brush, forded the stream, and fell into the steady lope that he used to cover ground. He was so tired. But west lay the land out of which he had walked in pride so many years ago that he had lost count, five or seven or nine. He meant to return there, or die. He would not remain a Quman slave any longer.

Dusk came, but the waxing moon gave him enough light to see by as he walked on, a shadow among shadows on the colorless plain. Stars wheeled above, and he kept to a westerly course by keeping the pole star to his right.

Very late, a spark of light wavering on the gloomy landscape caught his attention. He cursed under his breath. Had the war band caught and passed him, and did they now wait as a spider waits for the fly to land? But that was not proud Bulkezu's way. Bulkezu was honorable in the way of his people—if that could be called honor—but he was also like a bull when it came to problems: he had no subtlety at all. Strength and prowess had always served him well enough.

No, this was someone—or something—else.

He circled in, creeping, until in the gray predawn light he saw the hulking shapes of standing stones at the height of a rise, alone out here on the plain as though a giant had once stridden by and placed them there carelessly, a trifle now forgotten. His own people called such stone circles "crowns," and this fire shone from within the crown. He knew then it was no Quman campsite—they were far too superstitious to venture into such a haunted place.

He crept closer on his hands and knees. Grass pricked his hands. The moon set as the first faint wash of light spread along the eastern horizon. The fire blazed higher and yet higher until his eyes stung from its glare. When he came to the nearest stone, he hid behind its bulk and peeked around.

That harsh glare was no campfire.

Within the ring of stones stood a smaller upright stone, no taller or thicker than a man. And it burned.

Stone could not burn.

He would have prayed, but the Quman had taken his faith together with so much else.

A woman crouched beside the burning stone. She had the well-rounded curves of a creature that eats as much as it wants, and the sleek power of a predator, muscular and quick. Her hair the same color as the height of flame that cast a net of fire into the empty air. Her skin, too, wore a golden-bronze gilding, a sheen of flame, and she wore necklaces that glittered and sparked under the light of that unearthly fire.

Witchfire.

She swayed, rocking from heel to heel as she chanted in a low voice.

The stone flared so brightly that his eyes teared, but he could not look away. He *saw* through the burning stone as through a gateway; saw another country, *heard* it, a place more shadow than real, as faint as the spirit world his ancient grandmother had told tales about but with the sudden gleam of color, bright feathers, white shells, a trail of duncolored earth, a sharp whistle like that of a bird. Then the vision vanished and some stone snuffed out as though a blanket of earth thrown on the fire had smothered it.

Stone and fire both were utterly *gone*.

A moment later the lick and spit of everyday flame flowered into life. The woman tended a common campfire, fed it with dried dung and twigs. As soon as it burned briskly, she made a clucking sound with her tongue, stood, and turned to face *him*.

Ai, Lord! She wore leather sandals, bound by straps that wound up her calves, and a supple skirt sewn of pale leather that had been sliced off raggedly at knee-length. And nothing else, unless one could count as clothing her wealth of necklaces. Made of gold and beads, they draped thickly enough that they almost covered her breasts—until she shifted. A witch, indeed.

She did not look human. In her right hand she had a spear tipped with a stone point.

"Come," she said in the Wendish tongue.

It had been so long since he had heard the language of his own people that at first he did not recognize what he had heard.

"Come," she repeated. "Do you understand this tongue?" Then she tried again, speaking a word he did not know.

His knees ached as he straightened up. He shuffled forward slowly, ready to bolt, but she only watched him. A double stripe of red paint like a savage's tattoo ran from the back of her left hand up around the curve of her elbow, all the way to her shoulder. She wore no curved felt hat on her head, as Quman women did, nor did she cover her hair with a shawl, as Wendish women were accustomed to do. Only leather strips decorated with beads bound her hair back from her face. A single bright feather trailed down behind, half hidden. The plume shone with such a pure, uncanny green that it seemed to be feathered with slivers from an emerald.

"Come forward," she repeated in Wendish. "What are you?"

"I am a man," he said hoarsely, then wondered bitterly if he could name himself such now.

"You are of the Wendish kin."

"I am of the Wendish kin." He was shocked to find how hard it was to speak out loud the language he had been forbidden to speak among the Quman. "I am called—" He broke off. "Dog," "worm," "slave-girl," and "piece-of-dung," were the names given him among the Quman, and there had been little difference in meaning between the four. But he had escaped the Quman. "I—I was once called by the name Zacharias, son of Elseva and Volusianus."

"What are you to be called now?"

He blinked. "My name has not changed."

"All names change, as all things change. But I have seen among the human kin that you are blind to this truth."

To the east, the first rim of sun pierced the horizon, and he had to shade his eyes. "What are you?" he whispered.

Wind had risen with the dawning of day.

But it was not wind. It sang in the air like the whirring

of wings and the sound of it tore the breath out of his chest. He tried to make a noise, to warn her, but the cry lodged in his throat. She watched him, unblinking. She was alone, as good as unarmed with only a spear to protect her; he knew with what disrespect the Quman treated women who were not their own kin.

"Run!" he croaked, to make her understand.

He spun, slammed up against stone and swayed there, stunned. The towering stone block hid him from view. He could still flee, yet it wasn't it too late once you could hear their wings spinning and humming in the air? Like the griffins who stalked the deep grass, the Quman warriors took their prey with lightning swiftness and no warning but for that bodiless humming vibrating in the air, the sound of their passage.

He had learned to mark their number by the sound: at least a dozen, not more than twenty. And singing above the rest ran the liquid iron thrum of true griffin wings.

He began, horribly, to weep with fear. The Quman had said, "like a woman"; his own people would say, "like a coward and unbeliever," one afflicted with weakness. But he was so tired, and he *was* weak. If he had been strong he would have embraced martyrdom for the greater glory of God, but he was too afraid. He had chosen weakness and life. That was why They had forsaken him.

She shifted to gaze east through the portal made by standing stones and lintel. He was so shocked by her lack of fear that he turned—and saw.

They rode with their wings scattering the light behind them and the whir of their feathers drowning even the pound of their horses' hooves. Their wings streamed and spun and hummed and vibrated, lancing above their heads and then curving in over their helmets, which were painted white. Their armor had a dull gleam, strips of metal sewn onto leather coats, and on a standard fixed to a spear they bore the mark of the Pechanek clan: the rake of a snow leopard's claw. The Quman had many tribes. This one he knew well, to his sorrow.

At the fore rode a rider whose wings shone with the hard iron fletching of griffin feathers. Like the others he wore a metal visor shaped and forced into the likeness of a face, blank and intimidating, but Zacharias did not need to see his face to know who it was.

Bulkezu.

The name struck at his heart like a deathblow.

A band of fifteen riders approached the ring of stones, slowing now, the hum of their wings abating. From a prudent distance they examined the stone circle and split up to scout its perimeter and assess the stone portals, the lay of the ground, and the strength of its defenders. The horses shied at first, made skittish by the great hulking stones or by the shadow of night that still lingered inside the ring, but taking courage from their masters, they settled and agreed to move in closer.

The woman braced herself at the eastern portal with her spear in one hand and the other tucked at her hip. She showed no fear as she waited. The riders called out to each other. Their words were torn away on a wind Zacharias could not feel on his skin—audible but so distant that he could make out no meaning to what they shouted to each other, as though the sound came to him through water.

At once the whirring began again as all the riders kicked into a gallop and charged, some from the left, some from the right, some from the other side of the circle. Wings hummed; hooves pounded; otherwise they came silently except for the creak and slap of their armored coats against the wooden saddles.

Beyond the woman and the eastern portal, with the rising sun bright in his eyes, Zacharias saw Bulkezu as iron wings and iron face and gleaming strips of iron armor. The two feathers stuck on either side of his helmet flashed white and brown. The griffin feathers fletched in the curving wooden wings that were fastened to his back shone with a deadly iron gleam. Where the ground leveled off he galloped toward the waiting woman, and lowered his spear.

Zacharias hissed out a breath, but he did not act. He already knew he was a coward, a weakling. He could not stand boldly against the man who had first mocked him, then violated him, and then wielded the knife.

He could not stand boldly—but he watched, at first numb and then with a surge of fierce longing for the woman who waited without flinching. With an imperceptible movement she lifted her fingers from her hip. From within her uncurling hand mist swirled into being, spread, and engulfed the world beyond. Only the air within the stone circle remained untouched, tinted with a vague blue haze. An unearthly fog swallowed the world beyond the stones.

All sound dissolved into that dampening fog, the whir and hum of spinning feathers, the approach of the horses, the distant skirl of wind through grass. . . .

Kate Elliott

The Novels of the Jaran:

☐ **JARAN: Book 1**   UE2513—$5.99
Here is the poignant and powerful story of a young woman's
coming of age on an alien world, where she is both player and
pawn in an interstellar game of intrigue and politics.

☐ **AN EARTHLY CROWN: Book 2**   UE2546—$5.99
The jaran people, led by Ilya Bakhtiian and his Earth-born wife
Tess, are sweeping across the planet Rhui on a campaign of
conquest. But even more important is the battle between Ilya
and Duke Charles, Tess' brother, who is ruler of this sector of
space.

☐ **HIS CONQUERING SWORD: Book 3**   UE2551—$5.99
Even as Jaran warlord Ilya continues the conquest of his world,
he faces a far more dangerous power struggle with his wife's
brother, leader of an underground human rebellion against the
alien empire.

☐ **THE LAW OF BECOMING: Book 4**   UE2580—$5.99
On Rhui, Ilya's son inadvertently becomes the catalyst for what
could prove a major shift of power. And in the heart of the
empire, the most surprising move of all was about to occur as
the Emperor added an unexpected new player to the Game of
Princes . . .